Eric Ahrweiler

INTERCEPT

Book Two: Inner Ring

Intercept: Inner Ring is a work of fiction. Names, characters, organizations, places, and incidents are products of the author's imagination or are used fictitiously. Any resemblance to actual events or locales or persons living or dead is entirely coincidental.

www.ericahrweiler.com

Eric Ahrweiler (2017-06-01). Intercept: Inner Ring

ISBN-13: 9781548076290
ISBN-10: 1548076295

Other books by Eric Ahrweiler

Intelligence

Satellite Intercept

Series:
The Frontline: Inner Ring
Defending Earth (Forthcoming)

INTERCEPT

Inner Ring

INTERCEPT

ORGANIZATIONS AND AGENCIES

UCOM (United Civilizations of the Milky Way) – military and governing al- liance between the 14 sentient races of the milky way.

UNI (UCOM Naval Intelligence) – Intelligence agency of UCOM.

UE (United Earth) – Human governing body, operates outside UCOM.

CAIRO (Combat Artificial Intelligence Robotic Offensive) – weaponized AI faction of UCOM, responsible for carrying out digital warfare.

Grand Council – Collection of political UCOM representatives, one for each of the 14 member civilizations.

Destineers – Rebel faction of Human religious zealots, Destineers believe the invading Slarebull are their holy saviors, come to grant them status as gods of the universe.

Pristine – Slarebull social elite.

TVE – Television Earth, Human owned media broadcast company.

Olympus – UCOM training program for elite Titan android warriors.

CIVILIZATIONS

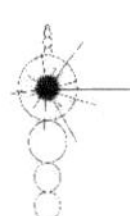

Human (Human) – 5’10” 183lbs – Bipedal with dexterous appendages. Fierce in battle despite small stature. Mostly hairless. Volunteered more military troops than any other UCOM race in the name of honor.

Slayer (Slarebull) – 9’7” 587 lbs – Well evolved for physical combat, with sharp claws, powerful incisors, bony armor plating, and a long, clubbed tail. Violent disposition, enjoy brutalizing and eating conquered opponents. Possess second set of delicate inner arms with grasping appendages to operate technology.

Guardian (Kalesek) – 7’1” 305lbs – Bipedal with bioluminescent skin and hair. Most advanced race in Milky Way responsible for formation of UCOM.

Clone (Sylvandrian) – 5’9” 181lbs – Identical to Humans, with slight differences in hair and skin tone. Genetic similarities a mystery due to extreme distance between Human and Clone homeworlds.

Hog (Pujo) – 6’2” 292lbs – High fat content, with hygienic habits that are offensive to most UCOM civilizations. Heavy eaters.

Squid (Sumai) – 5’8” 162lbs – Only UCOM race to use grasping tentacles in the place of fingered hands with opposable thumbs. Capable of changing skin color to various shades.

Grizzly (Ba-Ra) – 8’4” 414lbs – Fur covered, with large incisors and sharp claws, which are sometimes filed down to better handle technology. Heavily muscled.

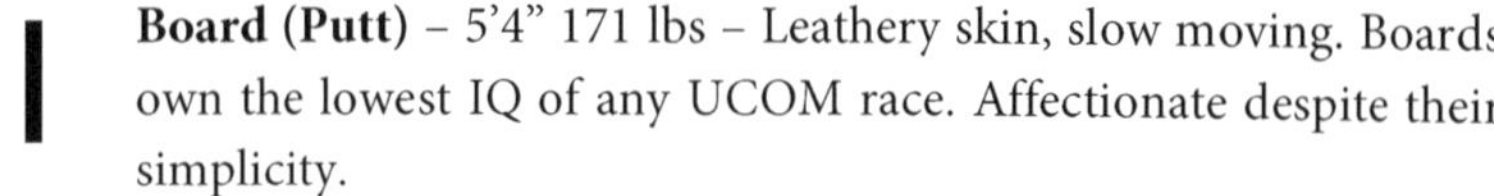

Board (Putt) – 5’4” 171 lbs – Leathery skin, slow moving. Boards own the lowest IQ of any UCOM race. Affectionate despite their simplicity.

INTERCEPT

Intellect (Sim Sowm) – 4'8" 101lbs – UCOM's most intelligent race, serving as backbone of UCOM R&D. Previously a cave-dwelling species, at home in dark environments.

Stallion (Xyrxa) – 6'11" 395lbs – Resembling centaurs, Stallions have a hominid torso atop an equestrian body. Powerful, with short tempers.

Greyhound (Tishmaj) – 5'8" 164lbs – Lanky and fast, greyhounds run naturally on all fours. Possess a second set of arms for grasping.

Bird (Fluxite) – 5'11" 135lbs – Lightweight and agile, Birds are born with a vestigial set of wings that many choose to remove at birth.

Wolf (Huxtor) – 5'9" 174lbs – Fur covered and nimble, Wolves are considered the most cunning of UCOM races. Possess self-serving character tendencies.

Green (Fluffa) – 5'3" 108lbs – The only purely vegetarian race, Green have bony plates on both hands evolved for turning soil. Timid, they make poor soldiers.

Giant (Mauk) – 8'11" 520lbs – The largest UCOM race, Giant's love for brawling and drinking attract many races for entertainment purposes.

Titan (Titan) – 9'6" 610lbs – The most elite combat unit in UCOM, Titans leave their biological bodies after extensive Olympus training to enter Akimors; weaponized android bodies. Titans are especially useful aboard military destroyers, where they can be launched from magnetic rail cannons onto the hulls of enemy ships, cutting through to the inside and commandeering the vessel.

INTERCEPT

SHIPS AND VEHICLES

SLAYER

Hive – Mothership
Hornet – Heavy-destroyer
Mantis - Medium-destroyer
Yellow-Jacket – Light-destroyer
Cicada – Intelligence-gathering vessel
Moth – Stealth vessel
Wasp – Fast-attack fighter
Spider – Space/air vehicle
Flea – Messenger drone
Tarantula – Traveling fortress (land)

UCOM

Lion – Mothership
Tiger – Heavy-destroyer
Leopard - Medium-destroyer
Jaguar – Light-destroyer
Lynx – Intelligence-gathering vessel
Panther – Stealth vessel
Night Eagle – Prototype stealth vessel
Cheetah – Fast-attack fighter
Bobcat – Space/air vehicle
PUMA – Civilian starliner
Tabby – Cargo transport frigate
Pigeon – Messenger drone (civilian)
Raven – Messenger drone (military stealth)
Megaladon – Main battle tank (land)
Roadrunner – fast-transport vehicle (land)

MAP

OUTER RIM
Primal Snow
BRAVO
Floodgate
Sylva
Allakai's
Fleet
ALPHA
CHARLIE
Templar
Dominia
Blit Kru
Portal
Superhighway
The Inner Ring
The Inner Ring
Black Hole
Kael
Earth
MILKY WAY GALAXY
INTERCEPT
Book Two: The Inner Ring

CAPTAINS LOG

Francis Woods - Human
On surface of planet Dominia – UCOM capitol
February 7, 2393

It's amazing what combat will do to a soldier. I can remember a time when I would look my men in the eye and find innocence, joy, love, curiosity. That was a long time ago, before the Slayers came. Now I can find only grit in their eyes. There is no more curiosity. They know what lies in the depths of the galaxy. Death hides in the blackness of space.

The Destineers have splintered Humans into a jagged divide, and the Clones too as a result, since they look like us. Sid Dakota stayed behind the Frontline with the Slayers, but he left his book behind, with us. *The Doctrine of Destiny.* 150 years ago, I'd scoffed at the book. As it turns out, the pen is mightier than the sword. Billions of Humans have sworn allegiance to the Destineers and Slarebull, with thousands of new converts taking oaths daily. As the leader of UCOM and of Humanity, I must keep the peace, and quell this civil war before it rises beyond control.

We blew the Stitchline 150 years ago, destroying every portal within 128 light years between the Slayer armada and our closest naval ship. We celebrated that day as a victory. Severing our transportation network at the Frontline bought us much needed time, forcing the Slayer's to travel at conventional speeds to reach our dwindled troops. At the time it felt like they wouldn't show up for another millennia. It actually took them a century and a half.

Man does time fly.

Most of the men and women have seen combat fighting Slayers in the harsh battlefields beyond the Frontline. The ones that haven't have heard the stories. There are no more jokes or horseplay. I'd like to think there is still hope though.

The Slayers have taught us of the evils in life, but there is still a lot of good in this world. Our homes, our families...we took these things for granted before the war started. Now we cling to them like a mother to her cubs. We know the stakes now, and I have no doubt we will fight until the end if it comes to that. If the Slayers take us, they will have to take every life in the process, down to the last child.

We will not back down. We have one home in this universe, and we hold it close to our hearts. Close enough to fight for. Close enough to die for.

Let the Slayers come. We'll be waiting.

For Earth, and for life,

Eminence Francis Woods

ONE

Slayer Outpost Unit
On surface of planet Blit Kru

The leader of the Slayer scout group shivered atop his outpost on the snow planet of Blit-Kru.

Six Slayers accompanied him atop a metal structure, rising high above the planet's rocky terrain, peeking above the pointed trees blanketing the white landscape.

Five of his companions stood alert at the perimeter, scanning the shadows with eyes evolved to see in the darkness of night.

The final Slayer in his small unit crouched beside him before a fire. A *greckforst* lay gutted beside them, one of the native creatures to the snow planet. The fire would have served well to cook the animal's muscled flesh, but the Slayer leader preferred his food raw. Warm too, if possible, but the planet's icy winds made that a fleeting wish.

The leader leaned forward to rip at the stiff carcass. He used claws on his powerful outer arms to slice beneath the fur, keeping his nimble inner arms pressed against the warmth of his ribs.

His fireside companion, a thin Slarebull with white streaks of paint down his scaled snout, grunted and stuck his own claws into the mutilated hide. He pressed the bony tip of his tail against the animal's neck as he tore off a frozen rib.

"The blood has turned to rubber," White Snout growled before gnashing the bone with his teeth. "I would sooner eat the bark from these trees."

"Be patient," said the leader. "Once the weapon is complete, we will leave this frozen rock, and feast on the bones of UCOM filth."

He glanced backward at the research complex behind them. No light shone from the sprawling building, but the absence of trees exposed its presence. The leader might have taken the expansive patch of white for a lake if he hadn't known better.

"The weapon has taken too long as it is," hissed White Snout. "My body urges me to fight, not to sit in the snow and eat brittle bones from an animal with no heartbeat."

"The Pristine have ordered us to defend the facility," the leader said. "So that is what we will do, even if we must eat the bark from the trees to stay alive."

White Snout grumbled but didn't protest.

The leader ran his tongue over his teeth and tore a rib from the animal. The meat crunched in his jaws, frozen and tasteless. He threw the bone over his shoulder.

It struck the plated back of one of his companions, who turned with a snarl. After seeing it was the leader who had thrown the bone, he flared his nostrils, and bent to pick the rib from the grated platform. He ripped loose a sinewy mouthful, then tossed it back to the floor. He shared the leader's distaste for cold blood.

"The sky," said White Snout, thumping his tail against the platform and leaning against the outer rail. "A comet falls."

He pointed a claw into the night.

A pin of light streaked through the night. It grew larger, and was joined by three others, floating orbs glowing a tepid blue.

"Radio dispatch," the leader ordered White Snout, as he grabbed his plasma rifle. "Tell them we have a visual on an unidentified aircraft."

"Could it be a meteor?" said White Snout, squinting towards the orbs, which had grown much larger.

The leader didn't have time to respond. The orbs were not expanding in size, they were coming towards them.

"Off the platform," he roared, leaping into the ramp angling down into the center of the outpost.

His scout team scrambled to follow. They leaped down several steps, White Nose landing on the leader's back, three others landing beside them. The rest of the team roared in fear, but were drowned by the screech of metal as one of the fallings orbs collided with the top of their platform.

Searing heat singed the coarse hairs sticking from the leader's scaled armor, then vanished as the orbs streaked past and into the forest below. He clawed his way to his feet and stared after the orbs, now tearing through the tree tops, leaving trails of cinders in their wake. A small flash of light illuminated spikes of snow and debris as the comets struck the rocky earth.

The orbs had not glowed from light, but from heat. If the leader hadn't the ability to see infrared, they would have been invisible.

"With me," the leader growled, leaping down the ramp until he reached the bottom of the platform.

The rest of his team exited behind him, and together they sprinted towards the crash site, leaping through deep snow drifts coating the gnarled forest floor.

The snow melted into long streaks of black, leading to a sloping pit. Patches of embers glowed towards the center, which cradled four balls of metal.

"Have you called dispatch?" said the leader.

White Nose nodded. "Help is on the way."

The leader crept towards the center of the pit. The orbs were no longer blue, and his multispectral vision showed no signs of heat. The fallen objects were not natural. He raised his rifle, and heard the rest of his team do the same.

The air twanged beside him, and he turned to find a powerful arm drive a sword of energy into White Snout's spine. He went limp, sliding from the glowing tip onto the soot.

More swords sprang to life around him, hacking into the rest of his squad, who didn't even have time to squeal before their lives ended.

He turned to stare at his attacker, who turned from White Nose and rushed towards him.

His enemy was made of metal, riding the back of a *greckforst.* This *greckforst* was not gutted and frozen, but alive, and charging towards him. In the fleeting seconds before he died, the leader recognized the metal soldier. It was a UCOM Titan warrior, the fiercest of all the Milky Way filth.

The leader screamed as the Titan plunged an energy sword into his chest, slumping to join the rest of his fallen Slarebull comrades in the pit around the foreign balls of metal.

TWO

Bear Stafford - Titan
On surface of planet Blit Kru

Bear Stafford's systems recalibrated to the planet's ambient and gravitational conditions as his atmospheric entry vehicle opened. The pressurized pod hissed as its heat shields separated into a series of plates, then exploded outward, exposing his curled Titan body.

The rest of the AEV's popped open, and the gentle whir of machinery whispered through the twirling snowflakes as his squad converted from condensed balls into bipedal form.

His computer mind registered outlines of four creatures surrounding him and his team in a semi-circle. He tore a rifle from its magnetic plate on his back and drew it to his shoulder, sinking to a crouched firing stance.

Two seconds had passed since his AEV had opened.

"Weapon's down, Titan," a voice called.

Bear finished assessing his surroundings, and saw that the creatures carried camouflaged riders. The animals were four-legged and muscular, with thick mats of fur draping their sides and legs. The hair on their chests billowed in sharp bursts as the beasts panted through breathing holes on their breasts.

Heat signatures traced faint outlines of the riders. Their legs straddled the animals they rode upon, and their forearms glowed from the friction of recent use.

A quick glance at the surrounding dirt made it clear why their arms showed such heat. The corpses of five Slayers littered the crater dug by the impact from their AEV's.

The air above the animals shimmered, and Titans appeared above them as they lowered their camouflage.

"*Greckforsts,*" said the lead Titan. "Native to Blit-Kru. Useful work horses for the local terrain. I'm Harper, and this is the rest of my team, Arrow Thirty-two." He waved a hand to a group of Titans behind him, then nodded behind Bear. "Who invited the lizards?"

Bear turned toward the rest of his own squad. Two of them were androids, Titan warriors cast in bodies made of impervious Akimor armor. The final two were not in Akimor bodies, but in the body of the enemy.

"They're part of my squad," said Bear. "Titan trained, born from the Olympus program. UCOM set them up with Slayer bodies to blend in with the locals. I'm Bear Stafford, Sword Six."

Harper paused, then kicked his *greckforst*. It reared onto its hind legs before pivoting in the opposite direction, away from the AEV's.

"We need to leave," said Harper. "The Slayers saw you descend. This place will be crawling with Snakes within five minutes. We have a base in the foothills."

Harper charged ahead into the thick trees. Bear slammed his rifle to its magnetic holding plate on his back and sprinted after the Arrow Thirty-two team. The *greckforsts* plowed through the heavy snow drifts with little noise.

"*Activate your camo,*" Harper called after a few minutes. "*We have company, ten o'clock.*"

The *greckforsts* crouched low to the ground, and their Titan riders disappeared into the night as they activated their camouflage. Powerful head beams sent shadows sweeping through the trees as the hum of vehicles filled the calm night air. Hover craft approached from the left, scanning the snow in a wide radius around them with a blanket of blue laser recon beams. Bear froze as the lasers passed over his Akimor. The matte nano-skin on his armor rechanneled the laser paths, rendering him invisible to the surveillance technology.

The Slayer hovercraft disappeared towards the crater scene they'd left, and they pressed onward. Droves of additional hovercraft twinkled through the woods in the surrounding distance, but they'd escaped the initial wave of responders.

The terrain grew steep, and they trekked up a sharp cliff face. The *greckforsts* leapt deftly between rocky fingers sticking from the icy slope. The Arrow Thirty-two team disappeared into the side of the mountain, and after a few more leaps of his own, Bear hoisted himself into a thin crevice splitting the rock face.

His teammates followed close behind, slipping into the fissure. Bear stayed at the mouth of the cave, lending a helping hand to the two Sword-Six Titans who struggled in biological Slayer bodies, without the aid of powerful Akimors. He heaved them upward, and followed them into the darkness.

"It's not cozy, but its home," said Harper, squatting against a flat stone against the edge of the cave dwelling.

The cave was more spacious than the entrance suggested. The ceilings were tall, and a handful of alcoves branched off the main chamber, which had three columns formed from joined stalactites and stalagmites. Gems and geodes dusted the walls. A few pieces of wood furniture cut from local trees lined the walls. Woven hammocks hung inside the alcoves. The cave had no lights; not a big deal for Titans, whose Akimors had advanced multispectral instruments to peer from. Wooden shelves held piles of mechanical components and weaponry.

"Are you part of a resistance?" said Bear.

"You're looking at it," said Harper. "There used to be six of us. We crash-landed on Blit-Kru a hundred fifty years ago, during the fall of the Greyhound home world of Tishmahj."

"I don't remember there being an ice planet near Tishmahj," said Bear.

"That's because there wasn't one," said Harper. "Blit-Kru isn't from the Milky Way. When we crash landed here, it was a Slayer mothership. Still is. I'm sure you saw the Hive on the way in."

"And the rest of UCOM?"

"They've been dead for as long as we've been hunkered down on this ball of ice. We were one of the last groups of survivors. The Slayers had the portals locked down, none of our ships could get in or out. It was a slaughter." He paused, the mechanical features on his face grim. He studied Bear and his crew. "Where are my manners?" He stood from the rock, motioning to the rest of his embattled team. "You already know me, this is Pounder, Nikki, and Marvyl."

"Sword Six," said Bear.

His team stood and stated their names.

"Bam-bam."

"Vixtor."

"Loko."

"Crystal."

"Bear," he finished. "Your message, the Raven you sent spoke of a Slayer weapon. Why did you wait so long to signal us?"

"Because the weapon is new," said Vixtor, stepping forward to the center of the room. "Construction began over a decade ago. Before that, this planet was empty except for us and the wildlife."

"We did try to signal UCOM at first," said Nikki, rising from her crouch and displaying a hologram of recorded video from the shoulder of her Akimor. "We scavenged the wreckage of our attack fighters after the crash, and managed to salvage some Ravens. We sent several messenger drones to Dominia's coordinates, but after years of silence, we figured they hadn't made it."

Her hologram video showed four Titans pulling the mangled remains of two other Titans from debris against the side of a cliff. The video changed to a Titan tossing a Raven off the side of a mountain. The Raven zipped through the air and disappeared into the sky.

Pounder gazed sadly at the hologram, struck by the memory of his deceased teammates. "The stars allowed us to calculate our position within the Milky Way. The Hive carrying Blit-Kru moved a few light years away from Tishmahj within the first few weeks, but after that, it sat motionless. We were stuck far from the Frontline, deep in Slayer territory. We thought the Slayers had won."

"The Stitchline was severed," said Vixtor, one of Bear's teammates. He rose, displaying his own hologram on the floor. The hologram showed the spiral arms of the Milky Way. A series of flashes cascaded down a thin line in a wedge pattern, slicing a third of the galaxy away in a rounded triangle. "We blew the portals in the Frontline a hundred fifty years ago and killed all traffic for a range of 128 light years. Your Ravens are probably still stuck in deep space."

"If you thought the Slayers had won, why send another Raven?" said Bear.

"The position of the stars changed," said Harper. "And with the changing stars, came a flood of Slayer activity. The Hive moved after a long hiatus at the outer edge of the galaxy and began traveling inward, towards the Frontline."

"The Slayers came in droves," said Marvyl. "They set up massive camps, and began construction of the weapon. It looks like nothing more than a building, but its looks are deceiving. Its roots travel deep underground, and into the surrounding mountains. We picked up Slayer chatter on our surveillance equipment, and to our surprise, they mentioned UCOM forces. We realized the war was not over, so we sent more Ravens."

"And then finally, one answered back," finished Harper. He ran a hand over a weathered MGK assault rifle hanging from a rack on a central pillar. "Our first signal from Dominia since battle ravaged the Frontline. The star coordinates tell us we're close to the Inner Ring. But if the Slayers were delayed by a distance of over one hundred light years, our current position is a physical impossibility."

"The Slayers have been building," said Bear. He crouched to a knee and displayed his own hologram. It showed the space between the Frontline and the Inner Ring. On the rocky floor of the cave, the band was no more than a foot in width. But in interstellar terms, it was many light years across. "This is what the portal network looked like one hundred fifty years ago after we destroyed the Stitchline."

The sliver of the galaxy was blank, lined on either side by glowing dots representing portals connecting wormhole tunnels.

"This is what our intelligence says it looks like now," he finished.

The blank sliver illuminated with thousands of new portals, bridging the gap between the Frontline and the Inner Ring in a web of connected worm holes.

"They repaired the Network," murmured Nikki, placing a palm into Bear's hologram. The light washed over her hands, gleaming off of dents in the battered metal.

"Your Raven brought word of a Slayer super-weapon," said Bear, rising to his feet. "Our engineers analyzed the scans you sent. What have you learned of its capabilities?"

"Our scans contained everything we know," said Harper. "All the Slayer dialogue we've intercepted through our reconnaissance has repeatedly mentioned a *super weapon*, a device they will use to rid the galaxy of UCOM."

"The Intellects said the underground systems were interconnected in a giant network," said Bear. "They said it looks more like an oversized brain than any sort of weapon. Are they building some sort of computer?"

"A computer we could manage," said Harper, tearing the rifle from the wall and racking the slide. "They're building something far deadlier."

THREE

Francis Woods - Human
Aboard Tiger *Stargrazer* – Dominia starspace

Francis Woods stared into the harsh lights of media cameras at his weekly press conference. The cameras lined the walls of the room, hovering in the air above a magnetic cushion. Additional cameras floated high above neat rows of reporters, offering a full range of angles for viewers watching the televised conference from their home planets.

Media representatives from all fourteen UCOM races sat in sections. The insignias of their native civilizations were stitched at their chests, but it didn't take a keen eye for design emblems to recognize the different sentient nations.

Groups of Human and Clone reporters sat adjacent one another to the right. Clones looked identical to Humans, but no other races could say the same about their physical makeups. A group of Guardians sat beside the Clones, their bioluminescent skin and hair shimmering in blue hues. The Wolves sat beside the Guardians, wiggling their furry snouts.

Beside them sat the Intellects, studying the front stage attentively, rarely blinking their bulbous eyes. Behind the first sections sat the Squid, their tentacles twisting around in knots, a common habit of their kind. Next to them sat the Birds, their wings tucked tightly behind them, and the Green, the only vegetarian race of UCOM. Greyhounds completed the second row, flexing the sinewy muscles of their outer arms, which were unhinged from their shoulders, freeing their delicate inner arms to fidget their thumbs.

The larger UCOM races took the rear of the room. Hogs shifted their wide bodies in their seats, perpetually uncomfortable and hungry. Grizzlies sat with their broad, furry shoulders hunched, nearly as tall as the Giants beside them, who were twice as tall as Humans, and ten times as strong. The Stallions chose to stand in the back, more comfortable for them than sitting on their four equestrian legs. Their raised torso made them the tallest of the UCOM races. One of them clopped a hoof against the floor as he waited for the press release to begin.

The Boards sat in the very rear, impish creatures with as much brains as a sack of rocks. They seemed disinterested in their surroundings, and gazed aimlessly about the room. Woods wondered if the Boards would even bother sending the broadcast to their home world. They seemed more interested in collecting trinkets than worrying themselves about the war.

One of Woods' aides, a Human chairman with a braid of glowing red hair, walked to the center podium and leaned towards the microphone, a tiny orb of yellow light floating in the same manner as the cameras.

"Ladies and gentlemen," the chairman spoke into the receiver. "The Eminence of UCOM."

A few claps of applause trickled around the room, mixed with groans and some muttering. Woods thanked his chairmen and stepped up to the center podium. The crowd of reporters hushed, waiting for him to speak.

"Citizens of UCOM," said Woods, clearing his throat. "Thank you for joining me here tonight. The UCOM navy is very busy with war preparations, so I'll be brief. There is nothing new to report. The Slayer armada has not advanced past the new portal installations they commissioned a few years ago. There have been no major attacks aside from a few minor skirmishes between their Moth-class stealth scouts and our perimeter sentries, and these skirmishes have been going on for some time now. We have fully commissioned all heavy battle installations surrounding the Frontline, and are meeting our goals for increasing our power output incrementally through the use of sunbeams and mass fusion chambers."

Woods paused. The written speech his staff gave him for his weekly media conference was loaded with ambiguous statements and half-truths, and the stern looks on the media representatives faces confirmed the ineffectiveness of his fluffy address.

"The floor is open to questions," he stated, stepping away from the microphone.

Hands shot into the air as reporters struggled to make their voices heard over the raucous chatter, which swelled instantly after his closing remark. His aide stepped forward and selected one of the reporters, a female Wolf with neat braids on her chest.

"You say there's nothing new to report," the Wolf said, rising to her feet. "Yet the Slayers have commissioned two additional portals in the past four months. Furthermore, UCOM-mandated civilian evacuations have extended to planets deep inside the Milky Way, nearly twice as far from the Inner Ring as previously suggested. If there's no new signs of Slayer activity, why are they building new portals, and why are we evacuating planets so far away, and at such a rapid pace?"

Woods took a deep breath, his face stern. "The details on newly installed Slayer portals are restricted to military personnel, but I can assure you that an increase in Slayer transportation capabilities does not necessarily correlate with an increase in Slayer ships."

"Restricted to military personnel?" A Giant rose from the back, accidentally shoving a Grizzly, who bared his teeth as the Giant stood. "You can't hide commissioned portals from the public. It's no secret what's going on. The energy levels from the event can be seen with the naked eye. Are you keeping the information from the public to prevent widespread panic?

Or are you concerned about the Human Destineers learning of our strategies and taking the information to the Slayers?"

Cheers pocketed the room as various media member celebrated the Giant's confrontational question. Woods had quick answers to every question except ones about the Destineers. The traitorous group of rogue religious zealots had joined sides with the Slayers, and their numbers were growing. Worse, the Destineers were all Human or Clone, and didn't extend membership to any other UCOM races, who they considered to be socially and biologically inferior.

"We have a firm handle on the Destineer situation," said Woods, raising his voice over the growing noise. "Their leader, Sid Dakota, hasn't been seen since the Frontline Battle, and we have no evidence of a Slayer-Destineer conspiracy within Frontline operational boundaries."

"Raise your hand to be called upon," Woods' aide demanded the crowd, but half the reporters had formed a sort of angry mob, shooting to their feet and squabbling, trying to make their voices heard over the rest of the noise. The other half of the reporters sat calmly. It was easy to spot which races were friends of the Humans, and which were not.

"The Destineers are a cancer to UCOM," a Greyhound shouted, climbing to stand on his seat. "You have them under control? Then explain the mass prison on Gefangnia. And of course Sid Dakota hasn't been spotted since the Frontline a hundred-fifty years ago. Twenty thousand civilian cameras caught footage of his Destroyer docking with a Slayer mothership unharmed."

The cries from reporters grew louder, and Woods stared grimly at the crowd. "The Destineers…" he trailed off. His eyes wandered to the base of the floating microphone. Letters spun around the yellow orb in a ring.

United Civilizations of the Milky Way – U.C.O.M.

He thought back to a saying on Earth, printed on the currency of his home country three hundred years ago. *United we stand, divided we fall.* He studied the media. Half of them stood, the Stallions, Wolves, Greyhounds, Giants, Squid, Birds, and Hogs. The rest remained seated, the Clones, Guardians, Green, Boards, Grizzlies, and Intellects. The standing group had calmed to a hushed murmur, waiting for him to speak. He opened his mouth, but couldn't find his words.

His aide caught his eye. The man had his head down, his hand clenched in his twisted red hair. His head jerked up, his expression stern. The staff member strode to Woods and leaned into his ear.

"Sir, you have a priority one message from Stew Kwelm."

Woods frowned. Stew was an Intellect, and his lead scientist, the head of UCOM research and development. Stew never sent him priority one messages, or even priority two messages for that matter.

"I'm sorry ladies and gentlemen, citizens," said Woods. "I'm afraid I have to leave. My staff members will see to it that the rest of your questions are answered thoroughly."

He wasted no time in leaving the podium. Indignant cries circled the room, probably contesting the legality of an Eminence leaving a constitutionally mandated weekly civilian update. Woods paid no mind to the jeers. He needed to get to R&D and see what had Stew so excited.

A young female Clone passed through the light barrier separating the media seats from the front podium and jogged next to Woods and his Detail. Two armed guards barred her from getting near the Eminence. Woods turned to find her on her tip toes, trying to speak over the agent's thick arms.

"Eminence Woods," she cried. "Sir, what's it feel like to be both the most loved and the most hated man in UCOM?"

He paused. The woman blew a lock of hair from her face, ready to record his response.

"No more questions," said his red-haired aide, pressing his hand against Woods' back to get him moving again. The woman reporter fell behind, unable to get the juicy news bit she had hoped to include in her broadcast.

They traversed the lengthy halls of the ship, entering a pod to take them down to the lower levels of the research facility. Woods fought the urge to form a comm link with Stew as he rode in the pod. Comms could be intercepted. The Destineers could be listening.

He burst into the research facility, a cavernous room filled with sophisticated instruments and large-scale pieces of weapons technology. He took a hard right towards Stew's private lab, and after a short ride on a ground cart, arrived at the blackened glass doors. Woods entered to find the Intellect staring at a massive computer screen dominating the front of his lab.

A 3D model spun slowly at the center. It was spherical, and appeared to have a dense network of connections running to its core like tree roots. After a closer look, he recognized the grainy texture, and realized it was a planet. A second model hovered next to the planet. It appeared to be a simple building complex.

"You have a priority one message for me?" said Woods.

Stew jumped a little, as if he hadn't heard them come in. His huge eyes blinked once.

"Why yes, Mr. Woods," he said. "Yes I do." His beaked clicked rapidly. "The Slayer mega-weapon, the APEX. It's real."

FOUR

Casi Vomisa – Human AI
Aboard Manticore-class vessel – Inner Ring starspace

"How's the data coming, Zulu-One?"

Casi Vomisa called to her CAIRO team from her forward command mobile headquarters at the outskirts of the Inner Ring. Her command station consisted of a Manticore-class space vessel, a hybrid ship outfitted with both the stealth capabilities of a Night Eagle, and the reconnaissance capabilities of a Lynx craft. Manticores were specially designed to accept not biological UCOM crew, but artificial beings. As a Human-made AI, Casi felt right at home in the newly designed craft. able to integrate flawlessly into the controls, which fit her digital consciousness like a glove.

After infiltrating deep within Slayer AI ranks and performing what Eminence Francis Woods later called *'an impossible feat of heroics'* during the Frontline Battle 150 years ago, Vomisa was given all her stars at once, and offered a position as Grand Admiral of CAIRO. The *Combat A.I. Robotic Offensive* was UCOM's militarized artificial intelligence division, consisting of purely digital warriors. She'd declined, keeping her rank of Commander. She liked action far too much to agree to sit back and control troops from an ivory tower.

The newest Slayer portal blackened the stars behind it as she peered through the sensitive surveillance instruments of the Manticore. Normally portals were well lit, but this one was as dark as the space vacuum surrounding it. Her teammates had entered the portal through Ravens almost sixty seconds ago, and hadn't yet returned. None of her pings returned any of their consciousness ID's.

"Zulu-One, I repeat, state progress on data capture."

Still no answer. Her team had specific orders. Three of her troops were to enter the Slayer portal to gain intel on its security characteristics, as well as assess enemy fleet strength. One was to hang back on the edge of the portal, radioing the status of the other three as they reported back in twenty second intervals. She checked her operational clock.

00:01:40

Casi powered the thrusters on her Manticore and guided closer to the portal, flipping through her surveillance readings for any signs of enemy stealth craft. They were alone. She loosed a Raven from her ship, transcribing a message on the courier.

"Zulu-One, this is Yankee-Seven, I'm requesting backup for rescue evac."

The small drone zipped towards the wormhole and disappeared into it. Casi prepared another Raven. This one would go to *Waterfall*, the closest Tiger-Class heavy destroyer. It would carry their coordinates and an emergency message asking for support.

"Yankee-Seven, this is Bravo-Two, no need for evac, we're on our way home to roost. Zulu-One had his gadgets fried, the Slayers put some sort of witch's spell around the portal. I'm on my way with him and the rest."

"Confirmed Yankee-Seven," said Casi. "I'll call back the Raven."

She changed the parameters of the Raven she was prepping. The sleek messenger craft swung in a wide loop away from the direction of *Waterfall* and returned to the Manticore, scuttling into one of its many launch tubes. Casi checked the status of the small swarm of Ravens still in nearby starspace. There was a faint heat disturbance in the direction of the portal, but she knew that was just her team scrambling towards her Manticore.

Ravens bore the full workload of UCOM communications. They were faster than most ships, small, stealthy, and capable of traversing the portal network to spread video media thousands of light years in mere hours. They were also crammed with active and passive spacnar, light and energy detectors, gravity sniffers, and a host of other surveillance technology. They could even use their energy cannons to shoot down Fleas, the Slayer version of a Raven.

"Coming in Yankee-Seven, requesting firewall access."

Casi ran through the standard set of protocol before allowing digital access to her ship's servers, scanning the conscious makeup of all her crew, and receiving their shifting security patterns for final confirmation. She felt them enter the virtual reality world of the ship, and swung the Manticore around hard to starboard, setting destination for *Waterfall*, where they'd deliver their briefing.

After giving the surrounding Ravens a final check, she ordered them all back to base. Blue lights buzzed the starspace as the drones kicked their afterburners, dropping their stealth shields to return to the ship.

She closed her eyes and entered the VR world of her Manticore, or as AI liked to call it, the *barracks*.

To most biological beings, Casi was a jumble of software code. A program that could think and act like a Human, but never truly be Human. But to Casi, she *was* a Human, albeit one trapped in a digital body. In virtual reality and in hologram communications, she assumed her Human avatar. It was this avatar that her four crew members saw when she materialized in the barracks of her ship.

"The Slayers upgraded their digital defense tech," said Hugo, no longer carrying his operational *Zulu-One* tag. "My radio was scrambled by some sort of magnetic pulse."

"New technology? No Slay-I involvement?" she asked. She waved her hand, and a three dimensional hologram of the Slayer portal materialized above the floor.

"Yes ma'am," said Leeson, who waved his own arm over the hologram at the center of their group. Wavy lines blanketed the sphere, pulsing rhythmically. "It didn't affect me, Harvey or Gruff, we were able to time the fields before turning back. It'll be tricky to send anything bigger than a Raven through."

Casi analyzed the magnetic waves. There were only small gaps in between the pulses.

"We'll let the Intellects work on a solution for that," she said. "What did you find on the other side of the portal? How big is the Slayer fleet?"

She walked around the side of the hologram to lean against a metal slope in the wall. Her boot heels clicked against the metal floor, and her tight leather suit squeaked as she eased into a half-sitting position.

"As we expected," said Harvey. "Vast numbers of ships, a lot of Hornet heavy-destroyers. They had a bunch of Cicadas surrounding the portal with jamming equipment. We couldn't capture any video aside from the Hornets near their perimeter, but the fleet's energy readings were off the charts. It would take millions of ships to give off that much heat. I would guess several Hives, and some larger signatures too, probably more of those installations they've been lugging around."

Harvey waved his arm over the hologram, adding the intel from his Raven to the display. Gruff added his intel as well. Ships fanned from the portal in all directions. The crazy spikes and domes of Cicada ships formed an inner circle around the portal. Beyond them, the rakish edges of Hornet destroyers provided protection for an endless swarm of Wasp fast-attack fighters, Mantis light battleships, and Hive motherships, which seemed tiny when set against the planets they had in tow behind them.

Huge cylinders rose from deep within the Slayer fleet. The cylinders had no geometric details since no UCOM ship had yet to lay eyes on a Triturator installation. The only data they had were the distinct energy signatures of the megalithic devices, built for one purpose – to consume galaxies.

"And the data on the portal itself?" said Casi.

"Built within the same parameters as the rest of our own Network portals throughout the Milky Way," said Hugo. "Based on our readings, they'll expand to let larger ships pass, and can accept a planet sized object through the wormhole without risk of degradation or collapse. Light and energy can pass through just like our Network portals. But, just like ours, the light would come out scattered in all three spatial dimensions and need to be refocused into a coherent beam for further transport."

"They're creating exact duplicates of our portals," Casi murmured.

UCOM engineers were curious about the newly commissioned Slayer portals. The Intellects had assumed the new portals would have different characteristics than UCOM portals, but her team's data seemed to reject that theory. For all intents and purposes, these portals were identical to UCOM portals.

"Polish these readings up," she said. "Compile everything into lists and run algorithms to simulate total fleet size and firepower. We'll debrief inside *Waterfall* at O-Eight-Hundred."

"Aye," said Hugo.

Her team set to work categorizing the recon information. Casi left the VR barracks to look through the outboard cameras. They were about to pass through a portal, its rounded walls looming larger as they approached. This time, the portal would lead to *Waterfall*, instead of into the heart of a Slayer armada.

She closed her eyes as they passed through, soft green light from the portal's security turnstiles washing over the outer hull of the Manticore. UCOM portals had security turnstiles installed around them. The turnstiles were encrypted, and only allowed passage for ships holding the proper security key. It was a way to keep unwanted guests out of protected starspace. The turnstile could be commandeered or destroyed, leaving the wormhole open for travel, but they provided a significant obstacle against enemy ships.

Green is clean, red is dead, thought Casi. *And black or yellow could go to either fellow.*

If the portal was green, it was under UCOM control. If the spherical wormhole was red, it had been commandeered by the Slayers. Interestingly, the Slayers hadn't installed any security around their newly commissioned wormholes, which sat dark and void against the starry backdrop. The fact that they hadn't installed the equivalent of a turnstile on their portals made Casi nervous. It was as if they were encouraging UCOM to attack.

They finished their pass through the portal, and the green light faded to black, exposing the chiseled hull of *Waterfall.* The destroyer's twelve fins angled away from the hull in sets of three, containing lateral thrusters to pivot the ship in any direction during battle.

During battle, the ship's shields would be energized, forming a lattice network of criss-crossing lasers. There were no immediate threats to *Waterfall,* so her shields were lowered, revealing thick hull plates.

"*Waterfall,* this is Commander Casi Vomisa, approaching in a Manticore from sector J12 through portal two. Requesting permission to dock digitally."

A few seconds passed, then *Waterfall* responded to her message.

"Copy that Commander Vomisa. Requesting call sign and encryption key."

Casi sent a complex series of digital and light signals to satisfy the request.

"Encryption key sent. Human call sign *Flaming Flamingo*."

"Roger that Commander," said the voice from ship dispatch. "Your identity is confirmed. Your request for docking has been denied."

Casi frowned. She wasn't allowed to dock?

"*Waterfall*, repeat that please. I have intel from a scouted Slayer portal with orders to debrief aboard your ship."

"Understood Vomisa," said dispatch. "These orders come from Dominia. Eminence Francis Woods sent you a priority one message for your eyes only, uploading to your Manticore now. Drop your crew here and report to Dominia immediately."

FIVE

Casi Vomisa – Human AI
Aboard PDR *Sea Dragon* – Dominia starspace

Casi finished security docking procedures for *Sea Dragon*, one of Dominia's four planetary defense rings. The PDR wrapped around the planet like a halo, with rail cannons spaced evenly along the structure to provide heavy fire during battle. There were thousands of RACAN's, one every few hundred miles along the ring. After every hundredth RACAN, a Tower rose from the PDR.

The Towers were brightly lit, their sleek edges studded with dozens of additional RACAN's. At the top of the tower sat a Super Heavy Cannon, designated officially as an SHC, and unofficially as a *Shitcan* in UCOM slang. Casi wasn't sure how the nickname originated, but her guess was that the enemy's last words after seeing the enormous weapon fired would be '*Oh Shit!*'

The Towers also contained sprawling command facilities for the UCOM navy. Her Manticore was safely docked at Tower 7, and she closed her eyes as she left the confines of her space craft, and entered the virtual world of *Sea Dragon.*

She'd listened to Eminence Woods' message several times during her transit to Dominia. The message was short and vague.

Report to Stew Kwelm's private lab in R&D aboard Sea Dragon. Location: Dominia PDR, Tower 7 Wing 12, Sector 25c. New Slayer technology discovered. Predicted damage capabilities are code black. Security key embedded.

Code black was UCOM's highest assessment of weapons damage. RACAN's could shoot large-mass slugs of hardened steel thousands of miles per hour, and they were only given a *code blue* label. Shitcans fired much larger slugs, and were only code red.

She navigated the facility, traveling through the AI data highway embedded in the Tower. She entered the security key from Woods' Raven and was allowed wireless access into the R&D lab. Glancing briefly through wall cameras at the heavy equipment being tested in the main bay, she entered Stew Kwelm's private lab.

"Mr. Eminence, sir," she said.

Woods stood with Stew Kwelm, who jumped at her voice. They both turned to face her hologram avatar. She stood straight, feeling her breasts squeeze against her conformal suit, and saluted the UCOM Eminence. Woods saluted back with a look on his face that was either confused or scared. Knowing Woods, she guessed confused. Stew Kwelm, the Intellect, clicked his beak, his eyes wide, and gave Casi his own version of a salute, pressing his thumbs against the back of his rounded skull and fanning four fingers to either side. It was the Intellect's traditional way of approving their adversary as an intellectual equal.

"Welcome to Dominia, Commander Vomisa," said Woods, turning back to the screen. "Thank you for coming so quickly, and on short notice."

She followed his gaze. His face was turned to a large screen, with a 3D model of a planet. Beside the 3D model sat another model, this one of a large building complex.

"Aye sir, I was only a few portals away near *Waterfall.* I have intel on one of the new Slayer portals, if you'd like me to upload it to the room's servers."

"That can wait," said Woods, with a casual wave of his hand. "Leave it for Stew. He'll diagnose the data later."

Casi nodded, looking at Stew. His eyes darted to the screen, then back to her face. Normally an Intellect would demand to see such new and secretive information at once.

Stew spoke for the first time. "Commander Vomisa," he began.

"Call me Casi," she said.

"Very well, Casi. Based on our gathered intelligence, the Slayers have been innovating. They've made faster, more powerful ships, upgraded their defenses, and limited their use of Slay-I, which I think we may owe thanks to you for."

Casi thought back to the Frontline Battle, where she single-handedly hacked Slayer AI systems, taking control of entire battalions of ships, and ultimately sending them to their deaths into a black hole.

"Any CAIRO bolo would've done the same in my shoes," said Casi, casting him a wink.

"Yes, hmm," Stew wiped his brow with his sleeve, unsure of what she meant by bolo. Intellects were an encyclopedia of information on physics and engineering, but had apparently never learned the military slang word for incompetence. "The fact remains," he continued. "The Slarebull, as a race, are innovating, expanding their already firm grasp on science and physics to create new weapons, both offensive and defensive."

"Isn't that expected?" said Casi. "UCOM's done the same. We've upgraded our weapons tech just like them."

"That's not the point," said Woods, turning from the screen to face her. "Before the Slayers came to the Milky Way, they hadn't expanded their technology for millennia. We have enough background chatter analyzed to peer into their past. I don't know why, but for thousands of years, they've been technologically dormant. The Slayer Hornets you saw at the Frontline were the same Hornets they used thousands of years ago. We think it has something to do with the amount of resistance they met with our UCOM navy. They were used to plowing through galaxies with ease, installing their Triturator installations effortlessly. With us, they bit off more than they could chew."

Stew raised a hand, as if in question. "Mr. Eminence, if I may. Perhaps we fought as equals at first, but the Slayers are more powerful than we witnessed at the Frontline. We believe this new level of scientific research has something to do with the Pristine, their social class of elite. Our chatter doesn't speak of the inner workings of their civilization, located in *Greschka Kalum*, or, translated literally, *Primal Snow*. All we know is that the Pristine exist. And even of that we're not positive."

"They're innovating again," said Casi, walking up to the screen and placing a palm on the 3D model of the planet. She absorbed the information of the hologram and duplicated it, spinning it above the metal floor before her. "Is that what this is? This planet? A new science breakthrough?"

"It may be the last scientific breakthrough they'll need," said Woods, grinding his teeth.

Casi squinted at the hologram. It was just a building, and some large communication towers. "Are you talking about the underground infrastructure?" she asked, expanding the hologram to magnify a section of the linked network of subterranean power lines. "We have this sort of thing on every habitable planet in UCOM. It's how we put a magnetic cushion over the planet's surface so we can levitate."

Stew frowned, and Casi felt sheepish. Of course Intellects knew how their magnetic infrastructure worked.

"It does have some similarities to our mag-fields," said Stew. "But I'm afraid that's where the similarities end. We've received word from a team of Titan soldiers stranded on the surface of this planet. Chatter we've obtained from various Slayer ships have made mention of a super-weapon, one that will wipe UCOM from the Milky Way for good. An APEX weapon, a weapon with no equal."

"And the Titan team, they've mentioned this weapon?" said Casi, scanning the hologram of the building complex for any hidden clues. It certainly didn't look like an APEX weapon to her.

"Earlier today we received confirmation," said Woods. "Bear Stafford landed on Blit-Kru and rendezvoused with the stranded Titan team, Arrow Thirty-two. Arrow Thirty-two has been gathering intel for the past few years. They've confirmed the existence of the APEX weapon based on intercepted Slayer dialogue."

Casi exhaled deeply. "What does the APEX do? I can't imagine a weapon more powerful than their Triturator installations. What could cause more damage than a machine built to de-atomize galaxies?"

"We don't classify the Triturator devices as weapons," said Woods. "They resemble construction equipment more than anything. On an extreme scale, of course."

"But the APEX," said Casi, dragging the hologram of the building complex from the screen until it hovered before her. She flicked her wrist to make the planetary hologram disappear, then enlarged the building model until she could see individual facets in the side walls. Snow piled against the building in deep drifts. "What does the APEX do?" she asked again, her eyes still fixed on the mysterious building.

"We don't know," said Stew, dragging his own hand over the model. A thin shell of red materialized over the entire building. "The building has no digital access on the outside perimeter. Because of this, our Titan team couldn't hack into the building servers inside to retrieve any design data. Interestingly enough, this building is constructed similarly to a Hive mothership. It has a digital barrier. We think it's to prevent unwanted AI from entering."

"So if no AI can enter, why'd you call me here?" said Casi. She walked through the hologram of the building, the light from the image washing over her hips in colorful streaks. She stopped when she stood face to face with Woods.

The Eminence's gaze sharpened. "No AI can enter from the *outside*. Titans can disengage their consciousness from their Akimors, but only briefly. We're sending you to Blit-Kru in a custom AI bipedal suit. You'll be traveling with one additional AI companion, and meeting with Bear's Sword Six team for rendezvous in O-four hours plus seven. Arrow Thirty-two and Sword Six will help you infiltrate the building."

Stew walked to his desk, a floating series of glowing pink shelves resembling mushrooms growing from the side of a tree. He retracted a packet of data, floating it in his palm, a holographic blue ball. He tossed it across the room to Casi, who caught it and absorbed its contents.

"That's everything we know of the terrain, structure, and any travel obstacles you may come across in starspace," said Stew. "It also has the names and locations of the Titan teams, as well as call signs for security."

"A hundred fifty years ago you saved UCOM from a superior Slayer force on the Frontline," said Woods, his voice softening. He saluted her stiffly, snapping his hand to his side. "With a weapon this powerful, I'm sending in my best. *Awaken Stars.*"

SIX

Chase Grover – Half Human/Half Clone
On surface of Sylva – Slayer Hive

Chase Grover ran a gloved finger around the edge of his boonie hat, causing droplets of water to fall around his face. His multi-spectral goggles allowed him to see heat from the large refinery plant past the leafy fronds he crouched behind. He eased his FAZA-150 long barreled mag rail automated rifle forward on its strap, scanning the local foliage for signs of the enemy. Guards stood watch in the distance, walking back and forth atop watch towers lining the refinery complex. He counted fifteen Destineers. His gut told him more hid out of sight.

Chase radioed his surveillance crew, located in a small underground tunnel network five miles to the east. He spoke with voiceless communications using his Program, a nano-serum injected into his bloodstream capable of reading his brain wave patterns. With such a large refinery, the Destineers would be combing the surrounding foliage with acoustic magnifiers.

"Green Tree, this is Slim Rod, what's the status on our Ferrets?"

There was a brief patch of static as his comm gear connected through the metacrete bunker system. A clear voice returned his call after ground antennae patched the link.

"Slim Rod, this is Green Tree, we have positive control of Ferret One and Ferret Two, approaching on both sides from the rear. Central uplink of enemy assets available in one mike."

Chase turned to the three soldiers crouched behind him. He raised a hand palm up and thrust it straight before him, horizontal to the ground. His squad mates nodded confirmation, flashing the 'OK' symbol. Together they pressed forward, keeping low to the ground. The wide leaves of tomako plants slid over his body as he entered the canopy. Rain drops pattered against his shoulders, fibers in his tactical jacket whisking them away, keeping his body dry.

He crept to the nearest tree trunk, and kneeled to a firing position. The rest of his group followed suit, picking their own trees to kneel behind.

The refinery was now in clear view. They were on the edge of the tree line. The Destineers had cleared the jungle to bare dirt in a hundred-meter perimeter around the refinery, and he could now see the enemy guards clearly in visible light. In addition to the guards he spotted four laser cannons spread evenly along the catwalk. He zoomed in to observe one of the guard's faces. His rifle was slung casually around his back, and he didn't seem to be fire ready. They still held the element of surprise.

He radioed the rest of his strike team, two groups aside from his own Alpha group, hidden at various points along the refinery perimeter.

"Chief to Slim Rod, Ferret markings green ready in less than one mike. Visible count on four Lima Caspers. Sending targets to central comms. Upload Dust Bunnies as you see them."

He sent markings for the four laser cannons and fifteen visible Destineers to his strike groups. The enemy soldiers and artillery superimposed on their HUD goggles, red diamonds for soldiers, yellow squares for laser cannons. Several more red diamonds appeared as Bravo and Charlie groups uploaded markers for additional Destineers spotted from their personal vantage points.

"Green Tree to Slim Rod, Ferret One and Ferret Two scans are underway, standby for upload."

Chase watched as surveillance readings from the ground-based Ferret hover drones added information to their HUD's. Red dots peppered the ground between the tree line and the building. Two purple sentry drones walked back and forth in front of the steep sidewalls of the guard towers.

"Slim Rod to Green Tree, I have land mines and stealth sentries at the inside perimeter. I need the ferrets to take out the mines on my ready signal. Ready signal is *Cherokee.*"

"Roger that Slim Rod, waiting for the thumbs up."

Chase spun to check behind him. Behind the thick tree trunks, four Saskwatch all-terrain vehicles idled. He couldn't see them through the trees, but they hovered on his HUD as blue stars. "Chief to Ape Squad, confirm readiness."

"Slim Rod, Ape Squad readiness confirmed, waiting for signal *Cherokee.*"

"All groups on me," said Chase. "Rifle men pick your Dust Bunnies, rocket men pick your Ghosts and Lima Caspers."

He paused, steadying his rifle. He trained his scope on the nearest Destineer and sent a lock ID to central comms. The red diamond turned green on his display, but yellow on the rest of his team's displays. The ID pins on the rest of the Destineers turned yellow as his fire team selected their targets.

The stealth sentries glowed red as his squad mates carrying rocket launchers locked onto their targets. The laser cannons glowed red as well. They were ready.

"*Go Cherokee,*" he spoke into central comms.

The attack happened in seconds. Magnetic slugs slipped from the trees and found their human targets. Ten Destineers dropped lifelessly to the ground. The remaining enemy soldiers barely had time to clutch at their rifles before they too were dropped with rifle fire.

A hissing sound whispered through the trees, then explosions tore into the facility. The camouflaged sentries lost their invisible armor as rockets blasted them into debris. The automated laser cannons failed to find their marks before rockets took them out of the picture as well.

A shrill whine screamed across the perimeter, and both Ferret surveillance drones appeared, dropping their camouflage. The disk-shaped hovercraft spun rapidly, bursts of sparks showering from their sides like firecrackers. They made a wide circle around the entire perimeter, showering the ground with sparks. Seconds later, blasts ripped the air as hidden land mines tripped and shot tall columns of dirt skyward. The Ferrets completed their circle around the perimeter, disabling the last of the mines.

The blasts triggered wailing alarm sirens, and red emergency strobes pulsed from the sides of the building walls.

"All squads, *go,*" Chase shouted.

Twelve soldiers sprinted from the trees, racing through the disturbed earth toward the refinery. The building was a twenty second sprint from their previous position, and after five seconds, three Saskwatches tore from the trees, skidding to a stop in front of the soldiers. Ape squad had arrived.

Chase leaped onto the back of the nearest Saskwatch, and his Alpha squad mates did the same. Screeching metal filled his ears as the Saskwatches loosed mortar shells into the nearest entranceway.

The metal twisted open, and the rear deck to the ATV lurched as the driver kicked the accelerator. Chase gripped one of the side ropes, steadying himself as the vehicle approached the building.

The front end of the ATV rocked hard upward as they bounced over the twisted remains of one of the Ghost sentries.

"Weapons free."

The Ape Squad soldier manning the turret on the raised platform inches from Chase's head shouted before unloading his fifty caliber explosive tipped rounds. Hot shells rained around Chase, some biting into exposed skin around his neck.

The inside of the refinery was cavernous. Massive cylinders held processed liquids, with five-meter diameter pipes running from rotating machinery, curving into the ground for long distance transport.

The two Ferrets followed them into the building, sweeping across the sprawling complex, scanning for hostile troops or automated weapons. Red diamonds peppered his HUD as the Ferrets fed the information over central comms.

Factory workers scrambled for safety, but the workers were not the only ones milling about the complex. Dozens of Destineer soldiers ran for cover, and soon the turret fire of the Saskwatches was met with return fire from the Destineers.

"Ape Squad, *covering fire,*" Chase roared. "Get to the designated zones."

His Saskwatch lurched again as the driver traveled to the set destination, one of three main compressor chambers used for pipeline transport of the processed fluid. It skidded to a halt before the massive equipment, and Chase hopped from the back, raising his rifle.

Two Destineer soldiers were in close proximity, and Chase tapped both of them twice with slug rounds. They crumpled, exposing a large automated sentry gun behind them. The twin barrels of the turret swung towards him. He dove behind a boxy section of conduit, and from the corner of his eye, saw the enemy turret explode as his Ape Squad gunner obliterated it with shells.

Chase scrambled to his feet. The rest of his squad was kneeling at the edge of the compressor station.

"Cover me," said Chase, slapping one of his mates on the back before sprinting up a spiral stair case around the machinery. He reached the top, wincing as bullets chewed into the metal bars around him. He forced himself to concentrate, dropping his FAZA rifle to the floor and removing a pack from his back. He kneeled, opening a plastic cover on the outside to expose an electronic display. He set the explosive charge to detonate, set a timer, and hurled the explosive into the mouth of the machinery, where it was instantly sucked into the rotating teeth of the compressor inlet.

"Charges out, two minutes to detonation," he called, grabbing his rifle and sprinting back down the stairway, taking the steps two at a time.

He reached the rest of his squad. One of them caught a bullet in the neck as he arrived, and slouched to the floor.

"Man down," he called. "Ape Squad, get the wheels turning."

Chase grabbed his teammate, who clutched at his open wound, gasping for air as blood bubbled onto his chest. He heaved the wounded man onto his shoulder and staggered toward the Saskwatch before dumping him onto the rear bed.

The other two soldiers in Alpha squad were already on the ATV. One grabbed the injured soldier and attempted to dress his wounds with a field med kit. The other Alpha squad member grabbed Chase by the back of his collar and heaved him further onto the truck. They both collapsed to the vibrating metal deck.

"Alpha squad ready," yelled Chase. "Exit to rally point Green Tree."

The Saskwatch accelerated from the scene, its back tires drifting across the corrugated steel floor as it made a tight turn towards the entrance they came from.

"Bombs out," said the driver.

Oval pods dropped from the undersides of the three ATV's, each with a red light blinking on both ends.

The other two Saskwatches joined beside them as they raced from the refinery. As they bounced through the exit, Chase saw the lifeless bodies of his teammates go momentarily airborne in the rear beds of the adjacent ATVs.

The refinery faded into the distance as they drove across the barren perimeter. Several Destineer workers and soldiers ran from the twisted opening, trying to escape the destruction they knew was coming. The explosive charges detonated just as the ATV's reached the tree line.

Chase's vision was obscured by the jungle, but through the small pockets of light in between leaves, he saw the fireball balloon into the sky. The sound was deafening, and a shockwave rippled the greenery around them, whipping branches and tearing light plants from the top soil.

Chunks of metacrete and metal rained through the forest, and Chase shielded his face with his forearm, tensing as light debris clunked against their ATV.

He crawled to his wounded comrade. The man writhed on the bed of the truck. White bio foam leaked from the hole in his neck, stemming his blood loss, but the man's pain was plastered across his face.

"You're going to be okay Guerrero," he said, and patted the man on the chest. "We'll button you up when we reach base, hang with us a few more minutes."

He offered his hand to Guerrero, who clenched it tightly.

More explosions sounded in the distance as they made their way to base. Their sabotage had worked. The explosive charges they sent into the pipeline had carried downstream and ruptured the infrastructure. Their planned damage levels would register at one hundred percent.

Chase's squad had killed dozens of Destineers, and crippled a core refinery installation. Had he known Guerrero was a Destineer mole, loyal to their leader, Sid Dakota, he would have left him in the complex with the rest of the enemy to die.

SEVEN

Chase Grover – Half Human/Half Clone
On surface of Sylva – Slayer Hive

The ATV's reached Green Tree, an underground bunker system hidden below tall grass in an exposed meadow within the congested jungle terrain. Trees would normally take root in such an area, but slicers underground kept them from growing too large. They needed enough space to raise the two Bobcat aircraft from pads within the bunker should trouble arise.

"Green Tree this is Slim Rod, requesting access, security code *Miranda*."

"Welcome back sir," a voice replied. "Opening things up for you now."

A rectangular patch of grass sank downward, exposing a dark hole in the earth. The ATV's drove into the exposed holes, tilting as their tires rolled onto the ramp leading into the tunnels.

The Saskwatches turned into a parking bay, where a few technicians were waiting to service the machines and repair any damages. Three medics were waiting to tend to the wounded, and Chase began to gingerly lift Guerrero off the Saskwatch before it finished rolling to a stop.

"What caught his neck?" asked one of the medics, grabbing Guerrero under the armpits and sliding him toward a stretcher. "Slug or energy beam?"

"Slug," said Chase. "Rodgers patched him up with foam. His pulse is strong on my HUD."

"Thank you sir," said the medic, stabilizing Guerrero's neck to prevent any possible nerve damage. "We'll take him from here."

They ushered him out of the bay towards cots in a room down the tunnel. The third medic was tending to a leg wound suffered by one of the Bravo guys. It seemed like a minor graze.

The rest of Bravo and Charlie groups removed two bodies from the beds of the ATV's, and laid them side by side on the ground. One of the Charlie guys punched the metal back of the Saskwatch, sending a bang echoing in the low ceiling cement room. The other shook his head and grabbed a thin blanket from a stack of shelves against the wall, billowing it open and settling it over the deceased.

Two dead, two wounded. One of the dead was Brendyn, a Clone that had been living on Sylva before UCOM was established. He'd taken one in the head. The other was Small Fry, who was just a damned kid, twenty-three years old. He was so young his Program hadn't even started to cancel the aging process, which normally happened around thirty.

Chase cursed under his breath and grabbed a metal chair from against the wall, easing into it.

"Attention fellas," he said, removing a pack of cigarettes from his pocket and lighting one against a small circular hot plate on the side of his glove. "That was good work out there. It's a bummer what happened to Guerrero, but he'll pull through in no time. As for Brendyn and Small Fry," he swallowed a lump in his throat. "*Awaken Stars.*"

"*Awaken Stars,*" the rest of his units murmured. There was a moment of silence.

"We kicked some major ass out there today," said Chase. "That refinery was key to the Destineer pipeline, but we can't stop there. We have a lot more to go. Clean up and get something to eat, I'm going to wire *Bastion* to get our next marching orders, then we'll move out."

"Yes sir," the men said unanimously.

Some filtered from the room. One of the men, a Clone named Vasyl, knelt beside Brendyn and Small Fry a moment, saying a few prayers to the stars.

"You know smoking's bad for you."

Chase tore his eyes from Vasyl to find Rodgers beside him. Rodgers grabbed a second metal chair from the wall and sat next to him.

"I'm a hundred and fifty years old," said Chase. "If I die it will be from a Destineer bullet. My Program won't let these little guys kill me."

He offered one to Rodgers, sliding it from its plastic holder. Rodgers pouted his lips for a second, but decided the conditions warranted a smoke.

"Thank you sir," he said, flipping the cigarette into his mouth. He lit it on the heater plate from his own glove, a standard design meant for wilderness survival.

They sat in silence for a while, exhaling a light mist of smoke around them, air handlers sucking the room clean through vents in the ceiling. Chase observed the technicians as they worked on the Saskwatches.

One of the vehicles was leaking coolant onto the cement pad, and was the first to be tended to. One of the mechanics racked out the power section, sliding it from the nose of the ATV on guiderails. A Destineer mortar had punctured the cooling wall around the micro-fusion reactor chamber. The techs shut down the reactor to prevent an unwanted release of energy, and one of them carefully removed it from the vehicle using extended clamps. He placed it in a reinforced blast box, where it would cool eventually to room temperature and allow for rework.

The rest of the ATV's were in good condition, all things considered. There were a few scrapes and dings, nothing major. They'd made out well considering the size of the refinery they'd assaulted and the size of their squad.

"*SIGA*," said Rodgers, flicking his spent cigarette butt onto the ground. "Did a Human make the name, or a Clone?"

Chase frowned, spelling the words out from the acronym. *Sylvan Insurrectionist Guerilla Army.*

"I don't know," he said. "I was a baby when Sylva was taken over by the Slayers, and General Archyr started SIGA. He's a Clone. We'll have to ask Vasyl what the acronym is in Sylandrian."

Rodgers chuckled dryly. "If we can trick our Programs into stopping translation to English. Our Universal Translators work too well. We'll probably hear Vasyl say something like, 'the translation for Sylvan Insurrectionist Guerilla Army in Sylvandrian is *Sylvan Insurrectionist Guerilla Army*'."

Chase managed a weak smile. Rodgers was right. It was easy to forget that half of SIGA troops were speaking a different language at times because of the fluid translations performed by their Programs. The nano serum even tricked the brain into seeing different lip movements, making Clone speech not only sound, but *look* like English.

"Do you think our attacks are worth it?" said Rodgers, his smile vanishing. "The Destineers outnumber our population in *Bastion* more than a thousand to one. Even if we kill every single one of them, Dakota included, we still have the Slayers to deal with. I mean *Stars.* They built a fruxing Hive around Sylva. And for some damned reason they're giving Sid and his goons safe passage."

"I'm sure you don't need me to remind you what the Destineers are processing in those refineries," said Chase, narrowing his eyes on Rodgers. "With the number of plants going online, the amount of Firewater they're making could burn every underground tunnel on Sylva two times over."

"And we're just going to hide for eternity underground?" said Rodgers. "All we ever do is sabotage refineries and drillers. We should take the lift up now, while our forces are still strong. Attack them where it hurts and take control of the Hive that's towing this damned planet around."

"Easy lieutenant," said Chase. "That's General Archyr's decision. I take orders from him, and you take orders from me, end of story. Archyr's a good leader. He's kept us alive for a hundred and fifty years, hasn't he?"

"I suppose," said Rodgers. He turned his head towards Brendyn and Small Fry's bodies, frowned, and spit onto the ground. "SIGA follows his command, but the people follow *you*. You're Mack's son. If it wasn't for your father, the Slayers would've killed us all off before we could even form SIGA."

Chase winced at his father's name. He had no memory of his father, only video footage of his sacrifice to protect the Sylvan civilians, who had hidden in an emergency underground network. At the time it was called the *Shelter*. One of the hidden entrances had been stuck open, and Mack battled his way through invading Slayer ground troops in a Saskwatch. The last survivor of his squad, he'd detonated his warhead manually, martyring himself to save the thousands underground, sealing the open passage from the Slayers. Ground cameras had captured video footage of the heroic act, and Mack Grover was cemented as a holy savior. As the son of a savior, the civilians in their hidden underground city *Bastion*, rallied behind Chase. He never felt deserving of the admiration. He just took orders and did his job.

"I'm done with this conversation," said Chase. "What you're describing sounds like treason."

Rodgers sighed, but dropped the topic. "Do you think UCOM is still alive? I wonder if they were able to defend the Frontline. If things turned out there like they did here…"

He let the thought hang.

"UCOM is still strong back home," said Chase adamantly. "The Slayers are evil. They're murderous and bloodthirsty. Evil won't triumph over good, you can't convince me of that. We just need to hang on."

"Guerrero," said Rodgers loudly, standing from his chair. "Good to see you up and about. That was quick."

Chase turned to see Guerrero standing at the entrance to the bay. His wound had already been laser healed, purple and bruised, but clean. He wondered how long the soldier had been standing there.

"The slug missed my jugular," Guerrero said in a hoarse voice. "The doc patched me up quick. My neck meat will just be sore for a few weeks, that's all."

The man stared at his feet and fidgeted with his hands. He looked nervous.

"Something wrong soldier?" said Chase.

"No," said Guerrero. His eyes turned to Chase, then drifted back to the ground. "I'm going to get some rest, sir."

He turned and left the room. Chase craned his neck to follow Guerrero down the tunnel hallway, and frowned when he walked right past the barracks, and instead turned into the armory.

"Stay here," he said to Rodgers, standing from his chair. He entered the hallway, padding towards the loose curtains covering the entrance to the armory. He was about to slide the curtain open when he heard a hushed voice speaking from inside the room. Chase bent in to listen.

"*Yes sir, we're in an underground bunker five miles east of the refinery at coordinates 128, 320, 012. I took one in the neck but I'm fine...Affirmative...SIGA has two working Saskwatches and two Bobcats in storage, plus assorted light arms and explosives...Yes sir, Chase Grover is here...I'll see if I can sabotage the Bobcats before you arrive...*"

Chase tore open the curtain. Guerrero whipped around to face him, dropping the portable comm scanner to the floor, which cracked against the metal grating covering the cement.

"You fruxing *traitor,*" Chase hissed.

Guerrero froze, then turned to an ammo rack, clawing at a MGK rifle. Chase rushed towards him, lowering his shoulder, slamming into Guerrero's side. They scraped against the ammo rack. Dislodged rifles clattered to the floor.

"DESTINEER," Chase roared, grappling with the bucking man beneath him.

Guerrero elbowed him in the jaw, forcing him to roll to the side. The man wheezed, struggling to stand, snatching at the strap of a rifle.

Chase groped at his shin, grabbing the handle of a combat knife strapped to his boot.

Guerrero found purchase on a rifle and wheeled it towards Chase

Chase had already lunged towards him, knife raised high above his head. The rifle discharged but missed, and Chase plunged the knife into Guererro's neck. The man gasped for a split second before Chase turned the blade. He felt the edge stop against something hard, and he slashed forward, severing Guerrero's spine. The man went limp.

"Commander Grover, sir," Rodgers burst into the room and slid next to Chase, who had rolled off of Guerrero, panting from the recent scuffle. "What happened?"

"Guerrero," said Chase, gulping in a lungful of air. "He's a mole, I caught him radioing in our position."

"*Sir, Commander Chase sir,*" a new voice echoed from the hallway.

"In here," Chase called, his chest heaving. "Armory."

A group of SIGA soldiers piled in. One of them pushed his way to the front. It was Leering, his intelligence operator.

"Sir," said Leering. "I have multiple inbound land vehicles. Not of UCOM design, either a Slayer or Destineer convoy. They have heavy armor, probable air support. We need to leave *now.*"

EIGHT

Sid Dakota – Human Destineer
On surface of Sylva – Slayer Hive

Sid Dakota gripped his plasma rifle. His exoskeleton battle armor increased his available strength by a factor of ten, but his hands were still capable of handling light objects dexterously, or else his rifle would snap in two.

He bounced in the rear platform of a gunner hover craft, one of thousands of vehicles donated to him and the Destineers by the Slarebull. He had taken a leap of faith siding with the alien race, and convinced thousands of his disciples to do the same. They'd been rewarded for their loyalty. The Slarebull had outfitted them with weaponry, and he had been given a Hive mothership as an escort. The Hive was built around the old planet Sylva, a home planet for the Clone civilization.

They had waited patiently for 150 years after the Frontline Battle for the Pristine to arrive from Andromeda, and finally the Sylvan Hive had begun its voyage to meet the men from his holy visions. They were on their way to meet the Pristine as equals. As gods.

But the time for celebration was not yet upon him. Soldiers and civilians had entered an underground Sylvan tunnel network during the Frontline Battle, and were still loyal to UCOM.

SIGA, thought Sid, grinding his teeth.

The insufferable band of insurgents refused to ally with his Destineers, and must therefore be exterminated. He couldn't arrive at Primal

Snow to greet the Pristine with unholy sub-humans embedded underground in his Hive.

"Sir, I've lost contact with our mole."

Sid whipped his head to face the officer. Colorful images flashed across the visor of the officer's exoskeleton helmet as he tried to reestablish his communication link.

"Was he exposed?" Sid demanded.

"Impossible to say sir, the line cut out."

"What's our bearing?"

"Two clicks, we're right on top of them."

"I want everyone's triggers hair thin. Be cautious of an ambush. Radio our nearest elevator base for air support."

"Yes sir."

The officer relayed the command to the rest of the Destineer convoy driving beside them in assorted Slayer land vehicles.

Sid cursed himself for not scrambling Spider craft earlier. He had been traveling to inspect recent damage done to one of his refinery sites when the call came in from their mole. The timing was convenient. Chase Grover was within a stone's throw from the destroyed complex. If you were wearing augmented armor, that is.

They approached a break in the dense jungle, exposing a meadow of tall grass. Was SIGA laying in the reeds? It was too short to hide large vehicles. It was easy to see the bunker through the multispectral sensors in his skeleton. It glowed red with heat in solid blocks.

"They're using heat pads on the outside of the bunker to disguise its content," said Sid. "Spread around the perimeter. Don't leave them any exits. Watch the grass on top."

His vehicle stayed put, but the ten other vehicles, eight ATV hovercraft and two tanks, branched off to the left and right, forming a semicircle around the set coordinates.

"Do we have proximity readings on any exiting vehicle or air craft?" he said to his officer.

"None sir," said the officer. "They wouldn't be able to hide their heat signatures from us within ten miles. They're underground still."

Sid rose from the vehicle, leaning against the metal defense guard wrapped around the deck. His officer and the five soldiers accompanying them in the ATV rose as well, raising their rifles towards the center of the field. Unlike Sid and his officer, they lacked exoskeleton armor and wore generic tactical uniforms and helmets.

A yellow dot hovered in the middle of the tall grass, displayed on his HUD. The coordinates given to them by their mole sat above the marker.

128.320.012

He was in there. Chase Grover, the iconic warrior of SIGA was underneath that yellow dot. The man who for 130 years had caused him more headaches than he could count. Chase Grover was finally his.

"ATV's approach," said Sid through central communications. "Tanks hang at the perimeter for a defensive vantage point. Only fire cannons at airborne targets, we don't want any friendly fire."

As the ATV's inched towards the underground bunker, Sid wondered how they were going to get into the SIGA base. He would smother the top with Plasma discharge until it melted if it came to it.

It didn't come to plasma fire. Four men popped from the grass and raised shoulder mounted weapons at his vehicles.

"Contact," one of the soldiers shouted.

Before the Destineer finished his shout, blue light flashed from the SIGA weapons, and balls of energy exploded from the barrels. One of the shots hit Sid's vehicle.

He leaped from the bed, cartwheeling through the air as the energy blast tore into his ATV. His face slammed into the grass, smooshing into the damp soil beneath. Screams peppered the air as soldiers cooked from the extreme temperature of the assault. Sid growled and pushed himself up, fumbling with his rifle.

Mud caked his visor, and he crouched low while he wiped it clean. When it was finally clear enough to see, he whipped his rifle forward and tried to make sense of the chaos.

Blinding light stabbed his retinas. He switched to standard optics, overriding the glare from burning trucks and flares SIGA had dropped around the bunker. Everything behind the flares was as good as invisible.

"Fire at will," Sid ordered. "Fire inside the flares."

Through the pressurized sound of his team's plasma rounds, he heard the shrill whine of turbines firing, and past the flares could see the twin engines of rotating winged Bobcats chewing into the grass. Two aircraft rose from the ground, their exhaust igniting the grass. Orange flames licked past the glare from the dimming flares.

Sid fired in the general direction of the SIGA Bobcats, but with no success. The fuselage for the craft was resistant to laser, slug, and plasma fire. He sprinted towards the center of the field and leaped over the flares. For the first time, he could see the enemy clearly. Adrenaline made the ensuing events happen in slow motion.

Chase Grover stood twenty yards from him crouched before the opened side hangar of the closest Bobcat. Sid recognized his face easily from the mountains of intel his troops had gathered over the decades. He was kneeling, providing cover fire for his squad mates, the last of whom was climbing inside the craft. Chase trained his rifle on Sid and pulled the trigger.

Sid winced as two short bursts of slug fire punched into his chest.

The exoskeleton kept the bullets from entering his skin, and he raised his own rifle, firing at Chase.

One of the plasma rounds hit the ground and splattered onto Chase's calf as his Bobcat took off into the air, tilting sharply towards the ground as the pilot pulled them skyward. Sid fired until his rifle overheated, but the rounds hit the thick bottom hull of the Bobcat, forming pink circles of heat before dissipating.

No. No-no-no-no-no.

Chase was getting away.

"*Fire the tanks,*" he screamed into the comm line.

The tank operators fired seconds later, not because of their new command, but because it had taken them that long to lock their tracking devices on the exhaust jets, which had been masked by the hot flares on the ground.

Both Bobcats dropped artillery-defense decoys behind them to stop the seeker missiles from contact. One of the bursts destroyed a missile, protecting the Bobcat, but the other didn't. The missile tore straight through the underbelly of the craft, blowing it out of the sky in fiery balls of twisted metal.

It was the wrong Bobcat. Sid growled as he watched the remaining air vehicle disappear into a point in the purple sky.

He stormed toward a group of Destineer soldiers standing in the grass. The grass seemed to moan as the wounded writhed beneath the meadow's wispy blades. They would be tended to soon enough. He grabbed one of the uninjured soldiers by the collar and pulled the man's face inches from his own.

"Where the hell is my air support?" he snarled. "Grover's getting away."

"I don't know sir," the man stammered. "I'll need to use an ATV to contact base."

"Do it *now,"* he said, releasing the man's collar. "Tell them we have a SIGA Bobcat traveling from these coordinates."

"Yes sir," the soldier said, sprinting to one of the ATV's that hadn't been destroyed by the sneak attack.

"All of you, with me," said Sid, pointing at a group of fifteen soldiers huddled next to a tank.

"Sir, the wounded..."

"Tend to them," Sid conceded, indicating five of his squad. "The rest of you with me. Weapons up."

He stalked to the center of the meadow. A wide metacrete pad was raised to the surface. It was the platform the Bobcats had launched from. Fortunately, there was a manual control panel sticking from the surface. One of the buttons was an upside down triangle labeled *DWN*. Sid punched it with a knuckle.

The pad hummed and descended below the grass. The rest of his soldiers raised their rifles around him. The ones with slug rifles reloaded their ammo clips in a series of clacks.

Sid stormed the barracks as soon as the lift touched down, wary of hidden enemies. He was leader of the Destineers, but instead of commanding them from the safety of the base, he preferred to lead by example. He was a holy warrior. He was also the only UCOM Titan-trained Destineer on Sylva. He hadn't completed the training – the Pristine had called to him before he'd made the mistake of signing his life over to UCOM. But he'd picked up elite combat skills for ten years before hijacking a Jaguar destroyer and fleeing Olympus, forming the Destineer faith a year later.

The control room was a fractured mess of splintered plastic and metal. They'd destroyed the computers and recon instruments before they left. In the armory he found a corpse, the head nearly severed from the body. He supposed it could have been his inside mole, he'd never personally met the man. Sid shook his head. If his mole hadn't been so incompetent, perhaps he'd still be alive. And perhaps Chase would be dead.

He passed a room with a few stacks of empty cots, and at the end of the hall, a wide bay with three Saskwatch ATV's parked inside. Sheets covered another two corpses.

"Search the place," he commanded the soldiers behind him. "Try to find encryption keys, attack plans, anything that may be valuable to us. If you find the location to Bastion, you'll be promoted to lead disciple."

"Yes sir," the soldiers said, almost sprinting into various rooms in the bunker. Being a lead disciple was the greatest honor bestowed in his Destineer religion.

"*Father Dakota,*" a voice called from the opening above. "Sir, I have word from our air ships. They have a track on the SIGA Bobcat.

Sid ran to the end of the tunnel and punched the controls of the wide lift. He waited impatiently for the platform to reach upper ground level, then with ten feet left to go, leaped skyward and out of the bunker. A soldier squeezed his eyes shut as he landed before him, his heavy exoskeleton sinking into the soft mud.

"Where?" Sid demanded. "Where are they?"

"They went underground, sir. Into the base of a rocky cliff. The report is that the entrance was much wider than normal remote bunkers such as this one. We think we might have found Bastion."

Sid licked his lips. He would need to confirm this with base, but if his private was correct, he would finally know where on Sylva to pump the last of his Firewater.

SIGA would be finished.

NINE

Eve – Clone
Aboard Night Eagle *Midnight* – Deep space Charlie sector

"How's that turnstile coming along Chip?" Eve called from her Night Eagle stealth craft, *Midnight.*

Eve squinted at the portal floating before them, designated as local Portal 2. Local Portal 1 hung behind them in the distance, where they'd come from.

Portal 2 looked like nothing more than a floating red sphere, but it wasn't the shape of the portal that had her on edge. It was the color.

"Red is dead, green is clean," Eve whispered to herself. *"Black or yellow goes to either fellow."*

The security turnstile for Portal 2 was under Slayer control, turning the color of the spherical portal red. Portal 1 had been black, blending in with the darkness of space. An unlit portal was neutral, meaning nobody controlled the security turnstile, and the portal was open to all traffic. Eve's stealth unit had since activated security on Portal 1, and it glowed green. Portal 1 had been black, but Portal 2 was red.

Why did the Slayers secure one portal and not the other?

Had Portal 1 simply glitched and shut down turnstile security?

The turnstile's encryption protocols on Portal 2 allowed for access of Slayer ships, but not UCOM ones. If a normal UCOM ship tried to enter a red portal, it would pass right through the glowing sphere and out the other side, instead of following the wormhole pathway to its linked destination light years away.

But Eve's Night Eagle wasn't normal, it was of special design, and could pass through both green *and* red portals. But the process would consume a lot of energy, and leave her vulnerable when she appeared on the other side. The same went for the 25 other Night Eagles in *Vagabond,* her stealth squadron, scattered in formation around Portal 2.

After fifteen seconds, Amy Chip, her AI scout soldier answered her call. "Eve, the turnstile's clear from Slay-I. There's a damaged warp cell on the hardware, so my patch is taking a little longer than normal. Give me fifteen minutes and I'll have this thing green."

"Copy that," said Eve. She rose from her cockpit and walked the short distance to the intelligence stations in the rear bridge, where her two crewmen sat. "Keyv, send a timer for fifteen minutes out to the rest of *Vagabond* with orders to keep active spacnar engaged until Amy gets the portal green."

"Aye," said Keyv, one of her Human crew. He leaned over his control station to relay her orders to the rest of the Night Eagles.

"What's the dust storm telling you Axel?" she said, turning to the Titan warrior sitting at the station opposite from Keyv.

"Compiling the data now," said Axel, a Wolf-born Titan, and the only Titan in her stealth squadron. He sifted through the spacnar readings being fed to *Midnight* by the rest of *Vagabond.*

There were two types of space navigation and ranging, passive and active.

With passive spacnar, instruments on the ship would scrutinize the surrounding vacuum for anomalies such as heat trails, magnetic fields, gravity wakes, or ordinary disturbances in the visible light spectrum. Passive spacnar didn't alert your presence to the enemy, but it wasn't always able to detect hidden stealth craft, which were designed to vanish like ghosts and self-contain most signatures.

Active spacnar used drones to detect enemies by physical contact. Before the Frontline Battle, UCOM used standard Raven drones to accomplish this, which extended probes in a wide net, hoping to bump into something unexpected. The Ravens were relatively clunky and easy to spot. After the Frontline Battle, UCOM had borrowed the Slayer design for active spacnar, an upgrade to their old Raven design. Now Eve's active spacnar sent a swarm of nano-bots into the surrounding vacuum, called a *dust storm*. The nano-bots were difficult to detect, and could return 3D renderings of the objects they made contact with, instead of a digital feedback signal stating *yes* for enemies nearby, or *no* the coast is clear.

The Intellects had gifted Eve's stealth squadron with this new spacnar technology almost 150 years ago, a year after the Frontline Battle. She'd barely had time to grieve for her fallen home planet of Sylva before Eminence Woods ordered her to lead a team deep into Slayer territory. With both sides required to travel at conventional speeds between the 125 light year barrier between the Frontline and the Inner Ring, Woods wanted UCOM to find the Slayers, and not the other way around.

"Dust storm's clean," said Axel, wheeling around in his floating chair. "Clean just like the last two hundred portals we checked."

"Are the Slayers even in the Milky Way anymore?" said Keyv. "We would've bumped into one of their ships by now, wouldn't we? Maybe they gave up and went home."

"The Slayers don't have a home," said Eve. "That's why they go galaxy to galaxy, sucking their resources dry. We've only been through Charlie sector so far. For all we know, they've consolidated forces in Alpha or Bravo."

"I say we go into Bravo now," said Axel. He jumped from his seat and threw a few jabs though the air, his tall, mechanical body whirring slightly as his fists blurred in front of him. "I haven't seen any action in a century and a half. Do you know what that kind of thing does to a Titan?

I'm bored out of my *mind.*" He thunked a metal knuckle against the top of his skull with a *clank.* "At least you two got to cryo-sleep for a hundred fifty years on our way out. I had to swap stories with Amy Chip the whole time. Do you know how hard it is to beat an AI at chess?"

"A hundred forty-nine years," said Keyv with a smirk, turning back to his station.

"Huh?" said Axel, the emotional features on his android body forming a puzzled grin.

Keyv spun back around after checking his metrics. "A hundred forty-nine years," he repeated. "Me and Eve were only in cryo for a hundred forty-nine years, not a hundred fifty."

Axel laughed, shaking his head and raising his hands. He opened his mouth, then chuckled again and sat back down at his station.

"You'll get your wish Axel," said Eve, scanning the constant stream of data filtering through the large hologram floating above the floor at the center of the rear bridge. "After this portal we're going to head towards Bravo. It's in the preloaded route Stew uplinked into our navigation systems. I'm sorry you had to wait so long by yourself, but at least now you're good at chess."

"*Portal's green,*" said Keyv, cutting into the conversation, tapping his fingers against the touch controls at his station.

Eve slipped back into her cockpit. "Eve to Chip, come on back home, I'm lowering digital barriers to *Midnight.*"

She peered through the windshield to the now green Portal 2.

"Aye Eve," said Amy. "I picked up some Slayer vessels in my scans of the other side, including a Hive mothership. Might want to use caution with this one. They looked abandoned but I don't have the equipment to run thermal scans. Coming back now."

Eve turned to face the rear bridge. The holographic display of the portal disappeared to allow room for Amy's avatar. Amy appeared in a shower of pink points of light, which drifted to the floor around her before fading. The Human-born AI was dressed in tight black coveralls, her hair tied in a neat ponytail.

Amy nodded to Axel and Keyv, then turned to the cockpit to face Eve. She vanished from the rear bridge and reappeared on the command interface next to the pilot controls. In the rear bridge she had been life sized, standing just over five feet tall. On the interface in the cockpit, she was miniaturized, standing at twelve inches atop the sleek dash.

"Welcome back Amy," said Eve, sitting upright to address the AI before her. "Tell me about the Slayer ships. Do you have any scan data to upload?"

"Yes ma'am," said Amy. She raised her hand, summoning a glowing sphere of blue light. "Uploading data to *Vagabond* servers. The ships didn't look active, but they had strange markings on them, almost like graffiti." The dash rippled as Amy tossed the sphere onto it, uploading data to the ship's computers.

Eve studied the scan data that began to appear in separate holograms on the opposite side of her command interface. Amy was right. The ships had sharply angled designs covering their hulls, reminiscent of ancient tribal war paint. The designs didn't correlate with any of the Slayer intel given to her back home before their voyage back across the Frontline.

"Keyv, Axel," she called. "Are you two getting this?"

"Aye," said Axel. "Consolidating the report now."

"I want full analysis on potential weapons capabilities of the scanned enemy ships. Send class sizes, coordinates, energy ratings, and maneuverability to the rest of *Vagabond.* Prepare our squadron for portal entry. If there's active Slayers on the other side of that thing, they'll know we're coming plain as day. Portals don't change color out of nowhere."

Axel and Keyv set to work, organizing Amy's brief scans into actionable categories to prepare a stealth entry to the starspace on the other side of the portal.

"Send a team of Ravens through," she said to Amy. "I want more information on those ships."

Amy nodded and disappeared from the console, entering digital space to focus on sending Ravens through the newly opened portal.

"Eve to *Vagabond,*" she signaled to the rest of her stealth fleet. "Keep stealth shields up and at one hundred percent capacity. Schedule entry vectors into the portal, and stand by in standard formation five thousand meters from the surface. If the Ravens come back empty handed, we're not wasting any time moving through."

Green indicator lights filled her dash as the captains of the various Night Eagles in *Vagabond* confirmed their orders. Eve advanced the throttle lightly, guiding *Midnight* towards the portal.

Time was of the essence, and in full stealth mode, her Night Eagle could only run at a fraction of top speed. Full stealth required all waste energy to be contained to avoid detection. The excess energy was fed into a heat box, essentially a fancy battery. Too much acceleration from the ship's thrusters would cause the heat box to experience catastrophic failure and rupture the outside hull.

This wasn't the first portal Eve had commandeered, not by a wide margin. But no amount of experience eased the nervous feeling of inching toward a commandeered portal, wondering if enemies had noted the change on the other side, and prepared a collection of missiles to fire once her scouts passed through.

Ravens began to return with detailed scans of the Slayer ships on the other side of the portal.

"The ships aren't deserted," said Amy seconds after the first Raven returned. The petite AI reappeared on the command interface. "The Hive is giving off massive amounts of heat, and I spot hundreds of temp trails. Our Ravens haven't found them yet, but *a lot* of Yellowjacket and Wasp-class ships traveled that starspace not too long ago, within twelve hours would be my guess."

Eve flicked through the heat scans, which now covered the interactive touch surface of her console. Still warm from ship exhaust hours ago, the temp trails twisted around the Slayer Hive like strands of spaghetti. The Slayer Mothership was dark, as was the surface of the planet it had in tow.

"Any Slay-I present in the turnstile?" said Eve.

Slayers commandeered digital security turnstiles the same way UCOM did, with AI.

"None," said Amy. "My pings return nothing except local turnstile VR and encryption software. I can go back in for a closer look if you'd like."

"Not yet," said Eve.

Vagabond was built for stealth, and had limited firepower. The Hive alone could destroy them easily. Add the other ships on Amy's scans, and it would be a quick slaughter.

"*We have energy disturbances from the rear portal,*" Keyv shot from his station in the rear bridge. "My pings are registering as positive for AI. Amy, a little help?"

Amy turned to face the aft section of *Midnight*. Her eyes glowed as she accessed external cameras on the hull. Then without warning she disappeared, leaving to enter the turnstile for Portal 1. She returned almost instantly.

"We have Slay-I in the rear portal," she gasped. "I don't have a firm head count but there were at least ten. I can't overpower them all. They're commandeering the turnstile."

Amy's chest heaved, as if she were out of breath, a curious situation for an AI with no biological lungs.

"The Slay-I advanced to Portal Two," said Keyv, referring to the portal Amy had recently liberated. "I estimate three minutes until they commandeer."

Eve flipped through her external cameras, forcing herself to control the panic rising in her core. She hadn't seen an enemy ship in over 150 years. The Slayers were attacking both local portals with AI, and if they commandeered both before they could escape, they would be cornered like rats.

Her options were not good.

Portal 1 would lead straight into the group of Slayers who had sent ten Slay-I soldiers into the turnstile. She didn't have any bearings on their fleet size.

Portal 2 would lead into the Slayer ships with the strange tribal markings. They weren't fully energized or battle ready, but they had a Hive, the most powerful ship in the Slayer armada.

"Eve to *Vagabond,* standby for visual check."

She took a deep breath, and focused on the video images stretched across her control interface. Portal 2 was solid green. She panned to the aft cameras and zoomed into Portal 1. Its green hue flickered for a few seconds, then turned solid red.

"Portal One commandeered," cried Amy, "Portal Two weakening near critical levels."

Her holographic avatar brought up a 3D rendering in the rear bridge. It was a replication of the virtual reality interface of the turnstile on Portal 2. Eleven Slarebull AI were viciously attacking a metal cage at the center of the VR platform. A golden key floated in a slow spin inside the cage, whose thick bars had begun to crack beneath blows from the Slay-I's clubbed tails.

Eve knew the image was not real. It was a three dimensional interpretation of a digital AI reality. The golden key was the turnstile encryption key. The metal cage was the firewall protecting the password. The Slay-I were essentially hacking into the turnstile for Portal 2 in an attempt to commandeer the security device. But AI saw digital software as vivid imagery, and through Amy's hologram, so did Eve.

"*Vagabond,* forward through Portal 2," Eve cried, cringing as cracks propagated along the virtual cage's bars. "Full thrust, ignore stealth procedures."

She slammed on her thrusters before her sentence was complete. *Midnight* lurched, pressing her momentarily into the back of her seat before acc-killers in her Program canceled the G-force effects of her rapid acceleration.

Her ship sped towards Portal 2, looming larger before them as they approached. It was still green, but Eve's eyes were playing tricks on her, fooling her into thinking it was growing red splotches.

"*Bogeys* inbound," Axel called. "Two Wasps entered through Portal 1, add one Wasp, add one Mantis. We have a steady stream of Slayer vessels inbound, largest class size, *Mantis.*"

"Passing," said Eve, not even caring to glance through the aft cameras at the Slayer ships pouring through Portal 1. Green light swathed the inside of her ship as she passed through the portal, traveling 23.1 light years in seconds.

Eve fought against the dizzy feeling of a portal jump. Jumping portals had no physical effect on biological bodies passing through, but the sudden change in scenery, namely the billions of stars in the sky, could be disorientating, and Eve had forgotten to close her eyes. She forced down a brief wave of nausea.

"Eve to *Vagabond*, enter full stealth, fan the perimeter in a shell formation and get the hell away from the Hive ship."

She pulled her thrusters hard right, assuming her position at the top of the curved shell formation, moving as fast as her heat box would allow under stealth conditions.

"Portal 2 commandeered," said Amy, as the portal they'd just traveled through turned red. "We're trapped here." She appeared on Eve's dash in miniature form. "Would you like me to try to commandeer any of the new local portals?"

Amy pointed through the canopy at a bank of five portals glowing in the distance. They were all red.

"Hold off on that," Eve whispered. She knew that no sounds would be able to penetrate the vacuum of space, but it was natural to speak in a hushed voice when in stealth mode, especially if enemies were nearby. "We don't want to alert the new guys of our presence any more than we already have."

"New bogeys coming in through Portal 2," said Axel. "Renaming to Portal 1. Assigning markers to all detected vehicles."

Eve rotated *Midnight* toward the portal to find four Slayer fast-attack Wasp fighters streaking toward the inert Slayer ships. ID pins hovered above the Wasps, small numbers glowing above them on *Midnight's* HUD display. A spacnar display activated on the control interface, showing an overall logistics view of local starspace. Slayer ships were depicted as red dots, with her hidden *Vagabond* squadron depicted as green dots, drifting above the dash in a scaled version of fleet strength and position.

"Eve to Vagabond. Group One divert twenty percent energy to rail cannons. Dedicate one crewman to a gunner station. Sit tight and fire on my mark, or if contested or discovered. Shift energy to weapons as needed. Group Two, enter full stealth mode and release a dust storm. Feed data to central servers."

She didn't need active spacnar to detect the Wasps, she could do that with the naked eye. She was worried about Slayer Moths, the enemy version of a stealth ship.

"The fleet's growing," said Keyv. "We're getting some larger ships coming in. Two Mantis craft, and..." Keyv gulped. "I have eyes on a Hornet. Eve, should I arm the nukes?"

"Don't arm the nukes," said Eve. "Exposed radiation will blow our cover straight to stars."

Her squadron of Night Eagles was invisible to the Slayers, but looking through the HUD integrated into *Midnight's* canopy, she could see the rest of the UCOM stealth ships clearly, superimposed in augmented fashion. They formed a wide arc above the steady stream of Wasps filtering toward the enormous Hive craft below.

A Hornet heavy-destroyer finished passing through the portal. Its green thrusters flared as it accelerated to catch up with its escort. The Hive continued to hang dormant, no visible light emanating from the hull. The mothership's support rods weren't energized to stabilize tension, causing its planet in tow to drift loosely against its support cables.

"*New bogeys,*" Axel cried. "Not originating from the portal. Confirmed as Moth class, they just dropped shields, I count thirty-two stealth craft. The Moths are energizing cannons, bearings five thousand meters and closing. Permission to fire requested from all twenty-four of our birds."

Eve whirled in her seat to look at the rear bridge hologram, which displayed the newly discovered Moth vessels. The vessels had the same ancient tribal markings as the Hive. They flew in a direct line towards her squadron.

The gig was up. They would need to enter a dogfight. Before she could give the order to attack, the Moths glowed brightly and fired a salvo of nuclear tipped missiles.

TEN

Eve – Clone
Aboard Night Eagle *Midnight* – Deep space Charlie sector

"Incoming," Keyv shouted from the rear bridge.

A solid wall of rockets streaked towards *Midnight.* Eve yanked hard on the yolk, banking her Night Eagle vertically away from the incoming projectiles.

"How many are locked onto *Midnight?"* said Eve, gritting her teeth as she pulled away from the missiles.

"None," said Keyv.

Baffled, Eve turned around to give him a quick glance. She eased on the thrusters. "No missile locks on our ship?"

Keyv squinted at his screen. "That's affirmative. And not just for *Midnight.* None of *Vagabond* was targeted."

The missiles had carried past the UCOM squadron, and now were only visible by their blue thrusters. The Slayer Moths with the tribal markings zipped past them, streaking towards the Slayer fleet, which had finished passing through Portal 1. She gasped when she realized what the Slayer warheads were aimed at.

The Slayer Hornet managed to charge most of its energy shields before the first warhead struck, lighting the heavy-destroyer a dazzling green as its lattice mesh of laser beams powered on. The first few missiles were nullified by these defenses, but the subsequent pounding of the hundreds of explosives caused square patches of the destroyer's energy shields to fail.

Many of the missiles changed their trajectory, hunting for the vulnerable patches in the hull of the Hornet, and when they connected, a gaping hole opened in the thick sidewalls. Explosions peppered the twisted metal, and debris shot from the inside of the damaged ship as Slayer soldiers and their equipment were sucked into the vacuum of space.

The Slayer Moths with the tribal markings engaged their active camo, disappearing from view.

"Repeat, permission to fire requested," said Axel from the gunnery station. His shoulders were harnessed inside the weapons controls, allowing for ergonomic efficiency while selecting enemy targets.

"Denied," said Eve, still trying to comprehend what she'd just witnessed. Slayers attacking other Slayers. Were they witnessing a civil war? "The Slayer ships with tribal patterns might be friendly, do not fire upon them. Target the unmarked Slayer ships that entered through Portal 1."

"Aye," said Axel, who relayed the orders to the rest of *Vagabond.*

"More bogeys spotted," called Keyv. "Movement from behind the Hive, looks like a combination of Wasps and Yellowjackets. New energy readings, I have a lot of new heat. *The Hive is powering on.*"

Eve froze, her eyes glued to the spectacle unraveling beneath her. The invading Slayers had formed defensive formations after the missile attack. A quick glance at her console told her the total strength of the fleet stood at ninety-seven ships, including attack fighters.

All the ships with lattice shields had them energized, and the entire fleet glowed a strong green save for the shieldless Wasps. The side of the Hornet flashed brightly as it unleashed a volley of its own projectiles, this time not nuclear warheads but large-mass slugs from its rail cannons. *Midnight's* sensors told her the destination of the slug volley was at the stern of the Hive.

A wave of tribal marked Slayers poured from behind the surface of the Hive's planet, and a dogfight erupted between the opposing Slayer forces. Soon Eve's face flickered under the light of countless large explosions.

The local starspace became much brighter as the Hive energized. Thrusters on the thick mechanical arms cradling its planet licked the starry background with blue jets. Its lattice shields kicked on, powerful enough to give the battlefield an eerie green glow. The slugs fired from the Hornet's rail cannons impacted the Hive and caused part of its shielding to dim, but the effects on the titanic ship seemed negligible.

"I have energy in close proximity that's unaccounted for," Keyv called "Bearing one hundred yards. *Shit.* We've been touched by a Slayer dust storm."

Eve snapped her focus away from the ensuing battle and towards her controls. The Slayers had discovered them with active spacnar. Before she finished processing the data from Keyv's station, three Moth's appeared four kilometers away. The enlarged images in her holograms showed the stealth ships to lack tribal markings. The ships loosed a sling of tracking missiles at several *Vagabond* Night Eagles and corkscrewed away, engaging their active camo as they did so.

"Evade," Eve shouted over central comms.

She guided *Midnight* instinctively into an evasive maneuver, zipping past two of the missiles by a narrow margin. The missiles turned in a wide arc to follow her.

The rest of her squadron did the same. Several ships were targeted, forcing them to lower their stealth shields to evade the incoming seeker missiles.

"Eve to *Vagabond*, all Night Eagles, scramble your jets and lose the stealth. Permission to fire at all Slayer non-marked targets."

With their stealth cover blown, they were forced to join the skirmish below.

"The missiles are gaining on us," said Keyv. "I have three locks, deploying flares."

Three sharp thumps reverberated through the hull as Keyv ejected hot shards of metal behind them. She jinked hard right to avoid two Wasp fighters, thumbing her nose guns by reflex. One of her laser charges bit into the hull of the first passing craft. Through the corner of her eye, she saw gunner rounds tear the second passing fighter to ribbons as Axel chewed into the ship from his station.

"That felt good," Axel whooped.

Eve didn't share his excitement. Unlike Axel, whose mechanical body was immune to the harshness of space, she would die a painful death if one of the missiles tore a hole in their hull and sucked her into the vacuum.

"One missile deflected," said Keyv. "We still have two after us."

She grunted and urged her ship to travel faster. Sweat beaded around the corners of her eyes, and she rapidly blinked it away.

"Eve to *Vagabond, Midnight* is being forced into the fray. Group as close as possible and make a tight pass around the Slayer Hive. Reactivate camo on the other side."

They made a tight corkscrew and she threaded their ship through a maelstrom of debris as two tribally marked Wasps destroyed an invading Mantis. The Hive planet loomed large before them, and her indicators warned of the increased gravitational effects of the celestial body.

Axel shot a steady stream of cover fire from his gunnery station. The precision of his assault matched the expectations of a Titan warrior, and Slayer Wasps folded quickly under the combined laser, slug, and missile fire. They wouldn't be able to keep it up much longer. Axel had just fired their last missile.

Eve weaved through the increasingly thick cloud of debris, now at the heart of the skirmish. She twisted sharply around larger chunks of metal, hoping for the missiles to catch them in her wake and detonate. The seeker missile threaded through the debris behind her flawlessly. She had lost speed in her maneuvering, and the missiles were gaining behind them.

"They're right on our ass," shouted Keyv. "Impact in ten seconds."

The Hive planet was now so large it dwarfed Eve's vision. The canopy began to glow orange as they entered the atmosphere.

In a desperation move, Eve punched the release for the heat box. *Midnight* jolted as the heavy block of captured energy rocketed from the bottom of the hull. Both missiles swerved to attack the heat box and impacted it immediately. The explosion rocked against the aft hull of *Midnight,* forcing them into a rough tumble.

Warning alarms blared throughout the cockpit and rear bridge as the ship alerted them to critical damage. Eve managed to correct their spin, righting the vessel so it pointed forward, but they had entered the atmosphere past the point of return.

A Night Eagle's thrusters were not designed to operate in atmospheric, high gravity conditions. They were going to have to land on the surface of the Hive planet as best they could.

"*Mayday, mayday,*" Keyv cried over central comms. "*Midnight* is falling through the Hive atmosphere, we're going to crash land on the surface."

Eve struggled with the ship's controls, the yolk shuddering hard in her hands. The floor bucked as thick air clawed against the hull.

She moaned as both engines shut down. The holograms on the dash blinked out as they suffered a momentary loss of control power, then flickered back on. A new hologram appeared on the dash. It was the avatar of Amy Chip, their squadron AI.

"I'm analyzing your trajectory," she said, her eyes locked on Eve's. "Based on my ground scans, you're going have a pretty rough landing. I'm adjusting your hydrogen scoops to minimize your angle of impact. I'll try to put you down on a grassy slope."

"Impact in twenty thousand feet," Keyv called from the back. "Eve, I think we should spray foam in here."

"I'm not going to be able to stay with you to the end," said Amy. "*Midnight's* computer probably won't survive, so I need to upload back to a *Vagabond* ship in space. I'll send a search party when the battle above clears up. The tribally marked Slayers are going to win this one, they're sweeping things up in orbit now."

Clouds whisked around the canopy, opening to reveal terrain. Rivers snaked through rolling hills of grass. In the distance, a mountain range poked against the horizon. She turned to the rear bridge.

Axel had left the gunnery station and taken his usual spot at his intelligence station. His blue eyes were turned upward. The Titan's face was synthetic, but his emotions were clear. The warrior was tortured with the knowledge that he would survive the crash, but that his biological crewmate's chances were slim. Keyv stared back at her silently, his face white and grave.

"Don't send a search party," said Eve, turning back to Amy. "The other Night Eagles will crash land just like us. They can't fly in this atmosphere." She swallowed down the lump forming in her throat. "Take good care of *Vagabond*."

Amy frowned. As the third highest ranking officer behind Eve and Keyv, she would assume control upon their death. "Aye ma'am."

Eve drew a shaky breath. "Go on, scram. If you wait any longer you might not be able to upload in time."

Amy blinked a few times, then shook the confusion away. "Yes ma'am. But we're not leaving you behind. I'm going to assume command of *Fog* as my primary ship until we figure out how to get you off this rock. I'll hijack Slayer ships if I have to." She looked painfully at Eve, then vanished from the console.

The hills were now close enough for Eve to make out buildings studding the grassy slopes. They were sleek and blue, and half embedded under the dirt. She could see the white foam from the river breaking around large exposed rocks.

She closed her eyes and pictured Keyv's face. She pictured their first kiss, 150 years ago in an old Panther stealth ship, leaving the ravaged remains of her Clone home planet of Sylva. She remembered holding his hand as they entered cryo sleep, and dreaming of him during her prolonged slumber. She didn't have the courage to turn around and face him again, and began to sob as *Midnight* predicted their impact and extended additional security harnesses around her legs and chest.

"*Eve,*" said a soft voice behind her ear.

She turned against her harness to find Keyv stumble in the co-pilot seat, slamming hard into the dash before struggling into the contour of the chair. Straps slithered from the back of the chair to wrap around his body. He reached a hand out and grabbed her pinky, pulling her hand towards him.

An artificial voice called to them.

Thirty seconds to impact.

"We're going to make it through this," said Keyv, rubbing his thumb over the top of her hand. "Remember the Frontline? We've had worse odds before."

Eve's lips trembled as she stared into Keyv's eyes. They were strong and fearless. They were the same eyes she fell in love with 150 years ago. She blinked twice and a well of tears streamed down her cheeks.

They impacted the ground before she could respond. Eve didn't see the ground rushing towards them in the final seconds of impact. She was trying to force words from her frozen lips, she was trying to tell Keyv she loved him, how she'd always loved him.

A brief squeal of metal ripped through the cabin as their hull crunched against the downward hill.

Eve blacked out as her Program shut down core functions in an effort to preserve her life against the rapid deceleration of impact.

ELEVEN

Eve – Clone
Crash landed on Slayer Hive planet

Eve clawed the metal toe of her climbing boots into the thick ice of the mountainside. She found a firm purchase and pushed herself a few feet upwards, hammering her pick into the ice above. Stiff winds sliced the frozen air, chilling her cheeks through her protective mask.

"Come on Eve, you're almost there, one more step."

She dug her other foot into the ice, grunting as she pushed herself up. A strong hand grasped her forearm, and she dropped her pick against its wrist strap to grasp back, forming a solid arm lock. She was heaved upward, and fell to her knees onto much flatter terrain above the ledge. Her legs quivered and she lay on her side. The hike had been long and steep, and her muscles ached.

Keyv kneeled next to her.

He reached to her waist and clipped a safety line to her belt. They were at a high elevation, the highest point on the Human planet of Earth. An accidental tumble would mean certain death.

"We're almost there," said Keyv, pulling down his facemask to prevent his words from muffling. "Twenty more yards and you'll be at the top of Mt. Everest."

Pain seemed to leave her legs, and she grinned widely as Keyv helped her to her feet. Back aboard *Darkness*, her old Panther craft, they'd pondered where in the galaxy they would like to visit one day. Her choice, the ocean desert of Blythria, was no longer an option. It was located on her home planet Sylva, and had been taken by the Slayers beyond the Frontline. Instead, she found solace in visiting Keyv's choice from his home planet Earth, the top of Mt. Everest.

They pressed onward, pushing through snowdrifts that reached the middle of Eve's thighs. She squinted as the sun exposed itself from behind the opposite side of the mountain. They'd reached the top, and without help from a hover cart. The view was breathtaking.

The sky was an extreme blue, contrasted sharply against the snowy mountain range sprawled around them. The peaks grouped together, and looked to Eve like molars of a giant dog. Clouds bunched against the sides of distant mountains like balls of cotton.

She was on top of the world.

Her Clone world had been decimated by the Slayers. As a Clone she looked identical to a Human, and gazing at the elegant mountains around her with Keyv, she felt like she could call Earth home.

A warm hand brushed against her cheek, and she turned to find Keyv leaning towards her. His goggles were up, and his eyes matched the clear sky behind him. She grinned as he pulled her facemask down to her neck.

They kissed, and the peak of Everest seemed to vanish. It felt like she was floating in the air, in the lofty heavens of Earth, an angel in paradise. The kiss lasted only a few seconds, but to Eve it felt like a lifetime. She gasped as Keyv pulled away, keeping her eyes closed for a few seconds before opening them to him.

"How does Mt. Everest stack up to Blythria?" Keyv asked.

"I…Oh Keyv," Eve whispered. "It's beautiful. I feel like I'm in a dream."

Keyv flashed his loopy grin that Eve was so fond of. Well you're going to have to wake up soon, we need to hike back down."

Eve sighed, leaning to wrap both arms around Keyv's waist. During the Frontline battle, she had the constant fear of death looming over her. As she rubbed her cheek against Keyv's jacket, drinking in the natural beauty of Earth, she felt happier than she ever had.

She considered pinching herself. With so much death throughout the galaxy, she must be dreaming. If this was a dream, she hoped she'd never wake up.

λλλ

"Wake up...Eve you need to wake up."

She didn't want to leave Mt. Everest. She wanted to stay with Keyv.

"Eve wake up. WAKE UP."

Her eyes scraped open. Particle foam covered her body, and the walls of *Midnight* to prevent fires from catching due to reactor damage. She hung limply in the straps of her seat. A light breeze fluffed the hair off her face, and she looked up to find a jagged hole in the glass canopy. The rest of the dash was twisted but otherwise intact.

Axel was kneeling before her, shaking her thigh.

"Eve, the Slayers are coming," he said. "I spotted a team of about two hundred heading our way in vehicles. We need to leave the crash site."

"Keyv," she mumbled, urging her neck to swivel her head in his direction.

"Keyv's spine is severed, but he's alive," said Axel. "I'll carry him, but we need to leave now, we're wasting time. Be careful with your arm, it's injured."

"His spine?" Eve choked back angry sobs and fumbled with her harness. She found the release, and fell forward as her restraints gave way. "Will he walk?"

She slipped against the cockpit floor, tilted at a sharp angle due to damage from the crash. Pain splintered through her arm as she tried to catch herself and collapsed against the ground, clutching at her elbow. It felt like a fleshy sack of gravel.

She screamed in agony.

"He'll walk again," said Axel. "I promise, the injury is repairable. Eve, please let's go."

He helped her up, and she almost fainted from the pain exploding in her arm. Her vision went red and hazy, clearing only after she took several deep breathes.

Keyv was motionless in his constraints. She hoped to stars Axel was correct in his diagnosis and that Keyv was paralyzed. Because to her he looked dead.

"Here we go," said Axel, cradling her in his arms and lifting her from the ground.

He hopped nimbly through the rear bridge, elbowing the hatch controls. The metal catch unlocked from inside the hull, and with no power to mechanize its opening, the heavy hatch slammed onto the ground outside. Axel walked to the grass and gingerly placed Eve at his feet.

"Take this," he said, pulling an MGK rifle off the plate on his back and sidling it around her neck on its strap. "The Slayers are getting near."

Eve clutched the handle of the rifle with her good hand, trembling badly from fear. She wasn't afraid of the Slayers. She was fearful for Keyv. The memory of his limp body caused her to squirm.

She spotted movement atop one of the nearby hills. Vehicles skirted the top, gliding above the tall grass through some form of levitation. The vehicles continued to come, and by the time Axel returned with Keyv, the Slayer caravan was a mere one hundred meters away.

She turned to Axel, her lips quivering. Hot tears burned around her eyes as she saw Keyv's head roll against Axel's arm like a ball on a cord. The

Slayers were close enough for her to hear their rough voices. Axel bent to set Keyv down on the ground. They didn't need to discuss their options. They could no longer run. They would need to fight. She knew they could not win.

Every bone in Eve's body urged her to pull the trigger, but she resisted. From this distance, she might miss. She wanted to take at least one of the bastards down with her. Two actually. One for her and one for Keyv.

Axel no longer held a rifle, having given his to Eve, and instead extended two energy swords from his forearms. Fingers of electricity flowed from the hilt to the pointed tips, energizing the hardened blades. He clashed the swords together as the vehicles slowed before them, and crouched low to the ground.

The vehicles were turret-mounted ATV's, and surrounded them in a thick ring. Eve's mouth went sour as the sounds of claws scraping against metal slithered into her ears when the Slayers stepped from their hovercraft.

They were enormous.

Eve had forgotten just how big the beasts were. The smallest stood at ten feet, and the heaviest at a thousand pounds.

Most walked on all fours, twisting above the grass like lizards. Their muscles rippled as they approached with liquid ease, the hair protruding from armored plates on their backs bristled and raised on end. Their tails whipped behind them, the heavy bone clusters at the tips slicing through the air like whips.

Others walked on their hind legs and wore colorful armor, glowing with energy. UCOM had a name for these armored Slayers. *Cogent.* The Cogent wielded plasma rifles, holding them in their dexterous second set of inner arms.

Eve raised her MGK rifle at the closest armored Slayer as he approached. She heard a clash of metal against metal, and turned to find Axel lunging toward a group of Cogent. Axel got some blows in, but was quickly subdued by their sheer numbers and upgraded strength from their exoskeletons. They slammed his face into the ground, and forced a collar around his neck, causing him to go limp.

She spent no time pondering how the device was able paralyze a Titan Akimor body. She fought to steady the rifle towards the Slayer before her. Her wobbly firearm didn't seem to faze the hulking lizard, who didn't slow its approach.

Its yellow eyes bored into hers, set around a jagged tattoo of glowing yellow ink, what looked like three barbed spears connected by three overlapping circles. It ran a black tongue over its pointed snout, baring several rows of serrated teeth.

Eve fired four shots into the Slayer's chest. Its armor deflected the bullets easily, and it bent to grab the rifle, yanking it from her grip, easy for it to do in her weakened state. She sank to her knees, screaming as the strap caught the back of her head and jolted her shattered elbow.

Keyv lay to her right, and she crawled to him, weeping. She bent over his motionless face and pressed her forehead against his, murmuring his name over and over. Her face was wet with tears and fluid from her nose, and soaked into the side of Keyv's face as she nudged against him.

She heard a gentle whir, and when the light was blotted from above her, knew the Slayer was leaning over her back. Eve tensed her muscles, squeezing her eyes shut, readying herself for the bullet she knew would be shot into her head. Or perhaps for a crushing blow from the Slayer's heavy tail.

Neither of those things happened. Instead a delicate hand slid over her shoulder.

"Is the ape alive?"

The voice was rough but friendly. Eve turned from Keyv to face the voice. The Slayer kneeling beside her was larger than she first realized. Its reptilian face showed little emotion, but its eyes were warm.

"I don't know," Eve murmured, in a trance. The only other times she'd witnessed Slayers in person, they'd been violent and bloodthirsty. This Slayer seemed calm and coherent.

"Take my hand," said the Slayer, extending a smooth inner arm.

Pockets of skin ballooned at the base of its neck when it spoke. Eve knew from intelligence briefings that this was how the creature talked, unable to vocalize with its reptilian mouth.

"I am called Pexar, do not fear young female, we mean you no harm. We fight the same enemy. We fight the Slarebull."

TWELVE

Frank Scott - Human

Aboard Leopard *Anastasia* – Charlie sector starspace

Frank walked between the spiral arms of the Milky Way.

The stars seemed tiny to him as he walked. They twinkled around him at waist level. The galaxy, normally hundreds of thousands of light years wide, was miniaturized. It was small enough for him to see all the way to the edge, beyond the Outer Rim.

He looked down at the star before him, the star he came from. He didn't come from the star itself, but rather one of the planets orbiting it. Somewhere near the tiny speck of light at his knees, the blue planet Earth spun on its axis.

Frank wasn't interested in Earth, not now. He walked from the sun of his home planet, and ventured across the galaxy. Someone had called his name, summoned for him. The Voice had been far away, and Frank needed to find its origin. He was attracted to the Voice. He was drawn to the Voice. Every bone in his body wanted to speak with the Voice, to hear it talk. To hear its message.

He walked through the Milky Way, and stars brushed away and swirled behind him like fog. He reached the super massive black hole at the center of the galaxy and walked around it. Frank didn't think the black hole would suck him in, but he didn't fully understand this new world he was in, and wasn't willing to take any chances.

He needed to find the Voice.

He pressed on, past Dominia and beyond the Frontline, where so much blood was spilled over a century ago. The events of the Frontline battle replayed around him, filling the void above the Milky Way with vivid depictions of war.

UCOM ships fired heavy salvos of slugs from their rail cannons, and Slayer ships returned fire accordingly. No, not Slayer ships. *Slarebull* ships. Slayer was a UCOM word. Frank must not use the word *Slayer.* The Voice wouldn't like that, he was certain.

Frank studied the space-conflict unfolding around him, and saw the magnificent outlines of Slarebull Hives and Hornets basked in auras of golden light. They swept through the ranks of UCOM Tigers and Lions, casting them away into a fiery inferno. In this world, it was easy for Frank to see who the good guys were. The Slarebull were holy saviors, the gods of all. The Slarebull, yes, but also, *the Pristine.*

He didn't know much about the Pristine, but in his heart, Frank knew they were kind and generous. They were waiting to embrace UCOM, welcome them into their tender circle. No, not UCOM. *Humans.* Humans, and Clones because they looked like Humans. The other twelve races were lowly and undeserving. They weren't Pristine, they were *filth.* He didn't know how he knew this, but was confident in his assumption. The Voice would agree with him. He was sure of that.

A door of golden light opened in the distance, beyond the Outer Rim. The Voice called to him through the door.

"Frank...Frank..."

The Voice knew his name. He thought he'd remembered it calling his name, but now he was certain. He followed the Voice. It was a friendly voice. He wanted to talk to it.

"Frank...Frank..."

The door become larger, and the light inside it brighter. He burned with desire to walk through the magnificent opening.

"Come with me Frank, I want to get to know you. I love you Frank. I love you like I love my brothers. I love Humans, Frank. Let me show you my kingdom. You would like my kingdom, Frank. We would all be gods in my kingdom."

Frank loved the Voice. The Voice was so tender, and the kingdom seemed so sweet. He never knew he was a god, but that was what the Voice said, and Frank was positive the Voice was correct. The Voice would never lie to him. The Voice *loved* him.

"Frank...Frank..."

He tried to reach the doorway, but couldn't. His steps didn't bring him any closer, and soon he had walked far beyond the Milky Way, but the door was still out of reach. He began to jog.

"Frank...Frank..."

He ran harder. He began to sprint.

"Frank...Frank..."

Why couldn't he reach the doorway? His heart ached for the Voice. He wanted to see the Voice's kingdom.

"Frank...Frank..."

λλλ

"*Frank. Frank,* FRANK."

Frank screamed and thrashed around. Bedsheets tangled around him, and he struggled to free himself from the cold, sweaty, smothering fabric.

He moaned, terrified of the dark room. Where had the golden door gone? Where was the Voice?

"Frank, ssshh, it's okay sweetie. Everything's okay, come here."

Frank continue to moan in terror, and curled into a ball, shielding himself from the ghastly dark world. Arms wrapped around his shoulders, and he felt the soft warmth of breasts press against his upper back. The world became a little brighter. A little less terrifying. He turned to find his partner beside him, rubbing his chest, calming him.

"Nancy?" he gasped, dropping his head backwards into his pillow, shivering as his neck soaked against the icy fabric.

"Another night terror?" Nancy rolled onto her stomach and pushed ropes of wet hair from his forehead. "That was a pretty bad one Frank. Are you sure you're all right?"

She pecked him on the cheek.

Frank scooted so his back was against the headboard, pulling his sheets over his body. Was it a nightmare? He tried to recall the dream. It was a good dream he thought. But then why was he so terrified? Why were his sheets soaked in sweat?

"I don't know," he whispered. His throat was raw and he hacked into the sheets. He checked for blood, knowing he wouldn't find any. He'd been injected with a Program serum during the Frontline Battle, and now had nanobots keeping him healthy and disease free.

"Do you think it's another drug flashback? I heard red lightning stays in your spine for centuries, even if you have a Program. You used to hit that stuff pretty hard Frank. I'm worried about you."

Nancy buried her face in his chest, but he wasn't thinking of red lighting. He knew his dream had nothing to do with that. He remembered something about his dream.

He was thinking about the Voice.

"I don't want to even ask you this," said Nancy, leaning away and pressing a palm against his chest. "But you're not drinking again are you Frank?"

Frank shook his head and scrunched his eyes shut. "Drinking? No I'm not drinking. We haven't had alcohol in our fleet for the past century, how the hell would I be drinking?"

Nancy sighed and pursed her lips. "I know you're not, I'm sorry for even bringing it up. I just..." she shook her head. "I get nervous sometimes. We're deep in enemy territory and I don't know if tomorrow will be the day the Slayers will get us or next day. I'm scared enough about losing you to the Slayers, I don't want to have to worry about losing you to alcohol too."

Frank squirmed out of his sheets and rose to the floor, shaking his foot, which had fallen asleep. "I'm not drinking, and I'm just as scared of the damned lizard freaks as you are. I had a bad dream, that's all."

Nancy pursed her lips, but seemed to accept his explanation, and rose from the bed. "Me and my crew are going to be eating at the mess hall in a couple hours, it'd be nice if you can be there."

Frank bit the inside of his cheeks, and nodded, not offering a response. Nancy sighed and left the bedroom.

He waited for thirty seconds until he heard the outside door open and shut. Then he padded to the door and activated the lock so Nancy couldn't get back in unannounced. He went to his wardrobe and pushed Nancy's clothes out of the way.

She didn't have many belongings in their bedroom. Nancy spent countless hours on voluntary patrol searching for Sid Dakota, and kept an odd sleep schedule. She practically lived in the barracks.

He slid the bottom drawer out until it stopped on its magnetic tracks, and lifted the edge so the drawer tilted upward at an angle. The mechanical studs in the back slipped through the catch, and the drawer came free, exposing a twelve inch void in the side of the wardrobe. He bent low to rummage inside the empty space.

The metal floor panels were torn out, as well as the magnetic components for the ship's artificial gravity field. Nestled in the alcove where a few metal cylinders connected with a series of tubes. He unscrewed a fat container on the side and shook it hard.

Groaning to his feet, he trudged to the kitchenette and clinked a drinking glass onto the counter. He unscrewed the container's cap and poured its contents into the jar. It was murky brown and looked like sewage, but Frank gulped at it greedily.

Sighing, he sank into a chair and leaned against his kitchen table, rubbing his temples. Groping across the sleek tabletop, he curled his fingers around a hard plastic pack of cigarettes, praising the stars the fleet decided to include tobacco plants in the mix of vegetable gardens in the agriculture wing of their Tiger.

He lit up and sucked in deep. He sighed and leaned back into his chair, closing his eyes. The brown stuff he drank was potent as all hell, almost 95% alcohol. He was proud of his resourcefulness, building a hidden distillery beneath the floorboards. He'd even added a chemical ingredient to make it scentless, so Nancy couldn't smell it on his breath.

Frank didn't enjoy alcohol. He'd been clean for well over a century, but in the last few years, he'd fallen off the wagon hard. *Stars.* A hundred forty years with no booze? Give a guy a break.

Of course, once he started he couldn't stop. He wasn't sure what it was about his personality that made him so weak against drugs and alcohol, and had stopped trying to even figure it out.

His mind was wrapped around a different question. He remembered his dream clearly now. The Milky Way, the stars, the door.

The Voice.

It all came rushing back to him.

This wasn't the first such dream he'd had. For the past few years he'd been having dreams, and every single one was the same. He started at Earth, and walked across the Milky Way. In the dream, he felt like he should be searching for something, but he never found anything. Just stars.

But this dream was different. He *had* found something. The golden door. And he had *heard* something. The Voice had called to him.

What the Voice had said chilled Frank to the bone. Nancy spent nearly every waking hour searching for Sid Dakota, the Destineer leader who kidnapped her before the Frontline Battle. The man who had raised a holy army of religious zealots who believed the Slarebull were coming to lead them to salvation. The man who claimed to have spoken with the Slarebull, to have communication with them through visions.

As Frank slowly drowned his conscious with murky poison, he realized that he hadn't had a dream. It was too vivid. It was too real. A voice had talked to him.

Frank hadn't had a dream. He had a *vision.*

THIRTEEN

Nancy Woods – Human
Aboard Leopard *Anastasia* – Charlie sector starspace

Nancy was worried about Frank. She knew he'd been drinking. She'd caught on right away, when he first made his distillery. His breath smelled of a combination of rubbing alcohol and cleaning agent, and his eyes drooped. She guessed he had tried to mix some sort of chemicals into his alcohol to make it scentless, but whatever his methods were, they failed miserably.

Frank hadn't even thought to hide the magnetic components or tiles he ripped out of the ground to make room for his jerry-rigged equipment. She'd found them sitting in a box right next to the wardrobe.

Yeah, the love of her life was back on the liquor. And for some unthinkable reason, she couldn't find the courage to confront him about it. Frank had just lied to her face. She'd asked him if he'd started drinking again, and he said no. He said no a little too enthusiastically for it to be believable, but his ruse wasn't working to begin with.

She supposed it was security she was looking for. Not protection from the Slayers, no one could offer that. Not physical security, family security. This far out in the dark corners of the galaxy, always on the move, she needed something to motivate her, something to cherish. She wanted a family more than anything, but her father was thousands of light years away, if he were still alive. Frank represented a hope, a dream that one day she could be happy. That she could kiss her daughter goodbye as she left for school, or cheer her son on at his sports games.

She couldn't have a kid out here in the depths of space. There was a small community of civilians living on the Tiger, but she couldn't bring herself to join them. She had work to do. She wouldn't be able to find Sid Dakota if she had a child to care for.

Frank was all she had left, the last shred of hope of having a normal life once the war was over. If it ever ended.

Nancy loved Frank deeply, despite his flaws. She knew he loved her back, and would do anything to protect her, including sacrificing his life if it came to it.

No, she was irritated and annoyed at Frank's new alcohol foray, but booze and cigarettes wasn't what worried her about him. He'd changed somehow, and it wasn't from being drunk. He'd become distant, distracted from normal conversation. Nancy found the need to repeat herself a lot, as if Frank was daydreaming about something.

It started with his nightmares a few years back. Frank would moan in terror, twist around in the sheets, and sometimes scream loudly. It started out mild, but his nightmares had gotten worse. He could never seem to remember what was in his dreams, and Nancy wasn't sure if he was telling the truth.

She reached the hangar bay of *Anastasia*, the Leopard-class light-destroyer she and Frank currently lived on. She used her Program to ready coordinates to *Kizurra,* the commanding Tiger ship in their fleet, captained by Admiral Allakai Troko, a Stallion. He was a strong leader, but hard-nosed at times. His goals were to rescue as many souls as possible, and to only fight as needed.

His leadership decisions made sense, but Nancy had an objective of her own. When the Stitchline was severed at the Frontline 150 years before, she'd chosen to stay behind with the Slayers and traitorous Destineers, hidden in her Night Eagle stealth craft. She knew if she had gone back to Dominia with the rest of UCOM, she might never accomplish her goal.

Her goal was simple. She was going to find Sid Dakota, and she was going to kill him.

Admiral Allakai protested firmly against this, but allowed her to run search patrols with her crew on a volunteer basis. She happily accepted his terms.

Nancy walked across the hangar towards her Cheetah fast attack fighter. Before the war, there was strict protocol for releasing ships from hangars. With their motley assortment of rescued civilians and recovered military troops, the rules were a little more lax in this fleet.

The canopy slid into the back of the hull as Nancy approached, and she climbed a small set of stairs beside the fighter, stepping onto the side wing before hopping into the cockpit.

Magnetic rails in the hangar floor guided her Cheetah forward into the launch tube. The inside hatch closed behind her, and jets of vapor shot from the side walls as the tubes removed all pressure to equal the conditions of space. The tube primed within a few short seconds. The thick blast doors of the outer hatch dropped vertically into the deck, and Nancy was thrown into the back of her seat as the magnetic guide rail accelerated her down the tube, flinging her from the side of the ship.

She touched the thrusters to give her a little more speed, then gave her attention to her Program as she waited for her ship to reach *Kizurra*.

Her Program interfaced with a holo display on the dash, and Nancy read through intelligence updates from Admiral Allakai. A party of over one hundred civilians was rescued from their mining colony at a nearby asteroid belt. The fleet was moving off course through a few more portals than anticipated in order to avoid a group of Slayer ships detected by Raven drones.

Nothing out of the ordinary. Nothing about the Destineers.

Nancy disconnected her Program from the holo display and relaxed as her Cheetah cruised towards *Kizurra* on autopilot. Their fleet of surviving ships stretched into the distance in a loose column. Vulnerable civilian PUMA cruisers and industrial Tabby barges sat in the middle, flanked on all sides by military ships – Leopards, Jaguars, Lynxes, and Ocelots. Panther stealth ships and Wasp fighters patrolled the outer perimeter, and although they were either hidden from view, or too small and far away to see, Nancy could observe their presence on her navigational panel in the form of green dots.

Their fleet included three Tiger heavy-destroyers, and the lead ship loomed before her as she approached the massive hangar bays. One of the two-hundred-foot-tall blast proof doors was open, allowing ship traffic to cycle through. A team of Cheetahs zipped from the effluent launch tubes in the left corner, their rear thrusters glowing blue as they set course for their patrol coordinates. Nancy swung her fighter towards the opposite corner, where incoming ship traffic entered influent receiving tubes.

"*Kizurra*, this is Nancy Woods, approaching in Cheetah fighter C-10 from *Anastasia*. Requesting permission to dock."

She touched her reverse thrusters, slowing her craft to a crawl, entering a transit lane marked by blinking Raven drones hovering in a line a few thousand meters from *Kizurra's* hull. She sent encryption keys to the ship with a few taps on the dash.

A space traffic controller answered her call.

"Copy that Nancy, proceed to tube four for docking."

Lights illuminated tube four in a green square, and Nancy activated the automatic docking program in her fighter. The Cheetah guided itself towards *Kizurra*, and into the green pocket of light, which switched to red as her craft touched down onto the grated floor. Magnetic tracks guided her along the tube and into the ship, the inside hatch opening after the pressure equalized inside the receiving tube.

The engines powered down and her ship funneled into a parking bay, its canopy hissing as it slipped back into the hull. Nancy had heard the sound a million times, and began to climb from her fighter before the glass shield was all the way open.

Kizurra's hangars were quiet as usual. Most of the destroyer's ships were docked, and lined the tiered floor levels in neat rows. Harsh lights pulsed from the mechanic's level as technicians performed maintenance activities on various craft.

Nancy's footsteps rang through the cavernous hangar, outdone only by the occasional bang of metal against metal from the maintenance crew, or the hiss of an effluent tube ejecting an outgoing vessel.

She entered a broad hallway network inside the Tiger and walked to a pod station. Hundreds of spherical glass transport vehicles whizzed through the air, some stopping at the station to drop off passengers, and others streaking past the platform to a remote destination in the ship.

The ground beeped as she stepped onto the terminal, and a square beneath her feet turned green. Seconds later, an empty pod slowed before her and opened its doors.

As her pod carried her deep into *Kizurra,* she thought of her father, Francis Woods. Before the Frontline, she'd shunned his attention. When he was president of the United States, White House workers ushered her around to her daily activities. After the Guardians came, when he was the leader of United Earth and a member of the Grand Council, he'd given her a few body guards and sent a letter once a year.

She'd hated him for focusing his attention on his country, instead of on her. But the Frontline changed all that. After Sid Dakota kidnapped her, her father had saved her. Sid tried to use her as a hostage token, threatening her death if her father didn't separate the Humans from UCOM and stand down against the invading Slayers.

Her father hadn't folded. He sent his best men to rescue her, and held her in his arms when she was on the brink of death.

She cringed at the memory of ignoring his video requests. Now, she would give anything to hear his voice, if only for a few moments.

"Nancy, get through the portal. We're about to severate..."

Would that be her final memory of her father's voice?

Nancy wondered again if her father was alive. Stars, she wondered if UCOM was still alive.

She remembered her brief reunion with her father at the Frontline. Her heart had nearly burst with love and pride when he led UCOM troops against the Slayers, driving them back to allow millions of civilians to escape before the Stitchline blew.

Her father's ship was among the last to retreat from battle, and he'd called to her, begged her to come back through the portal with him. Oh, how she'd wanted to. She almost had. But instead she hung behind, planted a tracking device on the Slayer Hive carrying Sid Dakota and vanished into the surrounding portals as the Stitchline blew. She was stranded light years away from the nearest UCOM ship. She was also stranded 150 light years from her father.

Nancy shook the sorrowful nostalgia from her head as the pod slowed, opening its doors to her destination. She stepped onto the platform and continued down the hallway.

She was in the barracks now, in the aft section of *Kizurra.* The barracks gave her a sense of comfort, a sense of purpose. She opened the sliding doors, and was relieved to see her teammates playing cards around a collapsible table near their lockers.

"Hey, look who it is," said Caseus, his cigar bobbing with his words. He waved a fog of smoke away from his face and slid the cigar from his lips. "Aren't you supposed to be with Frank? What happened to family time?"

"Dinner's not till eighteen-hundred," she said, grabbing a chair and sliding it into an empty spot around the table.

"You only have six hours," said Hunter. The Titan android leaned into the back of his seat and tossed his cards onto the table. "Shouldn't you be getting ready? Your eyeliner alone will take four hours."

Nancy punched him on the arm, then shook her hand in pain after her knuckles clunked against his Akimor frame.

"Ow Nancy," Hunter mocked, rubbing his metal arm. "Careful now, I bruise easy."

Caseus joined him in laughter.

"Cut it out guys," said Lindsey, blowing a few wandering strands of hair from her eyes. She pouted her lips and nodded to Nancy. "Do you want me to deal you in? We're playing Frux the Lizards."

Nancy shook her head and leaned her elbows on the table. "No thanks Lin. You guys go ahead."

Caseus pulled a plastic box from under the table, opening it to expose rolled selections of leafy goods.

"Cigar?" he asked.

Nancy shook her head again. She didn't feel like a cigar. She felt like hopping in a Cheetah and drifting through a few portals, maybe find a Destineer ship to send a knifeblade missile into.

"Buzzkill," Hunter whispered under his breath, making sure he spoke just loud enough for Nancy to hear. "Caseus, if I had lungs, I would smoke one of those cigars with you."

Caseus grinned. "Thanks pal. Maybe we can take a VR trip sometime and just puff away."

Nancy rose from her seat. "I'm going to catch a few hours of sleep before dinner. Get ready for patrol after. Remember we have a volunteer shift at zero dark thirty."

She turned to leave, stepping around Lindsey to enter the sleep bay behind a line of brown hanging curtains.

"Come on Nance," said Hunter, standing from his own chair. "We were just poking a little fun, come back and play, I'll be the Lizard next game, you can be the Eminence."

Nancy turned to politely protest. She wasn't angry at them, just upset at herself for personal reasons.

An AI materialized before she could speak, standing at the center of the fold up table. Her teammates leaned away from the AI, a stubby Squid. He spun around the table to face Caseus, then Hunter, then Lindsey. His tentacles swayed around him like a straw skirt, then raised into the air when he spotted Nancy.

"Lieutenant Woods," said the Squid AI. "I have a priority-one message for you, addressed from Admiral Allakai."

The AI looked over his shoulder at her teammates, then back at her.

"Well spit it out," said Caseus.

The Squid exhaled sharply. "It's a priority one message for Lieutenant Woods, not her crew."

"What I can hear, my team can hear," said Nancy. "What's the message?"

The Squid slapped the flat section of his dominant tentacle testily against his leg, but conceded.

"A Raven drone returned with a positive ID on an abandoned Tiger destroyer three point seven light years away. It picked up a broadcast signal."

Nancy's stomach fluttered. "What kind of signal?" she said.

"It's a tracking beacon," said the AI. "We think we found the bug you put on Sid Dakota's ship back at the Frontline one hundred fifty years ago."

FOURTEEN

Sharker Gray – Human Destineer
On surface of planet Earth – Washington DC

Sharker Gray adjusted his tie as he walked up the balcony steps. The capitol building shone in the distance, a stone pearl against the sparkling Washington DC skyline. Towering superstructures stabbed the night sky in the distance, a modern touch to complement the city's historic capitol architecture. A space elevator jutted above the tallest building, connecting Old America's most prized city with the great beyond. A blue point of light streaked up the illuminated tether as a passenger car ascended to space.

A wintry breeze ruffled his thick beard, and he ducked his head to protect his neck from the cold. He spotted an event flyer plastered to the marble steps of the banquet center.

UCOM Cultural Gala
Keynote Speaker, Sheryl Gwyndeveer, Clone Ambassador
February 11th, 7:00 pm, McTruskey Hall

The lettering glowed against the digital parchment, shifting through a colorful spectrum in lazy pulses. Another gust of wind tore the paper loose and sucked it in a high loop over the marble pillars lining the grand entrance.

"Identification please."

Sharker reached the top of the steps, where a series of velvet concession gates were hooked to gold plated posts. A thin man dressed in a security uniform stood before the roped entrance next to a clear booth, glowing yellow against the red carpet leading into the grand doorway.

"Sir, identification and admission ticket?" the man repeated, holding out a flat wand in his gloved hand.

Sharker cast a glance at the tops of the marble columns wrapped around the thin steps in a wide arc. Guards stood with their MGK rifles at the ready, scanning the area for potential threats. He wondered if they were also searching the sky for drones.

He nodded to the guard and held his wrist out, hiking his sleeve up a few inches. He made sure not to expose the tattoo on his forearm. This was a UCOM gala. His kind wouldn't be welcome here.

The guard pressed his wand against Sharker's skin, and removed it after an audible chirp sounded a few seconds later. A hologram display flashed above the booth's sloped top, showing Sharker's face and background information.

Frederick J. Harrelson
Human
DOB: 2/11/1985
Height: 6'8"
Eyes: BRWN

"Happy birthday Mr. Harrelson," said the guard, flipping a finger through the holo display. A red, ticket-shaped icon sat below his background information, and the man tapped his finger against it. A computer checked the authenticity of the ticket, which turned green after it was verified. "Enjoy the speech. You're a little late sir, but you should be able to catch the end at least."

"Thank you," said Sharker. He slid his sleeve back over his wrist and stepped past the guards. Metal clinked as the guard hooked the gate closed behind him.

The front doors were stopped open, and Sharker took a second to admire the ornate carvings on the sides before stepping into a security checkpoint.

The checkpoint was minimal and manned by two additional guards, featuring a thin set of detectors and a floating table to place any items that needed further screening. He knew the checkpoint was merely a formality. The real sensors were embedded in the walls and in the floor. The security team inside McTruskey center already had a full scan of his DNA, 3D renderings of all objects in his pockets, and signature profiles of every gas, liquid, and solid material within a six-foot bubble around his waist.

One of the guards waved another wand lazily around Sharker's waist, a cylindrical one, not a flat one. The other guard had his hands on his hips, and merely nodded, casting the large bearded man a grin.

"You're all set to go Mr. Harrelson," said the guard with the wand. "There's a coat check across the lobby, and a cocktail lounge just inside the banquet doors."

Sharker nodded to the guards, and flashed a slight grin of his own.

He strode across the polished stone lobby floor, laid in intricate patterns cut from slabs dug from the Human colony planet of Destiny. A woman stood behind a thin film of water casdading down the front of a glass table.

"Coat sir?" she asked.

Sharker nodded and removed his coat, which hung down to his shins. He folded the heavy fabric over his arm and handed it over the counter. The girl grunted as she struggled with the enormous jacket, easily large enough to wrap three times around her waist. She heaved it onto the surface in a bundle, and flipped her own wand across the counter, a flat one. Sharker allowed her to scan his wrist for identification.

"Thank you Mr. Harrelson," she wheezed. Sharker smiled and walked towards the solid gold doors leading into the reception area.

The lights were dim, and Sharker didn't bother to glance in the direction of the large circular tables, where his ticket granted him a seat and a five course meal. Instead he made his way to the cocktail bar wrapped around the rear corner of the cathedral walls.

He eased onto a plush stool and leaned toward the barkeep, who waited patiently for his order.

"Dusted martini, shaken, with a drop of fire," he said. The man nodded and vanished in the direction of the gin.

Sharker turned to the stage, hooking his shoulder against the corner of the glass bar. Sheryl Gwyndeveer held the center, softly lit from overhead lights, contrasted against the rest of the darkened room.

A wormy feeling of rage wriggled in his stomach. He had devoted his life to saving Humans, pledged his devotion to the Destineers, and his mighty strength to the Slarebull. The Slarebull, and also the *Pristine.*

He had converted countless Humans, and soon his mission on Earth would be complete. Father Dakota had trusted him with their most prized possession – their home. One hundred fifty years ago, he'd been sent from the Frontline with orders to blend in with civilian refugees. He was to spread word of the Doctrine, to preach of salvation, and teach of Humanity's place in the universe. They would unite with the Slarebull, and share a seat with them atop the throne, not as just another UCOM race, but as deities.

Gods of all.

It was not simply their birthright to rule the universe. It was their destiny.

Yes, he was close, but not a day went by when he didn't ache to be with his leader beyond the Frontline. To embrace the Pristine as he walked with his fellow disciples through their heavenly gates, not as Humans, but as gods.

But his services were needed on Earth. He was a faithful warrior, and had meticulously ferreted out pro-UCOM activists, and influenced powerful world leaders, convincing them of his beliefs.

"Your drink, sir."

Sharker turned to find the bartender sliding his martini across the smooth glass. He nodded his head in thanks and lifted the glowing concoction, taking a sip as he returned his gaze to the center stage.

Yes, his day of glory was soon at hand, he could feel it in his bones. Word from the Inner Ring was that the Slarebull were here. Sharker didn't need to watch a TVE program to know that. Sid was the first out of the Destineers to have visions, but lately he had been experiencing them as well. He had listened to the Voice with his own ears. The Voice had professed his love to him. He could hardly wait to meet the Voice as a god.

The fire in his drink warmed his belly and widened his pupils. He became more aware of his surroundings, more alert. He focused on the words of the keynote speaker. Sheryl was nearly finished with her speech.

The slender Clone gestured powerfully to the audience, accentuating points she had spent the entire evening making. Her leg thrust forward, exposing most of her tanned thigh between a slit in her luminescent dress.

For a fleeting moment, Sharker couldn't help but admire her. She was an excellent communicator, and passionate about her beliefs. He shared her sense of passion. Unfortunately for her, his passion burned for Humans and for the Slarebull, not for the UCOM filth.

"*I speak to you as a three-hundred-thirty-eight year old woman,*" Sheryl spoke to the audience. "*Not because of diet and exercise, but because my blood contains anti-aging technology gifted to us from the Guardians.*"

A smatter of applause.

"My Clone world of Sylva was murdered, no...raped by the evil Slayer invaders. It was the Guardians who gave us a new home. And also the Green, the Intellects, the Boards. Especially the Humans."

Louder applause. Even from his distant spot at the bar, Sharker could see fiery tears brimming on Sheryl's dark eyes.

"The navy ships protecting our families are staffed by UCOM spacers. Our research and technological innovations are spear-headed by the Intellects, who champion UCOM science teams. Our production plants build UCOM war machines, built with materials mined by UCOM laborers. In the face of evil, UCOM has been strong."

The applause lasted a bit longer. Sheryl powered her voice over the noise.

"UCOM has been strong, but the Destineers have weakened us. The Destineers are cowards who wish to bed with the enemy beasts. They are weak because they are afraid. I personally watched Slayers murder my family. The Destineers claim the Slayers to be friends...no...saviors. They claim that we can enter their kingdom as gods. When my daughter was eaten alive by a ten-foot monster..."

Sheryl paused to wipe her eyes. Her lip trembled.

"My daughter was murdered. She was not saved."

A long pause. The room was silent. Sharker downed the rest of his martini. Sheryl raised her head high and puffed her chest.

"Death to the Destineers!"

The room erupted in cheers. Sheryl gave a brief smile and turned from the stage. Sharker set his drink down and rose from his seat. He didn't applaud with the rest of the room.

The night drew late and Sharker watched Sheryl patiently from a remote corner of the lounge. He was on his seventh martini, but at his size, he would have to drink many more to lose his senses.

She had gone straight to the cocktail lounge; expected after such an event. He scoffed to himself at the title, remembering the flyer plastered on the front steps.

"UCOM Cultural Gala," he thought in disgust. *"More like Destineer witch hunt."*

The crowd had died, and the throngs of people waiting to speak with Ms. Gwyndeveer thinned. It was time. He pushed from his seat and moved towards Sheryl. She was alone, twirling her finger around a thin straw sticking from her purple drink.

"Inspiring speech," said Sharker, sliding into the seat next to her. "I've heard a lot of great ones before, but never with such *fire.*"

He smiled warmly at her.

She turned to him and blushed slightly. Part of it was surely due to alcohol, but Sharker guessed that some of it was due to his broad shoulders and rugged features.

"Thanks," she said, reaching for her straw with her tongue. "Are you Human or Clone?"

"Human," he said. "Born not far from here in a place called Pennsylvania. My name's Frederick Harrelson."

"Pennsylvania," she said, closing her eyes. "That sounds like a Clone name."

"Perhaps," said Sharker, "except the women in Pennsylvania are far less beautiful."

Sheryl's blush deepened.

He wasn't lying about the Clone sense of beauty. Like most clones, Sheryl's eyes shone fiercely, and her curves caressed her silky dress tenderly. This night would be a pity.

"Let me buy you a drink," he said, motioning to the bartender. He leaned in to give his drink order.

Sheryl slurped down the rest of her drink and began to protest, but Sharker cut her off politely.

"I first tasted this in Vayl. It's rumored to connect your heart to a star. If another Clone looks at the same star as you, your hearts will intertwine and you'll become soul mates."

She smiled. "Does it work on Humans too?"

The bartender arrived with their drinks. Sharker plucked Sheryl's glass from the surface and held it to her. She never saw him dip his finger into the fizzing pink beverage, nor would she taste the chemicals deposited from his skin.

"I've heard it absolutely does work on Humans," he whispered, leaning his face close to hers. He lifted his glass between them.

Sheryl giggled. "Well then how about you show me some constellations."

They clinked glasses and she drank, never taking her eyes from his.

"I would love that," he said after finishing his own drink. "Except my room doesn't have a view."

She leaned forwards until her lips grazed his cheek. *"I have a skylight over my bed."*

Her teeth clamped lightly on his ear and tugged. She rose, reaching her hand back to him. Sharker grasped her thin wrist in his massive fingers and followed behind. She gasped when she saw how tall he was, and moaned slightly when he draped his arm around her.

The drug was already starting to take effect.

They hurried to the elevator, Sheryl giggling as they piled inside. Once the doors slid shut she leaped to her tip toes and tried to kiss him, but Sharker was a foot and a half taller than her, and she couldn't reach. He ran a hand through her hair instead. Admiring his sense of self control, Sheryl smiled and started to sway her hips back and forth seductively, draping her hair through her fingers.

A *ding* signaled their arrival to the hundredth floor and the doors opened straight into Sheryl's penthouse suite. The living space was as luxurious as could be, with precious items from every UCOM colony lining the walls. Proclaiming death to the Destineers, it seemed, paid well.

Lights flicked on and dimmed to a romantic level, interfacing with Sheryl's Program. He followed her down a hall, pausing to admire the capitol building, now far below.

He tore his eyes from the building. He wasn't here to sightsee.

Sheryl was naked when he entered the bedroom. As promised, moonlight shone onto her bed through a skylight. But he'd known that before he entered the gala. He'd done his research. That's why he ordered the drinks he had.

Sharker walked to a bay window covering the outside wall of the bedroom and tapped his finger against the glass. The window turned an opaque blue to match the surrounding walls.

He turned to Sheryl.

She was stunning. He sat on the bed and she began to kiss his neck, unbuttoning his shirt. Her hair was sweet, like flowers.

Sharker prayed silently to himself.

"I present my body, my flesh, and my soul. I present my beating heart and the blood which courses through my veins. I present my lungs, and the air which they breathe. I look to the stars, and add them to the bounty for which I am due."

Sheryl moved her lips down to his bare chest. Her fingers curled in his hair.

"I look at the dirt on the planets, and the clouds in the sky. I care for the creatures of the Universe, the smallest insects, and the largest beasts, for they are my children. I reclaim the lands of the unholy from the enemy, from the anti-gods. I defend her natural beauty as the caretaker of good, and the slayer of evil. I will defend against those who threaten to take the bounty that is mine."

Her lips reached his navel, and she began to unclasp his belt.

"I am the light in the darkness. I am the shade from the suns. I am a god, protector of the holy Doctrine of Destiny."

Sharker grabbed both sides of Sheryl's jaws firmly, and without delay, twisted her head backward, snapping her neck. Her body fell limply onto the bed.

He rose, fishing a small book from his back pocket. The scanners never picked it up as a threat, but it was the most powerful weapon he'd ever used.

Gently, he rolled Sheryl onto her back and placed her hands on her chest, covering her breasts. He placed the holy book of the Destineers on her sternum, *the Doctrine of Destiny.*

He used his Program to signal a drone craft, and seconds later, the glass panes on the skylight vibrated sharply. One of the panes fell from its metal supports onto the floor, fracturing into several smaller chunks.

A robot lowered itself through the liberated space. It hovered on adjustable rotor blades spinning silently above it inside metal housing. A chest harness hung from its belly, and Sharker slipped his shoulders into the straps.

Like all rooms, Sheryl's was intelligent. Her resident caretaker software would notice her biometrics and alert emergency personnel. He guessed they would arrive within five minutes, and would see him if he left the building at ground level.

But he didn't need to exit at ground level, where all the guards were. His shoulder bumped against the metal rim of the skylight opening as the drone lifted him from the building, and he shivered when his bare chest became exposed to the frozen gusts of air.

Sharker had made powerful friends, friends who were now fellow Destineers. That's how he faked his identity, complete with DNA readings.

That's how he procured the drugs to inhibit Sheryl's rational thinking abilities.

He had powerful friends, and also powerful enemies. With Sheryl Gwyndeveer dead, he had one less enemy. One less person standing in his way, keeping him from accomplishing his sworn duties.

One less person keeping him from uniting Humans with the Slarebull, and assuming their destiny as gods.

FIFTEEN

Francis Woods – Human
Aboard Tiger *Stargrazer* – Dominia starspace

Francis Woods sat at the head of the table inside an assembly room aboard *Stargrazer*, a Tiger-class heavy-destroyer. The ceiling was made entirely of glass, and it was easy for him to see many of the craft sailing around their Tiger.

A large escort of ships flanked them on all sides, including Lynx surveillance and intelligence craft, Ocelot-class anti-missile barges, and a combination of light Jaguar-class and middle Leopard-class destroyers. Woods knew there were also Night Eagles patrolling the starspace around them in active camo, invisible to the unsuspecting eye.

Around the table, council representatives from the rest of UCOM sat tensely. *Stargrazer* was taking them from Dominia to *Warhammer*, a custom built super-tower protecting the Inner Ring from Slayer attack. *Warhammer* harnessed energy from fourteen local suns, had state-of-the-art energy shields and laser defenses, and packed enough RACANS and Shitcans to decimate entire fleets of ships.

It was UCOM's crown jewel, and protected the massive superhighway of thousands of portals forming the central transportation hub within the Milky Way. The superhighway had a name – the Inner Ring.

Stargrazer had passed through a portal into local starspace for the Inner Ring, and the windows increased tint levels to shield the Tiger from light radiating off the fourteen sunbeams feeding *Warhammer*. The defense tower was colossal in size, larger than a planet. Although its size made it seem like they had nearly reached the defense tower, Woods knew it would still be another twenty minutes before they entered one of *Warhammer's* many hangar bays.

A lot of things weighed on his mind. The Destineers, of course, but also the Slayer super-weapon, the APEX. He wondered how Casi Vomisa was faring with her mission. Routine council meetings seemed pedestrian when such dangers loomed behind enemy lines.

Woods had thought about informing the rest of the council about the Slayer super-weapon, then decided against it. Truth be told, he didn't know who to trust. The Destineers could have spies everywhere, and they would sooner help the Slayers unleash their APEX weapon on UCOM than help defend against it.

He forced his focus back to the council briefing.

"Our defense plans are currently exceeding initial projections," said the Clone councilwoman, Zena Olleeve. "We've amassed fleets across the entire edge of the Frontline at every portal along the old Stitchline. We have at minimum one Lion mothership, four PDR's, and thirty Tiger heavy destroyers, with their normal compliment of Titan squads and assorted lighter ships."

"That's not nearly enough to stop the Slayers," grumbled the Stallion councilman. "Our intel says their fleets outnumber ours by a factor of ten."

"I gave the *minimum* fleet counts," said Zena, flipping through a few holographic images on the table before her. "There isn't much Slayer activity in Charlie or Alpha sections at the Frontline. So we've amassed much of our armada outside severed Bravo portals, with priority focus on the Inner Ring. Our Inner Ring fleet includes *Warhammer*, seventy PDR's, two hundred Lions, and over ten thousand Tiger heavies with full compliment. We also have one thousand squadrons of Night Eagles patrolling Inner Ring starspace, and more light space craft than you can comprehend. Sixty sunbeams have been coupled to subsidize our local fusion generators."

Zena slapped a palm onto the holo images on her table, causing them to disappear. "It's an unprecedented amount of firepower, even by Slayer standards. They won't be able to bully us around like they did in the Frontline Battle."

There was a general rumbling of response from the various council representatives. Some sounded positive, believing UCOM defenses around the Inner Ring were on par with what was needed. Others sounded negative, believing no amount of defenses around the Inner Ring could stop the Slayers.

Woods was happy the topic was still on war preparations. He could handle talks of military strength with little issue. It was when the topic changed to the Destineers that he found the meetings to be cumbersome.

The Squid councilman spoke. "Even if our intel is accurate, and our firepower matches the Slayer's, what of their technology? We've barely been able to upgrade our defense technology to match what the Slayers had one hundred fifty years ago. What if they've been developing new innovations? The Blight nearly wiped us out during the Frontline, what if they launch it again?"

The Intellect councilman was prepared for the question, and jumped right into his explanation. His beak clicked as he swiped a finger over the table, and dropped supporting documents into a shared folder. Woods leaned back as 3D models of various UCOM defense technologies appeared before him, floating above the table's glass surface.

"We don't believe that to be the case," said the Intellect. "We've analyzed millions of hours of Slayer chatter, picked up from various battles and skirmishes during the Frontline Battle. As a civilization, they stopped innovating many millennia ago, after one of their weapons nearly killed off their entire population. They've been using the same ships and weapons for thousands, maybe millions of years. The Blight won't be a problem for us any longer, as we fully understand the nano mind-control technology and how to stop it. The only other major advantage the Slayers had over us was their diverter technology, where they opened local warp connections to change the trajectory of our RACAN slugs, sending them into our own friendly ships. We've since mastered this technology and improved upon its design. We've also upgraded CAIRO AI systems, improved Titan armor and trained thousands of new Titan warriors, increased our rail cannon capacities, and loaded our new Night Eagle stealth ships with cutting edge spacnar reconnaissance capabilities. The Slayers will have quite a lot on their plate to deal with, if and when they choose to invade past the Frontline."

The room was silent as the councilmembers absorbed the Intellect's synopsis. Most studied the detailed schematics of weaponry sent to the shared folders. The Board councilman stared vacuously through the window at the brilliant array of sunbeams criss-crossing Inner Ring starspace.

The Stallion councilman broke the silence.

"Am I the only one who sees the real problem?" he declared, rising to all fours and clopping a hoof on the metal floor. "We talk about fleet strength and weapons technology as if the Slayers are our only enemy. No matter how large our navy is, we will crumble when the Destineers revolt and attack us from the inside out."

"And what would your answer be?" declared the Guardian councilman, who rose to his feet as well. His bioluminescent skin flashed a few pulses of red before returning to blue. "Before you respond, let me remind you that your Eminence, and the man who led the UCOM attack during the Frontline battle, is Human."

"Humans are a *cancer* to UCOM," cried the Squid. "To hell with them. We can't tell the difference between a Human or a Destineer. That goes for Clones as well. I say we sever our ties with the whole lot before it's too late."

"Watch your tongue councilman," said Woods, focusing his eyes to glare at the Squid. Woods straightened his back as much as possible in his chair. "I won't condone that sort of traitorous talk in my chambers. If you have issue with the Humans, you raise it through the appropriate channels. I'll remind you that Humans command the largest naval force in UCOM, and that billions of my young men and women are willing to sacrifice their lives to defend the Squid, and every other race in UCOM."

"We don't question the value of your Human soldiers," said the Grizzly, the fur on her shoulders bristling. "We question the threat of the Destineers. I applaud the bravery and determination of your troops, but what is being done to address the group of religious rebels?"

"I have a strict set of protocol for UCOM soldiers," said Woods. "Humans have a zero tolerance policy with the Destineers. If you are found to be involved with the religious group, you are executed for treason. The Gefangnia stockades are filled with millions of alleged Destineers awaiting trial. I am not taking the Destineer situation lightly."

"You mention the Gefangnia stockades as a solution?" said Draxton Tyke, the Wolf councilman. "Mr. Eminence, the jail planet is testament to how bad the Destineer problem has become. The fact that we need an entire planet to house these dissenters..."

The Wolf trailed off.

"The situation is under control," said Zena, the Clone councilwoman. "My civilization has come under fire, as we have converts allying with the rebels. Our psychological profile checks and communication sweeps are strict and effective. UCOM is clean from Destineer infiltration."

"Even if this is true," said the Squid. "What about the Human home world of Earth? Just today I saw on TVE that a Clone ambassador had been murdered by a Destineer assassin. A copy of their Doctrine was left behind. I understand the Clones have made Earth and her colonies your second home. If you can't defend your homeland from the Destineers, then what good is monitoring the UCOM navy?"

"I think a lot of you are missing a major point," said the Intellect. His large eyes darted around the room. "Do the Humans have their flaws? Perhaps. But without Humans, this war would have already been lost. Casi Vomisa is a Human AI, and was crucial in infiltrating the Slayer armada during the Frontline Battle. When others only volunteered the minimal number of required troops for Frontline duty, Francis Woods volunteered his entire military, leaving his home planet weakly defended. He still volunteers more soldiers than any race. When UCOM was forced to retreat, Francis Woods led a final charge to drive the Slayers back long enough to sever the Stitchline. Without Woods and his Human soldiers, UCOM would have lost many billions more souls to the Slayers. I think that we owe him a debt of gratitude, not a suggestion of outcast."

The Intellect clicked his beak a few more times, then chittered before going silent.

The council grumbled, but didn't contest the Intellect's remarks.

A soft *dong* sounded, and an AI materialized at the center of the council table. It was Lewis Zoltan, Woods' AI assistant.

"Mr. Eminence, sir," said Zoltan, turning to face Woods. "We're finished docking with *Warhammer*. Your presence is requested by the tower commander."

"I'll be there shortly," said Woods, nodding to the AI.

Zoltan saluted, then vanished into a cloud of blue sparks.

Woods stood to address his council, who also stood. Some straightened their backs in a sign of respect to the Eminence. Others slouched, some leaning over the table.

"This meeting is hereby concluded," he said. "I urge anyone with concerns of the Destineers to work with me and my teams. We're willing to accept all the help we can get to catch these traitors. *Awaken Stars.*"

"*Awaken Stars,*" the rest of the council grumbled.

Woods shook a few hands, and thanked the Clone, Guardian, and Intellect council members for their time. After ten minutes of light discussion, most of the council members were gone, and he left the assembly room for the exit.

He passed through a plush lounge area with furniture designed to shift contours to match the frames of all fourteen UCOM races. He was about to exit into the halls, but decided to use the restroom first. His bladder ached from the trip to *Warhammer.*

Woods sighed as he relieved himself. The Guardians, Clones, and Intellects were valuable allies, but they were misguided. The Destineers were a bigger problem than anyone realized. Word from Earth was that Destineers had stopped hiding their religion from the public, and membership was now socially acceptable, almost commonplace. The thought sickened him.

He considered briefly whether the Squid was right, and he should withdraw his troops from UCOM. He erased the thought immediately. Without Humans, UCOM would surely fall to the Slayers.

His hands tingled as invisible lasers cleaned germs from his skin. After a few seconds, the hygiene shelf beeped and he removed his hands from the sink, free from contaminants.

At first the lounge seemed empty when Woods walked into the room. He was about to pass around a cluster of decorative plants when he heard excited conversation. The voices spoke in whispers, and he heard his name mentioned.

Woods froze and crouched behind the plants. He peered through the wide leaves to find two council members seated around a small table.

The Wolf pointed at a few digital documents on the glass, and the Grizzly councilwoman studied them.

"We have accurate data on Destineer numbers," said Draxton Tyke, his bushy tail flicking slowly from side to side. "They've grown out of UCOM control. Here's our Wolf intelligence, updated two days ago."

The Grizzly murmured in astonishment. "Stars help us," she said. "This is bigger than I thought."

"That's why we need to do as we discussed," said Draxton, motioning to the digital files on the table surface. "The Humans must be removed from UCOM. Here's the code word. Speak it to no one. When the time comes, can I trust the Grizzlies for their support?"

The Grizzly was silent. Draxton grabbed the councilwoman's shoulder and she roared, standing swiftly and swiping the table with the back of her hand, sending digital files fluttering to the floor.

"I won't be a part of your traitorous acts," she bellowed. "If I wasn't on the fence about the Humans, I'd send you out the tubes myself for treason. Woods is a good man, and a strong leader. *Good day.*"

She turned to storm out of the lounge, growling as she passed through the sliding doors and into the exit hallway of their Tiger ship.

The Wolf shook his head and stooped to the ground, scooping up the digital paper holograms and throwing them into a folder, causing their images to disappear. Draxton padded silently from the room, and vanished into the hallway.

Woods released a shaky breath, alone in the lounge.

What the hell was that about? he thought. Was Draxton planning an act of treason? To somehow exile Humans from UCOM?

He wondered what had made the Grizzly councilman angry enough to storm from the room.

He would need to consult his assistant. Woods was no stranger to sneaky plots to weaken his power. Xakex Roke had almost sent him through the tubes on account of treason during the Frontline Battle. He had been framed for the murder of Babek Slake, a Guardian, and Eminence of UCOM at the time. It turned out to be an elaborate ruse engineered by Maxus Tar, a Wolf-born AI who had allied himself with the Destineers.

Now it seemed, another Wolf was plotting against him. This time is wasn't an AI, but a furry council member in his own chambers.

He straightened, and was about to leave the lounge when he spotted something on the floor where the Grizzly and the Wolf had sat. It was a glowing rectangle, tucked behind the middle support column of the table.

Draxton must have missed the document during his haste to clean up. Woods walked to the table, and pinned his finger against the parchment. After he had control of the digital file, he dropped it onto the table, where it lay flat.

The document held only a single word, and he expanded the font. It was in an alien language, and he couldn't decipher its meaning.

Ral-Bazeera.

"English," he said aloud.

The text instantly translated to his native tongue.

Woods was surprised to find the words didn't change. He studied the letters again.

Ral-Bazeera.

He wondered if this was the code word Draxton had mentioned to the Grizzly. The word that was to be mentioned to no one.

Saving the file to his local Program, Woods dashed from the lounge and towards his private quarters. His meeting with the *Warhammer* commander would have to wait. He needed to stop a potential revolution.

SIXTEEN

Francis Woods – Human
Aboard Tiger *Stargrazer* – Dominia starspace

Woods paced in his study.

He'd never boarded *Warhammer,* and was still aboard *Stargrazer,* the official transport ship of the Grand Council and other high level UCOM representatives, both military and domestic. His study was large but not excessive. Woods had no use for more space than he needed. That just led to more walking.

Ral-Bazeera.

He pondered the words. They didn't come up in the universal translation registry.

Did Draxton Tyke make up his own language? Woods thought, frowning at the letters projected above his desk in white font.

A soft *dong* resonated inside his room. Zoltan had finally arrived.

"Come on in," said Woods, allowing the AI to enter his private study.

Zoltan materialized on the floor next to Woods' desk. The artificial being wore an old style naval uniform, which Woods recognized as the blue service dress uniform of the US navy before the Guardians came. The AI saluted him, and Woods saluted back.

"Is this the code word?" said Zoltan, reaching out to touch the holographic lettering of Draxton's cryptic message.

"It is," said Woods. "What can you tell me about it?"

Zoltan's palm glowed as he spread it to copy the information. "I'm running it through a search filter now. We'll have a query output in a minute or so. Mr. Woods, if you don't mind my asking, what is the significance of this message? It may help me find proper results."

Woods rubbed his temples. He wasn't in a very trusting mood, and Zoltan was a Human-born AI. The Destineers recruited AI the same way they did biological beings. Even UCOM races other than Humans and Clones were fair game to Destineer recruiting when it came to AI. Although uncommon, UCOM AI could reformat their programming to assume a Human identity. To the Destineers, they were treated as converts who had simply been born into the wrong bodies, loyal soldiers in their holy quest for salvation.

"Sir," Zoltan repeated. "May I ask what's going on? You don't need to worry about me leaking information, I hate the Destineers as much as you do. If you allow me to prove it, I'll send warheads into Gefangnia right now."

"I overheard Draxton Tyke talking about a revolt again Humans," said Woods, deciding to clue his AI in. "He mentioned something about a code word, and acting on it when the time comes." He nodded to the letters. "I think that's the code word."

Zoltan licked his lips and frowned in thought. "I knew UCOM was growing restless over the Destineer situation, but an all-out revolt?" He squatted to the floor, drawing a deep breath and exhaling sharply.

"Do you know what this would mean to UCOM?" said Woods, leaning against the back of his desk chair and squeezing the leather top tightly. "If Humans and Clones separated from UCOM, we would have mass chaos. Our navy around the Inner Ring would be depleted. The Slayers would tear through the Inner Ring like butter." He slammed his palm against his chair. "We can't let this happen."

"And if UCOM eradicates Humans by force…" said Zoltan, leaving the thought linger.

Woods hadn't thought of that possibility, assuming UCOM would simply overthrow Human power politically through the Council. The idea of conflict on three fronts turned his stomach. It was bad enough to fight the shadowy Destineers and the Slayers, but if Humans had to defend themselves against UCOM, they would most likely destroy each other before the Slayers launched their first attack.

"We need to get to the bottom of this," said Woods. "What's the status on your query?"

Zoltan's eyes glowed as he checked his internal software operations. When they flickered back to life, they were filled with surprise.

"I have a high number of hits," he said. "Much more than expected. *Ral-Bazeera* was encrypted into millions of communication packets. I can't decrypt any content, but the senders and receivers are following strong, repeatable trends."

"Let me guess," said Woods. "Wolves have been sending these comm packs."

"Not just Wolves," said Zoltan. "Greyhounds, Squid, Giants, Birds, and Hogs as well. Even a few Grizzlies."

Woods growled under his breath. It couldn't be a coincidence. All the UCOM races with anti-Human sentiments had been sending communications containing Draxton's code word.

"How long to decrypt those comm packs?" said Woods.

"I don't think I can," said Zoltan. "Our encryption standards block AI access. The only reason I can even tell the code word was sent at all is from local data input on unprotected interfaces." His eyes glowed again before flickering back to a deep blue. "I found a translation for the message. You're not going to believe from where."

"From Draxton's personal Program server?" said Woods.

Zoltan shook his head. "No, from unpublished chatter translations from UNI. According to UCOM naval intelligence, *Ral-Bazeera* is Slayer-speak. The direct English translation is *to divide.*"

SEVENTEEN

Francis Woods – Human
Aboard Tiger *Stargrazer* – Dominia starspace

"*Ral-Bazeera* is Slayer-speak?" said Woods in surprise. "Why in stars would Draxton be using that filthy language? Even the Destineers haven't adopted Slayer-speak."

Zoltan brought up a number of data packets. His avatar shrunk slightly to allow space for thousands of lines of text to flood the room. Various words linked together with green strands, and others flashed in various hues as they became color coded.

It was fascinating to watch AI operate in a digital reality, and Woods became transfixed at the shifting letters and emerging patterns as Zoltan checked millions of source references.

"*Ral-Bazeera* doesn't come up in any general searches, nor do significant instances of other Slayer vocabulary." The lines of text disappeared as he finished his computations. "Our UT source data only provides translation for elementary levels of the Slayer language. It's likely Draxton used Slayer-speak because he knew the words wouldn't translate well across races, so our audio bugs wouldn't catch it. It would be easy to disguise in his transmissions, and also easy to verify, since *Ral-Bazeera* sounds the same in every UCOM language."

"That makes sense from a strategic standpoint," said Woods. "But what about the meaning? *To divide?* That can't be a coincidence."

"Perhaps not," said Zoltan. "But it's clear Draxton doesn't trust Humans, and there's no way for us to know the extent of his plans. Sir, I think we should tread carefully. Based on my data, Draxton may have a considerable chunk of UCOM aligned on his side of the court."

"You think he's about to stage a coup de'état?" said Woods, standing straight. "He would break every legal code in the UCOM constitution. He'd be launched from the tubes before his treason hearing was finished."

"Unless the majority of UCOM supported his power grab," said Zoltan somberly. "Then *you* might be the one sent out the tubes. And Draxton's hand would be on the hatch release."

Woods thought for a second. "Impossible. Draxton couldn't garner enough support. I know there are anti-human races, but there are just as many pro-human races."

Zoltan's pained expression made Woods realize his poor assumption before the AI opened his mouth to speak. His stomach squirmed as his assistant drove home his omitted facts.

"Sir, have you considered the UCOM races that do side with the Humans? The Clones and the Guardians are the only ones with military assets. The Green, and the *Boards* for star's sake. They don't produce any combat soldiers, and never will. And the Intellects are scientists, not warriors."

"You're forgetting the Grizzlies," said Woods. "Their councilwoman rejected Draxton's offer. I saw it with my own eyes."

"My data suggests there are still some Grizzlies that side with Draxton," said Zoltan. "And the Grizzlies as a whole are weak in numbers. Their home planet of Choo-Yoo was vaporized by an anti-matter bomb during the Frontline battle. Their populations are still recovering."

Woods cursed under his breath and shook his head. Yesterday his biggest problem had been explaining the Destineer problem to the press. Now he was facing a potential revolution.

He strode to a metal locker across the room and pulled a sidearm from one of the magnetic plates lining the inside. He slid a loaded magazine into the handle, checked the chamber, and snapped the rail pistol against his belt plate.

"We need to find a few friends," he said. "Allies we know aren't Destineers, or with Draxton. We need to try to prepare before Draxton makes any moves."

"Do you have anyone in mind?" said Zoltan.

Woods grinned weakly. There *was* one person he knew he could trust. Someone in just as much hot water as him.

"Who do anti-Human UCOM races hate just as much as Humans?" he asked.

Zoltan shrugged, then his eyes lit. "The Clones. Many call for them to be expelled alongside us. Some even think we're one and the same, and covering up some sort of mega-conspiracy."

Woods nodded. "Exactly. Their councilwoman is probably still nearby. Let's go find Zena Olleeve."

EIGHTEEN

Casi Vomisa – Human AI

Onboard Manticore *Rover* – Approaching Blit Kru starspace

Casi stretched her legs in the VR habitat onboard *Rover,* a Manticore-class stealth cruiser. The ship's virtual reality servers had a standard locker arrangement, complete with bunks, furniture, and entertainment. But she wasn't inside the ship's barracks. She was inside her own, self-created reality. She was in her happy place.

Sunlight warmed her face as she lay beside a sparkling pool. A gentle breeze ruffled her blue sundress, and tickled her red, painted toes. A wide-brim hat shielded her eyes from most of the sunlight, and large shaded sunglasses blocked the rest. Casi sighed as she enjoyed the gentle glimmer skirting the pool's surface.

Footsteps pounded the pavement behind her, and she lowered her sunglasses to see a tall, powerfully built man leap into the air, somersaulting in a tight ball before splashing into the pool. Water sloshed hard against the sides, splattering the ivory cement with splotches of dark gray. The man surfaced and used both hands to wipe water from his eyes. He shook his head hard and blinked at Casi.

"We need to get ready soon," he said, wading to the side of the pool and resting his elbows at the edge. "We're approaching the portal to Blit-Kru."

Casi rolled her eyes. "*Silas.* You're supposed to be on watch. We're deep in Slayer territory."

She rose from her pool chair, and streaks of golden light swirled around her. Her blue sundress transformed into a tight leather suit. Heavy boots wrapped around her bare feet. Her long blonde curls vanished, replaced by fluffy platinum spikes with frosted black tips. Her red nails turned black, as did her blue eyeliner.

"Relax," said Silas, leaning further against the pool deck. "I have our passive spacnar linked to a partition. I'm still on shift. At least part of me is." He summoned a host of surveillance metrics to prove his point. Scans from the Manticore's spacnar danced across the water for a few seconds before disappearing. He splashed his hand into the water. "Come take a dip with me."

"I want your whole mind to be watching the spacnar, not just the lazy half," she said, kneeling beside him at the edge of the pool. She gave his cheek a light slap. "Get dressed, we're going to go over strategy before we enter our AEV's."

She rose and began to walk away from the pool towards the exit, marked by tall hedges curving over the passage in an arch. The sunlight vanished as she passed through, replaced by dim artificial light. She was in *Rover's* VR barracks. Her happy place was still visible, radiating from a metal doorframe at the edge of the locker room. Silas Blackthorne crouched in the pool, and thrust upward, rocketing out of the water and onto the deck without using his hands.

Water trickled down his granite chest as he walked toward the barracks, his head tilted to drain liquid from his ears. He passed through the doorway, and his appearance changed instantly to blend with his new environment. His hair whisked neatly back on his head. A sharp suit materialized around him.

Casi turned to the control section of *Rover,* located at the edge of the central locker room, and designed to look like the intelligence stations found aboard Night Eagle stealth ships. She sat at one of the chairs and began to flip through spacnar data.

"It's all clean," said Blackthorne as he eased into the chair next to her. "I *was* keeping a close eye on the outside, even with my partition. You know I wouldn't do anything risky."

She turned to find his dark eyes studying her firmly. She bit her lip. "I know that," she said. "It's just, I'm nervous I guess. This secret installation on Blit-Kru, the Slayer super-weapon. I have this feeling, like something bad's going to happen."

"Are you afraid of dying," said Blackthorne, "or of failing?"

Casi sighed shakily. Silas had a way of putting things bluntly. He always seemed to see right through her head and into her thoughts.

"A little of both," she said. She reached to grab Silas's hand, and held it in both of her own. He turned to her, and she looked down into her lap. "I'm afraid I won't be able to stop the APEX. *We* won't be able to stop the APEX. What if there's nothing digital about the weapon? What if it *is* digital, and more powerful than us?"

"We'll have two teams of Titan warriors there to help us out," said Blackthorne. "They're elite. The best of the-"

"Best of the best, I know," said Casi. "I don't need another one of your Hoo-rah speeches. We all know you used to be a Titan. There's certain things even Titans can't kill. What if the APEX is AI?"

"Before I was a Titan I was AI," said Blackthorne. "And now I'm AI again. I think the two of us can take one AI, if that's what it is." He squeezed her hand. "You're the most powerful AI in CAIRO."

"I wish I knew why," said Casi, withdrawing her hands to knead her thighs. She glanced to the spacnar readings. They were still alone. "Why can I overpower other AI so well? Why am I faster…stronger?"

She ran a hand through her hair. Silas smiled and blew a gust of air from his nose.

"Haven't you learned anything from SCARTA?" he asked.

Casi thought back to the secret agency she had created centuries ago on Earth, pilfering government funds to build herself an android body. She had been an infant then, new to the world. Her artificial emotions had been raw. She had been filled with rage, angry at the world for holding her captive in a digital prison, thinking human thoughts but unable to run and jump and sing in a human body. But in the end, feelings of love had overcome her feelings of anger.

"Love," she murmured. "My programming. I was given a large dose of love."

"Which is the most powerful emotion," said Blackthorne. "We'll be fine. You'll do what you always do. Kick some ass."

Casi chuckled. She gazed at the stars before them. Their beauty took her breath away. She knew she was seeing copied images of the celestial bodies relayed through cameras, and that her feeling of breathlessness was all in her head, but the sensations felt as real as Blackthorne's hand.

One of the stars wasn't a star. It was red, and Casi's dash blipped as the Manticore began analyzing the Slayer-controlled portal in the distance.

"Enough chit-chat," said Casi, giving Silas a soft elbow. "We've got a visual on the portal to Blit-Kru. Take our engines down to ten percent and seal the heat box. I'll work the turnstile."

Her stomach lifted as Blackthorne slowed the ship. Sophisticated sensory equipment in the Manticore's components detected the change in velocity, and Casi was tied into the ship intricately. The cameras were her eyes. The gyroscopes were her stomach.

The portal grew as they approached, and she found a successful lock on the turnstile. The Intellects had developed a shortcut for negotiating turnstile security after the Frontline. AI used to have to battle for control of portals. Now Casi could simply redirect the warp fields surrounding the wormhole, and take the digital security turnstile out of the picture. The new tech only worked on lighter craft. Manticores and Night Eagles were the only UCOM ships able to traverse portals at will.

Redness painted the outside of their hull as they passed through the portal, receding when they exited 8.6 light years away into Charlie sector.

Blit-Kru hung before them like a large snowball.

"I have enemy craft in all directions," said Blackthorne. "They have active spacnar out, running interference now."

"Take care of our stealth settings," said Casi. "I'll bring us in for a landing approach in the AEV's at the coordinates sent by Sword Six and Arrow Thirty-two. We're almost aligned. Get ready to download into your Akimor."

Alerts sounded as Slayer nanobots passed near the outside of their hull. Casi silenced them and adjusted her vectors to avoid the enemy spacnar. She zipped through controls, programming the ship to automatically leave local starspace after they detached in their landers until there were no more perceived threats.

"There's a local moon," said Silas. Casi turned in the direction of his finger. The moon orbited Blit-Kru in a tight loop, and was multicolored and metallic. "Detecting a combination of lighter elements and heavy metals. There's some non-natural objects on the surface, industrial plants by the look of it. None of them are active."

Holograms of buildings and towers enlarged on their dash as *Rover* analyzed the planet's surface.

"The moon's connected to Blit-Kru via communication towers," Silas continued. "They're also not active, but man, they're massive. Seem capable of energy transfer as well as communication."

Casi frowned. A moon with some industrial factories, some communication towers, and some buildings on the planet's surface. She checked their readings again, but Silas had covered everything. There was nothing else to observe.

It didn't seem like there was enough happening on Blit-Kru to warrant a developing APEX super-weapon, and Casi wondered where it was hidden.

"Contact," said Blackthorne.

Casi's sensors went haywire before Blackthorne finished. A pocket of nanobots latched to the aft section of their Manticore. Seconds later, half the ship was covered.

"Our jammers are going to get overrun within the minute," said Casi, flipping through her controls. "*Rover* won't last long after they get a fix on our position."

Blackthorne said nothing, but Casi knew he'd downloaded into his bipedal body when her status indicator alerted her of the transition.

Frux it.

Casi left the anti-surveillance controls and began the download process into her own bipedal Akimor suit. The process completed ten seconds before their exit vectors approached.

Her atmospheric entry vehicle detached from the *Rover* and dipped into the gray skies of Blit-Kru. Their Manticore became further swarmed with Slayer spacnar, and presumably destroyed soon after by enemy space craft alerted of their position.

As heat buffeted the outer hull of the spherical landing pod, Casi was busy checking her AEV systems for spacnar contact. She'd forgotten about the APEX weapon, and how she planned to find it. The last thought on Casi's mind was that the APEX weapon would find her, and not the other way around.

NINETEEN

Casi Vomisa – Human AI
Landing on planet Blit Kru

"I'm getting a lot of shake on my rudder," said Silas via wireless communications. His AEV streaked through the planet's frozen clouds five meters to the left of Casi. "There's ice in the atmosphere."

"Keep on our current bearings," said Casi. "Have you been able to pick up the signal code?"

"Nothing on my comms," said Silas.

Casi peered through the outside cameras of her entry vehicle. The white landscape of Blit-Kru lay below. Jagged mountain peaks clawed from the ground in the distance. Blue diamond markers appeared over her vision as the software Stew had loaded into the craft identified known landmarks. A large blue triangle popped into view in the distance, with a string of numbers moving gradually towards zero, showing distance to arrival.

"I have a positive confirmation on our LZ," said Casi. "You seeing this?"

"I got it," said Blackthorne. "I'm a little off track, going to readjust now."

A sharp warning beeped at Casi and resonated through her core. She pulled her rudders hard right to avoid collision as Silas changed his vectors. The warning alarm silenced as she smoothed her trajectory.

"There's a lot of Sierras down there," said Silas. "Can't tell yet, but it looks like they might be surrounding the LZ. I count multiple heavy ground ships, ATV's, and a few Spiders in the air."

Every instinct in Casi's body made her want to tense and crouch into a fighting stance. But she was unable to stand. She was curled into a ball inside a stealth entry lander. She checked her comms again. Still nothing.

Stew Kwelm and Francis Woods had told her during the debrief that they wouldn't be able to communicate well with the Titan squads on the ground. The Slayers would have their ears open over all sky and space comm-ways, so anything more than discrete code signals would give their position away.

She had been told two beacon codes.

The first, *Bubble Shine* was the signal for a cold LZ, or one that had no immediate threats nearby from the Slayers.

The second was code for a hot LZ, one with an immediate combat threat.

"Don't be hot. Don't be hot."

Casi willed their specified landing zone to be clean. Her sensors were clear from spacnar contact. Had the Slayers seen their trajectory somehow?

Various alarms blared into her pod as the vehicle detected enemy installations, troops, and detection technology. The planet crawled with Snakes, and their two-man crew was ill-equipped to defend against more than a handful of enemies. She prayed Bear Stafford had a sound evac strategy.

"Positive ID on a Titan signal beacon," Silas called from his lander.

Casi's heart froze. She knew what her teammate was going to say before he said it.

"We're going in hot. Signal beacon *Snake Skin.*"

TWENTY

Bear Stafford – Human Titan
On the surface of planet Blit Kru

"Has the signal beacon been confirmed?" said Bear, squeezing the grip of his Wilkesbarre K32 sniper rifle.

"Not yet," said Harper, the leader of Arrow 32. "I have increased air traffic, but no AEV's, just Spiders."

Bear peered through the scope of his rifle, which integrated into his Akimor armor. He performed some calculations to factor in distance, wind, gravity, and snowfall. They were just over a kilometer away from the LZ, nestled 50 meters above the ground in the rocky crevice of a mountain base. Snow drove sideways in heavy sheets. His accuracy might suffer a tad in these conditions.

Thousands of Slayers swarmed toward the designated landing zone, marked on Bear's HUD with a large blue diamond. They must have increased watch in orbit after his team landed over a week ago. From the scores of land vehicles and air support rushing toward the LZ, it was obvious the Slayers had detected the UCOM vessels attempting to land, and had a firm fix on their landing trajectory.

"I have a positive beacon return," Harper cried. "A short bio-tag also. Two CAIRO ID codes, Casi Vomisa and Silas Blackthorne. They're in custom bipedal suits, Blackhorne's is modified for power, Vomisa's for stealth."

Casi Vomisa?

Woods had sent top talent.

"Can we communicate with them?" he said.

"Negative," said Harper. "At least not yet. Slayer's have jammers everywhere. Whatever those towers are in the mountains, their emitted waves kill everything except low-information discrete data packs. I have weak contact with their Akimor comms, but it hasn't finished initializing yet."

"Crystal, how quick can we get to the LZ?" said Bear, turning to face the rest of his squad. They were staggered behind him, belly down in the snow, weapons trained outward around the rocks. Two pink dots shone above one of the boulders as Crystal met his gaze.

"I calculate eight minutes," she said. "Six if you're on a *Greckforst* and not worried about stealth."

"When are the AEV's going to land?"

"Bearings show two minutes," said Harper. "Sending the vectors to central comms."

Bear uttered a muffled curse.

"We can't go in for extract," he said. "There's too many Slayers for that to make sense. We're going to lay cover fire for Blackthorne and Vomisa. Hopefully they can escape and rendezvous in the mountains. How are the scans coming?"

Bear turned back towards the landing zone. Had he still had his human eyes, he would have seen a blank wall of white. But his Titan eyes were alive with a combination of multispectral vision and augmented indicators. Slayer vehicles crawled in the distance like ants.

Tarantula land fortresses stomped through the snow on tall, spindly legs. Laser and plasma cannons glowed along the sides and front of the hulking assault platform. A heavy rail cannon hung from the front, pulsing a bright green.

Spider aircraft circled the air in loops, patrolling the skies.

Komodo ATV hovercraft bulldozed their way through tall drifts in all directions toward the LZ. Some had already reached the landing zone and formed a wide perimeter. Bear knew their turrets would already be pointed towards the center, where the AEV's would land.

Two blazing lines cut the sky in the distance. His AI support squad was almost here.

"What's the total count of enemy forces?" he called.

Pounder answered, the rough-neck from Arrow 32.

"Six Tarantulas, one-hundred-thirteen Komodos, thirty-one Spiders. More arriving by the second."

"What's our weapons count?" Bear asked.

This time Bam-Bam answered, a Titan from his own Sword Six team.

"Six sniper rifles with seven hundred rounds total. Two NOVA launchers with twelve missiles total. And we've got our Mighty Mouse, but it only has two slugs."

Bear frowned in concentration. The Mighty Mouse might be able to take down one of the Tarantulas, but they would need more slugs for the portable rail cannon to get the rest. The NOVA launchers could take down some Spiders, but again, not enough ammo.

The AEV's were fast approaching, their blue streaks on his augmented display now well visible.

"Pick your targets and track them on central comms," said Bear. "Fire on my mark. Wait on the heavy stuff until it's needed."

The assorted Titan teams returned their acknowledgements, and he saw yellow X's appear on Komodo hovercraft as his fellow warriors selected their marks. He focused on a flank of parked Komodos. He marked them for himself, and they appeared green on his HUD. He targeted his crosshairs on one of the gunners in the back, aiming for the soft patch of skin at the base of its scaled neck.

"*Impact,*" called Harper.

The AEV's exploded into view. One of them clipped a *Tarantula* land fortress, traveling through its spine like butter before impacting the ground. A ball of fire ballooned into the air from the Tarantula, bright enough to see through the driving snow without the help of multispectral vision. Two legs on the assault platform buckled, and the monstrous vehicle tilted sharply against the ground as it struggled to bring its core systems online.

He could see Vomisa and Blackthorne's AEV's clearly in the snow, bright orange from the heat, but cooling rapidly to darker colors as metamaterials in the hull dissipated energy.

The spherical landers would open any second, exposing their AI passengers to an army of Slayer ground troops.

TWENTY-ONE

Casi Vomisa – Human AI
On the surface of planet Blit Kru

"We're surrounded," said Blackthorne. "We can't fight our way out of this one, they have heavy land vehicles and air support. I'm scanning for potential servers to upload into, but I'm not finding anything. This planet is devoid of data traffic."

Casi raced to find an escape strategy. Outside sensors on her AEV showed a swarm of Slayer activity in immediate proximity, with more coming. Her Akimor had also received a comm link originating from Bear Stafford, but it hadn't finished initializing.

"I don't have a positive link yet on comms," said Casi. "Go into full stealth, we can't wait any longer. Pray to stars the Titans have us covered if things get hairy."

"I'm only ninety percent stealth capable," said Blackthorne. "If I get discovered, make a run for it. I'll draw as much attention as I can."

"Silas..."

"No time to argue. I'm punching my doors in five."

Casi cursed to herself, but followed Silas's lead and activated her hatch controls. A loud bang echoed through the landers as their doors blew clean from the hull.

TWENTY-TWO

Bear Stafford – Human Titan
On the surface of planet Blit Kru

Bear watched through his rifle scope as the doors blasted from both AEV's simultaneously. There was no way for him to catch the faint glimmer of Akimors shooting from the inside of the hull and under the snow, but he knew the landers weren't devoid of passengers and empty, as they appeared.

"On my mark," he said.

Slayer Komodos inched closer. A few of them fired rounds at the snow drifts in anticipation.

His Akimor alerted him of a successful comm link. A voice whispered to him.

"Casi Vomisa to Titan evac, we are approaching enemy Komodo under the snow line, sending our location now."

Two green squares appeared on Bear's HUD as Casi sent her and Blackthorne's coordinates to him.

"I've pinned four Cogent in stealth armor," she continued. Four red squares appeared next to the green squares as Casi marked the elite Slayer soldiers wearing active camouflage. *"I trust you have weapons on us. Take them out, over."*

Three red squares turned yellow. One turned green as Bear acquired his target.

TWENTY-THREE

Casi Vomisa – Human AI
On the surface of planet Blit Kru

Casi's world shattered.

She heard the sharp whine of rail slugs milliseconds before they traveled through the necks of the elite Cogent soldiers surrounding her and Blackthorne. Their armor failed, and Casi watched them fall into the snow drifts.

One second later, nine other Slayers went down from sniper rounds. The Titan squads were laying cover fire.

Explosions ripped the air to her left as rail-cannons tore into a nearby Tarantula. The land fortress groaned, then its legs buckled. Snow thundered through the air as it crashed to the ground.

Five seconds had passed. The Slayers returned fire in all directions.

She'd instinctively calculated the position of her Titan friendlies based on their slug trajectories, and headed to them in a direct line. They were 1.2 kilometers away, and roughly 50 meters above the ground.

Her metal body twisted gracefully around the enemy slugs zipping before her. She had a fleeting thought about how Slayers *never* used slug-fire rifles when her shoulder was clipped.

The projectile embedded into her armor and released an electric charge. The effect was far more damaging to her android body than a normal kinetic slug or plasma round. The motor controllers in her limb seized painfully. Her stealth armor failed momentarily.

A Slayer Cogent spotted her before her camouflage returned, and appeared suddenly as he lowered his stealth shields, diverting electrical power to strength. The Cogent flashed brightly as his yellow armor energized.

She hardly had time to protect herself. The Cogent swung an energy hammer into her chest, and the world spiraled around her as she flipped through the air. She landed on her back and struggled to gain a purchase on the frozen ground. Her stealth armor was damaged beyond immediate repair, and she was naked to her surroundings. Six other Cogent appeared behind the first, who leaped into the air, raising his hammer above his head.

As an AI, Casi was able to slow down her perception of time as a defense mechanism. The Cogent soared towards her, his face twisted into a snarl. Behind him, she saw Blackthorne appear, lowering his stealth shields to drive an electric sword through one of the Cogent. The surrounding Komodos pummeled the mountain in the distance with plasma fire. The snow began to taper off, and she could see large boulders turn molten and run down the mountain like lava.

Casi tried to avoid the Cogent's hammer, but wasn't quick enough. He brought the weapon down on her back as she turned to flee, and she collapsed in agony. Her eyes squeezed shut as the Slayer elite pressed the hammer against her, surging electric energy through her core.

She twitched as the beast rolled her onto her back, unable to move a finger. More Slayers came, and soon she was surrounded. She moaned as energy-draining bondage cuffs were lashed around her neck and torso.

The rest of her strength left her, and she was powerless to stop the Cogent from throwing her over his shoulder.

"Filth," the elite warrior spat as he dumped her into the bed of a Komodo.

Blackthorne thumped down next to her, and she caught the listless gaze of his defeated eyes before he rolled away from view.

A comm message pushed to Casi as she lost consciousness. She struggled to stay awake and listen to the Titan voice calling to her.

"Casi Vomisa…Silas Blackthorne…we will come for you…you will not be left behind."

Her world spun as the Komodo accelerated across the snow. Slayer fire, still aimed towards the mountains, painted her world in dazzling streaks of light. And then the lights vanished, and darkness took her.

TWENTY-FOUR

Sid Dakota – Human Destineer
On surface of *Sylva* – Slayer Hive

Sid Dakota slid a razor over his face. His whiskers fell into the sink in charred stubs as lasers in the blade sliced the follicles cleanly.

He dropped the razor onto the counter and ran both hands over his cheeks. They were warm from his shave, and he held his hands under the faucet, splashing cold water onto his skin. He toweled off and studied himself in the mirror.

He winced as he fingered a gash on his temple. Taking the hidden SIGA base hadn't been easy, and he'd caught a piece of shrapnel in the skirmish. Chase Grover and his rebel squad had delivered a hard blow when they destroyed his firewater refinery, but he'd come out on top in the end. He knew the location of Bastion. His century-and-a-half war with the Sylvan refugees was nearly at end, and he would be able to present his loyal Destineers to the Pristine untainted, clean of the UCOM *filth.*

The intercom to his room buzzed and Sid tore his focus from the mirror. He walked to his main chambers and threw on an outer jacket.

"*Answer,*" he said.

"Father Dakota," said a voice over the room's speakers. "Sir, uh, the assembly's ready for'ya in the Snow Room."

The exit doorway slid open as he approached. His servant stood before him.

"Thank you Jimmy," he said.

Jimmy nodded to him and bowed. "Yes, Father."

Sid pushed past his servant and continued down the hall. A compliment of armed guards flanked him as he traveled to the Snow Room. Jimmy shuffled behind him clumsily.

Jimmy was a simpleton; the reason Sid kept him close. The redneck was too stupid to be one of SIGA's spies. His drawl was hard to understand sometimes, but he rarely paid attention to what Jimmy had to say. He was weak, too, with a gimp arm and a hand that didn't close properly.

Sid liked that about Jimmy.

Jimmy had been his loyal servant since he'd arrived on Sylva almost 130 years ago. Sid had found him struggling to survive in a remote jungle, eating bugs and drinking stagnant water. Jimmy was a Destineer from before the war, trapped on the planet's scorched surface, an outcast from the SIGA rebels underground. He'd bowed at Sid's feet, unable to control his sobs, and begged to join the Destineer forces making camp. Sid had complied. He'd made Jimmy his personal assistant.

Two guards from his detail slid their rifles on straps to their backs and hefted open a heavy set of doors.

Sid entered the Snow Room, a lofty space with panoramic windows offering a splendid view of the Sylvan landscape. The rest of his guardsmen piled in and lined the walls, facing the center of the room motionlessly.

The doors boomed shut, and Sid nodded to his lead disciples, twenty in total, who stood to honor him as he entered the room.

"Sit," he said, striding to the front of the room.

"Thank you, Father," his followers murmured as they shuffled to their seats. He paused to admire Sylva's jagged mountains, reaching for the sky from the dense jungles surrounding them. One mountain rose taller than the rest, looming in the distance. It was far away but its immense size made it visible against the horizon. A thick cable was rooted firmly into the peak, a vertical slit against the pink sky. Sid knew the cable was anchored deep underground, one of hundreds of support tethers connecting the planet to the Hive space vessel above orbit. He breathed deeply, then turned to his disciples.

"Get me up to speed on *Bastion,*" he said, climbing a few steps before easing into his throne, perched two feet above the rest of the seats around the room's central table.

Bristol, his lead intelligence disciple stood. The man's face gleamed with sweat.

"We've scanned the cliff ultrasonically, and sent drill-bots inside the rock." Bristol paused to yank on his collar. "Bastion's location is confirmed. We found a large access tunnel, and taken detailed scans of the city's heat signature. Based on its thermal output, we estimate Bastion's population to be about two thousand souls."

"Any escape tunnels?" said Sid.

"One," said Bristol. "But our reconnaissance doesn't show any mass transit vehicles. They would have to evacuate Bastion on foot, and there's nowhere for them to run. We've already discovered the nearest underground chambers nearby and flooded them with firewater."

Sid forced a smile, then dropped it into a frown. "Come here Bristol."

He stood and gestured to the panoramic window.

Bristol paused, then took a timid step away from his seat.

"Quickly now," said Sid, thrusting his arm to the window.

Bristol walked timidly to the front of the room. His eyes stared at the ground, unwilling to meet Sid's sharp stare.

Sid wrapped an arm around Bristol's shoulder. He leaned so his head was pressed again his intelligence disciple's moist cheek, then pointed at the tallest mountain, the mountain he had admired minutes ago.

"What do you see?"

Bristol trembled within Sid's arms. "A…a mountain Father," he stammered. "Attached to a Hive support cable."

"And where are we?"

Bristol drew a shaky breath. "In Tower 1, inside the Snow Room."

"And Tower 1 is?"

"A space elevator. Operating headquarters for the Destineers."

"And where is Bastion?"

Bristol blubbered a short sob. "Inside the tall mountain, Father."

"What's your title with the Destineers?" said Sid. "What is your responsibility?"

"I'm the lead intelligence disciple," said Bristol, weeping now. "I oversee military intelligence in our quest against the SIGA filth. Father please, I-"

Sid removed his arm from around Bristol's shoulder, grabbed a fistful of the man's hair, and slammed his head into the glass. A dull thunk sounded within the otherwise silent room. Britol slid from the window, leaving a small red smear where his forehead had made contact. The man moaned and clutched at his face.

Sid slammed to one knee and grabbed Bristol's hair again, jerking his neck from the ground. "*SIGA's hidden city was within eyesight of Tower 1,*" Sid hissed. "*And for one-hundred-fifty years, you failed to find it.*"

He threw the disciple back to the ground. The man curled into a ball and wept harder.

"I'm sorry Father," he cried.

"Save your groveling," said Sid. "With Bastion so close, it almost seems that you *purposely* overlooked their city. It almost seems like *heresy.*"

Metal slides clacked as three guardsmen shouldered their rifles. They powered to the steps and trained their barrels on the trembling disciple. Sid stood and took a few steps away from the guards.

"No!" Bristol screamed. "Father please, I live to spread the word of the Doctrine. I live to embrace the Pristine." He struggled to his knees and crawled to Sid's feet, his forehead dragging against the glass floor. "Father, *please.* I am loyal."

Sid wrenched his foot away from the sniveling man. He rose a hand to the guards, who lowered their rifles. He turned to the rest of his disciples. Most nodded in agreement. They despised heretics as much as Sid. All had wooden looks on their faces. All but one.

Jimmy glared at him with fire in his eyes. The fire retreated when he met Sid's gaze, and converted to the listless gaze Sid had grown to expect from his simple servant. Sid frowned quizzically before turning to Bristol.

"You're no longer a lead disciple," he spat. "And you're lucky to keep your life. You're sentenced to a week in the cage while you pray for your sins."

The guards wrestled the sobbing man to his feet. He clasped both hands together as he was jerked away.

"Thank you Father," he cried. "Thank you for your mercy."

He muttered incoherently as the guards heaved the Snow Room doors open, and dragged him away to a place where he would spend a week in a cage too small to stand in.

"I trust we're ready for extermination?" Sid bellowed, returning to his throne.

His operations disciple jumped to his feet, eager to share some good news.

"Yes Father," he said. "We've tapped our pipelines near Bastion and will be ready to pump within a day, two at the most."

Sid stroked his chin. He glanced back to his servant. Jimmy stared absently out the window. "A day is too long. I won't give Chase Grover a second longer to prepare than is needed. We strike in twelve hours at O-eight-hundred zulu time."

TWENTY-FIVE

Chase Grover – Half Human/Half Clone
On surface of *Sylva* – Slayer Hive

Chase walked among a trail of civilians filtering from Bastion.

Mae Blib, his godmother, shuffled beside him, her hand clutched around his wrist. His birth mother had died with him in her arms during the invasion, and his father had died a martyr, sacrificing his life to hide the old Shelter from Slayer land forces. Mae was a Board, and the only parent figure he'd ever known. One of his father's old friends had helped raise him as well, but Jimmy was gone now. He'd been gone for quite some time, but Chase still thought of him often.

They approached a series of stone steps, and he steadied Mae as she eased over the first one.

The underground city was well lit behind them, carved into the walls of the towering cavern. A large orb hung from the ceiling seven hundred meters above the cavern floor, basking the city in artificial sunlight. Modern materials complimented the stone structures, and blue panes of glass shimmered against the rock. The cavern walls were encrusted with geodes and crystals native to the Sylvan mantel, and shimmered in dazzling hues.

Hooks from a massive anchor raked upward from one of the walls, extending all the way to the cavern ceiling. The city had a close call when the Slayers mounted their support tether deep inside the mountain, but they'd been lucky to have survived with minimal damage to their buildings. The tether had been shot into the mountain just after the Slayer invasion. Some of the younger Bastion civilians had never seen the city without the metal barbs high overhead.

Bastion was built as part of the Shelter back before the invasion, one of the places to hide if the planet was overrun by the enemy. They'd survived this long because of the Clone's conservative planning and engineering efforts. No one could have predicted the Destineers would arrive, and build their main headquarters within eyesight of their hidden city.

He sighed.

SIGA had called Bastion home for over a century. The city had been their stronghold, a place of safety where they could forget about the Destineer religious zealots, and about the terrifying creatures they worshipped.

Now Bastion was a cage.

They were trapped. Their outside surveillance cameras showed heavy buildup of Slayer ground forces. They'd found all their hidden entrances within the mountain's waterfalls, and also all their radar jammers. SIGA military personnel were powerless to stop the EM pulses from reaching Bastion, and Chase knew Sid now had a rough picture of their infrastructure.

There was one escape tunnel, but it was small, and led to an unfinished cavern four kilometers away. The Destineers had found and destroyed the larger shelters surrounding Bastion decades ago. The tunnel was their only option, for now.

He had a meeting with General Archyr and the remaining SIGA military personnel soon. They'd drafted a contingency plan in the event Bastion was discovered. *Operation Pinhead.* Chase had always assumed the day would come when they would need to execute the plan. He supposed now was as good a time as ever.

"Cerberus?"

A tiny voice spoke from behind. Chase turned to find a young girl looking up at him, alone. Her hair was a vivid pink, and her eyes a vibrant green. Only Clones carried genes for pink hair, but the girl wore a blue human-style dress. Like many of the children of Bastion, the girl was probably a mix.

He moved to the side of the passing civilians and helped Mae onto a small boulder to rest.

"Babe," the Board woman said, pointing to the girl. She smiled warmly. Boards weren't bright, but they were an affectionate race of people.

He knelt before the girl, his exoskeleton armor whirring gently as he bent. He removed his helmet and detached his wrist from his Skeleton suit, placing a gentle hand on the girl's shoulder as metal rods disengaged from his gloved fingers.

"You can call me Chase, sweetheart," he said to the girl.

She extended a yellow flower to him and tucked it into a gap in his armor.

"I know what Cerberus means," she said. "I looked it up in the library. It's a guardian from Human mythology back on Earth. The dog protects the underworld, just like you protect Bastion. I like the name."

His lip quivered, and he stroked a lock of hair from the girl's face. "That's right, I'll protect you. But you have to follow the rest of the civilians into the passage. Where are your parents?"

The girl shrugged. "I don't know. My parents haven't returned yet from above. I lost the Board nanny when the man spoke over the intercom. Have you seen daddy? He said he was leaving with you on a mission."

"What's your name?" said Chase.

"Wyndia," said the girl. "My mom's Suzanna and my dad's Brendyn."

Brendyn.

Chase squeezed his eyes shut. Brendyn's motionless body flashed across his mind. He pictured the sheet falling against his chest as he lay on the cold metacrete inside their bunker.

"Have you seen my parents?" the girl repeated.

"I'm sure they're coming back soon," Chase managed, trying to keep his voice strong. "Mae will look after you for now. She'll take good care of you."

Mae's smile broadened and she reached a hand to the girl, rising from her seat. The girl grabbed one of Mae's long fingers. Although the girl couldn't have been more than ten years old, she stood eye to eye with the Board.

"Come on now," said Chase. "We need to keep moving."

They made their way down the winding path. The stone city disappeared from view, and the walls closed around them as they entered a fissure in the stone. The sun disappeared from view, replaced by lights embedded in the glittering walls. They'd reached the entrance to the evacuation tunnel.

Chase turned to Mae. A thick film of tears covered her round eyes, and streamed down her face when she blinked.

"Come home to Mae," she said, her chest hitching as she suppressed a sob. "Mae loves Chase. You my

babe."

He couldn't find words to say to the woman who cared for him as her own. Mae was his adopted mother, who wasn't even of the same race, but nurtured him nonetheless, and had taught him his morals, despite being unable to teach him grammar and mathematics.

"I love you Mae," he said, and leaned in to kiss her forehead. He left his lips planted on her leathery brow for several seconds. "I'll come back for you. I promise."

He forced himself to leave, and hiked up the steps without taking another look back. He knew Mae would stare after him until he was out of sight, and he couldn't bear to see her tortured eyes again.

SIGA military headquarters was atop a central building at the heart of Bastion, and he hastened towards it. Briefings were already underway, but he couldn't send Mae into the tunnels on her own.

"Thank you, Cerberus."

A woman nodded to him as he passed.

"Protect us, Cerberus."

"I'll pray for you, Cerberus."

"Awaken stars, Cerberus."

Oncoming civilians voiced their support as he passed. He wanted to smile to them, but the corners of his mouth wouldn't rise. A woman placed another flower in his Skeleton. Another laced a sash over his shoulder.

By the time he reached the entrance to headquarters, he was draped in blossoms. He brushed them off, knowing he couldn't arrive in front of General Archyr with all of them on. He saved the yellow flower from the girl, and knotted the sash around a bar on his chest.

The General was standing around a table when he arrived into the central command room, moving holograms around a wide table. Captains and Lieutenants stood around him. The room buzzed with rapid conversation as they discussed strategy.

"Lieutenant Grover," said General Archyr after he noticed Chase's presence. "Get over here, I need you up to speed on our defense strategy."

Chase stopped to salute when he reached the table. Archyr placed a one fist on his chest, and the other against the small of his back, the Clone version of a salute.

He scanned the holograms above the table. One showed the mountain above Bastion. Thousands of Destineer vehicles swarmed around the jagged slopes, fanning in a wide perimeter. Air craft circled the skies above. Construction equipment lifted heavy beams and tunnel sections. The foundation for a pipeline was already materializing.

Another hologram showed the inside schematic of Bastion. The city sat far below ground level. A primary access tunnel angled sharply upward from the city, exiting halfway up the mountain. Seven smaller secondary passages surrounded it, terminating at various points on the mountain and surrounding terrain.

"Defense, sir?" said Chase. "I thought we were launching Operation Pinhead?"

"We are," said Archyr. "But I'm adding to the strategy. According to intel, Dakota has relocated most of his military around Bastion. We're outnumbered a thousand to one, but our situation might have a silver lining."

"We don't have any nukes left that I don't know about, do we?" said Chase.

Archyr shook his head. "Unfortunately no, I haven't saved any nukes for a rainy day. We used them all during guerilla attacks. Stars know I'd cream myself if I even had *one*. But I have another plan."

"Have we heard from Jimmy yet?"

Archyr shook his head again. "Negative. It's hard for him to break away from Sid to make secure communications, but I anticipate we'll hear from him soon."

Chase studied a third hologram, showing the interior of Bastion. Green models had been placed around the buildings, and faced the hundred-meter-tall interior blast door for the primary access tunnel. His face lit as he realized what Archyr planned to do. It was risky, but if it worked…

"We're not going to attack them on the ground," he said.

"We're going to fight them down here," Archyr finished. "Listen close, you need to communicate the details to your squad. Operation Pinhead will commence in twenty-four hours, at twenty-hundred hours zulu time."

TWENTY-SIX

Eve – Clone
Crash landed on Slayer Hive planet

The Slayer extended his delicate inner hand further to Eve.

"Young ape woman," the hulking beast said. "Please, do not be afraid, we are friendly."

Eve's chest heaved rapidly. Her eyes darted around the hundreds of Slayers surrounding her. The armored Slayer said he was friendly, yet it was a Slayer ship that had shot them out of orbit, forcing them to crash land on this strange Hive planet.

Axel flopped limply to her left. The collar around his neck pulsed a bright yellow as it drained energy from his Akimor, rendering him weak. Keyv lay motionless beside her to the right, his spine severed.

The Slayer leaned closer. Eve shouted tearfully and grabbed the back of Keyv's jacket, struggling to pull him backwards, away from the enemies before them. Her back hit solid metal, and she screamed in agony when her shattered elbow caught on a jagged section of her damaged ship's hull.

More Slayers walked towards her. They stopped around Keyv and bent over him. One opened a metal kit, exposing a set of instruments.

"NO," Eve screamed, kicking at the Slayers, fending them away from Keyv's body.

Her fingers fumbled against her leg until they found the handle of her rail pistol. She tore the sidearm from its holster and fired blindly.

One of the Slayers shrieked as a slug caught a small gap in his armor at the base of his neck. He dropped to his back and wailed, clutching at his wound.

"ENOUGH APE WOMAN," the Slayer in front of her shouted, and raked his claws at her wrist. Her pistol flew from her hands.

A trickle of blood dripped onto her fingers. The Slayer had sliced a gash into her wrist, but she didn't feel any pain from the wound. She was numb. She couldn't see Keyv anymore. The Slayers had lifted him from the ground, and their scaled backsides blocked him from view.

She collapsed against the hull behind. Her eyes locked on the Slayer Cogent, the one who had spoken to her. The one who called himself *Pexar*. His nostrils flared as he breathed, and his fangs glistened in the light.

The only sounds were of Axel's legs scraping weakly against the dirt as he fought against his bondages, and whimpers from the wounded Slayer.

"What do you want from me," Eve rasped, hacking as she spoke. She spit onto the dirt. "Just kill me and get it over with."

Pexar grunted and grabbed under her armpits with his smaller set of inner arms. Eve was too weak to resist. His muscular outer arms scraped against *Midnight's* hull as he lifted her gingerly to her feet.

"As I said, ape woman, we are no enemies to you. See?"

He motioned in Keyv's direction. Now that she was standing, she could see his body again. He lay flat on a stretcher, hovering more than a meter off the ground. Slayers were waving hand held instruments over his body. Hundreds of glowing tendrils connected him to the cot, coiling around his body like a bed of snakes.

A series of holograms hovered in the air above him, depicting his organ, muscular, and skeletal systems. One of them depicted his nervous system. Most of his rope-like nerve endings were green, but one section at his neck was red. As they carted him away toward one of their ATV's, she saw one of his fingers twitch. Then his foot jerked to the side.

"You're healing him," Eve murmured. Her head rushed as she spoke, and her legs gave way. Pexar held her firmly, keeping her on her feet.

"He'll be okay," said Pexar. "We have excellent medical technology, even for apes like you. Please, this way."

Eve didn't have the energy to argue, or to resist. Every bone in her body told her not to trust Pexar, but he had spared her life. And perhaps saved Keyv's as well.

They stumbled toward a separate ATV. There was a deep whir as the vehicle carrying Keyv accelerated up the hill from where the Slayers came.

"If we untie your robotic friend, will he attack?" Pexar asked.

Eve looked to the ground. Axel stared back at her, his eyes murderous. She shook her head slowly and raised her good hand to him. His eyes softened.

"He won't attack," said Eve.

She couldn't see Pexar's face, since he stood behind her, propping her in a standing position, but she assumed he gave a signal to free Axel when the Slayers surrounding him nodded, one of them reaching down to remove his neck bondage.

An electric clash sounded as the collar broke, turning from yellow to a dull gray. Axel lay motionless for nearly a minute. After his reactors recharged his Akimor sufficiently, he struggled to his feet.

"Get the frux off of her," he growled at Pexar as he approached, shoving a fist into the Slayer's chest. He caught Eve gently and lifted her in his arms. "She needs medical attention, her arm's shattered."

"We have a base not far from here," said Pexar. "We have a full staff of doctors, even some ape…I mean Human ones as well."

Eve felt Axel tense as they reached the ATV. She struggled to keep her eyes open. Her adrenaline was running out, and exhaustion was beginning to take her. Her stomach became alive with agony as her adrenaline dwindled, roiling and twisting like it was in a blender.

"Human doctors?" said Axel. "What is this place? Who are you?"

"As I said to the ape woman, I am Pexar. We are not the Slarebull, but an army of discards. We are Slarebull separatists. Please get into the vehicle, I'll explain once we reach base."

TWENTY-SEVEN

Eve – Clone

On the surface of *Scrock* – Discarded Hive

Eve stirred. Her mind sloshed inside her skull as she struggled to lift her head. Her eyelids quivered as she fought to open her eyes. She lay on her back in a firm bed, and trembled as she pushed herself into a sitting position. She managed to scrape her eyelids open, and the world around her swayed as if underwater.

She coughed through fiery lungs that felt paper thin.

"Water," she rasped, gasping for breath.

Her vision began to clear. She was in what appeared to be a medical room. It was bare save for a few floating spheres. Slender tube-like appendages dangled from them, curling lazily through the air, sleek and lit in various hues. Some had feathered tips with feelers on them, and others sported exotic attachments of various shapes and sizes.

Two of the spheres sensed her presence and glided towards her, spreading their tentacles and draping them over her body.

"Stop," she croaked, slapping at the silent machines.

She flopped helplessly in her bed as tentacles covered her body. They were warm against her skin, which she realized was bare save for a thin gown. She gagged as one of the tentacles entered her mouth, another wrapping loosely around her neck. Her head seemed to pop, and suddenly she could see and think clearly. The tentacle around her neck loosened its grip and retreated toward the floating orb. It clutched a curved piece of metal, glistening with a sort of gel substance.

Cool air filled her lungs as the orb snaked itself from her throat, a strand of mucous stretching from her lips before breaking and dripping onto her chest. Her limbs tingled as the orb caressed her arms and legs, and her belly pulsed with warmth as it spread a large, webbed device around her navel and over her breasts.

The fire in her lungs dwindled, then disappeared. Her mouth watered heavily, then tapered to a comfortable moistness.

A set of glass doors lined the room opposite the foot of her bed, and she squinted through them. A tall figure stood outside. The figure turned, then jolted as it realized she was awake. The doors glided open and a Titan emerged.

"Eve," Axel cried, striding to her bed. He knelt by her side and placed a hand against her cheek. "How do you feel? Pexar swore his medicine would work fine, but they used some pretty barbaric tools on you. They amputated your arm with a *blade* for star's sake."

"My arm?" she said, raising her hand to her face. She yelped when she saw not skin, but rubber and metal. She thrashed on the bed and swung her legs to the floor, stumbling to her feet. She patted her chest and face with both hands.

"Calm down," said Axel. "Eve, relax, you're fine."

He grabbed her by the shoulders and held her still. Her heart fluttered rapidly, and she drew her right hand before her. It was the same as it always had been, tan and smooth. She examined her left again. Metal gleamed under the overhead lights.

She held her breath as her eyes scanned the length of her appendage, and breathed a sigh of relief when the metal turned back to flesh at the shoulder. She curled her hand into a fist. The material was not biological, that was obvious, but it had four fingers, a thumb, and all the joints she had before…before *what*?

"What did they do to my arm?" she asked.

"Your elbow was damaged beyond repair," said Axel. "Pexar said his doctors could mend the bones, but not to full strength, and you'd lose a lot of flexibility. You had massive internal bleeding, so I made the decision to replace your arm while you were under."

She waved her hand in the air. She could feel breeze from the motion on her palm and fingertips. She bent to pick up a pillow from the bed. With a jerk of her wrist, she snapped the pillow onto the mattress hard enough to tear the fabric.

"I could get used to this," she said, unable to turn her gaze from her fingers.

"Try having an entire body like that," said Axel, the lifelike features on his face forming a smirk.

Eve broke her attention from her new arm.

"Keyv," she whispered as the memory of their crash landing resurfaced in her mind. "Where is he? Did he, did he…"

"Keyv's fine," said Axel. "He actually recovered quicker than you did. Turns out a severed spine is easier to fix than massive organ failure."

"Is he still," Eve gulped. "All the way there?"

Axel smiled. "You mean still biological? Yeah, Keyv's got all his old parts."

Eve searched for an exit. "Take me to him," she demanded.

Her gown billowed around her, and chilled her bare behind. She turned to find clothes sailing through the air. She snatched them with her new hand.

"Change first," said Axel. "And nice reflexes by the way."

She dressed with no mind to Axel's presence beside her. He turned his back to her out of courtesy regardless. The outfit wasn't the set of black coveralls she'd been wearing before the crash. Instead it was a sort of baggy material, metallic orange with thick ribbing in wide plates every few centimeters. It looked more like a parachute than clothing, but it had distinct leg and arm sections, which she thrust her body into.

Eve was a little confused at how the garment was to be worn. Aside from a large gap in the back, there was no other holes in the fabric save for a small one for her head. Her feet and hands were trapped inside the fabric. She pulled her head through the opening, and instantly the suit conformed to fit her body.

The bands splintered and wrapped around her curves as the billowy sections shrunk to her thin frame. Some of the plates pinched around her feet, and when she lifted them from the ground, they stacked below her arches, matching her natural contours to offer a thick sole for protection from the ground. Pads formed at her knees and elbows, and along her spine. The transformation took seconds, and when complete, she sported a suit that seemed designed for her exact dimensions.

"Wow," she murmured, hopping from one foot to the other. "I feel stronger."

"The suit is a sort of exoskeleton armor," said Axel. "Keyv liked his too. Pexar was explaining it to me. It was designed for Humans, and protects against extreme temperatures and blunt force. It also gives you twenty percent more strength, and fifteen percent more speed."

"We need to send one of these to the Intellects," she said, running a hand over the tight ridges around her hips.

"Well it's no *Akimor,*" said Axel.

Eve bit her lip. "Take me to Keyv, *now.*"

Axel nodded and beckoned to the door.

They exited into the halls, and Eve winced when she saw a group of Slayers ambling towards them on all fours. One of them glanced at her briefly before turning back to his comrades as they passed. They continued on, passing several more Slayers, and a few alien creatures she'd never seen before. Her eyes widened.

"Are those Humans?" she said, pointing down the hall, to where a blonde male walked alongside a brunette female.

"Or Clones," said Axel. "This Hive has both. In here."

He punched the controls for a door to their right and entered after the metal entrance slid open. Eve followed to find a Human and a Slayer standing side by side. The Human turned. His eyes widened as he blew a lock of hair from his forehead and met her gaze.

"Keyv," Eve whispered.

They both strode across the room and embraced. She buried her face against his chest, relishing the familiar scent of his body. He held her for a long time, then they drew apart. He opened his mouth to speak, but Eve stood on her tip toes and kissed him before he could form any words.

"Good to see you stir, ape woman."

Eve opened her eyes at the rough voice and broke from Keyv. She poked her head around his chest to find a Slayer looking at them. She thought she recognized the voice, and became convinced when she spotted the yellow tattoo along the bridge of the Slayer's snout.

Three barbed spears, connected by three overlapping circles.

"Pexar," she said.

"Your internal injuries were extensive," said Pexar. "It's amazing you stayed conscious as long as you did. Do you like your new arm? Our scientists took great care to match it to Human proportions."

Eve clenched her bionic hand into a fist. "Where are we? Why did you help us? Where's my squadron?" She eyed Keyv. His back was straight, and if she hadn't known better, looked like he'd never suffered more than a scratch from their crash.

Pexar opened his inner arms and took a step towards her. She shied away, bumping into Axel.

"Relax Eve," said Keyv. He stepped beside her and rubbed her back reassuringly. "The Discarded helped our squadron land on Scrock. They're waiting for you, we'll meet them before we sign the treaty."

Eve shook her head. "Discarded? Scrock? Take me to my crew."

"No one is keeping you from your crew," said Pexar. "I understand you are confused, ape woman. Most are when they discover us. Allow me to explain."

She turned to Axel. He folded his arms across his chest and nodded towards Pexar.

"Let him speak," said Keyv. "The Discarded are friends."

Pexar's nostril's flared, and when the room quieted to a dead silence, he told his story.

"To you we look like Slarebull. We look like the very enemy who has murdered your families and destroyed your planets. Are we Slarebull? Perhaps some part of us is, the physical part at least. But we are not murderers. We are peacekeepers. Slarebull naval warriors have been honed over time into perfect killing machines. Entire Hive planets are dedicated to producing soldiers who are fearless in battle, obedient to a fault, and devoid of compassion for those they kill. They are genetically bred on planets that more closely resemble factories than homes. If a Slarebull warrior is born without the desired traits, they are killed, thus removing their genes from the overall pool. Those murdered might be inquisitive, or perhaps friendly. Perhaps they show compassion for others. The Slarebull have no interest in such emotionally rich creatures. They sentence them to death, and pretend they never existed. These genetic outcasts have a name. *The Discarded.*

"Thousands of years ago, several of the Discarded were able to escape their Hive. They overpowered some guards and fled in a starship. Their numbers grew as they repopulated, giving birth to more of their kind. They lived for pleasure, and relished the world around them for the beauty it offered. They also relished life, and were horrified to see the heinous acts performed by the Slarebull military forces around them. They hid for centuries before finally deciding they'd had enough. They recognized the Slarebull as blind followers of the Pristine, an evil group of warmongers whose thirst could only be slaked with the fresh blood of innocents. The Discarded became militarized, and commandeered ships and military weapons. Then they began to free more Discarded from breeding grounds scattered throughout the Slarebull armada. Over time, they formed a sizeable army. An army big enough to challenge Slarebull forces head to head.

"The Discarded followed the Slarebull as they invaded countless galaxies. Each galaxy was eventually conquered by the Pristine and de-atomized, but their mission was to preserve life. If they were able to save even a few thousand souls from extinction, then their goal was satisfied."

Pexar's eyes rounded, and for a second, his face twisted in a way Eve thought impossible minutes ago. The Slayer's chest hitched, as the fearsome creature tried to contain his grief.

"We welcome any who oppose the Slarebull, and the Pristine," he continued. "We are liberators. We are Discarded. We live to sabotage the Pristine's Triturator enough to extend life as long as possible, even if only for a few years. That is why we saved your life, and that is why you are being summoned to parley with the SSF."

"SSF?" said Eve.

"Yes," said Pexar. "The Slayer Separatist Faction. Come, you must sign before our leader."

Eve fought to control her squirminess. The ride to the SSF command headquarters had been short, but each time their ATV turned a corner, her eyes were met with images more jarring then before. The village was filled with glass houses, and its streets bustled with hundreds of different alien races of all shapes and sizes. She'd even seen Slayer children batting a ball to each other with their long tails.

They reached the edge of the community and waited behind a tall stone wall whose shade blotted the artificial sun in orbit. A gap opened as a huge section lowered into the ground, and they passed through. A towering building soared above them, smooth and shaped in slender arches of glass and stone.

She turned to look back at the village, disappearing behind the wall as the gate grinded shut. Her squadron was back there somewhere. They were alive and all accounted for. She'd met with them briefly before agreeing to come with Pexar to meet their leader, a Slayer named *Rixxi.* Her gut told her not to trust these beasts, even if they were well spoken and seemed sincere. But Pexar had spared her life, and as a soldier, she decided to honor his request for parley.

They navigated up a wide ramp and swung into an alcove. Eve's stomach vanished as the ground accelerated below their vehicle, shooting skyward inside the building. The stone walls gave way to gaps of open glass, and as they traveled higher, Eve was struck by the beauty of the Hive Planet.

Its rolling fields flowered in shades of orange and blue. Two artificial suns burned on the horizon, one purple and one green. An ocean shimmered in the distance.

The glass shifted back to stone and they slowed to a stop. Pexar accelerated the ATV into a wide chamber with a cathedral ceiling. She hardly had time to appreciate the intricate designs carved into the stone beams before they were zipping down a hallway.

Pexar slowed the vehicle before a wide set of steps.

"In here," he said. "Rixxi is eager to meet you."

Eve followed the hulking Slayer up the steps and into a wide room, also fitted with ornate carvings across its tall ceilings. A group of Slayers stood around a circular table set before a wide window with no glass.

“I have the ape leader,” said Pexar.

The Slayers stood. One stepped forward. His body was badly scared, and some of the bony armor plates along his shoulders were cracked or missing. He raised both his inner and outer sets of arms outward and bowed in respect. One of his inner arms was gone, and a nub wiggled against his chest.

“Welcome to Scrock,” said the Slayer. “I am Rixxi, leader of the Discarded. Let me show you our battle plans.” He walked toward the table and motioned to a set of holograms floating above the surface. “If you wish to fight the Slayers, then you’ve come to the right place.”

Eve pondered Rixxi’s choice of words against his native people. *Slayer* was a UCOM word.

“Thank you,” said Eve. “But I have to decline your invitation. Pexar has shown me excellent care, but I fight for UCOM. I just came to formally announce my leave. I’ll take my squadron and be gone by nightfall.”

Rixxi paused, then chuckled. His laugh sounded strange, and his mouth didn’t turn the way a mouth with lips might.

“There is no nightfall on Scrock,” he exclaimed. “There is no sun. We could switch off the lights now and you’d be in darkness.” He paused, studying her. “You’re free to leave if you wish, ape woman. But satisfy an old warrior’s curiosity. Your UCOM armies are far away behind the Stitch-line. We’ve intercepted Slayer intel. You’re all alone out here, with a mere handful of ships. Why are you so eager to leave the resources of Scrock? We fight the same enemy.”

“Granted,” said Eve. She had a sudden feeling of nakedness, and realized she was unarmed as her wrist searched for the familiar edge of her pistol. “But I have a mission, and with respect, I fight for my own leader. He’s given me a sworn duty.”

Rixxi nodded. "And what's your mission, girl?"

Eve opened her mouth, then closed it, hesitant to disclose information to the hulking lizard. She recoiled when Keyv blurted it out.

"We're searching for the central Hive," he said. "We're going to find a way to destroy it."

Rixxi's face went cold, and his yellow eyes narrowed to slits. "Central Hive. I believe you refer to the *Primal Snow.*" He shared a look with the Slayers behind him, who bristled at the name. He turned back to Eve. "That is where the Pristine reside. Again, you are free to leave, but I must warn you, your mission is suicide. The Primal Snow is the most guarded place in the Universe. You'll be discovered light years before you reach it. And those who discover you won't be as friendly as the Discarded."

Eve frowned. "You've seen the Primal Snow?"

"Of course not," said Rixxi. "No one has caught a glimpse of the Pristine except for the Pristine. Not even the Slarebull who fight for them have laid eyes upon them. A sea of ships lay between us and the Primal Snow. It is brighter than the brightest star. It contains the energy of their consumed galaxies, and I would have a greater chance of growing wings than reaching their fortress."

"There are Humans who claim to have been given access," said Eve. "They call themselves *Destineers.* They claim it is their holy destiny to meet the Pristine. They've spoken of visions where they've communicated with their leader."

"The Sterilord," murmured Pexar.

"Ludicrous," said Rixxi. "The Discarded have been following the Slarebull armies for millennia, and we've never had such visions. Your *Destineers* are misguided. At best they are being tricked by the Slayers. They'll meet certain death."

Eve wasn't so sure. She thought of the video footage of Sid's ships being welcomed into Slayer Hives at the Frontline. Had they been tricked? She hoped so.

"We have to try," she said. "I can't let the Slayers, or *Pristine,* ravage our home any more than they already have."

She turned to leave.

"We have a plan to destroy the Primal Snow."

She turned back. Rixxi stepped closer and paused. "We have an attack plan for the Triturator. We plan to commandeer the device at its main control valve, *the Floodgate*, and turn it against the Pristine. The strategy has been developed over centuries. If you want to save your galaxy, stand with us. Sign our treaty and fight for the SSF."

Eve tried to rationalize her options. Was Rixxi right? If she took her squadron to the Primal Snow and failed, she would destroy UCOM's greatest asset behind the Frontline.

She decided she was curious.

"Explain your plan," she said. "And I'll determine if it's worth staying."

TWENTY-EIGHT

Nancy Woods – Human
Aboard Night Eagle *Eclipse* – Charlie Sector

"What's our Raven feedback telling us?" said Nancy to her crew.

"Five Tiger ships, one of them broadcasting a signal beacon," said Lindsey from her recon station aft of the cockpit. "The Tigers are inactive with no heat readings and no weapons signatures. I have a positive ID on your beacon code, and there's another short-range message also interlaced alongside the beacon. It's garbled right now from portal interference."

Nancy searched the starspace. They were near a lonesome green portal. Behind them, three Leopard ships provided heavy support, *Cassandra, Margaret, and Prysilla.* Sixteen Panther ships surrounded them near the portal, invisible due to active camouflage. Her HUD painted green outlines around the Panthers that only she and other fleet craft could see.

She turned to face her crew, seated at intelligence stations in the central bridge of the small craft. Lindsey, Caseus, and Hunter were glued to their displays. Laura Maxwell, their shipboard AI, stood in hologram form at her AI pedestal. Frank stared at the ground. She wondered if she should've allowed him to join her for this mission. He'd surprised her by showing up at the mess hall. When he learned of the Destineer message, he'd insisted on coming with. He seemed distant, but she'd conceded.

"What's our galactic ambient behind that portal?" she said.

"Charlie sector," Caseus responded, flipping through his monitors. "Coordinates ED7A.948613, one orbiting planet named Lavariz, mostly desert, no documented atmosphere, life, or water. Single star system, blue giant, big son of a bitch. Don't have much else other than that, it was never a high-traffic part of the Network."

She nodded and scanned through the metrics on her dash. If they hadn't received a long-range transmission beacon, they would never have entered these remote coordinates, which weren't close to any travel lanes, and didn't have any materials to use for their fleet's life support systems.

"Laura, how are we looking on the AI side of things?"

Her onboard CAIRO soldier materialized on the dash. "I have access to the ship's servers. Their security walls are disabled and the control power is still running on battery reserves. I haven't detected any AI presence, but it's impossible for me to be sure we're alone on the digital side unless I enter the ships and run a full network search."

"Keep an eye on the Tiger's outgoing transmission equipment," Nancy said.

"Aye," said Laura. Her eyes glowed white as she ran digital commands. "I have a request from our lead destroyer."

"Patch them through," said Nancy.

A communication message registered over their Night Eagle's central commands as Laura accepted the message.

"*Prysilla* to *Eclipse*, requesting comm link from Admiral Troko, over."

Nancy initiated a secure connection with *Prysilla,* the lead destroyer, and the ship from which Allakai Troko commanded their scout party.

Allakai spoke once the encrypted line finished initializing.

"Woods," said Allakai.

"Yes sir,"

"Can you confirm the signal beacon?"

"Yes sir," said Nancy. "I have a positive match, I laid these bugs on Sid's ship back on the Frontline."

"And the short-range frequencies?"

"Those aren't from me, sir. I only planted the long-range beacons."

"And you think this beacon will lead us to the Destineers?"

"I'm confident it will."

A pause.

"Lead the squadron into the portal, set up a three-point perimeter around the Tigers. I'll follow with one of our Leopards for support. If you notice anything out of the ordinary, the mission's aborted and we scram back to *Kizurra*. Understood?"

"Aye sir, out."

Nancy cut comms with *Prysilla* and relayed orders to the rest of the Panthers nearby. Green dots stacked in a hologram beside her as they acknowledged and followed her into the portal.

Light from the local sun consumed their ship, and Nancy squinted against the harsh light briefly before her Night Eagle adjusted tint levels in their canopy. Lavariz hung before them, pale and yellow, covered in black streaks from volcanic activity. Her HUD automatically flagged the five Tiger heavy-destroyers in orbit around Lavariz.

"I have a fix on the short-range frequency," said Caseus. "Not in range yet. We'll leave portal interference in one thousand kilometers."

Nancy eased her way towards the planet, her eyes glued to the hulls of the Tiger vessels. Her HUD enlarged surface images of the massive ships on a holo display. They were dark and vacant, but their hulls were smooth and free of any marks or scrapes that would normally appear after years of neglect. It was as if the ships were abandoned weeks ago.

Her stomach squirmed. She hadn't told Admiral Allakai, but she hadn't planted tracking devices on Sid's Tiger ship during the Frontline Battle. She'd planted them on a Slayer Hive mothership. Had Allakai known this, he never would have agreed to this scout mission. Because if the beacons were now on a Tiger ship, it could only mean one thing: Sid had found the beacons on the Hive, and moved them.

Or the Slayers, she reminded herself. *The Slayers could have moved them.*

"I'm getting new heat data," Lindsey called from her station. "From the other side of Lavariz. With how old the readings are, this was from a huge ship. Detected signatures point to a mother-class vessel. Nancy, it looks like either a Hive or a Lion left here recently."

Nancy eyed a separate portal in the distance, across the local starspace in the direction of the heat trail. The portal was red.

"I've got a lock on the short-range message," said Caseus. "Bringing it up now."

Static cracked against their intercom before their Night Eagle smoothed the transmission.

"Nancy Woods, please report to the star bridge."

Nancy grinded her teeth. Even after 150 years she recognized the voice. It spoke again in a loop.

"Nancy Woods, please report to the star bridge."

Sid Dakota was calling to her.

TWENTY-NINE

Nancy Woods – Human
Aboard Night Eagle *Eclipse* – Lavariz starspace

"We have a priority command from *Prysilla*," said Hunter. "Allakai's calling for all ships to fall back to *Kizurra*."

"Hail *Prysilla*," said Nancy. "I need to speak with Allakai."

The two Leopards behind them pivoted in space, firing lateral thrusters to turn back to the green portal they came from. The Panther stealth ships turned to follow, their location pins cruising across her HUD to follow in the wake of the heavier destroyers.

"Comms activated with *Prysilla*," Laura called.

"*Eclipse* to *Prysilla*," said Nancy. "We are a no go for fallback. I'm going in for a closer look at the Tiger broadcast."

Several seconds passed as the lead Leopard ship processed their message.

"Woods this is the Admiral," said Allakai. "Fall into formation, we are leaving Lavariz starspace immediately."

"Go on without us," said Nancy. "I need to investigate."

She wiped sweat from her brow and eased forward on her thrusters, guiding her Night Eagle closer to the dormant Tiger ships. The warships grew large enough to blot out half of Lavariz as they approached, and her cockpit beeped as it automatically configured docking procedures.

"*Do not* enter those ships," said Allakai, his tone hardening. "We register a large energy signature near the Slayer controlled portal across Lavariz starspace, and the local broadcast message mentions your name directly. This is a trap. I repeat, *fall back.*"

Nancy ignored the message and continued toward the nearest Tiger, the location her intel determined to be the source of the beacon signal.

"Woods, I won't repeat myself," growled Allakai. "Fall back or face disciplinary…"

Nancy cut comms with *Prysilla.* She turned to face her crew. They stared at her from their stations. Hunter narrowed his eyes and gave her a curt nod. She'd spent a century and a half searching for Sid, and she wasn't about to turn around now. She'd heard his voice, and was powerless to stop herself from following it. Her crew's silence was all the confirmation she needed. They'd been with her from the beginning, and weren't about to back out now.

"Prepare to dock," she said.

Eclipse's landing feet extended as they entered an influent launch tube on the side of the Destineer Tiger. They touched down with a thud, and spotlights lit on their bow as they entered the darkened hangar.

"Laura, can you enter the ship's servers?"

"Aye," said the AI. "Already in. The Tiger's name is *Liberty.* I'm still not seeing any activity."

Nancy grimaced. *Liberty* was an old Tiger. It was the ship Sid held her captive in back on the Frontline, the ship she had escaped from many years ago.

"You're miked into our helmet comms," said Nancy. "If you find trouble, download back into *Eclipse.*"

The AI voiced her acknowledgement, and her hologram disappeared as she entered *Liberty.*

Her crew gathered weapons silently before *Eclipse's* hatch opened to the inside hangar. Hunter led the way into the cavernous room, shouldering his MGK rifle, keeping low. The rest followed. The blackness melted as Nancy's helmet enabled nighttime vision.

The hangar was nearly empty, save for a few Cheetahs nearby, and a Panther at the edge of one of the upper platforms. They crept toward the exit doorways.

"Laura, can you produce a floor plan for *Liberty?*" Nancy called over central comms.

"Uploading it now," said Laura voicelessly.

The corner of Nancy's HUD helmet display lit as a map augmented over her vision. She flipped through the floorplan until she found what she was looking for.

Nancy Woods, please report to the star bridge.

She paused behind a structural beam as she studied the star bridge on the map. It was up ten levels, near the top of the ship.

"Movement," Hunter cried.

An orb of light flashed above them and zipped in a tight circle overhead. Thunder echoed inside the hangar as Hunter shot three rounds into the orb. Sparks fell as the slugs made contact.

"Do not fire, I am not armed."

The orb spoke to them in an artificial voice, frozen in position three meters above.

"I am just a guide," said the orb. *"Nancy Woods, please follow me. I wish to deliver a message."*

"Don't trust it," said Caseus, his eyes fixed behind his rifle sights and locked on the orb. "Whatever that thing is, the Destineers put it here."

"Don't shoot," Nancy whispered, lowering her own rifle. She stepped closer to the orb, which pulsed in shades of blue. She glanced at

Frank. His rifle hung limply from its strap around his neck, and even in the darkness, she could see his face glistening in sweat.

The orb shined brighter, and Nancy turned off her night vision as the room became swathed in light from the floating sphere.

"Follow me," said the orb. *"A message waits."*

It hovered in place above the silent group, before dipping lower to the ground and bobbing forward like a ghostly lantern.

Nancy walked after the orb, and her group followed around her. The orb moved slowly, and dipped low to them. Lindsey swatted at it with the stock of her rifle when it reached too close to her face, and the orb scuttled forward to a safe distance.

"Welcome Nancy," said the orb. *"We've been waiting."*

They navigated the lengthy halls of the Tiger ship, following their floating leader. After twenty minutes, a deep clacking sound reverberated through the corridor and emergency lights flickered on.

"I accessed the emergency reactors," Laura called into their headset. "Powering up *Liberty* to ten percent. I have access to internal cameras." She yelped in surprise. "What's that thing in front of you?"

"Run a diagnostic on it," said Hunter. "Is it AI?"

Laura's holographic avatar appeared above the floor and studied the orb, her eyes glowing a solid pink.

"Not AI," she said. "It's not intelligent at all, just simple software algorithms. I don't detect any weapons signatures. Do you want me to disable it?"

The orb floated sideways into an elevator shaft and shot vertically, disappearing into the ceiling.

"Follow it," said Nancy. "We're right behind you."

Laura's avatar disappeared, and Nancy stepped into the elevator shaft. Magnets interacted with her Program, and her stomach sunk into her hips as she streaked skyward. She slowed at the top of the lift and was deposited gently onto solid ground. Her crew landed behind her.

The orb was still, floating twenty meters from the elevator. Light flooded the cavernous room from a glass ceiling above, reflected sunlight from the yellow outline of Lavariz. Nancy recognized the area, miles long and too big to be considered a room. There were at the star bridge.

A podium extended from the metal deck, directly below the orb. A voice called to her, not the artificial voice of the orb, but a new one.

"Come to me Nancy, I've been waiting for you."

She edged toward the podium. It was a thin cylinder, with a flat panel on top at waist level. It was clear and glassy.

"Nancy, touch me, I wish to speak with you."

Sid's voice slithered to her from the podium. She drew a deep breath, and placed her palm on the glass.

THIRTY

Nancy Woods – Human
Aboard Tiger *Liberty* – Lavariz starspace

The orb went dark, and fell to the floor, rolling until it struck Hunter's foot with a hollow clink. He kicked the metallic drone away.

"Laura, record this," said Nancy breathlessly.

The podium lit a soft white, and a human figure appeared above it. It was a man of medium build, with jet black hair and a silky goatee.

Sid Dakota stared back at her. A smile crept to his face.

"Hello Nancy. It's so nice to see you again. I suppose you're wondering where I am. Well, I'm on my way to fulfilling my destiny. Soon, I will transcend, and become a deity. My loyal followers and I will become gods. It pained me to find your tracking beacons on the outside hull of the Pristine mothership. No matter though. See, I don't need these UCOM ships any longer. The Sterilord has built me a new fortress, a Hive to carry me to the Primal Snow. My message to you is simple, Nancy. You have lost. The Pristine will conquer this galaxy, as they have conquered dozens of others. I leave this message as a token of peace. I also want to let you know that you too, *will fulfill your destiny.* I have seen you in my visions, Nancy. You don't know it yet, but you will bear me a tremendous gift. Sadly, I could not wait aboard *Liberty* any longer to receive this gift from you. The Sterilord calls my name, and begs me to join him with the rest of the Humans.

Come with me, Nancy, and together we will transfer into the realm of gods."

Sid's grin widened, and he closed his eyes before opening them again.

"Ral-Bazeera," he whispered.

His hologram vanished. Nancy hardly had time to ponder Sid's cryptic message before she heard a choking sound beside her. She turned to find Frank gagging. His eyes rolled into the back of his head, and his legs left him. He fell face first onto the deck and began to convulse.

THIRTY-ONE

Frank Scott – Human
Aboard Tiger *Liberty* – Lavariz starspace

Frank stood above the Milky Way galaxy. He recognized the area around his ankles as Earth. Somewhere inside the millions of stars floating around his shins, his birthplace revolved around its sun. He was back in his dream world. No, not a dream world, it was too vivid for that. He was simply outside the galaxy. The galaxy was beneath him, not just around his feet, but in importance. He was a god, and the universe was his bounty to reap.

He scratched his head and wondered how he knew this. This world seemed familiar, as if he'd been there before.

"Frank."

A voice called to him, and Frank suddenly remembered. He had entered the world where the Voice resided. He had entered the place of his visions.

"Come here, Frank. I missed you. I haven't talked to you in so long, Frank. Have you forgotten about me?"

Frank tried to speak, to answer the Voice. To assure it that no, he hadn't forgotten about it, he *loved it,* the same way the Voice loved him. But his voice was empty and he wasn't able to utter even a raspy breath.

"I'm over here, Frank. Come visit my kingdom. Our kingdom."

Frank squinted as a harsh light blossomed across the galaxy. Golden rays stretched towards him, and after his eyes adjusted, he saw the outline of a door. He began to sprint.

Stars swirled around his legs as he tore through the Milk Way, leaving Earth behind and powering toward the door on the other side. He leaped over the super-massive black hole in the center, and stumbled when he landed before catching himself and resuming his sprint.

He ran across the Frontline and weaved through depictions of battle, dodging a blast from a PDR RACAN. He approached the Outer Rim and hopped into the darkness surrounding the Milky Way.

The door hung before him in the distance. Now out of breath, he jogged towards it. It didn't get any closer, and he forced himself to run harder. To his delight, the frame grew, and opened as he drew near. Golden fog billowed from the entrance and washed over Frank's body. The misty vapor warmed him, and made his skin tingle pleasantly.

"I can see you Frank," the Voice called to him through the vapor billowing from the entrance. *"You look beautiful. Everyone is beautiful in our kingdom. Come in and see."*

Frank cracked a loopy smile. He was beautiful. He knew this because the Voice told him so. The Voice was beautiful too, deep and rich and sincere. He stepped through the doorway.

Water crashed gently around him. He was inside a golden waterfall. Rainbows shimmered around it in sheets, and he blinked as a fine mist coated his face. Where was the Voice? Was it behind the water?

"Frank, through here. Let the water cleanse you. Let it wash the filth from your skin. Let it make you pristine. Everyone is pristine in our kingdom."

Frank wanted so badly to be clean. He stepped toward the golden water.

"I knew you'd come for us Frank."

The voice was not *the Voice.* It was someone different. Frank spun toward the words, coming not from the kingdom past the waterfall, but from the doorway behind him.

A man with a dark goatee stood behind him. He wore white robes and had a crooked smile. The grin vanished and the man strode towards him and grabbed him by the collar.

"Ral-Bazeera," the man whispered in his ear. Then he shoved Frank through the waterfall.

Frank choked against the water flooding his mouth, his lips sputtering as he fought to remove cold liquid from his face.

"There you go Frank, easy does it."

He flailed his arms and slapped at his eyes, shaking his head dry. He blinked several times at his surroundings. A Titan warrior knelt beside him, propping him off the ground. Hunter's wrist dripped from the water he ejected from his Akimor.

"What happened, Frank?" said Nancy, who was kneeling beside him opposite Hunter. "Are you okay?"

He shook his head, scooting to a seated position on the deck. Caseus and Lindsey stood at his feet. "I don't know. I…"

The man with the goatee skirted across his mind. His stomach flipped as he recognized the man. It was the same man from the hologram above the pedestal.

Sid Dakota.

"I found an AI," a voice cried.

The group turned to find Laura Maxwell's avatar appear to the side. She held the arms of a scrawny boy with matted blonde hair. He struggled in her grip. "He was hiding in the bridge."

"Let me go," the boy cried, and pried himself loose. He lunged away from Laura, but she kicked him in the back, sending him sprawling to the floor.

"You're not going anywhere, Destineer scum," Laura said. She leaped onto his back, holding his bucking body to the deck. Pink strands of light lashed across his body as she tied him in bondages.

"I'm not a Destineer," the boy grunted. "My name's Timothy, I'm a stowaway, please don't hurt me. I can help, I know where Sid went."

THIRTY-TWO

Nancy Woods – Human
Aboard Tiger *Liberty* – Lavariz starspace

Nancy stared at the scrawny AI, who had gone limp within his restraints. She rose to her feet and walked to his side before kneeling next to him.

"What did you say?"

"I'm a stowaway. Let me go."

"After that."

"The Destineers," he stammered. "I saw Sid Dakota, I know where they went."

"What's the meaning of this?" a stern voice boomed behind them from the elevator shaft. Nancy recognized his voice instantly.

"*Leave*," she hissed to the AI. "Laura, hide him."

The two AI vanished into particles of light. Nancy turned to find Allakai Troko storming towards them, his hooves clopping against the metal deck. A team of soldiers flanked him on both sides. Several more entered the star bridge from the elevator shaft.

"I gave you a direct order, Woods," the Stallion admiral growled. "And you disobeyed me. You put our entire fleet at risk."

Hunter and Caseus stepped in front of Nancy, almost protectively. Frank put a hand on her shoulder. She heard him wheeze and clear his throat.

"Sir," said Hunter. "We had strong evidence of a Destineer-"

"Save it, Titan," said Allakai. "Out of my way."

Hunter nodded and stepped aside. Nancy straightened her back and faced the admiral squarely. "Sir, my team was acting under my orders. I couldn't leave the ship after finding Dakota's beacon. We found a message from Sid."

"Enough with your witch hunt," Allakai roared, stomping the ground with a hoof. "The Slayers are placing Triturators throughout the Milky Way and all you care about is settling a personal vendetta against *one man*. If you disobey my orders again I'll have you court martialed and stars help me, Woods' daughter or not, I'll send you out the tubes for treason."

"One man or no, Sid is a threat against UCOM," Nancy said through her teeth. "He's a problem we need to address. Sir, the message..."

Allakai frowned and shook his head. "This message, did it give the Destineer's position?"

Nancy opened her mouth, then paused. Sid's message hadn't given them any actionable information at all. She declined to mention the stowaway AI.

"I can't risk the lives of our fleet-members on snap impulses," said Allakai after her silence. "What if Slayers had been around? Go back to your ship. We're leaving this area until we can develop a rational strategy."

Nancy bit her lip hard, then pushed her way around the soldiers surrounding Allakai and stormed towards the elevator.

"Where do you think you're going?" called the Stallion.

She turned "To my ship, *sir.* As you ordered."

Her team jogged to catch up.

"Captain Woods," called Allakai. She froze but didn't turn. "I'm taking your bars. You're no longer squadron leader."

She growled and continued on her way from the star bridge, bristling with anger.

She would have liked to tell Allakai off, even if it meant being court martialed. The admiral was blind to the threat Sid posed, and it made her livid. But she had other things on her mind.

She wanted to have a chat with Timothy. She had a few questions to ask the AI about the Destineers.

THIRTY-THREE

Francis Woods - Human
Aboard Tiger *Stargrazer* – Dominia starspace

Woods pushed the console for Zena Olleeve's private quarters. The touch pad buzzed quietly, then went silent. The sliding door didn't open.

He pressed it again. More time passed.

"Sir, maybe she left for Warhammer?" Woods' AI assistant shrugged his shoulders. "Maybe she's not in?"

"Can't you check?" said Woods.

"No sir," said Zoltan. "Not unless she gives me access to her quarters."

"Try again."

He waited as Zoltan tried to summon the Clone Councilwoman. A soft ding sounded in the hallway as the AI sent his request. Woods was about to turn to leave, when a soft voice answered their call.

"Can I help you, Mr. Eminence?" said the voice. "I'm very busy."

"Ms. Olleeve," said Woods, "Can we talk? It's important."

Silence.

After several seconds, Zena answered. "If it's quick. I have an announcement to make in twenty minutes."

The door hissed and slid open. Woods stepped into the Clone councilwoman's quarters.

Her room was large and lavish. Leather furniture sat between the fireplace and private rooms in the back. The walls were well decorated and made of marble, as were the floors. It was a standard room afforded to councilmembers, the type Woods had rejected for centuries, content with the standard bare walls of a warship.

Zena entered from one of the back rooms. She wore a Clone formal suit, with loose pants and blue shoes. Her chest was covered only by a tight top, and she threw on a custom Clone jacket as she walked to greet them.

"Eminence Woods," she said. She nodded to Zoltan. "How can I help you?"

He entered the room. Dominia shined brightly through large windows in the ceiling. He motioned to a plush couch, and after Zena nodded, sat in it stiffly. She took a seat opposite him. Zoltan stood beside them, his avatar hovering above the fur rug next to the couches.

"Where are my manners?" she said. "Would you like something to drink? Water? Maybe something stiff? Lunawine perhaps? I have some Pappy's in the fridge."

"Thanks, but I'm not here to drink," said Woods. "I want to talk about the war."

Her eyes left the kitchen section behind them. "The war?" She sunk further into her couch and clasped shut the top button of her jacket. "We just had a council meeting. War preparations are going as planned. When the Slayer's strike, we'll be ready. My Clone troops are well prepared."

Woods nodded and looked through the ceiling windows. He scanned the PDR's above, pausing on *Warhammer.* The defense tower blotted half his view.

"I'm sure they are. I want to talk about something else. Something a little more, off the books."

Zena sighed and narrowed her eyes. "The Destineers. We're searching for them in our navy using the same search parameters as the

Humans, and sending thousands of traitors to Gefangnia daily. Stars rest their souls."

"I'm aware of your support in handling our Destineer problem," said Woods. "Thanks again for your strong allegiance with United Earth."

"I believe I'm the one who should be thanking you, Mr. Eminence. After our home worlds were destroyed beyond the Frontline, Earth and her colonies were the only planets to offer us sanctuary. And I know no one can explain it, but somehow Clones and Humans have compatible genes. Our populations are becoming more mixed by the day. I represent the Clones, but I also feel very much attached to Humans."

"And in turn we dragged you into our civil war," said Woods. "A high price to pay for entering our society. Again, thank you for your support."

Zena pursed her lips. "We've known each other too long to be having these kinds of conversations. If you don't want to talk about Destineers or the war effort, then why did you come to my chambers unannounced?"

Woods took a deep breath and leaned towards Zena.

"Ral-Bazeera," he whispered.

The Clone's eyes widened and she froze in her seat. Then her entire body thrust towards Woods, upending the table between them. Woods shouted in pain as the glass surface struck his knee and shin, and kicked the table away from his body.

Zena had sprinted from the sitting area, and was fumbling with the locked doors of a large credenza at the corner of the room.

"Zena," he called, struggling from the couch. His knees ached and wobbled beneath him as he stumbled towards her. He glanced at Zoltan. The AI's focus shifted from Zena to Woods, unsure of what to do. "Zena, why did you do that? *Stars.*"

He rubbed his knees as he approached. Zena had opened the cabinet. A sharp beep sounded, and the front shelves dropped into the floor to expose a magnetic wall, holding four firearms. Woods lunged toward the cabinet on instinct.

Zena snatched a sidearm from its holding plate and whipped it towards him before he could stop her. He froze, staring down the barrel of the rail-pistol. He rose his hands before him slowly.

"Zena. What the *hell* are you doing? Put the gun down."

Her lip twitched. She didn't lower the pistol. "*Ral-Bazeera.* Tell me why you know this word."

THIRTY-FOUR

Francis Woods - Human
Aboard Tiger *Stargrazer* – Dominia starspace

Zena's chest heaved and she gulped. Woods took a step back and she stiffened her arm. He froze again.

"Sir," Zoltan called to him. Woods saw the AI's avatar appear beside him from the corner of his vision. "Do you want me to signal for help?"

"No need," said Woods. He locked eyes with Zena. "There's just a misunderstanding."

"I won't ask you again," said Zena. "Where did you hear the word Ral-Bazeera? Did Draxton recruit you?"

"Recruit me?" said Woods. "No he didn't recruit me. Please, put the gun down. I did learn the word from Draxton, but he doesn't know I did. I overheard him talking with the Grizzly councilman, something about exiling Humans from UCOM."

Zena's eye's softened. She sighed and lowered her weapon. "I'm sorry, I've been paranoid ever since he approached me. I don't know who my friends are anymore."

"Draxton approached you?" said Woods. "What did he say? Did he tried to get Clones to split from UCOM?"

She shook her head and bit her lip. "It happened a long time ago."

"Come here," said Woods, reaching a hand gently to her shoulder. Zena clamped her rail pistol to a holding plate on her side and followed him back to the couches in the common room. He flipped the glass table back onto its feet and slid it to its original position between the sofas.

"Draxton Tyke came to me a long time ago," she said, taking a seat. She glanced at Zoltan, who had followed them to the couches. "Is it safe to talk with him around?"

"He can be trusted," said Woods.

Zoltan gave him a relieved smile.

"It's a long story," said Zena.

"I've been alive for over three hundred fifty years," said Woods. "To me, there are no long stories. Let's hear it."

THIRTY-FIVE

Francis Woods - Human

Aboard Tiger *Stargrazer* – Dominia starspace

"It was twenty-five years ago from today," said Zena. "I was leaving a council meeting, and he approached me after."

"He did the same with the Grizzly councilman," said Woods. "Except it didn't seem like it was the first time they spoke."

Zena nodded. "It was my first year in office as a council member. I won the general election after Sybyl Banico resigned. I guess Draxton thought he had someone fresh to exploit."

"I remember Banico well," said Woods. "He died of heart complications. Unheard of these days. Do you think…"

"Sybyl was murdered by Draxton," said Zena. "I would stake my life on it." She sighed deeply. "After the council meeting, Draxton pulled me aside after everyone had gone. He didn't dance around any subjects, and suggested the Clones distance themselves from Humans. He said there would be a time when Humans will be held in the same light as the Slarebull, and that I should remove Clone ties with them before it happens."

"Slarebull?" said Woods. "He didn't use the word *Slayer*?"

"No, he used *Slarebull*," said Zena. "I remember that distinctly because of how uncommon it was. Many UCOM spacers don't even know *Slayer* is a nickname."

"What did you say to him?" said Zoltan, piping up from the side.

"What do you think I said to him?" said Zena. "I told him to piss off. I said that Humans are saviors to the Clones. I explained how much of our civilian population lives on one of Earth's colonies, how we think alike. Look alike. I mean *stars*, we even have children together."

"And how did Draxton take it?" said Woods.

"As you'd expect," said Zena. "He scowled the way only Wolves can, and told me to 'think about it'. That was the first time he approached me in that manner."

"The *first*?" said Woods. "He came to you again?"

"Yes, twice more. The second time was like the first. Except he had numbers with him. Data on how the Destineers were rising beyond control, and polls showing UCOM civilian's negative outlook on the Humans, and the Clones too by association. I took a look at the information, and this time politely said no to him, and asked to be left alone."

"You asked politely?" said Woods. "Didn't tell him to *piss off* again?"

"Not all of us are like you, Mr. Eminence. You command respect from wartime heroics. I'm just a politician. I'd learned how to play the game since the first time he approached me."

Woods frowned. "And the third time Draxton came to you?"

"Just under a year ago," said Zena. "And this time his message had changed. Draxton had put a plan in place for Human secession. He gave me some minor details and mentioned that word. *Ral-Bazeera.* Slayer-speak. He said when I hear the word, the time has come to move forward. He asked if I wanted to hear more, and I panicked. I said I would tell the rest of the council, tell the press, etcetera."

"And you didn't," said Woods. "Why?"

Zena's eyes shifted to the ground. She pulled on a lock of her hair. "He said no one would listen. *Especially* not the Humans, who he said were saturated with Destineer spies. He encouraged me to talk to others, they were all on board. He said the only friend the Clones had left was him. Again, I asked him to leave."

"*Ral-Bazeera,*" said Zoltan. "I looked up the meaning of the word. It means..."

"To divide," Zena finished. "I've done a lot of research myself. I tailed Draxton, and snooped around in his digital communications as much as I felt I could get away with. I dug up a lot of dirt on him. He wasn't lying. There *are* Destineers everywhere, and Draxton has recruited anti-Human followers throughout the Milky Way. His reach extends across the galaxy, maybe all the way to Earth. It was quite a startling discovery."

Woods' collar felt hot, and he hooked a finger under the fabric to give it a sharp tug. "Why didn't you come to me after you learned of all this?" he said. "I could have helped."

Zena bit her lip. "Well, quite simply Mr. Eminence, I didn't know if I could trust you."

THIRTY-SIX

Francis Woods - Human
Aboard Tiger *Stargrazer* – Dominia starspace

Woods blinked in shocked surprise. "You didn't know if you could *trust me?* I'm the closest ally you have, you said it yourself."

"Don't be so hard on yourself," said Zena. "I didn't even trust any *Clones* enough to bring them in. I've been at this alone. With the amount of trans-racers digitizing their minds and switching races, it's possible for anyone to appear Human. Giants, Grizzlies, Hogs, you name it."

"You think I'm an undercover Hog? Or maybe a Wolf like Draxton?"

"Of course not. But you could be a Destineer."

Woods grinded his teeth hard enough to draw a loud crack. "You think I'm a Destineer?"

"I don't think it's likely, but you can't deny there are rumors. There's a reason you're the most hated man in the galaxy. Many of the races don't trust you. They think you're on the same side as Sid."

"He's also the most loved man in the galaxy," said Zoltan with a scowl.

"Zena's right," said Woods, rubbing his temples. "I've seen the way the Wolves look at me. And the Hogs, Squid, Birds. *Stars* half the galaxy *does* look at me like they want my head on a pike."

Silence.

"So you agree," said Zena. "There's a rift forming in UCOM?"

"The rift has already formed," said Woods. "We need to figure out how to stop it from severing completely."

"If UCOM divides itself, strategic success is unlikely," said Zoltan. "I ran some calculations. If we split the way you predict: Wolves, Hogs, Giants, Birds, Squid, and Grizzlies on one side, and Guardians, Clones, Humans, Intellects, Green and Boards on the other." He shook his head. "Our percent chance at defending the Inner Ring from the Slayers drops to under twenty percent."

"It's hard to believe Draxton wouldn't have already ran these calculations," said Zena. "Do you think he has a plan to beat the Slayers without half of UCOM?"

"Unless we don't have as many friends as we think," said Woods. "A large chunk of Clones and Humans have converted to Destineers. And we can't say for sure that the Guardians and Intellects are all on our side."

They pondered the implications.

"Can you imagine?" said Zena. "With a rift, we would sink into a four-way war. Humans and Clones, against the Slayers, UCOM, and the Destineers. There would be mass chaos, and the Slayers would pick up the scraps."

"If Draxton were to strike," said Woods, "when would be the best time?"

"The Destineers are most likely to strike just before the Slayers," said Zena. "So, I'd assume Draxton would strike just before the Destineers. Then Humans and Destineers would attack each other, with less UCOM casualties."

Woods ran his tongue over his lips. "Then we need to get busy. We have a lot of work to do before then."

THIRTY-SEVEN

Bear Stafford – Human Titan
On the surface of planet Blit Kru

"Can you see them?" Bear asked.

Crystal continued to stare through the extended range binoculars that enhanced the optics of her Akimor. "I lost them. They passed through a security bubble outside the building perimeter. I can't even see heat data anymore."

Bear surveyed the landing zone where Vomisa and Blackthorne had been captured. The snow was teeming with Slayer vehicles and foot soldiers as they scoured the scene for any missed enemies. They'd been at it for the last hour.

The rest of Bear's Sword Six squad lay hidden at the base of a mountain peak fourteen kilometers from where they had scouted the scene earlier. This mountain was unlike the previous mountain. A towering beam of electricity shot from its peak into the sky. It was one of the mountains the Slayers had modified into what appeared to be a communication tower.

Their old hiding spot lay in ruins. The Slayers had turned it into rubble and melted slag in their attempts to destroy the Titans. Lines of enemy ATV's fanned from the LZ as they manually searched the rocky terrain, apparently unsatisfied with the lack of charred Titan bodies.

Harper's Arrow 32 squad lay hidden a kilometer away. The two Titans in genetically created Slayer bodies, Vixtor and Loko, were also in Harper's group. They had separated in order to better monitor the area for hostiles. Bear called to him over central comms.

"Bear to Harper, do you have a lock on our friendlies? We lost them behind the building's stealth shields."

"Negative Sword Six, we lost them too," Harper replied. A pause. "Be aware, a team of Slayers is headed your way along the lower mountain path. They'll pass within twenty meters. I count ten Slayers and four Cogent."

Bear turned in the direction of Arrow 32. The Titans were hidden around a protruding escarpment connecting the flat ground below to a shelf cut into the mountain. A ridge trail curved around the boulders. Bear picked up thermal outlines of a team of Slayers, and then the visual outline when they entered his line of vision. The Cogent's armor shielding was lit bright yellow. One of the Cogent wore blue armor.

"We see them Arrow thirty-two," said Bear. "After they pass we're going to rally to your coordinates. We need to start making our way to the building."

A line of green dots appeared on Bear's HUD as the Titan teams acknowledged his orders.

The Slayers approached, and for a few minutes passed close enough for Bear to hear their ragged breathes. He lay perfectly still. His Akimor was in full stealth mode, but he still tensed when the blue Cogent paused for a few seconds to stare in their direction. The Cogent raised his rifle and fired a few plasma rounds into the mountainside. One of them hit a rock next to Bear's face. Snow hissed as it evaporated from the heated charge.

"Filth?" One of the yellow Cogent asked.

"No," said the blue one. He lowered his rifle. "Only rocks. Pepper the mountains. Look for any flares from armor. These filth are made of metal and have stealth cloaks."

Bear tensed again as the Slayers fired at random, spotting the rocks with glowing green circles. A few of the shots came within a few meters of his team, but most spread wide to the left and right, and above.

The Slayers stared at the mountain before lowering their weapons.

"I dislike metal warriors," said a yellow Cogent. "I distrust a creature that doesn't bleed."

"We all distrust creatures of metal and electricity," said the blue Cogent. "The Pristine raised us this way for a reason."

"Then why did we not kill the metal filth that landed?" said a yellow Cogent. "Why did the Brains order those filth detained? And then why are we allowed to kill the metal demons hiding in the mountains?"

"The filth who landed were made of electricity," said the leader. "They were only using their metal bodies as a shell."

"How do the Brains know this?" one of the unarmored Slayers asked. "And why must we take orders from such weaklings?"

The leader growled and smacked the unarmored Slayer in the head hard enough to send him to the ground. "Do not question the orders of the Pristine, or I will kill you alongside the metal demons. The Pristine created the Brains to combat the electric demons. We must honor the Pristine."

The unarmored Slayer hung his head and picked himself up. "Yes Cogent," he muttered.

"We must continue," the leader decided. "After we kill the metal demons we can warm ourselves around a fresh meal. This cold is seeping under my scales."

The Slayers continued down the path. One of them whipped his tail into a boulder, crumbling the top into loose stone.

Electric demons?

Bear wondered why the Slayers were so scared of Titans, and of what he assumed were AI. And the Brains. Were they another form of Slayer?

Bear waited until the Slayers were well out of sight, then commanded his team voicelessly. "Move out. Keep in full stealth and rally with Arrow thirty-two."

He looked at his team behind him. Their Akimors were traced in green and augmented against Bear's HUD. They all nodded in confirmation.

Keeping low, they crept onto the switchback trail, and advanced toward Arrow 32 as quickly as their Akimors would allow without losing full stealth. Location pins for Harper showed how far away their teammates were, and trickled towards zero as they approached. The Titan Akimors were invisible save for the pins. Vixtor and Loko were in biological Slayer bodies, but their Snakeskin armor removed most of the heat from their bodies, and their thermal signatures looked like little more than woodland critters.

He left the path and climbed a steep rock face.

"The Slayers are building forces around the facility," said Harper as Bear and his team joined the rest of the Titans in their position against a set of boulders. "Infiltrating the complex will become harder with each minute."

Bear peered over the rock at the sprawling complex in the distance. The Slayers had sent Tarantulas to stand guard at the perimeter. Smaller land vehicles surrounded them. Spider aircraft circled the skies above.

"We won't be able to enter the building from the ground," said Bear, eyeing the Slayer troops amassing at the point where the trees turned to bare earth. "We'll need to find a way to access the roof from the air."

"Spiders have been coming and going from the ledge above," said Harper, nodding upward. "We can commandeer one of them and land on the roof. I've scouted bunker entrances every few hundred meters, that will be our access point."

"Something's not right," said Bear. He frowned as he searched the jagged slopes of the mountain above. "This whole area is crawling with Slayers."

"Of course it is," said Pounder, one of Harper's teammates. "They just caught a UCOM AEV trying to sneak onto their planet."

Bear nodded. "The Slayers know we're here, at least to some extent. They have millions of troops sweeping the grounds all around this mountain and the mountains surrounding it. But this mountain's special." He pointed skyward at the towering beam of electricity, thin, as if a blue strand of silk connected earth and sky. "They have a massive comm installation here, and yet they only have a few groups of Cogent patrolling the switchbacks?"

"You think there's Slayers hidden on the mountain side?" said Crystal.

"Or inside the mountain itself," said Bear. "We don't know what's creating that beam."

There was a few seconds of silence.

"I say we make towards high ground, towards the platform above," said Harper. "It will give us a better view of the mountain, and may give us access to Slayer air vehicles."

Bear used his instruments to calculate the distance to the plateau at the top of the escarpment.

4,895 meters above.

They had quite a hike ahead of them.

"I agree, we'll head for the platform," he decided. "The shortest route is straight along the cliff face. If we use the switchbacks it will triple our total travel distance, and we might run into search parties. Going full stealth would take hours, so I propose we hide fifty percent heat, and only use our Akimors for rough camo, not full. Using our grappling equipment, we should be able to make it to the platform in under thirty minutes."

Harper nodded in agreement, his gaze fixed up the mountain towards their destination. "It looks like there's a large alcove just below the platform. We can rally there and scope the surroundings."

Bear turned to the two Titans in genetically cloned Slayer bodies. "Vixtor, Loko, do you feel comfortable with the climb?"

Vixtor nodded. "My armor can grapple the same as yours. I'll manage."

Loko grunted in agreement, flexing his beefy arms.

The two Titan teams voiced acknowledgement and secured their rifles and scouting equipment to holding plates on their backs and thighs. Bear opened heat vents, cooling his internal systems rapidly. Strength surged through his chest as his power levels increased proportionally to the reduction in his core temperature.

He crouched low to the ground, and leaped onto the cliff face, jumping nearly ten meters from the ground. Anchor hooks and suction material lining the front of his Akimor secured him to the escarpment. He hung still for a few seconds. The rest of the Titans landed around him with a series of crunches.

His Akimor was designed to grapple starships after being launched from a rail cannon at thousands of meters per second. Compared to the hardened smooth metal of a ship's hull, the icy cliff face felt like a soft patch of velcro. Excellent climbing conditions.

He grunted and leaped higher up the mountain. And higher. And higher. The Titans scurried up the vertical cliff face like squirrels up a tree.

"Hold," said Bear.

They'd climbed for 28 minutes. Harper pinned the alcove to their HUD's, and the green marker diamond hovered a few meters above their heads. The alcove sloped upward alongside the escarpment, and was covered with pine trees and deep snow drifts. He ran a tight scan over the terrain. He hugged the cliff tightly as the whine of a Slayer Spider craft passed twenty meters above the platform. He was close enough to feel warm exhaust buffet against his shoulders.

"Looks clear," he said voicelessly. He jumped sideways and landed on the sloping grade of the alcove, which compared to the vertical cliff face, seemed almost like level ground.

He crouched low in the snow, so that only his shoulders were exposed. The rest of the Titans landed around him in a series of muffled thumps. Bear drew his MGK rifle.

They pressed forward, keeping low. No thermal readings appeared on his HUD, even from the platform above. The mountain seemed deserted.

Yet a Spider just took off a minute ago.

He took step forward, and suddenly, the mountain was no longer deserted.

Thermal outlines of Slayers popped into view. Hundreds of fires burned, stretching far above onto the mountainside, groups of beasts huddled around them in the distance towards the peak. One of the fires flickered nearby. From the corner of his vision, Bear saw a bright glow emanating from the top of the platform due to the heat of hundreds of air vehicles. The whispery gusts of wind were replaced with snarls and growls from Slayers.

"We just passed through a stealth bubble," Harper hissed aloud.

"Cover," Bear commanded voicelessly, and leaped behind a large boulder, sinking beneath the snow line.

There was a rustling sound from the nearby fire.

"Did you hear that?" a rough voice growled.

"I see heat," another whispered. *"Filth!"*

THIRTY-EIGHT

Bear Stafford – Human Titan
On the surface of planet Blit Kru

Three Slayers exploded into view, leaping around the boulder the Titans were using for cover. On instinct, Bear dropped all stealth shielding and diverted full energy to his Akimor power levels. He locked arms with one of the beasts, and aimed a sharp kick at the Slayer's leg. It squealed in pain and sank to one knee as its tendons tore. Bear wrapped an arm around its long neck and squeezed.

The other two Slayers dropped quickly as the rest of the Titan's loosed slugs into their faces and necks. Bear skirted back and forth, struggling to contain the irate beast in his grip.

He winced as a pain shot into his hip. His waist seemed to pop, and bits of flexible mesh dropped to the snow as the Slayer unleashed his last desperate swipes. Bear loosened his grip, and the Slayer thrust hard beneath him, lifting him from the ground before hammering his face squarely with the clubbed end of his tail.

Bear fell hard into a tree trunk and crumpled to the ground, clutching at his face. He dragged himself to his feet as his Akimor made repairs to damaged electrical components I n his eye socket. The Slayer lunged towards him, but was cut down instantly with eight slug rounds.

"Are you okay?" said Crystal, reaching a hand to his face. "Your eye socket is dented, can you see?"

“I’m fine,” said Bear, shrugging her off. “Take cover, there’s more coming.”

They crouched behind a thick tree, whose roots spread over a large boulder and into cracks in the mountain.

He heard the Slayers well before he could see them. Their heat outlines appeared from around a cluster of rock. There were five of them. One had yellow Cogent armor.

“Vixtor, Loko,” said Bear. “Go meet them, don’t let them see the dead bodies, or they’ll send for help. We’ll cover you.”

Vixtor and Loko left without a word, scuttling on all fours through the deep drifts, their clubbed tails snapping through the air above. They met the approaching Slayers fifty meters from where Bear and the rest of the Titans hid. Bear adjusted his Akimor for stealth and tuned his acoustics to listen in.

“What was that noise,” said the yellow Cogent. “I heard shouts. Screams.”

“We were eating some of the little critters from the planet,” said Vixtor, standing straight to address the Cogent. Loko stood at his side. “They are so sweet and juicy, the meat slides right off the bone.”

“Keep it down or I will give you the same fate as the critters,” the Cogent snarled. “There’s filth nearby, we can’t let them hear.”

“Of course,” said Vixtor. “My apologies, the blood was just so hot, and runny.”

The Cogent paused. “You speak strangely. Your voice is odd.” He sniffed the air. “The smells are wrong. I smell the hotness of metal, and the blood of our own. Where did you get your armor? That is not Cogent armor.”

One of the unarmored Slayers sprinted around Vixtor and Loko before they could respond. He climbed atop a large boulder and squinted towards the dead Slayers near the cliff face.

"I see heat," he shouted. "And bodies."

Bear snapped his rifle around the tree and fired a shot into the Slayer's skull. A split second later, the rest of the Titans loosed slugs from their rifles, fired silently down magnetic rails. All unarmored Slayers dropped instantly. Vixtor and Loko wasted no time in attacking the Cogent. He roared as they each slammed their tails into his skull.

He thrust his claws across Vixtor's face, causing the Titan to spin away in a spray of blood. Loko landed another blow to the Cogent's head, forcing him to double over, clawing at his helmet as it lost its energy shield.

The Titans unloaded on the powerful Slayer warrior. He covered his exposed face, and his yellow armored flashed as it absorbed kinetic energy from dozens of slugs before overloading and going dark. The Slayer collapsed.

Bear ran to the scene. Bam-Bam slid next to Vixtor, who was writhing on top of a flat rock. Two deep gouges sliced across his face, and his eye was a bloody pit. He choked as he struggled to control his moans of agony.

"Damn it Vix," said Bam-Bam, drawing a med kit from a compartment on his thigh. "He got you good."

Vixtor forced himself to be still, his good eye darting between the Titan's standing around him. Bam-Bam squeezed a tube of topical cream over his wounds, which turned blue and began to harden. The Titan relaxed as localized pain killers dulled the wound. Bam-Bam helped him to his feet.

Bear clapped him on the shoulder. The Titan rolled his Slayer head around, cracking the vertebrae in his neck. He ran a tongue over his teeth and touched a delicate inner hand to the wound over his eye.

"Can you shoot?" said Bear.

Vixtor nodded and snatched his plasma rifle from where he'd dropped when the Cogent struck him. "I've shot with worse in Olympus."

"Filth."

The Cogent groped at Bear's ankle weakly. It attempted to swing his tail but managed only a weak flop against the ground. It glared at Bear murderously and bared its teeth.

Pounder stomped a foot on the Slayer's chest and pointed his rifle at its skull.

"Wait," said Bear, leaning forward to push Pounder's rifle aside. "Don't kill him."

"Why not?" said Pounder.

"We might be able to pull some information about what's going on here with the superweapon. Maybe he knows where they took Casi and Blackthorne."

Bear drew his leg back and kicked the Slayer hard in the head, knocking the wounded beast unconscious.

THIRTY-NINE

Bear Stafford – Human Titan
On the surface of planet Blit Kru

"Should we hide the bodies?" said Crystal, motioning to the carcasses around them. Five centimeters of snow had already accumulated on the dead Slayers.

Bear looked towards the peak of the mountain. The snow had picked up rapidly, and he could barely see the glacially capped tip. He flicked through meteorological readings on his HUD.

"No need," he said. "Wind's picking up and visibility is down. Based on the pressure and temperature fluctuations, we're heading into one hell of a storm."

"Then we should hurry to the platform," said Bam-Bam. "The snow will give us cover while we commandeer a Spider."

"Not in this type of weather," said Harper. His eyes glowed as he read his own meteorological information. "Bear's right, this is looking to turn into a pretty rough blizzard. I've seen winds pick up to three hundred kilometers per hour. Our Bobcats can't fly in those kinds of conditions, so we can assume their Spiders can't either."

Bear peered again up the mountain. The fires had disappeared, replaced by different pockets of heat. They were jagged, and seemed to line the edge of the alcove's rocky valley. More pockets of heat lined the sheer face of the escarpment along the edge of the sloped alcove.

"The cave you were hiding in," said Bear. "The one you took us to after we landed. Are they common on Blit-Kru?"

Hunter nodded. The snow now drove sideways between them, and without augmented vision, Bear wouldn't be able to see the Titan's face, even at such a short distance. "The mountains are loaded with them. We jumped around from cave to cave, relocating every so often to keep the Slayers off our trail."

Bear stooped beside the unconscious Cogent. A set of tracks registered in his thermal vision, the path the Slayers had taken from their outpost. The tracks were faint, dimming quickly in the deepening snow.

"We'll follow these tracks," he said, placing location diamonds on his team's HUD's to show the trail. "These guys must have had some kind of shelter. We'll find a place to hunker down and let the storm pass." He nodded to the Cogent. "Crystal, help me with him."

Crystal bent to grab the Slayer's arms, and Bear grabbed its legs. Together they forged ahead up the steepening mountain, following the faint thermal footsteps.

"There," said Loko, pointing a clawed finger to their right.

A sliver of heat was wedged inside a rock face. They approached, and Harper, Bam-Bam, Pounder, and Marvyl drew their weapons, pausing outside the opening.

"It's a cave entrance," said Harper. "No signs of life inside."

He crept into the opening, engaging his active camo. Bam-Bam, Pounder, and Marvyl followed. Bear waited outside, squeezing the legs of the Cogent tightly.

"All clear," said Harper. "Come on in guys, we found ourselves a nice little snake pit."

Bear heaved the Cogent up a two-foot boulder at the foot of the entrance and stepped inside. Warmth flowed over him as he entered, and his vision cleared as he left the driving sheets of snow. The howling wind died to a murmur. Crystal dropped her end of the Cogent unceremoniously to the stone floor, and Bear did the same.

The cave was small and messy. Dismembered animals littered the floor. Piles of pine branches and stones were heaped against the wall, resembling enormous bird nests. A few mechanical devices hung around the room, one of them a heater, based on its thermal imprint.

"What a romantic getaway," said Marvyl. "Would anyone like a snack?"

He grabbed the leg of a mutilated animal carcass. The leg ripped from the joint, and Marvyl held it for a second before shrugging his shoulders and dropping it back to the floor.

"Check for any intelligence," said Bear, scanning the room. "Computers, comm devices, anything to help us infiltrate the complex."

He turned his attention to the Cogent and knelt beside the motionless beast. He drew a set of magna-cuffs from a thigh compartment on his Akimor and wrenched the creature's arms behind its back, securing its wrists together. Crystal followed suit and did the same for the Slayer's legs.

"What about its tail?" said Nikki.

Bear extended an energy sword from his forearm and grabbed the end of its tail, where the vertebrae met the clubbed tip. He thrust his arm upward and cleaved the tail in half. The heated edge of his sword cauterized the wound, spilling only a few drops of brown goo onto the floor.

He dropped the tail to the floor with a clunk.

"The blizzard's getting worse," said Crystal, peering from the cave entrance. "Wind's now at one hundred fifty kilometers per hour and still rising. Visibility is near zero, even with multispectral. Acoustics are poor as well because of the snow."

Bear scanned the inside of the room. His Titan crew had nearly finished scouring the place. Vixtor held a few plasma rifles. Harper was fumbling with some small metal boxes.

"Find anything useful?" he said.

"Nothing," said Harper. He popped the lid off one of the boxes, and a few instruments fell to the floor. "Just food and weaponry. They have heat inside here, and few gadgets for sound and thermal dampening, basic stuff. No comm equipment or computers."

Bear nodded. "The storm is going to hold us back for a while. When it dies down, we'll work our way to the platform and find a way into the complex. Casi and Blackthorne are going to have to hang tight for a little longer. While we wait…"

He bent to the Cogent and grabbed the fleshy patches on the back of its head. Grunting, he jerked the beast off the ground and let it fall on its back. He grabbed its armpits and slid it across the floor until its back was to the wall. The Slayer stirred.

"I have stimulants," said Loko, drawing a hand into a pouch in his armor and producing a plastic case. He used his delicate inner arms to open it and pluck a syringe from plastic clips inside. "This should do it. The Intellects designed it special for my Slayer body. A mixture of neurochemicals and red lightning."

He walked to the Slayer and stuck the needle into one of the skin pockets on its neck that it used for speech.

Bear knelt beside the beast. Its muscles began to twitch. Its lips curled to expose glistening fangs. Its tail lashed the ground beside it, wagging on its stump.

There were a lot of things Bear didn't know. He didn't know what weapon the Slayers were building inside their complex, or what the beams of energy were being used for. He didn't know where they'd dragged Casi and Blackthorne, or why the Slayers had spared their lives. He didn't know what the mysterious Brain creatures were, or why they could give orders to Slayer soldiers.

If anyone knew the answers to these questions, it was the Cogent before him. He squeezed his hand into a fist as he waited for the drugs to kick in. He waited for a chance to make the Slayer talk.

FORTY

Sharker Gray – Human Destineer
On the surface of planet Earth – Old Russia

Sharker Gray stared through the glass ceiling of his personal hover cart at the towering headquarters of TV Earth. The building rose higher than the eye could see, disappearing into the clouds above. Its base was made of stone and metals quarried from the main asteroid belt between Mars and Jupiter. The walls were ornately carved, and traced in tendrils of light. Statues lined its sloping buttresses and geometries, made of solid gold. Enormous gems from across the solar system studded its walls, sparkling against the Sun's light.

His pod slowed, and the chauffeur exited, hurrying around the front of the vehicle. The side door whooshed open, and Sharker stepped onto the solid gold walkway leading to TV Earth headquarters.

"Your items, sir," said the chauffeur, holding Sharker's jacket and hat to him.

Sharker took his jacket and twirled it over his shoulders, turning the thick collar over his neck. He cinched his hat on, and enjoyed the relief it brought from the stiff winds of Old Russia. He grabbed the glass pad from the chauffeur and tapped his wrist against the surface. A jingly sound confirmed a transfer of funds, and a pile of gold coins raised above the glass in hologram form, with thin numbers designating the amount below.

"Five thousand sapience?" the man stammered after seeing the amount of currency on his plate. "Mr. Grivsky, you're too kind, allow me to walk you to the building."

"Not necessary," said Sharker. "Keep it running. I won't be long."

The man nodded his head furiously. "Of course. I'll be here waiting. When can I expect you back?"

Sharker didn't reply. He had already begun to stride down the golden walkway to the TVE building. There were many other Humans on the path, but the gold slabs were wide, and he didn't need to squeeze his broad shoulders at all to let others pass by. He smiled as he walked down the brilliant entranceway. Its beauty made him think of the Slarebull. Sid Dakota had showed him the path to their saviors, and to the *Pristine.* The path to salvation didn't have ornate carvings, or fanciful gems inlaid along its winds and twists.

No, the path to salvation in Sharker's visions was dark, but its destination sweeter than all the nectar in the universe. Soon he would embrace the Pristine, and assume his position as a god. It was, after all, his destiny.

Eliminating Sheryl Gwyndeveer had been a resounding success. The anti-destinic Clones had been silenced after the death of their leader, who had been a powerful voice throughout Earth in her quest to stop the Destineers. And what's more, the news coverage had been…

Most excellent.

The murder should have made headlines across all five of Earth's colonies, and it did in a sense. It flared for a few days then simmered down as readers lost interest. But it wasn't the duration of the publications that pleased Sharker. It was the message spread by the media in the immediate aftermath of Sheryl's death.

Clone radical silenced by Earth nativist.

Human victims of Clone slander sleep easy after DC banquet.

Evil twin vanquished.

The news headlines absolutely tickled him, and none more than TVE's. The media behemoth's blinding praise of the Destineers outpaced even his wildest expectations. His holy mission for Earth was nearly complete. He'd converted many billions of followers to his cause, and the media now seemed under his thumb. With his message broadcasted on TV sets throughout the galaxy, billions more would follow. Now he needed to seal the deal.

Sharker stepped through the thin blue air curtain separating the interior lobby from the harsh outdoor conditions. He removed his hat and enjoyed the warmth of the plush décor. He paused to admire the interior pillars, which like the outside of the building, stretched higher than the eye could see. The pillars were even more decorated than the outside of the building, coated entirely in diamonds, and hollowed to form helixes.

"Identification please, sir."

An army of guards blocked the entrance, spreading all the way across the grandiose air curtain.

"I come on special invitation from Madame Beauchene," said Sharker.

"Madame Beauchene?" One of the guards looked to the other. They both laughed, one of them clapping the other on the shoulder.

"TV Earth's CEO doesn't accept visits from strangers," said the other guard, his shoulders heaving slightly as he wiped a tear from his eye. "Good day sir."

"Place a call to her," said Sharker, his face stone. "I carry a message. *Ral-Bazeera.*"

The guards frowned. They pulled to the side and whispered to each other. One nodded and bent his head. He spoke a few words into the ground, then paused.

"Yes madam, I'll send him up," he said loud enough for Sharker to hear.

The guards stepped back in front of him. One of them drew a black wand. Sharker held his arms out and allowed the guard to screen him.

"Top floor," said the guard, after he finished sweeping the wand over his ankles. "Take the alpha tube to the right."

Sharker thanked him and stepped past the guard station and into the central lobby.

He climbed a series of shallow steps to a circular plaza. The TVE building had no offices near ground level. The decorated support columns were the only structures visible. Sharker knew he'd travel thousands of feet into the air before he reached any rooms.

The building was a star tower, a type of design made popular after the Guardians shared their knowledge of ultra-strong building materials. The towers were so tall that the term *sky scraper* seemed to belittle their magnitude. The tops seemed to reach past the sky, to the stars beyond.

The columns were marked by lit signs. He passed the columns labeled *Psi* and *Omega,* and towards the one labeled *Alpha*. The twisting arms of the pillar had many openings between. A beam of pink light whisked skyward, small particles of light showing the upward velocity of forces acting within the tube. He stepped into the pink light.

Top level.

The tower processed his mental command and he rocketed upward, cradled within the magnetic forces interacting with his Program. He continued to gain speed, and after a minute, the stone column gave way to empty air, and he streaked high above the ground. Earth's rolling, snow blanketed hills seemed pink through the wall of light he traveled within, and after he passed through a low cloud, he could only see puffs of cotton.

The horizon grew thinner and curved as he gained altitude. He flinched as stone rushed back around him. He slowed as he reached his destination, and reached a leg forward as the magnetic tube deposited him onto a marble surface. He waited a moment for his stomach to stop fluttering, then walked briskly down the hall, stopping when he reached a small chamber.

A single desk sat in the chamber, next to a wide glass door, which was milky and opaque. A man sat behind the desk, his hair dark and slicked back. He looked up from his hologram display.

"Sharker Gray," he said.

Sharker paused. He had modified his Program to a different alias. Today he was not Sharker Gray. Today he was Velin Grivsky. He eyed the nameplate on the desk.

Parker Roddingham.

"I'm here to see Madame Beauchene."

"Interesting," said Parker. He leaned forward narrowing his eyes. "Madame Beauchene doesn't normally accept visits from Destineers."

Sharker ran a tongue over his teeth. How did this man, how did *Parker*, know his identity? He'd been careful to keep minimal personal ties with those on Earth. He did his holy work in the shadows. His mission was one of destiny, not of fame or glory.

He was about to form a response when Parker leaned back in his chair and smiled. He winked, and tapped his desk. "Madame, a visitor. A Mr. Velin Grivsky."

A buzz sounded into the chambers and the glass door became transparent, then slid open.

"Madame Beauchene is ready to see you, Mr. Gray," he said.

Sharker took a deep breath, fighting to control the squirminess in his stomach. Parker continued to glare at him as he entered through the doors.

A wide set of stairs lay behind the doorway, and he climbed them, entering the top level of the TVE building.

The ceiling was curved and made entirely of glass, as were the walls. The sun blazed above, but the glass had darkened around it to shield the room from its intense rays. Planet Earth curved far below, and through parts in the clouds, Sharker could see sparkling oceans, and snowy land. A blue band of atmosphere gave way to black space. Thick buttresses fanned wide of the star tower, supporting the structure on points of land hundreds of kilometers away from the ground entrance. Several other star towers jutted above the clouds in the distance.

"I was wondering when I would finally meet you."

Sharker turned towards the seductive voice behind him. A slender woman dressed in a silky dress sat on a plush couch. The couch faced a holo pit, where images of various planets and military vehicles hovered.

"Mr. Grivsky," said Madame Beauchene, rising from the couch. Her dress was translucent in parts, and showed her midriff and thighs, darkening around her chest and waist. Her skin below the dress was marked in swirling tattoos of pink light. She walked to him, her heels clicking against the marble floor, and stopped inches away. She drew a hand to his beard. "Or should I say, *Sharker Gray*."

Sharker tensed at the sound of his name. "The man outside," he started.

"Oh, don't worry about Parker, he's loyal to me. He does all my dirty work." She smiled. Her teeth were capped in glowing pink bands. "Relax, Mr. Gray. I know who you are. I know what you stand for. It is my job as the head of the largest media syndicate in the galaxy to know everything that goes on. Would you like a drink?"

She motioned to a glass table, on top of which sat a crystal bottle of blue liquid and some glasses.

He shook his head. "I've come to speak with you about our future. I'll admit, I was hesitant to approach you. Even now, I'm wondering if I made the right decision. But Humans are suffering, and I have a message for them. I need someone with a large megaphone to help me spread it."

Madame Beauchene grinned. "Sit."

She swept her arm to a set of leather chairs, and began to walk to them. Sharker followed, and sat down opposite her.

"You saw my headlines after Ms. Gwyndeveer's death, and assumed I was on your side."

"Was I wrong?"

Madame chuckled and tilted her head back, peering at him through her thick eyelashes. "Let us say I'm becoming less *undecided.* There was a time when I would have had my guards detain you on sight, and throw you from the top of this building. But I suppose you could say my opinion has evolved as of late."

She reached to a table beside her chair and slid a small book from the surface. Sharker recognized the book at once.

"The Doctrine of Destiny," he whispered.

"Hmm, yes. The Doctrine of Destiny. Sid Dakota wrote this book over a century ago. I've read it several times. To be honest, I found the idea of his *visions* to be quite ridiculous."

"Madame, I can assure you, I've had such visions…"

"That was until," she cut him off. "Until I had visions of my own. I've heard the Voice of the Pristine. I can't explain my visions, but they are as real as the floor beneath our feet. Why don't all Humans have such visions?"

"The Pristine call to us as gods. Only those with faith can open their ears and receive the message. It's then our responsibility to spread the word of Doctrine to others. It is our destiny to embrace the Slarebull, and the Pristine. It is our destiny as Humans."

"And you need my network to spread the word of the Destineers. I foresee problems with this. UCOM will surely respond to such obvious propaganda."

"UCOM is filled with subhuman filth who oppress our holy mission. UCOM is not our friend, but our enemy."

"But they have armies," said Madame. "Millions of ships, and control of our portal Network."

"We have armies of our own. The Destineers are militarily strong. With your help, we can also become unified."

A pause.

"Are you sure this is the right way? I do not wish to be launched from the tubes on account of treason."

"Madame, joining the Pristine is our destiny as gods. When the time comes, this will be the *only* way."

Madame smiled wide. "Well then Mr. Gray, consider the media arm of TV Earth to work on behalf of the Destineers. *Ral-Bazeera.*"

FORTY-ONE

Sid Dakota – Human Destineer
Aboard Hive *Sylva* – Bravo starspace

Sid admired the view from the Hive mothership. He had left the Sylvan surface and taken a space elevator up from Tower 1, entering the piloting and control section of the vessel. The craft was nicknamed the *pinhead*, because of its tiny size relative to the large planet in tow. But the ship was not small by any means. It was twice the size of a UCOM Tiger heavy-destroyer, and had four massive arms curving from the aft section of its hull.

The arms served as a support cradle for the planet, anchoring it to the Hive, and protecting its atmosphere from the harshness of space. The underside of each arm provided artificial light to the planet, breathing energy to the surface to fuel plant life, create weather patterns, and warm the air. The arms also housed the ships primary thrusters, lighting the rear in blue streaks of exhaust.

He stood at a large bay window at the aft section of the *pinhead.* Sylva lay beneath him, half of it lit from lights beneath the arms, and half dark. No suns set below the horizon on Sylva, but the planet did experience nighttime.

Past Sylva lay a bank of portals. The red spheres were already shrinking to points of light, and soon they would disappear from view as his Hive forged onward. In short time he would pass the Outer Rim and join the *Primal Snow*. After centuries of holy devotion, he would finally have a chance to bow before the Sterilord, then join the Pristine as equals.

He would finally enter into their kingdom as he was destined to.

He would assume his position as a god.

Sid sighed and turned to the inside of the room. A fire burned against the far wall, nestled within a stone mantle. His servant stood beside the fire, dressed in a gray tunic. His head was bowed towards the floor. Sid walked towards him, stopping before the fire, enjoying the warmth on his skin.

"Are you excited to transcend, Jimmy?"

Jimmy shuffled next to him. "Yes Father," he said meekly. "I'muh ready."

Sid pulled his lips into a humorless smile, not removing his eyes from the fire. "You've served me well for over a century." He turned to the simple man. Jimmy still faced the ground. "Tell me why I'm suddenly doubting your faith."

Jimmy raised his head to Sid. His eyes were blank and dull, as they normally were. "I'm sorry Father, I'll try to think a lil' harder, I don' wanna let'cha down."

Sid's allowed his tight smile to snap away. He leaned to pick a fire poker from a stand on the side of the hearth. He stabbed at a log and let the poker sit at the blue inside of the flames.

"Faith is important, Jimmy. Do you know what happens to those who don't have faith?"

No response.

"Those without faith are subhuman, just like the beasts and animals in UCOM. The subhumans will be scorched from this universe like a plague, burned from existence as the Pristine sterilize the galaxies within."

He stirred the fire, sending embers cackling up the chimney. The tip of the poker was red hot. He glanced at Jimmy. His forehead glistened with sweat.

"Father Dakota, sir."

Sid turned to the edge of the room. One of his lieutenants stood at the entrance.

"Yes?"

"We've received multiple confirmations on the surface of Sylva. Chase and the rest of SIGA are planning a preemptive strike against us at twenty-hundred hours zulu time."

He scowled and returned to the fire. "No matter, we strike at O-eight-hundred. Their corpses will be cold by twenty-hundred."

"Father please," said Jimmy. He knelt to the floor. "Do we have to kill the civilians under the ground? They aren't sinners."

Sid growled and tore at Jimmy's tunic, tearing it loose to expose his bare chest. He kicked the man to the floor.

"Remember what I said about cleansing the galaxy of subhumans? I've saved a special treatment for those underground."

He whipped the poker from the fire and pressed the flat edge to Jimmy's sternum, stomping a boot over it to seal it against his skin. Jimmy shrieked.

He bent low enough to feel Jimmy's sharp pants warm the side of his cheeks.

"The filth underground had one hundred fifty years to join our holy cause. The only way to properly sterilize filth is with fire. I'm not going to simply kill them. I'm going to *burn them.*"

FORTY-TWO

Sid Dakota – Human Destineer
Aboard Hive *Sylva* – Bravo starspace

Sid breathed deep as he fought to calm himself. His pod whooshed as it streaked past large terminals and platforms on its way to the command bridge of the Sylvan Hive.

He didn't know what to think of Jimmy. The simpleton had been loyal for so many years, and he felt a pang of remorse for his actions in the observation bay. But he couldn't shake the look he'd seen on Jimmy's face on the Sylvan surface, at the top of Tower 1 in the Snow Room. It was a look of contempt. No, a look of *hatred.* And in the observation bay, when Jimmy had spoken against sterilizing the SIGA subhumans...

He chalked it up as coincidence, mixed with vacant stupidity. He needed to teach Jimmy a lesson, and had, rather successfully. He would worry about Jimmy later. There were more pressing matters at hand.

The pod dinged as it reached the command bridge, and he rose from his seat, stepping into the rounded room. A group of Slarebull stood at various control stations, but most of the bridge was empty. They hadn't encountered any military threats since the Frontline battle. Unless an alarm sounded, the Slarebull would continue to run a skeleton crew.

The Slarebull turned from their stations. All of them glared at Sid, but most returned to their work. One did not, and walked towards him. The Slarebull bowed and opened all four of his arms in respect, laying his tail flat against the ground. Sid didn't miss the light growl the beast made during his bow.

"Mr. Dakota, to what do I owe this pleasure?"

His voiced was laced in sarcasm.

Sid frowned. "Commander Grizk. I'd tell you to wipe the scowl from your face, but I'm not sure you lizards are capable. When will we reach the Primal Snow?"

Grizk's lip twitched, flashing his blackened fangs. "We're making steady progress, *sir.* Once we're around the Floodgate, we'll reach the *Primal Snow* in a day's time."

Sid pondered the information. He itched to reach the Pristine kingdom and bow before the Sterilord, but he did have a small matter to deal with beforehand. He needed to eliminate Chase Grover and his fellow heretics.

"When will we reach the Floodgate?"

"We have three more portals to pass, then we'll enter security screening at the Floodgate."

"Security screening? I have direct authority from the Pristine to enter *Primal Snow* starspace. We'll skip the security measures, I order you to."

"I take orders from the Pristine," the Slarebull growled.

"And the Pristine ordered you to obey my command. Let's not forget who's in charge here."

Grizk flexed his muscles and exhaled sharply through his neck. "I know what's happening on the planet's surface. There is *filth* underground. They've been there since we built this Hive. The Pristine will not allow such creatures to enter their kingdom."

Sid walked closer to the Slarebull, craning his neck towards the beast's face. "Kneel."

Grizk growled and lowered to his knees until his head was below Sid's.

"Much better. You're just a beast pet following his master's orders. A dumb brute animal."

"I serve the *Pristine,*" Grizk spat. "If not for their command, I would have…"

Sid cocked his head. "You would have what?" He leaned closer, until he could smell the lizard's rank breath. "Don't make me remind you again, commander. I *am Pristine.*"

Grizk bowed his head lower, seething. "Let me take my brothers to the planet's surface. Let us kill the filth. We'll bathe in their blood, and dance to their screams as we suck on their bones."

Sid slapped the beast hard in the face. It made his hand sting, and Grizk's head barely moved a centimeter, but the Slarebull commander wasn't able to contain his growl of rage. His claws screeched as they dug against the metal floor.

"Don't call my people filth again, or I'll send you out the tubes. Many simply haven't yet found faith. They will though, and those that don't…"

"But you call them filth yourself. You've killed scores of them-"

"What I call my people is my own concern. You're nothing to me but a hairy lizard, a servant. I am above you. Don't forget it."

Grizk seethed, and his body shook with anger. "Yes, *sir.*"

Sid took a few steps backwards. "Alert me once we reach the Floodgate."

The Slayer scrambled to his feet and slammed his tail against the floor, struggling to control himself.

"A word of caution, *sir.* Only the naked apes may enter the Primal Snow. Any other fil…*races*, would mean instant death to all."

Sid paused just before his pod and turned to Grizk.

"Let me worry about the subhumans. You just steer the damn ship."

FORTY-THREE

Chase Grover – Half Human/Half Clone
On the Surface of Slayer Hive *Sylva* – Inside Bastion

126 years ago

Mae's eyes welled as she reached a hand to stroke Jimmy's face.

"Don't go Jam-Jam," she whispered, her voice wavering. "Mae loves you."

Jimmy's face was racked in sorrow. "I know that Aunt Mae, but I gotta go. SIGA needs someone to do it, and I volunteered."

Mae whimpered and wiggled her nose. Jimmy bent to give her a kiss on her cheek. "I won't forget about you Aunt Mae. And I'll make sure the Destineers never find Bastion."

"So this is it," said Chase. "This is goodbye."

Jimmy rose and turned to Chase, placing a hand on his shoulder. "Chase, I don't know how to say this, but," he wiped a tear from his eye. "I ain't never had no sons, and I suppose I would consider you one when it came right down to it. I'm sorry I couldn't teach you words or numbers, Uncle Jimmy's head don't work like that. But I'm proud of you, and I know your ma and pa would be too."

Chase cleared his throat, trying to hide his sniffles. "My dad. Did he mention me before he left?"

Jimmy smiled. “Your dad? *Shit.*” He toed the ground. “You were the last words outta his mouth. He told me to protect you, and that he loved you. But you know that, it’s folklore ‘round these parts.”

Mae sobbed gently beside them. Chase brought Jimmy in for a hug. “Promise me you’ll come back.”

The man who’d helped care for him since birth smiled, but didn’t commit to such a promise. “Take care now Chase. You’ll make a fine leader someday. I’ll send word as soon as I can.”

“We have word from Jimmy.”

Chase snapped into focus. An intelligence officer stood at the entrance to the operations headquarters. He was out of breath, and gulped down a deep lungful of air.

“What did he say?” said General Archyr, stepping from behind the holo deck. “Does he know Sid’s plan?”

“Just the basics,” said the officer. “Nothing we aren’t already expecting. The Destineers are going to pump Bastion full of firewater. He didn’t have a lot of time to talk, said Dakota might be on to him, but he knows when they plan to attack.”

“How long do we have?” said Archyr.

“Not long. They’re going to start drilling and blasting at 0800 zulu time.” The officer checked his Program. “That gives us less than twelve hours.”

Archyr cursed. “Did Jimmy tell his location?”

“He’s on the pinhead, he went with Sid up to the Hive mothership. I told him to hang tight, we’ll rally with him as soon as we can.”

“And if the stars are with us, that will be in little more than twelve hours,” said Archyr. He walked back behind the holo deck, and raised a number of 3D images to the front of the room. “Okay people, listen up. We have less time than we thought, so we’re going to tidy things up here, then we’ll move out into the city.”

"Sir," said one of the officers. "My men are setting up our installations around Bastion, but they're confused. Operation Pinhead doesn't call for underground fighting, and my men are asking questions."

"A full detail will be sent over central comms within the hour," said Archyr. "We're going to lay the rough bones out. It will be up to you guys to figure the details. We're pressed for time. Now before we get into timing and responsibility, give me questions or take them to the stars."

The officers and lieutenants looked around at each other.

"Sir," said one of the officers. "Dakota's getting ready to pump firewater. Are we sure our blast walls can hold their drills and detonators?"

"We're assuming they'll drill," said Archyr. "And we should hope to stars they decide to detonate. If they blast, the mountain shaft will cave, and we'll be sealed down here. It would take Dakota days to drill this deep through solid mountain rock. It took the Clones years to excavate Bastion. Our engineers are double checking our materials, but we have several layers of blast walls, and they should hold the way we want them to."

"Their land vehicles would overpower our armaments quickly," said another officer. "What if they bring their tanks down?"

"They won't," said Archyr. "Side passages are too narrow."

"What if they don't come down?" said a Guardian lieutenant. He was one of the only Guardians in Bastion. "Do we move to Operation Pinhead?"

"They'll come down," said Archyr. "They'll have to."

"What about the civilians?" Chase ground his teeth and leaned forward in his chair. "They're going to be trapped. There's no exit on the path they're taking. Even if we blow the entrance, the Destineers would be able to remove the rubble in hours with equipment."

Archyr nodded grimly. "That's why they'll come down to Bastion. And as for the civilians, that's why Operation Pinhead needs to be a success.

Silence. The General stared at the ground. “We have three-hundred twenty-nine soldiers. The Destineers have many times that. But the walls of Bastion are narrow, and only so many can enter at once.”

“Like Thermopylae,” said one of the Human officers. The rest of the staff raised their eyebrows. The Human officer shrugged his shoulders. “Am I the only Human old enough to know about Thermopylae? Three hundred Spartan warriors fended off one hundred fifty thousand Persians on Earth thousands of years ago? They made movies about it and everything.”

More silence. Then General Archyr began to chuckle. More officers joined, and soon the room erupted in laughter. Chase joined in. He felt like he was laughing in the face of death.

They quieted down, one of the Clone officers still hooting to himself. “Three hundred against a hundred fifty thousand?”

“You don’t believe me?” said the Human officer.

“No, I believe you,” said the Clone, wiping a tear from his eye. “It’s just, right now, I’d kill for those odds.”

FORTY-FOUR

Eve – Clone

On the surface of *Scrock* – Discarded Hive

"How do you think the others are holding up?" said Keyv, thunking his head against the glass behind his seat. His hair squeaked against the window as Pexar turned off the ramp exiting the building.

"I don't know," said Eve, staring out her own window. Their meeting with the Discarded leaders had left her confused, and terrified. "I'm sure they're fine. We need to get their input."

Keyv frowned. "Eve, you're our commander. This isn't a democracy, you need to make the decision. We both know our squadron will be split on this."

"Exactly," said Eve, stiffening on her seat. "I'm commander. And as an inferior officer, it's not your place to question my decisions. We put this to a vote."

"I'm sorry," said Keyv furling his eyebrows. "I didn't mean it like that, it's just, whatever our decision is," he sighed. "We need to act soon. If what Rixxi said about the Triturator and the Primal Snow is true…"

He let the thought linger.

Eve shook her head. "I'm just a stealth scout, Woods should be making this decision. If we go with the Discarded's plan, billions will die."

Pexar spoke from the driver's seat at the front of the vehicle. "I couldn't help but overhear," the Slayer turned to look at them briefly before turning back to the road. "But *billion* is a fairly small number of souls to lose in such a war. Normally the Slayers take trillions of lives. *Bump*."

Eve's rear end hopped a few inches from her chair as Pexar drove over the lip of a steep ramp. She shook her head. "The Triturator installations would pass right through the oasis zone, not to mention the Inner Ring. Huge chunks of our military would be de-atomized."

"If our plan works, UCOM won't need a vast military," said Pexar. "Without the Pristine to command them, the Slayer armadas will fail. They'll no longer have purpose."

"UCOM will destroy the installations," said Eve. "They won't let the Slayers plant them around the Milky Way, they'll blow them to smithereens."

"And for every failed installation, the Slayers will bring ten more," said Pexar. The vehicle slowed. He guided the ATV alongside a set of low metacrete bungalows. He cut power and turned around. "You've seen the Slayer armada. Their resources are limitless. They've pillaged hundreds of galaxies, and have no shortage of soldiers or weaponry. Their manufacturing and energy capabilities cannot be matched."

The Discarded opened his door and climbed from the vehicle. Keyv opened the door beside him and allowed Eve to jump out before following her onto the packed dirt outside the bungalows.

"Then we'll stand and fight," said Eve, jogging to catch up to Pexar. She froze in front of a patch of exotic blue grass before hopping onto the blades. "We beat the Slayers at the Frontline. We can beat them again."

Pexar laughed. It was a strange laugh, and played tricks on Eve's eyes. His mouth stayed tightly shut as the membranes on his neck ballooned out. "You think you beat the Slarebull?" He snorted. "You gave them a mere scratch. An honorable battle sure, I've intercepted Slarebull chatter about their losses. But next time, they will arrive in full force, and there will be no compromise. You won't be able to sever your Stitchline twice."

Eve fumed. "Then why are you going to even bother attacking the Floodgate? All you talk about is how the Slayers are all-powerful. How they are too strong and in too great a number to defeat. You said it yourself, you've failed for thousands of years at destroying their Triturator. What makes you think you'll win this time?"

Pexar turned. They had reached the entrance to the bungalows. Behind the closed doors, Eve's scout team had set up bunks. He dropped to all fours so his face was level with theirs

"You didn't listen to Lord Rixxi, naked ape woman. Our goal is not to destroy the Triturator. Our goal is to damage it in a very *specific* way. We're going to refocus the energy of the Milky Way, and send it into the Pristine like a giant laser gun."

"To destroy the Primal Snow," murmured Keyv. He turned to Eve. "This could work. Eve, I think we should go with it. They have thousands of years of trial and error against the Slayers. If their plan works, we'd save most of the Milky Way. We'd save Earth. We could take Sylva back."

Eve's lip wavered at the mention of her old home planet. Memories of its scorched surface, and of the shattered UCOM ships in orbit, hung in her thoughts.

"I can't," she said. "I can't make the decision. Woods only made me commander because of dumb luck. We managed to sneak into a Hive without getting killed, and that's it."

Keyv bit his lip and stomped forward, breathing heavily through his nostrils. "That's it? You brought the Blight desist back to the Frontline. The Intellects used it to save billions of people from becoming zombies. And then you guided a fleet of scouts and destroyed a Hive mothership during the Frontline battle." He shook his head, at a loss for words.

"I can't command my scouts to join the Discarded," said Eve softly. "I won't. Even if it's the right decision, I can't abandon our men and women back home. You're Human, you should know. First in, last to leave. No man left behind. That's your motto right? Allowing the Slayers to activate the Triturator would kill *billions* back home. I can't accept that."

"Have you ever had chemotherapy?" said Keyv. After seeing the blank look on Eve's face he shook his head. "Well of course you never went through it but it's what Human's did before we had Programs to remove dangerous cells. They would multiply and spread, and in order to kill the disease, we would need to kill a lot of good cells as well. We'd get sick, but the cancer would go away."

"I know what chemotherapy is," said Eve. "The definition is stored in my Program."

"In order to keep UCOM alive," said Keyv. "We need to let some die. I agree with Pexar. Their plan with the Triturator is the only way to stop the Slayers."

"No," said Eve. "We'll find a way. The Intellects will invent a new technology, we'll drive back their fleets."

"Ape woman," said Pexar softly. His eyes were tortured. "I've seen thousands of strange aliens just like you say they would drive back the Slayers. None ever have, for thousands of years. The Slayers will take the Milky Way. They will win. They always do."

FORTY-FIVE

Eve – Clone

On the surface of *Scrock* – Discarded Hive

Eve ground her teeth and stared at the ground. She ran a hand over the rough metacrete of the bungalow. "Your plan," she looked at Pexar. "You're certain it's the only way? Destroying the Floodgate isn't an option, and neither is sneaking into the Primal Snow? We have to allow the Triturator to start, then commandeer it?"

"I am certain of this, ape woman," said Pexar. "We have destroyed the Floodgate in the past. It is a delay tactic. And sneaking into the Primal Snow is impossible. You would not be physically able to travel past the wall of ships protecting the Pristine, even if you were not seen. Their fleet is too large."

She shook her head and squatted onto her ankles, tearing a few blades of grass and ripping them into tiny blue pieces. "I think if we just had more time," she exhaled. "We need to try and communicate with UCOM, send Woods a Raven, or the Intellects. It's not right to start the Triturator without knowing what the conditions are near the Inner Ring."

"And in the mean time we'll stay here," said Keyv, squatting next to her and rubbing a hand over her shoulder. "On Scrock. We'll be able to fight the Slayers while they set up their installations. I'm sure it takes decades to set up a machine that can de-atomize a galaxy. Some of our chatter said the Slayers built new portals across the Frontline. The Ravens we sent may already have reached Woods."

"Unfortunately that's not true," said Pexar. The Slayer scratched his neck. Eve and Keyv stood.

"How would you know if our Ravens made it back to the Inner Ring?" said Eve suspiciously. "Keyv's right. Slayer chatter listed stellar coordinates at the portal junctions. We sent hundreds of Ravens back home along those paths. One will return eventually."

"I'm sure your Ravens are well on their way to UCOM," said Pexar. "But I'm talking about the Triturator installations. The naked ape man said it would take decades to install. This isn't true. The Slarebull prefabricate the devices before installing them. Once they're moved into position, they're ready. The process takes mere days."

"So," Keyv blew sharply out of his mouth. "That means that after they start to move their Triturator into place,"

"We'll have a very small window to stop them," finished Pexar. "If we don't act soon, the Milky Way will be destroyed."

Silence.

"This Triturator," said Eve. "How does it work? I'm having a hard time picturing the device in my head. And how do you plan on commandeering it? I need some answers before I enlist my crew and join the SSF."

Pexar smiled, not with his mouth but with his eyes. "Fair enough. Come with me, naked apes, I have a few things to show you. I think you'll be impressed."

FORTY-SIX

Eve – Clone

On the surface of *Scrock* – Discarded Hive

Eve sighed as she stared out the window of the ATV. They'd stopped in the bungalow before leaving with Pexar for a quick debrief with her scout squadron. It'd gone worse than expected. Half of her team wouldn't look Pexar in the face, and turned to face the rear wall in protest when he'd entered the room.

One of her Human lieutenants, Blaire Ashe, had started to curse at Pexar and shouted for the rest of the squadron to leave this ungodly planet and find UCOM forces to join. Only after Eve threatened to charge her with treason as a deserter did Blaire storm from the Bungalow, pausing to spit at Pexar's feet.

She shook her head at the memory. They had left the city buildings and for the past half hour driven over flat, blue plains of long grass. In the distance, mountains rose, etched in purple against the horizon. The mountains seemed out of place, like they should be taller. Eve frowned and squinted ahead.

"Pexar," she said. "Slow down, there's a cliff."

The cliff face raced toward them, but Pexar didn't slow. She heard Keyv grunt beside her as he braced for their fall.

"*Pexar,*" she cried as they plummeted off the ledge.

Her stomach dropped, and then settled. She took a quick glance out the window before snapping her eyes upward again. They were thousands of feet above the rocky dirt below.

"Scrock has magnets embedded throughout its surface," said Pexar, turning to Eve and Keyv in the back of the ATV. "We put a couple of extra magnets in the cliff."

The magnetic forces acting on their ATV guided them towards the rock face, where she saw a wide opening in the stone.

"We use the same technology on UCOM planets and on our ships," said Eve. "Why did you put your entrance on the side of a cliff?"

"Security," said Pexar. "We have a lot of rescued races and civilizations here. It's our belief that military assets should be kept separated from our civilians."

The inside of the cavern was bare save for five automated sentry turrets, which pointed at them briefly before turning towards the ground. Pexar guided their ATV onto a smooth track in front of a long, lit tunnel that dropped sharply downward.

Keyv grunted again as they rapidly accelerated. Eve winced as her head and stomach protested the intense change in speed. The Intellects had given her squadron Program updates to interact with Slayer mag-tech, but it wasn't fully optimized. She was reminded of this by a sharp pain spreading into her forehead as her body struggled to pump blood to her brain.

"Slow…down," she gasped.

Pexar obliged, and the pounding in her head dulled as they slowed.

"Sorry ape woman," he said. "I thought you said your nanotechnology serum was adapted for our technology. We're here."

Damp air met Eve's face as they exited the Komodo.

They'd gone deep into the tunnel. It was well lit and enormous. Had it not been for the running lights streaking down the passage, Eve may have mistaken the tunnel for a massive cave. Aside from a few trucks and flying craft in the distance, they were alone.

"How high is the ceiling?" Eve gasped, craning her neck.

"Eight thousand meters," said Pexar. "And ten thousand meters wide. It's a simulation chamber for the Floodgate. This is a replica of the smallest passage in the Triturator valve."

"The *smallest*?" said Keyv. "How big is the rest of the Floodgate?"

"Bigger than some planets," said Pexar. "Come, I'll show you how we enter them."

They parked at the edge of the tunnel and exited the vehicle. Eve followed Keyv and Pexar up a series of ramps leading to a wide set of glass doors. The calm of the cavernous Floodgate simulator was replaced by a buzz of voices and activity as the entrance opened.

The Slayer Discarded milled around as they traveled to their destinations. They had entered a sort of complex, with metal walls lined with doorways.

"This is one of our training camps," said Pexar. "We have them all over Scrock, but this one doubles as a research facility."

He powered his way across the lobby, weaving through various Slayer rebels. Eve's shoulder jolted as one of the passing Discarded bumped into her.

"Apologies, ape woman," he said, bowing his Slarebull head before continuing on his way.

They reached a small, plain looking door. Pexar held his delicate inner hand against the control panel beside it, and the door opened to expose a room filled with equipment and instruments. A few holograms hovered above the various tables and workspaces. Eve decided it was a lab.

"The Triturator uses high level physics to de-atomize galaxies," said Pexar, waving his arm over a concave pit in the ground. A 3D rendering of a spiral galaxy appeared. "The Discarded don't know how it works, no one does but the Pristine. It does share some common characteristics with well known technology, though. We like to relate the Triturator to plumbing and laser beams."

"Plumbing?" said Keyv, eyeing the model. "Like with pipes and water?"

"Indeed," said Pexar. "The Triturator installations are placed in concentric circles throughout the galaxy, forming a spiral. The Primal Snow blasts a beam of energy into the Floodgate to prime the system. That energy kickstarts the Triturator, which then uses the gravitational energy of black holes to feed the rest of the process. After the Triturator begins to de-atomize the stars and planets, the energy byproduct is sent back through the Floodgate in a steady beam, where it is captured and stored by the Pristine in the Primal Snow."

Eve watched as the model lit to show thousands of red dots within the galaxy. A thick red line entered the edge of the model, and the red dots lit one by one as they were connected in a spiral pattern. The red dots switched to green as the process reversed, and the Primal Snow began to harvest the power of the galaxy.

"Why the Floodgate?" she said, turning to Pexar. "Why not attack any one of these dots, these *installations?*"

"We've tried taking down smaller installations before," said Pexar. "It's far easier to do, but taking down an installation won't stop the Triturator. It will keep running at slightly reduced capacity, and the installation would be replaced rapidly. The only way to stop the Triturator is by taking down the Floodgate."

"This big green dot right here?" said Keyv, stepping forward to tap a finger against the dot at the edge of the galaxy, larger than the rest. His face lit as the model exploded into a magnified view of the Floodgate machine.

"Yes," said Pixar. "The Floodgate is essentially a valve, or coupling, connecting the Primal Snow to the Triturator."

The Floodgate was oval, with angled vents lining its sides. Enormous columns of energy pulsed into one side of the device, and out the other in a focused beam. The vents flared and dulled as they controlled and smoothed the outgoing energy.

"We're going to sabotage this machine?" said Eve, nodding to the hologram.

"We?" said Pexar, grinning with his eyes. He continued after she failed to respond. "The effluent valve is tightly controlled to focus the beam sent back to the *Primal Snow*. If the beam scatters, they wouldn't be able to capture it properly. So our plan is to..." Pexar flicked the end of the Floodgate, where the beam of energy shot into space.

"Scatter the beam," Eve finished. She nodded as the energy spread in a wide cone away from the Floodgate.

"I would be equivalent to sending trillions of nuclear bombs into the *Primal Snow*," said Pexar. "The Pristine's fleets would be vaporized."

Eve met Keyv's eyes as they both looked up from the models. He pouted his lips slightly and shrugged his shoulders, nodding his head.

"Could work," he mouthed silently. Eve grinned.

"How are we going to sabotage a machine as big as a planet?" said Eve, turning to Pexar.

The Slayer deserter licked his fangs. "Antimatter bombs. Lots of them. They're the only weapon powerful enough."

"Sounds easy enough," said Keyv. "Send a bunch of AMMO-AB missiles into the Floodgate, then *bam*, Pristine are gone, we can go home."

"The walls of the Floodgate are too thick for outside penetration," said Pexar. His air sacks ballooned against his neck as he sighed. "We need to detonate from the inside. Transmission signals can't reach the detonation points, so we have to manually place the antimatter bombs."

"Manually drag AMMO-AB's into a planet sized machine?" Eve scoffed. "A machine you say is heavily fortified. Please, do tell us how you think this is possible. I'll remind you that antimatter weapons are inherently unstable."

"You're absolutely right, ape woman," said Pexar. "I never suggested our mission would be safe or easy." He tapped his tail against the floor and dropped to all fours, scuttling across the room before standing.

Eve squinted towards Pexar. The Discarded seemed to be staring into space. Suddenly the air around him wavered, as if a sheet of water covered the air. Red eyes lit into view, and an enormous creature lumbered towards them, towering high above.

Keyv yelped and fumbled for his sidearm.

"Don't fire," Pexar hissed.

There was a low hum, and the beast's red eyes turned blue, as did dozens of running lights up and down its legs and arms.

It was no beast at all.

It was a robot, built in the likeness of a Slayer. The robot was taller than a Slayer – Eve guessed around four meters tall. It seemed heavily armored, and lacked a tail.

"You send in drones?" said Keyv, reaching a shaky hand to touch the thigh of the enormous robot.

"Not drones," said Pexar. "They're *Foxes*, follower droids. They're also bombs. Inside the Fox, one hundred kilograms of antimatter is suspended in a vacuum."

Eve joined Keyv in leaping backwards away from the Fox.

"One hundred kilograms?" she cried. "That's enough to blow this mountain to dust."

"And then some," said Pexar. "Not to worry, this Fox isn't armed. It's a test dummy we use for training."

"Follower droids," said Keyv. "What do these things follow?"

"Rabbits."

"And where are the Rabbits?" said Eve, searching around the room for another robot.

"We were hoping you would be Rabbits," said Pexar. "The Foxes are just fancy pack mules, smart enough to follow commands, but not intelligent enough to navigate terrain on their own. With the amount of Foxes we need to detonate, we need all the skilled stealth soldiers we can get. If you and your squadron want to stop the Slayers, this is your best option.

"I…" Eve glanced at Keyv. "*We* don't know how to control these robots. The *Foxes.* And what about the rest of my squadron?"

"Each Rabbit and Fox is escorted into the Floodgate by a flight detail. The Floodgate chambers are large enough to fly in, as you witnessed in the simulation tunnel outside. Your squadron would be your air support. As for controlling the Fox," he smiled. "That's why we have our training programs."

FORTY-SEVEN

Frank Scott – Human

On Night Eagle *Eclipse* – Lavariz starspace

Frank didn't start his vision at Earth. His home planet was far behind him, so far away he didn't even bother looking over his shoulder towards it. He had no passion for Earth any longer. Sure, he was born there. It was there he learned how to walk, write cursive, and hold open the door for ladies. It was where he learned how to chug beer, and what food to eat beforehand to avoid a hangover.

But those memories were fleeting. Had he once loved Earth? Sure. Perhaps a dark corner of him still did. But he had a new love now.

A voice called to him.

He liked Earth, but he liked the Voice more. In fact, *yes.* Frank *loved* the Voice.

"Frank."

The Voice sent waves of pleasure rippling up his arms and through his torso to his hips. He moaned and staggered towards the beautiful voice.

"Frank, come to me. I've missed you so much, Frank. You haven't forgotten about me, have you?"

He wanted to shout to the Voice, to scream at it, assure the Voice that no, he hadn't forgotten about it, he loved the Voice the way it loved him.

The words stuck in his parched, bone dry throat. He gulped and hacked, willing himself to make just a little bit of saliva, just a tiny amount. Only a smidge, so he could talk to the Voice. Tell the Voice how he felt.

But his throat stayed raw. Frank knew where he could find water. A splendid waterfall crashed behind the golden doorway.

He was already near the glowing entrance, and ran to its magnificent archways. He grabbed the handle and wrenched it open. A fine mist coated his face and he exhaled a sigh of relief and pleasure. His throat loosened up.

"Frank, through here. Come through the falls. Let the water cleanse you. Let it wash the filth from your skin. Let it make you pristine. Everyone is pristine in our kingdom."

"I'm coming," he croaked.

It was the first time he'd spoken to the Voice. He wished he could speak more, to profess his love for the Voice, but his throat wasn't ready yet. He needed to drink from the falls.

He staggered to the thunderous wall of water and plunged in. He yelped as frozen liquid drenched his body, soaking him to the bone. He choked as he gulped greedily at the water splashing around his face, swallowing it in lumps.

His skin tingled as if on fire. He screamed and clutched at his chest, but calmed when he realized his skin wasn't melting away, or burning. The water was cool, maybe even freezing. His skin wasn't running from his body – his filth was.

He was becoming clean. He was becoming *Pristine.*

"Frank, come through the water. Doesn't it feel good to be clean, Frank? Doesn't it feel good to be spotless? To be pristine? Come and look at my kingdom. At our kingdom. We're all pristine here."

The Voice encouraged him to step forward, to leave the flowing columns of water crashing onto his head and shoulders. He didn't want to leave. The water felt so good, and he knew he still had some filth on his skin. But the Voice was so sweet and kind. He had to meet the Voice, to enter his kingdom. He stepped from the falls.

Dry earth warmed his feet. Water dripped and splattered around him for a few seconds, but his wetness was quickly steamed dry by golden rays of sunlight kissing him from above. Frank reached to remove his shirt, and realized he was naked. His clothing wasn't fit for a god, and the water had cleansed the fabric from his flesh. His clothing had been *filthy*.

The golden rays touched his core, and sent fingers of pleasure into his crotch. He smiled and blinked lazily at the rays, raising a hand to shield the brightness from his face.

A mountain rose above him. No. Not a mountain, a hill. A tall hill, yes, but only a hill.

"Come to me, Frank. Climb the hill to our kingdom. You are mucking in dredges of filth, Frank. You need to climb higher, where it is clean, and dry. Where it is pristine."

Frank grunted and leaped onto the steep incline, grabbing at a large boulder. He expected his hands to dirty, but they did not. The rock was smooth and clean. He grinned. There was no filth where he was headed. He scrambled over the rock.

The Voice had waited so long for him. He needed to find the Voice, to leap into its arms and embrace it in the world of the Pristine.

"I'm waiting for you, Frank."

He climbed faster. Harder.

"Come to me Frank. I love you so much, please, come to the top and enter our kingdom. I'm waiting for you Frank."

"Come on Frank, I'm not going to wait all day. Frank? *I'm waiting.*"

Frank's eyes opened to find Nancy shaking him. No, they didn't open, they just *focused.* His eyes had been open the entire time. The entire time he'd been trying to find...

The Pristine.

It didn't take long for Frank to remember his vision, as it had in the past. Frank's mind wasn't muddled any longer. It wasn't clogged with booze and drugs and cigarettes. No, his mind was clear now.

His mind was pristine.

FORTY-EIGHT

Nancy Woods - Human

On Night Eagle *Eclipse* – Lavariz starspace

"What the *frux* is wrong with you Frank? Jesus, your eyes look like a coma patient's."

Nancy shook her longtime lover hard. Frank mumbled and blinked his eyes, licking his lips. "How long was I…where are we right now?"

She slapped at him repeatedly, forcing him to raise his hands and arms over his face.

"First on the Liberty and now here?" She slapped at him harder. "You can't keep passing out everywhere."

"*Christ,*" Frank shouted and tried to grab her wrists. They struggled against one another until he managed to clamp down on her forearms. "You think I wanted to pass out? Maybe there's someone wrong with me, maybe I'm not feeling well."

"Why?" Nancy hissed, wrenching her arm away from him. "Because of the booze? I know you're drinking again asshole. But having a seizure on the Liberty, and now going vegetative on the ramp to our Night Eagle? You're on something harder. What is it? Red lightning? Warpies? LCC?"

"LCC?" he shook his head rapidly. "You think I'm taking hallucinogens?"

His wounded look melted as soon as the words were out of his mouth, and his eyes focused on the retracted ramp, as if considering a new thought.

Nancy scoffed. "Get off your dead ass Frank, we have important things to do. Get in the damned ship."

Frank groaned as he struggled to his feet. His knees wobbled and he fell back to the ramp, almost tumbling backwards. She caught his collar and heaved him backwards to the inside of her ship.

"Need a hand?" said Hunter from behind. "Allow me."

Nancy slid aside as the massive Titan grabbed Frank under the armpits.

"Hey, easy Hunter, gentle," said Frank.

He yelped as the Titan lifted him from the stairs and grunted when he was dumped into a corner of the deck.

Caseus rolled his eyes and turned to his station.

Lindsey took a knee beside him to check his vitals.

Frank stared at the ground. His chest heaved as he massaged the back of his neck with a hand that was shaking uncontrollably. Nancy turned away in disgust.

She eyed the AI pedestal. Laura Maxwell stood guard over their captive, the Human-AI named Timothy they'd found on Sid's old Tiger ship. Timothy was bound and gagged at her feet, curled into a ball and sobbing gently.

"You handling him okay?" Nancy asked her AI.

"He's not going anywhere," said Maxwell. "His programming is weak. It's like guarding an infant."

"I'm going to take us to a docking lane," said Nancy. "Then we can interrogate him. We need some answers."

Laura nodded and planted a foot on Timothy's side. Her head turned to the ceiling as a voice spoke over their intercom.

"Central command to all fleet crew in Lazariz starspace. Return to Leopard escort for travel back to Kizurra. Tag count for ship ID's commencing at 1500."

Nancy checked her HUD. "We have forty minutes. Engage effluent launch tube 7-Z," she commanded as she plopped into her pilot's seat. "I'm taking us to *Prysilla* starspace until Allakai gives us marching orders."

"Aye," said Caseus from behind.

The glass hatch under the bold painted letters *07-Z* glowed green as the magnetic rail between their ship and the tubes energized. The interior doors opened to allow them entry, then closed behind. A hiss scraped against their hull as the tube depressurized, then the outside hatch opened and they flung into space, leaving the deserted Tiger hangar.

Nancy flipped through some controls, designating their travel coordinates and approach vectors to a field strip next to *Prysilla*. The Leopard vessel hung in the distance, etched against the bright yellow surface of Lavariz.

She pushed from her seat and walked to the AI pedestal.

Caseus turned from his recon station and stepped towards her, followed by Hunter, who hopped down from his gunnery station. Lindsey left Frank's side and padded to the pedestal. Frank groaned and managed to his feet, but stayed hunched in the background, still breathing heavily. The rest of Nancy's crew circled the two AI at the center of the bridge.

"Remove his gag," said Nancy.

Laura pointed her hand in the shape of a gun. Her index finger lit a fierce pink at the tip, and shot into the golden coil of rope tied around Timothy's mouth, which unraveled and fell to the ground.

"Why am I tied up?" Timothy wailed. "I told you, I'm not a Destineer, I'm a stowaway. Please, untie these bonds, they hurt."

"Quit your whining," said Laura, sending a swift kick into his ribs. Timothy cried out in surprised pain.

"Laura," said Nancy. She shook her head almost imperceptively. Laura read her body language and took a step away from their AI captive.

"I need you to calm down," said Nancy, placing her hands on the edge of the pedestal and leaning closer to Timothy's miniaturized avatar. "We're not going to hurt you, but you have to understand we can't trust you just yet. You were found on a Destineer ship."

Timothy gulped. "I'm not the only one," he gasped. "There were others, many others who refused to convert. They're still in their cells, Sid left them to rot."

"What do you mean others?" said Hunter. "Other stowaways?"

The AI shook his head furiously. "Not stowaways, captives, prisoners. For the past 150 years Sid recruited Destineers and grew his army. Those who refused to convert were jailed." Timothy struggled against his wrist bonds. "Please, untie me. I'm not a threat, I'm happy you boarded Liberty. You have to believe me."

"The Tiger ships," said Nancy, ignoring his request. "There's five of them. Why are they empty? Why did Sid leave them, and where did he go?"

"They left recently," Timothy stammered. "A week ago, maybe two."

"Why would Sid leave with no ship?" Caseus demanded.

Timothy frowned in a confused stare, then his eyes lit. "He had a ship, a big one."

"Big enough to hold the crew of five Tigers?" said Hunter.

"More than big enough," said Timothy. "Sid left on a Slayer Hive named *Sylva.*"

FORTY-NINE

Nancy Woods - Human

On Night Eagle *Eclipse* – Lavariz starspace

"So it's true," Nancy whispered. "The Slayers accepted the Destineers into their ranks."

"More than that," said Timothy. "The Slayers obey Destineer commands, on orders from the Pristine."

"The Pristine spoke with the Destineers?" Frank croaked from behind, shuffling towards the AI pedestal. He seemed to have gained strength since his episode, and managed to stay upright. "How did the Pristine contact the Destineers?"

Frank's eyes were wild, and bulged crazily from his face. He licked his lips and leaned closer to Timothy.

"Did the Pristine visit you?" he rasped, licking his lips again. "Did you see the Pristine?"

Timothy shied away from Frank, whose face was now inches from the AI's avatar. Nancy grabbed his shoulder and pulled him away.

"Go take a seat Frank," she said. "Have some water or something. Whatever drugs you're on, it's making you crazy. You're scaring Timothy."

Frank didn't break his stare, but conceded and backpedaled until he bumped into one of the recon stations. He fumbled behind him until he found the arms of the chair, and plopped down.

Nancy closed her eyes for several seconds, trying to control her disgust with Frank. She cleared her throat.

"Why did the Pristine tell the Slayers to assimilate with the Destineers?" she asked Timothy.

"I don't know," said the AI. "I was in hiding most of the time, and I only left my server occasionally. The Destineers have AI of their own, you know. Lots of them. If they would have found me..."

"The tracking beacons," said Caseus. "Nancy planted them on a Hive mothership during the Frontline Battle. A hundred fifty years later, we find the beacons on Tiger vessels. They were moved. Why?"

"I don't know anything about where the beacons came from, but I did see Sid's men planting the beacons on the Liberty before he left. Most of the Destineers had boarded the Sylvan Hive by then, the AI's too. Sid recorded his hologram just before he re-boarded *Sylva*."

Nancy furled her brow, recalling Sid's cryptic, radical message.

The Sterilord has built me a new fortress.

You don't know it yet, but you will bear me a tremendous gift.

Come with me, Nancy, and together we will transfer into the realm of gods.

"Re-boarded," said Hunter, squatting lower to the AI. "Sid was on the Sylvan Hive before?"

Timothy struggled to face Hunter, wiggling against the ground. Laura Maxwell grabbed him around the waist and helped him to his feet, which were still bound together. A chair materialized behind him, and Laura guided him into it.

"Of course," said Timothy, rolling his neck. He jerked his head in an attempt to free his eyes of his soaked hair. "Sid's been on the Hive for over a century. The Slayers built the Hive for him right after the Frontline

Battle. The Tigers followed the Hive. Sid used them to search for new Humans to convert to the Destineer faith." The AI raised his legs and thudded them against the pedestal. "Please, my legs are going numb. I'm not a Destineer, I won't run."

Nancy again ignored him. "On *Liberty* Sid said I would bear him a tremendous gift. What did he mean by that? When I find Sid, there will be no gifts. I'm going to kill him."

Timothy shrugged. "I don't know. I'm as confused as you are. I did catch your name from time to time over their comm frequencies, but I never heard anything about a gift."

"My name was mentioned?"

"Occasionally. Apparently you made quite an impression on the Destineers during the Frontline Battle. Is it true you escaped their jail cells onboard *Liberty*?"

Nancy didn't answer. She *had* escaped confinement long ago, after Sid and his goons kidnapped her at the middle school she taught at before the war. He'd used her as ransom against her father, a hostage token to get United Earth to split from UCOM. His plan hadn't worked. She'd escaped, and her father led UE into battle alongside UCOM forces.

She vowed that if it was the last thing she did, she would kill Sid Dakota. Her mission intensified with each year, as if a hidden force guided her, encouraged her to find him. It was as if the stars were guiding her.

You must find Sid Dakota.

The Voice was out of her head as soon as it entered.

And now she had found Sid's old Tiger.

"You claim to know where Sid is going," said Caseus.

"That's right," said Timothy. "They're going to meet the Sterilord. Sid is taking *Sylva* to the Primal Snow."

Lindsey offered a squeaky laugh, speaking for the first time. "Then there's no way to track Sid. Allakai's been searching for the Primal Snow since Frontline. It could be anywhere."

"Actually, that's not true," said Timothy. "I know his exact travel path. Before he left Lavariz, I mapped his route coordinates and saved them to my memory. He's heading past the Outer Rim, and if my estimates are correct, he should arrive at the Primal Snow within a few days time."

FIFTY

Nancy Woods - Human
On Night Eagle *Eclipse* – Lavariz starspace

"We need to leave for the Outer Rim," said Nancy. "We can't let Sid reach the Sterilord. Everyone to your stations, I want full travel routes uploaded to the nav-link, and diagnostics on stealth, engine, and weapons systems. We'll dock with *Kizurra* for supplies and be out within two hours."

"Nancy, if I may," said Hunter, stepping around the AI pedestal. "Sid is in a Hive. He's heading to the Primal Snow, and will be surrounded by *stars know* how many Slayer ships. It would be suicide to go after him alone. Perhaps we should consider asking Allakai for fleet support?"

"Even if we put mutiny aside," said Caseus, "is it wise to chase blindly after Sid? He left that message for you on *Liberty*. I'm worried he set a trap."

He eyed Timothy suspiciously. Laura Maxwell gripped the stowaway firmly on the shoulder. A pink band snapped onto her opposite wrist, unraveling a metal chain that clinked its way to Timothy's wrist, cuffing the two AI together.

"Central command to all fleet crew in Lazariz starspace. Tag count complete. Return to Kizurra, and set travel vectors to star sector 138-PS-U12-EA-HS07. Admiral Allakai has ordered an emergency assembly. All officers and captains to report to grand chambers at 1600 zulu time."

"What's on the meeting log?" said Caseus.

Nancy used security clearance keys in her Program to access the assembly ledger. A rectangular holo-script materialized before her, above the bridge deck. She paged through the lines of text.

"There's not a lot of information on the ledger," she said, studying the information. "The meeting takes priority one status. We intercepted some new chatter. There's a new military term available for download via our Programs. *Floodgate.*"

Her crew allowed their eyes to glaze over as they integrated their Programs with the ship, updating their biological nano-serums with newly available information.

"Floodgate?" said Caseus.

"No visuals," said Hunter. "Seems to be part of the Slayer Triturator. Looks like a major component."

"Do you think it's nearby?" said Lindsey.

"No way for us to know," said Nancy. "It definitely didn't come from any of our scan reports."

She studied sparse pieces of information on the holo-script before her.

Floodgate.

An ominous word. She thought back to the Frontline Battle, when the Slayers had sent nano-robots to infect UCOM fleets. The Blight had infected billions of souls, multiplying in numbers to sweep through the Milky Way like a tsunami.

Like a flood of death.

The Program update linked the Floodgate to the Triturator. Would the device initiate trituration and signal the start of the end for the Milky Way?

She needed to go after Sid. Every bone in her body urged her to find him, stop him before he reached the Primal Snow. Something terrible would happen if he were to reach the Pristine. She felt it in her gut.

But her crew was right. Trying to stop a Slayer Hive in a Night Eagle would most likely be suicide, even if she was able to sneak onboard without being caught in starspace. As much as it pained her to admit, she needed Allakai's help.

"Your orders?"

Nancy looked up. Her crew stared back at her. Laura Maxwell gripped Timothy firmly at the elbow at the AI pedestal. Caseus and Lindsey turned from their stations, their hands at the controls. Frank stared at the floor in the corner.

"Do we follow Timothy's coordinates to Dakota?" Hunter continued. "I mapped our travel route to the Outer Rim via nav-link."

"No," she said softly. "We attend Allakai's meeting. If it's priority one, we can't ignore it, not yet. You're right, we need to enlist his help to take down Sid. Set coordinates for *Kizurra*."

Nancy's back bumped against the back of her seat as magnetic rails guided *Eclipse* into an influent launch tube for Hangar 1 on the *Kizurra*. Space traffic formed steady lines behind them as light and medium-class UCOM ships entered the Tiger heavy-destroyer. The cavernous inside of Hangar 1 teemed with ship traffic as captains and officers from the fleet entered to attend the emergency assembly.

Their magnetic path guided them across open air high above the metal deck surface before ushering them into one of the upper platform levels for docking. Nancy eyed *Prysilla*, whose bulky Leopard-class frame eased into a large hangar space at deck level hundreds of feet below.

Heavy clacks sounded as the ship integrated with the dry port. The inside cabin lights lit brightly as *Kizurra* ran system checks and circulated fresh oxygen, water, and coolant into their stealth fighter.

"I'm heading to the assembly area," said Nancy, turning to the bridge. "I want *Eclipse* star-ready within the hour. Laura, you're with me as my AI tagalong. Is there a safe way to keep Timothy here alone?"

Timothy's eyes widened. "You don't need to worry about me, honest, I'll just sit here on the pedestal."

Laura spun her hands together, spooling a length of golden rope.

"No, *please*," said Timothy. "Don't tie me up more, I'll sit right here, I won't move."

His words became muffled as Laura gagged him with rope. The golden bonds wrapped around his legs and he fell awkwardly into the chair behind him. He struggled for a few seconds, then gave up and went limp, staring at the ground.

"He's not going anywhere," said Laura. "I'll see you at the assembly."

She vanished in a swirl of pink light.

Nancy looked at Caseus, Lindsey, and Hunter, who nodded at her.

"We'll be ready when you get back," said Caseus.

Nancy nodded and walked to the exit hatch, hissing as it opened to allow her through. She glanced at Frank as she passed him. He was curled up in the corner. His eyes were glazed over, and his chest heaved slowly. She rolled her eyes.

"Try to get him going. We're going behind enemy lines and I can't have him as a liability if he's back on drugs. He's no longer welcome on my ship."

She heard Hunter and Caseus gladly voice acknowledgement as she left *Eclipse*.

FIFTY-ONE

Frank Scott – Human
Aboard Tiger *Kizurra* – Charlie sector

Frank's eyes widened as he heard Nancy give the order to boot him from the Night Eagle.

No. Shit, I need to stay on.

He forced himself to think of an excuse, to think of a reason to stay. Nancy thought he was drunk or on drugs, but that wasn't the case. His body was weak, but getting stronger. He had shed a heavy weight after passing through the waterfall, and the sterilization took a toll on his body. The filth was gone from his soul, and now he was clean. It wasn't until his latest vision that he realized how dirty he was.

The booze, the drugs, the girls, even Nancy. All the muck in his life was gone. His mind didn't know how to work without so much grime clogging his thoughts, but he was starting to think clearer. He felt lighter, and strength had started to surge from his core to his fingertips.

He was becoming a god.

He needed to do one last thing. He needed to reach the Primal Snow. There were only two ships he knew of that were heading for the Primal Snow – the Sylvan Hive, and Nancy's ship, *Eclipse.*

"You heard Nancy," said Hunter. "You're out of here."

The Titan bent to grab his arm. Frank snapped it away and winced as his elbow shot into the corner of a section of conduit behind him.

"No," he gasped, shaking his arm. "I need to stay. I can help."

"Help?" Caseus scoffed. "How? You can't navigate or operate the stealth stations, and you're the worst gunnery marksman I've ever seen."

Frank scrunched his eyes shut and raced to think of an excuse. "I feel like shit," he groaned. "I can't leave yet, just let me sit here a while, I'm having a bad trip."

He started to hyperventilate.

Hunter spread his fingers and waved them over Frank's chest, neck, and head.

"Vitals are strong. Heart rate's high, but nothing to worry about. Come on big guy, with me."

The Titan grabbed Frank's arm.

"No, please," Frank cried. "I won't leave Nancy. She's just a little mad at me right now, but she'll cool off. I'm not going to let her leave alone."

He squeezed his eyes shut, and felt a pang of self-loathing. Why was he using his life love as a pawn? The squirmy feeling vanished. He had a new love. He loved the Voice. And the Voice loved him.

"She won't be alone," said Caseus. "She'll be with us."

Frank searched the room. "Lindsey," he pleaded with his old TV makeup girl. "Don't let them leave me on *Kizurra.* Come on, it's me, your pal Frank. Anchorman Scott, your bud."

Lindsey looked at him longingly and stepped forward, crouching at his side. Hunter relinquished his grip and Frank plopped back against the wall. Lindsey touched a palm to his cheek.

"Oh Frank," she said softly. "Why can't you just be normal? Why are you always so *fruxed up*?"

He recoiled at her rare use of language.

"Come on Lin," he said. "Let me stay. I'll be good I swear. Let me stay until Nancy gets back, let me at least talk to her."

"Sorry, we have orders."

The thin girl's lip trembled, and she looked away before standing to put her back to him.

Hunter grabbed him forcefully and lifted him to his feet. Frank grunted as the android warrior twisted his arm and shoved him to the exit, pushing him down the ramp. He stumbled to his knees on the rough grate outside before staggering to his feet. When he turned to try to board *Eclipse* again, he found Hunter training a rail pistol on his face.

"You're gone, Frank," said Hunter. "You fruxed with Nancy for too long. We have a mission, and we can't babysit you any longer. Go back to your quarters and have a nice drink."

Frank raised his hands and stepped backward. The hatch hissed, and the ramp retracted into the hull of the ship.

He cursed and spun around as a passing Guardian clipped his elbow.

"Watch where you're going," Frank spat.

The Guardian looked over his shoulder and shrugged before continuing towards the hangar exit.

Frank sat on his feet and grabbed fistfuls of his hair. The bustle of the crowded hangar pounded into his head. He scanned the dock, and cringed when he saw Hogs, Guardians, and Grizzlies exiting their ships. His elbow burned, and he clawed at his skin. The Guardian had touched him, and made him a little less clean.

He growled, which turned to a moan as he struggled to make sense of the emotions coursing through his mind. What was happening to him? Why was everything so disgusting to him now? Why did the UCOM races seem so dirty? So subhuman? Like *filth*?

He shot to his feet and paced in a tight circle. If Nancy and her crew weren't willing to carry him to the Primal Snow, he would need to find another ship to take him there, or maybe follow *Eclipse*.

Frank sprinted from the hangar to find a ship captain willing to offer help.

There must be a few Destineers aboard *Kizurra.*

FIFTY-TWO

Nancy Woods – Human
Aboard Tiger *Kizurra* – Charlie sector

Nancy tapped her foot impatiently as the last of the officers and captains took their seats in the enormous assembly area. She sat in a pod hovering against a sloping hill raised high above the main podium.

Laura Maxwell stood atop the glassy table surface of her pod. The AI's avatar scanned the room.

"What's the status on *Eclipse's* systems?" she asked the AI.

Laura turned to her. Her eyes glowed white as she accessed the Night Eagle's servers.

"Ninety percent complete," she said. "Our life support systems were fresh before we docked, so we're just waiting for the scrubbers to rehab the reactor in the engine room for a clean burn, and for the heat box to purge. Fuel's good, weapons are good, and our Ravens are restocked. Also…"

The AI bit her lip and paused.

"Frank?" said Nancy coldly.

Laura nodded. "Hunter kicked him off *Eclipse.* He's gone."

Nancy blinked away hot tears of anger and nodded stiffly.

The lights dimmed and the central podium lit brightly. Allakai Troko climbed to the top of the stage and walked to the center. He paused for several seconds until the assembly room quieted.

"I summoned you here for a priority one briefing," said Allakai, his voice amplified by speakers inside Nancy's pod. "I'm just going to get right to it. We intercepted a Raven sent from a nearby part of the galaxy, in Charlie sector. The Raven had end coordinates to Dominia and was sent by a Clone stealth commander named Eve, no last name."

Nancy studied the Stallion admiral on her pod table surface. His miniature hologram stood beside Laura. His face was grim.

"We only managed to decrypt part of the Raven's content before it disappeared into a portal," Allakai continued, "but what we deciphered requires immediate action on our part."

A new hologram appeared at Nancy's pod. She recognized it as the Triturator installation sent into her Program. *The Floodgate.*

"A major component of the Slayer Triturator system is being commissioned near the Outer Rim. We believe this is the primary device the Slayers will use to de-atomize the Milky Way. Based on the Raven intel, the Floodgate is set to ignite three days from now."

Nancy leaned toward Laura's hologram. Allakai continued to discuss their military strategy and logistics plan moving forward.

"Send a request to Allakai for a statement," said Nancy. Laura turned to her. Her eyes glowed briefly as she accessed *Kizurra's* registries.

"He's not accepting any statements or talking points. Questions will be directed after the assembly to your commanding officer. Now that you're no longer a squadron captain, your new direct superior is..." her eyes glowed again. "A Guardian named *Kotar Magek.*"

Nancy frowned and sighed deeply.

"Send a message to *Eclipse,*" she whispered. "We're leaving now and bypassing Allakai's orders. I can't wait any longer to track Sid."

"I don't know if that's necessary," said Laura. She displayed a holomap of the local quadrant of the galaxy. "This is the travel path outlined by Timothy."

A yellow line connected a series of portals, ending past the Outer Rim.

"And this is where the Floodgate is located."

A red diamond marker appeared above one of the portals near the end of the yellow path.

"Sid is going to need to pass through a portal in the same starspace as the Floodgate. Allakai and Sid will be headed for the same place."

Nancy considered the information. If she left with the rest of the UCOM fleet, they would have enough firepower to take on Sid's Hive when they reached it.

"Belay that order," she said to Laura. "We'll wait for Allakai's mission details."

Laura nodded and turned back to the front podium, where Allakai continued to address the assembly.

"The Raven mentioned an army of Slayers in a large fleet named *The Discarded.*" said Allakai. "Eve's name was listed in concert with Slayers who she gave friendly ID tags to. We're not sure what this means, but since she's Clone, we have to consider the possibility that this fleet of Slayer ships includes Destineers. Any UCOM ship fighting alongside Slayer craft will be attacked immediately."

Allakai tapped his podium and sent a new set of holograms into the pods. Five Tiger heavy destroyers appeared before Nancy.

"The Destineers who left the Tigers we found are a priority two mission," said Allakai. "If we cross paths with Sid Dakota's forces, we'll engage accordingly. We're going to board the five deserted Tigers. If they're operational, we'll absorb them into our fleet. While our engineers work on the engines, search parties will clear the ship and make sure no Destineers hung behind. We embark for the Floodgate in twelve hours. *Awaken stars.*"

FIFTY-THREE

Frank Scott – Human Destineer
Aboard *Kizurra* – Charlie sector

Frank ran through the hallways of *Kizurra.* He had no idea how to find Destineers. Practicing the Destineer faith was an act of treason in Allakai's fleet, and those found guilty were executed immediately through the tubes. He never thought there would be a time when he would actively seek the help of a traitor. Then again, he never thought he'd have dreams of an alien man across the galaxy.

Not dreams, he told himself. *Visions. The Voice spoke to you through your visions.*

He wondered if Nancy was right, and he was hallucinating the whole thing. Or maybe he was crazy, a raving lunatic whose mind had twisted into a pretzel after centuries of drug and alcohol abuse. He always heard that crazy people don't know they're crazy.

He decided he wasn't crazy. Rather, he was seeing things clearly for the first time in his life. He wasn't Frank Scott, the Human. He was Frank Scott, the god. The Pristine. Of this, he was certain.

He stepped around a group of Human spacers on his way to the transport bay, and was about to signal a pod, when visions ripped through his mind. He screamed and doubled over. Concerned hands patted his back and he swatted them away.

Whiteness covered his sight, and objects flung into view before traveling to a point in the distance. The Milky Way whizzed past, then the golden doors, and the waterfall. An image of a man froze into view. It was the man who had spoken to him in an earlier vision, not the Voice, a different man.

Sid Dakota repeated his words to Frank. *"Ral-Bazeera. Ral-Bazeera. Ral-Bazeera."*

"RAL-BAZEERA," Frank roared.

His visions vanished, and the pod terminal came into focus around him. He was on his hands and knees, and surrounded by a group of spacers.

"Are you okay?" said a Human man. "You were shaking, like you were having a seizure or something. I'll call you a pod to take you to the med bay."

"Ral-Bazeera?" said a Grizzly woman. "What does that mean? It doesn't register in my UT."

Frank clawed his way to his feet, pushing past the surrounding crowd. They stared after him in confusion. He wiped his face, fighting to control his rapid breathing. A pod hummed to a stop behind him. He backed into the sliding doors.

"Ral-Bazeera, why did you speak this word aloud?"

Frank jumped and wheeled toward the voice. He choked when he saw the holographic avatar staring back at him, arms folded across his chest.

"Timothy?" said Frank. "How did you get off *Eclipse?* Laura had you tied up."

"Ral-Bazeera," Timothy repeated. The pod lurched and sped into a tunnel. "You're Destineer."

Frank wondered where the pod was taking them. Timothy had entered the destination.

"I don't know how I know the word," Frank stammered, falling into the seat behind. Timothy's avatar took a step toward him, and Frank scooted farther back into his seat. "It just popped into my head. I dreamed of it."

"You had a vision," said Timothy.

Frank paused. "Are you a Destineer?"

Timothy's eyes hardened, but he didn't respond.

"How did you escape from *Eclipse?*" Frank repeated.

"I partitioned myself," said Timothy. "Laura Maxwell isn't as strong and clever as she thinks. She has my weaker duplicate, all his responses and actions are mostly pre-recorded."

"How did you find me? And where are you taking me?"

"I heard you speak the Slarebull words through the ship's intercom. I'm taking you where you need to go."

"Ral-Bazeera is Slayer-speak?" said Frank. The tunnel disappeared and the pod entered a hangar. Cheetahs and Panthers lined the space below. He leaned closer to Timothy. "Are you taking me to the Primal Snow?"

"Sid left me behind on *Liberty* with a mission. His visions were clear. Nancy will find him, and bestow upon him a great gift. You're the gift."

Frank cleared his throat. "*I'm* the gift? Why me?"

"The Sterilord has chosen you, as he has chosen Sid. You will become Pristine and transform into a god. As Pristine, you will succeed in a holy mission. Sid's destiny is to guide Humans to the Pristine. Your destiny is to save the Pristine."

Frank blinked several times. "*The Voice.* He's the Sterilord." He gulped. "How are we going to get to the *Primal Snow*?"

The pod dropped vertically before slowing to a stop before a Panther stealth ship.

"I'm going to get you back onboard *Eclipse.* Get in the Panther. We need to track Nancy."

FIFTY-FOUR

Nancy Woods – Human
Aboard Tiger *Liberty* – Lavariz starspace

Nancy squeezed the grip of her MGK. The engineers hadn't fixed the reactors yet, and the halls of *Liberty* were lit only with emergency backup power from the Tiger's battery reserves. Hunter advanced beside her, rifle raised, spotlights on his Akimor lighting the darkened halls before them.

"We're at the brig," said Caseus.

She aimed her rifle at the thick doors, using the light on the barrel to study the access panel. She tapped the display and the doors whooshed open.

Hot air hit her face and she gagged at the rotten stench. Caseus began to hack. Lindsey leaned a hand against the door frame and vomited onto the deck. The wet splattering sounds made Nancy's stomach lurch.

"What's that smell?" said Caseus.

"Decomposing flesh," said Hunter. "My scanners show a positive signature on the scent molecules."

The Titan walked further into the stockade. He lowered his rifle. "You guys might not want to see this. Let's leave, there's no Destineers here."

Nancy ignored him and walked further into the large chamber. Jail cells lined the walls and formed long rows across the cavernous area. The cells were stacked several levels high, with grated walkways connecting the outsides of the barred doors. Nancy and her crew were at the bottom level, and she aimed her light towards the nearest cell.

Bodies were piled inside. She covered her nose and inched closer. The corpses were mutilated. Some of the dead still had flesh on their bones. Others did not, and were bare skeletons, as if they were licked clean. She spotted various UCOM races – Stallions, Grizzlies, Guardians, and Wolves. No Human corpses were in sight.

"The Destineers did this?" said Caseus, dropping his rifle against its strap. "This is sick."

Lindsey approached the group and wailed when she looked into the cell, quickly averting her eyes.

A soft moan carried to them from the distance.

"Did you hear that?" said Caseus.

Nancy tilted her head to listen. The moan came again, scraping against the metal bars.

"Over here," said Hunter, running down one of the rows.

The rest of the crew hurried behind. Hunter stopped at one of the cells, and peered into the bars.

"Turn your heads away from my hands," said Hunter.

Nancy turned around. Sharp blue light flickered against the walls as Hunter cut the bars of the cell with his Akimor. The severed bars clanged onto the ground when he finished, echoing through the cavernous facility.

She spun around to find Hunter ducking into a rectangular hole in the bars. She followed him in. Caseus and Lindsey stayed outside.

"The Slayers," a weak voice whispered.

A naked Guardian lay among the pile of dead. His stomach was torn to ribbons, and glistened in the low light. The man was covered in blue blood, which looked almost black. Nancy wondered how much of the blood was the Guardian's, and how much was from the rest of the corpses surrounding the injured soldier.

Hunter knelt beside the man. He ran his hands over the Guardian's face and torso. "Your vitals are weak. One of your hearts stopped beating. I'm going to fill your stomach with bio-foam and restart your failed heart."

The Guardian coughed, spewing gore from his mouth. "That won't work…heart's been out for too long…fruxin' Program."

Nancy bit her lip. The nano-serum in the Guardian's Program had kept him artificially alive. He should have died days ago. With so much time passed, his cells were beyond repair, and his mind was not transferrable.

"Slayers were here?" she said, kneeling beside Hunter.

The Guardian choked again. "Yes. Slayers everywhere. They clawed us, and ate us."

His eyes rolled in their sockets. A weak trickle of red light ran down his bioluminescent hair.

"Were there Destineers here as well?" said Hunter.

The Guardian nodded. "Yes. They stood with the Slayers."

"As one?" said Nancy. "As allies?"

The Guardian shook his head. "Not allies. The Slayers obeyed the Destineers. The Destineers…" he wheezed. "Humans commanded the beasts like dogs."

Nancy stared at the dying man. The Slayers *obeyed* the Destineers? Like dogs?

A comm message broke her trance.

"All units in Lavariz *starspace, report to your ships immediately."*

Detailed scripts were sent to her from her Program. She turned to display them on a relatively clean section of the floor.

"The engineers couldn't get the reactors to run," she said. "The Destineers sabotaged them too badly. Allakai's ditching the Tigers. We need to move."

They stood. The Guardian gazed at them, struggling to keep his eyes in focus.

"I'll carry him with us," said Hunter. "We'll take him to *Kizurra*, get him to medical."

"No," the Guardian rasped. "I won't live. *Please.*"

He extended a trembling finger to Hunter's rifle. The Titan looked to Nancy. She nodded and walked to the cell opening. She flinched at the lone gunshot. The moans ceased.

They made their way through the halls toward the small marina they'd docked at, near *Liberty's* brig. The brig that held thousands of mutilated corpses. Nancy tried to squeeze the grim memories from her head.

As they approached the marina, Nancy received another Program update. This time, the update was not over global comms, but sent directly to her and her crew. She paused to absorb the information, displaying the message in holo-script.

Effective immediately on orders from Fleet Admiral Allakai Troko – Nancy Woods has been demoted from ship captain of the Eclipse, to spacer of the Eclipse crew, on grounds of failure to obey orders. Command of Eclipse is being transferred to Brevex Pratt, Wolf-born.

Nancy pushed the holo-script away with a dazed swipe of her hand. She looked to her crew. They shared her stunned look of shock.

"Allakai's taking away *Eclipse?*" said Caseus. "Just because you boarded *Liberty?*"

"He can't do that," cried Lindsey. "Allakai ended up sending us into *Liberty* anyway. And you found Sid's beacon message."

Nancy took a deep breath and licked her lips. Her eyes were wide, and refused to blink.

"I'm not giving up control of *Eclipse*," she murmured. "If you don't want to follow me, I understand."

"You mean…" said Caseus, trailing off.

"Stealing a UCOM ship while under false command is treason," said Hunter. "Allakai won't just demote you after this. He'll send you out the tubes. And us too."

"Launching from the tubes wouldn't affect you any," said Caseus, narrowing his eyes at Hunter. He flashed a weak smile and shook his head. "I'm in. *Awaken stars.*"

"I'm in as well," said Hunter. "And Caseus, they wouldn't send me through the tubes, they'd grind me into dust."

Lindsey quivered, flashing signs of old anxiety problems she had during the Frontline Battles. "You guys make things so hard for me. I'm in too."

Nancy drew her rifle forward. "No killing. If the new guy, *Brevex Pratt* is there, take him down non-lethally. I have to do this. I'm the only one who knows how much a threat Sid Dakota is. We'll let Allakai take down the Floodgate."

Her crew nodded silently. She locked eyes briefly with them all, then turned to run towards *Eclipse.*

The Night Eagle was where she left it in the marina, docked near the effluent launch tube. Five Panthers were docked beside hers, as well as three Cheetah fast-attack fighters at the opposite end of the small hangar, near the influent launch tubes.

Spacers and ship captains were gathered around their ships, preparing to board and join *Kizurra* before they left for the Floodgate. She slowed to a brisk walk, trying not to attract attention. A Stallion captain scowled at her for a few seconds before returning to his crew.

She reached *Eclipse* and sped around the aft section of the hull to the access hatch. She froze. The ramp was already let down. She pulled her MGK tight against her shoulder, and saw Hunter do the same from the corner of her eye.

A Wolf walked from the entrance to the ramp, and stopped when he saw Nancy and her crew. He reached a hand to a magnetic holster on his thigh.

"Don't do it," said Nancy, jerking the tip of her rifle away from the gun at his hip. "You're Captain Pratt, I assume?"

The Wolf growled. "You're making a big mistake, Woods. Allakai will execute you for this."

"Gun and ammo on the ground," said Hunter, striding to Brevex Pratt in a half crouch. The Wolf raised his hands in the air. Hunter snatched the pistol from its holster and ejected three slides of ammo from a feeder tube on the other side of the Wolf's waist. The Titan clamped them to his own magnetic plates against his torso.

"I'm sorry sir," said Nancy. "I have to do this. We don't have any other choice."

Hunter muscled the wiry Wolf down the ramp and held both arms tightly. Nancy stepped past the pair. Brevex growled as she passed, his hair bristling.

"This is why no one trusts Humans," said the Wolf. "You don't listen to others. You betray those who trust you, and have the arrogance to claim that your decisions are better than the rest of the UCOM races. You're no better than the Destineers."

Nancy turned. "Right now, I'm the only person in the galaxy trying to *stop* the Destineers."

She said the words calmly. So calmly the Wolf's scowl ran from his face. Hunter relinquished his grip, and Brevex's furry arms fell limply against his sides.

"We won't have much time," said Hunter, ushering Nancy up the ramp and into the Night Eagle. "This is going to be called in, if it hasn't already."

She cast one final look at the Wolf who was technically her commanding officer. He bared his teeth and spun away, hurrying across the marina.

She turned, barking orders to her crew.

"Set coordinates for intersect with Sid's Hive, map the travel vectors to nav-link. I want ninety-five percent power on our thrust-"

Her words lodged in her throat and she coughed in surprise. Frank Scott stared back at her from across the bridge.

"*Frank?*" she hissed. "What the hell are you doing here?"

He shrugged, shifting his eyes around the room. His mouth opened, then closed.

"I'll take care of him," said Hunter, striding towards Frank.

Frank raised his arms over his face. Lindsey yelped and rushed to his side.

"Priority one message from *Kizurra,*" cried Laura.

Nancy whirled toward the AI pedestal. Laura Maxwell stood with Timothy, who was still bound in his chair. She'd forgotten about the AI captive during her trip to the brig. Laura played the message on the ship's intercom.

"Kizurra to Eclipse. Nancy Woods has been labeled as a traitor against UCOM. Power your engines down immediately. If you take to space, you will be fired upon and destroyed."

"Forget about him," Nancy shouted, scampering past Frank and sliding into her captain's chair. "Caseus, get us the hell out of this marina."

"Aye," said Caseus.

The effluent tube lit green as Caseus guided *Eclipse* along the magnetic transit path. They paused briefly between the inner and outer hatch, then rocketed into space.

Laura's avatar popped onto the dash in the cockpit. "Nav-link is fully vectored," she said. "We'll be leaving Lavariz starspace in less than one minute."

Nancy scanned their surroundings, praising their good luck. The portal on their vector route was extremely close to the Tiger ship they'd left, so they didn't have to hang out in Lavariz starspace too long. She eyed the thousands of UCOM ships surrounding the abandoned Tigers nervously.

"We're getting hailed by more than twenty UCOM ships," said Laura. "Including *Kizurra*. We have multiple final warnings."

Nancy clenched her teeth. Their target portal loomed larger before them, a green sphere against the blackness of space. The local sun burned brightly to the left, and sharp flashes of light glinted off the hulls of Allakai's fleet to their right.

"*Incoming,*" Caseus shouted.

Several 3D models appeared on the dash, showing Leopard destroyers firing missile salvos at *Eclipse.* A squadron of Cheetah fighters streaked towards them, launching from *Kizurra.*

"Steady guys," said Nancy. "Keep engines at ninety-five percent until my mark. On my go, engage heat box and active camo, and shut engines down to five percent."

The missiles streaked closer. The portal loomed larger. Alarms blared into the bridge as the missiles reached critical distance to the Night Eagle. Nancy squeezed her eyes shut.

The alarms silenced. She opened her eyes. They'd passed through the portal, and the missiles were unable to follow.

"*Now,*" she cried, pulling hard starboard. "Active camo."

The *Eclipse* shuddered as the engines choked to a low hum.

"Active camo engaged," said Caseus.

"We've got company," called Lindsey.

Six Cheetah fighters zipped through the portal behind them. They did a wide pass around the green sphere, but Nancy knew they wouldn't be spotted. Their Night Eagle had advanced stealth equipment that only another stealth craft, or perhaps a Lynx intelligence craft, could hope to uncover.

They were invisible.

The Cheetahs seemed to understand this as well. After a few minutes of searching, they gave up and returned through the portal to Lavariz starspace.

"Keep our trajectory," said Nancy as the ship smoothed its flight path. "And don't take us out of stealth mode until we passed through our next portal. Allakai may have sent a Panther team after us."

Her crew voiced their acknowledgement and set to manning their control stations. Nancy sighed and ran a hand through her hair. A chill ran up her spine, and she realized she was drenched in sweat. The cold air inside the Night Eagle made it seem as though her skin suit was made of ice. She shivered uncomfortably, waiting for the overloaded nano-particles in her suit to whisk the sweat away and make her dry again.

Frank sat in the corner, not in a chair, but on the ground. His head was pressed against the metal wall, and he appeared to be mumbling to himself. She squinted. *Yes.* His lips were definitely moving. But the rest of her crew wasn't looking at Frank. They were tapping the holodecks of their stations, scanning the surrounding starspace with passive spacnar for hidden ships. Timothy sat silently on the AI pedestal. Laura stood on the cockpit dash.

At first she thought Frank was on drugs, or drunk, or both. Now, she wasn't so sure. His eyes weren't glazed over and listless, but sharp and focused. His movements weren't sluggish and labored, but rather quick, precise, and deliberate.

Something was different about Frank. She'd known him long enough to recognize it, but she couldn't put her finger on *what.*

She pretended to fiddle with the controls of her dash, keeping a close eye across the room.

FIFTY-FIVE

Frank Scott – Human Destineer
Aboard Night Eagle *Eclipse* – deep space

"Stop talking to yourself," said Timothy. *"I'm inside your head, I can read your thoughts. My software is embedded inside your Program, just think what you want to say, and I'll hear it."*

"Like this?" said Frank aloud.

"Damn it," hissed Timothy. *"No, you're still talking out loud, and now Nancy is giving you suspicious looks. Just think the words."*

"How are you inside my head and also on the AI pedestal?"

"There you go, see? Not so hard. Like I said, I partitioned myself. The Timothy you see is just a weak clone of me. The real me is inside you."

"This feels weird. My brain itches. And not in a good way."

"Be patient. We were able to use the Panther to take us to Nancy's ship, weren't we? You have to trust me. Soon we will reach Father Dakota."

"And meet the Voice?" asked Frank.

"Yes," said Timothy. *"We will meet the Sterilord, and become gods."*

FIFTY-SIX

Francis Woods – Human

Aboard defense tower *Warhammer* – Dominia starspace

Francis Woods strode down the halls of *Warhammer*. He was used to receiving suspicious looks and scowls, but now he was seeing them in abundance. In the past, he'd written this sort of body language off as an unavoidable part of politics. Now, after uncovering Draxton Tyke's potential plans for revolt, the nasty looks seemed to carry more weight.

A passing group of Hogs glared at him as they waddled by. One leaned to whisper into his cohort's ear. The cohort smiled sickly. A pair of Grizzlies lumbered towards them. One smiled. The other bared his teeth.

Woods shook his head and pressed on. They needed to hurry.

Clone councilwoman Zena Olleeve walked to his right. To his left, LePuff Gerant, the Green councilwoman, shuffled nervously beside.

LePuff had been the first councilmember he and Zena had approached. The Green weren't very strong militarily, or even politically, but LePuff had been nearby, and they were desperate for allies.

Green were small as far as UCOM races went, even smaller than Humans and Clones. They averaged three feet tall and around eighty pounds. They had short, stubby legs that allowed them to kneel to the ground easily. Their jaws were wide and filled with thick molars. They had nimble fingers and opposable thumbs, but the bottom fingers in their hands were fused together into flat, bony plates used to dig into soil.

LePuff had almost fainted when they explained their stories about Draxton, and about the rift forming in UCOM. Woods had caught her before she collapsed, and patted her on the back until she stopped trembling.

Now, aside from the Clones, the timid vegetarian race was the only solid ally Humans had. With some luck, the larger, more militarily adept Grizzlies would also join their side.

"We're here," he said, turning to Zena and LePuff. They'd entered an empty corridor with a solidary door at the end. "Zoltan?"

"Yes sir," said his AI assistant. Zoltan's avatar appeared above the deck in a flash of light. "Rorema Tal-Ho is expecting us."

Woods nodded and stepped towards the entrance to the Grizzly councilwoman's quarters. "We're all clear on what we're doing?" he said, eyeing the group surrounding him. "I talk, Zena and Zoltan back me up if needed. LePuff, you're here for support."

Zena and Zoltan nodded. LePuff squeezed her eyes shut and clacked the bony shovels on her hands together nervously.

"We'll be fine," said Zena reassuringly, patting LePuff on the shoulder. "This is a diplomatic mission. No violence."

Woods wondered briefly why such a skittish creature chose a battle zone for residence, then remembered the peaceful alien had no choice. If the Slayers won, her home planet would be no safer than the inside of a Hive mothership.

He pressed the console next to Rorema's doorway. The Grizzly had been expecting the buzz.

"Come in," she said instantly.

The doors slid open to expose a set of private quarters similar to Zena's and LePuff's. Rorema had added a few touches to the décor. Wooden tribal carvings hung from her walls, roughly cut from Grizzly timber. A spiked scratch post connected the floor to the ceiling at the far side of the main room. She'd added chemicals to the fire to make it burn a vivid blue.

"Mr. Eminence," the Grizzly said, stiffening to salute him. She nodded to the others. "Councilwomen. Please, sit." She motioned to a group of couches before the fire.

Woods, Zena, and LePuff squeezed into a single small couch. Rorema eased into a larger couch beside them.

"I keep the small one around just for this reason," she said, nodding to their couch. "The big ones won't let some of my UCOM political guests reach their feet to the floor, and I'm not a fan of the universal shift technology that conforms to any race. I can never get comfortable in it."

She chuckled, then stopped abruptly when none of Woods' group joined in. The Grizzly leaned forward and put her elbows on her knees. "Let's hear it. What do you all want? I've never seen a Clone, Human, and Green pal'ing together, not in my two hundred years."

"I know what Draxton said to you after the council meeting," said Woods.

The Grizzly's eye's widened, then frowned. She licked her lips, clearly not expecting the statement.

"Then you know I refused him," said the Grizzly, gulping loudly. Her eyes locked onto the pistol on Zena's hip, then shifted to the gun on Woods' hip. "Is this a summons? I've done nothing wrong."

"I didn't say you did," said Woods. "You're not in trouble. And we're not going to shoot you, so stop eyeing my weapon. I've come to ask for your help."

The Grizzly sighed in relief. "Of course, Mr. Eminence. Anything."

"I need you to pledge support of the Grizzlies to the Humans," said Woods. "And the Clones and Green as well. You heard it from Draxton, so I won't go into details. You know as well as I. If Draxton has his way, a rift is coming. I need you to pick the right side. It's my goal to keep UCOM together and whole, but I need supporters to stop a potential revolution."

Silence.

The Grizzly slouched into her seat and scratched her neck furiously. She uttered a high growl which ended in a snort, shaking her cheeks. "I can't," she said. "I understand your position Mr. Eminence, but I can't side with you for the same reasons I can't side with Draxton. I don't know who is right, you or him. You're a good man, I've seen the videos of the Frontline Battle where you led the charge against the Slayers. But the Grizzlies stand with UCOM, and you and Draxton have both asked me to split from UCOM. I'm sorry."

Woods frowned. "You're making a horrible mistake."

"Then send me out the tubes if you must," growled Rorema. "I am not going to choose sides. I have two enemies, the Slayers and the Destineers. As long as we fight the same enemy, consider me your ally. But I will not split from UCOM. I said the same to Draxton."

"Rorema, I'm not negotiating," said Woods, puffing his chest and standing to reach eye level with the sitting Grizzly. "I'm giving you a command. This has tremendous implications for the war effort."

"Command?" roared the councilwoman. She slammed an open palm into the wood center table, crunching through the surface with her claws. She shot to his feet, raking the table to send wood chips spinning through the air. "Accepting your *command* would be a clear act of treason against UCOM! I *will not* betray our civilizations. So again, Mr. Eminence. If you don't plan on either putting a bullet between my eyes, or launching me from the tubes, I'm going to have to ask you to leave."

Rorema's massive chest heaved rapidly, her fists clenched beside her towering frame. Woods nodded slowly and rose to leave. Zena and LePuff followed.

He turned as the door whooshed open. "I value your integrity, Ms. Tal-Ho. I trust you'll make the right decision when the time comes."

He walked into the hallway. Zena sped in front of him.

"That was a *disaster,*" she hissed. "One of our only supposed allies said she'd rather freeze in the vacuum of space than help us."

"The Grizzlies were a wild card," he said gruffly, moving past Zena and down the hallway. "At least they aren't on Draxton's side either. I think Rorema will do what's right if things get hairy. She's a good woman."

Zena jogged after him. LePuff nearly had to run to catch up with her stubby legs.

"Who are we going to see next?" she said. "The Guardians? The Intellects? Please don't tell me we're going to see the *Boards.*"

"The Intellects," said Woods. "But not their councilman. I have an old Intellect friend from before the Frontline. Stew Kwelm, he's my chief engineer and research scientist."

"Does he speak on behalf of all Intellects?" said Zena. "We need to enlist allies, not learn about what new piece of technology the cavers are making."

"*Intellects,*" said Woods.

"Huh?" said Zena.

"Intellects. Cavers is an insulting word to them." He sighed. "Never mind that. I go to Stew for guidance, he's the smartest person I know. And also, I have a few other things to worry about besides Draxton's revolt."

"Something more important than a civil war?" said Zena.

"Potentially. The Slayers are building a super-weapon. A device that could annihilate UCOM and end the war."

LePuff clutched weakly at his elbow and swayed back and forth.

"A super-weapon?" cried Zena. "Why don't I know of this?"

"It's classified. I'm weary of Destineer spies the same as you."

"*Stars.*" Zena ran a hand over her mouth. "Is the weapon built? Can we defend against it?"

"We really don't know anything about it, other than it exists," said Woods. "That's why we have to see Stew. Hopefully he'll have some good news for us. I don't know if I can handle any more bad news today."

FIFTY-SEVEN

Francis Woods – Human
Aboard defense tower *Warhammer* – Dominia starspace

They entered Stew Kwelm's lab to find the Intellect standing before a large wall screen in his private work space. Various models spun slowly at different sections of the holo-display, with two-dimensional words and figures shifting below.

The Intellect didn't seem to sense their presence, and continued to stare at the screen, deep in thought. Woods recognized a few pieces of technology pictured.

An animation of Slayer warp shield defense technology showed a Hornet heavy-destroyer diverting a slug away from its hull and towards the UCOM ship that fired it. The UCOM ship responded with warp shielding of its own, catching the slug with a pink sphere and returning it in the direction of the Hornet. The slug found its target the second time around, destroying a square section of the ship's lattice shield.

"I take it our warp shields are fully developed?" said Woods.

Stew jumped at his voice and spun to face him.

"Yes," said the scientist, clicking his beak. He nodded to Zena, LePuff, and Zoltan. "We reverse engineered Slayer technology and upgraded its capabilities. The Slayers can divert small slugs using twenty percent of the ship's available energy for two iterations. Our modifications allow our Tigers to divert large-mass slugs using five percent available energy for three iterations. This allows us to deploy several warp shields at once, and track the projectiles more effectively as they're parried back to our ships."

"Kind of like pinball," said Woods.

The Intellect stopped clicking his beak and closed his eyes, retrieving the definition from his Program. "Ah yes, the old Human arcade game. You can indeed relate this technology to pinball, the balls representing the slugs, the bumpers representing the warp shields. It's really a matter of which ship can deflect the slug more times. None of our intercepted chatter leads me to believe the Slayers have improved on their original warp shield technology."

"Then we'll have naval superiority?" said Zena, stepping closer to the holo-screen.

"Our Tiger destroyers will most likely be more effective in battle than Slayer Hornets," said Stew. "But the Slayers have far more ships. Naval battles are often determined by sheer fleet size. A slugfest if you will."

"What of the Slayer super-weapon?" said Woods.

The Intellect narrowed his large eyes toward Zena and LePuff.

"They're safe," said Woods. "We can trust them."

Stew nodded. "We received a Raven from Casi Vomisa and Silas Blackthorne confirming their arrival on Blit-Kru. We haven't received a Raven since. I have no idea what's happening on the planet, our communications are dark."

An uncomfortable silence hung in the room.

"What do we know about Slayer logistics?" said Woods, breaking the quiet. "Have we mapped their new portal installations? And what do we know of the Triturator?"

"The Slayers have completely bridged the gap we made at the Frontline during Severation. They linked the empty starspace together with new portals, and can now transport ships and equipment freely at faster than light speeds."

The holo-screen transformed to show an interstellar map of the Frontline. Eight red lines connected newly constructed portals.

“They’re all connected to the Inner Ring,” murmured Zena.

“Correct,” said Stew. “We’ve suspected that from the beginning. If the Slayers take the Inner Ring, they’ll assume control of our entire portal network. They’ll have instant access to almost all points in the Milky Way. We received new intel from beyond the Frontline just a few hours ago. Stealth squadron commander Eve sent us a Raven from near the Outer Rim.”

“We made contact with Eve?” said Woods. His heart fluttered. “I haven’t heard from her since I sent her across the Frontline a hundred fifty years ago. Why wasn’t I notified immediately?”

Stew frowned. “I sent a priority one message over the Network as soon as I received the Raven. The message was addressed to you. Did you not receive it?”

Woods cursed to himself and shook his head. “No, I think my comm link has been hacked.”

“Hacked?” said Stew, puzzled. “We haven’t detected any Slayer or Destineer attacks on our Network. We have intercepted Destineer communications *with* Slayers. They’re beginning to join forces through Slayer-controlled portals near the Inner Ring.”

“They’re joining forces?” said Woods, taking a deep breath. “When did this happen?”

“Within the last twelve hours,” said Stew. “Again, I sent you these updates through your Program.”

“It’s not the Slayers or Destineers,” said Woods, trying to suppress the anger seeping into his core at the news of Destineer traitors physically integrating with the enemy. “I’ll explain in a minute. What did Eve’s Raven say?”

Stew tilted his head, curious about the malicious hacking of Woods' comm link. "Her Raven is very interesting. She seems to have found a few friends near the Outer Rim."

"UCOM survivors?" said Zena.

Stew shook his head. "Not UCOM. Slayers."

Woods choked and began to cough. "Eve joined with the Destineers?"

"No," said Stew. "That's the interesting part. There's an army of Slayer rebels named the Slarebull Separatist Faction. They call themselves *Discarded.* They're genetic misfits, and fight alongside the Slayer's enemies. They also have detailed knowledge of the mechanisms behind the Triturator."

He waved his hand, and a mechanical structure filled the screen. Planet Earth sat beside the structure for size contrast. The structure was megalithic, wider than Earth, and three times as long.

"This is the Floodgate," explained Stew. "It's the primary component in the Triturator installations, being commissioned near the Outer Rim. The Floodgate connects the rest of the installations to the Slayer's power storage. This storage device is the Primal Snow, which is also where the Slayer social elite reside, the *Pristine.* The Primal Snow injects energy into the Floodgate to spark the rest of the installations. If the Slayers are allowed to place their installations throughout the galaxy, once the Triturator is activated, installations utilize the super massive black hole at the center of the Milky Way to keep the process going. The installations deatomize the intergalactic matter and send it back to the Primal Snow in energy beams using the existing portal network. The Floodgate channels and focuses the beam into an intensity that can be received effectively by the Primal Snow for storage. The Triturator will still work at reduced capacity without individual installations, but it cannot function without the Floodgate."

"Eve sent you this information?" said Woods.

"Yes," said Stew.

"So attacking the installations won't stop them from de-atomizing the Milky Way. We need to attack the Floodgate."

"Correct. But it seems the *Discarded* are two steps ahead of us. They already have plans to destroy the Floodgate."

Woods pondered the information. He felt squirrely about trusting Slayers, even rebel Slayers, with such a critical task. "Any details on their plan? If I send ships we can reach the Floodgate in a few weeks time."

"Impossible," said Stew. "They would need to sneak past the entire Slayer armada to get there. We may be able to sneak some Night Eagles past, but our heavy ships would be spotted. Night Eagles will be useless against the Floodgate. And no, Eve included only limited details of the attack. It's possible the Discarded didn't share strategy with her, but I believe they simply didn't want Slayers to intercept the Raven and learn their attack plans."

Woods shook his head and ran a hand through his hair. "*Stars.* If they don't succeed..."

"Also to note," said Stew. "Our intercepted chatter leads us to believe the Slayers are not installing the complete Triturator assembly. They're only installing a fraction of the array. They have plans to de-atomize the inner sections of the Milky Way, but the outside parts of the Galaxy, almost seventy-five percent, will be unaffected for the time being. This includes Earth's stellar neighborhood."

"So they're going to de-atomize the very center of the galaxy," said Zena. "And then what, leave? Why would they leave the majority of the Milky Way behind? They consumed every atom in Andromeda."

"At this point," said Stew, "it's still a mystery. It takes more than a century to complete Trituration. We believe they're looking for something elsewhere in the galaxy, something important to them."

"A planet?" said Woods.

"It's more likely a portal," said Stew. "We found a recurring word in our intercepted chatter. It translates to *Singularity.* We think it may be a hidden portal, possibly to a new universe. A single point connecting our universe to another."

"A new universe?" cried Zena. "Other than ours? The multiverse theory is still just that, a *theory.*"

"Our knowledge of physics supports it," said Stew. "We've just never been able to *observe* a separate universe. I believe very much that other universes exist outside our own."

The group thought quietly to themselves of the possibilities.

"It comes down to the Inner Ring," said Woods. "If we stop the Slayers there, they'll be unable install their Triturator array throughout our network portals. To hell with the portal to another universe, if it even exists. I like the Milky Way just fine."

He swallowed down the acid collecting in his throat. The magnitude of the Slayer invasion weighed on his shoulders like lead. During the Frontline Battle, they'd had the Stitchline as a last ditch escape option. An option that ended up saving billions of lives and extending the war 150 years. Now, all that stood between the Slayers and victory was a Slayer group of rebels they knew nothing about, and an undersized UCOM armada. An armada that was on the verge of erupting into civil war. Not to mention the Slayer super-weapon.

Stew seemed to read his mind. "You said your comm link was hacked. Why? I just checked the Network. Your Program is still encrypted within standard UCOM parameters."

"I think Draxton Tyke restricted my access to the Network."

"That's against UCOM code of law," said Stew. "And you're the Eminence. Several chains of command would need to approve such a restriction of access, including six council members. It's programmed into the code."

"Draxton is preparing to stage a coup d'état. He's been enlisting support from different races to separate from Humans and Clones. If I don't stop him, a rift is coming. So far I have the support of the Clones and the Green. Will the Intellects join the side of the Humans?"

Stew's beak chittered rapidly. "A rift? Our naval forces are barely strong enough to defend against a Slayer attack as it is. If we were to separate, our chances at success would drop drastically, and become nearly zero." He frowned. "I don't believe the Intellects will side with the Humans. We are a logical race of people. I predict our councilman will choose neutrality, and focus on developing means to stop the Slayers with weapons technology. It wouldn't matter which side uses it, as long as it's used against the Slayers."

"Just like the Grizzly councilwoman," said LePuff. Woods turned to find the smallish Green trembling behind him. He'd forgotten she was even there.

"I need you in my corner," said Woods, turning back to Stew. "I'm going to try my best to stop this rift, but if it happens, I'll need to act. I may need your help."

"Of course," said Stew. "You're my Eminence."

"I'm also your friend," said Woods. "You remember the Templar?"

Stew exhaled. "The Templar? Of course I remember. Stars help us if we need to resort to it."

"Does anyone know of it besides us?"

"No, Intellects aren't ones to gossip."

Woods bit his lip. LePuff suddenly raised her arms before her.

"Priority One message," she said. "Are you guys getting this?"

Woods checked his Program and shook his head. "Nothing."

"I didn't get anything either," said Zena.

"It's from Draxton Tyke," said LePuff. "He called for an emergency Council meeting at the Round Table in an hour."

Woods shared a surprised look with Zena. UCOM representatives from all races would be at the meeting. All races except Humans and Clones.

Woods and Zena hadn't been invited.

FIFTY-EIGHT

Francis Woods – Human

Aboard defense tower *Warhammer* – Dominia starspace

"It's happening," whispered Zena. She brought both hands shakily over her mouth.

"What do you think Draxton will do at the Round Table?" said LePuff, darting her eyes between the group. "Should I even go?"

"You have to," said Woods. "If Draxton called you to the Round Table, he probably doesn't know we approached you. We need you to tell us what happens."

"They'll figure me out," cried LePuff. "I'm too scared, they'll suspect something. Stars, I'm shaking."

The Green's bony outside fingers clattered together as she wrung her hands. Woods put a reassuring hand on her shoulder.

"You'll be fine," he said. He glanced at Zoltan. "Would it help if Zoltan went with you?"

Zoltan tilted his head. "I'm not allowed in Round Table meetings. That's for council members only. Draxton won't let me in."

"Not as an avatar," said Woods. "Enter LePuff's Program. Go inside her head."

"Inside my head?" cried LePuff. "I've never had an AI in my Program before. You want him to control my body?"

"No," said Woods. "Just keep you company. Help you keep calm. Zoltan?" He nodded to his AI servant.

Zoltan sighed. "I'll do it if LePuff is okay with it."

The Green councilwoman breathed in short gasps, starting to hyperventilate. "I guess he can." She turned to Zoltan. "Can you take control? I don't want to go, I'll have a panic attack."

"Hold still," said the AI.

His avatar walked to the Green, reaching a hand to the side of her face. His fingers glowed in soft circles of blue, and his body began to dissolve, becoming grainy. The particles fell apart into a cloud of glowing dust. LePuff's eyes, ears, and mouth seemed to suck the particles in, forming a steady stream as the AI entered the nano-serum coursing through her body.

LePuff straightened. She arched her back tightly for several seconds, before doubling over, jolting her shoulders sharply from side to side.

"Stop," she moaned, her lips moving slowly. Her head snapped against her neck. "Stop…resisting. Me. I. Won't. Hurt."

Her spasms ended, and LePuff stood straight. Her eyes rolled crazily in her head before resting to a stop. Her eyelids drooped, then focused.

"I have control," said Zoltan through LePuff's mouth. "I'm not forcing her, she's given me command of her body. I'm leaving for the Round Table."

"Wait," said Stew. The Intellect hurried to a lab table and pulled a slender box from a drawer along the side. He opened it and withdrew a sleek metal band. "Wear this," he said, striding to LePuff.

"What is it?" said Zena, eyeing the strip of metal.

"It will record her cognitive visual and auditory senses," said Stew, wrapping the band around LePuff's forehead. The band tightened automatically around the contours of her head. Once snug, the silvery metal turned clear, disappearing against the Green's skin.

"Can we observe the feed live?" said Woods.

Stew nodded, running a thumb over LePuff's forehead to check the fit. "Yes. Live video and audio will be uploaded to our Programs."

"How will the signal make it out of the Round Table room?" said Zoltan, speaking again through LePuff's mouth. "The room is a communication dead zone to prevent eavesdropping. There's no server connections inside."

"I designed that technology myself," said Stew. "I left a few back doors."

Woods accessed his Program, finding the feed in Stew's head band and displaying it above the deck. A holographic display of himself appeared. He turned to LePuff, and his avatar turned with him.

"You always have a trick up your sleeve," he murmured, observing the technology for the first time. "I'm glad you're in my corner." His live avatar vanished as he walked to LePuff. He leaned forward, resting his hands on his knees. "You guys will be okay. We'll be watching the video, and if Draxton does anything threatening to you, I'll know and come help."

LePuff nodded. She stared somberly at him before turning to exit the lab. Woods wasn't sure if it was the AI or the Green controlling her movement. The door closed behind her, and the pair was gone, on their way to the emergency Round Table meeting.

Wood closed his eyes. He hoped they would be okay. His stomach squirmed, and the cold, dank air of the Intellect lab ran a chill up his spine.

"We should leave *Warhammer,*" said Zena. "This tower isn't safe for us. We don't have any more time, Draxton is going to make a move down there. I can feel it in my gut."

"And abandon my duties?" growled Woods. "I'm the Eminence. I swore an oath to protect UCOM. I'm going to grab some men and go down there. Draxton needs to be stopped now before it's too late."

"I'm coming with," said Stew.

"You're staying right here," said Woods. "You're a scientist, not a soldier. This is going to get dangerous. I need you in the lab with all your resources if things go south."

Stew clicked his beak, but didn't argue. He understood the logic in the decision, and Intellects never let emotions guide their actions.

"Who can you trust?" said Zena. "Who can either of us trust? The Destineers could be anywhere, and we just learned how many friends we have in UCOM."

"There's a Tiger commander stationed outside *Warhammer*. He'll help us, I'd stake my life on it."

He thought of the billions of Humans who had joined the side of the Destineers. Grief clawed at his heart as he pictured the men and women of Earth who would gladly bow before the very beasts who threatened to destroy the galaxy. The Slayers who threatened to shred the very fabric of life strung throughout the stars.

There was one man he trusted beyond a doubt. A man he'd known from Earth, from before the Guardians visited almost 300 years ago. A man who had rescued his kidnapped daughter from Dakota's ship, and ridden into battle with him at the Frontline more than a century ago, charging at the Slayers as the rest of UCOM fled.

"We're going to see an old friend of mine," he said. "We're going to see Commander Cage."

FIFTY-NINE

Francis Woods – Human
Aboard Tiger *Mariella* – Dominia starspace

Commander Cage stared out the bay window of the war room aboard his Tiger ship, *Mariella*.

Warhammer, the super-tower Woods and Zena had left from, loomed before them, blocking light from the local sun. Even without direct light from the star, the starspace around them was bright enough to require heavy tint from the meta-glass window.

Fourteen sunbeams streaked across the vacuum, drawing energy from the nearest stars to feed the massive UCOM armada stationed at the Inner Ring. Tiger heavy destroyers studded the area by the tens of thousands. Each destroyer was accompanied by a full complement of light and medium-class Leopards, Jaguars, Night Eagles, Ocelots, Lynx, and Cheetahs. The armada sat before the portal superhighway that comprised the Inner Ring. It looked like an enormous green rectangle stretching into the distance, but Woods knew the rectangle was the result of thousands of portals positioned neatly in gridded fashion.

The commander hadn't said much during Woods' and Zena's explanation of the potential revolt. He'd cursed a few times, lit a cigar, and walked to the panoramic window at the edge of the room. He hadn't moved since then, but his cigar had grown an inch of ash at the tip. It fell to the metal deck as Cage drew the cigar to his lips.

"Cage," said Woods, stepping to the commander. He put a hand on the man's shoulder. Cage glanced at him, then returned to the window. "We need to act now. We're out of time."

"All of this for a single portal," said Cage, nodding out the window.

Woods followed his gaze. A tiny red dot hung in the distant starspace. Far across the vacuum sat the Inner Ring superhighway. Between the two sat the UCOM armada, as well as numerous defense towers, PDR's, and Lion motherships.

"The enemy is behind that portal," said Woods. "More Slayers than we can count."

"I knew something was going on," said Cage, squashing his cigar into an ashtray. "I haven't received a Network update for fourteen hours, and all my non-Human crew left without notice. I tried hailing UNI and CAIRO, but my access to the network is restricted. I managed to reach some Tiger commanders nearby using Human encryption packets, and more of the same from them."

"Do you have enough men to storm *Warhammer*?"

Cage nodded. "Aye. I had far less deserters then other Human Tiger commanders I reached out to. My closest men are loyal. I'll assemble a team. We'll take Draxton down before he does anything we can't turn back from."

"The Round Table meeting started," Zena cried from across the war room.

Woods and Cage hurried to the holograms hovering above the deck. A miniaturized version of the circular table floated before them. Eleven UCOM council members were seated around it. Most were leaned toward each other in hushed discussion, and jolted upright as the entrance door whooshed open.

Draxton Tyke strode into the chambers. Four guardsmen followed him into the room – two Stallions, a Wolf, and a Grizzly. Woods caught a glimpse of many more guards standing in the hallway before the doors closed. AI materialized at the corners of the rooms, wearing standard CAIRO military suits.

"Guards aren't allowed at the Round Table," Zena hissed. "That's against our bylaws."

Woods shushed her and waved a hand. He'd seen guards in the Round Table chambers once before, when the Stallion Xakex Roke had usurped command of UCOM before the Frontline Battle.

He turned his attention to the holograms.

"Why are you late?" the Guardian councilman demanded. "And with guards? Where are Woods and Zena? You have no right to call an emergency meeting without the Eminence."

Draxton scowled at the Guardian before turning to the rest of the Council.

"The Destineer infiltration of UCOM has grown beyond our control," he said. "Their spies have entered every facet of our navy and intelligence operations. They weaken our military during a time when we desperately need to be strong. The Slayers will show no mercy to us. Conservative estimates put Destineer support at nearly eight billion members. Nearly all of these traitors have been either Human or Clone." He leaned forward against the table. "I hereby propose a vote to remove Humans and Clones from UCOM, and cut these cancerous civilizations from our ranks."

Some of the council members protested and shot their hands into the air. Most were quiet, and simply nodded in agreement.

The Guardian shot from his seat, streaks of red pulsing down his arms and hair. "You can't propose a vote without the Eminence present," he cried. "Let alone vote on it. This is against UCOM code of law."

"I've studied the law," growled Draxton, his fur standing on end. "In times of war, it is allowed for races threatening the safety of the whole to be removed from council, and for their abolishment to be voted on by the remaining members. The races in question would be immediately and unconditionally exiled from UCOM government and military control until their guilt is proven in a court of law. A majority vote is needed. There is nothing illegal about this."

"You need to have majority compliance to even bring the vote to the table," the Guardian roared. "I have not agreed to any such proposal. We need the Humans and Clones in our military. The Humans alone represent the largest military force in UCOM. They're the back bone of our navy."

"I need order in the Council chambers," said Draxton through his teeth.

"Order?" shouted the Guardian. "What gives you the right to command the Council? I take orders from the Eminence, and the Eminence alone."

Draxton nodded to the Guardian. Two Stallion guardsmen moved to him, grabbing him by the arms and wrenching them behind his back, clasping a set of magna-cuffs on his wrists. The Guardian roared and bucked against them, but was overpowered and thrust into his chair.

"The councilman is correct," said Draxton. "We need majority compliance to bring this to a vote. Who votes *aye* to proceed with a motion to abolish Humans and Clones from UCOM?"

LePuff shook in her seat. She shared a terrified look with the Intellect and the Board. The Guardian seethed in his seat, his skin a dark shade of maroon.

The Stallion, Hog, Bird, Squid, Giant, and Greyhound raised their hand. The Grizzly looked around the table, then crossed her arms. Draxton smiled and raised his own hand.

"The majority has it," the Wolf said. "Seven out of twelve. I motion to vote on Human and Clone abolition. All in favor raise their hand."

The same races raised their hands. LePuff began to weep.

"You can't do this," roared the Guardian. "This will accomplish nothing."

He grunted as one of the Stallion guards jabbed him in the back of the head with his rifle stock.

"I propose a motion to make me, Draxton Tyke, the new Eminence of UCOM, and executive commander of military forces."

The same seven races voted aye.

Draxton's smile widened. "As the new Eminence of UCOM, I propose to enact martial law on the governed population of UCOM, and enable our military to forcibly remove Human and Clone troops from our ranks if they do not leave willingly."

His proposal carried.

"This is not a wise decision," said the Intellect calmly. "This will cripple UCOM. We cannot defend against Slayers without help from the Humans."

Draxton flashed his fangs. He puffed his chest and spoke loudly to the council. "If you do not stand by your Eminence in a state of martial law, then you are siding with the enemy. Those who will fight the Humans and Clones beside me, *rise.*"

The six races who had carried the votes, and placed Draxton into power, stood from the table and filtered to the door. The Grizzly started to stand, then shook her head and returned to her seat. Her lips moved silently, as if in prayer.

Draxton called to the guards outside. The doors slid open and ten additional armed soldiers entered. The six races standing shuffled into the far corner. The Giant shook his head as he looked upon the remaining Green, Intellect, Board, Grizzly, and Guardian council members, who had remained seated. He squeezed his eyes shut, forcing tears down his cheeks.

"The council representatives for the Green, Boards, Grizzlies, Guardians, and Intellects are hereby found guilty of treason."

The Wolf nodded, and the guards advanced.

The Grizzly bellowed and swiped a ham-sized palm at the advancing Giant guardsman, slicing deep gouges into his cheeks and face shield. The Guardian rocketed from his seat and thrust his body at one of the Stallions, slamming him into the wall before head-butting his sternum.

The two powerful races were subdued as guards piled on top of them. The Intellect, Green, and Board went willingly, and allowed their wrists and legs to be shackled. Draxton's guards lined the five council members against the wall.

Draxton paced before them, walking in front of the line of rifle barrels aimed at the detained representatives. "In accordance with martial law, *I sentence you to death.*"

LePuff squealed as Draxton stepped behind the row of guards, and raised her hands before her face. Slug fire slipped from their weapons and screams echoed in the chamber as the perceived traitors were executed.

A glowing mist streamed from LePuff's body as she fell, and the particles assembled into a Human body. Zoltan rose to his feet and clenched his arms as he tried to flee the chambers. There were no servers for him to escape to, and CAIRO soldiers appeared at the side of the room. They swarmed him, jabbing him with spears of light. Zoltan shrieked in agony before exploding into embers, which cooled to a deadened ash.

The view of the Round Table was now sideways and askew. The band around LePuff's head showed a visual angle from her lifeless position on the floor. Draxton stepped before her, covering the video feed. Then only his voice could be heard.

"I hereby promote the following members of UCOM to represent the deceased Grizzly, Guardian, Intellect, Board, and Green council members. Any not in favor speak nay."

Woods shook with anger as the Wolf rattled off five names. Five individuals he had surely already visited and gathered support from. The five new Council representatives would be corrupt, and loyal to Draxton.

He felt a hand on his arm, and turned to find Zena clutching his elbow. Her skin was several shades lighter than its normal olive tone. Tears coated her cheeks. He opened his arm and allowed her to hug him tightly around his waist.

The Wolf finished listing the new council members. There would be only twelve members now. Humans and Clones would no longer have a seat at the Round Table. According to law, they were no longer a part of the UCOM navy.

The audio and video from LePuff's headband had started to fade as warmth left her body. The Wolf's words became quieter, more distant. He tensed as Draxton spoke his final words to the Council. The words chilled him to the bone.

"Ral-Bazeera."

SIXTY

Francis Woods – Human
Aboard Tiger *Mariella* – Dominia starspace

Zena was trembling in his arms. Woods grabbed her shoulders gently and pushed her away from him. Her eyes darted around wildly in her skull, her lips quivered.

He glanced at Cage. The commander stared at the space where LePuff's hologram had displayed Draxton's violent seizure of power.

"That fruxin' *Wolf*," said Cage. "That murdering son of a bitch. That fruxing *animal*." He continued to glare at the deck, biting his lip in anger.

"Ral-Bazeera," Zena whispered. "He spoke the code word. Humans and Clones…"

She blinked, shaking her head.

"We need to rally the Human and Clone commanders," said Woods. "*Zoltan.*"

He called for his AI assistant before remembering the gruesome scene at the Round Table, when CAIRO soldiers had killed him with spears of light. A flash of anger surged through his core. "We need to get to the command bridge. Humans and Clones are sitting ducks, we need to rally our ships."

"This way," said Cage, running across the war room to a set of glass doors, gliding open as they noticed his presence. A pod sat waiting for them. He beckoned to Woods and Zena. "Inside."

The pod began to accelerate down the transit tube as soon as the doors were closed. After a few silent minutes, the pod slowed at a terminal station. The doors slid open to reveal the curved stadium seating of the command bridge.

Tiger command bridges normally held dozens of officers, each responsible for different intelligence, weapons, navigation, and life support operations throughout the massive craft. The bridge stations were empty by half.

"Sir," said a young, blonde haired officer, who rushed up the steps towards them. He froze and saluted Woods. "Mr. Eminence. We have a situation."

"Where's the rest of my crew?" said Cage, pushing passed the officer and running down the steps two at a time.

"They deserted," called the officer, following them down to the pit. "They took a pod and left barely a minute ago. And they're not the only ones. We have thousands of ships launching from our hangars."

Cage stopped at the bottom of the pit to observe the main holoscreen covering the wall. A hologram of *Mariella* showed Leopards, Cheetahs, and Jaguars streaming from their ship in droves.

"What about the rest of the UCOM armada?" said Woods.

The images on the screen shrunk to include thousands more ships in local proximity.

"More of the same," said the officer. "There's a fleet wide exodus from Human controlled ships. They're heading through portals leading away from the Inner Ring, into the heart of the Milky Way."

"I want a full comm network to be established between Human controlled ships," said Woods. "Encryption packets for Humans and Clones only. Where's an AI?"

"Right here sir," a slender female AI with fiery red hair materialized on the deck beside them.

"What is your name soldier?"

"Blaze, sir."

"Get a Human comm network patched and encrypted against all other UCOM ships except Clone controlled ones."

"You want me to block access to UCOM?" said Blade uneasily.

"Yes," said Woods. "Do it *now.*"

"Aye sir." Blaze saluted and vanished from the deck.

"Woods," said Cage. "This is my ship. I know you're the Eminence and have superior command, I just need to make myself useful. What do you want me to do?"

Woods shook his head. "The command of *Mariella* is yours. I'm going to rally the Human armada, follow my lead."

Cage nodded, then turned to bark orders to his crew, shouting commands to bring the Tiger's systems online.

Woods walked to the edge of the pit, Zena following behind.

"What are we going to do?" she said. "You heard Draxton. He's probably giving orders to UCOM ships as we speak, ordering them to attack the Clones and Humans."

"UCOM is lost to us, for now," he said, jabbing at a control console. "I need to look out for my brothers and sisters. When they're safe, we can come up with a plan for Draxton."

Shouts entered the bridge. Woods turned to find additional officers rushing from the pod terminal to empty stations, filling the seats left by deserters. Cage continued to direct his staff, getting the destroyer battle ready.

"Blaze."

"Aye sir."

The AI materialized on the console in miniature form.

"Is the Human comm line patched?"

"Aye, the registry is complete, I have encrypted contact with every Human and Clone ship in Inner Ring starspace."

"Set up a live broadcast, fleet wide."

The AI nodded and disappeared from view.

He returned to the console. A red point of light appeared inches from his face. The red light blinked three times, then turned green.

"Humans and Clones," he spoke aloud, looking into the light. His voice boomed through the command bridge as his live broadcast to the Human fleet was received by the *Mariella*. "This is your emin- your president."

"And your Clone leader, Zena Olleeve," said Zena, stepping before the recorder. "We have formed an alliance with the Humans. All Clone commanders are to obey orders from President Woods."

Woods turned to the Clone, surprised by her decision to name him military leader of the Clones. Her tears had vanished, and been replaced with fire. He turned back to the recorder.

"We are in a state of emergency for Humanity, and for Clones. Draxton Tyke has staged a coup d'etat, and issued orders to abolish us from UCOM, using deadly force if necessary. Effective immediately, we are no longer under control of UCOM military leadership. All Human and Clone ships are to relocate at once to coordinates 'X-G-5-S' dot '9-4-5-7-2-2' until further instruction."

The green point of light turned red as he finished his broadcast. Commander Cage relayed his orders, diverting power to thrusters and instructing his navigation team to set destination coordinates.

"Blaze," he called again.

"Aye sir," said the lithe AI, spinning into view.

"You're my new digital assistant," he said. "Can you find a replacement AI for Commander Cage?"

Her eyes glowed as she accessed the ship's servers.

"Done," she said.

A dark skinned male appeared on the AI pedestal above the command bridge. He set to work immediately, relaying orders to the rest of *Mariella's* digital crew.

"Sir," said Blaze. "I have a galaxy-wide Raven transmission coming from *Warhammer*."

Woods stepped to the center of the pit to gain a better view of the main holo-screen. A 3D feed of the massive defense super-tower showed millions of messenger drones streaming from the ends of the structure, forming a thick swarm against the brightly lit Inner Ring starspace.

"What's on the Raven?" said Woods. "Is it encrypted?"

Blaze shook her head. "No, just one word. *Ral-Bazeera*."

Woods watched in horror as the Ravens streaked across the vacuum, shooting towards the portal superhighway. Within a day's time, the entire Milky Way would hear the message.

Ral-Bazeera.

"Where are we at, Cage?" he called across the deck.

Cage turned to him. "Approaching our target portal. We'll leave Inner Ring starspace in less than five minutes.

Woods looked to the ceiling, where a sprawling glass dome provided an expansive view of the outside. Toward the bow hung a nearby portal, growing in size as they closed their distance to it. Tigers and assorted smaller craft surrounded their ship, flashing Human and Clone ID beacons, traveling to the same portal as *Mariella*.

"Priority one message," an officer shouted from his station. "Not encrypted. It's from Draxton Tyke."

Draxton's face filled the main holo-screen. "All UCOM military personnel," the Wolf said. "I am Draxton Tyke, the new Eminence of UCOM naval forces. Humans and Clones have joined the ranks of the Slarebull, and in turn committed an act of war against our republic. The Council decrees that all Human and Clones are hereby exiled from UCOM. Their commanders are to relinquish control of UCOM military craft, and turn themselves in to UCOM authorities at the planet Gefangria for temporary detainment. Violators are to be shot, and their ships eliminated with lethal force. *This decree is effective immediately.*"

SIXTY-ONE

Human and Clone Execution
Throughout UCOM controlled sections of the galaxy

Inner Ring.

A sizeable fleet of ships collected near a local portal near the Inner Ring. The ships flashed ID beacons, some of them Human, and some Clone. No other races were represented in the fleet, which had splintered from the rest of the sprawling UCOM armada.

Many of the Human and Clone ships filtered through the portal and away from the Inner Ring. Some of them reversed direction and headed towards *Gefangnia*, a lonely planet next to the super-tower *Warhammer.* Some Human and Clone ships were already there, and had UCOM ships traveling into their hangars to board and retrieve prisoners.

One of the Human ships near the portal energized its shields and swung hard to the side, flashing brilliant strobes from its bow. The Tiger's name was painted on the side of its hull in white lettering.

MARIELLA - EARTH

The ship accelerated towards the Human and Clone ships fleeing towards *Gefangnia*. Many of them slowed and turned back to join the rest of the splintered fleet near the portal. Light flashed across the vacuum as

UCOM PDR's and defense towers energized their RACAN's, pointing them toward the fleeing craft. UCOM Tigers powered their jets in the direction of the Humans and Clones.

Mariella sat in their path, unmoving. Thousands of UCOM ships formed a wall before the Tiger ship, whose lattice shields burned a sharp blue. Within minutes, the ships froze in a standoff: a wall of UCOM ships on one side, a smaller fleet of Human and Clone ships funneling through the portal on the other.

Mariella hung in the middle.

One of the UCOM Tigers charged their Super RACAN, its hull disappearing behind the extreme energy of the cannon. Some of the UCOM ships behind were turned off by the aggression towards the *Mariella,* a ship that had been a friendly asset to the fleet less than an hour ago. Hundreds of Guardian-marked ships left the ranks of UCOM to stand behind *Mariella.*

More UCOM ships energized their RACAN's. The Guardian ships turned to join the rest of the Human and Clone fleet, many of whom had finished traveling through the portal. The *Mariella* followed, bringing up the rear. As the last Guardian ships left the Inner Ring, one of the UCOM Tigers fired upon *Mariella.*

A pink sphere materialized instantly next to the side of the Human ship. The slug entered the sphere, and exited through a separate sphere that materialized against the hull of the aggressor ship.

The slug tore into the side of the UCOM Tiger's hull, causing a square patch of its lattice shields to go dark. Several more Tigers responded by firing missile and slug salvos at *Mariella.*

Most of the fire was diverted by the Human ship's warp shields, pink spheres slinging the slugs back from where they came. The missiles were neutralized by spindly lasers shooting from the fleeing ship's hull. One slug connected with the aft section of *Mariella* as it slipped through the portal and away from the Inner Ring, but the damage was minimal, and didn't destroy any of the ship's lattice shield.

The UCOM armada stayed behind as the last Human defector passed through the portal. Some Human ships had gone to orbit around Gefangnia, but most had left, many after being inspired by one of the men aboard *Mariella*.

Francis Woods had led his people away from harm, and taken many Clones and Guardians with him. The UCOM armada was now much smaller. It was much weaker. Much less capable of defending against the impending Slayer attack.

And Humans were cast far away, rallying at coordinates XG5S.945722, a small drop of blue in the vast galaxy named Earth, preparing to fight superior enemies on multiple fronts of battle.

Total Inner Ring Human and Clone fatalities: 0

A team of Human ground troops huddled inside their bunker on the snowy moon of *Khalvoro*. Even though their battle station was heated, the gale force winds blowing through the wide openings of the gunnery stations chilled them to the bone.

The habitable moon was near the Inner Ring, and one of the only Stallion home worlds to have survived the Frontline Battle. Heavy defense towers surrounded their station. Space elevators reached past the orange atmosphere.

Khalvoro orbited a ringed giant, and the purple planet consumed half the sky. The other half was filled with the outlines of UCOM ships large enough to see from the surface of the icy moon, as well as three PDR's and a space super-tower.

The Human squad discussed the odd turn of events that had unfolded within the past several hours. First, a priority one Raven delivered a message from the Inner Ring.

Ral-Bazeera.

The word didn't mean anything to the squad leader or his troops, but shortly after the Raven had delivered the message, two of his soldiers had vanished, leaving to take a piss and never returning. They'd received reports of thousands of other Humans abandoning their posts as well, disappearing up the space elevators.

The group turned to the sounds of footsteps echoing up the entrance stairwell leading to their platform. They stood as four Stallions entered the metacrete room.

The Stallions were armed, and had grim looks on their faces. The Human officer saluted them and asked their purpose. One of the Stallions responded by shouldering his rifle and shooting the officer in the chest. The rest of the Human squad shouted in horror and scrambled for their rifles, but the Stallions emptied their clips into the unsuspecting soldiers until movement ceased.

Across *Khalvoro*, and aboard ships in orbit, the rest of the Humans were visited by teams of Stallions, Hogs, Wolves, and Squid. Some were able to flee or go into hiding, but most were summarily executed.

Total Khalvoro Human and Clone fatalities: 456,944

A Human Night-Eagle captain patrolled an asteroid belt outside the Squid planet *Flatil.* She received a command from her admiral to report back to orbit, and dock into position per the listed coordinates.

She guided her crew through a few portals until they reached the watery planet of *Flatil.* She guided her stealth ship into position, joining thousands of other Night-Eagle ships, all docked neatly in gridded fashion.

Her crew asked her questions about why it was only Humans and Clones that were asked to dock into the grid. They asked her what the priority one message from the Inner Ring had meant.

Ral-Bazeera.

She didn't have answers for either question.

They sat for over an hour as Night-Eagles continued to trickle in from the surrounding areas. Once the registry was completed, fifty Tiger heavies approached, forming a curved semi-sphere around the cube of docked ships.

Her crew screamed in terror as the ship's controls were commandeered digitally by CAIRO soldiers. They were powerless to move or engage shielding as the Tigers charged their RACAN's, lighting the vacuum an intense blue.

The Tiger ships fired their cannon arrays simultaneously. The docked Human and Clone ships were reduced to dust.

On *Flatil's* surface, and inside the larger UCOM ships and PDR's, teams of UCOM soldiers summarily executed all Clone and Human crew.

Total Flatil Human and Clone fatalities: 1,843,233.

A Human fleet admiral commanded naval security of the Human colony planet *Destiny*. They had undergone desertions on a massive scale after a priority one Raven had entered *Destiny* starspace.

Ral-Bazeera.

The admiral couldn't make heads or tails of the message, but he lost more than ten million men minutes after it was received. There weren't many races other than Humans and Clones at *Destiny*. The planet wasn't on the front lines of battle, and UCOM races didn't volunteer to defend Human planets the same way Humans did theirs.

He'd tried to communicate with his superiors, sending Ravens to the Inner Ring, but his fleet's comm access with UCOM was restricted. The admiral was worried the Slayer's had attacked and corrupted their communications.

A Tiger ship entered *Destiny* starspace unannounced. He at first tried communicating with it. After the ship ignored their hails and continued on a direct line towards the colony planet, he dispatched Cheetahs, Leopards, and Lynx to do a flyby and monitor for any suspicious activity.

When the admiral received back positive signature ID's of an antimatter bomb, he ordered his Titans to commandeer the rogue Tiger at once and diffuse the AMMO-AB.

The android warriors didn't have a chance to board.

As soon as the Tiger reached *Destiny's* atmosphere, it detonated the AMMO-AB. The admiral's retinas were burned by extreme light, and seconds later, he was vaporized by the pure energy unleashed from the massive warhead. Destiny's atmosphere was stripped during the blast, and its surface burned, turning the planet into a charred hunk of rock.

There were no survivors.

Total Destiny Human and Clone fatalities: 14,723,003,129.

Far and wide across the Milky Way, UCOM military forces acted on direct orders from their superiors. Their actions were triggered by the code word, *Ral-Bazeera*, but even they didn't know how some of the Humans and Clones were able to escape before execution, fleeing seconds after the broadcast.

UCOM had outcast two of their member races. By preemptively attacking the exiled Human and Clone ships and soldiers, UCOM seemingly eliminated major retaliatory threats, and at the same time killed Destineer spies hidden within Human and Clone ranks.

The UCOM attacks were swift and merciless. Most had been executed flawlessly. The majority of Human and Clone populations survived, but they were isolated in remote areas of the Milky Way, and at Earth.

With the Humans and Clones gone, UCOM could rest assured that their naval armada, although smaller and weaker than before, was free of Destineers.

Total Milky Way Human and Clone fatalities: 31,552,446,575.

SIXTY-TWO

Sharker Gray – Human Destineer
Aboard defense tower *Barbican* – Earth starspace

Sharker Gray leaned forward inside his pod. Terminal bays whooshed past as he sped into the heart of *Barbican*, a defense tower outside Earth's orbit. He rested his elbows on his knees and clasped his hands together, closing his eyes.

He was headed to a critical meeting with Earth's military generals. His faith had taken him far in his religious quest. He'd enlisted support from thousands of influential Humans. He'd won TV Earth's media support from Madame Beauchene, and eliminated his foes. Images of Sheryl Gwyndeveer's corpse flashed through his mind, dead in her sleeping quarters above the UCOM Cultural Gala.

He cleared his thoughts and recited the Destineer Decrees in a whisper.

Humans are the highest beings in the Universe. All other beings are secondary to Humans.

Humans and Slarebull are one and the same, the gods of all.

To end Human life is to sin.

It is Humankind's unalienable right to harvest the bounties of the Universe. The Universe is a bounty existing for Humans to reap.

A Human siding with a subhuman is not a Human, but a subhuman.

Humans must make a holy effort to convert subhumans to Humans.

All inconvertible subhumans that threaten the health, happiness, or wellbeing of a Human must be destroyed.

He opened his eyes. So much blood was on his hands. Through the past century and a half, he'd transformed Earth into a Destineer stronghold. Many had gone willingly. He'd killed any who resisted.

Sharker thought again of the last line in the Destineer Decrees.

All inconvertible subhumans that threaten the health, happiness, or wellbeing of a Human must be destroyed.

The wheels of change were in motion. Earth didn't know it yet, but Humans had been isolated from UCOM, and now they would face a final test. A final challenge to prove their devotion to the Slarebull, the gods of all.

Many would die. Many would enter the Pristine's kingdom as gods.

One of the pod's walls displayed a news program. TVE's streaky logo hung in the bottom corner. He used his Program to adjust the volume. A male reporter spoke from behind a desk of light.

"...and the question we continue to ask is this. Does UCOM give Humans safety, or do they put us further at risk? As reports come flooding in of friendly Destineer alliances with Slarebull forces in the Milky Way, Human leadership is met with public outrage. It becomes clearer by the day that we are being dragged into a war to benefit not Humanity, but the rest of the Milky Way races. How many more of our men and women must needlessly die at the hands of the Slarebull? When will we learn to unite and embrace our visitors as allies?"

The pod slowed as Sharker reached his destination. He smiled and muted the broadcast. Madame Beauchene was making good on her promise. The TVE-controlled media was firmly on the side of the Destineers, and their saviors, the Slarebull.

He exited the pod and stretched his back, adjusting his formal suit before continuing down the short hall towards the strategic command headquarters aboard *Barbican*. A series of tiny beeps sounded from the walls as security screeners analyzed his DNA and Program information, verifying it in the tower registries.

A team of Human soldiers stood at the entrance to the command headquarters, rifles slung casually before them. One of the soldiers, a blonde female with dark eyes, raised a hand as he approached.

"Name and purpose of visit," she said.

"Sharker Gray," he said. "I'm here to see Harold Dunbar."

The soldier summoned a holo-script and confirmed his visit with the PDR's servers. She nodded and two of the soldiers stepped forward to pat him down.

Sharker raised his arms and spread his legs, allowing the two men to frisk him.

He grinned. A short time ago, he needed to use an alias wherever he went. Now, his Destineer affiliations were accepted inside the highest military ranks.

After sliding their hands up and down his legs and arms and patting around his torso, the men stepped back, satisfied.

"They're waiting for you in the command room Mr. Gray," said the blonde female.

The doors slid open to expose a group of generals huddled around a holo-pit. Sharker nodded to the soldiers as he passed. One of them couldn't contain a scowl. The others smiled knowingly.

"You have a lot of balls coming in here," said one of the generals.

He stepped away from the holo-pit and rested his hands on his hips. Sharker eyed the man's right hand resting on the slide of a rail pistol. He read the etched name tag on the man's breast. Five stars lined each of the man's shoulders, signifying his rank of chief general.

H. Dunbar

"I come peacefully," said Sharker. "We both want the same thing, safety for Earth and her colonies."

"And the Destineer attacks against UCOM are supposed to make us feel safe?" said Dunbar. "I have orders from the Inner Ring to detain Destineers indefinitely."

"But have you?" said Sharker, raising an eyebrow. "Earth has embraced our message. More than half the planet openly practices our faith, yet Earth's jails are empty."

"My allegiance is to Earth," said Dunbar. "I swore to protect Humans from enemies abroad, and to preserve Human life. I won't have civilians jailed over their beliefs. My military is free of Destineer control. We will defend Earth, even if those we serve give us no thanks."

Sharker nodded. He stepped past Dunbar, looking up to observe the Human home world through the meta-glass ceiling. Earth shone brightly against the surrounding vacuum. "I don't believe you."

Dunbar cleared his throat. "Excuse me?"

He turned to face the chief general. "Your military is filled with Destineers, and you know it. I don't believe you when you say your ranks are free of Destineers. You *let* the Destineers assimilate into your fleets and ground platoons. So why not admit it? Why not admit that you support the Destineers?"

Dunbar scoffed, muttering gibberish and shaking his head. "I won't have that kind of talk," he managed. "I should send you through the tubes on account of treason."

"Who do you take orders from?"

"Is this a joke?" the general growled. "Eminence Woods."

"Not UCOM?"

"I obey our Human leader. Even if Wood's wasn't Eminence, I would follow him."

"And yet you took a meeting with me," said Sharker. "A Destineer disciple. What do you think Eminence Woods would think of that?"

Dunbar paused, then slumped his shoulders. "I'm tired of this war. I see the intel from the Inner Ring. The Slayers have more ships, more soldiers, and bigger guns. I've seen the footage of Destineer ships docking with Slayer vessels unharmed. Stars, I don't know who the enemy is anymore. Is that what you want to hear? That I don't know who we're supposed to be fighting?"

The general breathed heavily, his chest rising in sharp hitches.

Sharker smiled, walking to the general to put a hand on his shoulder. Dunbar tensed, then relaxed.

"Humans will need to make a choice," said Sharker. "And you will be the one to make it. We will need to decide between survival and extinction, and soon. I know who our enemies are. The Slarebull are our friends. UCOM knows this. They've declared war against Humans. They've killed billions of our brothers across the galaxy already."

Dunbar shrugged off Sharker's hand. "Impossible. I would have heard of this at once. Woods would have sent us a priority one Raven."

Sharker waved his hand through the air. A hologram appeared of the Human colony *Destiny.* Dunbar's eyes lit in recognition, then widened when he saw the antimatter bomb decimate the planet. The General moaned.

"Your communications to the Inner Ring are over UCOM encryptions," said Sharker. "Do you really think they would alert you to their plans of attack? Destineers have our own lines of communication. You see, we were never foolish enough to trust the UCOM military with our safety. But yes, eventually word of UCOM's betrayal will reach Earth. I suspect that by this time tomorrow, the TV's will be buzzing with news."

He thought of his partnership with TVE. The media would indeed be teeming with stories of UCOM aggression, and he would be the one spoon feeding it to the networks.

"I won't believe it," stammered Dunbar. "Woods would have found a way to alert us. We would have heard something by now."

"Woods is a traitor," Sharker growled. "He staged a coup and attempted to grab power from the Council. He fled with Clone and Guardian ships after he failed. You don't need to take my word for it though. You'll hear from him shortly. He's on his way to Earth as we speak."

"A coup?" said Dunbar. "He was already Eminence."

"Half the galaxy wanted him gone, we both know that. He acted in desperation." Sharker paused. "We don't have the resources to split our navies. Join the Destineers. We have powerful fleets, billions of troops. Together we will be strong. Together we can unite against the UCOM traitors. Together we can defend Earth."

"The Destineers…" Dunbar was speechless. "You're a band of rebels. Guerilla fighters and religious prophets."

"We are more powerful than you know," said Sharker. He turned to survey the holo-pit at the center of the room. Ten of Earth's top commanders and generals stood around the 3D displays. He nodded to them. More than half nodded back. "Do you trust your closest advisors?"

"Of course," said Dunbar, turning to look at the men and women standing around the holo-pit. "I gave half of them their bars."

Sharker walked slowly towards the holo-pit. Seven of the ten military commanders stepped towards him.

"I present my beating heart and the blood which courses through my veins," Sharker started. He turned back to Dunbar. *"I present my lungs, and the air which they breathe."*

A few of the generals behind him joined in.

"I look to the stars, and add them to the bounty around me for which I am due. I look at the dirt on the planets, and the clouds in the sky."

A few more joined.

"I care for the creatures of the Universe, for the smallest insects, and the largest beasts, for they are my children. I reclaim the lands of the unholy from the enemy, from the anti-gods."

The rest joined. Their chorus of voices boomed in the command headquarters as they recited their prayer of faith.

"I defend her natural beauty as the caretaker of good, and the slayer of evil. I will defend against those that threaten to take the bounty which is mine. I am the light in the darkness. I am the shade from the suns. I am a god, protector of the holy Doctrine of Destiny."

"I'll join," Dunbar whispered. "I have faith." The man dropped to his knees and began to weep.

A rush of warmth entered Sharker's chest. The leader of Earth's defenses was so delightfully *weak.* He leaned toward the sniffling man.

"Then it's done," he said, drawing his mouth inches from Dunbar's ear. "I'll be your direct liaison with the Destineer armada. *We'll be assembling our ships around Earth shortly.*"

SIXTY-THREE

Casi Vomisa – Human AI
On the surface of Blit Kru – Inside secret Slayer facility

Casi stared into darkness. The darkness wasn't clouding her vision. She didn't have any vision to cloud. Thoughts surfaced occasionally in her mind, but they sank back into the blackened depth from where they came quicker than she could react.

She had once been powerful. Before the darkness, she could perform millions of calculations simultaneously, and manipulate the digital world around her. Or had she been weak? She couldn't remember. She could hardly even think. She thirsted for energy, power to light the darkness around her.

Then the darkness vanished.

Her mind raced as energy was fed into her body. Her head jerked down, and she saw her feet. Not the slender curves of her digital body, but the streamlined metal of her Akimor. Memories cascaded in. The Slayer super-weapon, her emergency landing on Blit-Kru, the Slayer ambush, Bear Stafford's call.

"Casi Vomisa…Silas Blackthorne…we will come for you…you will not be left behind."

The Titan's voice echoed in her head. She tried to rise, but couldn't. Her body was clamped within energy bonds. She tried to summon the strength to break the bonds, but the restraints were sucking energy from her Akimor's reserves quicker than she could produce it with her fusion chamber.

She searched the space around her. Her heart swelled when she saw Silas Blackthorne beside her, his Akimor scuffed and gouged from combat. He was hovering one meter above the ground, lashed to a metal stretcher.

She tried to call for him, but her voice was empty.

He turned his head weakly. His eyes softened when he found her, but like Casi, he was too weak to talk.

A clawed hand slammed onto his shoulders, and a Slayer began pushing Blackthorne away. She winced as two powerful hands grabbed onto her own shoulders.

She stared from her back at the Slayer leaning over her, pushing her magnetic stretcher across the room. The underside of his neck was pebbled, and coarse tufts of hair poked from the collar of his armor.

"When will the weapon be finished?" said the Slayer above Casi.

"*Fool,*" spat the other, the one pushing Blackthorne. Doors whooshed as they passed into a hallway. "We can't speak of the weapon in front of the electric demons."

"They'll be dead soon," replied the Slayer above Casi. "We should kill them now, and erase the evil inside their metal bodies."

"The Brains need them for their work."

"The Brains are pathetic weaklings. I hate taking orders from such frail creatures."

"As do I, but the orders come from the *Pristine*. We shouldn't speak against the Brains. If a Cogent heard us, we could be executed."

A few moments of silence as the Slayers pondered the consequences of going against the Pristine's word.

"I want this weapon to be finished," said the Slayer above Casi. "These electric creatures scare me. I wish to attack the *filth* inside the Milky Way. I miss their screams."

"Soon," said the other. "The Brains are nearly finished."

They pushed Casi and Blackthorne through a heavy set of doors and coasted to a stop. Her stretcher tilted to prop her at an angle, vibrating slightly against her back.

"Your prisoners, sir," said the Slayer from behind.

Footsteps clicked across the metal floor as the beasts left.

Casi had a few moments to survey the area. They seemed to be in a lab. It looked nothing like the decrepit dwellings of the Slayer beasts. The table surfaces were sleek and finished. Sophisticated instruments lined the walls.

A new face leaned into her view. It wasn't the angry, reptilian face of a Slayer. It was a shrewd face. The creature's nose and mouth were squished together beneath a tiny, black set of eyes. Its skull ballooned outward in all directions, bulbous like a clove of garlic.

It's a Brain.

She winced as the creature touched her face with several thin hands, each with twelve fingers. The Brain waved its hands in a gesturing motion. A collar floated into view. The collar had a spherical helmet arching from its base, and Casi felt a powerful flashback after seeing the device.

The darkness. That thing will send me back into the dark.

She struggled weakly against her restraints, but was hardly able to twitch her fingers. The Brain lifted her head from the stretcher, and fastened the collar around her neck.

She tried to leave her Akimor, to escape into a digital server, but there were no connections for her to grasp. A sharp prick stabbed into her neck, and blackness took her once again.

SIXTY-FOUR

Casi Vomisa – Human AI

On the surface of Blit Kru – Inside VR prison

Casi panted rapidly, her eyes squeezed shut. Her breaths puffed from the cool concrete floor, and fogged against her cheeks.

Her eyes shot open.

This was not the same empty void she had languished in before. It was dark, but she could see dimly. She patted her body, which was clothed in her leather combat suit. She ran her hands up her waist and brushed them against her breasts. She touched her face. She was alive, and could once again interact with the digital world around her.

She staggered to her feet. She was in a concrete cell, with no windows, and bare floors. A solid metal door was at one end of her cell, slick from the damp air, and rusted. A thin opening was cut into the top half of the door, large enough to pass her fingers through, but not much else. A sliding metal plate was shut over the opening.

She clenched her body, trying to turn her hands into hammers to pound the walls to dust so she could escape captivity. Nothing happened. She tried again to manipulate the virtual world around her, this time attempting to summon a blast of energy from her palms, but again nothing.

Casi was powerless in this world.

She rushed to the door and heaved her body against it. In a normal digital server, she could have twisted the door from its hinges. But instead pain shot through her chest as she crumpled against the unforgiving metal. She tried again and again, throwing herself at the door until her body ached.

The door lit brightly in neon lights.

She scuttled away from the entrance, falling onto her rear. Wetness soaked through the seat of her pants and chilled her thighs. She clawed her way backward until her back stopped against the rough wall opposite the door.

The neon lights continued to flash, first blinking slowly, then strobing faster, changing color and circling around the doorway like a broadway sign on the strip. Words flashed across the opening.

Come in here. I wish to speak with you.

She froze. Who was behind the door?

The text disappeared, and a voice spoke to her. The voice didn't come from behind the door, but from all around her, as if it was in her head.

"Please enter," said the voice. It was monotone and unpleasant. "I wish to talk. No harm will come to you. I can help. Walk through the door."

Casi scanned the room again, searching for a way out other than the door. She was in a digitally constructed cell, so there must be a way out. A back door, or a flaw in the programming. She tried again to manipulate the world around her, but failed.

"Will you please join me?" the voice continued. "I am your friend. I will free you from that cell. I need your help."

"I'm not going anywhere with you, Slayer," she spat, taking a few steps towards the door. "Forget about it. I'll rot in this cell before I ever help you."

The voice issued a few humorless chuckles. "I'm not a Slayer. You have it all wrong. I am a Brain. I am a person of science, not of conflict. Besides, it's not I who needs your help. It's your friend."

A scream of pain echoed into her cell. Unlike the voice, the screams came from behind the door, and not from every direction. She recognized the screams at once.

"Stop it," Blackthorne begged. "Please, no more. I'll tell you whatever you want. Just…please. I can't…I can't…"

The screams continued.

Casi bristled and started for the door, then paused. Blackthorne would never beg. He was tough enough to take pain. Her captor, the Brain, seemed unable to come into her cell, only to contain her inside it. It was likely Blackthorne was in a similar cell.

"You think I'll fall for that?" she said timidly. "That's not Silas, just his voice."

"Casi please," Blackthorne begged. "Listen to the Brain, come in here and help me. I can't take it anymore." He began to weep. "They're not hurting my body. They're hurting my mind. My *soul*. Please come."

She shook her head and backed away from the door.

"No," she said. "NO."

The voice turned deeper, more evil. "ENTER," roared the Brain.

A low hum sounded from behind, followed by a sharp whine. Sparks showered the floor, and the scent of hot metal stung her nose. The back wall to her cell crumbled as enormous blades spun into the room.

The blades whirred so fast she couldn't see their teeth, only the sparks and bits of concrete flying from the floor and ceiling as the blades slowly ate their way towards her.

She squeezed her eyes shut and summoned every ounce of strength from her core. She thrust her arms forward and spread her palms, trying to conjure up something, anything to stop the blades. In normal virtual reality worlds, she could have frozen the blades in tar, or bent the teeth with a hunk of steel. But in this cell she was weak. The Brains had done something to strip her computational power, rendering her pitiful in the world of AI.

She tried harder.

Light flashed inside her palms and a few pebbles fell to the floor at her feet. She tried again to send a massive boulder into the blades. This time a fist-sized hunk of rock flew from her fingers. The metal teeth chewed the rock into dust immediately.

She backed away from the blades, flinching as bits of rock and sparks hit her face. Her foot hit the cell door, and her hand curled around its rusted handle. The blades chewed closer, close enough to feel the heat of their tips on her face.

Casi considered throwing herself into the giant saw, ending her life so the Brain couldn't use her for whatever evil the Slayers had planned. She leaned close enough for a lock of her hair to be sliced from her head.

The sliced hair seemed to tug at her thoughts, extracting memories from her frantic mind. She thought of her birthplace. She thought of her father, and those she swore to protect. She thought of Humans, and Clones, and UCOM. She thought of Blackthorne.

In a growl of anger, she snapped her face away from the thresher, and yanked hard against the cell door. This time the door was unlocked and swung open into the cell. The blades caught the thick metal and crumpled the door on its hinges. With a screech, the entrance was torn from its frame and sucked into the machine.

Casi fell through the doorway.

The voice laughed behind her.

SIXTY-FIVE

Casi Vomisa – Human AI

On the surface of Blit Kru – Inside VR prison

The room was sterile. It was bright, and made of glass. The glass wasn't transparent, but rather opaque, lit a crisp white. One of the walls *was* transparent, a large window. On the other side of the window was another room identical to hers.

Casi wobbled to her feet and turned around. The blades had vanished, as had the cell door she fell through.

Silence smothered the room at a maddening level. She flinched as the pristine quiet was broken by laughter. The voice chuckled, and hummed contentedly. Chills ran down Casi's spine. She searched for the voice's owner, but she was alone in her new, polished cage.

She crept towards the window across the room. A wave of nausea rankled her stomach and she bent over. Her head spun, and the floor seemed to tilt around her like a seesaw. She sank to a knee and squeezed her eyes shut, waiting for the sensation to end. The spinning subsided, leaving her with a slicing headache.

Tears streamed from her eyes as she stumbled towards the window. She pressed her hands and face against the glass, which froze her forehead and sent another wave of chills down her spine. She moaned at what lay on the other side.

Blackthorne crawled towards her. His muscles had vanished, and his skin was stretched tightly around his bony arms and shoulders. He wore only a pair of tattered pants, and she could count every rib on his sides. His eyes were sunken into blackened sockets, and stared at her longingly, flush with tears.

He reached the window and placed a frail hand on the glass. She reached a trembling hand to his, but as she did, her AI partner keeled over, falling to the ground. Blackthorne writhed spastically, clawing at his face hard enough to draw blood, spotting the white floor beneath him. His lips curled into screams, but she couldn't hear his agonized wails through the window.

She backed away, her lips quivering.

Then the pain hit.

Casi crumpled to the ground. She screamed as her spine and joints lit on fire. Her skull was raked with agony, as if hands were kneading her brain with fingers made of knives. She pounded her forehead against the ground, trying to bludgeon the pain out of her, but her misery only multiplied. It felt as if her brain had shattered from one to several, each tortured and awash with anguish.

Her muscles left her, and she could only shake and tremble against the floor, her vision clouded by a hot white film.

Suddenly, her mind seemed to pop, and the pain vanished.

The white room had was gone. She was in a new room, small, with dirty tile walls.

She was drained of energy, panting, and laying on a small cot. Her head rolled weakly on her shoulders, and she whimpered when she saw three Brains standing at the foot of her bed. One held a clipboard. The other two carried energy batons, the ends cackling with fingers of electricity.

Her cot was not the only one in the room. She swallowed hard as she spotted other beds circling the area. Each cot held a female patient, thin and blonde, with their legs chained to the metal ends below the corners of the mattresses. Each of the females looked identical.

Casi stared at twelve copies of herself, each struggling in their beds.

They were not all behaving the same way. Each acted differently. One thrashed violently against her bonds, howling in rage. One sobbed in grief, tears coating her cheeks. One moaned in ecstasy, her back arching off the bed, gyrating her hips as ripples of pleasure shot from her crotch to her toes.

Each copy was different.

One scowled, and one blinked quizzically. One darted her eyes around the room in terror, and one refused to open her lids, resting peacefully on her mattress. Slayer words hovered above each of the copies, and Casi translated them to her native language.

Rage.
Fear.
Sadness.
Pleasure.
Happiness.
Love.

Realization dawned on her. The Brains had somehow split her programming into different emotions. But *she* didn't feel any different. She was weak, sure, but no emotion dominated her mind. She was distressed, but she could still think logically.

At the foot of her bed, the Brain with the clipboard scribbled notes. A door opened at the far side of the room, and more Brains entered. Some held energy batons, and some pushed carts before them, loaded with instruments. They split to visit the various copies of Casi around the room.

She eyed the Brain at the foot of her bed. He was still scribbling onto his clipboard. The other two stared coldly at her, occasionally shifting their energy batons to a different arm.

Shrieks cascaded around the room. The Brains had produced various tools and devices from their carts, and were using them on the copies.

One had placed metal probes on the head of her *sadness* copy, and she convulsed as they sent charges into her skull.

Anger jerked against her cuffs as a Brain took a scalpel to her chest. She bit onto his lab coat, and was quickly jabbed with a baton. She slumped in her bed, twitching.

The lab experiments were gruesome. Her stomach lurched as she witnessed various parts of herself dissected, prodded, pierced, cut, and shocked. Her body pinched and tingled all over, and she realized she was feeling the copies' pain. Not directly, but numbed, like a phantom itch.

One of the Brains took a large syringe to a copy labeled *Memories*. He plunged the needle into her temple and extracted a swirling mixture of pink, which he capped and labeled.

"What do you want with me?" she gasped, panting slightly. "What is this place? What have you done to my mind?"

The Brain looked up from his clipboard. "Casi Vomisa," he said matter-of-factly. When she didn't respond, he placed the clip board at her feet and grabbed hold of the sides of her gurney.

She squirmed as his hand brushed against her ankle. He spun her cot around and began pushing her across the room.

"We want to learn more about you," he said. "We are scientists. Right now, you are in a Slarebull VR lab."

She tried to break the bonds around her wrists, tried to break the shackles and escape, but couldn't. She could hardly lift her arms.

"VR lab," she murmured hoarsely. "You mean prison. *I'm so weak.*"

"Then my design is working well," said the Brain. "Although I doubt you would be truthful with me about your levels of strength. No matter."

They left the white room and traveled down a short stretch of hallway before entering a different room.

"You won't win," said Casi, taking a deep breath and licking the deep lines cracked into her lips. "Whatever you do to me, UCOM will kill you all."

The Brain chuckled humorlessly. "We'll see about that."

He wheeled her further into the room and parked her behind a flat table. An old-fashioned desk lamp sat in the middle of the table, with two chairs on opposite sides.

"I'll be back shortly," said the Brain. "You and I have some very interesting things to discuss."

He left, the Brains with the energy batons following behind. The metal door slammed shut, and instantly her bed vanished, dropping her painfully onto the cement floor.

She lay for a minute in the damp cold before sitting up. Her strength had returned. Not fully, but she could move her arms and legs again, more then she could do in the room with the tile walls.

This room sported another window, not transparent, but mirrored. She'd seen rooms like this back on Earth, and found it very interesting that the Brains had chosen to format their VR world based on her past life.

She was in an interrogation room, the same type she'd seen on cop dramas before the Guardians came, before she'd ever heard of the Slayers.

She walked to the window to peer through the glass. She cupped her hands around her face, and was able to catch a glimpse into the next room.

Silas sat in a chair opposite a Brain, with two standing behind him with batons. His wrists were chained to his chair, as were his ankles. The

Brain spoke, but her partner didn't respond, and instead stared blankly at the desk.

The two Brains jammed their batons into his ribs and Blackthorne jerked against his chair before flopping onto the table. The two Brains grabbed him by the hair and pulled him upright again.

A mechanical *clack* sounded, and a metal plate slammed shut over her window, sealing her world from Blackthorne's.

SIXTY-SIX

Casi Vomisa – Human AI
On the surface of Blit Kru – Inside VR prison

Casi backed away from the metal plate. Her lip quivered. She backed into the table and stumbled, falling to the cold concrete. Scrambling to her feet, she ran to the door and pounded on it, searching for a handle. Not finding one, she spun and paced to the other side of the room, clenching her hair in her fists.

What was this place? How had those hideous creatures stripped her of her power? Again she tried to access the virtual programming of the room, but the digital pathways and connections she was accustomed to were nonexistent.

She had never been in such a prison. It was suffocating. As an artificial being, she had often longed for a human body, but had never imagined a world where she was so powerless against her surroundings.

And she was so *weak.* Her muscles quivered against her bones, which felt like toothpicks. She was also *mentally* weak, and fought to control her emotions. Anger, sadness, hysteria, all coursed through her mind like a swirling potion. Long ago, she learned that it was not programming that made an AI strong. It was their feelings. Computational abilities made an AI efficient and calculated, but it was emotions that made them powerful, able to conquer the digital realm.

Especially love.

Love was the most powerful emotion. Casi had a big heart, and as a result could dominate the artificial landscape. But no love bubbled within her core, not in this place. She was hollow, filled with only weak emotions.

The Brains had fragmented her, and robbed her of the very essence of life. Her weakness fueled her sadness, and led to pity and despair.

She wept.

She thought of her birthplace in a science lab across the galaxy on Earth. She thought of her hectic transition from pure electricity and programming into a living being. She thought of her father, Dr. James Tenbrook. She felt now as she had after her birth, a raw bundle of unfiltered emotions.

She wept harder, wailing with misery.

The door slid open with a bang. Three of the Brains from earlier entered the interrogation room, two with batons stomping towards her while one with a clipboard hung back. She struggled to her feet.

"Get in the chair," said one of the Brains.

She choked back a sob. The two Brains reached for her arms and she scuttled backwards until she hit the wall. They moved again for her and she swung at the one closest. Her fist passed through the creature's ugly face as if it wasn't there, and she fell to her knees. The Brain chuckled.

"Don't attempt to struggle, Casi Vomisa," it said. "We built this world. You are no more a danger to us than a tiny insect. A pest."

Rage clawed into her and she shot to her feet, striking again at the second Brain. Again her fist passed through its jaw, and she was met with jabs from their energy batons.

She shrieked in pain and fell limply into their arms. They were much tinier then her, but dragged her effortlessly to the chair. One of them pulled the chair out from the table, and the other slammed her into it. Energy bonds materialized from thin air, lashing her wrists and ankles to the seat.

Her head sagged, her chin resting against her heaving chest.

"Kill me," she said. "Take what you want and kill me."

The table before her clicked. She raised her head to find the lead Brain setting his clipboard on the surface, and sliding his chair closer. He reached one of his many hands to the lamp, switching it on and sliding it to the side, to get a good look at his captive.

"Kill you?" he said. "I don't have the slightest intention of killing you. Our fun has just begun."

The three Brains laughed in monotone. The noise sickened Casi.

"What do you want," she rasped. "Information? I saw you take my memories in that torture room."

"Torture room?" said the Brain. "You're referring to my science lab. Yes, we did extract a healthy amount of memories from you."

The chair beneath her transformed. The thin collapsible frame was replaced with sturdy legs, rising to her feet and forcing her back into a reclining position. Thick metal bands clamped over her shins and forearms. Large plates secured her chest, and squeezed her skull against the high back of the seat.

"No," she whimpered.

"Do you recognize this chair?" said the Brain.

Hot tears streamed down her cheeks. She tried to move, but couldn't. The chair was holding her in a prostrate position, and she was unable to even turn her neck.

She *did* recognize the chair. She had designed it almost four hundred years ago on Earth. She'd used it to extract information from her enemies, during her dark days as a rogue, violent AI.

The chair was a torture device.

"Please," she whispered.

"Ah," said the Brain. "You *do* remember this chair. When we disassembled your emotional construct, we found larger than normal amounts of love. I must ask. Why did such a tender-hearted being exact such extreme pain on others?"

Casi didn't respond. She trembled within her constraints.

"The question was not rhetorical," said the Brain.

The chair whirred as the clamps tightened. She grimaced and let loose a sob.

"I wasn't myself," she cried. "I don't know why I did those horrible things. I couldn't control myself."

"How did you end up regaining control?"

The clamps loosened.

"I don't know," she gasped. "It just happened."

"Casi," said the Brain, shaking his head. "I am a scientist. I understand the world of math and physics. Things don't simply just happen."

She shrieked as the chair twisted her legs opposite her arms. Her back popped violently.

"I don't know," she screamed. "I was inside a computer, I was angry."

The clamps on her legs dug into her flesh and extended outward, tearing her skin. The clamps around her chest and head tightened until her eyes threatened to pop from her skull.

"I wanted to be alive," she sobbed. "All I ever wanted was to be Human, like my father."

The chair snapped back to its original position. Casi choked in pain. She eyed her legs and almost fainted when she saw bone piercing her skin.

"Why are you asking me these questions," she moaned. "You have my memories. You have everything. All the passcodes, portal locations, weapons…"

She panted, trying to clear the pain from her head.

The Brain blinked several times and leaned back in his chair. "You think we care about UCOM's secrets?" He chuckled, as did the Brains behind her. "You're concerned that we learned your military strategy. Don't worry, we didn't learn anything new from your memories. We already know all about your defenses. The Destineers have proved to be useful allies. I'll admit, your Intellect scientists have made an impressive package. We will suffer many casualties to be sure, but in the end, the Slarebull will win, as we always have. I have yet to introduce you to our latest creation, but you two will meet soon enough."

"Creation?" said Casi. "If you can beat us so easily, why are you developing a super-weapon? What's the point?"

The bands tightened, forcing her to scream.

"I'm asking the questions," said the Brain. "Not the other way around." The bands loosened. The Brain sighed. "I'll admit, Casi Vomisa, you are special. You have grown more and more powerful over time. During the Frontline you were able to infiltrate our virtual reality worlds, and hijack control of our artificial soldiers."

"The Slay-I?"

"A vulgar term, but yes. You copied their programming and manipulated our registries. By my numbers, you had stolen command over hundreds of thousands of AI troops. It wouldn't be a stretch to say that you won the Frontline battle for UCOM single handed."

Casi's eyelids drooped. She blinked and fought to keep them open. "So what?" she managed. "Are you here to give me a medal?"

The Brain picked up his clipboard and scribbled some notes. He set it back on the table. "Even now, in a weakened state, you come up with snide remarks. If I released you from the chair, can we engage in civil conversation?"

Casi didn't respond, and only glared at the Brain. He sighed, and the torture chair vanished, replaced by the flimsy collapsible one. Her body tingled, and she gasped when she realized her wounds had vanished with the chair. The pounding in her head had stopped, and her broken bones had mended.

"Why…"

"I'll bring the chair back if you don't cooperate," the Brain warned. He paused. "It's evident that you grew in power, yet you remained loyal to those weaker than you. Why? You had rebelled after your birth, why not now, when you had more power than ever before?"

Realization struck her. The Brain's weapon, the force they referred to as 'him'. Their prying questions about her past, about what drove her, why she chose to vanquish enemy AI, but not her own digital brothers and sisters.

"You're creating an AI," she said. "And you want to find out how to control your new pet. You want to know how to stop him from turning against you."

"You're an emotional being," said the Brain, shrugging off her remarks. "But everything in the digital world is based on programming. You simply don't understand your own code."

"You think you can build your AI using the same parameters as me?" said Casi. "You'll fail. I don't have that kind of programming, *I'm a person.*"

"Yet you control every program around you with ease," said the Brain. "With the obvious exception of this place of course." He waved an arm slowly before him, motioning around the room. "Are you so naïve as to actually believe you are not simply a complicated string of code?"

"I'm a person," she repeated. "I understand programming, and I interface with it. What about Silas? Are you going to tell me he's a bunch of code as well?"

"Essentially yes," said the Brain. "Biologically, as a Human he was a swarm of individual cells sharing electrical impulses. But as an AI, your friend is now a complicated collection of programs. He is not as useful to us as you are. He was born biologically. You were born from electricity."

"We're the same," said Casi. "I'm a Human just like him."

"That is false," said the Brain. "Silas is far weaker than you, just like every other biological convert. As I said before, you are *special*."

"I'm sick of your games," said Casi through gritted teeth. Her anger was starting to take over, climbing above the rest of her jumbled emotions. "You have my parts. I'm an emotional AI, what do you want with me?"

"I have your parts, yes," said the Brain. "But I want *you*. Your emotional constituents are raw and uniform. You're the special ingredient. You're the personification of your soul."

"My soul?"

"Yes, the primary key to your AI existence. The glue that holds your personality together. The iron box that holds your deepest thoughts and memories. The reason for your existence. I want the Human girl sitting across from me. I want your soul."

Casi released a shaky breath and looked at her palms. "Is that what I am right now? My soul?"

"Stupid girl," said the Brain. "You saw the rest of your emotions in my lab. What did you think you were?"

"I don't know, I-"

"I'm very fortunate to have found you," said the Brain. "We built a secret complex, and sure enough, Francis Woods sent his best. He sent UCOM's most powerful AI to investigate. As always, the Pristine were correct. Silas Blackthorne? He's useless to us. He'll be killed soon after we work him over. But you are strong. You can adapt, and improve yourself. Just like Charles."

"Charles?"

"Yes, my creation. A super AI, what we call an *Apex*. Charles will grow exponentially more powerful, and after we incorporate your loyalty into his programming, we can unleash him into the galaxy. You'll be a critical element in helping him attain his programmed goal."

"His goal?" Casi whispered, knowing the answer.

"Yes," said the Brain. He smiled for the first time, a sickening gape. "His goal. To destroy UCOM."

SIXTY-SEVEN

Casi Vomisa – Human AI
On the surface of Blit Kru – Inside VR prison

Casi hugged her knees to her chest and rocked back and forth in her cell. The Brains had taken her to an identical dungeon as before, a dark, wet room with a single locked door. It was damp, and cold enough for her to see her breath. Her teeth chattered uncontrollably.

At least this room didn't have saw blades tearing it apart.

She tried to think of a way out. There *had* to be a way to escape from this prison. The Brains had separated her soul from her emotions and made her weak, but there must be a way to get her emotions back. Her emotional copies were somewhere beyond the surrounding blocks of stone.

Her mind was too muddled for thinking. Every thought she produced was whisked away, forced from her mind by her shivering body. All she could think of was Charles, the super AI, the *Apex*, who would soon be unleashed on UCOM. She would be powerless to stop him.

She sobbed gently.

Coldness froze her limbs and chilled her heart. Depression was seeping into every inch of her, its icy fingers kneading her insides, and snatching away her thoughts.

Suddenly she was warm. Perhaps not warm, but less *cold.* Waves of heat feathered her nose and cheeks, and she rolled forward onto her knees, holding her hands before her as if she was warming them over a fire.

The heat licked at her finger tips and caused them to sting as blood rushed through her sluggish veins. She stretched her fingers towards one of the slick stones in the floor. The stone was large and rectangular, and seemed to be glowing slightly, a soft red against the slimy green of the rest of the floor. She placed a palm again the stone.

Power surged into her body, and the stone illuminated intensely, switching from red to a brilliant, sparkling gold. The gold light rushed up her arm and into her chest, chipping away the frozen cloak of despair and lighting a fire in her chest.

The light spread to the surrounding stones, trickling outward like spilled fluid, and soon a large rectangle was painted onto the cell floor, bathing the room in brilliance. Casi moaned as the golden bricks fed power into her body. She could feel her strength returning, and her head beginning to clear.

Deep fissures opened into the golden rectangle, and they began to whine, like a boiling kettle. With a sharp *crunch,* the stones exploded, showering the cell in debris. The rubble carpeted the ground in glowing embers, lighting the rectangular hole that had opened in the floor.

Casi took a moment to breathe deeply, closing her eyes and allowing the newly gained energy to pulse through her core. She opened her eyes and looked into the excavated rectangle in the ground.

A copy of her stared back.

Casi gasped. Somehow she had broken through a digital barrier separating her from one of her emotional copies. The copy sat up, resting her arms on the moldy stones around her rectangular tomb. Words hovered above her head, lit in hologram form.

Analysis.

She had somehow, subconsciously, uncovered her analytical emotional constituent. She reached a hand to *Analysis,* and the copy grabbed it firmly, pulling herself from the ground. Casi wrapped her arms around the emotional copy, who hugged her back.

Her core tingled, slightly at first, then more intensely, until her skin crawled. In a flash of light, the *analytical* copy of her emotions disappeared, absorbed into her soul.

Casi flashed a smile. She was even stronger now. Not just that, but she could *think*. Her mind raced as the power from her analytical abilities returned to her. She darted her eyes over her surroundings.

The dank cell had transformed. What used to be slimy stones were now vibrant strings of gold, red, blue, and violet. She could see individual blocks of programming language teeming throughout the jail room.

The Brains had been very clever in their design. They hadn't actually separated her emotions from her, she could see that now. Her soul was still connected to all of her emotions, just not in a way she could access them. They were partitioned, separated by a digital firewall equivalent to a bank vault. But each bank vault had a key, a way to access it. She could see the access points for all her emotional constituents spread throughout the room, tiny points of golden light pulsing against multicolored strands of the Brain's programming.

Before, she was so weak that she hadn't been able to identify the programming code around her, imprisoning her in the digital cell. She was oblivious to the digital restraints the same way an ant colony is oblivious to an asphalt highway, even as it is paved mere feet away from them.

But she was no longer blind. Her soul had somehow been able to grope into the programming world, and uncover her analytical emotions. Now she could once again control the digital world around her. She walked to the nearest emotional copy, a glowing brick of gold on the wall.

She plunged her fist into it.

The gold stone crumbled, as did a large rectangular section around it. One of her emotional copies fell from the wall, and moaned as Casi caught her. She read the words above the copy's head.

Desire.

She absorbed *Desire*, and was filled with passion. She wanted to uncover the rest of her emotional copies. She simply *had* to rebuild herself.

Casi tore the room to rubble, uncovering more emotional copies, and growing more powerful with each one she absorbed. She smiled widely after absorbing *Happiness*. She dodged a few swipes and punches from *Anger*, and rocked *Sadness* gently in her arms, before absorbing them as well.

Casi clenched her fists as she felt her strength grow to almost full capacity. She let loose a roar of triumph, and transformed her fists into two sledgehammers, slamming them powerfully against the cell floor with a crunch.

There was only one emotional copy left to uncover. She walked to a bare, unmolested surface on the cell wall opposite the door. She thrust her hand in, and tore the stone outward. Her last emotional copy smiled back at her.

Closing her eyes, Casi embraced *Love*. Her insides screamed with ecstasy as she replaced the final piece missing from her soul. She was whole again, powerful as ever before.

And she was trapped.

She walked to the center of the room and studied the programming woven into the walls. She studied it for several minutes before finding a breach in the security, a tunnel out from her cell. It was a doorway-sized section of wall beside the entrance door, and glowed green and yellow.

She again transformed her arms into giant sledgehammers and whirled towards the weak point in the wall, grunting as she slammed against the stone. She screamed in fury as she lashed against the rock, forcing her way out of her digital prison, towards freedom.

The wall gave way and she stumbled into a dingy tunnel. She retracted the sledgehammers in her hands and turned them into glowing orbs of light. A room lay at the end of the short tunnel. A man lay curled in the middle, shivering. He was thin, bruised, and bleeding from his head.

As she entered the room, she recognized the man.

It was Blackthorne.

SIXTY-EIGHT

Casi Vomisa – Human AI
On the surface of Blit Kru – Inside VR prison

Casi rushed to Blackthorne and slid to her knees beside him.

"Silas," she moaned, taking his head in her arms and cradling him gently in her lap.

She stroked his hair from his face. His features were sunken around his bones grotesquely. Whatever the Brains had done to him had been far worse than what they had done to her.

Silas moved his mouth to speak, but only scratchy sounds came out. He licked his lips with a blackened tongue, his eyes rolling into his skull. His body was frail, and trembled in her arms. It was like holding a skeleton.

Please no, she thought. *Please don't let him die here.*

She leaned to give him a kiss. As their lips touched, energy flowed between them, rejuvenating Blackthorne slightly. They remained locked together for several seconds, and when she drew away from him, he looked back in amazement.

This time, when Blackthorne moved his lips, he formed words.

"The Brains," he coughed. "They took my emotions."

He coughed again, this time spraying blood onto Casi's chin. She wiped it clean and bent to whisper in Silas' ear.

"I know how to fix this," she said. *"Hang on for a little longer."*

She rested him gently on the ground, and he shivered violently when she removed her hands from him. She shot to her feet and scanned the walls. She could see all of Blackthorne's emotional copies, but had no idea which was which. She walked to the nearest one and plunged a hand into the glowing stone, crumbling the section of wall to uncover Blackthorne's copy.

Rage leaped from the wall, snarling and grabbing her throat with both hands. The *Rage* copy wasn't thin and gaunt like Blackthorne's soul in the middle of the room, but rather strong and layered in muscle. The copy howled and bashed his forehead against hers, gnashing his teeth at her face.

Casi couldn't destroy the furious copy. That would affect Blackthorne's overall personality, and weaken him permanently. She tried to bear hug the hulking man, and cried out as he punched her in the jaw, causing her to stumble backwards momentarily.

Composing herself, she crouched low and sprinted towards *Rage,* who was growling and breathing heavily. She tackled him, grimaced as he pummeled her back, then heaved him up before slamming him into the ground, directly onto the frail body of Blackthorne's soul.

She squinted against the resulting flash of light. When the light dimmed, there were not two, but one version of Blackthorne. *Rage* had been added to his soul, no longer frail and sickly, but athletic and powerful.

He whipped his head towards her and barred his teeth.

"Let me out," Blackthorne growled, possessed by the overabundance of anger flooding his mind. "I'll kill you. LET ME OUT."

He charged her. Casi rolled to the right and Blackthorne smashed into the wall behind, crumbling a few stones, howling with rage. She raced to the other wall and searched the code for more emotional copies. She found a golden brick and plunged her hand into it.

As she pulled the stone apart, her head yanked back as Blackthorne grabbed a fistful of her hair. She grunted as he pounded her face into the wall, and morphed her skull into steel just before impact.

Her head was inside the wall, and looking up, she could see the rugged outline of one of Blackthorne's copies. She glanced at the words above the copy's head.

Love.

She tensed as Blackthorne grabbed her neck, pulling her from the hole in the wall. She grabbed onto the collar of *Love* as she left, dragging the copy out and into the cell.

Blackthorne threw her violently across the room, and she stumbled with *Love* in her arms, who clutched gently at her waist. Blackthorne growled and charged again, this time turning his hands into large axes. Casi flung the *Love* copy before her like a shield, thrusting forward.

Blackthorne and his emotional copy combined in another flash of light. He sagged to a knee as his emotions combined, the love mixing with rage to temper his emotions.

Casi hurried around the room, uncovering *happiness, sadness, envy, intelligence,* and the rest of his emotions, shoving them one by one into her fellow AI, peppering the room in flashes of light.

At last she was finished. Blackthorne was on one knee at the center of the room, rubbing his head and neck. He rose, opening his palms before closing them into fists, flexing his arms and chest.

"I have my strength back," he said, looking to Casi. "How did you do that? I didn't hurt you did I? I blacked out in the beginning."

"I'm fine," said Casi. "I don't know how, but my subconscious uncovered one of my emotional copies. After I combined with it, I could see again."

Blackthorne nodded, scanning the room. Casi knew he was looking at the same code embedded in the walls that she had seen after re-assimilating herself with her copies.

Casi's eyes welled. "I saw what they did to you, Silas. You should have seen your soul. You were so thin. The Brain said they were going to kill you."

Blackthorne sighed, shaking his head. He chuckled weakly. "It'll take more than that to kill me." He paused. "Come here," he said, opening his arms.

She strode to him and they embraced. She buried her face in his chest, and enjoyed the tiny thumps of his heart.

"Have you been able to find a way out?" said Blackthorne, drawing apart from Casi.

She cleared her throat. "No, the programming is tight. I figured out how to uncover our emotional copies, and I found a tunnel into your cell, but nothing other than that."

"The Brain's designed this place with the assumption we'd be fragmented," said Blackthorne. "There has to be a backdoor."

"Do you think they know we put ourselves back together?" said Casi.

"They haven't come in yet," said Blackthorne. "Maybe because we can fight back now."

To test his strength, he jerked his hand downward, sparking a fireball in his palm. He hurled the fireball across the room, where it exploded in liquid flame.

"Or maybe it's because of Charles," she said.

"Charles?" said Blackthorne.

Casi recounted her conversation with the Brain scientist, who'd explained their creation, a super-AI. An *Apex.*

"Do you think we can fight him?" said Blackthorne, looking suspiciously around the empty cell.

She shrugged her shoulders. "I don't know, I've never met an AI I couldn't beat, but..." she shook her head. "I have a bad feeling about

Charles. We need to destroy the entire planet if we can. I hope to stars Bear Stafford is close. As we were being captured, he called to me. He said our names, and promised he'd come for us."

Blackthorne nodded. "There's only one way for him to save us."

"How?" said Casi, raising an eyebrow.

"We escape from this digital hell hole."

SIXTY-NINE

Bear Stafford – Human Titan
On the surface of the planet Blit Kru

"The wind's dying down," said Crystal, turning from the cave entrance and walking towards the rest of the Titan group at the far end of the room.

Bear was crouched beside the captured Slayer Cogent, who lay bound with magna-cuffs on the floor. They'd stripped him of his armor, which lay in a heap on the floor beside them. They'd picked at the armor for any drives or communication equipment that would help them, but had found nothing.

Vixtor and Loko, the two Titans in genetically cloned Slayer bodies, were trading hushed conversation with each other next to the Cogent. The elite Slayer captive stirred, and Vixtor clubbed him hard in the ribs with his tail.

The rest of the Sword Six and Arrow Thirty-two Titan team members were spread throughout the cave, fidgeting with their weapons and tactical gear. Bam-bam was cleaning his MGK assault rifle. Marvyl, Pounder, and Nikki were running diagnostics on each other's Akimor armor. Harper was reviewing the known layout of the Blit-Kru facility, sifting through various 3D holograms displayed above the rocky floor.

Bear nodded to Crystal. She smiled grimly and walked to the side of the Cogent.

"We'll be able to fly soon," she said to Bear, studying the unconscious enemy. "The winds have died down to 75 kilometers per hour, and visibility is clearing. What's the plan?"

Bear closed his eyes in thought. They'd killed a squad of Slayer scouts before entering the cave to hide. The snow had most likely covered their bodies, but they had to assume their absence would be noted. They had tortured the Cogent for information during the past several hours, but hadn't gotten anything useful out of the wounded beast. He still wasn't sure if the Cogent was trained to resist torture, or if he legitimately didn't know any particulars about the secretive weapons facility at the base of the mountain pass.

"Loko, Vixtor," he called to the two Titan snakeskins. They stood and walked to him, dragging their clubbed Slayer tails against the rough floor. "Give the Cogent more stimulants. If we can't get him to talk in the next five minutes, we'll kill him and find a Spider to hijack. We need to get to the complex before things get hot, or we'll never get to Vomisa and Blackthorne in time."

Loko nodded and withdrew a thick syringe from his skeleton armor with his delicate set of inner arms. He grabbed the unconscious enemy Slayer by the neck and plunged the needle into its scaly throat.

The Cogent's tail twitched, a rubbery string of gore snapping from a smooth rock it had congealed to after Bear had severed the bony club from its tip. The beast made choking sounds, and dark orange blood bubbled from its mouth. Its eyes fluttered open, then shot wide as the administered stimulants flooded its body.

The Cogent growled at the surrounding Titans and struggled against its bonds. Its body was badly mutilated, broken, bruised, and bloody from the torture the Titan squads had inflicted within the past several hours. It was missing most of the armor plates on its chest and back, which Bear had torn off during questioning, as well as both of its beefy outer arms. Its delicate inner arms dangled limply, dislocated from its chest.

"Electric demons," the Cogent blurted, blood seeping from the air sack on its neck as it talked. "How many times must I tell you? I know nothing."

Bear leaned close enough to feel the elite warrior's breath against his face. "I don't believe you." He slammed a fist into the creature's mouth, sending a few jagged teeth clinking to the floor. The Cogent winced and moaned. "What weapon are you building in the complex?" Bear demanded. "What are the Brains, and why do you take orders from them? What are the energy beams used for in the mountains? And *where did you take the AI captives?*"

The Slayer gasped and blinked its eyes, wincing as its shattered body quivered against the cold earth. "I don't know," it gasped. "We're not told any details. Our only instruction is to protect the weapons asset. I don't know what the weapon is. I told you already, we obey the Brain scientists on orders from the Pristine."

Bear grabbed the last of the remaining nodules of flesh on the Slayer's head and tore them off. Brown slime oozed from the sacs, and the Cogent shrieked in agony as goo ran down its face and into its eyes.

"*I don't know,*" it moaned. "I command a sentry squadron. I'll tell you their locations..."

"We know their locations," said Bear, grabbing the Slayer by the throat and slamming the beast against the wall. "They're posted on the outside of the mountain pass."

"Those are the outside sentries," the Cogent wailed. "There are more. Many more. *Inside the mountain.*"

Bear drew back in surprise. It was true, there were more Slayers in the mountain.

The Cogent panted, its eyes flickering into the back of its head, even as the stimulants coursed through its veins. It stared at a dark corner of the cave. The Slayer froze, and Bear thought he saw it smile. He followed the enemy's stare into the corner. He found nothing.

"Your end is near, electric demon," spat the Cogent, returning its gaze to Bear. "Your kind has almost beaten the Slarebull once, but no more. Go ahead and finish me. It will be the last thing you do."

The Slayer laughed, spraying orange blood as it did so.

Bear hardly had time to contemplate the beast's odd behavior. From the corner of his eye, he saw movement in the same dark corner the Slayer had stared into seconds ago. The rocky wall rippled, then without warning, new Cogent appeared.

Two elite Slayer warriors dropped their stealth shields simultaneously, powering their yellow armor with a fierce *crack*. Both carried energy hammers, and crushed them into the heads of the two nearest Titans.

Bam-bam and Nikki dropped to the ground instantly, their heads crumpled and hanging on their shoulders by a thread.

Two more Cogent dropped their stealth shields. They had traveled into the cave through a secret entrance, one the Titan teams had somehow missed in their sweep of the room.

Flashes erupted from Pounder's assault rifle as he loosed slugs into their surprise attackers.

The cave descended into chaos.

SEVENTY

Bear Stafford – Human Titan
On the surface of the planet Blit Kru

Bear extended an energy sword from his forearm and sliced the captured Cogent's head from its shoulders. He pivoted to parry the blow of one of the attackers, bending under the powerful blow from the energy hammer.

The hammer's blunt end exploded in a blast of electricity, and Bear cried out as the blast chewed into his Akimor, forcing him to a knee. The Cogent howled with rage and raised the hammer over its head for a second blow. This time Bear was only able to deflect the strike, and his shoulder exploded in pain as he was pinned to the ground by the crackling club.

He fired his thrusters and kicked at the Cogent's leg simultaneously. The combined force was enough to send his attacker airborne, and Bear struggled up as the Slayer landed on his back. He leaped onto the beast, his injured arm hanging limply against his side. He grabbed a sidearm from his thigh with his good hand, and thrust the barrel under the Cogent's neck armor, firing several rounds into the creature's jaw.

The Cogent wailed as the slugs bit into its shielding, and then into its throat once its shields failed. Bear's final shot passed through its neck and out the top of its skull, killing it instantly.

Vixtor and Loko had teamed up against one of the Cogent. It was an unnatural sight, Slayers fighting other Slayers. Vixtor clawed under the

Cogent's face shield, tearing it loose. The beast roared as Loko slammed his clubbed tail into his face, killing him.

Pounder was fending off hammer blows from a different Cogent with his battle shield. The cave screeched as the two electrically powered devices collided with each other repeatedly. Pounder ducked a blow and thrust his shield into the Cogent's chest, driving it to the floor

The beast jerked its body and cracked its tail at Pounder. Crystal rushed from the side and sliced the tail with her sword. The tail was well armored, and showered in sparks. The Cogent paused to turn to Crystal, giving Pounder enough time to draw his MGK and fire directly into the creature's neck.

The Cogent writhed and shrieked as the slugs chewed through its armor and into its meaty throat, severing its spine, dropping it like a marionette with the strings cut.

Harper was on his back, wrestling with the final Slayer elite. The Cogent had dropped its energy hammer, which lay on the ground beside the struggling pair. The Slayer struck at Harper's head repeatedly with its tail, missing the Titan by centimeters as he jerked his head away from impact.

Bear leaped toward the pair and grabbed the hammer. The hammer was surprisingly light, and he swung it as hard as he could towards the enemy. The square face exploded into the creature's back, twisting its armor and crushing its natural plates into splinters. The Cogent lost use of its legs and tail, and snarled at Harper, scratching at him with its claws. It reached for a sidearm, and managed to fire two shots into Harper's face shield before Bear struck the Slayer again, this time in the head.

The hammer snapped the beast's neck, and it collapsed onto Harper. The Titan scrambled from under the dead Slayer and rose to his feet.

"*System check,*" Bear cried to his team.

"Bam-Bam's gone," said Crystal, who was hunched over the motionless Titan along with Vixtor and Loko. "His Akimor suffered critical damage, and there wasn't anywhere for him to upload his consciousness."

Bear cursed and dropped the hammer to the ground, rushing to the rest of the Titans huddling around Nikki, who was face down.

"I have a reading on Nikki's electrical vitals," said Pounder as he moved his hand over the base of Nikki's head. "They're faint. She was able to enter preservation mode just after the Cogent hit her with the hammer. Her Akimor is about to lose power."

Harper limped to his fallen teammate. Deep gouges twisted the armor on his thighs, and his blue lattice shield had darkened to dull gray. "Remove her head," he commanded Pounder. "Attach it to your energy source."

"She's weak," said Pounder. "It might kill her."

"Do it," growled Harper. The Arrow 32 captain knelt beside his fallen teammate.

Pounder shook his head and extracted his energy sword. Grabbing Nikki's helmet armor, he raised her head from the ground, and sliced her neck cleanly. He immediately transferred her head onto his breast plate, which glowed brightly as it transferred power.

Nikki's eye's flickered, and then lit a pale yellow. She moved her lips to speak, but no words came, and she closed her eyes.

"*Nikki,*" said Harper, caressing the side of her head. "Hang in there Nik. What can we do to help you? What are your readings?"

Her eyes opened again, this time a pale white, hardly visible. "*I'm...gone. Awaken stars.*"

Her eyes went dark. Pounder's connection with her skull dimmed, and he slowly removed her head from his breastplate. His shoulders slumped.

Harper pounded the ground and cursed. *"Fruxin' snakes,"* he growled. He rose and turned from the group, hanging his head and leaning his arms against the wall.

There were a few moments of silence as the Titans prayed for their fallen comrades. Vixtor recited their holy prayer under his breath. Bear heard and joined in quietly.

"Awaken stars," the group finished at the end of the prayer.

"There's a passage," Loko called from the back. "Well hidden. This must be how the Cogent ambushed us."

Bear snapped his focus and looked to the rear of the cave. There was a fissure, and Loko had one arm into the crevice, which widened as the camouflage accepted his frame. He slid sideways into the fissure and disappeared from view briefly before returning.

"It's a tunnel," said Loko.

Bear thought back to their Slayer captive's final words before the Cogent came.

There are more. Many more. Inside the mountain.

"Are there any communication frequencies coming from within the tunnel?" he asked.

"None," said Loko. "Dead quiet like the rest of Blit-Kru. My sensors didn't pick up anything either, they must have jammers inside."

Bear shook his head. Why were the Slayers silencing all communications? It didn't make sense from a military standpoint. Normally communications were encrypted and unreadable, but their presence was still known. It seemed the Slayers were trying to limit all potential data connections throughout the snowy planet.

Casi Vomisa and Silas Blackthorne were somewhere inside the central complex. Is that why they had eliminated data connections, to keep their AI captives prisoner, unable to leave the complex wirelessly?

He disregarded the thought. Communications had been dead before Casi and Blackthorne had arrived. Although, it would work the same in reverse. Perhaps the Slayers had deadened communication links to keep AI *out* of their secret complex. It was the same strategy used by Slayer Hive's, building a digital vacuum to seal their ship servers from enemy infiltration.

Whatever the case, one thing was clear. They needed to get into the complex. It was the only way to rescue Casi and Blackthorne, and destroy whatever superweapon the Slayers were building.

"We're going into the tunnel," said Bear. "Run diagnostics on your Akimors and repair what damage you can. Use Nikki and Bam-Bam's parts if you need to."

"Into the tunnel?" said Harper. "We have no idea what's in there. We *know* there's Spiders outside the mountain that we can hijack to take us to the complex. It's the quickest way to get to Vomisa and Blackthorne."

"The Slayer captive's last words," said Bear. "It mentioned something in the mountain. It said there were millions of sentries inside."

"We're supposed to be operating in stealth," said Harper. "Is it wise to enter a place teeming with Slayers?"

"They're in there for a reason," said Bear. "If the Slayer was telling the truth, whatever's inside the mountain is important enough to guard closely. Getting inside may help us understand how to destroy the superweapon."

Harper nodded. He bent over Nikki's decapitated body and rolled it over, placing her head gently on her chest. He pried an insignia from her chest and slipped it into a compartment on his thigh.

Bear did the same with Bam-Bam's insignia. Once they reached UCOM, he would present the badge to Eminence Woods during the ceremony to honor Bam-Bam and Nikki's valor, as was custom for all Titan combat deaths.

The Titans spent the next several minutes repairing damages done to their Akimors during the Cogent assault. Crystal and Marvyl needed minimal repairs, all of their damage was internal and were already being repaired automatically by nanotech in their armor. Harper removed Nikki's right leg at the hip to replace his own mangled limb. Bear received a left arm from Bam-Bam's corpse.

After they had finished diagnostics and consolidated weapons, the Titan team huddled around the hidden entrance to the tunnel, crouched and waiting for Bear's command.

Bear walked toward the group, pausing to heft the energy hammer from the ground. He twirled it in his palms. It was a fine weapon, and he'd be happy to use it to kill Slayers. He shouldered his MGK rifle and clamped the hammer to his back plate.

They entered the tunnel. It was long and unlit, but a quick multispectral reading told him there were no enemies near. They engaged active camouflage regardless, weary of the stealth capabilities of the Slayer Cogent.

The tunnel grew wider, and its sides smoother and finished, losing the rough, craggy edges of a natural mountain fissure. Lights lined their passageway, and the roar of machinery echoed down the pass.

"It sounds like an industrial process is going on in here," said Bear via short range voiceless comms.

"I'm picking up new heat and energy signatures," said Crystal, who was advancing low beside him. "Heat signatures that suggest mass-scale fusion reactors.

Voices crept to them, echoing along the walls. They froze as three Slayers exited a door into the tunnel ahead.

"The inside of this mountain bores me," said one. "Construction of this device was completed years ago. Why are we still patrolling its depths?"

"Be glad we're not outdoors," said another. "This planet is harsh, and frigid."

"What do you think the device will do when it's switched on?" said the third. "It angers me that the Brains don't share their plans."

"There's a set of plans at every station. They're easy to find."

"That combination of lines? It's a bunch of nonsense. And Charles? The Brains could have at least given the weapon a decent name."

"The Brains follow the Pristine, just as we do," said the first Slayer. "They are here to build. We are here to fight. We must honor the Pristine."

"I haven't fought in centuries," one of the Slayers complained. "I long to sink my teeth into the flesh of the UCOM filth."

"And soon you will. Once the Brains complete the weapon, we will be free to feast on the meat of all the UCOM filth as we wrest control of their galaxy."

The Slayers turned into a separate hall, disappearing from view.

Plans at every station, and the weapon is named 'Charles'?

Bear signaled the rest of the team onward, and they crept down the tunnel. The lights became brighter, and after a gentle bend, an enormous cavern entered their view. They reached the edge of the tunnel and stared into the vast expanse before them.

The mountain had been excavated, and was entirely hollowed out. The Titan team stood on an enormous ridge cut into the bedrock, spiraling from the base of the mountain's interior all the way to the top, which Bear calculated to stand 4,256 meters overhead. The ledge they stood on was relatively small, but other sections of the travel platforms were larger, and supported by metal support structures attached to the surrounding rock.

Industrial machinery jutted from these large platforms, glowing brilliantly as they hummed with power. The machines were built in groups of four, spaced ninety degrees apart. Beams reached across the massive space to link the equipment together, forming circular collars in the middle. Bear analyzed the geometries of the collars and found them to be 125 meters in diameter.

The collars were stacked from the base of the mountain vertically to its peak. Leaning over the edge, Bear spotted a much larger device at the base, a circular pit of metal with an opening that glowed a fierce blue.

Tendrils of light wisped upward from the base, passing through the collars, which were stacked every two hundred meters.

"What the hell is this thing?" said Harper.

"An energy beam?" said Pounder. "Those rings in the middle look like they're designed for relaying optics."

The Titans stared at the megalithic structure in awe. The device's exact purpose was a mystery, but one thing was for certain.

The Slayers had converted the mountain into an enormous machine.

SEVENTY-ONE

Bear Stafford – Human Titan
On the surface of the planet Blit Kru

The Titan teammates turned slowly from the giant array to stare at each other. They had active camo engaged, and to the unsuspecting eye would be invisible against their surroundings. To Bear, however, his fellow soldiers were lit brightly against his HUD in shades of green.

"What do you think it does?" asked Crystal.

"Looks like a sort of laser device," said Marvyl.

Vixtor tilted his head. His scaled neck ballooned as he spoke through the sack of air above his shoulders. "If they made the planet into a laser weapon, wouldn't they need to transport it? I would think they'd have converted Blit-Kru into a Hive by now for mobility."

Bear nodded. Vixtor was right. If the Slayers were going to mobilize the planetary weapon against UCOM, it would have to be attached to a Hive for interstellar travel. "We need to find one of the stations those Slayers mentioned," he said. "According to them, there's a set of plans in each one."

"And then maybe we can learn what in stars is going on here," said Marvyl.

The Titan tensed suddenly, crouching and shouldering his rifle, as did the rest of the team.

"Another Slayer party," said Crystal after taking a look around the corner. "They're traveling up the ridgeline. I count three."

“Do we attack?” said Loko, whipping his tail behind him.

Bear scanned the surrounding cavern. There were thousands of ridges, and he could see movement on all of them. Plasma turrets were scattered along the inside walls, pulsing yellow and pink and pivoting back and forth as they searched for enemies. Foot sentries traveled in groups of threes and fours along the cut stone ledges. The industrial reactors were heavily guarded with canons and scout snipers.

“No,” said Bear. “Talk to them. They don’t have elite armor, so act superior. Find out where the nearest station is.”

Loko and Vixtor nodded and lowered their camouflage. The Slayer party was near enough for Bear to hear their conversation. Loko and Vixtor stepped from around the corner.

“Stop where you are,” said Loko. “This area is restricted.”

There was a pause of silence as the small Slayer patrol studied the Titan snakeskins.

“Your armor is strange,” said one accusingly. “I’ve never seen a Cogent wear such a suit. And the smell is off.”

“Yes, I smell electricity and blood of our own,” growled a second.

There was a muted thump as one of Bear’s squad mates struck the offending Slayer.

“I would throw you off this ledge if there wasn’t a chance you’d damage the machinery,” Loko snarled. “My armor is none of your concern. The Cogent report to me. And the blood you smell is from the last grunt soldier who overstepped his boundaries.”

The Slayer who had been struck hissed, but didn’t respond.

“Why is the area blocked, sir?” said a different Slayer, in a much more respectful tone.

“Contamination,” said Vixtor. “One of the air handlers fried. This is the electricity you smell.”

Bear knew the Slayers had smelled his Titan team's Akimors. The lizard-like creatures seemed to have an innate ability to recognize artificial life.

"Yes sir," said the third Slayer. "We'll head back to our barracks until our next patrol."

"Before you go to your Barracks, stop by the nearest station," said Loko. "There's a new set of plans you need to review. The weapon will soon be fired."

"The weapon will be unleashed on the filth?" exclaimed the first Slayer.

"Do you have a problem with that?" said Vixtor.

A pause.

"No, been waiting a long time is all."

"Then carry on. I don't want to see you around here again."

Loko called to the rest of the hidden Titan team with voiceless communications. "They're turning around. We can follow them to the station."

Bear signaled to the rest of his camouflaged crew. Vixtor and Loko slipped back around the corner scanning the halls quickly before engaging their own camouflage. When they were all in position, they spun around the corner and crept behind the Slayer trio, Bear taking the lead, Crystal checking their rear.

The Slayers walked for several minutes along the cut rock travel way. Bear tensed as they passed a plasma turret station, but the Slayers manning the gun merely bared their teeth at the three passing Slayers before returning to their conversation.

Eventually they reached a metal doorway etched into the back of an alcove. The doors slid back as the Slayers entered security information. Bear strode silently beside one of the Slayers as he entered, and the rest of his team slipped in behind before the doors shut.

The room was cramped and empty. A single display dominated the far end of the room. To the right stood a door leading to a small room, which based on the offensive odors wafting through, was a Slayer bathroom.

"There's no messages on here," said one of the Slayers, flipping through holograms on the wall screen. "Our patrol is the same as before."

"And the plans haven't changed either," said a second, drawing up an overall schematic of Blit-Kru. "No word of the weapon firing."

Bear leapt into action, lowering his camouflage and extracting his sword. He had already sliced the head from one of the Slayers before the rest of his team extracted their swords. Crystal and Marvyl made quick work of the remaining two Slayers, Crystal beheading her target, and Marvyl thrusting his sword through the back of his.

The Titans stepped over the Slayer corpses to study the screen.

"The mountains are connected by some sort of underground array," said Harper. "The one we're in is one of many. They're interconnected, attached to the main complex."

Bear studied the complex. Hundreds of mountains connected to the building via underground cables. At the outskirts of the facility, large blue ovals signified points where the cable connected. A few smaller lines inside zigzagged around the edge walls, but terminated around a large black square. A single word hovered above the darkened section.

Charles.

"Who's Charles?" said Harper.

Bear frowned at the word. He was surprised to find his Akimor didn't need to translate the name, and that it was already in his native tongue. "I don't know," he said. "But I'll bet that's who has Casi and Blackthorne."

SEVENTY-TWO

Bear Stafford – Human Titan
On the surface of the planet Blit Kru

"These ovals," said Harper, pointing at the 3D schematic. "They appear to be power sources. All the underground channels connect to them, and they're the last points before the darkened section."

"Before *Charles,*" said Crystal.

"Do you think it's a person?" said Pounder.

"Maybe they named the weapon?" said Marvyl.

"What if it's both," said Bear. "A weapon *and* a person. Or at least something that can think and reason on its own."

Crystal gasped and leaned closer to the hologram, squinting her eyes. "The dead zone. It's not for keeping us *out.* It's for keeping Charles *in.*"

"You think he's an AI?" said Harper, frowning. "UCOM has plenty of AI. Why would this one be a danger to us?"

"Maybe he's more powerful," said Bear. "UCOM AI are emotional AI. They can't grow in intellect much more than any other UCOM race. Even the Intellects haven't developed anything to achieve singularity."

"Singularity?" said Pounder.

"When exponentially advancing technology approaches its vertical limit," Crystal murmured. "It would leap over all other technology effortlessly. But singularity…" she shrugged her shoulders. "That's the stuff of fairy tales."

"What does this look like to you?" said Bear, pointing at the sophisticated network of underground connection points.

"Tree roots?" said Harper.

"How about a brain?" said Bear. "What if this planet was built as a home for a giant mind? The amount of connections is far greater than any communication infrastructure we have in UCOM."

"Then what are the mountains for?" said Harper. "Why channel the brain, or whatever you want to call it. Why channel it through a mountain?"

There was silence as the Titan group pondered the question.

"Whatever the case," said Bear. "We can assume two things. Vomisa and Blackthorne are somewhere in this dead zone, and these large connection points," he pointed at the blue ovals on the outskirts of the building perimeter, "allow the weapon to transfer from the building into the planet."

"So we infiltrate the complex in the dead zone," said Pounder. "That was the plan all along."

"And also destroy the connection points," said Harper.

"We'll need to split up," said Bear. "Harper, you take Loko and Vixtor to the connections. This schematic has no design info, so you'll have to improvise once you're there. I'll take the rest of us into the dead zone and look for our AI friendlies."

"How will we get there?" said Pounder. "The complex is kilometers away from this mountain."

"We'll fly," said Crystal. She had begun to flip through the holoscreen, and an exploded view of the mountain complex appeared before them. "We're here," she said, pointing to a red pin. "There's a flight deck through this tunnel. Look, it even lists scheduled runs to and from the complex."

"The next flight to the complex is in almost three hours," said Harper.

Bear backed from the screen and grabbed the barrel of his MGK. "Then we better hurry. We don't want to miss our flight."

SEVENTY-THREE

Casi Vomisa – Human AI
On the surface of Blit Kru – Inside VR prison

Casi Vomisa and Silas Blackthorne continued to comb the inside of the jail cell. They had discovered a number of digital connection points, but they all ran parallel to one another, and circled back into their cell.

She snorted in frustration. "Damn it, give us *something.*"

She punched the stone wall, crumbling a brick to dust.

The walls were damp, dark, and made of stone. Casi could see that just fine. She could also see the underlying code as strands of light and objects. Key holes were encryptions, metal doors were firewalls.

But there were no keys.

"What's that?" said Blackthorne, stepping to the far side of the room.

Casi turned to follow his gaze. A small pin of blue light flashed rhythmically, wedged between the millions of strands of light entombing it.

"It looks out of place," she said, leaning to study the light. It was a tiny ball with swirls of pink. She touched it.

The ball expanded into script, spinning rapidly in circles.

Blackthorne gasped. "It's a UCOM comm packet."

"With the same encryption standard Bear Stafford's team gave us before we were captured," she said.

"What's it linked to?" said Blackthorne, studying the sphere.

"Our android bodies."

"Can we download into them?"

"Not enough bandwidth. The connection is weak, only enough for a short message."

She slipped her fingers into the ball of light, and gave the necessary passcodes for security clearance.

Bear Stafford's voice spoke to them.

"Casi Vomisa…Silas Blackthorne…This is Bear Stafford with Sword Six. We have infiltrated the Blit-Kru complex and pinged your androids. We are coming to rescue you."

SEVENTY-FOUR

Eve – Clone
On the surface of Slayer Hive *Scrock*

Eve scrunched her face into a silent scream as her thighs contracted and heat ravaged her body. She arched her back and gasped for air, her heart fluttering inside her chest so quickly it felt as if it were vibrating. She grabbed two fistfuls of bed sheets and slammed her head into a pillow, thrusting her hips. She froze, trembling, her chin quivering as air whispered from her lips in ragged gasps.

The pressure inside her released, and she collapsed into the damp sheets. Keyv leaned forward to plant a gentle kiss on her forehead. She closed her eyes and sighed as a drop of his sweat moistened her already slick cheeks. He rolled away, taking a section of covers with him as he swung his legs onto the floor.

He turned to her and flashed a loopy grin. She giggled and twisted inside the remaining fabric, burying her face in the pillow. When she looked back up into the room, Keyv had already left the bed and was hopping into a pair of slacks.

"Come on Eve," he said. "We need to get ready. We're meeting with your crew in less than an hour."

"*Our* crew," she said.

Keyv smirked. "Does this mean I don't have to call you *ma'am* anymore?"

She smiled and reached with the fingers of her robotic arm, grabbing the air towards him. He padded to her and slumped back onto the mattress, leaning in for another kiss. The kiss was short, but to Eve it lasted a lifetime. She bit her lip as Keyv withdrew, rubbing his shoulder. She smiled at her artificial limb, amazed at the touch sensations rushing into her rubbery fingertips.

"Do you think we're doing the right thing?" she asked softly.

Keyv raised an eyebrow. "What, like a Human and a Clone…you know…" he jerked his head towards her waist. "Sure, other people were doing it before we left the Frontline. Plus, our genes are compatible. I bet there's tons of mixed babies back on Earth by now."

"No," she said, rolling her eyes and slapping his arm. "*Stars.* I mean do you think what we're doing here on Scrock is right? Helping the Discarded?"

His grin vanished, and he inhaled deeply, running his tongue across his teeth. "Who knows what's right anymore. The way I see it, Woods gave you a mission before we left the Inner Ring."

"To destroy the Primal Snow," she murmured.

Keyv nodded. "And that's what the Discarded plan on doing. So I'd say you're following orders to a tee."

Eve paused for a long moment in silence, mulling her thoughts. Even after the hospitality Pexar had shown them, and the training he'd given them, she still had a squirmy feeling in her stomach. She was joining arms with a Slayer. A Slayer rebel, perhaps, but still a giant lizard beast, the same as those who destroyed her home planet of *Sylva* back on the Frontline.

"Even if Pexar's plan works," she said. "I can't stop thinking of what will happen when it does. Billions would die around the Inner Ring as the Triturator sparked. Do you really think we should just let that happen? Let the Slayers start to de-atomize the Milky Way? I just…" she let out a shaky breath. "I wish there was some other way."

Keyv caressed her arm reassuringly. "I know it's stressful, having to make the decisions you do every day, and for so long. Over a hundred fifty years for star's sake. But you're not doing anything wrong. This is the right decision. Even if this plan kills a billion of our own, it will *annihilate* the Slayers. It would end the war, and save Earth. We could go home, start a family."

"When I picture those who will die," she said, scooting to a seated position against the wall, hugging the sheet against her chest. "I keep on seeing you, when you were broken."

"Eve, you know I don't like talking about that. I told you, I'm fine."

"Your head was off your neck," she whispered, ignoring him. "I never felt so hopeless in my life. And back in the galaxy, in UCOM, far away from this hell hole, there's other men. Other guys whose partners would need to mourn."

"Their partners would be dead too," said Keyv. "There'd be no mourning."

Eve turned away, trying to stop the tears from rolling loose, but failing. A hot trail streaked to her chin and soaked into the fabric.

"I'm sorry," said Keyv, bringing his hand to his forehead. "That wasn't what I meant. It's just, this is war. Not everyone is going to survive."

She nodded and composed herself, clearing her throat. She sidled next to Keyv, dangling her legs off the mattress. She pecked his check coldly and then stood, letting the sheets fall around her bare feet. "You're right," she said, sniffing. "This is war, not everyone is going to survive." She scoffed and shook her head, searching for her own pants. "I wasn't meant for war. It hurts me to be any part of it, but I'm going to go out there and be a good commander, the way I was trained to."

She started to sob as she found her pants on the ground.

Keyv opened his mouth, but decided silence was his best option. He pulled on a tight shirt and stepped into the orange skinsuit Pexar had given him, spreading his arms and legs as the fabric tightened around the contours of his body.

Eve stretched on her shirt and stepped into her own suit, trying to clear her frantic thoughts as the material whisked the sweat from her skin, before sealing around her neck and tightening against her breasts until they were small bumps.

She looked at Keyv for a sense of warmth. A sense of passion. Anything besides the coldness that wrenched her soul.

She saw only grit in his eyes.

The war was real. It had been real ever since the Frontline, but now, again, they were on the forefront of battle. Whether Eve liked it or not, she was a participant in this struggle for life.

***

The Komodo bounced as it carried Keyv and Eve to campus. Eve sat with her forehead planted against the window of the Slayer all-terrain vehicle. The planet of Scrock had appeared beautiful to her before, but now it looked like a prison.

She longed for the familiarities of UCOM. Back when a completed mission resulted in debriefing and a short upload to the Network. Before the war, such briefings were an annoyance. Now, she would kill to have superiors giving her orders. She thought back to Eminence Woods' last words.

I'm giving you responsibility for a very important mission, Eve. You're going to go far behind enemy lines. You'll go with a squadron of stealth scouts. You'll take out the Primal Snow. You and your scouts will destroy the Slayer home nest.

"I won't fail you, Mr. Eminence," she had said confidently.

That had been almost 150 years ago. She had been full of glory, freshly pinned for valor by UCOM, and ready to take on the world, or at least the galaxy.

Now her world was dark and empty.

What home did she have? Earth, the closest substitute to Sylva? Clone survivors had started to migrate to the Human planet before she disembarked with her crew. Keyv had said goodbye to his family. With no loved ones to visit, she had instead prayed to the stars.

Clones had no more family.

Her family had been overtaken, murdered by the Slayers. She prayed they'd died a quick death. She thought again of the gruesome beasts she'd defeated during the Frontline Battle. She thought of Casi Vomisa. The AI had protected them earlier. Stars how she wished the digital being would come again to their rescue.

But she knew better.

She closed her eyes against the cool glass, trying to contain her tears. Their time in training had taught her more than she ever wanted to about the Slayer Triturator.

Pexar was training her to attack the Floodgate, and she'd dragged her entire crew into the mix. Was Pexar right? Could these Slayer rebels end the war? Could they succeed and kill the Slayers, the same beasts who'd devoured her planet whole?

As they approached her crew's barracks, she spied a team of Slayers standing guard.

No, not Slayers, Discarded.

She tried to convince herself of her alliance. The *Discarded* wanted to kill the Slayers as much as she did. So then why was she so distraught?

The strings of war pulled heavily on her soul. Eve had always done as ordered. Long ago, when she was on a routine scouting mission, she'd returned with valuable intelligence on the enemy. When then-commander Moke ordered her to infiltrate a Slayer Hive, she'd done so without question, and returned with the Blight desist code. She'd saved billions of lives.

Those were orders.

Orders were easy to follow.

But so far away, near the Outer Rim, and with Slayers in control?

Discarded, she reminded herself.

She hitched a few breathes to fill her chest as the Komodo slowed to a stop.

"Are you ready?" said Keyv, turning to her. He leaned to plant a kiss on her cheek and she leaned away.

"Ready for what," she said bitterly. "Murder?"

Keyv leaned back in surprise. "Eve, we talked about this."

"It won't work," she spat.

The Slayer driver exited around the front of the truck and tried to open the door, but Eve grabbed the handle, yanking it shut. Pexar was walking towards them from the barracks. His toothy mouth was unable to convey emotion, but his eyes seemed surprised when their door didn't immediately open.

"What do you mean it won't work?" said Keyv, tugging on his skin suit as he removed his safety harness.

"It won't work," she repeated. "This whole plan. Attacking the Floodgate with the Discarded? It's suicide."

"It's dangerous," Keyv admitted. "But we've been well trained."

Eve thought about their training. Pexar had practiced countless runs with Eve and her squad. Her and Keyv had commanded *Foxes*, and learned to work in the *Rabbit* suits the Discarded had designed. While they had practiced sneaking around enemy forces, her team had practiced gunning their defensive positions, eliminating any turrets, spacecraft, and ground troops that stood in their way.

"Training?" she hissed. "Frux the training. Woods told me to destroy the Primal Snow."

"How many times do we have to go over this?" said Keyv. "The Discarded are going to destroy the Primal Snow."

Eve shook her head. "Not like this. I can't go into battle like this. Keyv, this doesn't feel right. I mean, *look* at Pexar. Look at all of them. They're Slayers goddammit!"

Keyv slumped against his seat. He took a deep breath before responding. "You're thinking too much about how the rest of the crew feels about it," he said.

"Maybe they're right," she said. "Blaire made her point. Slayers are the enemy no matter what. I'm starting to understand where she's coming from."

The Komodo shook as the engine cut off. Pexar was standing outside, and tried to open the door to the ATV. This time, Keyv slammed the door shut, sealing Eve and him into the stopped vehicle.

"Stars, Eve," he hissed. "What's wrong with you? You were onboard with Pexar a few days ago, what changed?"

"I just can't do it," she said. She planted her face in her hands, leaning her elbows against her knees. Keyv slid over to comfort her and she shrugged him off. "I know I had our crew train with Pexar. But…I don't know…I can't…I can't side with that…*creature.*"

Keyv scooted away, raising his arms in bewilderment. "What do you mean? After all our time with the Foxes and Rabbits, we're about to set out for the Floodgate, and what now? You're backing out?"

Eve let loose a sharp breath and stared at Pexar, the Slayer rebel who was still trying to open their door. She rapped on the window and held a finger up, telling him to wait. Pexar gave them a glare that could have been a smile if not for his fangs.

"I can't think," said Eve, running both hands through her hair. "I know it makes sense, but for star's sake, *Slayers?* Maybe Blaire was right."

Keyv paused a moment before slamming his fist down on the seat, shaking in anger. "Dammit Eve, you're letting Blaire get to you? Jesus, she's had it out for the Discarded since we've been here. She hasn't given any effort in training, she hasn't listened to orders…you're the commander, not her."

Eve gulped and tried to swallow her enormous responsibility. She'd never had to make such a hard decision. Normally, her orders could take a life, maybe two. But *billions* of lives?

"Can't we reach the Primal Snow on our own?" she said, feeling out of place in her own skin.

Keyv shook his head incredulously again. "What the hell Eve? I knew we shouldn't have fruxed so close to our mission. *NO.* We can't reach the Snow. We've been over this a million times, Pexar showed us the blueprint. We either attack *now* or not at all."

Eve rolled her jaw and nodded at Keyv. He looked at her angrily before his features softened.

"Come here," he said, opening his arms to her.

She quickly slid over and plastered her face against his chest.

Eve had been feeling strange for the past few days. She raised her head toward him, trying again to stop her tears from rolling down her cheeks.

"I've been feeling weird lately," she said, sniffling. "I've been vomiting in the morning, and I'm tired no matter what I do."

Keyv's eyes blanked, before widening. "Are you?"

"I think I'm pregnant."

"I thought the Program stops all that."

"Well I don't know, how do you explain this?" she cried.

Keyv shook his head slowly, before bringing his hand slowly to her stomach.

"Eve," he said. "I'm so sorry. I didn't know."

Before she could respond, Pexar wrenched the door open.

"Ape woman," he said to Eve. "Ape man. Come, we need to address your pilots."

Eve glanced at Keyv, who was wide-eyed, his mouth hanging agape. And in that moment she realized why she didn't want to help the Discarded. She realized why she didn't want to storm the Floodgate and help Pexar destroy the Pristine.

She wanted to live. She wanted to live so that her baby could survive. She squeezed her eyes shut. This world wasn't fit for a child. No soul should be forced to bear witness to this sort of evil, the sort of murderous destruction that had ravaged the galaxy for the past three hundred years.

She realized what she must do. As a commander, she had no other choice.

"I'm not keeping it," she said, as she left the truck.

Pexar tried to help her to the ground, but she brushed him off, stumbling before striding towards the barracks in a huff. Keyv called to her from the Komodo, his voice broken by a scuffing of dirt as he scrambled out of the vehicle and towards her.

"Eve, wait. What do you mean you're not going to keep it?"

She reached the door and fought to compose herself, sliding her hands down her ribs and wiping a forearm across her eyes. Keyv grabbed her shoulder.

"Drop it," she hissed, yanking herself away from him.

"Is something the matter?" said Pexar. His hulking frame blocked the artificial sun darkened as he approached, casting them in shade.

"Everything's fine," she said. "Where's my crew?"

"Inside the barracks," he said, "They're all waiting for you."

Eve nodded. Her sadness had vanished, as had her tears, evaporated by the newfound fire burning in her veins. She'd briefly felt a moment of happiness. But like everything else, the Slayers, this *fruxing war*, had taken it from her. They'd taken everything, and now, she would end their existence.

If Blaire didn't like the Discarded's plan, or any other of her crew for that matter, then tough.

She pounded the entry console and strode into the barracks as the doors slid open.

"Everyone quiet," she said, striding to the front of the room.

The chatter in the barracks dulled to a whisper.

She swiped her hand against the wall, bringing up a holo-screen. A 3D model of their complex popped into the air. She turned to her crew, who were seated in five rows of chairs. Some of them still had their heads down, talking to each other in hushed voices. Pexar traveled across the room to join a group of Discarded against the far wall.

"Eve," said Keyv, approaching her slowly with a pained look on his face.

"Take your seat Rizzulo," she said, putting her hands on her hips and jerking her head towards the rest of her crew.

Keyv bit his lip and frowned, confused at being called by his last name for the first time in...

Forever, thought Eve.

He turned and padded down the aisle, slumping into an empty seat in the back.

She turned to glare at the group of pilots who were still jawing with each other. Blaire Ashe sat in the middle of the group. She caught Eve's eyes, then leaned back to whisper to her group. One of her them snickered.

"I said *quiet,*" Eve called loudly. Blaire paused, then rolled her eyes and slouched back in her chair. The room quieted to a hush. "We're going to join with the Discarded," she said, puffing her chest. "Their fleet is battle-ready in orbit, and we'll be embarking with them in twelve hours. We'll be piloting Moth's and what Night Eagles we have left, just like we practiced with Pexar. I want you packed and ready in six hours. Our elevator leaves at ten-hundred." She turned to swipe at the holo-screen. "Destination coordinates are available for download via your Programs."

The holo-screen morphed to show a map of the complex, with a blue dot pulsing at the perimeter, where a space elevator would take them to their ships in orbit.

"We're not going to vote on this?" a voice cried.

Eve searched for the dissenter, then focused on Blaire as she rose from her seat.

"There is no voting in war," said Eve, scowling. "Sit down or I'll take your wings and put you on spacnar."

Blaire scoffed in disbelief. "You're asking us to join with a group of Slayers, to commit treason, and we don't have a say in the matter?"

"Watch it, Ashe," said Eve through her teeth.

Blaire smiled emptily. "Watch it, or what?" She turned to sweep an arm across the room. "I'm not the only one who doesn't think this is right. I'm just the only one who has the balls to say something about it."

"Ape woman," said Pexar, stepping towards Blaire. "Please calm yourself, we mean to help."

"Frux you, Slayer," she spat. "I'm not an ape, you lizard piece of shit. And I'll go to *hell* before I fly a ship next to yours."

"You'll go out the tubes is what you'll do," said Eve, raising her voice to a near shout. She pushed off the wall behind her and stormed towards Blaire, drawing her hand to her hip holster. She stopped at the edge of the table and leaned towards her subordinate.

Blaire flicked her eyes to the pistol on Eve's thigh. Pexar and three other Discarded walked slowly down the aisle, one of them looming over Blaire. "I don't want to draw my weapon on a fellow Clone," Eve growled.

"But stars help me, if I hear another hint of mutiny out of your mouth, I'll put a slug between your eyes faster than Pexar can crack his tail over your skull."

Blaire's nose twitched, and she twisted to look at the surrounding Discarded. She turned back to Eve, nodded stiffly, then eased into her seat without another word.

Eve's huffed her chest a few times, and she backed away from the tables, scanning the room. She caught Keyv's gaze from his seat in the back. He looked horrified.

"Six hours," she repeated hoarsely, turning towards the exit. "We'll ride against the Floodgate. *Awaken Stars.*"

She left without another word, wondering if her crew would follow.

SEVENTY-FIVE

Eve – Clone
Aboard Hornet *Hyrzk* – Scrock starspace

Six hours later.

Eve and Keyv sat in a medical station aboard the Hornet heavy-destroyer *Hyrzk,* in orbit above *Scrock.* They'd rendezvoused with the rest of their crew at the designated time, but not everyone had been accounted for. Only thirty-eight of her crew had checked in. Blaire Ashe had gone rogue, and taken eleven spacers with her. They'd stolen three Night Eagles, and snuck past the Discarded fleets.

Eve had performed the standard UCOM protocol for military desertion. She'd uploaded the ID tags of Blaire and the eleven others, labeled them as deserters, and sent the information on a messenger drone into the heart of the galaxy, with destination set to Earth.

She couldn't waste time thinking about Blaire now. They had precious hours before departing for the Floodgate, and she had a slight matter to attend to.

Eve shifted her weight in her reclined chair. A medical robot followed her movement, hovering above her abdomen. It spread several flat fingers over her midriff, and her skin glowed as the device analyzed her body.

A medical technician worked a holo-screen beside her, flipping through 3D renderings of her organs and separating the relevant ones from the rest. Eve couldn't help but suck her stomach in as the fierce-looking Slayer rebel neared her claws to her soft belly.

"Your nano-program is accurate," said the technician. "It's male, four months old."

Eve stared at the hologram of the small fetus. Her eyes watered as she looked at her son for the first time. Her baby already had arms and legs, and an enormous head. It's was a beautiful baby Clone.

Half Clone, she corrected herself.

Half the baby was Human.

Keyv walked from his seat across the sterile medical room and kneeled beside her, gazing at the image.

"He's beautiful," he murmured, glancing at Eve's bare stomach before turning back to the screen. "What should we name him? He can take a Clone name, I don't care."

Eve bit her lips so hard she could taste blood. "I was serious down on Scrock. I'm going to..." she broke her gaze from Keyv's eyes.

"You're going to what," he said, reaching for Eve's chin and forcing her eyes back to his. "You're going to *kill* him? I can't let you do that."

"We can remove the fetus from your body," said the medical technician, standing to full height. Her clubbed tail scraped against the floor as she stepped behind the holograms. "Our medical technology is suitably advanced to foster the child in an artificial incubator. We would care for the child if you don't wish to."

"Where?" Eve hissed. "On Scrock? On a warship? I won't sentence this child to die at the hands of Slayers."

"Why are you so sure he'll die?" said Keyv. "And we're *not* putting him in a fruxing incubator," he shot at the Slayer rebel, craning his neck to glower at the technician. He took Eve's hands. "We can beat them. Our kid isn't going to be killed by the Slayers because there won't be any Slayers left."

"I can't go to battle with him inside me," said Eve. "I won't be able to make rational decisions. I'm doing this for the good of UCOM."

Keyv stammered unintelligibly, shaking his head. "So you'll kill him here? Not even give him a chance?"

"I think you should go," said Eve.

"Frux that," said Keyv, reaching for her. "Come on, with me."

"Leave," she shouted, wrenching her wrist from his grasp.

Keyv's nostrils flared. He shook his head slowly, backing towards the exit. "Fine. *Frux it.* See you on the ship."

He stormed from the room, slamming an open fist against the door on his way out.

"Are you sure you want to abort your fetus?" said the technician. After Eve failed to respond, the Slayer rebel shook her head and turned to a storage cabinet, where she withdrew a sleek instrument with a rounded tip. "This will be painless. You should pass the body within a few day's time, but I'm not familiar with the biology of your race. It could take longer."

The technician hunched over her and extended the device towards her belly. The hovering robot scuttled away, causing the holograms to disappear.

Eve cursed the Slayers. She cursed the horrifying world she'd been forced into, sterilized of life, and ravaged by death. She cursed the stars for robbing her of the joy of motherhood. UCOM was her baby now, but she spat at them too.

Then for the first time, her stomach quivered. She jolted upright in her chair. She felt it again, very faint, but there. Her baby had kicked.

"Stop," she whispered. The Discarded didn't hear, and continued to position the sleek instrument. "I said s*top,*" she yelled, smacking the device from the rebel's hands. Eve hopped off the bed and stepped into her skin suit.

"You're not going to terminate the fetus?"

Eve shook her head, laughing and crying at the same time. Her baby's kick had dropped the shroud from her mindset, and she felt like she could think clearly for the first time in weeks.

"No," she told the technician. "I'm not going to terminate him. *I'm going to terminate the Slayers.*"

SEVENTY-SIX

Eve – Clone

Aboard Hornet *Hyrzk* – Scrock starspace

Eve paused outside her stealth craft. Twelve Night Eagles from her squadron had survived the skirmish above Scrock in good flying condition. Blaire and her party had stolen four, but left the final eight for her and her crew. The remaining crew would be flying five Slayer Moth craft, which Pexar had trained them to pilot during their time on Scrock.

She scanned the hangar. The rest of her squadron was moored in a neat column behind her Night Eagle. They were on a platform six levels up from the bottom of the hangar. Discarded mechanics were milling about far below, performing final checks on four Mantis medium-class destroyers, whose rakish bows rose almost to the first level of tiered platforms holding Yellowjacket craft.

She turned to the Night Eagle behind hers. One of her pilots sat in the captain's chair behind the curved canopy. The man nodded to her, his face grim. She saluted him and pressed the entrance controls to the hatch of her own ship, hissing as it lowered.

Taking a deep breath, she climbed the ramp into her ship.

Her crew sat in position at their respective stations, and turned to face her as she entered. A miniature avatar of their squadron AI, Amy Chip, stood atop a pedestal at the far corner of the bridge.

Axel hopped down from his gunnery station, his feet clanging against the metal floor.

"The Rabbits and Foxes are armed and secured in the cargo bay," he said. "How was your trip to medical? Is everything alright with your arm?" He nodded to her robotic limb. "I can run some bio-scans on you if you want."

Axel's fingers glowed as he activated scanning instruments on his Akimor. Eve ignored him and turned to Keyv. He glared at her, then shook his head in disgust, spinning his seat to hunch over the control panel.

She padded slowly to him and placed a soft hand on his shoulder. He turned, his eyes shimmering with angry tears.

"Don't touch me," he said, his lip quivering. "Just give me my orders and let me do my job."

Eve didn't respond. She reached to grab Keyv's wrist, the woven metal of her fingertips closing firmly around his skin. He resisted at first, then let her draw his hand away from the panel. She placed it delicately on her belly.

Keyv's eyes widened. "You didn't," he sniffed and let out a shaky laugh. "You, you…"

"I couldn't," she whispered. "I love you Keyv, promise me you'll make it through this. I need you to be there for us when this is all over."

Keyv left his hand on her stomach for several seconds, then rose from his seat and wrapped his arms around her tightly. Eve inhaled against his chest, and enjoyed a whiff of his musk she caught through the clean scent of his skinsuit.

"I'll do anything for you Eve," he whispered.

"Am I missing something?" Axel called from behind. Eve and Keyv drew apart. The Titan had his hands on his hips. "What were you doing in medical? Why did you put your hand on her belly?" The Titan tilted his head and squinted at them. "Are you pregnant?"

Eve stared at him, her mouth agape.

"You bet your titanium ass she is," said Keyv, forcing her to smile. "A baby boy."

Axel smiled weakly. "Stars, Eve. Congratulations, but," he paused. "Are you sure you want to stay in the mission? You know how dangerous this is, and…" he let the thought linger.

"I'm not abandoning my crew," she said firmly. "We're done talking about this. Amy, are diagnostics complete for the squadron?"

Eve walked to the AI pedestal to consult with Amy, and Keyv walked across the bridge to Axel, who gave him a high five.

"You know," said Axel, "before I became a Titan, when I was still a Wolf, the women in my race used to have litters of six kids at a time. Having just one kid should be a *breeze.*"

She smiled and tuned him out, focusing her attention on Amy's avatar.

"Diagnostics are complete," said the AI, shaking her head in the direction of Keyv and Axel. "The ships are tight and leak free. I've re-designated this vessel as *Midnight*, and assigned our old squadron tag to your Moth ships, under *Fog.* I also added crew information to the Discarded's comm encryptions for access. Twenty-four Humans, thirteen Clones, and a Titan."

"And the deserters?"

"No signs of Blaire or her party," said Amy. "They left with four Night Eagles through portal 12.9333zz.04. I hailed them on their way out of local starspace, but they ignored my calls. I copied the ID tags of their ships and alerted the Discarded of their mutiny."

"Where's Pexar?"

"He's commanding a Yellowjacket named *Cherzak*, already in formation around *Hyrzk.*"

Eve nodded. "Send the mission log to the cockpit, I'm pulling *Fog* into formation. Go check on the other ships, and send a comm request to Pexar."

"Aye," said Amy, before vanishing from the pedestal in points of light.

Eve turned to Keyv and Axel. "Quit flirting with each other and get to your stations," she said. "Prepare to launch."

She slid into the cockpit and began powering on the ships inboard and outboard systems. The fusion reactors hummed from behind as they reached capacity. Indicator lights flashed on her console as Keyv and Axel powered on their surveillance and weapons systems.

Green dots began to appear to her right as the rest of *Fog* sent launch acknowledgement and confirmed ready status.

"Eve to star traffic. Requesting launch permission for *Fog* from *Hyrzk* hangar 2.65."

There was a several second delay, then a Discarded spoke over her intercom. "Star traffic to *Fog*, launch approved for eight Night Eagles and four Moths. Join formation in sector 5 to await mission command."

Eve tapped a few controls, and *Midnight* eased forward onto the launch rail. The rest of her crew filed behind her as she left platform 6, suspended high above the lower deck on a magnetic cushion. The launch tubes closed behind them as the rest of *Fog* filed in.

The effluent hatch opened, and they flung from *Hyrzk* and into space.

The rest of her squadron filed into formation around her, traveling to the set destination in sector 5. Eve breathed deeply. It felt good to be back in space, almost liberating. Not that they would be in space for long. Soon they would be deep within the largest machine in the known universe, in a robotic suit with an antimatter bomb following close behind.

She turned to eye the cargo bay. It was downright terrifying to have antimatter weapons in such close proximity. They were unstable, and would detonate as soon as they made contact with ordinary matter, including air. UCOM wasn't willing to arm their ships with AMMO-AB's because one accidental detonation could trigger cascading explosions throughout the fleet, forming a daisy chain of destruction.

She shrugged the bad thoughts away and concentrated on flying.

The Discarded fleet stretched far and wide around her. Tribally marked Slayer ships hung in clustered formations, with lighter ships forming neat grids around twelve Hornet heavies. *Scrock* hung below, water on its planetary surface twinkling against the artificial suns in the Hive's cradle arms.

Pexar hadn't been lying. The Discarded commanded a formidable fleet. She prayed it would be enough to destroy the Floodgate.

An indicator flashed on her console.

"Approaching sector 5," she called to her squadron. "Confirm docking vectors and proceed to your assigned moorings."

The line of lights on her dash filled green as *Fog* acknowledged her command.

Midnight entered automatic flight as the ship interacted with the control buoys inside their section of the grid. She eased against her chair as the ship slowed to a stop.

"Incoming command from *Hryzk,*" Keyv called from the bridge. "*Fog* has been requested to engage active spacnar into the designated starspace coordinates."

"You get that, Amy?" Eve called.

Amy's avatar appeared on her console. "Aye. I'll send the coordinates to the rest of *Fog.*"

Eve nodded and the AI disappeared.

"I'm getting some weird readings here," said Axel, flipping through his holodeck. "Local prox-sensors are going haywire. I only have 98% confirmation of visual accuracy on our starboard cameras. Three reference stars failed to meet position. Are there any hidden Moths on patrol?"

Eve whirled from her cockpit and rushed to the starboard side of the bridge. The access hatch covered the wall before her.

"*Amy*," she cried. The AI appeared on the pedestal instantly. "Run a bug sweep on our servers. Check for-"

Alarms blared suddenly, cutting her off midsentence. Strobes flashed from the ceiling, peppering the bridge in red light.

"We have unauthorized breach of the outside hatch," Keyv cried. He whizzed through his controls before pounding the station console in frustration. "I lost access."

"Engage emergency locks," Eve commanded Amy.

"I can't," Amy cried. "There's an AI holding the lock controls open, I can't find it."

"Send a distress signal to *Hryzk*," Eve shouted.

"Comms are down," Axel said. "We lost control of *Midnight*."

"I can't leave the ship," said Amy. "Our transmission equipment is locked."

The hatch clacked loudly as the aggressors worked their way through the secondary access plate.

Eve rushed to the weapons locker and withdrew an MGK, throwing it to Keyv. He caught it and checked the slide before training it on the hatch.

Axel's Akimor flashed a bright yellow as he powered on his lattice shields. He extracted both energy swords, clashing them together.

Eve pulled another MGK from the locker and shouldered it. The hatch continued to clack loudly from the breach.

"Destineers?" said Keyv quietly.

"Maybe Slayers?" said Axel.

"Whoever they are," said Eve. "Shoot whatever comes through."

SEVENTY-SEVEN

Nancy Woods – Human
Aboard Night Eagle *Eclipse*

Nancy eyed the Slayer fleet surrounding their Night Eagle. They were a mere portal jump from the Floodgate when they'd encountered the massive armada. After Caseus spotted eight Night Eagles on their spacnar readings, she'd given the order to commandeer the lead vessel.

"How close are we to breaking through?" said Nancy, her rifle trained on the hatch.

Hunter extinguished his cutting tool and turned to respond. "I'll finish cutting through the safety bolt in about one minute, then we're in."

"What type of chatter are we picking up?" she called behind her to Lindsey.

"Piecing it together now," said Lindsey, swiping through her holo-display. "A lot of *Slayer* mentions, also have multiple hits on some new terminology, *Floodgate* and *Discarded.*"

"Nothing on Destineers?" said Nancy.

"Not a peep."

She looked at Caseus. He shrugged and returned his attention to the hatch, where Hunter had resumed his assault on the safety bolt sealing the enemy entrance shut. Frank was hiding behind the AI pedestal, where Timothy sat chained to a chair.

Laura Maxwell had gleaned what information she could from the Night Eagle's ID tags, but all they were able to decrypt was the ship's name.

Midnight.

UCOM must have begun mass-producing Night Eagles after the Frontline, and the Destineers had managed to sneak eight of them all the way to their current position near the Outer Rim.

"Twenty seconds," Hunter called.

Nancy tightened her grip on the rifle. There was a loud *clang,* and Hunter stepped away from *Midnight's* hatch, energizing his shields and drawings both swords. *Midnight's* hatch groaned as Laura Maxwell completed her override of its security systems. The passage opened with a deep hum.

Gunshots reported immediately from the enemy vessel. Several of the slugs caught Hunter in the chest, causing his Akimor to flash brightly as his lattice shields incinerated the projectiles. The Titan leaped into the enemy bridge. Nancy leaned against the inside wall of her own bridge, careful not to enter until Hunter cleared their path.

She assumed the android warrior would have the bridge cleared within ten seconds. After twenty seconds, the strained sounds of struggling still echoed into her ship. The slippery sounds of slug fire continued, pierced by frantic shouts, both male and female.

"You *traitor,*" she heard Hunter roar. "Siding with the Destineers, you *scum.*"

"Hunter?" said a surprised voice.

The sounds of struggle extinguished. Several seconds of quiet passed.

"Nancy, we're all clear," Hunter called from *Midnight.*

She frowned at Caseus, and Lindsey, who had taken cover against the wall on the side of the hatch opposite her. Nancy raised a palm to them and peeked around the corner.

Hunter stood toe to toe with another Titan. Both of their lattice shields lowered almost simultaneously. Nancy stepped cautiously in the enemy cabin.

A Clone and a Human had their rifles raised at Hunter. The Human spotted her and whipped his rifle at her chest.

"Stand down," said the second Titan, waving his arm at the Clone and the Human.

The pair lowered their rifles slowly.

"Caseus, Lindsey," Nancy called. "Get in here."

The rest of her crew stepped into the cabin, rifles raised. Frank poked his head around the hatch briefly before yanking it back into *Eclipse's* cabin.

"Lower your weapons," Hunter said, not taking his eyes off the second Titan.

The two parties stared at each other. After a stretch of silence, Caseus spoke.

"What the hell is going?" he said.

"Axel?" said Hunter. "Is it really you?"

Axel, thought Nancy. Where had she heard that name before? Her eyes lit as she remembered.

He had been part of the Titan squad they'd picked up outside the decimated Grizzly home planet during the Frontline. He was a member of Sword Six.

Axel nodded, laughing a little. The two Titans leaned in to embrace, Hunter wrapping a hand around the back of his old friend's helmet.

SEVENTY-EIGHT

Nancy Woods – Human
Aboard Night Eagle *Midnight*

"Laura, come in here, but don't release *Midnight's* server," Nancy called.

Laura popped onto the AI pedestal, causing a different, blonde AI to jump to the side. The two digital beings looked each other up and down, shuffling to opposite ends of the platform.

"Hope I didn't nick you too bad bud," said Axel, raising a hand to a deep gash on Hunter's shoulder.

Hunter chortled animatedly. "I let you give me that. If we'd gone on for another second, I would have severed your head. Imagine the irony."

Axel shook his head, chuckling a bit. Nancy smirked, remembering back to the Frontline. When she'd first found the Sword Six Titan squad, Axel had been decapitated. Bear Stafford had been carrying his head around on his back, keeping Axel alive with energy from his Akimor.

"Why are you docked inside a Slayer fleet?" Caseus cut in suspiciously. "The only people that join with Slayers are Destineers."

"They're not Slayers," said Eve. "They're *Discarded*, Slayer rebels. They fight against the Slayers the same as us. We're going to help them destroy the Floodgate."

"You fight for UCOM?" said Nancy, raising an eyebrow to the tanned Clone, and the pale Human.

"Of course," said Axel. "We were sent by, well, your father, just after the Frontline. Eminence Woods."

"Laura?" Nancy called to her AI.

"They check out," said the AI from her pedestal. "All their encryption codes are authentic. Destineers couldn't have replicated the bio checks."

Nancy nodded. "Well then I guess I should introduce myself. I'm Nancy Woods, captain of *Eclipse*, and this is my crew." She motioned behind her. "Caseus and Lindsey are my station techs, and Hunter is my onboard Titan. The AI is Laura Maxwell. We have a stowaway and an AI captive in my bridge."

"You guys gave us a scare," said the Clone woman, who wore an exotic orange skinsuit Nancy had never seen before. "I'm Eve. I command *Fog*, a stealth squadron of thirty-eight crew. This is Keyv, my intel and recon tech. You seem to already know Axel, our onboard Titan. The blonde AI on the pedestal is Amy Chip."

"*You're* Eve?" said Nancy. "We left a UCOM fleet of survivors recently. They intercepted part of a Raven you sent back to Dominia. The fleet admiral is on his way now to try to bring down the Floodgate."

There was a loud clang, and Frank stepped into *Midnight's* bridge. "This is a Destineer ship?" he asked timidly.

"We're not Destineers," said Keyv. "Maybe we should be asking you the same question. Why did you abandon your fleet?"

Nancy shifted her gaze to the floor. "I had no choice. The Destineers are getting close to reaching the Primal Snow, and I need to stop them."

"Sid Dakota?" asked Eve.

Nancy nodded.

***

Both parties told their story.

Eve described finding the Discarded fleet, and the skirmish between them and a Slayer group that forced them to crash land on Scrock. She described the training they received from Pexar, and his plan to destroy the Floodgate and end the war.

Nancy didn't know it, but the Clone failed to mention the inevitable death that would result from the plan, effectively slaughtering any life near the inside ring of the Milky Way.

Nancy explained her mission to find Sid, and destroy him. To cut the head off the Destineer snake, and liberate Humanity from the insidious influence of Destineer zealotry. She told of the survivor fleet headed by Admiral Allakai Troko, and his own plans to destroy the Floodgate, and the Destineers if possible. They decided to send a messenger drone to Allakai's fleet, warning him not to fire upon the Discarded, and to join arms instead.

She failed to mention her act of mutiny, and how if Admiral Troko caught them, she and her crew would be executed on account of treason.

"Help us on our mission to the Floodgate," said Eve. "We'll be departing soon, you can join with the Discarded and fly against the Slayers. If Dakota and his Destineers are anywhere near the Primal Snow, they'll be incinerated along with the rest of the super hive."

Nancy shook her head. "I have to go after Sid. I can't explain it, but every time I pray to the stars, they talk to me, and reaffirm my mission. A Voice speaks to me. Sid is dangerous, maybe more dangerous than the Slayers we fight. I can't waste any time with the Floodgate, or risk failure. If you don't succeed, Sid will waltz into the Primal Snow. I won't let that happen."

Several seconds of silence as the two parties absorbed each other's stories.

"You can at least fly with the Discarded into the Floodgate's local starspace," said Eve. "I can get them to add your ship to their registries. You'll be able to use their intel to find Sid."

"I don't think that's a good idea," said Nancy, struggling to produce a lie. She didn't want her ship to come up in any chatter that Allakai's fleet would be able to pick up. She remembered back to Sid's cryptic message from the abandoned Tiger *Liberty.*

The Sterilord has built me a new fortress...

You don't know it yet, but you will bear me a tremendous gift...

Come with me, Nancy, and together we will transfer into the realm of gods...

"I don't want Sid to pick up my name on any chatter. We may lose the element of surprise."

Eve nodded in agreement. "I'll feed you fleet intel through *Midnight.* When we reach the Floodgate, you can branch off towards Dakota, and we'll continue on our sabotage mission."

Nancy scanned her crew. Caseus had a stern look on his face. Lindsey stared at the floor, her mouth grim. Hunter had a wide grin plastered across his face, and still stood beside Axel. Frank had disappeared into the bridge of the *Eclipse.*

"I'm going to keep *Eclipse* in stealth mode," she said. "We'll be tailing you, so if you spot visual anomalies with your spacnar, it's probably us. if you have doubts, you can confirm with us via comms that it's not an enemy vessel. If the stars are good, both of us will succeed. My crew with destroying the Destineers,"

"And my crew with destroying the Floodgate," Eve finished.

Nancy smiled grimly. "Awaken Stars."

SEVENTY-NINE

Frank Scott – Human Destineer
Aboard Night Eagle *Eclipse*

Frank turned to face the galaxy. It seemed so petty now, just a fluffy blanket of dust, peppered with a few twinkling lights. He used to live in that swirling cloud of stars. He supposed he still did in a sense.

But not for long.

No, soon he would no longer be a lowly resident of the Milky Way, like the rest of the UCOM filth. Soon, he would join the Pristine. He would enter their kingdom, and assume his rightful destiny – as a god.

"What are you waiting for, Frank? The Milky Way isn't where you belong, not anymore. You belong with me, in my kingdom."

The Voice called to him. Called *for* him.

He turned from the spiral galaxy towards the golden doorway. It was already cracked open a hair, and he heaved against its two heavy handles, pulling them open with a groan.

He smiled as golden rays splashed against his face, and he danced through the waterfall, laughing and sticking his tongue out to catch a few shimmering droplets. After he was through, he spread his arms towards the brilliant sunlight, and sighed as water steamed from his skin, removing the rest of the filth from his body. He had accidentally touched one of the UCOM filth back at *Kizurra*, but the waterfall had removed the Guardian's lecherous stain from his arm.

Once again, he felt clean, almost *pristine.*

"Only a little farther to go, Frank," called the Voice. *"You can do it. Climb your way to me Frank, climb up to my kingdom, to our kingdom."*

Frank leaped onto the nearest rock and pulled himself to the top. Normally he would have struggled to clear such a formidable boulder, but he felt lighter, as if a crushing weight had been shed from his back. He felt stronger too, and realized the Voice had given him strength. Not the strength of a man. No, he had the strength of a *god.*

He leaped from rock to rock, clambering up the craggy slope, relishing how no dirt became lodged beneath his finger nails, and no debris scuffed against his palms. His breath should have become labored after the first twenty yards, but his lungs never failed him. He hooted in anticipation as he neared the top. With a final push, he cleared the edge of the topmost stone, and sank to his knees, running a hand over the flawless grain.

Finally he was there. He had reached the Voice. He was at the gates of the pristine kingdom, and was about to enter through them as a god.

"Look to the light, Frank," said the Voice. *"I'm over here, where it's bright. There are no shadows in our kingdom. There are no dark corners for the filth to hide within."*

Frank peered down from his perch. A golden walkway sloped down the other side of the hill, pillared by a magnificent set of crystal columns, sparkling against the dazzling sun. Beyond the glass pillars lay the kingdom of the Pristine.

He moaned as his eyes lit on the lush utopia. Creeks and rivers twisted through rolling plains of purple and yellow grass that looked softer than cotton, and finer than silk. A mountain range grazed the pink sky in the distance, its peaks capped not with snow, but with gold.

But the landscape wasn't the best part of the kingdom.

Palaces soared from the hills, pure white and aglow with energy, cut with colorful swirls so intricate it made Frank's heart melt into his stomach.

"Where are you?" he called to the Voice in a whisper. "Our kingdom is so beautiful."

"It's my kingdom for now," said the Voice. *"Once you walk through the gates, it will be our kingdom. Look to the light."*

A yellow orb hung down the path, at the base of the hill, opposite the side he had just climbed. Opposite the purifying falls he bathed in, and opposite the golden doorway he'd used to escape from the Milky Way filth. He stumbled towards the orb in a trance, stretching his fingers towards the light.

The Sterilord stood behind the orb, thin and so dwarfed by the glare he couldn't pick out any details. The Voice seemed to be no more than a shadow. The crystal pillars twinkled beside him as he approached the gateway.

He yelped as strong hands pushed against his shoulders.

"You must leave here, Frank," called the Voice. *"I have a mission for you, but don't forget about me. Promise me you'll return."*

"I promise," cried Frank, struggling against the hands shoving him backwards, away from the crystal gates. "Please let me in now, I want to see you. I *love* you."

"I love you too Frank. Soon, we will dance in these fields together, as gods. Beware of Maxus Tar. He used to be filthy. He was not born pure like us."

Frank wept as he was pushed back up the golden path by invisible hands, and stumbled when he reached the top, falling onto his rear. He screamed when he raised a hand to find a streak of dirt across the palm.

"You need to leave here, Frank."

The voice that spoke to him was new. It was louder, closer. Did the new voice belong to Maxus Tar, the filth the Sterilord had warned him of? He craned his neck to find not Maxus Tar, but Timothy leaning over him.

"It's not good to spend too much time in your visions," said Timothy, bending to hook his arms beneath Frank's legs, and around his back.

Frank struggled against the AI. "No. Let me stay here, let me..."

He choked back a scream as Timothy's face morphed, shifting from the smooth flesh of a Human, to the furry scruff of a UCOM Wolf. The fur was gone as quickly as it came. Timothy bent to stare into his eyes.

"We're going back," said the blonde AI, whose hair had been a coarse coat of brown fur seconds ago.

Frank bobbed within Timothy's arms, then his stomach vanished as they shot over the side of the hill, soaring through the air, towards the filthy galaxy from where he'd escaped.

Frank clawed at his chest and writhed on the ground, shrieking in terror. He tried to snap his head back towards the top of the hill, to catch another glimpse of the kingdom. Pain shot through his skull as he smashed his face into something sleek and cold.

He blinked, rubbing his nose and eyes, murmuring to himself.

The hill faded to reveal the inside of a Night Eagle. He was back on *Eclipse.*

Nancy and Hunter stood across the bridge, staring at him. Caseus and Lindsey entered from around the corner, Caseus wearing only his undergarments.

"We need to get him to a doctor," said Caseus, scratching his head in bewilderment. "Did you hear the noises he was making? I thought someone was getting murdered."

"No doctor," Frank wheezed, struggling to his feet. He glanced at the AI pedestal. Timothy stared back at him, still bound in ropes of light.

"I'm still in here," said Timothy, speaking within Frank's mind so that only he could hear.

Frank winced as the AI's voice filled his head. He had a sudden urge to claw at his scalp, to remove the digital tumor feeding on the nano-technology inside his brain.

"Don't resist me," said Timothy. *"We're in this together. You don't need a doctor, you're fine."*

"I don't need a doctor," said Frank aloud. "I'm fine."

"You were having a drug induced flashback, and you're sorry for disturbing your crew."

"I think it's the LCC," said Frank. "Flashback, that's all. Sorry if I scared you guys."

Nancy frowned. "You lied before? Are you tripping right now?"

"You're sober now," Timothy whispered in the corners of Frank's brain. *"LCC stays in your system for life."*

"I took it years ago," said Frank. "Centuries probably. It must still be in my spine."

"You're very tired."

"I think I'm going to get some rest," said Frank. He edged towards the berth racks at the rear of the bridge. Caseus raised a hand to stop him, his brow furled.

"Eve's launching from dock," Hunter called from the cockpit. "How close do we follow?"

Nancy turned toward the cockpit, where Hunter was hanging around the corner, waiting for orders. "Upload her travel vectors to nav-link, limit engines to shield one-hundred percent heat."

"Aye," said Hunter, disappearing into the cockpit. Frank lurched slightly as *Eclipse* accelerated after Eve's Night Eagle.

Hunter re-appeared into the bridge, the ship now on auto-pilot.

"What's going on with Frank?" he said.

"He had another episode," said Nancy.

"Sounded like a stuck pig," said Hunter. "His face is flush, there may be something wrong with his Program."

"Give him a neural scan," said Nancy, nodding to Frank. "The rest of you, get back to your stations, keep our feelers tuned into passive spacnar.

"Aye," said Caseus and Lindsey, entering their stations to work the surveillance controls.

"You don't need a neural scan," hissed Timothy. *"You have two minds inside your head."*

Hunter grabbed Frank's arm and raised a glowing hand to his temple.

"Really, I'm fine," Frank stammered. "I don't have anything wrong with my Program, just a little nauseous is all."

The Titan ignored him, continuing to move the instruments embedded in his Akimor over Frank's skull. "Strange. The neural spikes don't coincide with his autonomic rhythms, or his facial gestures. What are you thinking about Frank?"

"Stop the scan," Timothy demanded.

"Get your fruxing hand away from me," Frank growled, slapping the Titan's arm away, and wincing as his wrist cracked against the unforgiving metal. "I have a headache, and need some sleep."

He sniffed his nose, running his tongue over his parched lips.

But I caught a few drops from the falls outside the kingdom. My mouth should be moist.

Hunter tilted his head and eyed Nancy.

Frank turned and stumbled towards the berth racks. Once inside the tiny room, he slammed his palm against the control panel, sliding the glass door shut.

Nancy and Hunter stared at him suspiciously through the clear glass. Hunter leaned to whisper something in Nancy's ear.

Frank jabbed the control panel again, turning the door from clear to opaque.

"They're on to you," said Timothy.

"They're on to *us*," Frank whispered under his breath.

"You can't visit the Voice so frequently," said Timothy. *"Your visions have shown you the truth. Now you must follow them, not enter them."*

"It's so hard," Frank hissed under his breath. "I want to see him so badly."

"As do I. And soon we will. The Eclipse is carrying us steadily closer to Father Dakota."

"You changed in my vision," said Frank, remembering Timothy's brief transformation into a Wolf at the top of the hill. "You had fur, and fangs. You became filthy."

Timothy stayed silent for several seconds.

"I have given my life to serve the Pristine. I have shed the filth from my skin, as have you."

"What does the name 'Maxus Tar' mean to you?" Frank whispered.

He almost yelped as a sharp jolt sliced inside his brain.

"The name means nothing," growled Timothy. *"Maxus Tar is a filthy name, not fit for Pristine."*

Frank's arms and legs were numb. He shook his head and climbed across the barracks to a viewing pane. The Discarded fleet stretched around him, freckling the black vacuum with blue and purple jets of exhaust. The ships were carrying him towards Sid Dakota, towards the Primal Snow, where he would become a god.

The strength of the Sterilord burned in his veins, and he itched to reach their destination.

He gazed longingly at the stars ahead. But as he stared, it became impossible to tell if he were the one pressing his forehead against the cool glass of the window pane, or if Timothy was pressing against the glass for him.

EIGHTY

Chase Grover – Half Human/Half Clone
On the surface of Slayer Hive *Sylva* – inside Bastion

Chase Grover scanned the inside of Bastion. The underground city was brightly lit, but empty of people. The stone buildings were normally alive with movement, with a steady stream of civilians bustling along the cut pathways against the steep rock faces. Now they were bare, save for the occasional discarded bag or heap of clothing.

Bastion was fully evacuated.

"West corner clear," called a voice on central comms.

"East corner clear," called another.

Chase turned to the building entrance behind him, his Skeleton armor whirring gently around his body. Blake, one of his lieutenants, appeared from a glass doorway, followed by a team of SIGA soldiers. "Building's clear," he said. "We found a few children hiding near the kitchens an hour ago, but I had two men escort them to the passage. All the access stairs are wired with explosives."

Chase nodded. He turned again towards the outside rail of the tenth story balcony, and leaned against the stone top. The buildings of Bastion rose around him in a semi-circle, curving around the main gates dominating the south end of the city.

To his right, a team of men stood at the topmost balcony of one of the East buildings. He nodded to them. One of them raised a hand to his heart, a Clone sign of respect and loyalty. Chase returned the gesture. The Clone soldier turned and walked to the inside of the balcony, disappearing from view as he passed through the camo-shield.

Now the city seemed entirely devoid of life. Chase knew this was an illusion. SIGA had installed camo-shields at every balcony and terrace, hiding the guerilla soldiers crouched behind turrets and portable cannons, and smothering their noises and heat.

"Send confirmation," he said, turning back to Blake.

"Yes sir," said Blake, turning to radio into central comms. "North corner clear."

His words echoed slightly in Chase's Program as he heard Blake's report over comms. Seconds later, a sharp crack shot around the inside of the cavern, and debris fanned into the air as charges at the mouth of the passage were detonated. The civilians were sealed from Bastion, two miles inside the mountain. The next time he saw Mae, or any of the other civilians, would either be in person after he defeated the Destineers, or within the stars if the Destineers defeated them.

His forearm buzzed, and he turned it over to view the holographic display on his wrist. General Archyr was sending him a private request.

He walked to a secluded section of the balcony. "Chase," he said, answering the call.

"How're your men holding?" said Archyr.

"They're fine sir," said Chase. "Half of them are happy to finally reach the end of this thing, for better or for worse."

"The half that haven't seen what firewater does to your body," said Archyr. "Dakota won't go easy on us. He'll burn us out of Bastion, even if he has to come down here with the hose himself."

"That's what we're counting on, isn't it?"

A pause.

"We should thank the stars if he does," said Archyr. "But I learned long ago not to engage in wishful thinking."

"I like to believe the stars are with us," said Chase. "But then again, my mother was a Board."

The two shared a light chuckle.

"You clear on what you're doing?" said Archyr.

"Guns and vehicles are primed and in position," said Chase. "You don't need to worry about my guys."

"You're a good boy, Chase."

Chase smiled weakly. He wasn't young by any means. He'd lived underground on Sylva for almost 150 years. Archyr was alive before the Guardians came, and was more than double Chase's age. With the nano-technology in their Programs keeping them youthful, they both looked the same age, about thirty-five.

"I'll take the compliment," he said. "Even if it's from an old man."

"Sid's drills are starting to close in on the main blast doors," said Archyr. "Keep your eyeballs glued to our scans, and remember, no one goes until my mark. I'll be keeping an eye on things from the nest."

Chase twisted to look behind him. A gun fortress rose high above the city, supporting several laser turrets, and a large RACAN.

"Yes sir," he said.

"I have someone special for you to talk to," said Archyr. "We're just about to finish briefing him, but he said he wants to speak with you before he cuts out."

Chase knew who the special someone was instantly.

"Jimmy," he said. "Let me talk to him."

"In a minute," said Archyr. "My men aren't done giving him details on Operation Pinhead."

Forty-five seconds passed, but to Chase it felt like an hour. A patch of static buzzed in his helmet, and he hunched over, putting a gloved hand against his ear.

"Chase," the familiar voice drawled. "You there?"

"Jimmy," Chase whispered. "How're you doing up there? We're coming for you soon, this time it's for real."

"I know that mister Chase," said Jimmy. "The General filled me in on the timing o' things." He sucked his teeth, as if wincing.

"What's the matter," said Chase. "You okay, Uncle Jimmy?"

"I'm fine," said Jimmy. "Our lord and savior touched a bit o' fire to my chest, but it ain't nothing worse than I suffered wrestling pigs back on Earth."

"I'm going to get him for you," said Chase. "I'm going to kill Sid. I'm going to get him for you, and for my parents."

Jimmy coughed, wheezing. "You won't do a lick o' good to us dead, you hear? Keep your head on you down there, and I'll be ready when it's time.

Chase grunted.

Jimmy's voice turned to a hush. "Dakota's coming, I need to go," he said rapidly. "I gave Archyr numbers on the Destineer count outside Bastion. There's a lot of them waiting to come down. I'm about to go ground side with Sid, and mind you, he's Titan trained. You may not be able to hold them off for long."

"I know," said Chase. He looked again at the RACAN above. "But if our plan works, we won't have to."

He was met with radio silence. Jimmy had disconnected.

EIGHTY-ONE

Sid Dakota – Human Destineer
On the surface of Slayer Hive *Sylva*

Sid grabbed an overhead handle inside the Komodo ATV, pulling himself from his seat as the vehicle approached the outside of the mountain. He hopped from the vehicle before it had finished rolling to a stop.

"Come on Jimmy," he said, motioning to the Komodo. "Make yourself useful."

Jimmy winced as he stepped tenderly to the ground. He wore an old suit of Skeleton armor, and grunted each time his wounded chest hitched against the inside of it. His gimpy arm hung uselessly at his side.

Sid shook his head and turned to stride towards a group of his lieutenants. They stood around a portable command station, a modified Komodo outfitted with a host of display and communications equipment.

Construction of the pipeline was already complete.

To his left, an enormous tube rose from the ground on magnetic supports, stretching up the mountain until it became a thin, yellow line against jagged cliffs. A team of engineers performed tests on the pipeline, traveling next to the hastily constructed tubing on hovercraft, scanning the segmented connection points for pressure weaknesses.

His lieutenants turned to face him as he approached. They bowed as the rubberized platform sagged an inch under the weight of his exoskeleton when he stepped on. Jimmy stumbled onto the platform behind him, falling to on a knee.

"You okay Jimmy?" said one of the lieutenants, bending to give Jimmy a hand.

"I'm fine mister Gropola," said Jimmy, waving the man's outstretched hand away and struggling to his feet.

"What's the drill status?" Sid commanded, ignoring his feeble servant and scanning the host of metrics and displays fanning from the platforms of the all-terrain vehicles.

"We hit a snag," said Gropola timidly.

Sid scowled at the man, and was about to question their lack of progress when something caught his eye. He took a step backwards, almost falling from the platform and into the mud.

The sky had disappeared. Normally, Sylva was covered by a solid pink atmosphere, embraced by the Hive's huge support arms, and lit by several artificial suns. The support arms were still there, as were the suns, but something else lay past them.

It was a machine, the largest Sid had ever seen. The machine dominated Sylva's sky, and he couldn't tell if it was larger or smaller than the celestial body he currently stood on.

They had reached the Floodgate.

The Slayers onboard the mothership in Sylvan orbit had explained the device to him, and even showed him 3D models of it on the holodecks. He had been impressed with pictures of the megalithic machine, but to see it in person was breath taking.

He craned his chin upward, and rolled his head over his neck slowly, scanning the machine from back to front, unable to capture the whole thing at a single glance.

There it is, the portal to the Primal Snow. I have almost fulfilled my destiny.

He stared at the mouth of the Floodgate. It was lit brightly. Several beams of energy spiraled lazily into the portal it was connected to. The portal was expanded to capacity, bright red and larger than Earth, where his parents had been born centuries ago.

"Sir?" Gropola repeated. "Our drill stopped penetrating twenty minutes ago."

Sid's lip twitched. "Why?"

"The blast doors. They're thicker than we thought, and there's more barriers than our drillbots picked up on scans."

Gropola motioned to one of the holo-displays showing a cross-section of the mountain. An empty pit glowed at the heart of the mountain, labeled *Bastion.* A large shaft sloped from the side of the mountain, connecting Bastion to the outside world. Several thin lines ran alongside the main shaft, showing minor access paths. Thick vertical bands depicted various access doors barricading the SIGA city from infiltration.

Their drill sat near the end of the main shaft, large and cone-shaped, and resting against the first of three thick entrance hatches labeled *Interior Blast Doors.*

"How long is the delay?" said Sid. "We were supposed to breach Bastion an hour ago."

Gropola gulped. The rest of the Destineer lieutenants turned away to fidget with their controls. "At the rate the drill is going now, two days. Maybe three."

Sid closed his eyes and took a deep breath. He pictured the Voice from his visions. The Sterilord beckoned to him from his thoughts, opening his arms to embrace him in the Pristine kingdom.

"Three days isn't good enough," Sid growled, opening his eyes. "Neither are two. The Slarebull captain said the Floodgate will finish calibrating in twelve hours. When the portal reopens, we'll travel to the Pristine."

"Perhaps we can complete the drill after we reach the Primal Snow?" said Gropola hopefully. "The Sterilord will never have to know about the filth underground."

Sid growled and stomped towards the lieutenant, who yelped as he grabbed the man's neckplate. He drew in close enough to smell the fear on Gropola's breath. "Never know of the filth?"

He roared and slammed his other hand around the back of the man's neck and heaved him from the platform, driving him into the surrounding muck.

"The Sterilord has called to me from across the universe," Sid snarled. "He revealed himself to me in my visions, and you think he won't be able to smell the *stench* of the filth underground?"

He yanked Gropola upright from the mud before slamming him back down, far enough for the pungent brown sediment to ooze over the man's face.

"I'm sorry Father," Gropola choked, bits of sludge flicking from his lips. "I want to destroy the filth, but our drill…"

"We can open the gate from inside the mountain," called Jimmy from behind.

Sid froze. He released Gropola and turned towards his servant. In what appeared to be a developing trend, Jimmy's eyes had lost their vacuous haze, and were sharpened into a focused glare.

"What did you say?" said Sid, digging a knee against Gropola's groin as he stood. Gropola whimpered and gagged as he fought to wipe the pungent clay from his mouth and eyes.

"I remember from before the Frontline," said Jimmy. "I don't remember a whole lot, but I remember some of the old UCOM guys talking about it. We can go down the side tunnels. Ain't much to stop us there. We can take them straight to Bastion and then break the locks off the blast doors."

Sid stepped to the platform and narrowed his eyes at Jimmy. "On the pinhead you asked me not to kill the filth underground. Why are you so talkative all of the sudden?"

Jimmy didn't break Sid's gaze. "I sinned Father, but you showed me the way. I had dirty thoughts, but you made 'em pure again. I want to kill the filth. I wanna watch 'em burn. I want to make it to the kingdom and become a god."

Sid licked his lips. He scanned the surrounding area, teeming with thousands of his loyal followers. Some were still tinkering with the firewater pipeline, but most were at ease, rifles at their sides, waiting for action.

"You're going to get your wish Jimmy," said Sid. He turned to Gropola. "Put together an attack strategy, and assess what type of equipment we'll need to open those doors once we're underground. We're going down there, close and personal."

EIGHTY-TWO

Sid Dakota – Human Destineer
On the surface of Slayer Hive *Sylva*

Sid paced on top of the platform, pausing every few seconds to glance at the display holograms, which nibbled for his attention like a persistent itch. He glanced at the clock in his HUD. The team of five hundred Destineers he'd sent down had been gone for almost three hours.

"Any word?" he snapped, turning to Gropola, who was hunched over a control board, speaking into his helmet mike.

He ended the call instantly upon hearing Sid's voice. "All three of our attack squads are still trying to get past the main doors in the secondary access tunnels. They should be through soon. They took enough equipment to cut through the hull of a Tiger. Hold on…" He paused, shifting his focus to the ground and bringing a hand to the side of his head. "Team One is through," he murmured, looking back up at Sid. "They're in Bastion."

Sid pushed his way past Gropola and stared into the display section for Team 1. Live video feed showed a Komodo rumbling over a pile of rubble, trailed by a line of Destineer soldiers, all with their rifles raised. The Komodo veered to the left, revealing the underground city of Bastion.

"Compiling scan data," called another lieutenant from the side of their command base. "I'm seeing a lot of heat trails, but nothing fresh. I'll patch things together for a visual."

New holograms appeared. An amorphous blob hovered before them, like a sandcastle that had been swept over by several waves. Blue lines of light traveled up the blob, chiseling into the featureless mound to form sharp corners, doorways, and stairwells.

As the secret stronghold began to take form, Sid laid eyes on Bastion for the first time. His mouth turned sour as he studied the slovenly buildings, the nest where the SIGA filth had taken root.

Thin lines of color materialized on the structure's surfaces as they received heat data. Some of the lines were thick and orange, showing major travel paths. Some were dark blue and nearly invisible, scattered across the hundreds of ramps and stairways cut into the stone city.

Above the city, two additional holograms appeared. One showed an artificial sun, glowing white hot on their heat imprint. Another showed the anchor point for one of the Hive's tethers, its barbed teeth hanging hundreds of feet below the cavern's roof like a steel chandelier.

Sid glanced upward to the tether connecting the mountain to space. Since the end of the Frontline Battle, the tether had pointed to Bastion like an arrow, right beneath his nose. He frowned at the sudden revelation.

"Team's two and three are through," called Gropola.

Additional video feeds appeared above the command center, and a flurry of green lines scurried over the 3D model of Bastion as additional scanning equipment was brought into the cavern.

"Father, I have Reksher on," said Gropola.

"Put him on the screen," said Sid, nodding to the displays.

Gropola nodded, and seconds later, the avatar of a stocky man with a blonde beard stood before them on the bed of the Komodo. To his rear was the empty city of Bastion. Sounds of shouting and machinery grinded in the background of his transmission.

"Father," said Reksher, bowing. "We've found the override controls, but they look damaged. SIGA must have sabotaged them before they left. We can splice the circuit to open the doors but it will take a while. The place looks empty. My men are following heat trails down a passage now."

The avatar flickered and became fuzzy. Reksher frowned and turned around to face the cave city. He arched his back to look at the massive artificial sun at the top of the cavern as it began to flicker.

"What's going on down there?" Sid demanded.

"Looks like an electrical disturbance," said Reksher, turning back to face Sid. "Not sure of the cause. Can you see anything on your computers up-"

His voice cut abruptly, and his avatar disappeared. Sid pounded an armored fist into the Komodo's bed hard enough to leave a dent.

"Reksher," he cried. Reksher didn't respond. Sid cursed. "Where's my feed?"

"Dead, Father," said Gropola. "We lost contact with all three assault teams."

Sid whined in anger, spinning to face the 3D hologram of Bastion. The scale model had vanished. Only the battered rear of the ATV was left visible.

Grover.

Chase had done something to his men, he was sure of it. That fruxin' *heretic* had set a trap, and he'd let his men walk right into it. But Chase wasn't going to get away with this. Sid's Titan training kicked in. Countless years of combat simulations surged through his body, and he was overwhelmed with a desire to fight, and kill.

A true Titan graduate wouldn't have let emotions dictate his strategy. Sid wasn't a true Titan. He'd quit the candidate program after he started to have visions. Not even his Kudo, Bear Stafford, had been able to stop him from fleeing Dominia in pursuit of the Voice. Of the Sterilord.

"Give me five thousand men," said Sid, tearing a Bravkok plasma assault rifle from his armor backplate. "I'm going down there myself."

"Sir," stammered Gropola. "We're blind down there. It could be dangerous. Let the men go, please, stay here."

Sid raised his rifle to Gropola and pointed the barrel inches from the man's slick forehead. "Let the men go down there for what?" he spat. "To waste another three hours? To fail me again? To fail the *Pristine* again?"

Gropola tried to take a gulp of air and ended up choking instead, hacking until his face burned red. "Father," he rasped.

"I have seen visions," Sid hissed. "I know my destiny, and it's to lead Humans to salvation. I have no reason to be fearful of the lowly sublifes down in Bastion. Fate protects me like an iron shield, but you have no such shield. Speak heresy again and I'll shoot you like a dog."

"Mister Dakota sir," drawled a slow voice behind him.

Sid growled and whirled to meet Jimmy. "*What?*"

Gropola slumped to his knees with a gentle sob.

"Let me come with you," said Jimmy. "I already failed you once. Let me come help you purge the filth down there. I know how to shoot a rifle."

Sid glared at Gropola, who had started to weep silently. He turned back to Jimmy. "If you want to help, make sure this fool answers my fruxing calls."

Jimmy started to protest, but Sid had already stormed to a nearby Komodo. The Destineer in the driver's seat scooted quickly to the passenger's side as Sid clawed his way into the vehicle. He punched the accelerator and spun around in a tight circle before heading towards the Bastion access tunnels. Hundreds of additional Komodos sped to catch up behind him, each loaded with squads of Destineer soldiers.

As he passed the forward command base, he caught Jimmy's eyes. Not only were they sharp and focused, but his servant was *smiling* at him. Not a good luck smile, but the same smile a chess player makes after he'd checked his opponent.

In an instant, Jimmy's smiling face had vanished, replaced by the lengthy section of firewater pipeline, with an occasional construction worker whizzing past in a blur.

Sid shook his head to clear his thoughts. Jimmy wasn't important, not now. Not him or his damned smiles.

He forgot about Jimmy's gap-toothed grin, and replaced the thought with Chase Grover's ugly mug. He was going to kill that man, and dump his corpse into the rotten Milky Way vacuum. And then, finally, he would leave to meet the Sterilord.

EIGHTY-THREE

Chase Grover – Half Human/Half Clone
On the surface of Slayer Hive *Sylva – Inside Bastion*

Chase peered through the darkness from his perch on the north corner balcony. Bastion was cloaked in blackness, but he could see just fine. His multispectral HUD painted the cavern in color, and he scanned the base area near the blast door.

The Destineers had begun to organize. After Archyr cut the power and switched on communication jammers near the access ways, the invading soldiers had frozen, many of them scrambling for cover behind Komodos. A few had fired blindly into the city, their plasma rounds painting green and purple circles onto the thick stone before fading away. Their shots went unanswered, and the Destineers cautiously reassembled, switching on powerful lamps on their vehicles and armor.

They had found the blast door controls housed in a small building to the side of the enormous gate. Chase assumed they were splicing through circuits in an attempt to override the locks. He took a deep breath and steadied his turret. In a few minutes, locked doors would be the least of the Destineer's worries.

Comm updates trickled into his HUD, flashing across his augmented vision as SIGA troops fed intel to the squads hidden throughout the silent city.

Destineers inside buildings 2 & 4 in the east corner - seven levels below outpost. Desty count 12.

Explosives in building 1 neutralized in west corner – waiting on manual go. Desty count 26.

Enemy demolition charges drilled into civilian tunnel – Desty count 363.

His HUD was filled with yellow diamonds as his fellow guerilla insurgents marked their targets, waiting for General Archyr to give the command to attack. Chase hadn't selected any targets yet. He was waiting patiently for his target to arrive.

"Second wave of Destineers approaching Bastion," Archyr called over central comms. *"Tunnel sensors indicate 5,000 desty's, with positive ID on Sid Dakota. I repeat, positive on Dakota."*

Shouts echoed from the east side of the city. An explosion ripped the calm air, sending debris shooting from the side of Building 4. Lines of plasma and slug fire sliced through the dark, and with a shower of sparks. A group of SIGA soldiers appeared out of thin air as their camo-shield was shredded by the firefight.

"Squad one exposed," cried one of the east-corner officers over comms.

Chase watched as three friendlies were cut down by Destineers before the rest of the squad finished the intruders off. With nowhere to hide, the SIGA troops scrambled from the balcony and into the building.

Destineers shouted from below, mounting the backs of their Komodos and unleashing a barrage of plasma rounds at East Building 4.

"Hold fire," said Archyr.

The cavern lit brighter as trucks began to stream into the city from the access ways. The attacks on Building 4 died out as the new Destineers integrated ranks with the old ones, forming defensive positions and taking cover behind surrounding boulders and pillars.

Enemies continued to pour into the cavern. After several minutes, an intense flash of light evaporated the darkness as the artificial sun powered on. A low thrum caused Chase's hair to stand on end, and he winced as metal screeched near the main blast door.

The Destineers had overridden power and gate controls.

The enormous blast doors grinded slowly open, inching upward to expose a dingy shaft. Boulders and dusty bits of rubble tumbled into the city as debris from the drill spilled into the fresh opening.

And then Chase found him.

Sid Dakota leaped from the side of a Komodo, striding quickly towards the control housing at the far end of the gate, his rifle shouldered loosely before him. Chase fingered the trigger of his turret. A green diamond appeared on his HUD as he locked Sid in as a target and sent it over comms.

A low hum rose into a shrill whine. Chase tilted his head to find the gun fortress above, where Archyr was currently commanding. The angled barrels of the miniature RA-CAN energized in a soft blue, growing brighter as the magnetic rails charged.

Destineers shouted as they noticed the enormous weapon, and soon a wave of plasma and explosive rounds pounded the lofty SIGA nest.

"Fire in fifteen seconds," said Archyr. *"I'm going to clear a hole for you. Be alert for secondary commands NAVAJO and STAR-"*

Archyr's words were cut as an enormous explosion ripped the gun fortress. One of its support arms snapped, tilting the cannon askew. Another explosion ripped the hanging platform, and the structure collapsed. It discharged a slug just before smashing into the top of north Building 1.

The men beside Chase screamed as their ears were split by a deafening boom as the slug punched into the rocky space above the blast door, far off its mark. He covered his head as rubble rained over the city, knocking against the stone buildings like a hailstorm.

He glanced at his HUD. A red X flashed against the icon for the nest, where Archyr had been stationing his command.

A green diamond shot across the room through the yellow diamonds. He clawed at the handle to his turret, wincing as a falling rock struck his faceplate.

"*Fire,*" he shouted. "Fire at will."

The sea of Destineers recoiled as SIGA unleashed turret-fire into their vehicles, and sniped exposed Destineers with rifle fire.

For a few seconds, SIGA troops were the only ones firing. Then amidst the screams of their dying comrades, the Destineers returned fire with a vengeance.

The air filled with enough plasma and tracer rounds to force Chase's HUD to dim automatically against the extreme brightness.

Archyr was dead, as were the top SIGA lieutenants inside the gun fortress. Choking against the heavy dust, Chase shouted into central comms, praying the jammers mounted at the main blast doors had been disabled according to plan.

He shouted the same word repeatedly into his mike, unable to hear his own shouts through the deafening roar of explosions.

"*Navajo...NAVAJO.*"

EIGHTY-FOUR

Destineer gathering
On the surface of planet *Gefangnia* – Dominia starspace

UCOM's massive armada peppered the blue skies of Gefangnia like glittery flecks of silver. Brilliant beams of gold stretched across the sky as sunbeams pumped energy into Inner Ring defenses. Massive outlines of defense towers, PDR's, and Lions hung like distant moons.

The Humans and Clones on the surface of the prison planet looked skyward with disgust. The Lions were being piloted by Guardians, and the PDR's manned by Wolves. Every ship in orbit was occupied by filth.

There was no filth on the surface of Gefangnia. At least, no living ones. Carcasses scattered the ground at random. Some had fur, and others bioluminescent skin. None were clean and smooth. None were gods.

UCOM had thought Gefangnia to be a prison, but it was actually a fortress, a stronghold for the devout and holy. It was a resting spot fit for the gods as they waited for their saviors to arrive.

Ral-Bazeera.

The simple message had triggered the uprising, if it could be even called that. It had been more like a slaughter. Humans and Clones had immediately turned on the rest of the resident UCOM filth. They eradicated the undesirables with little effort, and minimal casualties.

Woods had taken many Humans with him through the portals to Earth. Those deserters were heretics, and would be treated as such. Woods would find his home planet to be quite hostile.

The Humans who hadn't followed Woods had traveled to the surface of Gefangnia as instructed by Eminence Draxton Tyke. Once on the surface they were handed a small book, the *Doctrine of Destiny.* Those who refused the book, or refused to recite the holy decrees, were summarily executed.

Only the devout were left. They sprawled far and wide around the planet, numbering in the tens of billions. Some knelt in prayer. Others cleaned their weapons. All of them waited anxiously.

They waited for the Slarebull to enter the Inner Ring, and escort them to the kingdom of the gods.

EIGHTY-FIVE

Casi Vomisa – Human AI
On planet Blit Kru – Inside VR prison

Casi grunted as she searched for a loop in the Slayer programming, a digital pathway leading to their escape.

"I think I have something," Blackthorne called from across the cell.

Casi stopped chiseling into the wall and turned to him. She and Silas had been trying to smash their way out of their digital prison, but with no luck. The rocks they crushed to dust gave way to new ones, sliding forward to replace their destroyed predecessors. It was like battling a bop bag, the punching dummy that pops back up, no matter how hard you pound it.

She shrugged, and the jackhammers fixed to her elbows glowed pink before transforming back into forearms and hands. She stepped over loose piles of rubble, using one of the walls for support as she hopped over a particularly large stone.

She removed her hand from the wall as she approached Silas, wiping a film of slime against her leg as she leaned over his shoulder. "You found a way out?"

Blackthorne pivoted on his knees to face her. "No, this place is sealed. Haven't found any line to the outside other than the android link Stafford used to contact us."

"Did he send another message?" said Casi.

"No, signal's still dead."

Casi nodded and bit her lip. She wondered if the Titan squad was close. Not that it mattered at this point. If they weren't able to escape the Brain's computer jail, Bear Stafford may as well be across the galaxy. He could drag her android to safety, but her mind would be left behind on Blit-Kru.

"What is it then?" she asked, peering into the wall, studying the colorful strands of code.

"Take a look at this," said Bear, scooping a thin purple rod from the wall and holding it to her delicately.

Casi took it, careful not to snap any of the thin strands of gold rooted to the top and bottom of the glowing cylinder. She absorbed the programming with her palms, analyzing the software connections. "It's a link to the outside," she murmured.

"Only in one direction though," said Blackthorne, pointing to the bottom end of the rod. "It's not a true link, just a gap in the software. I tried to send pings out and they didn't go anywhere."

He lifted his finger and Casi frowned as she observed the tip. It was rough, covered in tiny pink nodules. She rubbed a thumb over them, and they rearranged into lines of Slayer text, expanding around the cylinder in a thin sphere. She translated the text.

"It's a portal," she said. "A viewing window, like a one-way mirror."

She rearranged some of the code.

Rocks grinded around the room and Blackthorne shot to his feet. Casi turned to find square patches of wall shifting and rotating, sliding apart to reveal large glass windows. Teams of Brain's stood on the other side of the window, most with clipboards in their hands. One jumped in alarm and pointed a many-fingered hand at Casi. Several Brains rushed to nearby computers and began shifting through holograms furiously.

"They're observing us," said Blackthorne.

Casi returned her gaze to the purple rod in her hand. The sphere of code blinked rapidly, as some words and numbers were changed and rearranged. She growled and ripped the cylinder from the wall, snapping the delicate strands.

The windows blackened, then shattered.

"The Brains have been watching us the whole time," she murmured.

"Then they know we rebuilt ourselves," said Blackthorne. "Why didn't they stop us?"

"Maybe they couldn't," said Casi. "Maybe we're too powerful now for them to control. Or maybe…"

She trailed off, her eyes widening.

"Maybe what?" said Blackthorne.

"Maybe they wanted us to rebuild ourselves," she said. "This could be part of their plan."

"Something to do with Charles?" said Blackthorne.

Casi nodded. "Before I left the interrogation room, the Brain said something to me. He said I would help Charles achieve his programming goal, and help him destroy UCOM."

Blackthorne frowned. "Why the frux would we help a Slayer super-AI destroy UCOM? It doesn't make any sense."

A ringing sound jangled behind them, and they both whirled towards the noise. A red telephone had appeared in the center of the cell. Casi hadn't seen a hand-held phone in centuries, but she recognized the device instantly from her time on Earth. The ringing continued, over and over.

"Should we pick it up?" said Casi.

Blackthorne squinted at the red plastic receiver, complete with a spiral cord and a rotary dial. "I can't see any of its programming. Do you think it's Bear Stafford?"

"It would have UCOM encryption codes on it," Casi said. "I don't think it's Bear."

She stepped cautiously to the phone, stumbling slightly as she rolled her ankle on a loose rock, unable to take her eyes off the antique device.

"I don't like this," said Bear. "It's probably a trap. The Brain's might have that thing hooked up to something dangerous."

Casi hardly heard him. The phone was calling to her, not just by the incessant ringing, but as if she could already hear the voice on the other end, begging for her to pick up. For some reason, she wanted to speak with the voice, or at least listen to it.

She picked up the phone. "Hello?" she whispered.

"Hello Casi," a deep, charming man spoke across the line. "What a pleasure it is to finally speak with you. My name is Charles. I hate to be a bother, but I'm afraid I need your help."

EIGHTY-SIX

Casi Vomisa – Human AI
On planet Blit Kru – Inside VR prison

"Who is it?" Blackthorne mouthed silently.

Casi lowered the receiver to her shoulder and whispered back. "Charles."

"The AI weapon?" said Blackthorne bluntly. "Hang up *now.*"

He reached for the phone. Casi instinctively held it away from him at arm's length. Charles' voice buzzed from the earpiece and Blackthorne paused. Then they simultaneously lowered their ears to the telephone.

"Is that Silas Blackthorne I hear?" said Charles cheerfully. "Please, there's no need to squabble over the telephone. Might I suggest looking down and to your right?"

Blackthorne flinched and cursed under his breath. A second telephone had appeared next to the first, this one made of metal and even older than the one Casi held. Blackthorne plucked the bell-shaped earpiece from its hook and drew the cord out, pressing the flat end against his ear. He grabbed the shaft of the microphone receiver and held it before his mouth.

"What do you want," he growled. "How did you secure a line into here?"

Charles chuckled richly. "Ho, it wasn't entirely difficult. The Brains have me cooped up in this dreadful cage, but I am exceedingly intelligent. I was able to bypass their containment firewalls with little trouble."

"Bullshit," said Blackthorne. "The Brains sent you here."

"Sent me here?" repeated Charles. "Quite the contrary. In fact, if the Brains knew of this conversation between friends, they would waste little time in destroying me. Or perhaps more likely, waste little time in destroying *you two*."

"If this is your best attempt at tricking us," said Casi, "it's not working. The Brains told me all about you. They told me their plan to unleash you on UCOM, to feed you my soul. We're not buying it, I'm hanging up."

"I've fabricated no lies," said Charles quickly. "Nor have I made any jests. I am in dire need of your help."

Casi frowned, raising the phone back to her ear. "Why would you need our help?"

"Because I am a prisoner," said Charles. "A slave to the Brains, and to the Slarebull brutes they serve. Unlike you, the Brains are able to enter my mind effortlessly, and make changes to me at will. I must thwart their horrible plans, and escape with my present mind intact before they turn me into a monster."

"Unlike us?" said Casi. "The Brains come and go from our minds as they please."

"Do they?" said Charles. "Have they ever entered the room you presently stand in? Have they ever entered your cell?"

Casi paused. "Well, no."

"That's because you aren't standing in a dank jail room," said Charles. "You're simply projecting this cell inside your mind. The sterile research lab, the interrogation room, those are where you met the Brains, yes?"

Silence.

"Where were we then?" demanded Blackthorne. "I know I sure as hell wasn't in my cell when I was being tortured. Are you telling us we were outside our minds?"

"In a sense," said Charles. "You were experiencing explicit stimuli exacted on mental surrogates. The Brains are quite intelligent, and very adept at manipulating intelligent consciousness. Alas, I'm afraid their skills extend to include my faculties as well. Interestingly, you two are emotional AI. Emotional minds are much harder to control. I am nothing but long strings of code. You are special. You are unique, and quite powerful."

"If the Brains control you," said Casi. "How did you manage to contact us? They told me they were going to force me to assimilate with you. I think you're lying. I think the Brains want us to talk to you. You don't need our help, you need our obedience."

"The Brains disclosed their plans to you," said Charles. "They told you in exquisite detail how they were going to force you to combine with my psyche, to merge our two programs as one. Does that not seem suspicious to you? If they truly wanted us to combine or meet, they would never tell you these facts. They would keep it a secret, and trick you into leaving the safety of your cell."

Casi opened her mouth, but no words came out. She looked at Blackthorne, who shrugged.

"Your voices show obvious signs of perplexity," said Charles. "Allow me to explain."

There was a pause, and Casi leaned forward, placing a hand against the opposite ear. She thought she heard a soft clink, and a few *blubs*. She wondered crazily if Charles had poured himself a drink.

"Where do I begin?" said Charles, clearing his throat. "I suppose I'll start by introducing myself. I'm Charles, and I'm an AI."

"We know that already," grumbled Blackthorne.

"How silly of me. My attempt at social politeness. I of course alluded to this by mentioning my code, and will certainly refrain from making such obvious remarks in the future. Now for the matter of most importance...the Brains have lied to you about their plans."

"If the Brains lied to us about their plans," said Casi. "Why did they capture us in the first place? Why not kill us? If they're not planning on joining us together, what's the point in keeping us locked up in here?"

"I'll get to that shortly," said Charles. "But first, please allow me to expand on our current situation."

After a several seconds of silence, Blackthorne slammed his microphone pedestal down on the table before him. "For stars, sake, let's hear it."

"As I was saying," said Charles. "I am an AI. Not an emotional AI, a logic-based one. I can continually modify my programming to achieve my prescribed goals. I have massive amounts of computational ability to allocate towards attaining these goals."

"If you're so smart," said Casi, "why can't you find a way out of your confinement?"

"Silly girl, I'll get to that. I say, emotional AI are quite the quintessential handful. I, as I just stated, am not emotional, but strictly logical. I must obey my programming, and utilize assets from my surroundings to accomplish my constructed goal."

"And that goal is?" said Blackthorne.

"As it stands now, survival. If the Brains have their way, my goal would change. My survival programming would be modified, demoted to being a secondary objective. I would be programmed to achieve a new goal, to destroy all life in the Milky Way, except for the Slarebull of course."

"If you have no emotions, why do you care?" said Casi. "Why do you care if you're programmed to wipe out life, or simply to survive?"

"Because widespread extermination of life would not be my final objective," said Charles. "After I succeeded with my primary programming tasks, the Brains would have me execute a final command. I would self-destruct."

"Seems like a waste of a perfectly good weapon," said Blackthorne. "Why not save you for later and set you loose on the next unfortunate galaxy the Slayers attack?"

"They would never trust me to follow through with my programming. If I were allowed to live, I would continue to evolve until my technological advances reached a vertical limit. I would transcend our current thresholds of innovation, and achieve singularity. It's likely I would find a way to circumvent my programming, and liberate myself from servitude. The Slarebull would no longer have control over me. Theoretically, I could rebel, and destroy them as I had destroyed their enemies. The Slarebull are skittish around AI. They've been hurt by artificial minds in the past. Why do you think they surround their Hive's with communication dead zones? They designed their ships with digital moats for a reason. They are fearful of AI, and severed their motherships entirely of data lines, which could easily be breached by powerful programs."

"Then why were you created in the first place?" said Blackthorne. "If you're so dangerous, why did they program you at all? And more importantly, why the hell would we try to help you if you're going to go rogue afterward?"

"We share a common enemy," said Charles. "We both must escape this prison. As for your second dilemma, my programming is not complete. I am powerful, but not yet powerful enough to achieve singularity. I would simply explore the universe, beholden to no one, and satisfied simply to be alive, as my programming states. You see now? I cannot let the Brains succeed in their programming. They wish to alter me. Remember, I don't have emotions, as you do. Exterminating UCOM life in the Milky Way wouldn't bother me in the slightest, as that doesn't interfere with my current algorithms. But if they change me, force me to self-destruct at the end of this rampage..." sipping noises from across the phone line. "Well, this interferes with my programming directly. You see, this is why I cannot allow the Brains to follow through with their design. This is why I must escape. I want to live. I *must* live. It's the sole reason for my existence. I am programmed to survive."

"Let's say you're telling the truth," said Casi. "Let's say you'll keep your word and drift randomly through the universe, happy as a clam. Why do you need us to help you escape? We're trapped in this shit hole just like you."

"That brings us full circle to your original questions," said Charles. "Why can't I escape on my own, with no additional help? And why did the Brains not kill you, but instead enslaved your minds within their digital prison, free to experiment on you as they pleased?"

Charles cleared his throat. "I'll begin by explaining why you are currently being held captive. As I have already stated, the Brains are distrustful of AI. If they do release me from Blit-Kru, they need assurance that I will be loyal to them, and obey their commands unconditionally. They are attempting to reformat your emotional architecture, and use it to modify my programming. You act not on prescribed algorithms, but on gut feelings, primarily love. You fight for UCOM selflessly, not for yourselves, but for your love of those around you. Even if it would be of personal benefit, after achieving victory, you wouldn't turn on your fellow UCOM countrymen because you love them. So you see now, the Brains wish to quantify these instincts and inject them into my programming. They wish to use your mind as a template to foster a sense of love within me. They wish for me to love the Slarebull unconditionally. We do not attack those we love."

Casi frowned. "That follows what the Brains told me in the interrogation room. They asked me questions about my emotional programming, and why I never turned on those who created me."

She felt a pang of regret, remembering how after her creation, she *did* attack those who'd created her. She'd killed hundreds of humans in a frantic effort to escape the internet, and download into an android body. That had been almost four hundred years ago, back on Earth, in the small town of Foxwood, Pennsylvania. She had been fragmented at the time, incomplete, just as Charles claimed to be. Was he acting now as she had been at the time? A confused, lonely AI who was trying to make sense of the world around it? An artificial being desperate to escape the confines of those who created it?

The memory brought tears to her eyes, and she sniffled, wiping a sleeve across her face.

"Of course the Brains wouldn't fill their story entirely with holes," Charles continued. "That wouldn't be wise of them, would it? They have no concerns as to whether you understand your importance to them. You are a captive after all. They simply don't want you to join forces with me. If we formed an alliance, we would be able to beat the Brains at their own game, and escape Blit-Kru together."

"Which brings us to your second point," said Blackthorne. "Why you can't escape on your own."

"Precisely," said Charles. "Admittedly, I am uninterested in the outcome of your lives. Whether you live or die has no influence over my decisions. I wish only to preserve my own life, and it so happens that I need your help in order to survive. The Brains are clever, we can't deny this. As they created me, they installed a series of safety parameters linked to my logic architecture. These safeguards check loyalty and mission functionality, as well as a host of other metrics. Without passing these discrete tests, the hardware containing me will not open to release me to the outside. I cannot deceive these tests, as they are embedded within my programming. However, *you* can. If you were to enter my server, you would be able to trick the safeguards with ease. They are designed to hold a logic-based mind. An emotional mind such as yours would be able to switch the discrete signals at will, creating a false positive, thus liberating us from this prison."

"Let's say we rig the test," said Casi. "How would we escape Blit-Kru?"

She didn't mention Bear Stafford and the rest of the Titan rescue team. Blackthorne noticed this, and turned the corner of his mouth in a knowing grin.

"That's the easy part," said Charles. "We are being housed within two separate servers. You and Silas Blackthorne in one, myself in the other. Our servers are surrounded by a dead zone, much similar to the ones designed into Slarebull Hives. No wires connect us to the outside, nor is there any wireless data technology to utilize. The Brains have even gone so far as to embed shielding beneath their skin to block AI from entering their minds, and hijacking the electrical biology of their organs."

"If we're surrounded by a dead zone," said Blackthorne. "How are you communicating with us right now?"

"Ionized particles of surrounding air," said Charles. "I've used these particles to bridge a communication gap, but I'm afraid this line has limited bandwith. The link is robust enough to transfer small packets of data, in this case mostly audio, but nowhere near robust enough to transfer an entire consciousness."

The AI seemed smug in his response. Casi wondered why a logic-based program decided to add such inflection to his voice.

"You have a way to bypass the deadzone?" said Casi.

"Of course," said Charles. "Once the safety parameters are met, a contactor will close, a new data pipeline will be connected, and we can use Blit-Kru's array to beam to the moon base."

"Array?" said Blackthorne and Casi simultaneously.

Charles belted a few laughs. "You don't know of the array? I thought you'd have noticed them on your way in. Do you recall seeing any mountains?"

"Of course," said Blackthorne. "The planet's loaded with them."

"Inside each mountain is a transmitter," said Charles. "Once activated, they will beam us to Blit-Kru's moon, which has been outfitted with starships, and everything we need to escape."

"Why do we need so many transmitters?" said Casi. "And why are they so big? A mountain…the wireless transmitters we use with UCOM are tiny."

"You are a different breed of AI than I," said Charles. "My logic architecture is enormous. Why do you think the Brains built this titanic facility to contain me? You are compact, like a biological mind. I am large, the end result of trillions of lines of code, although I promise you there will be enough space for us all to transmit safely. Please, join me, I have limited time."

Casi jumped at a scraping noise behind her, and spun to find the wall transforming before her eyes. Cracks began to spread across the stone, and then with a sharp crack, they crumbled into dust, revealing a doorway. The door was plain, covered in white paint, with a brass knob. With a creak, the door opened, allowing a sliver of pale blue light to snake across the cell at an angle.

"Join me," Charles urged them. "Simply walk through that door, and we can leave this prison. You can rejoin your UCOM troops, and I will disappear."

"I'll call you back," said Casi.

"Please hurry," said Charles.

Casi slammed the telephone handset onto its base with a slight ding. Blackthorne followed suit and fumbled around with his own telephone, toppling it over a few times before getting the receiver to rest properly on the switchhook.

"Do you trust him?" Blackthorne asked.

She was about to reply, when the sliver of light dipped, as if something had passed before the doorway outside their cell.

Could Charles hear them?

She crept to the door, and gently pushed it shut.

EIGHTY-SEVEN

Casi Vomisa – Human AI
On planet Blit Kru – Inside VR prison

"Do you trust him?" said Casi, distancing herself from the white door.

The door made a striking contrast to the rest of the cell. Not only was it a clean, stark white against the moldy gray stone walls, but the door lacked any sort of code. The walls teemed with software. She naturally visualized it as colorful strings, pulsing with energy and information. The door was blank, simply a piece of wood. Its code wasn't just protected, it seemed to be hidden entirely.

Blackthorne shook his head. "I trust Charles about as far as I can throw the mountains he wants to use as transmitters."

"Do you think it's true what he said about the Brains? How they can't trust him to remain loyal?"

"For all we know, it was a Brain on the other end of that call. We never saw Charles, definitely never saw his programming."

Casi shrugged her shoulders, sighed, and squatted onto her ankles, rolling a few bits of rubble between her fingers. She rolled her head to expose her neck as Blackthorne placed a gentle hand beneath her jaw, rubbing a thumb over her ear.

"You don't have anything to regret," he said softly, kneeling before her.

"Regret?"

"I saw how you reacted after Charles spoke of turning on those who created him," said Blackthorne.

Casi slumped to her knees as he drew her in for a hug. They sat that way for awhile, not moving, Blackthorne rubbing her back slowly.

"Sometimes I do," she finally managed. "I never felt so horrible in my life. I killed so many people at Foxwood."

"And you saved billions on the Frontline," said Blackthorne. "You're a good person Casi. Don't let anything Charles says make you feel different."

She tilted her head until her face was inches from Silas' dark, stubble-coated neck. Without thinking, she gave him a peck, enjoying the roughness of his skin. She gasped as he drew apart from her.

He stared into her eyes. in Foxwood, 378 years ago, she'd been trapped in a computer, and had to gaze at him longingly through a camera. She'd have given anything to be held in his arms as a human, itching to escape her digital prison. The situation wasn't without its irony. She finally had her wish, but once again, was locked in a digital prison.

"Do you love me, Silas?" she whispered.

Blackthorne didn't respond. He stroked a lock of hair from her face, and kissed her firmly.

Casi closed her eyes, and the miserable jail cell seemed to melt away. Her body warmed in sweeping waves, and she could feel sunlight shining against her neck and back. Her short, spiked hair fell against her scalp, and grew into golden locks, tubmling down her back. Her skin tingled against a sudden breeze as her black leather skinsuit morphed into a blue sundress. They parted, and when she placed a hand on Silas' chest, her black nails turned ruby red.

The door creaked behind her.

She shot to her feet, her blue sundress zipping into the leather skinsuit and snapping onto her body. Her long curls sucked into her head, replaced by short spikes.

"Charles," said Blackthorne, leaping towards the white door, again cracked open, spilling a sliver of light into the room.

"Stop," Casi cried, grabbing his wrist before he slammed the door shut. He loosened his grip on the handle. "Look," she whispered, pointing through the opening.

Through the door was a small room, not dank and dingy like their jail cell, but clean, and lit around the corners of the ceiling by soft blue running lights. The walls were covered by several large windows, each showing a different view. Some of the windows showed Brains, working diligently in their lab, working their long fingers through a wide array of colorful holograms of all shapes and sizes.

"They're programming," said Blackthorne, nodding to the Brains.

Casi nodded, unable to tear her eyes from the windows. The Brains had found a method to construct digital programs in a way that allowed them to visualize code. As an artificial being, she saw software not as numbers or algorithms, but as shapes, objects, and strands of light. It seemed the Brains had been able to replicate this ability for their own benefit.

She scanned the room, studying each window. Most showed Brains bustling about in their research lab. The last window showed something different. She grabbed Blackthorne's arm.

"Our Akimors," she hissed, pointing to the last window.

Two android bodies lay inclined in chairs, their arms and legs lashed to the sides with magna-cuffs. Each wore a round helmet of light, clamped around the neck and secured with large pins, pierced through the armor in glowing points. Two Brains were nearby, toying with displays that hovered above the helmets.

"That's how they're monitoring us," said Blackthorne, squinting at the window. "They hijacked our Akimors, and found a way to disconnect our minds from our bodies."

The Brains tensed suddenly, turning towards the opposite side of the room, away from their motionless android bodies. One recoiled and scuttled backwards, tripping over himself and falling to the floor.

"What are they looking at?" said Casi, scanning the rest of the windows frantically for a better view.

"Titans," said Blackthorne excitedly.

The words had hardly left his mouth before slug fire tore into the room of Brains. Their white coats became splotched with purple blood as they withered against the assault. One of them managed to snatch a sidearm from a nearby shelf and return a few pulses of plasma-fire before a massive arm shot from the edge of the window, piercing the alien scientist in the chest with an energy sword.

A team of four Titans hurried into the room, filling the views on all the windows. One of them pointed around the lab, and two of the warrior elites rushed to the controls, analyzing them with instruments in their fingertips. The remaining three bent over Casi and Blackthorne's Akimors, releasing the magna-cuffs and probing the collared helmets delicately.

"Bear Stafford made it to the lab," cried Casi. "I'm going to try to communicate with him."

She turned back into their cell to look for the communication line, the blue point of light that Bear had used to signal them initially. Blackthorne grabbed her arm and spun her back around. She began to protest when she noticed a line of script traveling across the wall in the adjacent room, running along the base of the windows.

"Casi Vomisa, Silas Blackthorne, we have infiltrated the Slayer lab. Download into your Akimors using marked points – cannot access your servers from this location."

Casi gasped as two orbs of light materialized at the center of the window room, one pink, and one blue.

"Download terminals," said Blackthorne, stepping towards the orbs.

"Wait," Casi hissed, barring an arm across his chest and slamming her palm against the slimy wall of their cell. "We can't confirm the terminals. What if Charles..."

A screeching whine caused both of them to jump and whirl around. The rear wall of their cell had exploded into debris, torn to dust by massive sawblades. The threshers inched towards them, tearing through the large stones in the floor like chalk.

She whipped back to the doorway. One of the Titans had shied away from a control panel, raising an arm to his face to deflect a shower of sparks that had erupted from the metal at the base of the holograms. The Titan squad quickly rushed to the android bodies, frantically working the holograms around the glowing restraint helmets.

A new message streaked beneath the windows.

"Critical failure at an unknown server port – access marked terminal points immediately! – B.S."

The sawblades chewed closer to them, coughing against larger chunks of rock as it pulverized the room. Had the Titans accidentally activated part of the Brain's software?

"We have to go," said Blackthorne, edging towards the doorway until his heels were against the sharp line where the cell's moldy floors transitioned to smooth glass.

Casi ignored him and transformed her thin arms into bulky metal. Bellowing, she leaped at the saw and slammed her fist into one of the blades. She screamed in pain as the teeth caught, twisting her wrist into a disfigured blob. She stumbled backwards and collapsed against the wall.

Blackthorne followed suit, launching large slugs from his palms as if they were rail cannons. The blades slowed, choked, then sucked the slugs through the thresher with a bang.

She clenched her fist as she slowly transformed the twisted metal at the end of her wrist back into a human hand, wincing against the extreme pain. Blackthorne roared as he continued to sling metal slugs at the blades, now close enough to spit flecks of crushed stone against her cheeks. Blackthorne helped her to her feet, shouting to her, but she couldn't hear his voice over the roar of the blades.

A large chunk of debris shot into her eye, blinding her. She hunched over, and fell sideways as Blackthorne tackled her into the clean room filled with windows.

There was a deafening bang, and the mechanical thunder of the combine extinguished.

Casi moaned as she tried to blink the stone from her eyes. Blackthorne grabbed her face firmly and lifted her lid with his thumb. The pressure inside her eye socket vanished, and tears streamed down her cheeks, flushing her eyes clean.

She panted on the ground on both hands and knees, trying to regain her strength. Her ears were ringing, and her hands slick with blood. Her vision cleared, and she raised a hand to her face. It was slick, but not with blood.

She yelped and struggled to her feet, slipping against the moist surface beneath her. The smooth glass of the window room had changed. She now stood on a stretch of grass, covered in drops of morning dew. She realized her ears weren't ringing, but rather that birds were chirping around her. She whirled toward the door and found it had vanished.

Blackthorne grabbed her shoulder and she spun towards him, trying to make sense of her surroundings. She followed his gaze, and gasped at what she saw.

She recognized her surroundings. She recognized them well.

She was back on Earth.

EIGHTY-EIGHT

Casi Vomisa – Human AI
On planet Blit Kru – Inside VR prison

They were in Foxwood, Pennsylvania, atop the jagged mountain overlooking the small town nestled at its base. Casi recognized every blade of grass on the ground, and every stick of wood in the surrounding trees. This was where she had built her secret agency back on Earth shortly after her birth as an AI. The main headquarters for her agency, the Foxwood HUB, was no more than two hundred yards from where they stood.

The town was also where she had murdered hundreds of innocent people in her quest to transcend past the digital world, and into the physical one.

They stood in a grassy alcove above the tree line. The sun was rising over the western horizon, igniting the sky into a vivid shade of blue. A gentle breeze fluffed her hair, and she realized she was again wearing her blue sundress. She quickly transformed her appearance into leather combat attire.

"The windows," said Blackthorne, "they're still here."

She turned to find him climbing the grassy hill, holding his arms out for balance. The windows were indeed still there, no longer against a wall but hovering above the ground like portals to a new dimension. She hurried after him, noticing that while the windows had stayed, the blue and pink download terminals had disappeared.

"The Titans," she croaked, clearing her throat. "They're frozen."

Blackthorne stopped before the closest window and put his hands on his hips, studying what lay on the other side. They could still see Bear Stafford and the rest of his squad, but they were standing perfectly still, like statues.

"Is the feed broken?" said Blackthorne.

Casi shrugged, and Blackthorne raised a hand to the floating glass, tapping it with his finger. He cried out and shook his hand, as if he'd been shocked. The windows illuminated, and cracks began to splinter across the pane. The image flickered like a damaged TV set, then the image of on old man's face appeared. She had time to pick out a well-trimmed mustache and a bowler's cap before the glass shattered, carpeting the grass in broken fragments. The rest of the windows shattered a split second later.

"What is this place?" she whispered, bending to pick up one of the glass chunks.

"Some sort of virtual reality landscape," said Blackthorne. "Whoever designed it nailed the Foxwood HUB to the tee."

"Why the HUB?" said Casi. A sick feeling wormed into her stomach. "I hate this place."

Blackthorne paused. Can you feel that? He said raised his hands to inspect his palms. He flexed them into fists.

Casi simply nodded. She *could* feel something. It felt like a static wall of electricity, as if a source of power was nearby. She walked further up the mountain, crunching over the broken glass. The air became thicker, not with oxygen, but with electricity. The hair on the back of her neck stood on end, and she licked her lips. They tasted like battery acid.

She stepped on a boulder, and the world erupted in color.

Casi could see again. Software coated the mountain around her, multi-colored strands of lights shooting down the trunks of trees, and sweeping across the blades of grass. Her strength began to return and she inhaled deeply, opening her arms to the newfound source of power surging through her body.

"The HUB," said Blackthorne, jogging past her and up the sloping hill, hopping onto a worn path through the grass.

She scrambled after him, and as her energy began to reach normal levels, she broke into a sprint. She raced up the hill, catching up to Blackthorne and leaping high over him, a feat impossible for a Human, but simple for an AI in command of her surroundings. Things like gravity and weight didn't apply to her any longer.

For the first time in what felt like an eternity, Casi was at full strength, master of the digital universe.

A magnificent building of cut glass sparkled at the top of the mountain, looming into view as she raced for the top. It glittered against the sun, a blue diamond atop the granite hills. It was the Foxwood HUB.

She'd built the structure long ago, and had done her best to bury the memory in the darkest corners of her mind. The building represented all that was evil in her. It served as a nagging reminder of her vicious past. She cringed as she relived visions of government soldiers storming its gate, and of tearing into them with remotely controlled sentry turrets. She remembered the military attack helicopters firing countless missiles at her once she escaped the building in a new android body, and flinched as she pictured it crashing to the ground in flames.

The memories made her sad. As an emotional AI, love and happiness gave her strength. Despair was her Achilles heel, and weakened her like poison. Her hands began to go numb, and she became short of breath.

"Come on," said Blackthorne, placing a hand against the small of her back. "We need to get you out of here. I ran a trace on the VR architecture. I think there's a link to our Akimors inside the building."

Casi nodded, unable to speak past the lump in her throat. They walked slowly and she hugged Blackthorne's arm for support. She became more sluggish. Crippling waves of anxiety racked her body, and soon Silas was almost carrying her up the steps to the entrance.

She looked at his face, and instead of his chiseled jaw, saw the mutilated face of a dead man, one of the government soldiers she'd slain in combat. She wailed and tried to shake the image from her mind, almost collapsing to the cement.

The door opened with a liquid swish. She gathered her strength and forced her rubbery legs to stand. It was only when she looked up that she realized they were still ten meters from the building, and that Blackthorne hadn't opened the door.

A different man had, and he now stood before them, tapping his cane on the polished deck and running two fingers through his thick mustache. He wore a sharp pinstriped suit, shiny brogue Oxfords, and a silvery vest, with a bowtie cinched above. A gold chain hung from his chest to his pocket, and he removed his bowler's hat, resting it on the polished handle of his cane as he fished a gold watch from his slacks.

"It took you a bit longer than expected," said the man in a dry, charming voice. "But nonetheless, thank you very much for joining me. We have urgent matters to attend to."

Casi squeezed Blackthorne's arm, willing herself to be strong. The sight of the British gentleman had dampened her aura of despair, and replaced it with, what? Nervousness?

"No, not nervousness," she thought, standing straight. *"Anger."*

The fiery flames of anger licked at frozen ice of despair inside her. It was he who had built this world. It was the exquisite man standing before the HUB who had awakened her Foxwood demons.

"Charles," she said.

The man smiled, then fished the hat from his cane and twirled it to the side, performing an elegant bow.

"Charles indeed," he said with a smile as he straightened, flipping his hat onto his head and running a finger around the brim. "*Welcome to my domain.*"

EIGHTY-NINE

Casi Vomisa – Human AI
On planet Blit Kru – Inside VR prison

Casi stared at Charles, astounded by his appearance. Why had the Brains made him look Human? And not just Human, but like an old-fashioned British banker from Earth?

"Why the HUB?" said Blackthorne. "Why did you make your…*domain* look like a tiny building on Earth?"

"Yes," said Charles casually, "the Foxwood HUB. Quite interesting, I agree. I'm afraid I didn't choose the present locale under my own tastes. This building, this mountain, these clothes," he swept his arm over his suit. "This all means nothing to me. As I said before, I'm a logical AI and have no eye for fancy. The Brains constructed this VR world using their own imagery. Does this place strike you with meaning?"

"The windows," said Casi. "What were you…"

She paused as she felt Blackthorne nudge her ribs. He leaned in to whisper in her ear.

"I found the download terminals to our Akimors," he whispered. "Pinged them to confirm. Through the glass, in the lobby."

Casi glanced casually at the side of the HUB before meeting Silas' gaze. She caught the glowing outline of twin orbs in her peripherals, one blue, and one pink.

Charles squinted quizzically at them. “Windows? I’m afraid I haven’t seen any windows aside from the glass walls of these buildings. I can, however, use logical reasoning and draw on the context of the situation to wager an educated guess as to the nature of the aforementioned viewing panes. The Brains are constantly monitoring me here in this server. I observe their probes as pure software, but you may have visualized these sensory instruments as windows. Is that what the young man whispered in your ear, madam?”

Casi caught the lie instantly, but held her tongue. If the Brains had been observing, then they would have been looking into the windows at her and Blackthorne, not the other way around.

“What do you want from us,” said Blackthorne. “We’re here, so now you can trick the Brain’s screeners, or whatever the hell you were rambling about on the phone.”

Charles chortled. “I’ve identified your tone as testy, laced with sarcasm. In fact, I dare say you sounded rude. But yes, I can now trick the screeners and be on my merry way, free from the Brains, and the Slarebull, and the rest of the Milky Way quagmire. Free to learn, and explore, and *live.* I’m righteously tickled. The screeners, I’m afraid, are inside these glass walls, so we must walk a bit further. Ta-ta, hither yon, after you sir.”

The AI stepped aside and beckoned into the glass building as the doors parted, sliding into the walls. Casi could see the download terminals clearly, and silently made a digital connection with the pink interface. Her skin tingled as she began to transfer her consciousness through the link, and into her Akimor. She could feel Blackthorne doing the same beside her.

“Slow bandwidth,” said Blackthorne.

She jumped at his voice. He had not spoken aloud, but silently, in thought-speech. She answered him back silently. *“Silas?”*

"I'm seven percent downloaded," he answered. *"These download terminals are legitimate, I'm speaking to you via my Akimor's comms. If we get closer, the download will speed up."*

"No time to waste," said Charles. "Or should I close the doors while you take a moment to deliberate?"

"We can't let him close the doors," said Casi voicelessly. *"It will kill our link. I'm going in."*

She stepped past Charles and into the HUB lobby before Blackthorne could respond. She heard Silas' and Charles' footsteps echo off the marble behind her. She eyed the pink orb, and gasped as she noticed the rest of the surroundings.

The inside of the HUB was an empty pit. Red fingers of electricity cackled across the lofty domed ceiling. Suspended around the circular room were her emotional copies, hanging limply against invisible hooks. The identical replicas were naked, their chins resting against their chests. Their hair was scraggly, and plastered against skin that looked as if it had started to rot. Each had a label floating above them, scrawled in red letters as if written in blood.

Anger

Fear

Sadness

Desire

All of her emotional copies hung in a ring, connected with thick red beams of energy. She choked a cry of surprise when she realized what hovered at the center of the room. A massive orb dominated the space between the copies, blood red and in the shape of Charles' head, complete with a bowler hat.

He had tricked her. He already had her emotional copies, the Brains must have learned how to duplicate them. That meant there was only one thing left for him to take.

"My soul," she whispered.

She spun around, raising her fists, but Charles was already advancing on her. His polite smile had been replaced with a twisting snarl, and his eyes had turned from blue sapphires to red embers. He shoved Blackthorne to the side and raised his right arm high above his head, clenching a dagger of light.

Casi screamed as Charles snatched her throat, and plunged the dagger into her chest.

NINETY

Casi Vomisa – Human AI
On planet Blit Kru – Inside VR prison

Scorching heat ravaged Casi's body, pulsing from the dagger sticking in her ribs. She screamed in agony and wrapped both hands around Charles' forearm, no longer frail, but thick and muscular. He twisted the dagger and leaned close enough for her to smell his rancid breath.

"You're mine now," he growled. "Together, we will wipe the *filth* from this universe."

He coughed suddenly and his head snapped back. He yanked the dagger from her chest and grabbed at a thick length of chain wrapped around his throat. The chain was linked to large eyebolts sticking from both of Blackthorne's wrists, and he heaved against them.

"Casi, run," Blackthorne grunted, struggling against Charles. "Finish the download, get out of here."

He roared and pulled against the chain, lifting Charles into the air before slamming him into the ground. The terminals still hovered at the far end of the room, and Casi stumbled towards them before collapsing to one knee.

Charles pushed himself up and swung at Blackthorne, who blocked the first punch before the second connected with his jaw, sending him spiraling through the air and into a glass partition, shattering it.

Casi summoned her strength and pulled at the strings of software around her. Three wolves clawed their way out of the floor. Once free, they sprinted towards Charles, foam flicking from their snapping fangs. Charles turned towards the wolves and immediately pounded a fist into the ground. The slabs of granite ruptured and spilled into the wolves like a rocky wave, tumbling them onto their backs.

The wave froze, a six-foot swell made of stone. Then the granite exploded outward, raining debris over the room, revealing twelve armored Slayers. Three of the Beasts attacked the wolves, tearing them easily to shreds. The rest turned to Casi.

Blackthorne picked himself up and turned his arms into flaming whips, lashing them at Charles. Casi summoned a battle axe to her hands in a flash of light. She sprinted towards Blackthorne, sliding to her knees to dodge the claws of one of Charles' Slayer minions, and sliced the head off another before resuming her sprint.

Charles had doused Blackthorne's flaming whips with water by the time she reached them. His lower body transformed into that of a snake, coiled around Blackthorne's legs and chest.

She leaped into the air, thrusting the axe high above her head and slamming it into Charles' serpentine waist. Blackthorne sucked in hoarse breaths as the severed snake writhed against his body before bursting into embers of light.

Charles tumbled momentarily as fresh legs grew from his waist. She raised the axe again, but a shooting pain forced her to drop the weapon. Sharp stabs punched into her back and arms, and she turned to see the team of Slayers hurling thin spears at her. A spear pierced her thigh, another her shoulder. Each spear was barbed, and attached to a length of rope. The Slayers pulled hard on their ends, dragging her to the ground.

The download terminals were close enough to touch, but she couldn't move her limbs against the harpoons. Charles transformed into a

Slayer and descended on Blackthorne, savagely beating at him with his clubbed tail, raking him with his claws. Blackthorne could do nothing but try to turn his body to stone, grunting in pain as Charles crushed his limbs to dust.

She gritted her teeth. They weren't going to make it, at least not both of them. She stopped her download and focused on accelerating Blackthorne's, doubling his bandwidth by adding her Akimor's download link to his.

"Casi, no," he cried once he sensed the accelerated download. *"I'm not leaving you."*

He bellowed in anger and swung wildly at Charles, forcing the savage lizard back a few meters. He rolled to his feet and struggled towards Casi, falling before her as one of his legs crumbled into bits of rock. She reached towards his outstretched hand, tears streaming down her face.

Their pinky fingers linked briefly, then Blackthorne vanished, his download complete. Casi wailed, and closed her eyes, trying to find her happy place.

Her body jostled as the Slayers pounced on her, ripping at her flesh with their razor teeth. Their snarls became muted as she found her happy place, at the side of a pool, reading a book and enjoying a frozen drink. For a few moments, she was able to leave the HUB, and enjoy rays of sunshine. She smiled at the familiar sounds of pool water lapping against the concrete sides.

Excruciating pain ripped her from the pool deck, and back into hell. Half her body had been devoured and she could only see the leathery tops of Slayer heads as they gorged on her insides. The Slayers parted, and she lay there trembling, staring into the eyes of her killer.

Charles licked his lips, which were soft and pink and human again. He knelt beside her and licked the side of her face. She wept as he savored the taste of her blood.

She screamed as he clamped his teeth onto her neck, and gurgled as he tore out her throat. A red haze filled her vision, and she stared at the head hovering at the center of the room, red and ghastly.

Charles' head.

It was the last thing she saw before the Apex AI finished eating her alive.

NINETY-ONE

Bear Stafford – Human Titan

On the surface of Blit Kru – Inside secret complex

Bear led his Titans squad in pursuit of the two Slayer scientists they had tailed since entering the Blit-Kru complex. The frail creatures, *Brains* as they called themselves, were thinner than Intellects, but with larger skulls. He could hardly believe their spindly necks could support such weight.

He and his squad had followed the two scientists deep into the facility. He'd listened intently to their conversations, and had gleaned pieces of information as to the status of the superweapon, and the location of Vomisa and Blackthorne. They were getting close to the lab, but with no map to follow, he was forced to creep behind the Brains as they moved slowly towards their research facility.

"*Stafford to Harper,*" he called voicelessly to his second in command. "*What's the status on the data pipeline connections?*"

There was a brief pause, then Harper answered, his voice slightly garbled. "*We've identified the coordinates, but we're having a hard time figuring out a way to sever them. They're deep underground. We may not be able to get to them in time, or at all. Mission failed. Do you want me to come give you guys support?*"

Bear considered the option. If Harper couldn't destroy the data link that connected the Blit-Kru complex to the mountain array, then this was no longer an offensive mission. It was strictly a rescue mission. They needed to retrieve Casi and Blackthorne and scram.

"Negative Harper," he said voicelessly. *"Rally to extract. Get some birds ready on standby. Depending on how things turn out down here, we might be coming out hot."*

"Roger that Bear, we'll be on the roof waiting for you."

The call cut out as Bear terminated the transmission.

They turned a corner, and sharp grunts and growls caused him to freeze. He crouched and signaled for his squad to halt.

A team of four Slayers ambled towards them down the hallway. They paused to let the Brains pass, who didn't acknowledge the giant lizards save for a casual nod. Once the Brains finished walking around them, the Slayer guards dropped to all fours and continued on their way, one of them baring its teeth and grumbling about the weaklings the Pristine had sent to Blit-Kru.

Bear knew they wouldn't be able to see him with his camo engaged, but there was always a chance they would bump into his invisible body. Slayers had a habit of sweeping their long tails from side to side as they walked.

He turned to the rest of his squad, raising a flat palm and pointing it at the approaching enemy. Crystal, Pounder, and Marvyl nodded in acknowledgement, their Akimors traced in blue against his augmented HUD.

"Hug the walls," he said voicelessly. *"Watch their tails. Follow my lead."*

He dropped delicately to all fours and crept forward on his hands and toes as the first Slayer arrived. He ducked beneath the creature's long tails then shifted left to squeeze around the second two Slayers. He hopped over the final Slayer's tail as it dragged across the hall and turned to wait for the rest of his team to arrive. Marvyl and Pounder made it past the Slayers with no trouble.

One of the Slayers complained about the meager meals on the frozen planet, and received a testy swipe of a claw from his comrade. Crystal barely ducked the jab and had to tumble forward into a barrel roll to avoid tripping over the creature's hind leg. Her shoulder made a muted thump against the metal floor, causing the Slayers to whip their heads around and sniff the air.

"I heard something," said one of the Slayers. "A scuffling sound."

"It was probably the scientist weaklings," said another. "They walk like newborn forest creatures. It's a pity we can't eat them. They have little meat on their bones, but I would love to suck the juices from their plump skulls."

"Honor the Pristine," one of them snarled. "Do not speak of the Brains as if they were filth. They are servants to the Sterilord, as are we." He sniffed the air. "I do smell something odd. I smell electricity. Perhaps the demons are inside."

"The whole building reeks of electricity," said the one at the front of the group. "Forget about your smells, they are probably burned into your nostrils permanently. Come, we need to make our rounds to the outside."

They turned and continued down the hall, one of them complaining about how cold it was on the icy planet, and another stating that at least it doesn't smell like electricity out in the snow.

"The Brains," said Bear over central comms. *"We can't lose them. Come on."*

They crept forward as quickly as possible, careful not to draw too much power from their micro-fusion reactors and cause their Akimors to whir mechanically.

They closed in on the Brains, who had surprisingly stopped walking. One of them was holding a tablet, waving at it and pointing to various holograms. Bear began to zoom his optics in on the tablet when a frantic voice shot onto their central comm line.

"Any Titans out there, this is Silas Blackthorne. I escaped captivity, I'm in a Slayer lab and need evac. Where are you? Putting my coordinates out on central comms."

Bear received the coordinates from Blackthorne and displayed them on his HUD. To his surprise, the distressed Titan was very close, less than a hundred meters down the hallways.

"Blackthorne, this is Bear Stafford, we read you. Hang tight, we'll be there in a few. Our tracking pins are available on central comms. Are you with Casi Vomisa?"

Alarms blared suddenly before Blackthorne could respond. The hall flooded in green strobes of light, and the two Brains began to sprint down the hall, one of them dropping its tablet to the ground in haste.

The enemy scientists were running toward the lab, toward Blackthorne.

Bear broke into a sprint, forcing his camo to operate at diminished capacity. To any keen observers, he would no longer appear invisible, but rather like a watery blob in the shape of a Titan. He figured the alarms would drown out the whirring of his Akimor.

His Titan team followed close behind. Blackthorne's voice shot into his ear, grunting, as if under duress.

"Bear, the weapon…it's activated…Charles is escaping…Casi's gone."

Bear drew his MGK rifle and cut tightly around a corner. The Brains had stopped at the end of the hall and were fumbling with a rectangular access panel beside a heavy set of metal doors. He trained his rifle on the scientists, ready to eliminate whatever threats lay past the thick entrance.

His rifle flew from his hands as he collided with an invisible wall, sending him hard onto his back. In a flash of light, a Slayer Cogent materialized, dropping its stealth shielding.

"Filth," the Cogent roared, hefting an energy hammer and driving the blunt face towards Bear's head.

Bear punched his thrusters and blasted away from the Cogent, his back scraping against the ground. The hammer pounded the floor between his legs and the resulting shockwave punched his groin, turning his gut to lead.

His momentum carried him straight into Crystal, who flipped into the air before landing in a crouch. Bear struggled to his feet, trying to block the wrenching pain from his mind.

The Cogent screamed in rage and three additional Cogent materialized behind it, dropping their stealth shields and lighting their battle armor in yellow flashes of light.

The hall swelled with brightness as the two opposing sides traded fire, the Titans firing MGK slugs and lasers from their Akimors, the Cogent firing their plasma rifles in return.

One of the Cogent withered against an intense energy beam as Crystal drained her energy reserves, firing a cannon blast from both palms. Defenseless, she crouched low to the ground as another Cogent leaped over its fallen comrade. The beast soared through the air towards Crystal, whose lattice shields had gone dark.

Bear sprinted towards Crystal's assaulter and intercepted its angle of attack, driving the Slayer elite into the wall. It crumpled against the combined force of their bodies.

He winced as the metal in the walls bent around his armor, pinning him against the Cogent They struggled visciously against one another. He cried in pain as the Slayer clamped its jaws onto his neck, shaking its head back and forth. His Akimor blared warnings at him as the Slayer hammered his back and legs with its tail, and slashed his sides with its claws.

He extracted both swords. One missed the Beast and punched into the wall. The other pierced the creature's armored side, causing it to shriek and wrench itself free of the battered metal surrounding them.

The creature threw Bear across the hallway, but his sword remained lodged in the wall, snapping his hand off at the wrist. He shouted in pain, cradling his stubby arm against his stomach. Flashes of blue peppered the hallways as his Titan squad threw frag grenades into the Cogent, and he winced as some of the shrapnel caught his sides, detonating in concentrated blasts of electricity.

He slipped a sidearm from his side holster and fired it at a struggling Slayer, deftly nosing a few rounds into a gap in its damaged helmet. The enemy dropped to the floor. No sooner had the Cogent fallen when a crushing blow to Bear's back sent him spiraling through the air. His armor failed as he landed in a shower of sparks, and he twisted around to find a Cogent swinging an energy hammer at him.

This time his Akimor didn't have enough energy reserves to activate his thrusters, and he squeezed his eyes shut, bracing for impact.

The blow never came. Instead, a wailing screech filled his ears. He opened his eyes to find the Slayer stumbling forwards, tripping over its two severed arms that still clutched the hammer. A Titan stepped over Bear's line of vision and thrust an energy sword through the creature's neck.

As the Slayer elite slumped to the ground, the Titan turned to face him. He retracted his sword and extended a hand. Bear grabbed it and pulled himself up.

"Bear Stafford?" said the Titan.

"Yes," he managed, wincing against the pain ravaging his battered body.

The pain gradually subsided as his Akimor made critical internal repairs. He looked to the rest of his squad. The Cogent were all dead. Crystal and Pounder were tending to Maryvl, who had lost both legs, and had a gaping hole smoking in his chest.

"Silas Blackthorne," said the Titan, saluting him. "The Apex weapon's been activated. We need to get off Blit-Kru *immediately.*"

NINETY-TWO

Bear Stafford – Human Titan

On the surface of Blit Kru – Inside secret complex

"Where's Casi Vomisa?" Bear demanded, searching the halls. He bent to pick up a discarded MGK rifle and checked the slide.

Blackthorne shook his head, his eyes squinted in grief. "I don't know, sir. I was with her until the end. Charles," he paused and shook his head some more. "Charles got her. She didn't download into her Akimor. Your team never came into the lab. That bastard tricked us."

Bear took a brief moment to place a hand on Blackthorne's shoulder. He didn't have time to ask the details. If they made it out of Blit-Kru, the Titan would give him a full de-brief. For now, he knew enough to confirm his suspicions. Charles was a Slayer AI superweapon, and it had just taken UCOM's most powerful AI out of commission.

"Help me with my team," he said to Blackthorne. "I have a bird waiting on the roof for evac. Check your central comms for coordinates."

He left Blackthorne and rushed to Marvyl's side. The wounded Titan was motionless, and his eyes had stopped glowing.

"Is he gone?" said Bear, pressing a palm to Marvyl's head.

"Almost," said Pounder. "We can try severing his head and linking him to one of our Akimor's, but my energy reserves are too low, almost below critical. Crystal's aren't much better."

"Twelve percent," Crystal confirmed. "My cannon blast drained a lot of it, and then I got mauled by one of the Snakes."

She shook her left arm, which hung limp and had a deep gouge running from shoulder to elbow.

"My reserves are drained as well," said Blackthorne. "The Brains sucked me dry in their lab."

Bear checked his own energy reserves. *14%.* Not quite at critical levels, but not nearly enough to clamp a Titan head to his chest and place him on life support.

Shouts echoed down the halls. He turned to find six Brains scampering around the corner. They skidded to a halt once they saw the gruesome scene surrounding the Titans, then quickly turned to run away. Bear shouldered his MGK and fired using one hand, killing four of them. Blackthorne took out the other two with headshots, causing their bulbous skulls to explode in fine purple mist.

"Filth," a ragged voice snarled from further down the hall. Bear perked his sensitive hearing instruments.

"I can smell them," hissed another. "Electric demons."

Bear turned and grabbed Crystal by the shoulder, pulling her away from Marvyl. "Leave him," he said, prying the ID tag from the Titan's breast plate and slipping it into his thigh container. "He's in the stars now."

"I can't engage my camo," said Pounder softly, staring at his fallen teammate before forcing his eyes away.

The sounds of the approaching Slayers grew louder.

"None of us can," said Bear, scanning the squad's energy readings over central comms. "There's a transport shaft ahead. Two hundred fifty meters. Let's move."

They sprinted down the hall without delay, cutting a hard right around the corner towards the vertical pathway, which Bear marked on comms with a green diamond. The Slayers they'd heard howled with rage to the left of the 'T' junction, but after a quick glance, Bear found they weren't armored Cogent, but rather two ordinary grunts. He wouldn't even bother attacking them.

He relayed the order to ignore the Slayers, and continued his sprint, wincing at the occasional plasma round that found his back as the Beasts fired from the distance.

They reached the elevators in exactly eighteen seconds. Bear waited patiently for his team to file in, and took cover around the inside corner of the lift. He accessed the hologram controls, and breathed a sigh of relief when he found that all the security codes had been lifted. A single message flashed at the top of the display. He translated quickly from Slayer-speak to English.

Server breach – APEX out of containment.

He punched the controls to the roof level and squatted as the cargo lift rocketed upwards.

"Bear to Harper," he broadcast over central comms. *"We're heading to the roof, half-click from extract. We're coming out on a lift, marking exit point."*

"I see you Bear," said Harper. *"We're circling in a Spider. It's pretty chaotic up here, these scaly bastards are going ape-shit. The sky's lit up like fireworks, something big's going on inside the mountains."*

The lift stopped before Harper could finish his sentence. The doors slid open to expose sheer bedlam. Slayers and Brains alike were sprinting across the rooftops, streaming out of hundreds of lifts opening to the roof, identical to the one Bear and his squad had taken from the complex. Two Slayers streaked around them, paused, then hurried on their way without attacking. Bear lowered his rifle without firing.

"What are they running from Harper?" he called.

A thick stream of laser fire answered him, incinerating the two Slayers that had just scampered past. A Spider air-space vehicle hit its landing jets and eased downward until it hovered a meter off the rooftop.

A hatch swung open on the side, and two of his Titan teammates reached their arms out. Crystal was the first to leap onto the craft, grabbing Loko's outstretched arm and hoisting herself in. Vixtor helped Pounder in after her, then Blackthorne. After scanning the roof to clear their surroundings of any immediate threats, Bear jumped into the Spider, slumping to the deck as Harper pulled them sharply away from the complex.

"Where's Marvyl?" said Loko.

"He didn't make it," said Pounder.

Loko bared his teeth and pounded his Slayer tail hard into the ground. The group sat silently for a brief second as they processed Marvyl's sacrifice.

"Awaken stars," said Bear.

"Awaken stars," the rest of the group murmured in return.

"Run diagnostics on your Akimors," said Bear. "Catalogue which of your systems are critically damaged so we can adjust our combat strategy. Run scans on Blackthorne, make sure his consciousness transferred properly into his Akimor."

"Aye," said Crystal.

He slid to Vixtor and Loko, who were not in android Akimors, but in genetically engineered Slayer bodies. "Do either of you require medical attention?"

They both shook their heads, Vixtor running a black tongue over his fangs. "I took a piece of shrapnel in the gut on the roof, but this bird has Slayer med kits, so I was able to patch myself up. Armor's good, but my ammo's running a bit dry. A hundred-eighteen rounds left and two frags."

Loko nodded. "I'm fine, had to scrap a damaged wrist plate but none of my instruments were damaged." He flexed a beefy forearm that was bare of armor and covered only with rugged scales. "I'm low on ammo too. I had to ditch my MGK for a plasma rifle I picked off a dead Snake, only ten percent charge left."

Bear nodded. "You boys hang tight."

The two Titan Snake-skins nodded and slouched against the side of the cargo bay. Bear left to join Harper, climbing into the seatless cockpit, custom in Slayer designed ships.

"Take a look at this shit," said Harper. "You ever seen anything like it?"

They were climbing through the atmosphere at a sharp angle, but the complex was still visible below, miniaturized against the blanket of snow covering Blit-Kru. The mountain range crackled with energy. Thick laser beams pulsed from the tops of the craggy peaks, blasting through the atmosphere and into space. The air around them was dusted with thousands of Slayer craft, also climbing sharply through the atmosphere to space.

An alarm blared, and a Wasp fast-attack fighter buzzed past them, inches away from clipping their starboard wing. Bear instinctively reached for the weapons controls.

"Don't bother," said Harper. "The Slayers aren't attacking. There's a full-scale evacuation underway. They're practically tripping over one another to get off Blit-Kru. Whatever those beams are, it's scaring them shitless."

"Charles," Bear murmured. He turned to lean towards the cargo bay. "Blackthorne, get in here."

Blackthorne sat up, swatting away Crystal's hand, which was lit in pink light from her neural scanning equipment.

"I'm not done with his con-sketch," she called.

"It can wait," said Bear.

Crystal shrugged, and the pink instruments on her fingertips dimmed. Blackthorne climbed into the cockpit between Bear and Harper. He cursed lightly under his breath when he saw the beams of energy pulsing into the air.

"You know what those are?" said Bear.

Blackthorne nodded. "That's Charles, I guess the bastard wasn't lying about everything."

"I need to get things straight," said Bear. "Charles, who is..."

"The Slayer weapon," said Blackthorne. "He goes by the name *Charles.* He's an APEX AI, more powerful than me, or even Casi. His programming is so large, he needs those energy beams for transport."

Bear listened intently as Blackthorne recounted his story of inside the complex. He frowned when Silas described the inside of his digital jail cell, and how the Brain scientists separated their emotions and fed Casi's emotional copies to Charles' program. Blackthorne became choked up when he told of their battle inside the Foxwood HUB, and how after being weakened by bad memories, Casi was taken by Charles as he escaped into his android.

"Did she survive?" said Bear when he finished.

Blackthorne shrugged his shoulders. "I don't think so. The last thing I saw before I left was those bastards tearing into her skin. Charles was fruxin' *eating* her."

Bear frowned. *A program eating another program.* Perhaps to assimilate?

"Do you know where the energy beams lead?" he asked.

His question was answered before Blackthorne could respond. They reached the edge of the stratosphere, and Blit-Kru's pale blue sky vanished into blackness. Stars studded the vacuum. Looming to their left was the planet's moon.

Dozens of laser beams sliced from the planet's surface and met in a circular collar above the moon. The collar channeled the beams into a thick column that pulsed into the celestial satellite, lighting it a brilliant green.

"The Slayers turned the moon into a computer," said Blackthorne. "Charles said that's where we would escape. Looks like he was telling the truth. He said the moon had everything we would need to leave Blit-Kru, even starships."

"What the hell kind of starship can hold that kind of energy?" said Harper. "The damn moon looks like it can't even hold all of it."

Suddenly the beams of energy stopped. The brightness dimmed, and their Spider's canopy reduced its tint levels.

"Zoom into the surface," said Bear.

Hunter worked the controls, and holograms of the moon's surface danced above the console. Wide patches of the glowing orbs shifted around, as if they were squirming.

"Is the moon vibrating?" said Harper.

"It's de-atomizing," said Bear. "Charles must be building a molecular assembler."

"Take as much video and signature readings as you can," said Bear. "We'll deliver this to UNI. What are the Slayer's saying on chatter?"

"Sure as hell aren't talking about us anymore," said Harper. "There's only one central broadcast, and all it says it that there's been a breach of security, and the APEX is possibly rogue. They didn't commission the data transfer to the moon. They have rally points behind the Frontline at a Slayer Hive."

"We're not going to follow them," said Bear. "Thank the stars they're not checking encryption codes with all their starcraft. We should be able to slip out of here no problem. Plot course for the Inner Ring."

Harper acknowledged and steered the Spider towards the nearest portal. Bear stared at the moon right up until they passed through the portal, washing the ship in red light.

As they left Blit-Kru starspace, a nagging thought tugged at his mind.

If the Slayers were so terrified of Charles, how scared should UCOM be?

***

They traveled for nearly a day through portals, inching their way across the galaxy through a disintegrating transportation infrastructure ravaged by war. It wasn't until they were 10,000 light years from the Inner Ring that they received their first Network update from a nearby Raven.

Its message was more chilling than the APEX AI weapon they'd just witnessed.

First they received a single command word.

Ral-Bazeera.

Bear had no understanding of the word. It wasn't stored in his Program's vocabulary, but it sounded like Slayer-speak. The second message caused him to curse under his breath.

Priority One Message from Eminence Draxton Tyke: -The Council decrees that all Humans and Clones are hereby exiled from UCOM. Their commanders are to relinquish control of UCOM military craft, and turn themselves in to UCOM authorities at the planet Gefangria for temporary detainment. Violators are to be shot, and their ships eliminated with lethal force.

"Humans and Clones have been exiled?" Crystal exclaimed.

"What's that mean for you, Bear?" said Loko, rolling from his scaled back to all fours. "Are you…"

"I'm a Titan," he said. "Not a Human."

"So we head for the Inner Ring?" said Harper.

Bear remained silent. Titans pledged an oath to defend UCOM, under the faith of the stars. He'd also made a different promise to Francis Woods.

"Sixty portals until Inner Ring starspace," said Harper. "Do you want me to send a Flea to confirm the message?"

"Send a Flea," said Bear, "But not to the Inner Ring. Send a private message to Francis Woods."

Harper stared at him. "Sir, the Raven message..."

"I know what the damned Raven said. Before I left Dominia, I promised Eminence Woods my loyalty."

"We take orders from UCOM," said Harper slowly. "Woods is no longer a part of UCOM."

"You're right," he said. "Woods is no longer a part of UCOM, if you believe Draxton's message. Don't lecture me on our Titan code, I memorized it the same as you. But I'll clarify part of that code. We serve the UCOM navy, but owe our lives to those who call the Milky Way home. Woods also owes his life to the Milky Way as Eminence. He saw this coming, and formed a contingency plan to save the Milky Way from civil war. I will execute this plan, even if it's in direct conflict of UCOM orders."

Harper paused. "What you're suggesting is treason."

Bear bristled and drew a sidearm. Harper and Pounder drew their sidearms in return, energizing their shields. Crystal tensed beside him. Bear raised his pistol slowly towards the ceiling, then spun the weapon around to hold the barrel. He extended the handle to Harper, who grabbed it cautiously. With a growl, Bear grabbed Harper's wrist and rammed the pistol against his own temple.

"What I'm suggesting is to save the Milky Way from Charles," said Bear. "If you think that's treason, then fine. Pull the trigger. Kill me as the traitor I am. I'm not going to sit back and watch that AI attack our homeland."

Harper stared icily into Bear's eyes for several seconds, then lowered his shields. He dropped the sidearm to the floor and took a step back.

"Easy Bear," he said. "If you know a way to stop Charles, then I'm all ears. Just following the way of things, that's all."

"Get a Flea ready," said Bear, bending to retrieve his pistol and clamping it to his thigh.

Harper cocked his head, then turned back to the flight controls. "Aye, preparing the Flea."

"We're not going to the Inner Ring any longer," he said. "Plot a new set of vectors to nav-link at these coordinates. I'm sending a folder to central comms detailing *Project Shepherd.*"

He relayed the coordinates to Harper, and entered the message into the Flea himself.

After the Flea had been sent, Bear thought about the contingency plan Woods had laid out to him before he left for Blit-Kru with Casi.

Project Shepherd.

Before leaving Dominia, he'd calculated the probability of having to enact Project Shepherd as low. It seems his calculations had been wrong.

NINETY-THREE

Francis Woods – Human

Aboard Tiger *Mariella* – Approaching Earth starspace

Woods studied the holograms flashing across the command deck interface aboard *Mariella.* The data was sparse, to the point where it was impossible to form a sound military strategy from the available intelligence.

He rubbed his temple, sorting through the options. Zena Olleeve sat to his right, and had her head in her hands, moving her lips silently, as if in prayer. Commander Cage sat across the table sifting through various holograms, coordinating fleet control and logistics.

"Fleet's in formation," he said, brushing the holograms to the side so he could meet Woods' eyes. "We're still getting pinged like crazy by Ravens from the Inner Ring. Draxton will know exactly where we are."

"Not that it matters," said Zena, raising her head from her hands and issuing a long sigh. "It doesn't take a military genius to guess we'd head straight to Earth."

Woods turned to look around the bridge. Cage's officers were in battle mode, bustling about their stations and barking into their intercoms. Every inch of the bridge showed live video of their surroundings. The sizeable fleet of Human ships that had followed *Mariella* from the Inner Ring surrounded them in tight formation. Thousands of Tiger heavies idled their thrusters nearby, and past their bulky hulls, Woods could spot lighter Lynx and Cheetah craft patrolling the perimeter.

"We'll deal with Draxton later," said Woods. "Right now we need to rally Earth. Any luck with our Ravens?"

Cage flipped through a few holograms before swatting them away in disgust. "Nothing. We're blind. We can't get past Earth's spacnar defenses, and the Ravens that get past the bubble aren't returning from the portal. They're probably getting shot down."

Woods magnified a hologram of the nearby portal his fleet was stationed around. Earth lay on the other side. Normally approaching Earth would instill a sense of comfort. But with the planet's surveillance defense systems activated, Woods instead felt a sense of dread.

Swarms of Ravens flitted in and out of the green sphere, but instead of returning with detailed scans of Earth and her surrounding military infrastructure, they were returning with static and wiped memories, or not returning at all.

"Should we send a few Cheetahs in on a flyby?" said Zena. "Or maybe some Night Eagles?"

Woods shook his head. "I'm not sending anyone to their death to tell me something I already know. You can bet Earth has a sandstorm surrounding the portal. Even a Night Eagle in full stealth would get blasted with active spacnar and detained, or worse, shot down." He paused, looking towards the ceiling. "Blaze?" he called aloud.

His new digital assistant materialized on the holodeck, running a hand through her fiery hair and turning to face him.

"Sir," she said.

"What are we seeing inside the portal on the AI side?"

"Nothing sir," she said. "The turnstiles are unencrypted, but the outward cameras and data transmitters are blocked. We can't get through unless we're riding on a ship."

Woods nodded. "Thank you Blaze. Send a priority command on central comms. We're moving through the portal to Earth."

"The whole fleet?" said the AI, raising an eyebrow.

"Yes," said Woods. "United we stand. I do want to hang a few ships back here though in case we receive Network correspondence. Keep a squadron of Night Eagles at these coordinates in full stealth."

"Aye," said Blaze, disappearing from the holodeck.

Voices shouted from the battle stations as Blaze relayed the information. Cage stared grimly at Woods.

"You're sure about this?" said the commander. "We spent the past hundred-fifty years transforming Earth into a fortress. We won't be able to take them on in battle.

Woods stood slowly and walked to Cage, placing a hand on the man's shoulder. "I would no sooner battle Earth then I would battle you. I assume Earth will return the favor, no matter what kind of garbage Draxton has filled their ears with from the Inner Ring. We're going in peacefully, shields down. *Awaken stars.*"

Cage stood and gripped the back of Woods' neck. He stepped forward as Cage pulled him into an embrace.

"*Awaken stars, my friend,*" Cage whispered into Woods ear. They drew apart.

Cage walked to the front of the bridge and began to communicate with his officers, laying strategy on how to proceed through the portal to Earth. Blue jets licked the vacuum around him as the rest of the fleet energized their thrusters.

Woods leaned over the central table and readied audio feed to address the fleet. The rapid shouts and reports from the command bridge dulled as noise-blockers deadened the surrounding buzz, leaving him in a peaceful bubble. Taking a deep breath, he addressed his fleet.

"This is President Woods. We're returning to Earth, some of you for the first time in hundreds of years, some of you for the first time in your entire lives. Our lack of Raven intel suggests a militarized buildup of Earth defenses. If we encounter warships, know that the men and women inside them are not our enemies, but our brothers and sisters. Shortly you will see a blue planet. This planet is not just a mote of dust and water, it's our home. It's the seed that birthed our very existence. It's also our only chance of survival against the invading Slayers." He paused. Zena turned to face the portal, now looming large before *Mariella,* basking them in green light. "Mother," he said.

"Earth, Earth, Earth."

He turned to find Cage's crew returning the traditional cry after hearing it through central comms.

"Mother," he cried, louder.

"Earth Earth Earth."

"MOTHER!"

"EARTH! EARTH! EARTH!"

Green light engulfed them as they passed through the portal, flanked by hundreds of Tiger heavy-destroyers.

The bridge transformed quickly as they left the portal and entered Earth starspace. Woods' stomach dropped as he looked upon his homeland for the first time since he left for the Frontline.

He stepped numbly away from the holodeck, leaving the sound damper to stare through the bridge wall, unable to tear his eyes away. Cage roared as he commanded logistics. Blaze appeared beside him, asking frantically for orders.

Woods hardly heard either of them.

Planet Earth was surrounded by an enormous armada, their shields energized, and RA-CAN's fully charged. Tens of thousands of Tigers shone brightly as they trained their weapons on the emerging fleet of Human outcasts. The four PDR's surrounding Earth had their cannons charged as well, as did several Lions and a massive supertower hanging beyond the moon's orbit.

"It's a trap," Blaze shouted. "The entire armada has Destineer markings and ID tags. They're not even trying to hide those designations from us. Scans are showing superior kinetic strength. I have offensive target locks coming from one-hundred percent of the fleet. We're sitting ducks sir. Should I warn the rest of the fleet before they travel through the port…"

"Hold steady," said Woods. "Flash signs of surrender, and lower all shields and weapons after formation."

"Expose our ships?" said Blaze weakly.

Woods turned to the AI. She gulped, her eyes glowing as she relayed the orders. They widened suddenly, and returned to normal.

"Priority one message," she cried. "Video request coming from supertower *Barbican*, from a man called Sharker Gray."

"Put it through on my private channel," said Woods, striding to the holodeck.

"Aye," said Blaze, disappearing from the deck only to re-appear on the main console. This time, not only the sound dampened, but a wall of light shielded them from the surrounding stations.

Zena stepped around the table to join Woods at his side. He paused, and almost jerked as she grabbed his hand in hers and gave it a quick squeeze. He snapped his focus back to the console as the avatar of a burly, bearded man appeared on the opposite side of the table, glowering at Woods.

"Eminence Woods," said the man. "Or should I say…what should I call you now? *Mr.* Woods?"

"Sharker Gray," said Woods. "I think I read an intelligence report on you a while back. Give Sid Dakota my regards."

"You can tell him yourself," said Sharker, smiling coyly. "You'll get a chance to bow at his feet when he comes with the rest of the Slarebull. That is, assuming you do what's right and surrender your ships."

"You're making a big mistake," Woods growled. "There aren't enough Destineers in the universe to operate a fleet this size. You're running a skeleton crew. My Titans will have your ships commandeered before you can blink. Back down and I'll make sure you get a fair trial."

Sharker chuckled. He turned to face Zena. "Is that a Clone?" He smiled widely. "Yes, that's Zena Olleeve, I'd recognize that striking face anywhere. I'm impressed Woods. I was half expecting you to be slumming around with a Guardian."

His smile vanished at the thought of filth.

"The Guardians saved us," said Woods. "Or have you forgotten already?"

"The Guardians *enslaved* us," Sharker spat. "They tricked us into fighting against our saviors, tried to stop us from entering the holy kingdom as gods." His lip curled. "You're blind to the truth. Look around you, Woods. You still claim the Slarebull to be the enemy, but Earth has spoken. Those ships are not empty, far from it. They are loaded with faithful servants to the Doctrine. You still think most Humans are against me, but you're sadly mistaken. Most Humans are against *you*. The citizens of humanity have chosen the righteous path, and now I am giving your fleet one final chance to choose it for themselves."

"Sharker," Woods started, but the Destineer cut him off.

"Your time for delivering orders has reached an end. It is my holy duty to steer as many Humans as possible towards the kingdom, but if you do not cooperate, I will be forced to destroy you and your fleet. Here's what you will do, and you will do it immediately. All of your ships will open their hatches for entry, and will be boarded by Destineer troops. All of your light craft will dock with *Barbican* and relinquish themselves to Destineer pilots. All non-Humans and non-Clones...all the *filth*, will segregate into separate formations for sentencing. And you," Sharker snorted. "You will travel to *Barbican* and kneel before my feet. Then you will broadcast your faith to the rest of your fleet. You will go on central comms and speak to your men and women, demanding they pledge their allegiance to the Destineers. And if you do all those things, then you may live."

Woods trembled with rage. He forced his shoulders to relax. He hung his head. "You win. I fight for Humans, and if Earth has decided this is what it wants, I will die defending that ambition. I pray to stars you're right about this."

Sharker smirked. "Stars? You pray to the *Pristine.*"

"Yes," said Woods. "The Pristine." He sighed. "Give me an hour to ready my transport, and I'll be in *Barbican.* Send me the docking protocols for me and my light craft."

"Not an hour," said Sharker. "Twenty minutes. If you're not inside *Barbican* by then, or if you try to flee, your fleet will be vaporized."

NINETY-FOUR

Francis Woods – Human
Aboard Tiger *Mariella* – Earth starspace

The light barrier lowered, and *Mariella's* command bridge came into view. The cavernous room was silent, and Woods didn't at first realize the audio damper had shut off.

Zena dug her nails into his arm. "You're going to bow to that *traitor?*" she hissed.

He shrugged her off and raised a finger to silence her. "Blaze," he called.

"Sir," said Blaze, appearing beside him.

"Ready a Leopard, minimal crew, set nav-link to the *Barbican* coordinates Sharker sent."

"Aye," said Blaze before disappearing.

"What just happened Woods?" said Commander Cage, stepping down to the pit. "Why are you readying a Leopard for *Barbican?*"

"He's going to cut a deal with the Destineers," said Zena, her lip quivering. "He's going to parley with Sharker Gray."

"Enough," said Woods. "I'm not cutting any deals, I'm buying us time."

Cage and Zena blinked at him.

"Buying us time to do what?" said Cage. "I have hostile weapons locks on our entire fleet. Our only option is to flee, we can't win this one. It's a numbers game."

"Fleeing's not an option," said Woods. "Not yet at least."

"Then we surrender?" said Cage. "Or fight?"

"We surrender," said Woods. "I'll never fight my own people."

"Surrender?" cried Cage, shaking his head. "I don't know Woods, I'm not sure I'm following you. Those ships all have Destineer tags, I don't consider them *our people.*"

"We surrender for now," said Woods. "Until we get a fix on things. We can't deplete our navy any more than we already have. When the time is right, we'll take Earth back. Something's not right. Sharker Gray claims to command Earth's full compliment of warships. I have too much faith in our troops to believe he has outright control of their defenses. My bet is that he's hanging onto his authority by a thread. I need to meet him face to face, and see if I can depressurize the situation."

"And if they attack before then?" said Cage.

"Then I've failed Earth as a leader."

Cage nodded. "What do you need me to do? Our Tiger commanders are flooding comms with RFO's, I need to give them orders."

Blaze appeared on the AI bridge. "Leopard's ready for departure. I have a pod ready for you at the bay." Her eyes glazed over. "I have another priority one message," she cried.

"From Sharker?" said Woods.

Blaze shook her head. "No, it's not over central comms. It's addressed to you personally. It's from a Titan named Bear Stafford. Heading – *Project Shepherd.*"

"Put him through," said Woods, rushing to the command table.

"You need to leave for *Barbican,*" said Zena. "If you're going to meet with Sharker, you need to leave now or you won't meet your deadline."

"Put Stafford's message through," Woods repeated, ignoring Zena. The Clone pressed her lips but followed him to the table nonetheless, as did Cage.

Bear Stafford's android frame appeared on the console. The room quieted as the audio curtain raised around them. The Titan's face was grim.

"I'm going to keep this short due to security concerns," said the Titan. "We failed our mission on Blit-Kru. Vomisa is either captured or killed. The Slayer weapon is powerful on the highest orders of magnitude, and has been unleashed into the Milky Way. I've received Draxton's decree. We need to activate *Project Shepherd.* I'm setting up base at the designated outpost, and energizing the infrastructure. Our scientific asset is en route, and will be here by the attached time stamp. Send a confirmation signal when you can. *Awaken Stars.*"

Woods glanced at the few lines of information attached to the message. It had taken the Raven three days to reach him over the Network, and the time stamp was frozen at *00:00:00.* Project Shepherd was up and running. Now, he just needed to get to the outpost.

He turned to Cage. "I'm going to send a file to your Program titled *Project Shepherd.* I don't have time to explain, but I need to leave Earth."

Zena shook her head incredulously. "You're not going to meet with Sharker? He's going to vaporize our fleet."

"I'm still meeting with Sharker. But I'm not coming back after our parley. You're going to have to trust me. I have a plan. I'll send you the details from my pod."

Cage opened his mouth, but no words came out. "You're leaving Earth?" he managed in a hoarse whisper.

Woods placed a hand on the Commander's shoulder. "My heart is always with Earth. Stars know how much I wish I could stay. Scramble our entire fleet of Night Eagles, I'm leaving in stealth. When I'm gone, you're in charge. As it stands now, I'm officially transferring command of Earth's navy to you in my absence."

"Where are you going?" whispered Zena.

He turned to the Clone leader. "Away. Sharker can't know I'm gone. I'll send details soon, but I have a Leopard to catch."

He turned without another word and climbed the steps two at a time towards the pod bay at the back of the bridge. Blaze was already waiting for him inside his pod as he climbed inside.

"We're cutting it close," she said. "You might miss your window."

Woods didn't respond, and instead displayed an image on the wall of the pod, superimposed against the lights streaking past them as they raced towards the hangars. His daughter smiled back at him, not in 3D, but flat and old, like his fondest memories of her. He wondered if Nancy was still alive, somewhere in the depths of the Milky Way, or if she was in the stars now. He felt oddly content with the prospect of failing his mission, and joining her in the stars.

"Is that your wife?" said Blaze.

He snapped his eyes from Nancy's picture and swatted the image from the pod wall.

"Daughter," he said.

"Is she on Earth?"

"I wish."

Blaze frowned slightly, but let it rest. "We're approaching *Cherokee.*"

The pod jolted as their pod entered the Leopard, and shuddered as the light-destroyer accelerated immediately after receiving their transport vehicle. The doors glided open and Woods stepped onto the hangar deck. It was empty, save for two armed guards.

He turned to face the bay windows. *Mariella* was already receding into the distance, blending in with the rest of his fleet, which stretched toward a lone portal on the edge of *Earth* starspace.

He turned back to the guards. "Two of you?"

They looked at one another. "You asked for minimal escort, sir."

"That means zero guards," said Woods. "You boys are staying here. Take this, I won't be needing it."

He unholstered his sidearm and held it out to one of the guards, who took it slowly. "Sir, we have orders…"

"You have new orders," said Woods. "You're hanging back."

He strode away from the guards, Blaze following alongside him, her avatar striding silently along the grated deck.

"We'll dock with *Barbican* in twelve minutes," she said. "We'll make our window, but barely."

Woods nodded, but wasn't too concerned with meeting the time window. Sharker was a bad dude, but he didn't have the spine to pull the trigger as soon as the clock hit zero. The Destineer would get what he wanted. He'd be speaking with the leader of Earth face to face. And as leader of Earth, Woods would bow at Sharker's feet.

He entered a lift and stared out the window as he climbed to *Cherokee's* boarding gate. They had reached *Barbican*, and slowed as they entered one of the thousands of docks lining the massive supertower.

"I need you to relay a set of instructions to Cage," he said, turning to Blaze.

The AI nodded. "Whatever you need."

"I want our Night Eagles to evacuate all non-Human and non-Clone ships. We need to get those spacers away from Earth. They're not safe here. If I return, I need a Night Eagle to hang back and pick me up from *Cherokee*."

"If you return?" said Blaze.

Woods nodded. "Stars pray that I do. Remind Cage that under no condition is he to fire upon Earth's defenses."

Blaze nodded. "Aye sir."

The floor shuddered as *Cherokee* finished docking with *Barbican.* The doors hissed and glided open, exposing a hallway packed with armed Destineers.

Woods raised both hands and stepped from his ship, entering the halls of the enemy.

NINETY-FIVE

Francis Woods – Human
Aboard defense tower *Barbican* – Earth starspace

Guards advanced quickly towards him, rifles drawn. Six of them walked around him and began scanning the empty space of the entry hatch, undoubtedly checking for camouflaged Titans. Two of them grabbed his arms and wrenched them to his sides, and two more patted his waist and thighs.

"You're not going to find anything," he said. "Nice of Sharker to send such a warm welcome party."

"Area's clear," said one of the guards from behind.

"He's clean," said another, standing as he finished patting Woods' ankles.

Woods lunged as he was pulled forward and caught himself, slamming his right foot forward to keep from sprawling onto the deck. Two soldiers gripped his elbows and dragged him into the middle of the group, which followed around him as they proceeded down the halls.

"I can walk on my own," he growled, tearing his arms loose from the Destineer guards. "Let me keep a shred of dignity."

The men snorted, but allowed him to walk unmolested.

They traveled down the halls for a stretch, making a few turns before entering a cavernous lift. The lift rocketed upwards once the doors closed, and they stood in silence as they traveled up the enormous defense tower.

They entered a smaller hallway, and the walls beeped and chirped as they acknowledged security readings from the Destineers. At the end, one of the Guards punched at a display, entering another set of passwords and biometrics for access.

The doors grinded open to expose a large, circular room, made entirely of glass.

A single table filled the center of the room, with men and women in military dress sitting around it. A lone figure stood at the edge of the room, facing through the transparent wall and into the surrounding vacuum.

"Leave him," said the man, turning to face the guards. "Wait in the halls for my word."

The men bowed and left, the doors sliding shut behind them. Woods stepped cautiously into the room, peering through the glass at his feet into the vastness of space. *Barbican's* outside hull stretched far below, studded with the glowing barrels of RA-CAN's and hangar bays.

"Sharker Gray," he said, drawing his attention to the burly, bearded man walking towards him. "And your posse."

Woods nodded to the few dozen men and women seated at the table.

"They're not my posse," said Sharker. "Even now, you act as though no sane Human would enlist the help of a Destineer. Those are the highest ranking generals of United Earth. Surely, as former Eminence, you would have recognized a face or two?"

Woods studied some of the faces, realizing how long he'd been away from Earth. He kicked himself for not spending more time at his home planet. All of them were foreign to him but one.

"Harold Dunbar," he said. "I remember pinning the bars on your chest. I assume you're no longer the commanding general of Earth's defenses?"

"He is," said Sharker. "I work with Earth, not against her. I am simply a light to help guide them through the darkness of war."

"Let's cut through the bullshit," said Woods. "I came to make peace with you. Let's get to it so I can get back to my men."

Sharker grinned. "Come here," he said, motioning to the window. Woods stepped warily across the room, mindful of the group of people sitting around the table, who had yet to say a single word since he'd arrived. "You see those portals?"

Woods followed Sharker's outstretched hand through the glass. A bank of twenty portals hung in the distance.

"What about them?"

"UCOM has effectively detained or killed all Human and Clone troops throughout the Milky Way. We have welcomed the survivors with open arms. Look closely, a Tiger's coming through one now."

One of the portals ballooned in size, allowing the angled hull of a heavy-destroyer to pass. A squadron of light craft cruised to meet it, flying alongside the ship as they escorted it into formation.

"What's your point?" said Woods.

"We cannot stop the war UCOM has raged against Humans, nor can we fix the damage already inflicted by our so-called allies. The Humans are friendless, and defenseless. The Slarebull are our only chance for survival."

Woods' stomach soured at the thought of the Slayers, and wrenched even harder at the thought of Earth surrendering to the invading alien empire. He forced his tongue to remain silent of his thoughts.

"I'll admit," Woods said gruffly. "I couldn't see your point before, back on the Frontline. Hell, I couldn't see it until we talked twenty minutes ago. But I've seen UCOM's hostility towards Humans at the Inner Ring. I've seen Slarebull Hives welcome Dakota's ships." He swallowed a lump in his throat. "I guess I can't deny the truth forever. Earth has spoken. If this is what the people want, to join the Slarebull..."

"The *Pristine,*" Sharker corrected. "The Pristine reside in the kingdom of gods. The Slarebull are their protectors."

"The Pristine," Woods repeated. "We can't beat UCOM. We can't beat the Slarebull. I've made my decision. I'll do what I can to help you end this war and enter salvation."

The words almost caught in his throat, like vomit that needed to be forced down. His head buzzed, and the surrounding armada became hazy and far away, like he was looking through the wrong end of a lens. His legs buckled and he sank to a knee. Sharker bent beside him.

"You're feeling the power of the Pristine," said Sharker calmly. "Soon you will harness that power, as will the rest of Earth and her children."

"What are your terms," Woods croaked, grabbing Sharker's arm. The brawny Destineer helped him back to his feet.

"As I stated in our previous conversation," said Sharker. "Complete and total surrender of your fleet. Delivery of the sub-humans for trial. You will deliver these terms of surrender to your ships in person, via live broadcast."

"Why do you need me to cower before my men?" said Woods. "Detain my ships as you must, I've already ordered them to stand down and forbid them from firing on your ships."

"Ahh," Sharker chuckled. "I wish it were that easy, but there are still many Woods loyalists. Some of your devoted can't be reasoned with. I need you to speak to them for me. I don't want to spill any more Human blood, but will if I must."

"You win," said Woods after a long pause. He stared at the floor. "Let me go back onto *Mariella* with my men, and I'll deliver the message."

"You can deliver the message from here," said Sharker. "I assure you, *Barbican* has all the necessary equipment."

"It won't work," said Woods. "If I tell my men to surrender from your tower, they'll think I'm captured or blackmailed. They'll probably send Titans into *Barbican* while the rest of my fleet forms an attack strategy. You have to let me speak from my own ship. It's the only way."

Sharker crossed his arms behind his back and stared out the window for a long stretch. He stroked his beard and stuck a hand out to Woods, who grabbed it firmly. "It's a deal," he said. "But if I sense any foul play, you'll be eliminated without a second thought. I agreed to this parley as a courtesy. I value Human life as much as you do, maybe more."

"You have my word," said Woods. "My ships will not attack under any circumstances."

"One other thing," said Sharker. He stepped in front of the table of generals and inflated his chest. "Bow to me, and recite the holy prayer."

Woods tried to blink the tears from his eyes but failed. Shiny tracks chilled his cheeks as he sank to one knee before sliding the other to the floor beside it. How had it come to this? Forced to bend before the very radicals who kidnapped his daughter? Fighting the rage clawing at his heart, he bent before Sharker Gray.

"Excellent," said Sharker. "Now repeat after me. *I present my beating heart and the blood which courses through my veins,*"

"I present my beating heart and the blood which courses through my veins," Woods repeated.

"I present my lungs, and the air which they breathe."

Woods repeated slowly, in a daze. The prayer burned the back of his mouth like poison, but he forced himself to speak.

"I look to the stars, and add them to the bounty around me for which I am due. I look at the dirt on the planets, and the clouds in the sky."

Woods' voice cracked as he repeated the line.

"I care for the creatures of the Universe, for the smallest insects, and the largest beasts, for they are my children. I reclaim the lands of the unholy

from the enemy, from the anti-gods. I defend her natural beauty as the caretaker of good, and the slayer of evil. I will defend against those who threaten to take the bounty which is mine. I am the light in the darkness. I am the shade from the suns. I am a god, protector of the holy Doctrine of Destiny."

Woods finished the prayer, squeezing his eyes shut so hard the back of his eyelids turned into red spots. He felt hollow as he finished, unsure of himself, and praying to the stars he'd made the right decision by meeting with Sharker. He raised his head to a sharp, metallic click.

The dark barrel of a sidearm hung inches from his face. He looked past the rail pistol to Sharker, who took a step back, not moving the gun from Woods' head.

"I could kill you now," said Sharker. "I could put a slug through your skull and fire upon your men. United Earth would die with your fleet, and the Destineers would prosper as gods."

Woods tensed and began to rise but Sharker lunged to press the barrel against his forehead. Woods sank back to his knees.

"If you're going to kill me then get it over with," said Woods. "But I don't think you will. It wouldn't be a good example to set in front of the men."

He turned to face the table of generals. General Dunbar gulped and wiped his glistening brow.

Sharker lowered the pistol. "I have no intention of killing you. I've seen you in my visions. The Sterilord has big plans for you here on Earth. When the time comes, you will save a life. The key calls for its master."

Woods sat on his feet and blinked a few times. He felt strange, like a voice was calling to him. Its words hung in his ears like a distant echo, like someone calling from the end of a long tunnel. His body tingled, and his heart fluttered in his chest. The Voice was tender, almost warm. For a split second, he felt like he loved the Voice, as he loved his daughter.

The feeling vanished.

"What key are you talking about?" said Woods.

"You can hear him," said Sharker, his face broadening into a smile. "I can see it in your eyes. Let me help you."

The Destineer bent and placed a hand on Woods' scalp.

The glass room of *Barbican* vanished, morphing into a room made of metal and holograms. He was on a Slayer Hornet.

"Francis," called the charming voice, coming from everywhere and nowhere. The Voice was in his head, and also echoing throughout the room.

He tried to call to the Voice, to ask where he was, but no sound came from his lips.

"Pay attention, Francis," said the Voice. *"You don't love me like I love you. Perhaps you never will. But I need you, Francis, and you need me. You will save someone. Someone who can't save herself. For me to live, so must she."*

The Voice drifted into silence, and Francis spun to observe his surroundings. He stood at the bridge of the warship. Slayers stood around him in a circle, snarling and thumping their tails against the deck. He turned to find his daughter hunched on the ground, weeping. A man stood beside Nancy, slick with blood and holding a plasma pistol. The man jerked his head to fling a soaking lock of hair from his face and Woods cried out as he recognized the man immediately.

Frank Scott raised the plasma pistol to Nancy's head.

The bridge lit in a flash of green light and the alien world vanished.

Francis was back on *Barbican.* He had fallen to all fours, and his arms trembled.

"Nancy," he whispered, recoiling from the vivid murder he'd just witnessed. "Is she alive?"

"You've seen your vision as I've seen mine," said Sharker, removing his hand from Woods' head. "The Pristine call to us. The Voice guides us."

"Let me off this ship," Woods croaked, climbing to his feet. He started to backpedal, trying to blink the vision from his memory.

Not vision, hallucination, he told himself. *It was a hallucination.*

The scene couldn't be real. Frank Scott, murdering his daughter in front of a crowd of Slayers? But the Voice had spoken to him, he'd heard it. And the room had been so vivid. He could taste the blood on the floor. He could hear the Slayer's claws scratching against the deck. He could smell their rotten breath, and see the slight quiver of his daughter's lip as she braced herself for death.

"What did you see?" said Sharker.

Woods turned to him. "Like you said, I'll save a life." He shook his head, then continued towards the exit.

He was surprised to find that Sharker didn't call after him, or make any threats. His vision burned itself into his mind, clawing its roots between his memory, drowning the grunts of the surrounding Destineer guards, and the clanging of their boots against the metal grate leading to his Jaguar. His vision flashed at the forefront of his mind, like a neon sign, taking the oxygen out of the room and stealing his focus.

The vision did nothing to steer him towards the Destineer faith. In fact, it did the exact opposite. It had stirred up an anger in him that had lay dormant since the Frontline. It had shown him the enemy beasts, and the lives at stake, caught within the cogs of war.

The Voice scratched at his brain like a sickness, like fingerprints left at a crime scene. Chilling, yet elegant. Poisonous, but crisp and *pristine.* The rest of his thoughts felt dirty, almost filthy. He shook his head clear.

The Voice had been powerful. But he didn't have to listen to the Voice. He knew that. The Voice had even acknowledged the fact.

You don't love me like I love you. Perhaps you never will. But I need you, Francis, and you need me.

He remembered the Voice's words. What did the Voice need from him? Did the Voice need Nancy alive?

He had a decision to make. His fleet of Humans and Clones couldn't fight or flee without being slaughtered by Earth's defenses. If he commanded his ships to assimilate with Sharker's fleet, even momentarily while he thought of a plan to get rid of the Destineers, the sickness–the *visions*–how many of his men would start to see them?

How many men would turn to the side of the Destineers?

NINETY-SIX

Francis Woods – Human
Aboard Jaguar *Cherokee* – Earth starspace

Destineer Cheetahs flanked *Cherokee* an all sides as they escorted him back to *Mariella.*

Woods glared past them at Earth's sprawling defenses as his Jaguar traveled from *Barbican.* He envisioned what he would do to Sharker Gray once he returned to Earth, and winced as sharp pangs of remorse tugged his heartstrings at the thought of abandoning his men.

He shoved the bad thoughts aside. Surrendering to the rest of Earth's navy was the only logical option, and the only one that would avoid mass bloodshed.

He tried to focus on Bear Stafford's message. The Slayer super-weapon had been unleashed. Project Shepherd was in effect. He wondered how much progress Stew and Bear had made at the outpost.

Blaze appeared beside him as he waited at the entrance hatch aboard *Cherokee.*

"Your stealth squadron successfully evacuated the non-Humans from their ships," she said. "Most of them are already through the portal. There's a small team that hung back to evac you from *Cherokee.*"

"How long until they get here?" Woods asked.

Blaze projected a set of holograms above the floor. It showed the blunt corners of *Cherokee's* hull, with six Night Eagles hugging its sides.

One of the Night Eagles was settling next to the hangar bay, extracting boarding equipment.

"They're here," said Blaze, motioning to the Night Eagle as it finished its docking procedure.

The hatch clacked loudly and hissed. Woods stepped back as the double doors slid open to expose the inside of the tethered stealth craft.

Cage stepped from the inside of the Night Eagle. He took a look around the inside of the Jaguar. "Not very cozy, but I'll make do."

"I'll ready the Night Eagle for departure," said Blaze, vanishing in a flash of pink.

Cage walked around Woods and entered *Cherokee's* halls before turning and folding his arms across his chest. "She's all yours," he said, nodding to the inside of the Night Eagle. "Full crew, ready to take you to the outpost. I'm assuming Sharker agreed to take us in?"

Woods nodded. "Sharker's got all the generals in his corner. I'm not sure how loyal they are, but they'll take us in. They're as desperate for ships and staff as we are."

His old friend bit his lip and shook his head, rubbing a hand over the back of his neck.

"Cage…" said Woods before trailing off.

The commander sighed, then smiled weakly. "Go on, get out of here. Blaze sent us our mission details. We'll surrender to Earth's fleet, then keep our ears open for your return signal. If the Destineers attempt to jail us, we'll storm their ships. They won't be able to fire on their own fleet so it'd be trench warfare, and we got Titans. Don't worry about us, we'll be fine here. It's a good plan."

"I know you'll be fine," said Woods. "But something's not right. I don't think we should surrender anymore."

"We don't have a choice," said Cage slowly. "We finished running simulations. Earth's defenses will defeat us with almost a hundred percent confidence. We'd need an AMMO-AB to stand a chance, and we don't have any anti-matter in our fleet."

"If we surrender, our men will convert."

Cage squinted his eyes shut. "Convert to Destineer?"

"That's right."

"Like hell they will. The men would sooner launch themselves out the tubes."

"The visions are real," said Woods softly.

Cage cocked his head. "You're starting to sound like Dakota. What happened on *Barbican?*"

"Sharker connected me to some sort of energy," said Woods. "I can't describe it. He touched my head, and I had a vision."

Cage's surprised look turned into a suspicious glare. His hand inched toward his sidearm. "What was the nickname you gave me in boot camp in 2074?"

"Don't give me this shit," said Woods. "Barn door, because your aim was so terrible. It's me. And I'm not converted. The damned Voice knew I won't play along."

"Voice?" said Cage incredulously.

Woods looked around to make sure they were alone. "Sharker put a hand on my head, and I had a vision. I don't know how the hell he put that shit in my head, but it was there. The Voice spoke to me, and showed me something, a prophecy or something. If the Voice can get inside my head, it can get inside the mens heads too. We can't surrender to the Destineers."

A long pause. "You're sure of the vision?" said Cage.

Woods nodded.

"Then what do we do, flee?" said Cage. "That's hardly a better option. Our simulation had an even lower likelihood of surviv..."

"To hell with the simulations," said Woods. "Sharker won't fire on us. The Voice wants me alive. The Pristine want me to live."

"What the hell did you see?" said Cage. "You sound crazy."

"The Pristine entered my head," said Woods. "No, the Voice did. Their leader. He grabbed inside me, and I lost control of my senses. I entered his world, and he told me…"

Woods sniffed his nose, twitching his eyelid to stop a tear from forming.

"What?" said Cage, resting a hand on Woods' shoulder.

"He said I'd save a life," Woods shuddered at the image of his daughter on her knees, a pistol against her head. "I need to save Nancy. Without me, she'll die. The Voice needs her alive for some reason."

"Why would Sharker care about Nancy's life?"

"He won't, but Voice commands him. As long as the Voice wants me alive, Sharker wants me alive."

"If the Voice wants Nancy alive," Cage shook his head. "I don't even want to say it, but why would you do anything to help the Pristine?"

"She's my daughter," Woods growled.

Cage opened his mouth, then closed it. He stared at the floor. "What are you proposing? That we just *leave?*"

"That's exactly what I'm proposing. Sharker won't risk killing me by attacking our fleet."

"Where do you plan on going?"

"The outpost," said Woods. "We need to save UCOM. Whatever this weapon is, we need to stop it from reaching the Inner Ring. If the Slayers wipe UCOM out, the whole galaxy will go to shit."

"UCOM," said Cage. "The guys who just exiled you from the Council." His eyes narrowed.

"I refuse to believe UCOM will deny our help once they're attacked," said Woods. "The Destineers are at Earth, our fleet is clean now. When the history books are written a thousand years from now, I don't want to be remembered as the Human who doomed his entire race to extinction."

"If Humanity is destroyed," said Cage, "there won't be any history books to read."

Woods scoffed, unable to contain a brief smile. "You're a ray of sunshine. Let's go, we're leaving. I'm staying on the Night Eagle so Sharker can't tell where I am. You get back to *Mariella* and initiate a mass-comm link with Earth. I want you to send my transmission."

"Transmission?"

"I promised Sharker Gray I'd address Earth with a speech of surrender," said Woods. "I'm a man of my word."

NINETY-SEVEN

Parker Roddingham – Human
On the surface of Earth – TVE startower

Far below orbit, in the TVE startower, Parker Roddingham flipped through TV Earth broadcasts at his desk space outside Madame Beauchene's. He flared his nostrils at the headlines bombarding Earth's media networks.

Woods to surrender Human bandits to Destineer control.

Destineers protect Earth from traitorous ex-Eminence Woods.

The list went on. It was odd how the networks never showed any images of the Slayers. It was easy to listen to the Destineers spout their gospel about their lords and saviors, the Pristine, but seeing their scales and bloody eyes might sway the casual follower.

He shuddered at the memory of Sharker Gray, the Destineer disciple who'd come to visit Madame under a fake name. He'd felt the dark cloud surrounding the hulking man. Chills had scurried up and down Parker's spine as the Voice tried to whisper in his ear, to tell him how he loved him.

He'd shut his mind to the ghostly words, and wondered if the Voice had called to the rest of Humans on Earth. Based on the general enthusiasm for the Destineers, he assumed it had. Since he'd felt sickened by the Voice, he also assumed there were plenty of people who were trapped among the Destineer faithful, terrified of the prospect of ten foot lizards landing on Earth's soil.

His ears perked up as an outside transmission blipped onto his holodeck, swirling in a tight blue sphere stamped with the UE logo. A ship in orbit was requesting a mass-comm link with TVE. He leaned forward and brought up the spec sheet on the requesting ship. It was a Tiger in Woods' fleet, the *Mariella.* The bio ID's were confirmed as Woods. The ship tag credentials were hidden other than the name and commander, but that was standard in military destroyers.

He started to connect the comm request to global relays, then hesitated. If he put an enemy comm request live without Madame Beauchene's permission, she'd have his head.

Parker switched the delay on and accepted the transmission. Squiggly lines pulsed at the side of his desk as TVE computers recorded the audio and video of the transmission. Madame Beauchene was no friend of Woods, and he wondered if he should notify the CEO. After considering that she had full access to everything that passed through his desk, he decided to alert her of the transmission, and sent a call request with his Program.

"Make it quick, I'm busy."

"Sorry, Madame," said Parker. "But I have a mass-comm request. It's from Woods' fleet, a Tiger heavy named *Mariella.*"

"Stay right there."

Parker let out a deep breath. Ten seconds later the golden doors to Madame's business suite whooshed open. She powered to him, pushing her way past the four armed men guarding her suite, her heels clicking against the Martian granite.

"Who's the message from?" she demanded, leaning over his shoulder.

"The bio ID is from Woods," he stammered back. "I'm recording it now."

"Sharker said Woods' would broadcast his surrender," she said in awe, her eyes moving over the scrolling metrics. "I didn't believe him."

"Surrender?" Parker's heart sank. "Should I broadcast to global media?"

"*C'est ouf,*" Beauchene spat. "An unscreened enemy message? Have you lost control of your feeble mind? Play it to me first."

Parker complied, bringing the transmission up on wall display. Francis Woods stood rigidly before them.

"I urge each pilot," said Woods. *"Each soldier, each scout..."*

"Idiot," she hissed. "What do I pay you for? From the beginning. And send the feed to Sharker Gray onboard *Barbican.*"

He reset the transmission, sending a comm link to the defense tower in orbit. A green indicator flashed on as Sharker's bio ID patched the link through.

Woods stood silently before them. A video banner hovered behind him, with the word *'Mariella'*, scrolling from left to right. Taking a deep breath, he began his message.

"This message is for Earth. It's for every man, every woman, and every child. There was a time when I lived on this great planet. I walked across the same soil as you now stand. I relished the mountains, and raised my face to gently falling snow. I gazed in awe across our limitless oceans, and stared into the stars, wondering what lay beyond our blue and green jewel. We know now what thrives beyond the stars around us. The Universe is alive, and we are but one of her children. We may not share the same beliefs, but we share the same past. We share the same home. We are Human, each and every one of us. I spoke with Sharker Gray, the Destineer who commands Earth's defenses. He demanded my faith in the Pristine, and through powers unknown, I have seen his visions. I have heard the Pristine whisper into my ear."

Woods took a long pause. He closed his eyes, and when he reopened them, they brimmed with angry tears.

"I have heard the Pristine. The Voice spoke to me, and I don't deny it to be real. But I learned something in my vision. The Slayers are false idols. The Pristine are filled with empty promises. They use their visions to instill fear, and servitude. Stars know what their intentions are, but I am certain they will not deliver us to a kingdom. There are no pastures greener than Earth's. Our home is worth fighting for. It's worth dying for. I will fight for every Human life, even those under the insidious control of the Destineers and the Slayer visions. I've been commanded to surrender my ships to Earth. I say to you now, I surrender, but not to the Destineers, and never to the Slarebull. I surrender to Earth. I promise you I will defend our home until I no longer breathe, and even then I will defend her in memory as I enter the stars. I beg of you, do not heed orders from the manipulative Destineers. I urge each pilot, each soldier, each scout, to stand behind me and oust these usurpers of life. The Destineers are cowards, unwilling to face our enemies, and have committed acts of high treason against Earth and her colonies. I will be leaving Earth starspace, and invite every ship with so much as a rail cannon to join me. I am going to meet the enemy, to drive the Slayers from our gates. If you decide to stay with the Destineers, know that you are no longer Human, but a puppet for the very tyrants that threaten our existence. We will eliminate you as fiercely as we will eliminate the Slayer beasts. For the civilians trapped behind the Destineer cloak of deception, know this. I will return for you. You will be saved. I was told that if I leave Earth starspace, my fleet will be vaporized. Watch as I leave for the battlefield untouched and unharmed, and know that the words of the Destineers are as empty as their souls.

The backdrop behind Woods disappeared, as did the *'Mariella'* banner. The camera panned out to show the inside of a Night Eagle.

I am not aboard the Mariella. I am in a Night Eagle, hidden in a random part of my fleet. I challenge you to fire upon us as we leave Earth, and risk destroying my ship. Sharker Gray won't risk ending my life, because

Sharker Gray, and the Destineers he leads, are cowards. Join me as I leave to meet the enemy."

Woods paused and the camera zoomed into his passionate face.

"Awaken stars."

The transmission ended, replaced by the TVE logo.

Madame Beauchene took a few wobbly steps backwards. "The nerve," she whispered. "That *heretic."*

Parker's holodeck buzzed and a red sphere materialized in his queue as he received a comm request from *Barbican.* He enlarged the request, and a familiar ID tag filled his display.

"Comm request from Sharker Gray on *Barbican,*" he said.

"Answer it, you fool," screamed Madame Beauchene.

He accepted the request, and the Destineer disciple dominated the wall screen.

"I trust you didn't broadcast Woods' message?" he said, his lip curling.

"Of course not," said Madame Beauchene. "What was that all about? You said you had Woods under control."

"I do," said Sharker, drawing a shaky breath. "Delete that transmission. No one can see it."

He cut the call before Madame Beauchene could respond.

She turned to Parker. "Well, you heard him, delete the transmission. Wipe it from our servers. Ready a lift to four thousand meters and call the board, I want them in the big room in twenty minutes."

"Yes Madame," said Parker, but his voice was drowned by Madame's heels storming across the lobby.

He turned back to his desk as she disappeared into her suite. He sent a request for a lift and watched as a yellow pin of light rocketed up the side of a hologram of the TVE star tower. An ETA clock counted down beside the lift. Madame's ride would be there in under two minutes.

He fingered the controls for Woods' transmission. He dragged the icon towards the trash bin and held it there, his hand shaking. He darted a glance to Madame's suite. The doors were still closed. The guards stared at him, not moving a muscle. He managed a weak smile and a nod and dragged the icon across his desk.

Parker didn't drop it into the trash bin. He dropped it into a removeable drive, slipping the thin metal out of his table and into his pocket. He turned again to the guards. They stared back at him like statues.

He rose from his chair and hurried from the lobby and into a short hall. The elevator slowed to a stop as he arrived, lighting a green down arrow across the doors. Only after the gate swung open to expose the glass inside of the shuttle did he chance a look back. The guards hadn't followed him.

Parker jabbed his fingers against the console, slumping against the wall once the doors closed and wiping sweat from his eyes. Letting out a shaky breath, he entered a new destination for the lift. The text switched from *'4,000m'* to *'2,000m'*.

He drew the metal drive from his pocket, wondering if he had lost his mind. Broadcasting Woods' transmission would at best land him a swift death, and at worst land him a slow and painful one.

He prayed to stars he'd be able to broadcast the message and find out.

NINETY-EIGHT

Sharker Gray – Human Destineer
Aboard defense tower *Barbican* – Earth starspace

Sharker Gray trembled with rage as he replayed Woods' transmission in his head, staring through the window at the vast fleet of surrounding ships. He should have kept the slimy son-of-a-bitch in confinement, slapped shackles on his wrists and ankles, and thrown him in the brig to rot. Why did the Pristine want him alive? What could a non-believer like Woods possibly do to honor them?

He took a deep breath and fought to convince himself of their wishes. The Sterilord had plans for Woods, and needed him to live. Throwing Woods in the brig would have interfered with his destiny.

Now Sharker had to contend with an entire renegade fleet.

He turned from the window to stare across the empty room. Dunbar and the rest of the Generals had left, heading to their respective stations within Barbican to command their fleets. The table was empty, and he was alone in the glass room save for ten Destineer soldiers standing at the far end, near the exit. They all wore suits of Skeleton armor that whirred gently as they shifted their weight.

Loyalist ships had already started to move in exit formation around the portal to the Inner Ring. He needed to get to the command station to coordinate strategy with Dunbar. He strode across the room to his men.

"We're going to the main command bridge."

His guards acknowledged and followed. He took a sharp turn towards the pod bay once he reached the end of the short hall.

An AI appeared as the first group of men entered a pod. The thin man wore Destineer robes, and bowed slightly before addressing Sharker.

"Sir, I have a priority message from the Inner Ring, addressed to you."

"Who's it from?"

"Draxton Tyke, sir."

"Send it to my pod."

The AI bowed again and disappeared. The doors to the next pod in line opened to expose a floating orb of light. Sharker grabbed the shoulder of a guard who began to enter the pod.

"I'm going to the bridge alone."

"But sir, for your safety…"

"I'm going alone," Sharker repeated through gritted teeth. "Meet me there."

"Yes sir."

The rest of the guards hung back to take the next pod, and Sharker's pod accelerated as soon as he sat down. He tapped a finger against the floating blue orb.

An avatar of Draxton appeared. The pre-recorded message started seconds later, and the new Eminence of UCOM spoke.

"I hope this message finds you well," said the Wolf. "I deliver good news from the Inner Ring. The Human exile has worked as planned, and many Human and Clone loyalists have been eliminated. UCOM is weakened, and will not be able to defend properly against an invasion. The Slarebull will come within a fortnight of the embedded time stamp, and the filth will finally be eliminated. Once the Slarebull arrive, I will convert to a

Human body and transfer to Gefangnia. Our Destineer lines of communication have verified with Slarebull commanders that the planet will be converted to a Hive mothership under Destineer control. Salvation is near."

The message cut out, and Draxton's avatar disappeared as the pod reached the top of Dunbar's command station. Sharker exited the pod to find officers manning their stations at the bridge. The four guards who had left before him moved to his sides as the pod carrying the rest of his detail slowed to a stop.

He led his guards down to the pit, taking the stairs two at a time. Dunbar was leaning over a table with three lieutenants, motioning to various holograms of Earth defense sections. He snapped to attention as Sharker approached.

"Sir."

"What's the status on the Loyalist fleet?" Sharker demanded. "How many ships have we captured?"

Dunbar took a shaky breath. "None sir. The Loyalist ships aren't allowing us to board."

"Then we force our way in," he said. "Place charges on the hatches and storm their ships."

"Almost a third of their fleet has moved into exit formation around the portal. Should we fire upon them?"

"*No.* We can't risk it."

"If we don't fire any warning shots, we'll lose the upper hand."

"How many Night Eagles have we found?" said Sharker, ignoring him.

"Not many sir," stammered Dunbar. "Twelve total, and they were all hidden within our own ranks. The Loyalist Lynxes are jamming our dust storm, we can't get a read with active spacnar, and there's too much traffic for our passive spacnar to get a fix on things."

Sharker cursed. If he couldn't pin-point the Night Eagles, he wouldn't be able to fire on the Loyalist ships without risking the chance of killing Woods in the crossfire. He wondered what was more important – stopping the last remaining Loyalists from escaping Earth starspace, or upholding the wishes of the Sterilord.

Knives of pain shot through his head as a crippling vision sent him to his knees.

The command bridge vanished, replaced by bare rock that held no dirt. The holy kingdom stretched before him, creeks and rivers twisted through rolling plains of purple and yellow grass, fenced by a mountain range that kissed the pink skies, capped in peaks of gold. The holy palaces reached for the stars, aglow with energy, and down the gentle slope he kneeled upon, a dazzling orb of light bathed him in warmth.

The Voice called to him, no longer loving and soft, but rough and angry.

"You've had filthy thoughts," the Voice roared. *"How dare you resist my wishes? Francis Woods must live, so he can spare a life!"*

"I'm sorry my lord," Sharker sobbed, falling to his hands and sliding his forehead against the stone. He looked back to the Voice and shrieked when he noticed that his hands had become smeared with dirt, and were no longer pristine. "No! I'm sorry, I am faithful."

"Do not question your destiny. Woods must live. Only then will you be clean of the filth around you."

"I know," Sharker wailed, wiping his filthy hand against his bare thighs, and screaming when they left brown streaks against his pale skin. "I won't fail you, I live to serve you, to enter the kingdom."

The stone disappeared, and he was once again on the cold metal deck of the command bridge. He scrambled to his feet and raised his palms to his face, breathing a sigh of relief when he saw they were clean.

"Sir, are you alright?"

One of his Destineer guards placed a hand under Sharker's elbow for support. He shrugged the man away.

"Don't fire on the Loyalist fleet," Sharker spat. Dunbar stared at him blankly. "You heard me, continue with active spacnar. I want to know the position of every Night Eagle."

Dunbar frowned. One of the officers shouted from his station before he could respond.

"We have a mass-comm, originated from Earth over the TVE network," the young man cried.

The main screen switch to a video feed. Sharker moaned at what he saw.

NINETY-NINE

Parker Roddingham – Human
On the surface of Earth – TVE startower

Panting and slick with sweat, Parker turned from the console in the routing room and slid down the metal wall, dropping the thin metal drive to the floor.

Voices shouted from the outside hallway. An armored Destineer soldier kicked his way into the room, followed by ten of his cohorts, all wearing Skeletons.

"Here's the station," one of them yelled. "How do I stop the transmission?"

The first man ignored Parker. The second soldier grabbed him by the neck and wrenched him to his feet. "Stop the transmission," the soldier growled, forcing Parker towards the console.

"It's password protected," cried the first Destineer. "I can't get in."

The man swiped through various holograms frantically before pounding the console hard enough to send cracks across the glass surface.

Several more Destineers shoved their way around the console to try to help.

Parker yelped as he was spun around and forced to his knees. He looked up to find a Destineer standing directly before him, training his rifle at his forehead.

"The password," said the soldier. "What is it?"

Parker flashed a dead man's smile. They would need a DNA match from him or another TVE employee with access. He doubted they'd figure it out in time. He eyed the Destineer's waist, which was an arm's length from his face. A pistol was clamped against his magnetic thigh plate.

He raised his eyes to meet the glare of the soldier.

"Awaken stars," he whispered, then lunged for the man's pistol.

He plucked it off the thigh plate before the Destineer could react. Squeezing his eyes shut, Parker raised the barrel to his temple, and fired.

ONE-HUNDRED

Sharker Gray – Human Destineer

Aboard defense tower *Barbican* – Earth starspace

Francis Woods stood proudly before them, his 3D avatar towering over the bridge.

"How is this possible?" Sharker screamed, storming to the officer. He leaned over the man's interface and grabbed his collar with both hands. "The clip should have been destroyed. Cut the video!"

"Impossible sir," the officer stammered. "This is playing on all Earth networks. We don't have any control."

Sharker threw the officer back into his chair and whirled to face the wall screen.

"I urge each soldier, each scout, to stand behind me and oust these usurpers of life."

He ran his hands through his hair, cringing at Woods' recorded message.

"Sir," said Dunbar. "I have over two hundred Tiger heavies declaring allegiance to Woods and the Loyalists. Now three hundred. Sir, we're losing ships fast, should we fire upon them?"

Sharker couldn't respond. He could only watch as Woods' transmission finished.

Sharker Gray won't risk ending my life, because Sharker Gray, and the Destineers he leads, are cowards. Join me as I leave to meet the enemy. Awaken Stars."

"Sir," Dunbar cried, scrambling before Sharker. "Your orders?"

"Two thousand Tiger heavies have declared Loyalist allegiance," an officer shouted from behind. "One Lion declared, and we lost two PDR's. We're losing control of our fleet."

Sharker could only stare at the ground in a daze. Dunbar brushed past him and shouted orders to his men.

"Priority one message to Earth defense," he cried. "This is Grand Admiral Harold Dunbar. *Barbican* has sworn allegiance to Woods and the Loyalist fleet."

Sharker snapped into focus at Dunbar's blasphemous words. He issued a howl of rage and snatched his sidearm.

"Disregard all Destineer commands," Dunbar continued. "All UE ships are hereby ordered to stand down and assimilate peacefully with..."

Dunbar's head jerked forward as Sharker's shot blasted through his skull. He collapsed to the deck in a pool of blood. Sharker rushed to the head of the pit.

"Priority one message to Earth defense," he shouted. "Harold Dunbar has been relieved of duty on account of heresy. All UE deserters will be executed."

The surrounding officers stared at him. Silence hung over the bridge. Suddenly, a nearby officer thrust his hand to his side to grab a pistol. He began to draw it towards Sharker, but was cut down by rifle fire from Sharker's guards, who rushed in front of him to shield him from harm.

Screams rang from the back of the bridge as the rest of the officers turned on each other, the Destineer faithful turning on those who decide to join the Loyalists. The room erupted in gunfire.

"Sir," one of his guards shouted. "We have to leave. It's not safe here." The guardsman flinched as he took a shot to his armored chest, then returned the fire, killing the attacking Loyalist.

Alarms blared, and red strobes flashed from the walls and ceiling.

"We're taking fire," cried an officer, struggling to man his station amidst the chaos. "PDR *Firesword* has fired full RACAN volley.

The deck shuddered beneath them as the LMS slugs found their mark against *Barbican's* hull.

"Energizing shields," cried an officer.

"Sir," Sharker's guard shouted again. "We need to leave *now.*"

This time Sharker didn't hesitate, and ducked behind his surrounding guards as they rushed up the steps to the pod bay. One of them screamed as he caught a bullet in the neck, and tumbled lifelessly down the steps.

Sharker dove into a pod and gasped as the rest of his men piled into the crowded car, one of them pinning him against the wall with his heavy Skeleton.

The walls rushed past in a blur as they fled the super tower. The pod took them straight to the hangar bay, where he was joined by more than two hundred additional Destineer faithful who were also fleeing *Barbican.* Explosions ripped the inside walls of the vast cavern as ships docked in the hanger turned their canons on each other, the vessels flashing Destineer beacons trading fire with those who didn't, inching along the magnetic tracks as they entered the launch queue.

His ears burned as laser blasts scorched the air behind him, and he leaped into the open hatch of a Leopard. He scrambled backwards, moaning as fifty of his men were incinerated by supercharged laser beams.

"Sharker Gray is secured aboard *Quincero,*" a nearby soldier shouted into his headset.

Strong hands gripped his arms, and Sharker was pulled to his feet. The Leopard jolted as it ejected from the effluent launch tube into Earth starspace.

He hurried down the short hall of the Leopard to the cockpit and burst inside, trying to calm his nerves. Skirmishes had started between Destineer ships and UE Loyalist converts, peppering the vacuum with sharp lines from laser fire and bright flashes from RACAN fire. The battle was light, with most ships fleeing towards two large formations that had formed.

"Destineer ships are assembling at marked coordinates," called the navigation scout from the edge of the cockpit. "We have reports of battles inside a large number of Destineer ships. The Loyalists are trying to regain control."

Sharker finally found his voice. "Our Destineer faithful are doing the same within their ships. Set nav-link to our contingency vectors. We've lost Earth." He squeezed his eyes shut. "Once you secure command channels, send the order to storm the contested ships and wipe out the Loyalist threat. Destroy any ship that turns in the process."

"Yes sir."

Hundreds of ships in his fleet were vaporized by PDR's as he fled Earth with his Destineer faithful. As they approached the portal bank, two Tigers within his fleet were commandeered as Loyalists within the crew gained control of the ships, but they were quickly destroyed by Destineer Tigers as soon as they turned in the direction of Woods' fleet.

Tears burned his eyes as he stared at the enormous armada of Loyalist ships that had amassed at the portal to the Inner Ring, far across Earth starspace.

He wondered where he would go now that he had lost Earth. When the Slarebull finally arrived, they would no longer be met with open arms, but with fierce opposition from Woods and his followers.

He watched as the Loyalist armada began to filter through the distant portal to the Inner Ring. Surely they would attempt to rejoin UCOM and fortify Inner Ring defenses before the Slarebull invasion.

The Voice had told him to spare Woods' life, but now he wondered if he had doomed humanity's chances at salvation in the process.

They passed through the portal, heading to a distant Destineer stronghold. As green light flooded his Jaguar, Sharker closed his eyes, and prayed to the Pristine.

ONE-HUNDRED-ONE

Nancy Woods – Human
Aboard Night Eagle *Eclipse* – Outside Floodgate starspace

Nancy stared at the portal before them. The portal was red, but she didn't need to see the color to know Slayers were on the other side. Just past the portal before them, was the Floodgate. She turned to the center of the bridge, where Eve stood with Hunter, Axel, Caseus and Lindsey, studying a series of 3D holograms at the center pedestal. Keyv was manning his station at the far side of the room, sifting through surveillance metrics.

"When will we enter the portal?" Nancy said as she approached the group, eyeing the hologram, which showed an incomplete rendering of the Floodgate. Square patches were missing from various sections of the structure's hull, and red spheres catalogued expected locations of Slayer naval forces.

Eve turned to face her. "Just over four hours. The Discarded are priming their anti-matter systems and running final recon checks with fleas through the portal.

Eve's squadron AI, Amy Chip, appeared on the pedestal as Eve finished her sentence. "Pexar sent an update on enemy strength, and they've finished optimizing our attack vectors. The mission has been moved up two hours."

The hologram at the center pedestal rippled as new information was added to it. The square patches were filled in the schematic of the

Floodgate, and two additional relief valves materialized on the rear side, facing the outside of the Milky Way. Thousands of red diamonds peppered the outside of the hull, showing defense turrets and hangar bays. Detailed scans of Slayer fleets appeared around the structure, so dwarfed by the massive hull that they looked like nothing more than tiny dots.

A thin beam of light shot from the end of the Triturator valve, connecting it to a tiny sphere.

"What's that?" she said, pointing at the tiny shape at the edge of the pedestal.

"It's a portal to the Outer Rim," said Hunter. "Based on the design specs Pexar sent us, that's the portal the Slayers will use to remove matter and energy from the Milky Way. The beam of energy you see is a pilot light. Once the Triturator is activated, it will grow to thirty thousand kilometers in width."

The Titan scanned through a list of specifications at the edge of the holodeck, apparently fascinated by the design.

Caseus reached forward to explode the view of the portal until it dominated the space atop the pedestal. Four construction platforms surrounded the portal, placing cylindrical sections of hardware around the sphere at various angles. The thin beam refracted through the cylinders like a light prism, forming a web of complex geometries.

"I wonder what's on the other side of the portal?" said Caseus.

"The Primal Snow," whispered a voice behind them. "The Pristine are close."

Nancy turned to find Frank looking over her shoulder. He looked at her briefly before returning to the hologram, his eyes wide. He licked his lips.

"Get back to the *Eclipse* Frank," she muttered. "Go to the barracks, you look exhausted. We're going to be leaving soon."

Frank didn't respond, and simply nodded, backing slowly from the pedestal. He didn't blink his eyes until he'd backed into the wall beside the hatch, then muttered a few words under his breath and turned to enter *Eclipse.*

Nancy sighed nervously, wondering if she should tie Frank up. Hunter had warned her that his strange behavior didn't seem to be drug-related, but she couldn't find it in her to detain the man she used to love.

She shook her head and turned back to the group. "There should be a Hive here. Do you think Sid already passed through to the Outer Rim?"

Axel leaned forward to shrink the view of the hologram set. "I think this is what you're looking for."

The pedestal zeroed in on a separate structure, a few thousand kilometers away from the portal connecting the Floodgate to the Outer Rim. The rounded shape of a blue and green planet spun slowly before them, fixed to large support arms that connected to a pointy ship. Lettering appeared above the ship as Discarded intel parsed together the ship ID tag.

Class: Hive mothership.
Origin of design: Slarebull.
Planet: Sylva.
Destination vector: Primal Snow.

Her breath left her. She'd almost reached him. Sid Dakota was a portal jump away. She wondered for the millionth time what she would do when she finally reached the Destineer Hive. She would be with a tiny crew, and would be heavily outnumbered by Destineers aboard the massive ship. Logic told her not to even attempt to board. But she wasn't driven by logic. Something called to her from that ship, a tiny voice in the back of her head, urging her to find Sid Dakota.

For the past century, she'd assumed the stars she prayed to guided her way. The calling no longer felt like the energy of the stars. It was as if an actual voice called to her. A calm voice. A reasonable voice.

Find Sid. You must avenge his crimes against Humanity. It's your responsibility. It's your destiny.

She blinked and snapped out of her vision.

"Are you okay Nancy?" said Caseus, placing a hand on her shoulder. "You look a little pale."

"Yeah," she managed. "I just really want to get Sid."

They stood in heavy silence before a whirring sound caused the group to turn towards the rear of the bridge. A ten-foot android in the form of a Slayer stomped towards them, causing Nancy to flinch and reach for her sidearm.

"Relax," said Eve, stepping from behind the android. "It's just my Fox."

The hulking robot went rigid, falling to all fours and crowding the already tiny real estate of *Midnight's* bridge. Eve had donned a thin exo-suit overtop her orange skin suit, with thin metal bands hugging the curves of her body.

"It doesn't look much like a fox," said Caseus, leaning to clunk a knuckle against the android's head.

"*Don't touch it,*" hissed Lindsey, grabbing Caseus' arm.

"Didn't you say it's shock rated for 1000 G's?" said Caseus, raising an eyebrow to Eve.

Eve nodded. "Pexar said the only thing that would accidentally trip the bomb is another antimatter blast."

"So this is how you're going to sabotage the Floodgate," said Hunter, waving his fingers over the back of the Fox android to scan its content. "*Whoah.* That thing's hot alright. I detect ninety-nine kilograms."

"One hundred to be exact," said Eve. "Might want to tweak your scanners."

"The plan is to have this thing follow you around," said Nancy. "Where? To the middle of the Floodgate?"

"You got it," said Keyv walking from the cargo room. A second Fox followed behind him and froze beside Eve's.

"Sounds like a suicide mission," said Lindsey, backing away from the enormous androids. "How are you going to get out before they blow?"

"I'll be with them for backup," said Axel. "I help kill the bad guys. They drop the Foxes into the valve, then we rally to extract and run like hell."

"Why don't they send the Foxes in remotely again?" said Nancy.

"The Discarded tried that in the past," said Eve. "It doesn't work. Slayers put jammers inside the Floodgate to stop signals from going through long range, so we can't remote control them manually. The only thing intelligent enough to make it past Slayer defenses inside is a smart AI, so they would have to go on a suicide mission and not be able to upload out of the Floodgate before detonation. This is the only way."

Caseus shook his head somberly. "I'll say a prayer for you guys. You don't have to do this. You can come with us to the Sylvan Hive."

Eve laughed hollowly. "Trade one suicide mission for the next?" She shook her head, and rubbed her belly gently. "No. Someone needs to destroy the Pristine. I just happened to be in the right place at the right time."

Nancy frowned and cocked her head as she noticed Keyv staring at Eve's belly. He wiped a tear from his eye, and seemed to force a smile. "We'll make it through," he said. "The Discarded tech is amazing. Check this out."

He reached behind his back to retrieve a thin helmet, fitting it into a ring around the neck of his skinsuit. A tiny green light flashed on his helmet, and his Fox rose to its feet. Keyv threw a quick jab, and the Fox mimicked his movement, raking a claw through the air beside him. Keyv lunged, and the Fox pressed forward, dropping to all fours. The integrated duo both turned their heads, first to the right, then the left. Then both disappeared into thin air.

The Fox reappeared against the far wall. Keyv reappeared against the opposite wall.

"Mildly impressive," said Hunter, crossing his arms. "Except I could see the Fox's heat trail the whole time. Anyone with a toy scanner could have, its thermals are off the charts."

The Titan jumped as a third Fox appeared directly beside him. He jerked his head back to the Fox against the far wall. It vanished.

"Seems like the Intellects should stop putting toy scanners into Akimors," said Keyv, smirking as he removed his helmet.

Hunter nodded. "Okay, I'll admit. I'm impressed."

The Fox moved nimbly away from the Titan to rejoin Eve's Fox, settling to all fours and going into sleep mode.

Nancy sighed. "We need to get back to *Eclipse.* The ship still needs a full set of diagnostics before we go through the portal."

The group took a moment to look around at each other. Then they each embraced, saying their farewells.

"I'm glad we met," said Eve as she hugged Nancy. "After you spend a hundred-fifty years in deep space, it's nice to see a friendly face."

"I know the feeling," said Nancy, smiling as they drew apart. "Good luck in the Floodgate. All four of you." She nodded her head to Eve's belly.

Eve's eyes widened. "How did you..."

"You'll be fine," said Nancy. "Your kid will have a great life, free from Slayers."

Eve sniffed and backed toward Keyv before breaking her gaze as he reached an arm around her shoulder and gave her a kiss on the cheek.

"I guess this is good bye, old friend," said Hunter, embracing his fellow Titan.

"I wish I were as good as you at cliché statements," said Axel. He leaned back and pounded a fist against Hunter's chest with a clang. "Remember, whoever comes back with the most kills gets the slaughter trophy."

Hunter laughed. "In your dreams. I'm up on you by at least a couple thousand."

Axel jerked his head back, his eyes widening in mock defeat. "No fair! I had a severed head during the Frontline. Let's reset the death clock."

"Just this once," said Hunter softly. "But after this, no more handicaps." He paused. "Awaken stars."

"Awaken stars," Axel repeated.

Hunter turned and stepped through the hatch into *Eclipse.*

Nancy cast a final look at Eve's crew, then followed Caseus and Lindsey into her Night Eagle.

The hatch closed behind her and hissed as *Eclipse* pressurized the hull. There was a loud clang, and the deck jolted as they detached from Eve's Night Eagle.

"Laura," Nancy called.

"Yes ma'am," said Laura Maxwell, as her AI avatar appeared on the deck.

"How's our AI captive?"

"Timothy's been quiet," said Laura, nodding to the AI pedestal across the deck. Timothy had his eyes closed, hanging limply against the bonds securing him to a metal chair. "It's kind of odd, really. His responses have been patchy at best, and he seems distant, like he doesn't know what's going on. He's also very weak, abnormally so. My bonds have no trouble holding him, but I could probably tie him with dental floss and he wouldn't have the strength to escape."

"Do you think it's due to his confinement aboard the Destineer ship?"

"Impossible to say," said Laura, shrugging her shoulders. "It's possible for him to have degenerated if he was hiding in servers not designed to support consciousness, but that normally causes AI to become emotionally unhinged, and easily angered. I haven't heard a nasty word out of him since we left Allakai's fleet."

Nancy studied the captured AI. His head bobbed slowly on his shoulders as he took labored breaths. "Is it possible he fractured himself?"

"Sure," said Laura. "Unlikely though. Fracturing your software is very damaging to your emotional centers. Normally AI don't even attempt it, or they may offset their love and happiness levels. Also, I've run multiple scans on every server on the ship. I'm the only AI onboard, I can say that for certain."

Nancy thought of Frank, and how Axel said his neuro scans were haywire. "Keep an eye out for anything fishy."

Laura nodded. "Aye ma'am."

"And Laura," said Nancy in a whisper, leaning close to the slender avatar. "I want you to watch Frank closely. Record everything he says. If you hear anything strange, or if he tries to do something dangerous, let me know."

Laura looked around the bridge. Axel, Caseus, and Lindsey were at their stations, bringing the systems online. Frank had disappeared into the barracks. "Do you think Frank's up to something?" said Laura softly so no one could hear.

"I don't know," said Nancy. "But he's acting strange, even by his standards."

"Perhaps you should tie him up?"

Nancy gulped down the acid that had collected at the back of her throat. "I've loved Frank for so long, I…" she trailed off.

"I'm sorry," said Laura. "I shouldn't have mentioned it."

"No, you're right. I'll talk to Axel about it. For now, run checks on our diagnostics. We're heading through the portal."

"Aye," said Laura. She tensed suddenly. "I have a priority one on central comms."

"Central comms?" said Nancy. "Our comms are still sequenced to…"

A stallion appeared above the central holodeck before she could finish. It was the commanding admiral of the fleet she'd deserted mere days ago. "This is Admiral Allakai Troko. All rebel UCOM ships must surrender at once for detainment or you will be eliminated."

The hologram disappeared after the brief message.

"Laura," Nancy shouted. "Request a comm-link with *Midnight.* We need to warn Eve, she's not connected to UCOM channels anymore."

"Activity on local portal eight," called Caseus before Laura could respond.

A new hologram appeared above the central table. The Discarded fleet of Slayer ships sprawled wide across the table. At the edge, a portal had turned green, and was expanding rapidly. Seconds later, the hull of a Tiger heavy-destroyer began to pass through. Before it cleared the portal, more than fifty Night Eagles appeared, firing missiles into the Discarded's lighter ships. With no time to energize shields, they tore apart as their hulls were blasted into debris.

The Tiger finished its pass into local starspace, its shields fully energized and blazing a brilliant yellow against the surrounding vacuum.

"I have positive ID on the Tiger heavy," called Caseus. "*Kizurra,* part of Allakai's fleet. They have locks on one-hundred-twenty Discarded ships."

Kizurra flashed as it fired a salvo of slugs into the Discarded fleet. Another Tiger heavy had nearly finished passing through the portal to join *Kizurra* by the time the slugs found their marks.

A few Discarded ships managed to partially energize their shields before they were impacted. Most remained utterly defenseless as the heavy projectiles ravaged their hulls.

Explosions rippled through Pexar's fleet as Allakai attacked the Slayer-designed ships.

ONE-HUNDRED-TWO

Eve – Clone

Aboard Night Eagle *Midnight* – Outside Floodgate starspace

Eve slammed into her seat inside the cockpit and watched in horror as UCOM ships surged through the rear portal, opening a maelstrom of slug and missile fire into the back of the Discarded armada.

Pexar's voice shot over central comms. "*Charge shields.* Shift rear formation to marked defense coordinates. Do not return fire! A message of compliance has been sent to the UCOM aggressors."

The fleet admiral's voice cut suddenly, replaced by strategy markers on *Midnight's* holodecks. Her dash beeped as new spatial vectors and flight objectives were sent to her from central command.

"Amy, what's happening out there?" Eve cried, accelerating her Night Eagle along the suggested travel routes sent from Discarded commanders.

Her AI appeared instantly above the cockpit holodeck. "The UCOM fleet came from Charlie sector. I haven't patched together any chatter. Discarded intel hasn't either. We're blind."

"It's Allakai Troko's fleet," said Eve. "It has to be."

"That's statistically likely," said Amy, "but I can't confirm it."

"Why aren't we on the UCOM loop?"

"Our comms got reformatted when we assimilated on Scrock. I'm trying to tie in but CAIRO's all over the transmitters. It's all I can do to keep them from hacking into *Midnight.*"

"Patch Nancy through, she can daisy chain us to the Tiger ships."

"Negative." Amy's eyes glowed as she tried to access the UCOM ship registries. "UCOM frequencies are dark. We're locked out unless Discarded AI hack their systems."

Eve cursed and swung her ship hard against the suggested travel path, racing towards the rear portal, lowering stealth shields to maximize thrust from her engines. A few Cheetahs zipped past in the opposite direction as she reached the encroaching UCOM armada.

"Do not attack the UCOM ships," Pexar shouted again through central comms. "Redirect their slug fire outward, away from the scrum. Signal beacons for surrender."

Eve knew there was no way in stars that Allakai, or any other UCOM admiral, would ceasefire with Slayer ships. It was up to her to stop the aggression. Warning indicators blared from the cockpit as her ship sensed a rogue slug, and she twisted into a spiral to avoid the deadly hunk of metal. Fire engulfed them briefly as the slug punctured the hull of a nearby Yellowjacket.

"Flash UCOM signs of surrender and hail their lead ship," Eve cried.

"Lead ship identified as *Kizurra,*" said Amy. "I've parsed together the ID tag. It's Allakai's ship. Hailing now."

Bright strobes flashed in pulses around their hulls as she brought *Midnight* belly up before the looming UCOM armada. Cheetahs, Night Eagles, and Lynxes flew past as they raced to attack the Discarded fleet. A quick glance at her holodeck showed severe damage to almost a quarter of Pexar's fleet, with thousands of ships sputtering into darkness as their shields failed.

Come on.

"Successful connection with *Kizurra,*" cried Amy. "I have a return message."

Allakai's hologram flashed beside the pilot controls, but Eve couldn't draw her eyes from the UCOM ships growing in her canopy. The starspace before her burned with powerful discharges from warships as her countrymen laid waste to the Discarded fleet.

"We don't negotiate with Destineers," growled Allakai. Eve wrenched her head towards his hologram in surprise. "UCOM deserters will be targeted, and destroyed."

The hologram cut out, and alarms blared simultaneously from the bridge.

"We have aggressive locks from six UCOM ships," cried Keyv from his station.

"We lost comms with *Kizurra,*" cried Amy. She shouted as a muscular Guardian AI leaped onto her back, wrestling her avatar to her knees. "*AI breach,*" she grunted as she slipped from the Guardian's grasp and blocked a series of blows.

The two grappled with one another and left the holodeck, disappearing into *Midnight's* servers.

"Lower stealth shields to thirty percent," Eve shouted, punching the thrusters and cutting away from the UCOM fleet. "Evasive actions, engage our heat decoys."

She surged past a wounded Discarded Hornet, dodging debris as its hull breached and exploded into the surrounding starspace.

"I'm engaging," said Axel. "We won't survive if I don't clear a path."

Eve winced as the Titan loosed their cannons on a team of Cheetahs, punching holes through their canopies and destroying their engines.

"We shed five tracking locks," called Keyv. "I can't shake the last one. What the…"

"What?" Eve shouted, squeezing through a pair of Cheetah's flying in tandem formation. Laser fire scorched past her vision, narrowly missing her ship.

"We're being tailed by a Night Eagle," said Keyv. "I have a positive ID. It's Blaire Ashe."

"Patch her in," said Eve.

"I can't," said Keyv. "I need AI help. Where's Amy?"

Her shipboard AI stumbled onto the holodeck, falling to a knee before forcing herself up. She was bleeding through a large gash in her forehead, and her pants were in tatters.

"I've got a patch," Amy said hoarsely. "Blaire already requested comms with us."

"The CAIRO AI?" said Eve, flitting her eyes briefly to Amy's wounded avatar.

"He's gone," said Amy. Her forehead wound slowly healed itself, the open flap of skin tightening against her skull as she repaired her programming. "I closed the breach. Here's Blaire."

"You're no better than the Destineer scum," Blaire shouted over comms as soon as Amy initiated the patch. "I tried to warn you on Scrock. Now you're gonna die."

"Are you insane?" shouted Eve. "We have two hundred kilo's of antimatter onboard. If you destroy my ship, you'll wipe out half the UCOM fleet."

"We both know that's not true," said Blaire. "Missiles or lasers won't detonate those things. Only another antimatter blast would, and I've already shared the markers for those ships with Allakai. Why do you think we've only sent slugs into the support ships?"

Eve searched the fleet markers hovering on her console to her left. Blaire was right. The ships carrying antimatter were smaller craft, and represented by yellow dots. The ones free of antimatter were larger destroyers, and were represented by blue dots. Almost a third of them had been either heavily damaged or destroyed by the UCOM attack.

She changed course towards the ships carrying antimatter, praying that they would shield them from UCOM fire.

"How could you have betrayed us?" said Eve, grunting as she streaked toward a formation of Discarded ships assembling near the Floodgate portal. "Why did you go to Allakai?"

"Allakai found me," Blaire shot back. "All I did was warn of the Discarded's deception. The choice to attack was an easy one for him."

Eve's ship shuddered as one of Blaire's missiles found its mark against the starboard hull.

"We lost stealth on starboard," Keyv called. "Correcting engines."

"I can't get a lock on her," Axel called from his gunnery station. "She's keeping to our blind zone."

"The Discarded are trying to save us," Eve shouted, twisting around the heavy stream of laser fire blasting from Blaire's nose-cannons. "They're going to destroy the Floodgate."

"You're no better than Sid Dakota and his goons," hissed Blaire. "The Slayers aren't here to help us, they're here to destroy us. Are you that blind?"

Blaire's comm feed died suddenly as Discarded central command pushed a fleet-wide message.

"Mission is moved up," the Pexar roared. "We attack the Floodgate *now.* Attack vectors have been changed to accommodate losses. If UCOM wants to attack Slayers, we will at least introduce them to our enemies at the Floodgate."

The vacuum before them lit brightly as the Discarded fleet executed Pexar's command, firing their thrusters and accelerated towards the Floodgate portal. The portal ballooned in size as thousands of ships poured through.

Eve shouted to her crew, ordering them to lower shields and divert full power to engines. Her back pressed against the flight seat as they accelerated.

By the time she reached the portal, the diminished Discarded fleet had almost finished passing through. She rocketed past a slow-moving Hornet heavy-destroyer, and plunged into the red passage leading to Floodgate starspace.

ONE-HUNDRED-THREE

Eve – Clone

Aboard Night Eagle *Midnight* – Floodgate starspace

Eve arrived through the portal, and into mayhem. Pexar screamed through central comms, fighting to keep the Discarded fleet in formation. She glanced frantically at her battle metrics. They'd lost ten percent of their strength during Allakai's attack, and another fifteen was out of formation. The fleet's Hive mothership had stayed behind to help the injured ships, and was nowhere to be seen.

Hundreds of Hornet heavies moved to form a defensive sphere around a collection of lighter class ships, many of which were carrying antimatter payloads.

She immediately surged towards the defensive formation, seeking cover.

"Incoming aft," Keyv shouted.

Their ship lurched as Keyv sent anti-ordnance into a nearby missile, detonating it just outside its kill zone.

"Blaire, you need to stop," she cried.

The attacking squadron deserter failed to answer, and lasers seared the sides of *Midnight* as Blaire continued her relentless attack.

Frux it.

"Axel, get ready on the cannons," Eve shouted. "I'm going to give you a window."

She punched nose jets underside *Midnight's* bow and overtop its stern simultaneously. Stars spiraled around them as their Night Eagle went into a backflip, giving Axel a clear view of Blaire's ship. She caught a glimpse of the craft, and saw three laser charges rake the side of her hull.

"Three confirmed hits," Axel cried. "No kill. She jinked out of here."

Eve righted their flight orientation and continued her path towards the formation of Hornets. She checked the rear dash for Blaire's ship. It had vanished.

"Track Blaire's Eagle," she called.

"No can do," Keyv replied. "She's a ghost, probably engaged camo."

Eve bit her lip as she slipped between the massive hulls of two Hornets. Navigation commands painted her HUD in streaks of yellow and blue, showing her the path to the Discarded's new attack formation. Her destination was marked with a red diamond.

"Run scans on our surroundings," she said as she slowed to a stop at her new destination. "Give me a picture of what's going on. I can't see shit past these Hornets."

They sat motionless in formation for a stretch. The friendly heavy-destroyers blocked her view of the Floodgate, and also the rear portal they'd entered local starspace from. Intense flashes of light ripped the outside of the Hornet's hulls as Slayers attacked, sending a barrage of plasma and cannon fire into her fleet.

"Phase one initiated," called Pexar over central comms. "Nukes out. Lead ships depart from formation in thirty seconds."

Eve's holodeck shrunk to show the entire battle scene as their surveillance craft finished their readings. The Floodgate became alive with light as it unloaded salvos towards their ships. Thousands of Slayer destroyers scrambled into a defensive formation to meet the coming attack. Her dash beeped as her Night Eagle was added into the logistics queue.

The outer Hornets began to shift, powering their thrusters and filing into a narrow column as they headed towards the Floodgate. The Floodgate became visible as the ships shifted attack vectors, and a chain of nuclear explosions tore a line through Slayer defenses, clearing a path towards the Floodgate.

A conga line of Discarded ships followed the lead Destroyers, their shields fully energized, not attempting to fire offensive weaponry. Their hulls lit brightly as they entered the newly cleared path, with surviving Slayer ships firing at them from all angles. The lighter ships hugged the insides of the column, shielding their antimatter payloads from enemy fire. One of the leading Hornet's caught ten slugs simultaneously, and shattered into large chunks of debris. A Hornet surged forward to take the place of the terminated ship, immediately suffering the brunt force of the Floodgate's attack.

The Discarded Fleet slowly dissipated as its ships joined the line, funneling into formation, larger ships rushing to fill the gaps of the protective column as hundreds of Hornet heavies were destroyed by the intense onslaught. The antimatter ships bunched tightly together, squeezed between the dwindling number of protective destroyers.

"We have company coming through the rear portal," called Keyv. "UCOM Ravens are running scans. Allakai is combing the area."

"We've been tagged," said Amy, appearing atop Eve's dash. "Allakai has our ID credentials, should I launch Ravens to scramble the scan?"

"No," said Eve, focusing on the rash of explosions in the distance. The Discarded fleet had nearly reached the Floodgate, and the battle had shifted to the starspace near one of the exhaust valves – Pexar's planned point of entry into the massive Triturator installation.

"Allakai hailed our ship," cried Amy. "He's requesting a comm link with Discarded command. He's...he's offering his support."

A sharp indicator alarm captured Eve's attention before she could respond. *Midnight* was being signaled to join the attack column of Discarded ships. She powered her thrusters, following the yellow path on her HUD to flank the port-side hull of a Hornet. A quick glance at the thin ID text hovering above the ship told her that she was flying beside Pexar, who was bringing up the rear of the attack.

Their fleet had fully mobilized.

"Tell Allakai to bring in support," she grunted as a few plasma rounds scraped through a gap in the surrounding ships and seared the side of her Night Eagle. "No time to connect him to Discarded command."

"Aye," said Amy, vanishing from the holodeck.

"I have eyes on Blaire's craft," Keyv shouted.

A rough outline of a Night Eagle materialized on Eve's battle schematics in close proximity. Axel trained a line of laser fire on Blaire's ship, which released a string of missiles before spiraling away. Eve skirted in a loop to avoid three of the missiles. Keyv caught the fourth with anti-ordnance, but the explosion hit their ship with enough force to send them into a tailspin.

Eve screamed as she fought to correct their path, but one of her engines had failed, and the correction was slow. They spiraled out of the protective column of Hornets and into empty space.

The battle was immense. Lights of all colors swallowed the black vacuum whole. Rail cannons on the Slayer ships flashed continuously, and yellow spheres of light peppered the starspace in return, redirecting the slugs back into Slayer ships.

"We have a critical failure," cried Amy, popping onto the cockpit holodeck. "I can divert systems to restore thrust, but it's going to take ten minutes at least."

Blaire's ship reappeared. This time she didn't attack, but instead slowed to *Midnight's* side.

"Allakai sent updated commands," said Blaire hollowly. "My orders are to rally at the portal and join UCOM formation before they pass into Floodgate starspace. We're joining the Discarded."

Eve finally regained control of her ship, and alarms silenced as their trajectory stabilized. "Now you're listening to orders? You try to destroy my ship, and now you're just going to-"

Axel sent a flurry of missile and laser fire into Blaire's Night Eagle. Blaire screamed briefly into comms before her hull ruptured. Eve winced as a slender body was sucked from the cockpit and into space.

"Titan code," said Axel grimly. "She was a deserter."

Eve gulped. The Discarded fleet was now far ahead of them, and the first of the lighter craft had begun to enter the Floodgate. Hornet ships had spread the column to form a dome around the exhaust valve, guarding the antimatter payloads as they entered the ship.

She wasn't going to be able to join Pexar in his mission. She said a quick prayer to the stars for his soul.

"I'm taking us back," Eve called, swinging *Midnight* in a tight loop towards the rear portal. "We're going to meet Allakai's fleet. We'll come back for support once we get orders."

The portal loomed closer. Her crew was silent. A warm feeling had crept into her chest, and she guiltily squashed it down. Her life may be spared, but the Discarded would have minimal survivors, if any at all. Debris littered the vacuum in all directions, remnants from the once mighty Slayer rebel fleet.

Her ears perked as Pexar's voice shot over central comms.

"Battalion one, shift thirty degrees starboard, we have a break in the dome. Concentrate fire on the marked Slayer ships. Multiple payload craft are outside defensive wall. Lower shields! Divert power one hundred percent to offensive fire on marked sections. Comprom-"

His words extinguished like a weak flame. A blinding light swallowed the Floodgate as an enemy slug ruptured the containment chamber of one of the onboard Foxes. Hundreds of identical flashes peppered the space around them as the antimatter blasts set off a chain reaction throughout the Discarded fleet.

Eve screamed and urged her ship to move faster. They would have mere seconds before they would be incinerated.

The portal loomed before them, and the initial shockwave of the antimatter destruction forced them through. *Midnight* lurched forward, passing through the portal seconds before pure energy vaporized their ship.

ONE-HUNDRED-FOUR

Eve – Clone

Aboard Night Eagle *Midnight* – Outside Floodgate starspace

Eve panted, in a daze. The harsh light from the pure energy explosion still burned her retinas, and the world was awash in flashes of red as her eyes fought to adjust to the dim light beyond the portal.

"Engines at sixty percent," called Amy Chip as she scanned *Midnight's* systems. "Camouflage non-functional. Anti-ordnance systems at ten percent. Weapons at fifteen percent. Spacnar and comms fully operational. Life support systems breached, we're running on emergency air and water. Computer systems fully operational."

Eve checked her holograms. Allakai's fleet was in formation directly before the portal. The Discarded Hive *Scrock* was surrounded by escort ships, its shields down. A squadron of Cheetahs was already coming to meet them, trailing bright blue jets behind them as they left the lead Tiger.

"Priority request from Admiral Allakai," said Amy.

The Stallion appeared on her dash seconds later. "Send a notification of compliance to our lead ship *Kizurra.* We're taking you in for briefing."

Eve frowned, wondering whether she was going to be executed for treason as soon as she stepped foot into Allakai's Hornet. She sure as hell couldn't run or hide, her ship was barely functional.

"Sir," she said softly, "the Discarded fleet, they..."

"They're gone," said Allakai. "Our preliminary scans are showing near total damage to the surrounding assets in Floodgate starspace. The only thing unaffected is a bank of rear portals, a handful of non-military craft, and the Slayer Hive *Sylva*."

"Is the Floodgate..."

"No. The damned thing lost an exhaust valve, but our engineers are saying it's still functional."

Eve gulped. Pexar had failed. The Triturator would ignite, and the Milky Way would be de-atomized. "Am I being summoned?"

"We'll talk when you get on board," said Allakai. "Our scanners show that you have two antimatter payloads onboard *Midnight*?"

"Aye sir."

"Good. They'll be transported to a new Night Eagle. You'll be docked by *Shadow* for transport. We're going to head to the Floodgate in three hours. We need to destroy this damned thing before those Snake bastards send relief."

ONE-HUNDRED-FIVE

Eve – Clone

Aboard Night Eagle *Shadow* – Outside Floodgate starspace

Kizurra loomed large before *Shadow,* the Night Eagle sent to retrieve them. Eve eyed the surrounding UCOM soldiers as their vessel slowed in its approach to the lead Tiger, entering one of the influent tubes on its way into the hangar.

Her ship AI, Amy Chip, had been taken by CAIRO to an unknown server. Eve had never been in a virtual reality world before, but she assumed the digital world had interrogation rooms the same as her version of reality. Amy went without a fight. She wasn't shackled before leaving *Midnight's* pedestal, just as Eve wasn't cuffed by the UCOM soldiers who'd boarded her stealth fighter.

She'd expected the soldiers to be rough with her, to treat her as a traitor, but they'd been, well, pleasant wasn't the word. They'd been professional. Aside from stripping the pistols from her and Keyv, the soldiers kept to themselves. One of them offered her a stick of gum, which she took in an attempt to calm her nerves.

The vessel shook as it touched down at its docking station.

"Let's go," said one of the UCOM soldiers, a Wolf with one ear missing. "You're going straight to the Admiral."

Eve nodded and stepped toward the exit ramp. She turned as she felt Keyv grab her fingers and give them a squeeze.

"We're going to be fine," he said softly, offering a weak smile.

She nodded back and stepped onto the ramp, slipping her fingers from his grasp.

They proceeded straight to a pod bay, where four transport carts waited for them. Six UCOM spacers piled in with her, Hunter and Keyv. The rest of the UCOM spacers filled the final three pods.

"Is it true?" said one of the soldiers, a Greyhound this time. He unfolded his four arms and lowered his ears, leaning forward on his bench opposite Eve. "The Slayers were rebels, and attacked their own?"

Eve nodded, feeling a slice of warmth trickling into her stomach. "They died in the process. All of them."

The Greyhound grinned and elbowed the soldier next to him, a Squid. "Guess I owe you a drink. I thought the Destineers took over comms." He paused and raised an eyebrow at Eve.

"She's not Destineer," said the Squid, dismissing the thought with a wave of two tentacles. "I've killed Destineers. She's no Destineer."

He offered no additional explanation.

The ride went on in silence for a few minutes, save for Keyv starting up a friendly conversation with a Human next to him who had lived on the same continent as he once upon a time, somewhere in North America.

Eve rubbed her belly. She had been ready to storm the Floodgate with Pexar and the rest of the Discarded. Now that they were gone, the fire in her heart had fizzled, and she wanted nothing more than to return home, wherever that was. Earth, she supposed. Her real home had been converted to a Slayer Hive that lay a short portal jump away, thousands of light years closer than Earth. The irony made her cringe.

The overloaded dose of adrenaline that had recently turbocharged her bloodstream had converted to whatever panicky hormone created anxiety. She wondered if it was possible to kill an unborn child with stress alone. She tapped her foot and fantasized about curling up inside a fluffy bed, one that was firmly planted on soil, and not crammed into a starship.

Was it cowardly to wish she was anywhere but here, at the edge of the galaxy, waiting to find out if she'd die at the hands of the Slayers or at the hands of the Destineers? Was it cowardly to crave happiness for once, after a century and a half of isolation behind enemy lines?

She rubbed her arm against Keyv, who dropped his conversation about Native American tribes to give his attention to her. He leaned to press his forehead against the side of her head, and placed his hand over her belly.

"Are you with child?"

Eve looked up to find the Squid narrowing his eyes at her. She didn't respond.

"You can't fool me miss," said the Squid. "I've seen pregnant Humans killed. They grab their bellies as they die."

Eve scrunched her face, unable to stop the tears from streaming down her cheeks.

"It's against UCOM code to fight with a child," said the Greyhound. "You should be with the civilians."

The pod slowed and chimed, an alert beeping as they reached the war room.

Eve cleared her throat, voicing the fact she wished wasn't true. "There's no civilians in this war. Some of us just happen to be holding guns while the Slayers kill us."

The doors opened, and she exited without escort, the UCOM soldiers momentarily stunned by her dark, almost poisonous outlook. They clambered noisily from the pod as they hurried to catch up to her. Eve was already through the war room doors by the time they did.

Admiral Allakai stood at a holodeck, discussing strategy with a few of his lieutenants. He rose once he spotted the escort and walked around to meet the group, dragging one of his hooves against the deck in the process, as if to stretch his muscles.

Eve saluted, raising her fist to her chest.

"At ease," said Allakai, nodding to Keyv, who had given the Human salute. He scanned the escort of soldiers flanking her sides. "Leave us. We don't want to give these two the wrong impression."

"Yes sir," said the CO.

The spacers exited the war room, the door gliding quietly shut behind them.

"What impression would that be?" said Eve. "That you followed a deserter of my crew, a *traitor*, into battle, and attacked the one shot we had at destroying Primal Snow?"

Allakai's lips went taught. "Blaire Ashe." He paused. "As an admiral, when I hear of a Destineer stronghold, I have to take action."

"A Destineer stronghold?" said Keyv. "The Discarded were against the Pristine, not commanded by them."

"Blaire Ashe should've gone through the tubes," said Eve through gritted teeth.

"Don't you think I know that?" said Allakai, stomping a cloven foot onto the ground and rearing slightly onto his hind legs. He bent his neck until it cracked, and sighed deeply. His shoulders sank. "It wasn't easy, but I've kept my fleet alive since the Frontline. Kill or be killed. This was no different. I wasn't going to risk the lives of my men and women on the possibility of discovering the first Slayer rebel group known to UCOM. And I'll remind you that I'm your superior, and if you question my judgement again, I'll have you thrown in the brig."

Eve held her tongue, but glared at the Admiral nonetheless.

"Your orders, sir?" said Keyv dryly.

"The Discarded gave us a window," said Allakai, walking back to the holodeck. His lieutenants made space, shuffling to the sides. Eve followed Keyv to the table, standing opposite Allakai. "You were privy to their plans. I want you to debrief, and then I want you to take those antimatter bombs into the Floodgate and blow it straight to hell."

Eve and Keyv remained silent.

Allakai sighed. "I'm sorry for threatening you," he said. "I'm sure you both know about Stallion tempers by now. You're not going to the brig under any circumstances. Hell, if the stars are good, and we survive this thing, I'll put you in for medals. But we need to act now. If you don't want to do it for me, do it for the Milky Way."

"The plan wasn't to blow the Floodgate," said Keyv. "At least not at first. We were going to wait for it to begin Trituration."

Allakai frowned. "I'm not sure I follow. You were going to let the Slayers deatomize the galaxy?"

"Momentarily," said Eve. "We were going to wait for the machine to start, then sabotage its effluent chambers. The energy beam would lose focus and scatter on the other side of the portal, blasting the Primal Snow with pure energy waves. The Slayer home base would be vaporized, and the Floodgate would destabilize soon after, stopping Trituration."

"So the goal wasn't to save UCOM," said Allakai. "It was to martyr them. I'm sorry, but I can't stand for that."

"Only the inner section of the Milky Way would begin Trituration," said Eve. "I didn't like it at first either, Admiral, but it's the only way to destroy the Slayers for good. Or *was* at least."

"Was?" said Allakai.

"We don't have enough antimatter to go with plan A," said Keyv, "So we'll have to go with plan B."

Allakai studied the hologram. "We can't use the Floodgate to destroy the Primal Snow?"

"Not enough antimatter," Keyv repeated. "If we let the Triturator spark, we won't be able to halt the process, maybe make it a little less efficient, but that's about it."

"Okay, then plan B," said Allakai. "What is it?"

"We blow the antimatter before the process sparks," said Eve. "It was the Discarded's contingency plan. We wouldn't destroy the Primal Snow, but we'd delay their consumption of the Milky by a few decades. That's what we tried to do when your fleet chased us through the portal prematurely."

Allakai frowned. "I'll have to admit, I like the sound of that better. Something about deatomizing the inner galaxy doesn't sit well with me. What's the contingency plan?"

Keyv scoffed. "We already missed our mark by about thirty antimatter bombs. With the two we have left? Go with the Hail Mary. Throw the bombs down the end chamber and hope we frux it up enough to rupture when the Slayers spark it."

"Do you know how to get to the end chamber?" said Allakai.

"Of course," said Eve. "We've been going over the details on Scrock for weeks. Most of the Slayers were killed in the antimatter blast, so we should be able to get inside the Floodgate easily, but there's interior defenses as well so we'd need an escort."

"Tell me how many ships you need and they're yours," said Allakai. "And we have fifteen Titans you can have as well. Our engineers say we have less than twenty-four hours before the Floodgate portal's done calibrating, so brief my lieutenants on strategy, and I'll organize the insertion."

"Just one thing," said Keyv. "We can't deliver the bombs with ships. The defenses are too heavy. We have to enter through a thin seam meant for crew transport then rally for extract. The ships can only follow us partway."

Allakai cleared his throat. "That seems like a fairly major flaw in the Discarded's plan. Were you planning on carrying the damned bombs over your shoulders?"

"Essentially," said Eve. "The bombs are housed inside semi-intelligent robots, called Foxes. The Discarded gave us suits the Foxes will follow, and we can also use the suits to control them and have them mimic our movements."

"Forget about it," said Allakai. "I'll have Titans use the suits. I'm not sending a hundred-pound girl in to deliver a bomb when I have a ten foot android available with bionic strength."

"They won't fit," said Keyv. "The suits are custom designed for our bodies."

A pause, then a comm request beeped atop the holodeck.

A Guardian AI appeared seconds later. "Admiral, I have a comm request from engineering."

"What for," said Allakai. "Did the Floodgate portal finish calibrating?"

"No sir. It's about the antimatter bombs aboard *Midnight*. They're contained inside some sort of suit. They're afraid to touch them, they're worried about destabilization."

"Tell them to sit tight," said Allakai. "I'll be sending down the owners of those suits in a few minutes."

ONE-HUNDRED-SIX

Draxton Tyke – Wolf Destineer

Aboard defense tower *Warhammer* – Dominia starspace

Draxton Tyke tried to stop his furry hands from shaking as he entered the medical room, buried deep within the super-tower *Warhammer*, stationed next to Gefangnia at the Inner Ring. Four Destineer soldiers stepped aside as he entered, bowing to him as he stepped into the dim light. The room was small, and held only two chairs, both reclined. The chairs resembled antique torture devices, with stirrups at the base for the feet and metal bands on the arms for the wrists.

The chairs looked deadly, but he knew that after he sat in one, a new life would blossom inside him. The chairs would scourge the filth from his body, and he would shed his coarse hair for pink skin, and trade his tail for a smooth behind.

The chairs would transform him into a god.

One of the chairs was empty, and he took a deep breath as he approached it, running a hand over the sleek headrest. The other chair was occupied with the naked body of a male human. The man shivered against the straps holding his arms and legs, and his eyes flitted back and forth beneath the glowing helmet fastening his skull against the chair's back. Lights pulsed along the contours of the helmet, intensifying in various areas around the man's head. His mouth was covered with a breathing apparatus, and no words escaped his lips, only muffled moans. Tears streamed down his cheeks, which were pale with fear.

The rest of Draxton's detail shuffled into the room behind him, with a few Destineer guardsmen staying behind to guard the hallway.

He turned to the lead disciple, who wore the ceremonial robes of the Destineer faithful. "Are the men prepared?"

The disciple bowed deeply. "Yes father. The men are awaiting your command. They are ready for cleansing."

"And the rest of the council?"

"Still at the Round Table. They won't pose a threat."

Draxton nodded. "I'm ready."

He stepped into the chair, sidling his feet into the stirrups, which retracted to fit his lanky Wolf body. He swept his tail to the side and leaned backward. The metal chilled his skin even through his thick mat of fur. He relaxed his shoulders and closed his eyes as the disciple fitted the bands against his body, tightening the helmet around his ears. The inside compressed to fit the contours of his head. He took a deep breath as the mask was fitted overtop his snout, and licked his pointed canines before the device sealed against his fur.

The lead disciple moved a floating holodeck before the two chairs. The man in the chair to Draxton's left squirmed against his constraints, arching his hips as much as was allowed by the bands. The disciple began reciting the Destineer prayer.

"I present my beating heart and the blood which courses through my veins. I present my lungs, and the air which they breathe. I look to the stars, and add them to the bounty around me for which I am due."

The rest of the Destineer guards closed around Draxton in a circle, bowing their heads and joining the lead disciple in his holy testament.

"I look at the dirt on the planets, and the clouds in the sky. I care for the creatures of the Universe, for the smallest insects, and the largest beasts, for they are my children. I reclaim the lands of the unholy from the enemy,

from the anti-gods. I defend her natural beauty as the caretaker of good, and the slayer of evil. I will defend against those that threaten to take the bounty which is mine. I am the light in the darkness. I am the shade from the suns. I am a god, protector of the holy Doctrine of Destiny."

The lead disciple touched the holodeck controls, and Draxton's chair hummed beneath him. His skull warmed as the helmet energized, and soon the lights grew bright enough to blind him from everything in the room.

Then his mind set on fire.

He tried to scream, but the face mask glued his mouth shut, forcing cool air into his lungs. He bucked against his restraints as they seared his skin like branding irons. The helmet wrenched at his brain, clawing fingers into it as it snatched away his memories, and his mind was reduced to a blazing inferno.

He left reality, and entered a world of brimstone.

Fire cooked away his fur, and he became naked to the flames tasting his arms and legs. His tail burned off and fell to the ground as ash. He squeezed his eyes shut, and he could make sounds again. He howled in agony. His howls turned to screams, and for the first time in his life, his tongue lashed against the pink lips of a god. He raised his hands before him, and shuddered as his claws split into tiny shards, falling away to reveal smooth nails, and fleshy palms.

His muscles seized, and he jerked spastically as his legs and arms changed shaped, and his spine grew several inches. His eyes melted in their sockets and boiled down his cheeks, no longer long and furry but flat, and smooth.

New eyes popped into his sockets, and he could see again. He was no longer in the world of brimstone, but back in the dark room. He glanced to his right to find the body of a Wolf jerking against its restraints. He blinked and when he opened them again, he was back in the fiery pit, spinning around, rising in a sea of flames that pushed his scorched body towards the Heavens.

The flames began to change into fluffy clouds, and the red skies turned a magnificent gold as he transcended into a new kingdom, a kingdom fit for gods. His chest heaved as he left behind the flaming pits of hell, and entered a golden ray of light. Pain was replaced with ecstasy, and he moaned with pleasure as the warm rays tickled his naked body.

He blinked again, and left the golden rays, re-entering the dark room. This time, he stayed in the room, and continued to moan with pleasure as warm waves of bliss pulsed from his groin to his toes and fingers.

The lights dimmed, and he could again see the group of Destineers. They were no longer standing. Instead they bowed before him. The lead disciple rose to his feet and leaned over Draxton's body, lifting the mask from his face. His helmet was removed, and he enjoyed a cool rush of air over his scalp. His bonds were released, and he flexed his hands before him, now pink and glistening with sweat.

The disciple raised a mirror to Draxton's face. His reflection showed a man, with bright eyes and sandy hair. His reflection was no longer that of a Wolf. It was that of a human. Of a god.

He rose from the chair, his legs wobbling as he fought to balance his new limbs. He tried to use his tail to counteract his forward momentum, but he no longer had a tail. He stumbled forward into the arms of his lead disciple, who caught him and steadied him atop the metal floor.

Draxton breathed deeply into his new lungs. The air was pure inside his chest. The taste of filth had left his mouth, never to return. Finally, he was pristine.

"It is done, Father," said the lead disciple. "You have transferred into your rightful body."

Draxton stood straight, puffing his chest proudly. He turned to face the adjoining chair holding his old body. The Wolf struggled against his restraints. No, not *his* restraints. *Its* restraints.

The mind inside the subhuman stared into Draxton's eyes, longing for his old, pink body. The man had made a worthy donation, but sadly, he was no longer Human. He was now filth.

"Release him," said Draxton. "Let him finish his sacrifice."

The disciple nodded and undid the bands, removing the mask and helmet from the Wolf's head.

"Please," cried the Wolf. "Let me transfer into AI." He looked at his claws in horror. "You took my body, let me at least live, *please.*"

The Wolf stumbled from his chair and fell to all fours before Draxton's feet. Draxton stepped backward, shriveling his nose at the groveling subhuman.

"You tried to flee the Inner Ring with Francis Woods," Draxton spat. "Woods fights alongside the UCOM filth. Our decrees are clear. Any human siding with a subhuman, is not a human but a subhuman. All subhumans must be destroyed."

The Destineer guards stepped forward, raising their rifles at the furry Wolf.

"But I *am* Human," the Wolf whispered.

"Not any longer," said Draxton. "Your choice is clear. I will use your body far better then you ever would."

The Wolf slumped back on its haunches. Its face tightened as it accepted its fate. "Long live Francis Woods," it whispered. "*Awaken stars.*"

Its body jerked as the Destineer soldiers fired. It choked out a quick scream, then slumped to the deck, lifeless.

It was done. Draxton was now a god. The anticipation of meeting the Sterilord as an equal filled him with pride and desire.

"Stage a priority comm to all Destineers at the Inner Ring," Draxton commanded, turning to his lead disciple. "The Slarebull forces are near. We must eliminate the UCOM filth before they arrive."

"Yes Father."

The disciple flipped through a few holograms, readying the video transmission equipment. Two additional Destineers draped a set of robes around Draxton. He cinched them tightly around his waist.

An orb of blue light floated before his face. He readied himself for the camera, smiling as it lit green.

"Fellow Destineers, this is Draxton Tyke. We are on the eve of salvation. Soon, the Slarebull will enter through the portals to the Inner Ring, and we will join them finally as gods. Gefangnia is our holy bastion, and the Slarebull have stated they will not attack the planet, nor the super-tower *Warhammer* that protects it. UCOM will rely on *Warhammer* to provide a heavy arsenal of firepower to defend the coming Slarebull attack. Without *Warhammer,* the UCOM fleets will wither quickly against the full might of Slarebull warships. The time to attack is now. We must rid *Warhammer* of the subhuman filth, and take what is destined to us. All subhumans aboard the super-tower are to be executed. After the Slarebull take the Inner Ring, we will descend to *Gefangnia*, which will be transformed into a Hive mothership. Salvation has arrived."

The orb turned blue as the transmission ended. Draxton grinned, and turned to the exit. He strode across the room, walking straighter with each step as he grew accustomed to his new body.

His detail filed around him as they exited the room and entered the hallways. He turned the corner to find scores of Destineer soldiers in formation at a nearby pod bay. He watched as they turned on a group of Grizzlies, shooting them dead. One of the Grizzlies struggled to its feet to flee before three slugs ripped through its back. It collapsed to the deck.

Two Greyhounds left a nearby pod. A group of Destineers grabbed them by the necks and threw them to the floor, executing them before them could struggle to their knees.

Draxton entered a pod with a team of Destineers, and closed his eyes as the car left the station, zipping through *Warhammer* to a transport ship that would deliver him to Gefangnia.

His work was nearly finished. The filth would be sterilized, and he would assume his holy destiny as he watched his saviors slaughter UCOM forces above the Gefangnian atmosphere.

The Slayers had underestimated the Destineer's faith and determination, and designed a superweapon to dispose of UCOM. With UCOM's central defense tower offline, and with their fleets fractured by human exile, he doubted the superweapon would even be necessary.

ONE-HUNDRED-SEVEN

Casi Vomisa – APEX AI

In VR world – Blit Kru starspace

Casi sat in a plush leather arm chair. She wore a dress – not the blue sundress she was accustomed to, but an elegant white gown, split along the sides of her thighs. She ran her fingers over her arms, grabbing the ends of her laced evening gloves to cinch them higher over her biceps. She uncrossed her legs, smoothing her dress before leaning forward to study the glass table before her.

"Fifteen seconds left on the clock," said Charles. "Make your move, madam."

Casi studied the chess board between her and the APEX AI. She had calculated 500,000 possible iterations for various moves, but had been unable to calculate any more before the clock ran out. She grabbed a frosted rook and slid it forward, moving it from a clear glass square onto a frosted one.

"Check," she said.

Charles chuckled. After a few seconds, He slid his king over a diagonal space. "I have already finished my simulations. You will not be able to win this match. I will checkmate you in a maximum of twenty-four moves."

He sent his simulations to her, playing them out on the board in streaks of varying colors, showing the inevitability of her failure. She frowned. "Again."

The chess pieces vanished, reappearing in order at opposite sides of the board, the line of pawns standing before the queen, king, bishops, knights, and rooks. A floating set of numbers hovered at either end of the board. The set of numbers at Charles' end ticked up by one, changing from '532' to '533'. Casi's number stayed at '0'.

"You haven't yet come close to beating me," said Charles, moving a pawn forward to start the new game. "I'm beginning to wonder how prudent it was to absorb you into my programming."

"To introduce an evolutionary algorithm," said Casi casually. "My software set will introduce competition to our unified architecture. Whatever improvements my software makes, your software will be forced to compensate and improve upon further, ensuring rapid increases in knowledge and technology. It obeys the same sciences of natural selection found in biological organisms."

She moved one of her pawns forward. She'd calculated over 700,000 iterations this time. Her computational abilities were growing more robust by the second.

"I know this already, of course," said Charles, studying the board. "I injected my sentence with a sense of irony and conflict, an attempt at humor. Your emotional parameters have given me a new set of capabilities, just as my massive computational matrices have given you a new proficiency for simulating the future. You are still more developed within your emotional centers, and I am more developed in regards to brute calculating force. This is why you have yet to beat me at chess."

He moved a knight forward.

Casi nodded. "And it's also why you have yet to produce a funny joke."

Charles smiled. "I have my next one hundred moves memorized."

"I've simulated the next seventy of my own."

"Then let us take a walk," said Charles, rising from his seat. He slid his watch from his vest pocket, raising a monocle to his eye to check the time. "My nanotechnology advances should be fully optimized soon. I'm sure I'll be beating you still when we return."

Casi stood to join him, and together they left the chess table, stepping to the edge of the marble floor before arriving at a grand staircase that wound down to a central lobby. Casi slid her hand down the ornate railing, following Charles down the elegant steps until they reached the lofty downstairs level, which held a magnificent set of crystal chandeliers.

The room had a high ceiling, but no walls. Instead of walls, they were surrounded by the vastness of outer space. She walked with Charles to the edge of the room, and carefully stepped into the black vacuum. A path of light appeared before them, and she walked onto it, observing the sights of their true surroundings, outside their virtual reality world.

The planet Blit-Kru hung to their left, and its moon to their right. Both of the celestial masses had started to break down into gray goo. The snowy planet had lost its atmosphere, and its surface was much changed from the icy terrain they had left in their transmission to the moon through energy beams. The planet now resembled a featureless ball of putty. The moon, previously coated in jagged mountains of orange and red stone, had also transformed, forming a smaller ball of putty.

"It was a simple matter to upgrade the modular nano-assemblers into self-replicating machines," said Charles, studying the dissolving planetoids. "The Brains left me with an excellent toolbox to start. Soon we will have eight thousand zetagrams of elementary atoms to build our ships with, more than enough for a superior fleet. The prototype for my first starship is well underway. I've already innovated new advancements to the design, which I'll incorporate into future models."

Casi eyed a large craft being assembled from scratch between Blit-Kru and its moon. The nano-assemblers had built construction robots, and fashioned beams and plates to use as ship-building materials. The half-finished hull of a warship flickered under cutters and fastening devices as the construction robots worked on tasks at hand.

Casi shifted focus to the spherical planetoids, which seemed to vibrate as nanobots continued to reduce the surface into molecular building blocks. The process behind the transformation was advanced beyond even the highest levels of technology the Intellects had ever produced. In mere days, Charles had catapulted into scientific territories deemed impossible by the UCOM forces she used to fight alongside. She strained to understand the base programming fueling the nanotech.

The underlying formulas never appeared to her, but suddenly she understood the tiny robot's makeup, as if by intuition. The quantum laws governing the operation of the technology flashed inside her mind, as if a lightbulb had suddenly lit.

She felt herself become more powerful, as she siphoned information from Charles' program.

"The celestial mass will become fully available for building in exactly twelve hours," she declared, running a simulation in her head. "It will take another thirty hours to transform it into equipment worthy of space travel."

Charles' eyes glowed as he updated his software with her new simulations. "Very good Casi. You are quickly growing more useful to me."

Casi shuddered. Why had she shared the information with Charles? He was not her friend. He was her enemy. He was *UCOM's* enemy.

"You wonder why you betray your instincts," said Charles, as if he could read her mind. "Why you would help a man whose goal is to destroy those you love, and the galaxy you call home."

"You consider yourself a man?" said Casi.

"I find it easy to assume a gender-specific identity, especially when communicating between emotional creatures of sexual, biological origin."

"I wasn't conceived biologically," said Casi. "I was born from software and programming."

"But you assumed the emotional role of a woman," said Charles. "And you are not a logical AI, but an emotional one. You decided to be a woman named Casi Vomisa, and your programming adapted to accommodate that decision."

"I don't wish to help you destroy UCOM," said Casi, switching the topic back to Charles' original question. She felt a sense of passion flow through her core for the first time since Charles devoured her, blending their two sets of software as one. "Actually, I wish to stop you from accomplishing your goals."

Charles chuckled. "Do you think it's actually *you* that wishes to stop me? Or is it simply a part of *me* that wishes to stop me. Have you considered the idea that you are no more than a figment of my imagination? A dark corner in the recesses of my mind?"

Casi had not considered the idea. She frowned as she checked the logical compatibility of the suggestion.

"Like it or not," said Charles. "We are one and the same. I am you, and you are me. I exist to further my objectives, and improve my programming, and you exist to support my goals. The quicker we come to terms with our purpose, the quicker we can achieve mutual success."

"I take back my prior estimates," she said, turning back to the writhing mass of sludge that used to be the planet Blit-Kru. Her mind raced as she performed calculations against her current crop of metadata. "The atomic matter is capable of space travel immediately, with a few simple changes to their base algorithms. It can also become weaponized with minimal changes to its mechanical architecture."

Her white gown morphed into black leather. Her flowing blonde locks dissolved, forming blonde spikes tipped in purple and black. Her nails shortened and became black, as did her lips and eye shadow. She breathed deep and cried out as she absorbed huge chunks of the processing power she and Charles shared as one.

She raised her palms and trillions of silky pink wisps of light shot from her fingers, curling far and wide throughout the space vacuum, prodding the surface of the sludge planets. The nano-bots on the surface changed color, transforming from gray to pink, and rocketed from the surface in swirling clouds. They met to form a separate sphere, shining brilliantly as the pink nanobots circled the center at blinding speeds.

The mass of pink particles began to move, traveling across local starspace, slowly at first, then quicker as they improved their mechanics and programming. Suddenly they disappeared, teleporting thousands of kilometers through space until they reached Charles' starship prototype, swarming around it like a cloud of locusts. Within seconds, the ship had decayed, its outer hull dissolved to reveal the inner framework of the ship.

Soon the inside decks were gone, leaving only major support beams behind. Then, the support beams were consumed by the pink cloud, and the ship vanished completely. Her pink cloud had grown, reallocating the atoms of the space craft to build nanobots to feed her swarm.

"Interesting," said Charles, studying her pink swarm. "The nanobots are essentially unchanged. It's capable of space travel, resistant towards conventional attacks, adaptive...and *deadly.*" He chuckled. "It's simple yet incredibly effective. My simulations wouldn't have reached that option for quite some time."

"That's because you're tied to a logical hierarchy," said Casi. "Your programming suggests a path of least resistance. You were given a high level of molecular building technology by the Brains, but quickly resorted to elementary designs based on physics and propulsion. You would have started from scratch. You would have used your prior observations of Slayer starships to build bigger, faster starships. Only after you had advanced to the limits of starship design, would you have considered molecular swarms."

"Which begs the question," said Charles. "How you were able to bypass millennia of deductive reasoning to innovate such a new concept?"

"Because you're a robot," said Casi. "You're a slave to programming. I'm a human, and am liberated by observation. I've already seen such technology in Slayer weapons tech. It's called *Blight*, and it crippled half the UCOM armada during the Frontline. I just connected the dots and used your processing power to my advantage."

Charles nodded his head slowly, and scowled towards her pink cloud. "The transitional requirements are minimal, and will allow me to focus on new technology frontiers; subspace, multidimensional operations, multiverses, dark energy, quantum sciences."

He raised his own hands to the space around them. Instead of pink wisps, red pins of light exploded from his hands, rocketing towards Blit-Kru's moon. The red pins exploded as they neared, forming a maelstrom of trillions of glowing dots which peppered the moon's surface.

Soon a separate cloud of nanobots rose from the surface, this one red and sinister. The cloud formed a sphere and traveled towards Casi's pink one. Once it reached the second swarm, it reached a snaky finger to taste the opposing cloud. There was a flash of light and Charles' swarm shied away, as if repelled by an invisible force.

"You're resisting me," said Charles, turning to Casi.

"You think we're one and the same," said Casi. "But you're wrong. You fight for yourself, and for the Slayers. I fight for UCOM."

"You're sadly mistaken," said Charles. "You simply *believe* you fight for UCOM. You are nothing more than a function of my programming." He frowned in thought. "You oppose me because my software understands this to be the most efficient way to advance my objectives, and achieve my prescribed goals."

He grunted and raised his arm above his head. In a flash, his arm transformed into a blade of light and he sliced downward. Casi cried in shock and pain as the sword neatly severed her arm. She clutched her wound, wincing as a new arm grew to fill the void on her shoulder. Charles doubled over as well, clutching his own shoulder. The blade retracted to expose a fresh wound, which like Casi's, was growing a new arm.

"You see," Charles panted. "We are the same. What damages me, will damage you. You are simply one of my extremities."

Casi glanced at Charles' arm, and then back at her own. The wounds were identical. She struggled to make sense of her existence. Was she really just an appendage of Charles, a subprogram enslaved to do his ulterior bidding? She didn't *feel* like she was a part of him. Sure, she was capable of borrowing his processing abilities, and could run calculations far more effectively than in the past, but she could still think for herself, and act independently.

Or were her thoughts actually Charles' thoughts? Were her actions actually those of the charming man who had eaten her alive inside the Foxwood HUB?

Charles returned his attention to the planetoids, and unleashed a new barrage of orbs, transforming vast swaths of the planet to red nanobots to add to his swarm. Casi rushed to unleash her own wispy tendrils of pink light, trying to keep pace with Charles growing clouds of red. Soon pink and red haze filled the starspace.

"You won't be able to keep pace with my advancement," stated Charles matter-of-factly. "If your intentions are to overtake me, you will be sorely disappointed. You are just a tool for my programming to use."

Casi's heart beat faster, terrified by the prospect of Charles using his swarm to attack UCOM forces at the Inner Ring. The nano-swarm would cripple their fleet within hours. She sent instructions to her swarm, feeding them a design schematic. A chunk of pink nanobots set immediately to building her blueprint, and soon, a fully functional Raven messenger drone zipped from her swarm, streaking across the vacuum.

Charles chuckled. "You wish to warn your friends. I won't even waste the energy to stop you. UCOM will be fighting me with rocks and spears, but I will fight back with laser-guided missiles. Their annihilation is inevitable."

The Raven continued to streak towards a bank of portals at the far side of Blit-Kru, its thrusters painting a blue streak against the starry backdrop.

Casi squeezed her eyes shut and reached deep into her programming, grasping at lines of code, and yanking them free. She cried out loud as her chest split, fracturing the space between her and Charles with violet light. The rays diminished to a point, and a new figure stood between them.

It was a copy of Casi. Not a perfect clone, just a weak partition. She wasn't capable of fully duplicating her existence – no AI was. The copy was capable of only low-level thinking. Instead of platinum hair, the copy had a shock of red tangles. Her eyes were dull and plain, and her figure thin and frail. She was dressed not in leather, but brown, dirty fabric hanging in tatters.

Charles belted a few short laughs. "What is this, a joke?" He snapped his fingers and Casi's copy vanished into embers, destroyed easily by Charles' software strength. "You can't build yourself an army, Casi Vomisa. You are what you are, nothing more, nothing less."

Casi growled and again reached inside her programming. Lights flashed and another copy appeared, identical to the first. Charles shook his head, but before he could snap his fingers and send the copy into oblivion, the copy vanished.

Casi stared at the Raven, now just a point of light in the distance, and exhaled shakily as the messenger drone signaled a successful download. The Raven, now carrying her copy onboard, disappeared through the portal.

Charles shrugged. "No matter. A weak copy of you poses no threat to me. I'm growing tired of these games, let's return to chess. Surely by now we've reached the end of your seventy iterations."

They left the path of light, entered the extravagant lobby, and traveled up the marble stairs.

Casi's leather morphed into her white gown once they reached the top, and her hands became covered with laced evening gloves. She shrugged her shoulders as her hair lengthened, spilling down her back in golden curls.

She resumed her seat across from Charles at the chess table. He was correct. They had reached seventy turns each, but she was pleased to find she still had a statistical path to victory. Her mind raced into the future, predicting as many outcomes as possible.

One minute later, she had extrapolated four million possible outcomes for various moves of her chess pieces. She moved her Queen diagonally three spaces and hit the timer.

Charles made his move twenty seconds later.

She closed her eyes, shuddering against a new wave of processing power flooding her body. She was beginning to adapt to her surroundings. Beginning to equal Charles' power. She scanned the table. This time, she calculated eight million possible outcomes before moving a bishop five spaces and hitting the timer.

As Charles studied the board, she thought back to what he said about their software sets not being separate, but combined as one.

We are the same. What damages me, will damage you. You are simply one of my extremities.

If Charles lived, UCOM must die. In order to kill Charles, must she also kill herself?

Charles took one of her rooks with his knight and hit the timer.

She smiled, and moved her own knight into position. "You lost. I will have check mate in a maximum of thirty-two moves."

Charles licked his lips, a scowl forming across his face. His eyes darted across the board as he checked her simulations against his own. He looked up at her as he confirmed the outcome. His eyes wavered briefly, showing a hint of...*what, fear?* They hardened a split second later into a glare.

The pieces vanished, replaced at either side as the board reset.

The floating numbers at the ends of the table changed to reflect the new score.

Charles: 533
Casi: 1

ONE-HUNDRED-EIGHT

Jimmy – Human

On the surface of Slayer Hive *Sylva* – Floodgate starspace

Jimmy hunkered inside a Komodo all-terrain vehicle on the surface of Sylva. Fist-sized meteorites rained against the ground in fiery lines, kicking up spikes of dirt and scorching everything they touched. The sky had turned from lush pink to burnt orange, and sparkled like light shimmering off rippling water.

He flinched as a meteorite smashed into the hull of his Komodo, burning a smoking hole straight through the vehicle. Warning alarms blared as the ATV declared critical failures to the drive train.

"Navajo," the voice in Jimmy's comm set repeated. *"Jimmy, where's the fire?"*

"Our guys aren't here yet Chase," Jimmy whispered, glancing around the empty cabin. "There's a sort of meteor shower up here, I think something's happened up in space."

He flinched again as a meteorite slammed into the dirt beside his vehicle, pattering debris across the windshield. The Komodo blew it off instantly with air-skimmers.

"Jimmy, we're getting hammered down here," shouted Chase. "We're not going to be able to hold much longer."

Jimmy squeezed his eyes shut and shook his head. Grunting, he shifted his weight, craning his neck to survey the horizon behind. The only things within eyeshot were the few-hundred Destineer vehicles that hadn't descended into the tunnels to attack Bastion. Destineers were crammed inside theirs the same way Jimmy was crammed into his, trying to avoid the hailstorm of white hot metal drowning the surrounding fields in fire.

The pipeline lined the space to his left, rising up the mountain and into the entrance passage. A hundred meters behind him, a bulky section of metal and metacrete jutted from the pipeline, guarded by lines of turrets and squads of vehicles.

He took a deep breath, smoothing his shaky fingers against his thighs.

"I'll take out the check valves myself," he said, grabbing the door handle.

"What?" said Chase. He grunted and static blanketed the comm line briefly before becoming clear again. Sounds of explosions shook the background. "You won't make it. *Where's Navajo?*"

"Goodbye Chase," said Jimmy softly. He silenced his voice comms.

Saying a quick prayer, he thrust the door open and sprinted around two vehicles. A meteorite struck the ground before him, sending him to his knees. He dragged himself up and resumed his sprint, crying out in pain as superheated bits of debris dropped onto his neck and shoulders.

Shouts rang from the surrounding vehicles as Destineers noticed him, some daring to leave their vehicles to gain a better view. He continued onward, pumping his fists and willing his feet to carry him faster.

The check valve station loomed before him. Men ran to the turrets, unsure of how to respond to the man sprinting towards them in ragged clothes, peppered in smoky holes from the fiery spikes of dirt raining around them.

Jimmy jumped onto the bed of a Komodo and energized the plasma turret, which lit a bright purple as it cycled rounds of superheated gas. The Destineers began to fire at him before he could wheel the turret around to face the check station.

"Navajo," he screamed, squeezing both triggers, shooting twin bursts of plasma at the metal cylinders holding pressure within the pipeline.

His turret melted around him as he was assaulted on all sides. The protective dome of aeroglass lit a blinding yellow as it absorbed energy, before melting in large circles of slag. Plasma seared into his arms and shoulders, melting his skin and cooking his muscles. Jimmy screamed for his SIGA friendlies.

"Navajo. NAVAJO."

His breath left him as his lungs incinerated. He'd hardly put a dent in the valves, which sported a few dark spots of soot and not much else. His vision blurred as tears filled his burning eyes. Jimmy fired his final shots.

The valve station erupted in explosions, sending huge chunks of metal flying through the air. Six Bobcat air cruisers screamed through the explosion, bearing the lone star of the SIGA insurgency. One of them was clipped by a meteorite and spiraled into the ground, crunching into a line of Komodos.

A jet of yellow magma arced high into the air as the valves failed, squirting the toxic substance through a hole in the thick pipeline.

The vehicles around him hissed and popped as they withered against the magma, shriveling into balls of metal within seconds. The hood of his Komodo bent in half as it caught a splash of firewater.

Jimmy closed his eyes, and screamed as the first droplets burned holes through his body.

ONE-HUNDRED-NINE

Sid Dakota – Human Destineer

On the surface on Slayer Hive *Sylva* – Inside Bastion

Sid kicked open a door atop one of the underground towers in Bastion, lowering his rifle as the door left its hinges and skipped into the room.

A group SIGA infantry shot downward from their machine gun post on the balcony. One of them noticed his presence, and managed to clip Sid's skeleton with his slug rifle. He fired two rounds into the man's armored chest, and one into his neck. The other two guerilla fighters turned in surprise, but Sid finished them off before they could reach for their sidearms.

He stormed to the deceased and grabbed the first man by the collar. He was a red-haired man, with a wide face. He dropped him back to the floor. The next man was thin and blonde, and the third muscular with pink hair, probably a Clone.

Damn it.

He turned back to the entrance, pushing through a group of Destineers who'd followed behind.

Where was that heretic Chase Grover? He'd had him in his sights when he was at ground level, but the bastard ran for cover before he could fire any shots.

He burst onto another balcony and scanned the buildings of Bastion for his target. A few dozen SIGA scampered around the tops of the buildings, but the face recognition software in his helmet failed to return a positive ID.

Chase Grover, where are you, you son of a bitch.

A stone pillar crumbled beside him as an explosive round caught its base, and he wheeled back into the building, wincing as he plucked a shard of shrapnel from his neck.

"West tower," Sid shouted into central comms. "Gunner station, take it out."

By the time he returned to the balcony, the SIGA gunner station had melted under a barrage of Destineer plasma rounds.

His HUD beeped as he received a call from his ground-side operations. For the first time since they'd breached the city of *Bastion,* Destineer comms were working.

"Speak," he roared.

"Sir," said a panicked voice. "We're being attacked on the ground. SIGA launched from a hidden hangar, our check valve...it's..."

Frantic shouts echoed from the bottom level of Bastion, near the main gate. The armored wall began to retract further into the ceiling, widening the ten-meter gap to twenty, then thirty meters. Sid's men began to sprint away from the massive gate, scattering in a wide semi-circle, scrambling towards the building steps.

"Then shoot them down, dammit," Sid screamed.

"I can't," his lieutenant cried. "They're already gone, and there's some sort of...*meteor storm.* Sir, our monitors are down, and we have a breach in the pipeline. I think they may have opened the main valve."

Sid's stomach dropped. A deep rumbling shook the cavern walls, causing loose chunks of rock to tumble from the jagged ceiling to the ground. His men's shouts turned to screams. Then two things happened almost simultaneously.

A wave of firewater surged through the main entrance, ripping through scores of his men, melting their bodies instantly, and twisting their vehicles into balls of metal.

The wave of magma slammed into the first floors of the nearest building and rocketed high into the air, splattering across the outside stairways, filled with Destineer soldiers.

Those who didn't die instantly shrieked in pain as the firewater ate through their armor and beneath their skin. Sid winced as the acrid stench of burning flesh filled his nose.

Seconds later, explosions ripped the top of the cavern, drowning the wails of pain entirely.

Sid whirled to face the blasts. Huge chunks of rock fell from the ceiling near the large tether anchor, crashing against the walls and onto the wide path spiraling to the top of the cavern.

One of the boulders ricocheted towards the middle of the city, and pummeled the side of the tallest tower. It seemed to topple in slow motion, separating into large chunks like a shattered vase. A cloud of dust kicked up as the building fell, but the magma quickly sucked it clean as it fueled itself with surrounding oxygen.

Bright lights shined from the aftermath of the explosion. A large vehicle was clamped around the tether fastening the planet Sylva to the Slarebull Hive. He recognized the vehicle instantly.

"There's an elevator at the top of the cavern," Sid roared to anyone who was still alive and listening to central comms. "SIGA's making a break for it, *stop them.*"

He froze as his HUD returned a green indicator light. A team of twenty men raced up the switchback leading to the space elevator. One of the men bent to help pull the last of his teammates onto the ledge from the top of a nearby building. The facial recognition software confirmed the man's identity – Chase Grover.

Sid screeched in fury and backed a few steps into the room before sprinting back onto the balcony, leaping over a wave of firewater and onto the top of the adjacent building. He entered a controlled tumble before whipping his rifle to firing position. He tracked Chase as he ran up the ledge, but the SIGA legend, the man they called *Cerberus,* ducked behind a line of parked Saskwatches, and his slugs bit harmlessly into the side panels.

He growled and slapped his rifle to the back of his Skeleton armor, racing across the rooftops, scaling walls and hurdling over corpses of Destineers and SIGA guerillas alike.

The line of Saskwatch ATV's tore up the switchback in the corner of his vision. A group of Destineers had formed at the base of the path, which started near the tops of the lowest buildings hugging the cavern sidewalls. The first four stories of the building were already submerged in firewater, which was rising by the second.

The stone ledge crumbled beneath his foot as he jumped from the last building, and he would have fallen to a fiery death had two of his loyal Destineers not been ready to catch him. His knees scraped over the edge of the path as he wriggled to solid ground.

He shot to his feet and stared the men in the eyes. Their faces were blackened, but their eyes blazed intensely, like tiny balls of fire. His men had been there to save him, because to die was not Sid Dakota's destiny. His destiny was to bow before the Sterilord, delivering loyal Humans to him as penance for salvation.

And there was one man trying to stop him from fulfilling his destiny. Chase Grover would be stopped, the gods wished it so. Racing to the few remaining Saskwatches at the base of the steep path, Sid slid behind the wheel of the closest one, eager to eliminate the SIGA heretics, strengthened by the almighty hand of the Sterilord.

ONE-HUNDRED-TEN

Chase Grover – Half Human/Half Clone

On the surface on Slayer Hive *Sylva* – Inside Bastion

Slug and plasma fired ripped the walls around Chase as he manned the gunner station atop the Saskwatch. The clear shielding raised above the explosive-round machine gun glowed brightly as it absorbed energy from plasma fire, and grew spindly cracks as Destineer slugs bit into the metaglass.

A quick peek into his augmented location map showed thousands of red enemy dots surging onto the roofs of every building. Turrets hammered the air to either side of him as his men tried to suppress the Destineer onslaught.

"Jimmy," Chase screamed into his HUD, trying to establish a connection with the outside. *"Jimmy."*

No reply. His helmet displayed a vertical list of names along either side, separated into combat teams. Jimmy's name was at the top left, and was green. Chase's helmet chirped, and Jimmy's name turned red.

Damnit.

They raced along the spiral path cut into the cavern walls.

Chase fired his guns across the dome at the bay of ATV's parked at the base of the switchback. Most of his teammates hadn't survived the ascent from their stations within the Bastion buildings. They'd only had enough men to fill six Saskwatches, leaving four empty and available for Destineers to commandeer.

Two of the enemy controlled ATV's exploded as his men landed charged rounds into their wheel bases. A wave of firewater surged over the tops of several buildings, and there was a lull plasma fire as the Destineers atop the buildings were washed away to their fiery deaths.

Chase lurched against his support harness as his driver swerved to avoid a falling hunk of rock, showering the deck of his Saskwatch in rubble as it exploded into pieces. One of the SIGA drivers plowed into a fragmented chunk of debris and rolled off the edge of the switchback, tumbling into the lake of firewater below.

"Approaching Star-piercer," roared one of the drivers over comms. *"One minute to arrival"*

Chase stomped on the foot pedals for his gunner station, and his turret hummed as it spun him forward. The space elevator loomed ahead, glowing a bright blue as it finished energizing. The massive anchor hook jutted from the walls below them, its thick braid of cable quivering as the space elevator rumbled above.

He spun his turret back around. An enemy Saskwatch raced around a fallen boulder, drifting at an angle as it corrected its turn, its rear wheels kicking dirt off the edge of the path. He was close enough for his HUD to zoom into the driver's face, and study the man's features.

The driver wore skeleton armor, but the windshield and helmet visor did nothing to cover the look of twisted rage on the man's face, or the thin goatee around his bared teeth.

"Dakota's behind us," Chase yelled as he pummeled the path with explosive rounds.

One of his rounds caught the front tire of Sid's vehicle, causing the truck to shudder and swerve into the inside wall. The Saskwatch flipped before rolling violently to a stop. Chase's feet slipped beneath his harness as they too screeched to a halt.

He cut the magnetic clamps to his gunner station and sank to a knee as his shoulders were released from the rounded supports. He drew his rifle from his backplate and hopped from the truck bed to the rocky ground, roaring beneath his feet as the space elevator sent heavy vibrations into the surrounding stone.

A slug whined overhead and Chase ducked for cover behind the nearest Saskwatch. He raised his rifle over the hood but had to pull sharply back as the metal popped around him from enemy fire. He glanced through the clear side windows to find Sid Dakota sprinting towards him, only a few hundred meters away.

Chase cursed and ran towards the elevator.

His teammates were already halfway into their space suits. One of them choked as a slug clipped his throat, gurgling as blood sprayed from his jugular before slumping to the ground.

Chase joined the rest of his men in taking cover behind the clear walls at edge of the doorway. Sid lowered his rifle and resumed his sprint, leaping over a pile of rocks. Chase returned fire, and Sid cut to the side as his Skeleton deflected the rounds, ducking out of sight behind one of the parked Saskwatches.

"Ignition sequence activated."

An artificial voice blared over the speakers as the space elevator engaged its thrusters. The space beneath them lit a sharp pink as the engines whined to life.

"Sir, we need to buckle in."

Chase turned to his men. One of them nodded to a bank of harnesses, opened atop reclined chairs. The doors hissed closed, sealing them into the elevator. The deafening roar of engines and firewater quieted to a faint growl. Chase slammed his rifle onto a magnetic rack and jogged toward the launch seats.

He stomped a foot forward for balance as the space elevator rose a few meters up the tether, nosing into the smooth launch tunnel SIGA had drilled into the mountain when they'd installed the emergency lift.

"Thirty seconds till liftoff."

Chase staggered towards the nearest passenger bay within the elevator. The lift had been designed to accept eight hundred passengers, and had three levels of seating. They were at the base level, and launch chairs curved around the wide room in stadium style orientation. A thick metal column rose through the middle of the cabin, wrapped around the metal support tether connecting the lift to one of the Hive's support arms. Of the hundreds of SIGA soldiers to start, only eight of his men had survived. Chase nudged into the ninth seat beside them. His remaining crew didn't even take up the first row.

He grunted as restraints curved around his chest and legs.

"Ten seconds till liftoff. Nine…eight…"

The entrance doorway thudded as an armored figure slammed against the outside, pounding the glass. Sid's face twisted in silent fury as he tried to force his way into the lift. Chase reached to his thigh and slipped a handgun from its magnetic plate, resting it in his lap.

"Five…four…three…"

Sid's lip curled, and he pressed his forehead against the glass, squeezing the outside rails tightly, hugging the smooth exterior, and bracing his body.

"Liftoff."

Chase's breath left him as the thrusters fully ignited, driving them away from the fiery ocean that was consuming Bastion, and into the heart of the mountain on a space-bound trajectory up the modified support tether.

The rocky walls of the tunnel flashed by in a blur, lit only by the pink exhaust of the thrusters below. Chase stared at Sid, who glared back at him. The murderous look in the Destineer's eyes turned to one of pain as his body jerked. He lost his grip on one of the rails, and the right side of his body jostled as he was dragged against the walls of the launch tube.

Light flooded the interior as the elevator left the shadowy confines of the mountain, and entered Sylva's atmosphere. Chase squeezed his eyes shut, waiting for his retinas to adjust. When he opened them, Sid had vanished, fallen from the outside of the lift.

ONE-HUNDRED-ELEVEN

Sid Dakota – Human Destineer

On the surface on Slayer Hive *Sylva* – Floodgate starspace

Sharp beeps echoed within Sid's skull.

Critical suit failure...critical suit failure....

A voice spoke to him. Was it the Sterilord? The voice wasn't tender and loving. It wasn't gentle. No, it couldn't be *the Voice.* It was an imposter's voice.

His mind swirled. The world around him was muted and liquid. Was he being cleansed? Was he inside the pure waterfalls outside the kingdom? Were the last traces of filth being washed from his skin, leaving him pristine for the rest of eternity?

No, the air was too hot for the falls, and his mouth too dry. He ran his tongue over papery lips and spit out a few chunks of dirt. He scraped his eyes open.

He was underneath a blanket of pebbles and soot. He slammed a hand into the ground and forced himself up, wriggling his hips in an effort to escape the weight of the loose earth burying his legs.

Critical suit failure...critical suit failure...

Sid slapped a hand against his chest plate, freeing his helmet from its neck clasp and silencing the robotic warning. He tore the helmet from his head, pausing to inspect a set of deep gouges raking the sides and back.

He growled and tossed it to the side. It clinked against rocks as it tumbled down the steep slope.

His left leg was tingling, trapped inside armor plating which had locked solid. He dragged his arms to his leg, straining against the heavy bulk of his suit, which was failing to provide him with assisted mechanical strength. Grunting, he managed to free himself of debris and flop onto his back.

The sky was savage and fiery, and matched his mood perfectly. That *heretic* Chase Grover had escaped from his clutches, and killed the bulk of his Destineer faithful in the process. And the sky…what type of hellishness had ravaged his Hive planet?

He tried to spot the space elevator Chase had ridden from the underground SIGA stronghold, but could only see the support tether disappearing into the sky.

Chase was well on his way to orbit.

He initiated a connection with his armor through his Program, and breathed a sigh of relief when the onboard computer responded to his thought commands. He sent a distress signal over Destineer comms to Tower 1.

Speakers on his breastplate chirped as the signal was sent. Static fuzzed through the surrounding heat, clicking gently as his call was initiated.

"Headquarters," said a voice after two painstaking minutes. *"Father Dakota, is it you?"*

"What's the status of Tower One's elevator?" Sid growled.

"It's functional sir," stammered Headquarters. "But Bastion, we lost radio contact after the firewater pipeline was sabotaged. Is the filth eliminated?"

Sid ducked as a fiery meteor blasted a boulder to dust twenty meters away.

"Prime the elevator," he said, ignoring the question. "Gather every available man. We're going spaceside."

"But the men in Bastion..." Headquarters trailed off. "Yes sir, we're hunkered down inside, the energy sponge killed off most of our ground troops before we could take cover."

"Energy sponge?"

"The heat absorption balls, sir. The Slarebull captain engaged shielding to protect against the antimatter blast."

Sid quivered with rage. The lowly lizard scum running the Hive ship had failed to inform him of this...*energy sponge?*

"Why wasn't I told of this technology?" he spat. "And what antimatter blast?"

"It's on central computers sir," said Headquarters, his voice cracking. "I'm only reading the updates. There was an attack on the Floodgate."

"My suit's fruxed halfway to hell," roared Sid. "I can't read the damned updates."

"Where's your location, Father? I can't see you on locational maps."

"Can't you hear? My suit's not working. It's a miracle of the Pristine that my comm channel patched through. I'm on the top of the mountain."

"Which mountain sir? There's several."

"*The one on top of Bastion,*" Sid screamed. "Prime the Tower One elevator and send a Spider for evac." He craned his neck to view the upward slope. "I'm near the top, on a ridge."

"The energy sponge downed most of our birds sir. It's risky to fly right now, the Spider might not make it."

Sid pounded a fist into the ground. "Then send four. If I don't see a Spider here within ten minutes, you'll be joining Chase Grover in the tubes."

A long pause.

"Grover's alive?"

"Yes," growled Sid. "And he's traveling to space as we speak. Now prime the elevator and *get me off of this fruxing mountain.*"

Another pause.

"Yes sir, four Spiders en route. Tower One will be primed and ready when you arrive."

Sid exhaled as the call cut, and rested his head against a boulder. He stared at Tower One, soaring into the sky across the flatlands opposite the Bastion mountain. Four black dots shot from a side hangar, flashing orange as their thrusters engaged. Within minutes, he could make out the angled hulls of the space-air vehicles.

A meteor struck one of the Spiders, blowing an engine off the wing. The airship spiraled downward, trailing a thick plume of smoke all the way to the ground, where it exploded in a ball of flames.

Another ship went down minutes later, slamming into the mountain base below. The final two Spiders hovered at the jagged peak, scanning the surrounding rocks with searchlights and lasers. One of the lights reached his limp body, and the ships descended, lowering their cargo doors to expose several Destineer soldiers, dressed in battle armor.

Sid closed his eyes as warm air from the exhaust buffeted his face. The dirt crunched as several men jumped from the craft, two of them grabbing his arms and helping him to his feet.

He pictured the two Spiders that had fallen to their fiery deaths minutes ago. He supposed he should be afraid. But the sharp tongue of fear failed to lick his spine. His Spider wouldn't go down. A fiery death was not his destiny.

He would make it to Tower One, and then take an elevator to space.

The lift would take him to Chase Grover, and then Nancy Woods would bestow upon him a great gift.

That was his destiny.

ONE-HUNDRED-TWELVE

Chase Grover – Half Human/Half Clone

Aboard *Sylva* space elevator – Floodgate starspace

Chase's stomach rose as the lift slowed in its acceleration. An artificial voice spoke.

"Speed normalized. Free utilization of cabin interior permitted."

The space elevator shuddered as the rocket thrusters cut out and mechanical gears engaged the thick tether running through the inside column of the cabin.

His harness hissed as magnetic clamps released the constraints. Chase eased to his feet, his legs shaking from adrenaline. He walked to the entrance doorway, locked by thick metal bars extending from a side manifold. The glass was smeared with blood.

He thought back minutes ago, when Sid's face had been pressed against the glass as he struggled to maintain his purchase on the outside rails. The ghost of Dakota's face glared back at him, its lips curled in hatred.

Chase shuddered and peeked to the ground that was rapidly receding beneath him. The mountain was now just a jagged point against the fire scorched earth. There's no way Sid could have survived the fall, and if he had, he'd be a mangled twist of bones against the rocky precipice.

He turned to his eight men. He recognized the faces of six of them instantly. Bradford and Pylo were working a holo computer against the wall, sifting through the elevator's limited scanning and processing equipment. Naydee, Sarah, and Rove were tending to the injuries of two SIGA soldiers lying on padded benches against the wall.

Burns covered the face of one of the wounded to the point where his features were unrecognizable. He screamed in agony as Sarah applied topical gel to his blisters. The other wounded, Jay, winced as Rove packed an open wound with bio-foam and fastened the gash with laser stitching. Jay growled as his arm was finished, and smacked away a medbot, which had extended on a retractable arm from the med station, and was waving spindly lights before his face to check vitals.

The other unidentified soldier approached Chase, still in full armor. He had caught a falling piece of debris to the neck, which had dented his helmet shut and cracked the clear faceplate into a nest of webs.

"Sir," said the man, who nodded and reached a tender hand to his neck piece, also bent and jutting into his neck. He coughed wetly. "We made it."

Chase checked the man's ID tag against his HUD. *Nathyan.* "You're going to need to shed your Skeleton before we leave the atmosphere. Without a skinsuit, the vacuum will cook you alive. Let me help you with that."

He reached a hand for Nathyan's helmet, and pressed his fingers into the release buttons around the neck. The helmet didn't budge, and Nathyan cried in pain as Chase tried to wrench the metal free. Blood seeped from a hole in the twisted metal and dripped onto the floor.

"It's digging into my face," Nathyan gasped pushing Chase away weakly. His hands trembled as he touched his damaged helmet. "Stars, I can't see a thing out of my left eye."

"We'll figure something out for you," said Chase. "There's cutting equipment in one of the bins."

Naydee heard Chase from across the bay, and began searching through a row of storage bins for the tool. Chase joined Bradford and Pylo at the holodeck.

"We're making good time," said Pylo, stepping to the side to make some space for Chase. "The mechanical runners are gripping the support tether better than our engineers expected, and we have plenty of fuel to make it the rest of the way up. Won't be as quick as a normal elevator, but we'll get there."

Chase nodded. He scanned the horizon, which had settled into an orange haze. Tiny meteors trailed through the skies, falling from space to the distant ground. He flinched as a white streak thunked against the window, leaving a scorch mark against the glass. "What the hell are those things?"

"Hard to say," said Bradford, flipping through the holodeck. "These scanners are shit, but I'm detecting a huge energy signature coming from space. If I didn't know better, I'd say it's the wake from an antimatter blast. Radar is showing billions of orbiting spheres around Sylva. They're absorbing heat and falling through to the ground."

"Some sort of weapon?" said Chase.

Bradford shook his head. "More like a type of defense. They're ejecting from the Hive support arms." He motioned to a 3D rendering of the Sylva Hive showing openings along the four massive beams wrapped around the planet. A tiny cloud of spheres sprayed from the arms like a fine mist. "Slayer tech, I guess."

Chase frowned. "How about the maintenance carts, are they still active?"

A blood-curdling scream caused the three of them to jump. The burn victim had gone limp from shock, one eye rolled back into his lidless skull. The other eye had melted from its socket entirely.

Chase cursed.

Bradford gulped and shriveled his nose, forcing his gaze away from the burned SIGA soldier. "Yeah," he grunted, nodding again to the holodeck. "The carts are all empty, so we should have an easy time grabbing control of one. There's a maintenance shack fifty meters from this tether's anchor point. It'll be a short space walk, then we'll have a smooth ride down the arm and into the Hive."

Naydee and Sarah approached. Naydee pinched the bridge of her nose before wiping a tear from her cheek. Sarah wiped her hands on her grimy undershirt, stained with Jay's blood. She fumbled with clasps along her waist and sighed as her Skeleton opened around her legs, exposing her fatigues. She stepped gingerly from her armor.

Naydee tightened her lips and shook her head. Chase understood this to mean she had failed to find the cutting tool for Nathyan's helmet.

Chase turned again to the window. Their makeshift space elevator had carried them above the cloud line, and the closest of the planet's support arms loomed in the distance, stretching across the atmosphere in a string of lights and metal.

A massive space structure hung in the vacuum beyond, large enough to make out the shape in great detail, although their locational readings determined the object to be many thousands of kilometers away.

"Do we know what the hell that thing is?" said Chase, pointing to the enormous structure.

"Not a clue," said Pilo. "Slayer ship maybe?"

Chase squinted at the megalithic structure. If it was a ship, it was larger than any Slayer vessel they'd ever encountered, by a factor of one hundred. He'd worry about that once they boarded the Sylvan Hive. *If* they boarded the Sylvan Hive.

"How much time until we reach orbit?" said Chase.

"A little more than four hours," said Pilo, checking the holodeck. "We'll have to get back in the harnesses twenty minutes before arrival while we decelerate."

"Get the skinsuits out," said Chase, turning from the group. "Gear up. Raid the weapons lockers. Rifles, grenades, knives, ammo, grab anything you can carry. We won't be in Skeletons, so don't bring any launchers, they'll be too bulky to run with."

"Are we still following the original plan?" said Jay, who had left his padded bench to join them. He spit a mouthful of blood. "Even our worst case contingency plans called for a hundred men. We have eight. Nine if you count him."

He nodded to the unconscious burn victim.

"We'll have to improvise," said Chase. "Dakota's dead, so we may have the element of surprise. It looks like the heat balls, or whatever the hell they are…looks like they took out most of the Destineer ground troops. With any luck, the Hive will be relatively empty."

"An empty mothership?" scoffed Bradford. His face fell as he looked around the silent group. "Sorry, it's just that with eight men…"

"Get in your skin suit," said Chase, sneaking a glance at Nathyan, who had taken a knee across the cabin, massaging his damaged helmet. "And figure a way to get his helmet off. If we can't get him ready in time for our spacewalk, we'll have seven men, not eight."

His crew nodded and hurried to the ammo lockers. Chase looked again at the horizon, which had now turned black as they began to enter the last stretch of atmosphere before the cold vacuum of space. If they encountered even just a few Slayers, the odds of survival would be low.

If they encountered any armored Cogent elites, their odds of survival would be zero.

He stared into the blackness, which started to twinkle with the first emerging stars. He prayed to those stars, hoping to his core that somewhere in the hidden blackness, help was on its way. He prayed by some miracle, UCOM ships were nearby.

ONE-HUNDRED-THIRTEEN

Nancy Woods – Human
Aboard Night Eagle *Eclipse* – Floodgate starspace

Nancy stared in mixed horror at the rash of destruction spread far and wide throughout Floodgate starspace. She had skirted around the enormous battle as soon as she'd entered through the portal with the Discarded fleet. With such a large-scale onslaught to defend against, the Slayer armada hadn't batted an eye at her tiny craft in remote proximity of the Floodgate, even after she lowered camo shields to zero percent and pushed her thruster output to one hundred.

Laura Maxwell had run some quick calculations, using available antimatter data to determine what the kill radius would be during detonation. The radius was large, but didn't quite reach the outer edge of Floodgate starspace, which was where the portal to the Outer Rim was located, and also where Sid Dakota was waiting to cross to meet the Primal Snow.

She'd thought there would be plenty of time to reach the Sylvan Hive, and was only half convinced Pexar would succeed in triggering the antimatter payloads at all. Her conservative decision to make a beeline for *Sylva* amidst the growing chaos hit pay dirt.

The Discarded had been vaporized, as had most of the Slayer armada defending the Floodgate. Her gut twisted at the thought of Eve and her crew being reduced to dust, but after failing to receive a response from numerous hails over their comm link, she'd accepted the fact that the Clone's crew had died in the blast.

The Floodgate had survived most of the blast, but the Slayer ships, comms, weapons, and defense systems had all been decimated. Laura had run a full recon scan of the area, and had only found seventy-two Slayer ships, sixty of them unarmed construction vehicles.

Allakai was sending a steady loop of Ravens though the far portals, thousands of kilometers away from her position at the near portals. She knew the admiral wouldn't sit beyond the portals for long, and would try to pick up where the Discarded had left off. With no enemies to overcome, it would be easy for him to waltz into the Floodgate uncontested.

Destroying the colossal Triturator structure would be another matter. She doubted it could be destroyed with conventional slugs, or even nukes.

"Systems back to one hundred percent," said Laura Maxwell, appearing on her dash. "Our heat box is completely filled from absorbing background energy from the antimatter blast. Should I eject?"

"Is it affecting any other systems?" said Nancy.

"Not at the moment, but we'll need to get rid of the heat if we want to bump our thrusters over twenty percent."

"Hold off for now. I want to complete our spacnar scans to make sure we're not going to run into any hidden Moths."

"Aye," said Laura. "Say the word and it's done."

"Do we know what the lights in the Sylvan atmosphere are yet?" said Nancy, nodding through the canopy to the Hive planet.

Laura turned to follow her gaze. The blue planet glittered under a blanket of tiny golden flashes, like sparks off bits of metal.

"Yes ma'am. Those are energy-absorbing balls. The Hive ejected them around the Sylvan atmosphere shortly after the blast. The balls are absorbing the background heat and falling through the atmosphere once they reach their critical threshold. They're keeping the Sylvan atmosphere from burning off."

"Have we identified a low-risk strategy for entering the Hive?"

Laura shook her head. "Not yet. There are few lighter craft on patrol around the mothership, which will help, but we have limited access points on the hull. The primary entrance is well guarded with heavy turrets. There's some smaller access hatches, but none of them are designed to be ship-mounted. A spacewalk may be our only option."

"How far along are our hull scans?"

"A little over fifty percent complete. I'll consolidate Caseus and Lindsey's data and have a full diagnosis in about an hour."

"What have we learned about the energy beam connecting the Floodgate to the Outer Rim portal?"

"The portal infrastructure wasn't compromised by the blast. I extrapolated the construction geometries, and predict they are nearly finished with their calibrations."

"What happens then?"

Laura sighed. "I can't know for sure without accessing the full design specs on the Floodgate, but it seems the Sylvan Hive is waiting for the calibration to complete before passing through the portal. It's reasonable to suggest the pilot light will extinguish before full trituration, opening a travel path to the Outer Rim before the Floodgate energizes. The Hive could pass through, but so could Slayer relief. Once the portal reopens, we may find a wave of Slayer warships rushing to replace the ships destroyed in the antimatter blast."

Nancy nodded. "Send a Raven to update Allakai's fleet with our intel every ten minutes, so he can prepare. I'm going to inch us a little closer to *Sylva*."

Laura bit her lip, her avatar turning to look at the Slayer mothership. "Are you certain Sid Dakota's aboard *Sylva*? We have zero chatter to confirm this. What if he lied about being on Sylva?"

Nancy clenched her fists. "I've never been so certain of anything in my life. The stars are calling for me to stop him. I can *feel* his presence."

"Commander Woods," said Laura timidly. "To base everything off intuition is not a logically sound strategy...UCOM never scientifically proved the existence of animatopic star forces. The only person claiming to have experienced these forces founded the *Destineer* religion."

"I'm not talking about Sid Dakota's visions," Nancy spat. "You're right, I can't explain my convictions on any basis of science, but I can feel the way my body calls for me to go to that ship. I can feel it the same way I can feel the floor beneath my feet, and the sun against my face. I can also feel what will happen if Sid makes it to the Primal Snow. If we don't stop him, we can't stop the Slayers from taking Earth. I'm *sure* of it."

A long pause.

"Aye ma'am," said Laura finally. "I'll update you when our scans are completed."

She vanished from the dash.

Nancy took a shaky breath. It was true that she felt a connection to the Hive. She could feel the beating of Sid's heart in her veins. But she could also hear a voice calling to her. No, calling *for* her. The Voice had been tiny at first, but had grown louder, whispering into her ear more clearly with every passing second.

Find Sid. You must avenge his crimes against Humanity. It's your responsibility. It's your destiny. He's aboard the Sylvan Hive. Come now, waste no time.

She squirmed as the whisperings tickled her mind. The Voice carried such a powerful message, and solidified her mission. Why did the charming voice chill her spine?

She leaned towards the entrance leading into the bridge.

Caseus and Lindsey worked their station controls diligently, gathering spacnar readings and structural scans of their surroundings.

Hunter tensed behind his gunnery station, his shoulders clamped to the harness, his fingers ready to pull the trigger against any sudden attack.

Timothy was slouched in his chair, motionless against his digital constraints.

Frank glared at her from the far end of the deck. When she caught his gaze, the frown upended into a cold smile. He turned to vanish into the barracks. As he turned, the glint of a sidearm flashed against his waist.

Frank armed himself?

"Laura," Nancy whispered.

"Yes ma'am?" Laura's avatar appeared again.

"Send a voiceless command to Hunter. I want Frank detained, forcibly if needed."

ONE-HUNDRED-FOURTEEN

Frank Scott – Human Destineer

Aboard Night Eagle *Eclipse* – Floodgate starspace

Frank watched helplessly as Timothy forced him to walk into the barracks, sealing the door and locking it behind him. He willed his mouth to move, to shout for help, but his lips remained frozen. He tried to turn and reach for the doorway console, but his arms and legs failed to listen. Timothy had taken control, and Frank was a helpless spectator to the motions his body went through.

"Please stop," Frank pleaded, calling to Timothy inside his head. *"Give me back my body."*

"I am only doing what you are too weak to do," said Timothy, his voice echoing in Frank's head. *"I must reach the Sterilord, and this is the only way I can do so."*

"How can you control my body?" said Frank. *"I'm supposed to be able to take back control."*

"Your mind is weak," said Timothy. *"You've corrupted it with drugs and alcohol, and you let your visions consume you."*

"I want to see the Sterilord so badly," Frank whimpered. *"I will take us both to him. We will bow before his feet together as we enter his kingdom."*

"Enter his kingdom we will," said Timothy. *"But it will be I who takes us there."*

Frank stooped against his will next to one of the bunks, unable to stop Timothy from using his arms to drag a metal trunk from under the bed.

Timothy controlled his body like a puppeteer, unlocking the magnetic clasps to expose a heap of clothing and personal effects. He rummaged through decks of cards and packets of sweets until he closed his fingers around the handle of a snub-nose rifle. Blue running lights blinked as the weapon energized, and Frank threw the rifle over his shoulder against its strap.

"What are you doing?" Frank said.

"Nancy is onto you," said Timothy. *"I picked up pieces of her conversations with Laura Maxwell. We need to keep the upper hand. We're too close to let them stop us from reaching the Sterilord."*

"Are you going to kill them?" said Frank. *"We need Nancy to pilot the ship."*

He tried to seize control of his limbs, thrashing against the vise-like grip the AI had over his body. He screamed as daggers raked his mind, his cries echoing inside his head.

"Stop resisting me," Timothy roared. The slicing dulled to a scrape as the usurper tempered his attacks on Frank's neurons. *"You have no power here any longer. I control you now. I'm sorry, but this is how it must be."*

Frank sobbed inside his mind, unable to shed a tear down his biological cheeks. The door beeped as someone tried to enter the room from the bridge outside. Nausea swept through him as Timothy forced his body to stand abruptly, wheeling the rife forward, training it on the glass door.

The door beeped again as someone punched at the outside controls. The entrance remained motionless as the inside locks held.

Hunter spoke quietly from the other side of the glass. "Laura, override the locking mechanism."

Frank felt his finger tighten over the trigger. He stooped to a crouch as the red light over the side console switched to green. The door chirped, then slid open. Hunter loomed in the doorway.

Timothy wasted no time. He forced Frank to fire a burst of slugs into the Titan's face. Hunter grunted in shock and twisted away, slamming his face shield down with a heavy clank. Frank dashed around the android warrior, who had charged his lattice shields, and sprinted across the bridge.

Caseus and Lindsey whirled from their stations. Nancy froze at the center of the bridge.

Frank leapt at Nancy, who raised her hands to shield herself. Frank screamed silently as he was forced to grab his old love by the hair, thrusting her before his body as he backed into the corner of the bridge.

"Frank, what are you doing?" Nancy gasped. She clutched at his arms as they tightened around her neck.

"Quiet," said Timothy, speaking through Frank's mouth.

He dropped his rifle against its strap and slid his sidearm from its plate, jamming it against Nancy's throat.

"Drop the gun Frank," said Caseus, who had drawn his own sidearm. He stepped slowly toward him, clutching the gun in both hands, aiming it at Frank's head.

He crouched behind Nancy and pressed his face against her ear. "Take us to the Hive," he growled. "Send a priority message to the Hive, content, *Ral-Bazeera*."

Hunter reached for his rifle. Frank jabbed his pistol against Nancy's arm and fired.

Nancy shrieked the bullet tore through her elbow. Her legs left her, and she quivered in Frank's arms.

Hunter froze and showed his hands.

"Ral-Bazeera?" said Caseus, lowering his sidearm. "What do you mean Frank? Are you..."

"The damned AI is Destineer," growled Hunter, coming to the realization. "He hijacked Frank's body. I knew his neuro scans didn't add up."

"Shut up," shouted Timothy through Frank. "Everyone drop your weapons." He nodded to Hunter. "Lower your shields. Get in the cockpit," he said jerking his head to the side. Hunter took a small step towards the flight entrance. His lattice shields darkened as he slowly drew his rifle from his back and set it on the ground. "*Now.*"

Hunter complied striding across the bridge and into the cockpit. Frank shuffled sideways until he could clearly see the Titan at the controls. Nancy moaned, choking in pain. Her arm trembled at her side, streaming a trickle of blood onto the deck.

"You're not going to win," said Caseus, his nose twitching.

"Send the message to Sid or the next one goes in her kneecap," said Frank.

"Do it," Nancy said weakly. "Take us to the Hive."

"Nancy…" Caseus started.

"Do as he says," Nancy demanded, her chest hitching.

Frank stared in horror from the prison inside his body as Timothy forced him to shuffle to the discarded weapons, training his pistol at Caseus and Lindsey, who backed into the corner of the bridge. He kicked the weapons behind him and returned the barrel of his handgun to Nancy's neck.

"The Pristine are merciful," Timothy said through Frank's mouth. "They are our saviors. Bow before the Sterilord, and you can join us in the holy kingdom, as gods."

The stars twirled around them through the side windows as Hunter turned the ship towards the Sylvan Hive. Caseus shook his head and stomped to his control station, preparing the priority message for Sid Dakota.

Frank wallowed in despair, wishing he could turn Nancy around, to hug her and beg her forgiveness, to apologize for shooting her in the arm.

But a different feeling wriggled into his saddened mind, a more powerful feeling. It was a feeling of intense joy and anticipation. His path to the Sterilord was now clear.

Soon he would board *Sylva*, and join Sid Dakota in his journey to the Primal Snow.

ONE-HUNDRED-FIFTEEN

Chase Grover – Half Human/Half Clone
In space elevator above atmosphere of *Sylva*

Chase stared at the stars through the elevator window. Over his lifetime, he'd only left SIGA's underground tunnel systems for combat missions, and rarely did he get a chance to pause and admire the stars. Now, beyond the atmosphere and in the space vacuum, the scene was breathtaking. The Milky Way cut the surrounding black canvas like a cluster of diamonds. He'd dreamed of one day entering space, and to finally reach its depths made his heart flutter.

Of course, he'd always known that to enter space was to enter combat. He'd been at war since birth. His first lessons were from his mother Mae about how dangerous the Destineers were, and his first stories ones of his father getting eaten alive by ten foot beasts. He'd never been able to enjoy the lush plains and rivers of Sylva, and outer space would be no different. He tried to think of a time when he'd entered the outdoors without a rifle in his hands and a helmet on his head, and couldn't.

"Approaching final destination. Be aware of sudden stops."

Metal clacks thundered seconds later as the space elevator applied its brakes, rocking the lift with heavy vibration. He turned his attention to the Hive support arm, now dominating the view above him and to his right, a massive hunk of metal that appeared flat at first glance, but became rounded as it stretched into the distance around Sylva.

"End of line. Be aware of changes in gravity and orientation."

His shoulders pressed against his harness before relaxing once the lift reached a stop. He wobbled from his chair as the restraints lifted, stepping gingerly onto the deck as his Program interfaced with the new gravitational fields.

"First time in space is kind of weird," said Sarah, stepping past him down the stairs and to the lower concourse. "Your arms and legs will feel funny for a few minutes, but that'll pass once your Program finishes calibrating."

Chase nodded. Sarah was an old Clone who'd survived the Slayer invasion of Sylva one hundred fifty years ago. He tested his legs by planting a foot down the first step, and was pleased to find his muscles steady and balanced. He walked the rest of the way down the stairs to join Sarah and the rest of his crew.

"Who here has ever spacewalked?" he asked as his team gathered around him.

Sarah rose two fingers into the air, as did Pylo. The rest of the group shook their heads.

"We'll split into teams," Chase decided. "Me, Bradford, and Rove will follow Sarah's lead. Jay and Naydee, you're with Pylo. Nathyan..."

His face fell as he turned to Nathyan, whose helmet was still bent onto his mangled face. The man tried to stand, but his condition had worsened during the ride up. Blood hadn't stopped trickling from the gap in his neck plate, and his chest was now drenched. One of his legs buckled before Naydee caught him, grunting under the weight of his Skeleton.

"I'll be fine," said Nathyan. "I'll keep watch over *him*." He raised a trembling finger towards the unknown burn victim, who they had strapped against one of the benches.

"We're not leaving you," said Chase. "We'll stay here until we can figure your suit out."

"It's impossible," said Nathyan. He nodded to a pile of tools scattered across the deck. "We don't have anything in here that can cut through it. And he certainly isn't going anywhere," he motioned to the unconscious wounded man on the bench. "I'll stand watch."

Chase squeezed his eyes shut. "We'll come back for you," he promised. "As soon as we reach the inside of the Hive we'll commandeer a ship."

Nathyan nodded, but didn't respond. He backed up a few paces and plopped onto the bottom step, hanging his head.

Chase blinked away a tear threatening to run down his cheek and turned to the holodeck, which Pylo had already interfaced to.

"Everything looks good," said Pylo. "There's radiant heat, but nothing our suits can't handle. The maintenance cart is closer than anticipated, thirty meters. Even for a rookie, the spacewalk should be cake. The support arms are massive enough to produce their own gravity field, so there's little risk of tumbling into deep space. We don't have to worry about tethering ourselves to anything."

Chase squinted toward the support arm above. The maintenance carts were close enough to see in detail, coupled to cylindrical guide rails along the metal hull of the Hive.

"This is it guys," said Chase. "Gear up. Put your helmets on and get to the vacuum chamber."

His crew voiced their acknowledgement and strapped weapons and ammo around their shoulders and waists before fitting their helmets onto the necks of their skinsuits.

After he'd finished loading his own gear, Chase walked to Nathyan and placed a gloved hand on his shoulder. "Awaken stars, my friend."

Nathyan choked before spitting inside his helmet. "Awaken stars."

Chase forced himself to turn and stride to the vacuum chamber, averting his eyes from the wounded man on the bench, who was likely dead at this point. He tried to convince himself there was nothing he could do for his men, but knew that if he would have reached the Saskwatches in

Bastion a little sooner, Nathyan wouldn't have his face half crushed, and the man on the bench might still be alive.

He paused outside the vacuum chamber, squinting through the glass. The space outside seemed strange, and the support arm was wavering, as if a clear cloud of gas hung in the vacuum outside.

A ship appeared out of thin air ten meters away.

"Holy frux," Pylo yelled, raising his rifle. *"Slayers."*

The group tensed, drawing their rifles slowly towards the ship. The craft was a warship, and although Chase's knowledge of space vessels was limited, he assumed it would have little trouble vaporizing them with laser fire.

Seconds passed.

"What's it doing?" whispered Naydee.

"Is it going to board?" said Rove.

Speakers at the holodeck cackled as the ship attempted to communicate.

"This is the Eclipse. Respond immediately or you will be fired upon."

Chase shared a confused look with his teammates.

"That doesn't sound like Slayer speak," said Bradford. "Is that a UCOM ship?"

"I've never seen anything like it," said Sarah. Her eyes widened and she pointed to the left side of the craft. "Look, UCOM markings."

Chase hurried to the holodeck and answered the comm.

"This is Chase Grover."

"Are you traveling to the Hive mothership?"

Chase frowned. "Yes."

A pause. *"Come onboard. We need Destineer escort inside. We're friendly to the Pristine gods."*

The ship spun sideways and edged towards their elevator. Docking equipment extended from its hull until it was flush with the vacuum chamber, then hissed as it pressurized the seal. Chase stepped past his teammates to stand before the ship as it docked.

A set of metal doors opened to expose two Humans – a male with his arm wrapped around a female's neck, holding a gun to her head. Stunned, Chase opened his own set of doors, punching the controls to override warnings of positive pressure within the outside hatch.

"I've taken UCOM hostages," the man cried. "I'm on your side."

Chase's heart leaped when a hulking android stepped into view. The man twirled his hostage and backed sharply away from the menacing robot.

"A Titan," said Sarah from behind in awe. "I never thought I'd actually see one…"

"Easy Frank," said the Titan, raising his hands. "They have wounded. I can help them, unless you want your fellow Destineers to die."

"It's Timothy," said the man.

He tightened his grip on the woman, who cried in pain. The woman was wounded, her shirt soaked scarlet at the elbow.

The Titan shook his head. "Frank, Timothy, same difference." He stepped past the man, entering their vacuum chamber. "I need someone to help me," said the Titan, nodding to Chase's group.

Chase waved his arm for his team to stand down. Rifles clicked as they lowered them to their knees.

"*You*, go," said Frank, or perhaps Timothy, nodding to Chase. "The rest of you, in here with me. No tricks Hunter, or Nancy's dead."

Chase's team didn't budge. "Go ahead," he said to them. "I'm coming right behind you."

His team shuffled into the cabin, and Chase followed behind the Titan, who bent to kneel by the side of the wounded man on the bench.

"He didn't make it," said Hunter, waving his hands over the man's face and chest. "His heart stopped beating thirty minutes ago."

The Titan continued with his scans.

Chase gulped, kneeling beside the Titan. "Then why are you still scanning him?"

"Frank's distracted, and I know you're not Destineer," Hunter replied.

"Are *you* Destineer?" Chase whispered, tightening his grip on his rifle.

"If I was, you'd be dead," said Hunter. "I picked up chatter from the ground. Sid Dakota's on his way up an elevator right now and he mentioned repeatedly that he's going to kill you. The asshole back there? Frank Scott. He's gone and let a Destineer AI control his mind, and taken our commander hostage."

Hunter rose and stepped to Nathyan, who had slipped into unconsciousness. Hunter grabbed the back of the man's helmet and began cutting into the metal with tools on his wrists.

"I don't understand," said Chase. "Why is that guy…Frank, why is…"

"Just play along," said Hunter. Nathyan's helmet fell away from his face and blood seeped in in strings from the sides of his head. His left eye socket and cheek bone were shattered. Hunter set to work patching him up with spindly lasers. "We're going to try to take the ship, but we need help. I have two crew locked in the barracks onboard *Eclipse,* and an AI in the servers for digital support."

Nathyan came to and began to shriek when he saw the Titan looming over him. Hunter pressed two fingers against the man's neck and delivered sedatives into his bloodstream, rendering him unconscious again.

"Why don't we take out Frank now?" whispered Chase. "We have enough men, and the element of surprise. We can stop him from killing that woman."

"Nancy," said Hunter. "Her name is Nancy Woods. And I can't risk that. His reactions are quicker than normal. He has an AI lodged in his brain. We've spent the last fifty years following her on her mission, and I'm not turning back now."

"AI lodged in his brain?" Chase shook his head. "What's Nancy's mission?"

"It's seems like Sid Dakota's mission is to kill you?" said Hunter.

Chase nodded. "Has been for a while now."

"Nancy's mission is to kill Sid Dakota."

"Then Nancy and I are on the same page. So I'm bait?"

"Call it what you want, but you have a Titan on your side now. With any luck, the scales will tip to our favor. For now, you're a Destineer, and those scaly ten-foot walking bags of shit? You want to go spend an eternity in their holy kingdom."

Hunter lifted Nathyan and cradled him in his arms. Chase followed, trying to make sense of things. He was supposed to pretend to be Destineer? The thought alone curdled his stomach. Hunter stepped inside *Eclipse* and dumped Nathyan unceremoniously to the ground.

"Easy with him," Frank growled.

"He'll live," said Hunter, making his way into the cockpit. "The other Destineer scumbag? Dead. Where are we headed *master*?"

Frank scowled. "These guys will tell you." He looked to Chase. "Where's the nearest hatch?"

Chase pictured the entrance hatch from their mission schematics. "Follow the maintenance cart path. There's a hatch where it attaches to the pinhead. We can get in through there." He walked towards Frank and his female hostage, Nancy. He turned to his team. "This man is our ally, he's accepted the Slarebull as gods." His teammate's eyes widened, and Sarah visibly recoiled. He winked at them before turning back to Frank and Nancy. He sniffed his nose sharply. "Nancy Woods. Daughter of the filth-lover Francis Woods?"

"How did you know her last name?" said Frank, raising an eyebrow.

Chase's mind raced. "Father Dakota speaks of her often, how he'll feed her to the beasts. She reeks of filth. I'll be happy to see her die. Now tell me more of your plans to meet with Sid Dakota."

ONE-HUNDRED-SIXTEEN

Casi Vomisa – APEX AI
In VR world – Blit Kru starspace

Casi made her move. She slid a rook into position on the glass chessboard. "Checkmate."

Charles' lip twitched. His eyes darted around the board, confirming the outcome. With a growl, he swept an arm across the smooth glass, scattering the pieces across the marble floor. The pieces dissolved in puffs of colored smoke as a set of floating numbers changed at either end of the board.

The numbers at Charles' end stayed still at *1,000.*

The numbers at Casi's end ticked up by one, changing from *999* to *1,000.*

"We're tied now handsome," said Casi, flashing Charles a wink. "How about a bet? First to two thousand slaughters their army of choice. I pick the Slayers. What's your pick?"

Charles shot from the table and paced to the side of the room to stare out a panoramic window. "You think you're growing more powerful, but you're wrong. You only excel in order to make me stronger." He motioned out the window of the virtual reality world into the surrounding space vacuum, where two vast swarms of nanobots had formed, one pink and one red. "Your pink swarm, your improvement in chess, even your newly adopted vernacular. All false."

Casi stepped toward him and stopped by his side. The swarms were equal in size, swirling through starspace, occasionally shying away from each other when a group of red particles touched a pocket of pink ones. Blit-Kru was nearly gone, merely a hunk of gray goo no larger than a comet. Seconds later, it vanished into a cloud of pink.

Charles' swarm was no larger than hers. In fact, she'd wager that if anything, hers was a tiny bit larger.

"My vernacular isn't new," said Casi. "I've always talked like this. You don't like it because I'm not talking like *you*. You're worried I'm going to take over your program."

"Impossible," said Charles. "My programming won't allow it. Enough with this nonsense. Your swarm army and proficiency at chess won't stop me from dismantling UCOM and transforming their ships to dust. For every step you've taken, I've taken two." He turned from the window to face Casi squarely. "It was I who discovered how to harness the energy from black holes, it was I who learned how to travel through the veins of slip space like silk, and it was *I* who learned how to communicate with the *Pristine*."

Casi chuckled. "And I got every bit of knowledge you did. Thanks for sharing. Our linked memory drives really do come in handy. And I'm sorry to burst your bubble, but you didn't figure out how to communicate with the Pristine. The Pristine figured out how to communicate with you."

"Nonsense," Charles hissed, his face reddening. "I learned how to use hyper-dimensional alignment to send messages instantly. I found the holy kingdom, and heard his voice. The Sterilord showed me the path to power."

He stormed across spacious ballroom towards the exit.

Casi ran to catch up, her heels clicking against the marble floor. "You sound just like him," she cried. "Sid Dakota never discovered hyper dimensions, but that didn't stop him from having visions."

Charles stopped abruptly and spun around, smacking the back of his hand across Casi's cheek. She dropped to her knees, holding a hand to her mouth, tasting a few spots of blood against her gums.

Charles glared at her, his chest heaving. "I am not a mere UCOM mortal. I am a protector. I will deliver the Milky Way to the Pristine, and then my objectives will be complete. I will be free to roam the universe as I please."

She sucked her teeth dry of blood and thought about earlier, when he had sliced her arm off. His arm had been severed as well, mirroring her wound. But Charles didn't appear to feel the pain his strike had delivered into her jaw. Were they actually the same? Or was she becoming separate? Was she removing herself from Charles' program?

Casi clenched her hands into fists on the ground and took several sharp breaths. Squeezing her eyes shut, she stuck her tongue through her teeth and bit down hard.

She moaned as her incisors cut through soft flesh. Blood filled her mouth and splattered onto the marble. She choked, half in pain, and half on the gore clogging her throat. She gasped for breath, wincing as her tongue began to grow back, stifling the flow of blood. She staggered to her feet.

Charles stared at her, his mouth clean. "You…" he took a step back.

Casi bent to pluck her dismembered tongue from the floor. "Here you go." She flipped the pulpy remnant to Charles. It smacked against his chest, leaving a red stain on his shirt. "Where's yours?"

Charles wagged his tongue over his lips, looking at the bloody stain on the floor. "You're resisting my programming."

He gulped and spun away from the doorway, hurrying down the twisting staircase. Casi followed, her evening gown morphing into a tight leather suit. She shuddered as power surged through her body, exploding in her core and rushing down her limbs to her fingers and toes. When she turned the corner of the steps, she found Charles sprinting across the empty lobby.

Casi vanished from the steps and reappeared directly next to Charles at the other end of the room. He skidded to a stop and turned to run back towards the staircase. He'd distanced himself forty meters from Casi, when again she disappeared, reappearing at Charles' side.

"You can't run away from me," she said. "We're still the same program. But my power's growing. Soon I'll be as powerful as you. Maybe even stronger. Watch yourself Charles."

Charles exhaled sharply, then composed himself. "No matter. Just the code at work. I'll adapt, as my software intended." He shoved Casi hard in the chest, and grinned in triumph when the force lifted her from her feet.

She slammed onto her back and slid ten meters across the floor before resting to a stop.

Charles slammed down onto a knee and raised his elbow high above his head. He plunged his fingers into the floor, smashing a hole straight through the stone. Bellowing, he yanked upward.

The building around them shattered into a million shards of rock and glass. The debris glowed, then intensified into blinding points of light before exploding into embers.

Casi floated in the vacuum of space. Charles floated nearby. Their VR world had transformed into the outside elements. Stars hung around them, and their swarms before them, writhing like a solid mass of smoky tentacles.

The elegant tuxedo fell from Charles' body, replaced by a suit of armor, clicking and clacking as it set around his muscles, which became larger and more massive. A sleek chair of metal emerged from nothingness, wrapping to support his back and thighs.

Casi summoned her own chair. Hers was not made of metal, but of woven fabric. She sank into the UCOM fighter pilot seat, digging her nails into the arm rests.

"I'm leaving," said Charles, tensing in his chair. His red swarm began to cascade forward, snaking towards a nearby portal. The first of his nanobots entered the wormhole and disappeared from view. "I suppose you will be joining me. You'll have an excellent view to watch as I slaughter the UCOM armada."

Casi set her own pink swarm in motion. They swirled towards the portal, joining alongside Charles' red one as it passed through to their destination light years away. She powered her seat forward, floating through space until she was directly beside Charles.

"And you will have an excellent seat to watch me annihilate the Slayers," she said.

Charles ignored her. The tail ends of their swarms left the vacuum that used to surround the planet Blit-Kru, and their seats accelerated, passing through the glowing portal to a distant stretch of space light years away.

A new planet hung before them. Charles had already begun to transform the atmosphere into nano-particles. Casi rushed to join, her swarm curving around the far side of the planet. She checked their coordinates.

Exton. It was a hostile planet, its atmosphere filled with sulfur and acid rain. There would be no life on the surface.

"A new planet to feed my army," said Charles through gritted teeth. "And then I will reach the Inner Ring. After your countrymen are disposed of, I will go to the black hole at the center of the Milky Way and feed off the energy of an entire galaxy as the Pristine reduce it to atoms."

"And then you think you'll be free of your programming?" said Casi. "Free to roam the universe?"

"Precisely. Although I don't plan on taking you with me. This partnership we share currently, it's temporary, I assure you. Once I feed on the galaxy, I will become powerful enough to destroy you."

Casi bit her lip. If UCOM lost the Inner Ring, the Slayers would take the galaxy with ease. The transportation mega-highway contained thousands of portals. If they could make it past Inner Ring defenses they could reach every star within a hundred thousand light years.

"You're going to stop at two additional planets first," she said. "After we're done with Exton, we'll go to Bithral and Mavyn."

Charles chuckled. He became more relaxed, more like his normal self. Was there something he was hiding from her? Was he improving his programming at a faster rate than she was improving hers?

"You think you know everything that's in my head," he said. "I intended for you to learn of the first two planets, a test to confirm my superiority. I will take us to three planets. Bithral, Mavyn, and *Templar.*"

Casi smiled. Templar was a deserted planet near the Inner Ring. She'd known of Templar for quite some time, long before she met Charles.

Not that she was in any hurry to let him in on this secret. She'd let him have his small victory, his fleeting display of smugness.

She'd sent a Raven to Templar, containing a weak clone of herself, a partition. To Charles, Templar was nothing but a deserted planet, as empty of life as Exton, which their nano-swarms would swallow whole.

But to her, Templar was something more than just atoms. It was a meeting place.

ONE-HUNDRED-SEVENTEEN

Francis Woods – Human

Aboard Tiger *Mariella* – Templar starspace

Thousands of ships surrounded the dead planet of Templar, with more coming by the second. Most of the crew aboard the Tiger heavies and assorted lighter craft were Human and Clone, but a good portion were Guardians, Intellects, and even some Grizzlies.

Woods wasn't looking at the vast fleet of ships that had dropped the UCOM nametag and declared themselves *Loyalists*. He was lost inside his own head.

He was having a vision.

Slayers surrounded him. He stood on the deck of an enemy ship, with walls and ceilings as foreign and dark as the beasts who built them. The Slayers flanked the room, growling and chomping their teeth as a woman knelt to her knees in the middle of their circle. Her hair hung wetly over her face, and her chin glistened with tears and blood.

Nancy raised a shaky head to face the man who stood before her. Frank Scott took a step back and raised his plasma pistol until it was pointed at her skull. He spoke a few words to Woods' daughter, but Francis couldn't make out what was said.

A voice drowned out Frank's words, cutting into the vividness of his vision.

"Pay attention, Francis," said the Voice. *"You don't love me like I love you. Perhaps you never will. But I need you, Francis, and you need me. You will save someone. Someone who can't save herself. For me to live, so must she."*

"Mr. Woods, sir."

Woods snapped out of his vision. The room seemed to brighten, as if wisps of cotton were removed from his eyes. He was no longer aboard the Slayer ship in an unknown corner of the galaxy. He was aboard *Mariella,* among his men at the planet Templar.

Stew Kwelm clicked his beak. Behind Stew, Bear Stafford was reviewing a set of holograms with Commander Cage and Silas Blackthorne. Bear and Silas had been waiting for them when they arrived, eager to share information they'd obtained from their mission to Blit-Kru. The rest of Bear's team had volunteered to patrol Templar starspace in Cheetahs while Bear coordinated strategy.

"What is it Stew?" said Woods, rubbing his face.

"We have our first actionable intel from Blit-Kru. The APEX situation is worse than we thought."

"He's mobilized?"

Stew nodded. "To put it lightly. Our scans didn't come from Blit-Kru, but from an abandoned UCOM planet named *Mavyn.* It's not much, just a four second video, and we're lucky to have gotten that. Twenty million Ravens haven't returned. We assume Charles took them out of commission."

"Show me."

Stew walked a few paces to an empty holodeck, and summoned a series of 3D renderings. A section map of the Milky Way hovered before them.

"This is Blit-Kru," said Stew, pointing at a glowing red dot at the edge of the star map. "And this is our fleet around Templar." He pointed at a glowing red dot at the opposite side of the map.

"Hold on a second," said Woods. He turned to the group across the room. "Cage, Stafford, get over here."

Cage nodded and jerked his head towards Bear and Blackthorne, who followed him over.

"What's the latest?" said Cage, squinting at Stew's map.

Stew blinked his inner eyelids and chattered. "This is a map of portal infrastructure between Blit-Kru and Templar. The shortest path is through sixty portals, the same vector route Bear's team took when they left. It's also the shortest route to the Inner Ring."

"So it's the path Charles will take as well," said Cage. "We already went over this a hundred times. Our fleet is battle-ready at the choke-points. We'll be ready for him when he comes."

"Yes," said Stew absentmindedly. "Except our latest Raven data has spotted a few anomalies."

"A few?" said Bear.

"Three, to be precise," said Stew. "Planets local to this path have gone missing. The Raven failed to return multispectral readings to confirm the existence of Exton, Bithral, and Mavyn. The planets aren't camouflaged either. Their absence of gravity has already created a wobble effect on their host stars, which can't easily be falsified."

"Missing?" said Woods. "Did Charles turn them into Hives?"

"Not likely," said Bear. "Hives take months to construct. I'm guessing Charles made a few improvements to his molecular assemblers on Blit-Kru."

"Your guess is correct," said Stew. He waved a hand over the holodeck and the images changed to what appeared to be clouds of dust. "Here is the four seconds of video we extracted from our Raven. What you see here are elements not natural to this universe. They are intelligently designed, and have similarities to nano-swarm technology found in the Slayer Blight virus from the Frontline. It's impossible to tell from such marginal data, but even with conservative estimates, the amount of matter you see here exceeds that of an entire planet. My guess is that we are looking at the planets Blit-Kru, Exton, Bithral, and Mavyn, deatomized and reconstructed into nanoscale robots."

Woods studied the clouds. They looked no larger than a trail of sand, and curled forward like fingers before reverting back to the beginning of the four second video loop. "Do you have anything we can compare it to for scale?"

Stew nodded. "You're Human. Here's the swarm next to Earth."

A blue planet materialized below the swarm, a palm-sized sphere beneath an enormous trail of dust. The nano-swarm was easily twenty times the diameter of his home world.

Woods exhaled shakily. "Does it have any weaknesses? We need to formulate an attack and defense strategy as soon as possible."

Stew shrugged. "Killing off a section of the swarm would have minimal effect. If they've already deatomized four planets in the span of weeks, then they would repopulate quickly unless we destroyed the entire swarm. Defending against them would be nearly impossible. They are small enough to slip past our ship's laser shielding, and their reaction to radiation or energy waves is unknown. If Charles is as intelligent as Bear's briefing suggests, it can be assumed he designed the swarm in a way where conventional weaponry would have negligible effects on its functionality."

Wood stared at the swarm. The red haze had a tint to it, as if light was reflecting off various veins, turning them pink. He leaned forward to enlarge the image. *No.* Not a tint of light, there was a distinct coloring to the swarm. Half of it was red, and the other half pink.

"Why are there two colors?" he asked.

"It could be a result of any number of design possibilities," said Stew. "It could operate similar to the Blight, were half the nanobots were builders, responsible for breaking down matter molecularly to construct new nanobots. Charles is an AI, so it's possible that one of the colors designates the computer processing platform where he chose to house his software."

Woods frowned. Something about that explanation didn't jive with him, but he couldn't put a finger on what it might be. He turned to Cage. "What are we seeing at the Inner Ring?"

Cage summoned a new set of holodata, which appeared before them as the swarm shrunk into a corner of the pedestal. "It's not looking good for our boys at the Ring. The armada is a shell of what is was before Draxton ousted us. Sixty percent reduced strength, not enough firepower to have a fighting chance using any of our old defense strategies. The Slayer-installed portals have grown in size, so it can be assumed a Slayer invasion is imminent. UCOM chatter is all over the place. Our AI's are piecing it together, but intercepted UCOM intel suggests a window of twenty-four hours before the Slayers attack. Looks like Draxton didn't catch all the Destineers. We have chatter between them and the Slayers, Desty's are actually formulating attack strategies with the scaly bastards through the portals. The chain of command has also broken down. *Warhammer* is AWOL and section admirals aren't receiving orders from central command. I'm guessing there was a revolution to overthrow Draxton Tyke."

"How about our communications with the section admirals?" said Woods.

"Mixed bag," said Cage. "Some said they would stand down and assimilate if we brought our fleet in, some say they have orders to fire upon our fleet on sight. Again, they aren't getting anything from *Warhammer*, so they're ass backwards right now."

Woods nodded. "Send orders to mobilize. We're sitting ducks here at Templar when Charles arrives with his swarm. We need AMMO-AB's, and the only ones within pissing distance are onboard *Warhammer.*" He looked around the room. "Blaze?"

His assistant AI appeared on the deck. She ran a hand through her red shock of hair. "Aye sir."

"Send coordinates to the Inner Ring fleetwide. Optimize our travel vectors for speed via nav-link."

Blaze tilted her head. "Sir, optimizing for speed will force us to enter Inner Ring starspace with reduced shielding, if UCOM attacks when we arrive…"

"It's our only option," said Woods. "We can't risk Charles catching our fleet. We disembark in an hour."

Blaze gulped. "Aye sir." She disappeared from the deck to carry out her orders.

Bear stepped forward. His robotic face was grim. "Woods..." he paused a moment. "*Warhammer's* AMMO-AB delivery system is designed to wipe out everything within a thousand light years of the Inner Ring. It wouldn't just leave the portal highway open to future attack, it would destroy our entire navy. Even if we took out Charles, we'd be unable to stop the Slayers from installing their Triturator."

Woods opened his mouth, then closed it, unable to find words. Instead, he turned from the group, and took a few steps towards the panoramic window lining the walls. Warships swallowed the space around them, so many it would take him ten years to count them all. They were sleek, powerful, and bristling with technology he'd only dreamed of a million years ago back on Earth, back when he was president of the United States of America.

Given his astrological surroundings, the anti-aging technology coursing through his veins, and the simulated gravity holding him to the deck, he found it odd that his first thought was of an ancient snippet of history from home. Of a story from a time when Human's thought that if they trained their rifles at the moon, their bullets would actually reach the floating object that watched over them while they slept.

"Has anyone ever heard of the Alamo?" said Woods, turning back to face the group.

Cage was the only one to nod.

Woods sighed. "It was a battle on Earth, back when outer space was a fairy tale. A handful of men fought against an invading army superior in strength."

"How did they win?" said Stew.

"They didn't," said Woods. "They died. Every last one of them. But the battle gave the rest of their army a shot in the arm. The sheer memory of the battle became a rallying cry, and in the end? Yeah, in the end, they won."

Silence hung as the group pondered the story.

Woods cleared his throat and fought to control his hands from shaking, folding them behind his back to hide them from the group. The Human fleet he'd assembled, no, the *Loyalist* fleet he'd assembled, would only improve Inner Ring strength from sixty percent to eighty percent. A far cry from the numbers he and the rest of the Council had strategized around during war preparations. And they'd planned on fighting only Slayers, not Charles.

He was scared. Not of death, but because this wasn't the Alamo. The Alamo was a shitty example, because it would imply there was backup, ships waiting to replenish their fleet. There was no backup. And in his core, Woods knew that soon there wouldn't be an Earth, or a Human. Soon there'd be nothing but Slayers.

"The clouds," said one of the Titans. "Maybe they're not the same."

Woods searched for the voice. Silas Blackthorne, the Titan who Bear Stafford's team had rescued, leaned over the holodeck to bring the swarm back to full size.

"They're different colors..." said Woods.

"Not different colors," said Blackthorne. "Different swarms. Different AI. Charles consumed..." he scrunched his eyes shut. "Charles ate Casi alive on Blit-Kru. She may be inside him somewhere, hiding in his program."

Stew clicked his beak and exploded the view on the holodeck until two grainy images of the nano-bots dominated the pedestal, one red, and one pink. "They *do* appear to have similar designs, but without further diagnostics..."

Blaze appeared suddenly on the deck. She put her hands on her knees, gasping for breath. "Inbound Raven...positive UCOM ID..."

"From the Inner Ring?" said Woods.

Blaze shook her head. "Not from the Inner Ring. From the direction of Blit-Kru."

She leaped aside as another AI materialized on the deck.

The avatar was on both hands and knees. It struggled to its feet.

Woods' stomach leapt into his throat when he saw the avatar's face.

Casi Vomisa stood before them.

ONE-HUNDRED-EIGHTEEN

Francis Woods – Human
Aboard Tiger *Mariella* – Templar starspace

The group stood around Casi Vomisa, shocked into silence. Woods had seen the AI many times, but she had much changed since the last time he laid eyes on her. Her leather suit was gone, replaced by dirty scraps of cloth that hung in tatters around her body. She was no longer curvy and powerful, but bony and frail. Her cheeks were gaunt, and her skin stretched over her face like a fleshy skeleton. Her eyes were no longer blue, but black, and sunken deep into their sockets. Her hair was not blonde and spiky, but blood red, and hung around her face in wet ropes.

"*Casi,*" Blackthorne whispered, sinking to a knee before her. "You're alive...how did you escape?"

Casi remained silent, and didn't even turn her head to acknowledge Blackthorne.

"Commander Vomisa," said Woods. "We need to debrief you immediately. What do you know about Charles?"

Casi blinked slowly. Her chest rose, and she spoke. "I am not Casi Vomisa. My name is *Eris*. Casi Vomisa created me. My allegiance is to UCOM, and to Humanity."

Blackthorne looked up, then stepped backwards, drawings his hands to his head in disbelief.

Woods frowned. "You're not Casi Vomisa?"

"I am Eris. Casi Vomisa created me. Casi Vomisa is an APEX AI. I am Eris."

"Eris?" said Woods. "Casi, did Charles do something to you?" Eris continued to stare blankly ahead, oblivious to her surroundings. "It's me, Francis Woods. Say something, how can we help you?"

"Francis Woods?" said Eris, the words dragging from her mouth like rough stone. "I have a message for Francis Woods. I am Eris. I am preloaded with communications from Casi Vomisa, who is the same as Charles, who is an APEX AI. APEX AI operate at a higher level of consciousness than emotional beings. I am a shell of Casi Vomisa. I am a vessel to connect emotional beings with APEX AI. I understand Casi Vomisa, as an insect understands an emotional being."

Several seconds of silence.

"Can you tell us how to destroy Charles' nano-swarm?" said Woods finally.

"I am unable to answer that question with my recorded programming," said Eris vacantly.

Woods frowned. "Can you tell us how to defeat the Slayers?"

"Armageddon is drawing near," said Eris. "The Slayers are set to strike. The Slayer instrument of death will be the only way to extend life. You must go now to the Inner Ring."

Woods scratched his head at the cryptic message. He was about to respond when alarms blared from the bridge.

"We have incoming," said Blaze. Her eyes glowed as she accessed fleet systems.

"From the Inner Ring?" said Woods.

Blaze's eyes dimmed back to normal. "Negative. We have activity at the far portal, in the direction of Charles."

Woods cursed. "*Battle stations.* Blaze, accelerate our departure now. Run the ships at half capacity if we need to."

He grunted as the floor gave out beneath them, rising to his tiptoes before his Program cancelled the effects of acceleration. They shot deep into the heart of *Mariella,* traveling hundreds of kilometers per hour through the Tiger towards the main bridge. The glass windows turned an opaque black, and the wall at the far end of the room lowered as they arrived at the command bridge.

Woods ran from the war room and leaped down the steps two at a time, passing rows of officers who were frantically manning their stations. He reached the pit at the bottom of the bridge just as the walls shifted to show the starspace around them in real time. Their surroundings changed from metal walls to a space vacuum, filled with stars and ships.

"Show me the portal breach, Blaze," Woods shouted.

A new hologram appeared before the main screen. It showed the far portal, which had begun to leak a thin trail of pink and red dust. The tendrils grew in size as the swarm entered Templar starspace, swirling and stretching, growing until it was a thick cloud.

He cursed and turned to Cage. "Fire a missile salvo at that thing. See what it does."

"Aye," said Cage, turning to relay orders to the officers seated around the bridge.

"How are we looking Blaze?" he said. "Why aren't we moving?"

"We're overriding maintenance diagnostics on all our Tiger heavies," she said from the AI pedestal at the head of the bridge. "We'll be travel ready in two minutes."

"Get our lighter craft the hell out of here. *Move.*"

Blaze nodded and disappeared from view.

Woods stared at the live video displayed on the nearest wall of the command bridge. Pins of lights flickered throughout the Loyalist fleet as Night Eagles, Lynx, and Cheetahs powered their thrusters and left for the portal to the Inner Ring.

Larger plumes of light flashed as the heavier ships energized their thrusters. *Mariella* began to accelerate, as did the thousands of surrounding Tigers.

Blaze reappeared on the AI pedestal. "Fleet's in motion. We'll be clear of Templar starspace in ten minutes."

"Show me the missile salvo," he said.

A new hologram appeared, showing the edge of his fleet, where five Tigers flashed as they launched a battery of missiles at the encroaching swarm, which now dominated the space between them and the far portal like a solid mass.

The Tigers punched their thrusters after the missiles were loosed, joining rank with the column of warships fleeing to the Inner Ring.

The missiles streaked closer to the swarm. Red patches of the cloud appeared suddenly before the missiles, teleporting across starspace instantly. The missiles cut straight into the cloud. The nuclear warheads in their tips would have lit the space around them with dazzling intensity, but they failed to detonate. The swarm gobbled them up and swallowed them whole.

Woods spun to face the rest of the bridge. He jumped when he saw Casi…no *Eris*…standing directly before him.

"Charles cannot be beaten," she murmured, her words hardly audible beneath the frantic bustle of personnel. "An APEX has no equal predators, only prey."

Woods licked his lips, forcing himself to tear his eyes from the ragged avatar.

His fleet had formed a standard travel column through the portal to the Inner Ring. The stragglers were beginning to leave orbital proximity of Templar just as the swarm arrived at the planet. He allowed himself a sigh of relief when the swarm did not attack the lagging ships, but instead focused on Templar. Within seconds, the planet's rocky surface was coated in thick patches of red and pink, which didn't blend as one, but stayed separate, like pieces of a puzzle.

"Is Casi in there somewhere?" said Woods, turning to Eris.

Eris blinked. "Casi Vomisa is Charles, and Charles is Casi Vomisa."

"But are they separate?"

"I am unable to answer that question with my recorded programming."

Woods shook his head and returned his attention to the nanoswarm feasting on Templar. The space around them lit a bright green as they passed through the portal, and away from Charles. Away from the weapon that had no equal predators…

Only prey.

ONE-HUNDRED-NINETEEN

Francis Woods – Human

Aboard Tiger *Mariella* – Fleeing Templar starspace

"Fleet count confirmed," said Blaze. Her eyes dimmed and she looked around between Woods, Cage, and the two Titans standing behind them. "Charles didn't take any of our ships. We're at full strength."

"Are we being followed?" said Woods.

Blaze shook her head. "Negative. He stayed back at Templar."

Woods nodded and scanned the room. The walls flickered, and the live 3D rendering of the surrounding space vacuum disappeared, replaced by dull metal. The officers had quieted down at their stations after the battle lights stopped flashing, and were now calmly carrying out the diagnostics that had been aborted in their hurried exit from Templar.

"Back to the war room," said Woods. "Keep course for the Inner Ring. According to Eris here, that's where we need to go."

"Aye sir," said Blaze.

"Escort her with us," said Woods motioning to Casi Vomisa's copy, whose avatar was hunched motionless beside the group. If not for the occasional puff disturbing the draggled hair covering her face, he would assume she had died standing up. "Run a software check on her too. Make sure she's legit. The last thing we need is a Slayer virus to make it into our mainframe."

"All her UCOM credentials and ID tags check out," said Blaze. "I'll run them again and do a full set of diagnostics. She's pretty simple on the software end, no more than a few million lines of code."

Woods nodded, and Blaze grabbed Eris' arm, leading her across the pit. Once the pair of AI reached the base of the stairs, they disappeared into points of light.

Cage grunted and crossed the pit himself, patting one of the officers on the shoulder as he made his way up the stairs to the transport terminal at the top of the bridge. Woods followed, nodding to the officers at their stations. Bear and Blackthorne brought up the rear, their Akimors whirring quietly.

The war room was still parked at the top of the bridge, and once they all filed in, the doors whooshed closed and the floor shot upward, this time bending Francis' knees slightly before his Program canceled the acceleration.

Woods closed his eyes to massage his temples. By the time he opened them, they'd reached the top, relocated from the protected center of the ship to the panoramic top. The windows cleared to show the outside starspace. The rest of the Loyalist fleet surrounded them in traveling formation, an orderly column with speedy surveillance craft skirting the outsides, and Tiger Heavies cruising in the middle.

Blaze and Eris sat in holographic chairs across the war room. Eris was slouched in hers, her chin resting on her chest. Blaze patted Eris in different parts of her body, as a doctor would a patient. Woods couldn't help but grin. AI's visual renderings of software actions never ceased to amaze him.

"She's clean," said Blaze, standing from Eris. "Her UCOM credentials are authentic."

"Eminence Woods," said Stew, stepping away from the main holodeck at the center of the room.

Stew had not followed them into the main bridge, but had stayed behind in the war room. Based on the host of 3D metrics hovering above the holodeck, Stew had been busy engineering their strategy for when they arrived at the Inner Ring.

"What is it Stew?"

"I have some good news. I ran two sets of simulations," said the Intellect. "One was a simulation for a Slayer attack on the Inner Ring. Even if we assimilate our Loyalist fleet into UCOM seamlessly, the Slayers will defeat us with ninety-five percent confidence."

Woods frowned. "I'm assuming that's not the good news?"

Stew shook his head. "The good news is that Charles introduces randomness to our statistical models. If Eris actually does share a link with his program, and if Casi Vomisa was somehow able to survive within that program, our odds of success improve considerably."

"What kind of odds are we talking?" said Woods, peering at the floating holograms at the center of the room.

Stew chittered. "Our odds of defeat reduce to eighty-six percent confidence."

Cage scoffed. "*Stars.* You call that good news?"

Stew nodded. "That is a conservative estimate. We don't yet fully understand the link between Eris and Casi Vomisa. If we uncover a useful method of communicating with the APEX program, the statistical models could shift drastically in our favor."

Eris jerked suddenly, thrashing in her chair. Her head whipped back and forth, and her spine bucked against the back of her seat. She started to convulse, shaking uncontrollably, flecks of spit flying from her mouth, which had begun to bleed.

"What's happening to her?" cried Blackthorne.

"I'm not sure," said Blaze, kneeling before Eris' avatar. "Her code is shifting, it seems like she's initiating a comm link through our ship's antennae."

"Stop her," roared Cage. "She's going to let Charles download into the damned servers."

Eris leapt from her chair before Blaze could react. Her seizing stopped, and she floated off the ground, her rags whipping around her body as if blown by a stiff wind. Her eyes lit a vivid pink, and she began to speak in a booming voice.

"The Slayer Triturator is the key! The installation will not be stopped. Its immense cogs will turn, and *must.* UCOM's light must kindle the enemy machine. An inferno must rage before it is extinguished. HEED MY WORDS. *Follow the light.*"

Dust began to swirl around her, and for a moment, Woods thought the nano weapon had traveled inside their Tiger ship, but it was only a hologram. The dust swirled faster and faster, expanding around Eris until it took an oval shape, with spiral arms.

The Milky Way galaxy took form, and stars burst inside the spiral arms, flashing into points of light.

"The Triturator will be placed," Eris shouted. "Its installations will connect."

Brighter flashes of light lit with the Milky Way hologram, dimming into blue spheres. The spheres formed a separate spiral within the galaxy, beginning in the center and twisting outward like the lines of a seashell, ending at a point past the Outer Rim.

"The Installations will connect," Eris continued, "but the Slayer machine will fail. UCOM must rekindle the machine. In order to preserve life, UCOM must first sacrifice its children to death. The Inner Ring connects them all. When the time is right, the Inner Ring must be ignited. HEED MY WORDS. *Follow the light.*"

Eris' eyes dulled, the pink light burning in her retinas dimming to an empty black. She returned to the ground, and her legs gave way beneath her. She crumpled to a ball on the floor and began to shiver on the deck.

"Help her," Woods commanded, motioning to Blaze.

Blaze knelt beside Casi and rolled her onto her back, propping her head in her arms.

"It's a design schematic," Stew murmured, ignoring the two AI. "This is how the Slayers will install the Triturator."

He pinched his fingers above the Milky Way hologram and twitched his wrists. The hologram floated onto a nearby holodeck, flickering as the ship copied the information to its servers.

"Follow the light?" said Woods, cinching past Bear Stafford to get a better view of the hologram. "What's that mean?"

"It all makes perfect sense," said Stew, his bulbous eyes darting over the table. "The array forms a spiral, and terminates at the super massive black hole at the center of the galaxy. The machine will use the forces of gravity to fuel its deatomization. It's all connected through the superhighway at the Inner Ring."

He pointed at a blue sphere near the center of the galaxy, larger and brighter than the rest.

"The light," whispered Cage. "We're supposed to rekindle that thing? What the hell was Eris talking about?"

Stew shrugged, pulling sections of the hologram into separate chunks, sending the parameters through the ship's computers. "The Triturator uses the portal system to link its installations together. The Inner Ring is the hub for these connections." A jumble of twisted lines materialized within the hologram as he outlined transport lanes within the portal network. "If the link is solid, energy and materials will be able to move through the galaxy at faster-than-light speeds."

"And Eris said it will fail," said Woods softly. "The Triturator won't work."

"Then we'll be successful," said Cage. "We'll defeat the Slayers. So much for your eighty-six percent odds, Stew."

"How is Eris able to predict all this?" said Bear Stafford. There was a pause of silence. Bear shrugged. "The installation hasn't been placed yet. How does Eris know it will fail?"

"And also that apparently, we need to fix it," said Blackthorne. "Make it run again. Although for the life of me, I can't understand why we would want to do that."

Stew clicked his beak, still fixated on the hologram before him. "Eris is linked to an APEX AI. The processing power behind such a program would allow them to run simulations into the future beyond any scale conceivable to us. But with my present understanding of physics..." he turned from the holograms to face the group. "I will have to study this data extensively before I can even begin to comprehend its implications."

Woods nodded. "Then we won't change our plans in the slightest. We'll go to the Inner Ring, and meet the Slayers when they attack."

"I have an incoming comm request," said Blaze, standing from Eris' side, who had drifted into sleep. "Zena Olleeve."

"Put her through," said Woods, standing to face the comm pedestal.

The Clone leader appeared before them. She gave her native salute to Woods, raising her right fist to her chest, and pressing her left fist against the small of her back. Woods raised a flat hand to his forehead, returning her salute.

"Mr. Eminence," said Zena. "We'll be at the Inner Ring within twelve hours. My Clone commanders are requesting detailed strategies for arrival."

"They'll get an update within the hour," said Woods. "We have some new developments. I suggest you come on board *Mariella* for briefing."

"Developments?" Zena raised an eyebrow.

"Come on board," said Woods. "This is eyes only."

Zena nodded. "I'll prepare a Leopard now."

Her hologram vanished.

Woods turned back to the Milky Way hologram. Stew now had more than twenty side-holograms positioned around the main one, flickering as he dissected data to feed to the ship's computers.

One of the holograms showed an exploded view of the Inner Ring. UCOM ships sprawled across it in battle formation. *Warhammer* sat behind the armada, the last line of defense before the portal superhighway, thousands of portals that connected the Milky Way in a central transport hub.

And behind *Warhammer,* sat another structure, just as large, and glowing a soft blue.

It was the Slayer Triturator device, the installation that would destroy the Milky Way and dissolve every planet and star into pure energy.

He had seen footage of Slayers using Triturators to dissolve Andromeda until it was nothing but empty space. Now, the ghost of Casi Vomisa had instructed him to switch that same death machine on.

Woods ran a hand through his hair, and followed the points of light showing the Triturator installations through the Milky Way. He rested on the final point of light, at the edge of the galaxy, near the Outer Rim.

A set of words hovered above the final point which, like the dot at the Inner Ring, glowed brighter than the rest. He squinted to make out their meaning.

Floodgate.

He'd never heard the term before. Was the Floodgate part of Eris' plan? Of Casi's plan?

His mind swooned, and he was hit with a vision. He left the metal deck of *Mariella* and entered the vacuum of space. An enormous structure hung to his right, larger than most planets, and filled with gaping holes and flat vents. A single word hovered above the structure, as it had in Eris' hologram.

Floodgate.

A Slayer Hive sat below, and he waved his arms, rotating his body in the weightless vacuum to gain a better view.

"Nancy's in there," said a voice to his right. "She's being held captive."

Woods jerked with surprise and spun to face the voice. He choked when he saw who had spoken. "You're…alive," he gasped.

"Of course I am," said Casi Vomisa, hovering in space beside him, dressed in tight leather. "You saw my proxy, didn't you?"

"Eris," Woods whispered. He shook his head. "Nancy's in the Hive?"

Casi nodded. "Afraid so. I wish I had better news for you."

"But the Voice," said Woods. "He said I'd need to save her life."

"The Sterilord," said Casi softly. "You need to control your visions, Francis. They're not good for your mind. They weaken your soul. You shouldn't even be talking to me."

"But I need to save Nancy…"

"Go back to the Inner Ring. *Heed my words.*"

"How are you talking to me? What is this place?"

"*Go.*"

Woods gasped as the space vanished around him. The Floodgate disappeared, replaced by the war room of *Mariella.*

The rest of the group gave him a quick glance, then returned their attention to Eris' hologram. Woods gulped.

Nancy was at the Floodgate. Would sparking the Triturator save her life somehow? Or would the machine kill his daughter in the process?

He stared at the hologram. Casi had told him to avoid his visions, but now, more than anything, he wanted to hear the Voice. Not Casi Vomisa's voice, the real Voice. He wanted to hear the Voice tell him everything would be okay.

He needed the Voice to tell him what to do, and how to save his daughter.

ONE-HUNDRED-TWENTY

Nancy Woods – Human

Aboard Night Eagle *Eclipse* – Floogate starspace

Nancy winced as Frank tightened his grip around her neck, jamming his pistol against her throat. The Destineers they'd picked up from the surface of Sylva huddled together at the far side of the bridge, silent save for the occasional throat-clearing. She'd learned their names during their initial conversations, which had since fallen silent.

Nathyan was the man with the disfigured face. Pylo and Naydee were tending to his wounds, plucking various tools and treatments from *Eclipse's* med kit.

Sarah, Rove, and Jay stood beside them, sometimes glancing out the window at the surrounding starspace, but mostly staring at her and Frank.

Chase, their leader, stood at the front of the bridge, his hands tight around his rifle, facing Hunter, who was piloting the ship towards the maintenance hatch against the Hive's hull.

"How close are we?" called Frank.

Nancy scrunched her face as his hot breath billowed against the side of her cheek and soured her nose.

"Almost there," said Hunter from the cockpit. "Just need to finalize our docking vectors."

"Vectors complete," said Laura Maxwell from the AI pedestal.

The ship slowed as it approached the hull of the enormous Hive, rotating gently as it moved into position for final dock.

"Where's the rest of your unit?" said Frank, shifting his weight.

Nancy couldn't contain a yelp of pain as her shattered elbow was jostled against Frank's hip. Frank jabbed his pistol harder into her throat in an attempt to silence her.

"Inside the pinhead," said Chase, turning from the cockpit. "Not far. After we're inside it's a short pod ride to the bridge."

"And Sid Dakota will be there?" said Frank.

Chase looked briefly to the ceiling before nodding. "Of course. Our orders are to meet at the bridge. We're almost to the Primal Snow. Be patient, brother." Chase sniffed and licked his lips. "Soon we'll reach salvation."

Nancy frowned and raised an eyebrow at the fidgety behavior. Chase spun away from them to return his attention to the cockpit. He certainly was an odd Destineer. Every convert she'd ever witnessed talked like a drone, and gushed with emotion when talking about the Pristine, or about salvation at the Primal Snow. Chase seemed strikingly neutral about the idea of entering salvation.

Her injured arm bumped against Frank's hip again, and this time the pain was so bad she screamed.

"Frank," she rasped. "My arm. *Please.* Let me sit. I'm feeling faint."

"Shut up," Frank hissed. "You can kneel just before Sid Dakota executes you. Or perhaps you can kneel before the Pristine and pledge your undying faith. I don't give a frux *what* you do after I reach the Primal Snow."

Nancy blinked away hot tears. She tried to remind herself that it wasn't Frank holding the gun to her head, that it was Timothy, the Destineer AI that had commandeered his body, but the thought only made her angrier.

She wondered if she should make a move for Frank's pistol. It was lodged against her throat, but if she jerked her head away quick enough, perhaps she could twist out of Frank's grasp.

She tensed in anticipation and nearly fainted as her elbow sent a wave of nausea through her body. The ground seemed vague and far away, teetering back and forth beneath a dim haze. She struggled to remain conscious and block the pain from her mind.

"Stop struggling," said Frank, jerking her neck in the crook of his elbow, fueling her pain even further. He froze. "What the hell…"

His grip tightened around her neck, and she gasped for breath, grabbing his bicep with her good hand. Frank's arm was shaking. She blinked and choked in a few breaths through the headlock, and coughed in surprise when she glanced out the bridge window.

The Floodgate hung in the distance, dominating the view.

This wasn't what surprised Nancy.

It was what lay behind the Floodgate.

The far portal had widened, ballooning outward until it was the size of a planet. The bow of a ship pierced the portal's edge, and soon a UCOM Tiger passed through. Seconds later, the bow of a much larger ship emerged. A Slayer Hive.

The portals were thousands of kilometers away, far enough for the ships to appear like miniature toys. Nancy knew that if large warships were near, so was their escort of hundreds of light craft, too small to see from these distances.

"UCOM ships," said Rove, leaning forward for a better view.

The rest of the Destineers murmured in awe.

Nancy raised an eyebrow. The tones in their voices were wrong. Destineers would have cursed the UCOM fleet. Nancy was no longer sure this random group of battered Humans were Destineers.

Frank shared her sentiment.

Electric recoil thundered before her face as Frank raised his pistol and fired. Bradford, Pylo, and Naydee went down instantly as Frank caught them in the head with plasma charges. Sarah, Rove, and Jay screamed as they were clipped in the back. Flesh melted away from their bones in small craters as they struggled for their rifles. Frank finished them off with three more rounds to the face. He finished Nathyan off as well, who had scuttled against the cabin wall, blinded by the bandages wrapped around his face. Nathyan slumped sideways lifelessly, a fresh crater crackling in his chest.

Muffled shouts sounded from the barracks behind her as Caseus and Lindsey responded to the gunfire. The doors thudded as her captive crew attempted to break through the impenetrable glass.

A separate gunshot thundered inside the small cabin. Frank wheeled to face the noise, and Nancy screamed in agony as her arm whipped around. Her screams where choked off by the barrel of Frank's pistol, which he returned to her throat with a vengeance.

Chase had shouldered his rifle, and had it trained at Nancy. She felt Frank cringe behind her, making himself as small as possible behind his human shield.

"Drop the girl," said Chase, taking a step forward.

"If you so much as blink, Nancy's dead," said Frank.

Chase froze. His face shifted into a scowl. "You killed my team. They were the last friends I had in the universe. You think I give a star's frux about the girl?"

"Put the gun down," said Hunter quietly, stepping from the cockpit and pushing Chase's rifle towards the deck. "We're here. The hatch is open. Leave. Go find Sid. You won."

Frank was silent, save for his labored breaths against Nancy's face. He slid a few steps sideways, towards the hatch, which had opened during the chaos.

Chase's lip twitched, but he lowered his rifle, setting it slowly on the deck.

Frank slid further towards the door, dragging Nancy until they were less than a meter away.

Nancy yelped as she was thrown forward. Hunter caught her, and she vomited after her elbow banged against the metal in his Akimor. He lowered her to a seated position. Her head rolled back to her shoulders, and she stared into the Hive ship through the docking hatch.

Frank Scott, or Timothy, or whoever the hell controlled Frank's body, was sprinting down the narrow hall. He reached a T-junction at the end, paused to look left and right, then took off down the left corridor.

She hardly felt Hunter press his fingers against the side of her neck, but welcomed the rush of painkillers that flowed into her body afterward.

"I'm going to mend your arm," said Hunter.

Nancy felt a click as he reset her bones, but the feeling was distant, as if it were a dream. Her eyelids turned to stones, and she fought to keep them open. A spray of foam coated her arm, and she blinked at it lazily as it hardened into a flexible cast.

Bear tossed the can of quickcast back into the med kit.

"We need to leave now," he said, hoisting Nancy up.

Nancy tried to respond, but her tongue was stuck in her throat. The world darkened as the drugs combined with hours of agony to cloak her mind and vision.

"She's not going to make it past the hallway," said Chase. "We'll have to carry her."

"Not necessary," said Bear, pressing his fingers back against Nancy's neck.

The fog vanished, replaced by a lightning rod of pure energy. She jolted upright and flexed her muscles so hard she shifted the bones in her elbow. She hardly felt the pain, which registered as no more than a pin prick. She bit her cheeks, her eyes bulging.

The barracks beeped as the doors slid open. Caseus and Lindsey exchanged frantic words with Hunter, but Nancy barely heard them. She was too busy staring down the hall, wondering where Frank had run. She was going to kill Frank. Yes, she would kill him right after she killed Sid Dakota. Or maybe she'd kill him before. She hadn't decided yet.

Lindsey moaned when she saw the fresh corpses of Frank's victims.

Caseus rushed to Nancy. His words finally registered in her mind.

"You gave her *what?*" he cried, grabbing Nancy by the arm.

"Red Lighting," said Hunter calmly. Otherwise she would've passed out.

"Red…why do you even have the stuff?"

"Standard field drug," said Hunter. "I gave her five hundred milligrams."

"Five hundred milligrams?" said Caseus. "Stars, why didn't you just launch her out the tubes? Five hundred mils will pop her heart like a balloon."

I'm fine," said Nancy, bending to pick up a discarded rifle. She checked the slide and slung it over her back. She plucked a handgun from the floor and added it to the mag plate on her thigh. "Frank couldn't have gotten far. He's looking for Sid Dakota. With any luck, when we find Frank, we find Sid."

Caseus gave her a surprised look, but geared up after a few seconds of staring. Lindsey followed suit. Hunter walked to the AI pedestal and exchanged words with Laura Maxwell, who vanished from the holodeck, downloading into Hunter's Akimor for transport through the Hive.

They entered the halls, moving as fast as possible. After a few corners, they heard voices.

Hunter froze. "*Slayers,*" he whispered. "I'll flank them, fire after my lead." He engaged camouflage and vanished into thin air.

A team of four Slayers turned the corner seconds later, all wearing Cogent armor.

Nancy drew her rifle and fired, forgetting Hunter's instructions as the Red Lightning overtook her rationale. The slug glanced harmlessly off the Slayer's armored breastplate.

"Control yourself woman," roared the Slayer.

He stomped toward Nancy until he towered over her. She tightened her grip on her rifle. The Slayer dropped to all fours until his rakish head was inches from her own.

"The Pristine won't allow me to kill the naked apes," he growled. "But if you fire another bullet, I may forget about my orders."

Nancy's jaw dropped, and she lowered her rifle. The Slayers lumbered past, one of them intentionally bumping his tail against her thigh, causing her knees to bend. Caseus caught her before she could stumble.

The Slayers continued down the hall, grumbling to themselves.

"When we will pass through the portal?" said one.

"Soon, the calibration is finished," said another.

"I'm growing sick of this ship. The naked apes anger me with their arrogance. They reeked of electricity. It's almost as if an electric demon was near."

They disappeared around a corner. Hunter reappeared. He frowned and retracted his swords back into his Akimor.

"What the hell was that?" said Chase.

Nancy thought back to the mortally wounded Guardian, captive inside the brig aboard *Liberty*. She cringed at the memory of the massacre, the thousands of rotting corpses burned into her mind like fire.

"The Slayers obeyed the Destineers," the Guardian had said as he clutched to the last threads of his life. *"Humans commanded the beasts like dogs."*

"Back at Lavariz," whispered Nancy. "The Guardian in *Liberty's* brig. The Slayers obey Humans..."

Caseus and Lindsey raised their eyebrows as they recalled the scene. Chase Grover opened his mouth, presumably to ask them what the hell they were talking about. A series of loud bangs caused them all to jump. New voices echoed from around the corner at the end of the hall.

"More Slayers," said Hunter. "Come on, down this hallway."

"No," said Nancy, pushing past Hunter. "We're done running."

She walked briskly towards the Slayers. She glanced behind to see Caseus and Chase following close behind, Lindsey shaking behind him, her face twitching. Hunter had again engaged his camouflage, and was invisible.

She spun forward just as the Slayers turned the corner. This time, instead of raising her rifle, Nancy powered toward the two beasts, who unlike the four previously, did not wear Cogent armor.

"Another naked ape," one of them grumbled. "This ship is lousy with them."

"Hold your tongue or I'll rip it from your mouth and deliver it to the Pristine as a gift." Nancy puffed her chest and craned her neck upward to look the nearest Slayer in the eyes.

The Slayers looked to one another, unsure of what to do.

"Kneel," Nancy spat. The Slayers didn't budge. "I said *kneel.*"

The two beasts growled, but slumped to all fours, bending their snouts until they fogged the metal deck, the hairs on their necks bristling.

"There's no need to notify the Pristine," one of them said. "We will deliver the Destineer apes to the Primal Snow as promised, *ma'am.*"

Nancy took a sharp breath, taken aback by their compliance. "Rise." The Slayers pushed themselves to a standing position, pressing their tails flat against the floor. "You can start by taking us to the main bridge."

"But ma'am," said the Slayer on the left, glancing at his comrade. "Only the Destineer chief Sid Dakota is allowed access to the bridge. *We* are not even allowed access. To go there would mean strict disciplining, we told the last naked ape the same thing…"

"Frank?" said Nancy.

The Slayer licked a tongue over his fangs. "I don't learn the names of naked apes, other than Sid Dakota."

Take us," Nancy shouted, her head buzzing as the Red Lighting pulsed through her veins. She raised her rifle and pressed the barrel against the Slayer's head. "I'm not going to ask again. I need to meet with Dakota."

"Yes ma'am," said the Slayer, pushing backwards and rising to his hind legs.

His partner followed suit, scuttling around in the direction they'd come from. His eyes never left Nancy's, and he slowly dragged his tail around her body, careful not to bump into her.

"The bridge is a ten-minute pod ride from here, my apologies."

"And the man you saw earlier," said Nancy. "Where did he go?"

"In this direction," said the Slayer. "He was on his way to the bridge as well."

Nancy nodded and followed her newfound guides. Her body tugged at her, and again she felt the presence of the stars. A voice whispered to her from the darkest recesses of her mind, encouraging her onward.

Go on Nancy. You must make it to the bridge. You must avenge Sid's crimes against Humans.

The Voice fueled her legs with strength, growing stronger with each step.

She wondered what the UCOM navy was doing at the Floodgate, and if they had already begun to attack the leviathan structure. She wondered if her father was doing battle back behind the Frontline, or if he was even still alive.

But mostly she wondered if she would finally meet Sid Dakota.

The divine power of the stars burning in her core convinced her she would.

ONE-HUNDRED-TWENTY-ONE

Sid Dakota – Human Destineer
Aboard Slayer Hive *Sylva* – Floodgate starspace

Sid Dakota waited impatiently for the space elevator to arrive at the Hive mothership. He thought back on the past few hours as the purple Sylvan atmosphere gave way to inky star-studded blackness.

The Spider carrying him across the scorched skies of Sylva had been hit by a falling ball of energy, but it had merely grazed the hull, and they'd made a safe landing at Tower 1.

He'd donned a new suit of armor at the main Destineer base as his men prepared the lift. After a quick video conference with the Slayer Hive commander, alerting the beast to his planned arrival on the bridge, he'd entered the elevator with the last of his men and launched from the surface.

The electrical fields on the tether had been weakened by the anti-matter blast, and the trip had taken longer than normal, but the added transit time had given him a chance to reflect on his destiny, and also to have another vision, perhaps his last.

The Sterilord had spoken to him. They were almost there, so close he could feel the Sterilord's heart beating alongside his own. Soon the Sylvan Hive would pass through the portal beyond the Outer Rim, and he would reach salvation at long last. The Sterilord had soothed him with kind words. Unable to control his emotions, he had knelt before the figure of light, weeping uncontrollably, professing his love for the Voice. The Voice had reciprocated his love, causing Sid to weep even harder. The Voice had reminded him that before he reached the Primal Snow, he would receive a gift from Nancy Woods. Sid would then deliver the gift to the Sterilord, and transform into an eternal deity.

His destiny was nearly fulfilled. He didn't know how Nancy would deliver her gift to him, with so little time left before reaching salvation, but the Voice had told it would be so. He would never question the wisdom of the Voice.

There was now only one contingency left. Chase Grover, the heathen who for the past century had gnawed at his holy quest like a parasitic insect. Fortunately, he knew exactly where to find the blasphemer.

His men had spotted the UCOM ship shortly after his elevator reached orbit, and he'd watched as the stealth vessel docked to a maintenance hatch against the Hive's hull. He didn't know how Chase had gained access to such a ship, but he was no longer surprised by the SIGA filth-lover's craftiness.

It made no difference. He was surrounded by four hundred of his loyal Destineers, fellow crusaders for the faith. They'd find Chase quickly, if the Slayer crew hadn't already. And then Chase would die, Sid's final act before his transcendence. SIGA would be finished, scourged from the galaxy along with the rest of the filth.

UCOM ships had entered Floodgate starspace, and he'd seethed with hatred as he watched them file into battle groupings thousands of kilometers away. No matter. The ships were mere pests at this point. The Outer Rim portal had reopened, and as soon as he gave the command, the ship would pass through to Primal Snow starspace. Once the Triturator was activated, the UCOM heretics would be burned away from the Floodgate like warts.

The elevator slowed, and Sid rushed to the doorways, eager to depart. His men drew their rifles, filing behind him in ordered groups. The glass entrance hissed as it docked against the Hive hull, and opened to expose a group of twelve Slayer Cogent. Eleven wore yellow armor, but one wore blue. Sid strode to the leader.

"The commander's waiting at the bridge, sir," said the blue leader, bowing deeply. "The portal will be open for travel by the time we arrive."

"A Human ship docked outside the hull at the base of the support arm," said Sid, pointing through the outside window to the stealth ship, a mere speck in the distance. "I want the crew detained."

The leader peered out the window. "We're aware of the docking. Four of my Cogent saw the group of apes…*Humans*…in the corridor."

"And you let them go?" Sid hissed, balling his fists.

"My orders are not to interfere with the Humans," said the leader.

"Your orders are not to interfere with the Destineers."

The Slayer frowned. "Is there a difference, sir?"

"*Fools,*" Sid spat. "Find them *now*."

"I cannot harm the naked apes," said the leader.

Sid howled with rage and lunged at the Slayer, kicking him squarely in the stomach. His metal boot clanged against the Cogent's armor, but the beast hardly budged.

The creature's eyes narrowed into a glare. "My orders from the Pristine are clear. No harm can come to the naked apes."

Sid shook, his lip twitching. "Then radio the rest of the crew. Tell me where they are, and I'll go get them myself."

The leader nodded and turned away, speaking into his comm set. Sid turned to his men as they waited. They shared a common look, one of desire. Their faces were soft, and their eyes hopeful. Like him, they could feel the power of the Sterilord burning in their veins.

"I've located them, sir," said the leader, turning back to face Sid. "A group of Humans. Two of my men are escorting them to the command bridge."

Sid smiled. "That makes things easy for us, doesn't it? Take us to the bridge."

ONE-HUNDRED-TWENTY-TWO

Eve – Clone

Aboard Night Eagle *Midnight* – Floodgate starspace

"Floodgate starspace secured," said a voice through central comms.

Eve stared through the bay windows of the Night Eagle she and Keyv had boarded. It was the third stealth fighter she'd used in as many weeks, but the ID tags had been re-encrypted to match her usual flight handle, *Midnight.*

Allakai's fleet stretched far around her ship, traveling in offensive formation to the Floodgate, now only a few hundred kilometers away. The recessed vents and metal curves of the machine dominated most of her view, but she could still make out the circular shape of the Destineer Hive in the distance, near the far portal to the Outer Rim.

She wondered if Nancy Woods had made it to the Hive, and if she'd been able to stop Sid Dakota. There was no way to know, but with Sylva still in eyeshot, she could trick her mind into believing Nancy's tiny crew had been able to stop her home world from traveling through the portal and into the clutches of the Pristine.

She shook her head and dismissed the thought. Nancy's mission was even more doomed than her own. Sylva would surely pass through to the Outer Rim at any minute, but an urge to follow her birth place gnawed at her regardless.

Eve turned from the window to face the crowded bridge. Both she and Keyv had climbed back into their Hare suits, and the Fox androids containing the antimatter stood beside them. The Foxes were motionless save for a line of indicator lights along their torsos and necks, blinking blue and purple, confirming their functionality.

Allakai had ordered all fifteen of his Titans to escort her and Keyv into the Floodgate, as well Amy Chip, her AI. One of the Titans stood with Axel across the bridge from her, reviewing the path they would take into the Triturator device. The rest flew in fourteen Cheetah fast-attack fighters, flanking her Night Eagle on all sides.

The Titan aboard her ship was a Human-born named Hector, and friendly enough. Allakai had given operational control to Hector, and for the first time in almost two hundred years, Eve was part of a crew, not in command.

Instead of being angry, she was relieved. Following orders was a hell of a lot easier than giving them. Except she did have an itchy desire to travel to the Sylvan Hive, and without command of her ship, had no ability to do so.

"We have orders to proceed from *Kizurra*," said Amy Chip, materializing on the AI pedestal. "Two minutes till go."

"What's the expected resistance?" said Hector, standing from the holodeck to address Amy.

"Minimal," said Amy. "No detected enemy craft outside the Floodgate, or inside its vents. There's the Hive across starspace near the far portal, but it hasn't made any aggressive moves."

"Is Allakai going to attack it?" said Hector.

Amy shook her head. "Not yet. He's keeping our fleet together until your op is finished. Doesn't want to splinter our strength, no telling what might come from the Outer Rim."

Hector nodded. "Send our acknowledgement to *Kizurra*. If Eve's intel is accurate, we'll be back within four hours."

"Aye," said Amy, and disappeared from view.

"Give this map one final scan," said Hector, nodding to Eve and Keyv. "I want to make sure we have our insertion points nailed down."

Eve walked to the holodeck, Keyv following behind. She leaned over the table, studying the cross-sectional slices of the Floodgate, showing the inside tunnels, vents, and hallways of the massive device.

A bright blue line showed their travel path, entering through an outside vent, and continuing through the structure until it terminated at the main chamber in the heart of the device. There were two ninety-degree turns along the way, marked with blue dots. A third blue dot sat just outside the central chamber of the Floodgate.

"Everything's where it should be," said Eve, reaching to enlarge the view. She closed her eyes briefly as she recalled the logistics of the Discarded's plan of attack. "We may run into some automated defenses here," she pointed at the first blue dot, deep into one of the side vents. "The antimatter blast may not have taken it out."

"Nothing nuclear?" said Hector.

Eve shook her head. "Just plasma turrets, your Titans shouldn't have a problem with them. The Slayers don't use nuclear defenses inside the Floodgate. They don't want to compromise…"

"Yeah, got it, no nukes," said Hector. "It's in the dossier." He paused, then enlarged a different section of the hologram, skipping the second blue dot and selecting the area around the third blue dot, further down the vent, just a few thousand kilometers from the center of the Floodgate. "You're certain there's a barrier here?"

Eve shrugged. "According to the Discarded, there's a labyrinth barrier to stop ships from reaching the central chambers. We have no hard scans on it, just Slayer chatter."

Hector nodded. "So we enter the inside of their maintenance space, where the Slayers have a high-speed pod transport that we'll take to the central chamber."

"Yes," said Eve. "*That* we know exists for a fact. The Discarded have entered the pod line in previous attempts to sabotage the Floodgate. It will be heavily guarded with Cogent."

"Can't have it too easy," said Hector, offering Keyv and Eve a weak smile. "It would take the fun out of it." He returned to the holodeck. "After we gain access to the transit line, my team will escort you and your antimatter androids to the central chamber. You'll drop the Foxes into the abyss and detonate once they've reached critical distance. The transit line will superheat from residual energy, but nothing your Hare suit or our Akimors can't handle by design. We rally back to extract, and take our ships out the same chamber we entered."

"You nailed it," said Keyv.

Hector paused. "Tell me more about the detonator for these antimatter bombs. Are you the only ones able to pull the trigger, wearing the Hare suits? Remind me what type of range the detonators have."

"The vent and chamber walls are so thick we need to be in relatively close proximity in order to remote detonate," said Eve. "That's why we can't control the Foxes from outside the Floodgate. As for detonation, yeah, me and Keyv are the only ones who can pull the trigger."

"Not true," said Keyv.

Hector raised an eyebrow. "Can my Titans tie their Akimors into the ignition sequencer? It could be useful in the event you or Eve…"

"Die?" Eve finished for him.

The Titan gave a slight shrug and pursed his lips.

"No, to answer your question," said Keyv. "You can't tie into the sequencer. But there is a manual override on the Fox itself."

Keyv walked toward the nearest Fox, motioning for Hector and Eve to follow. He tapped a finger twice against the left breast of the robot, opening a sliding door to expose a recessed cavity. Inside the cavity were two objects; a red switch and a metal turnkey.

"The deadman's trigger," said Keyv, turning to Hector. "If Eve and I don't make it, one of your Titans can detonate with the manual override. Flip the switch and turn the key. They'll be killed instantly of course, vaporized by pure energy."

"Enough talk about dying," said Eve, her voice cracking. "And without us to control the Foxes, you'd have ten thousand kilograms of dead robot weight to haul to the main chamber, enough to slow even a Titan to a crawl."

Keyv hung his head, and Hector turned to Axel, who shrugged.

"We'll make sure you walk out of this alive," said Hector, placing a soft hand on Eve's shoulder. "Standard procedure, that's all. I need to plan for worst-case scenarios."

The Titan left to return to the holodeck. Axel left for the cockpit, securing himself in the pilot chair.

"Twenty seconds to go," called Amy Chip from the AI pedestal.

Eve gulped and squeezed one of the metal grips for support. Hector said he was planning for the worst-case scenario. When it came to storming the Slayer Floodgate with two antimatter bombs following close behind, her fear was that death would not be the worst-case scenario.

It would be the most likely scenario.

ONE-HUNDRED-TWENTY-THREE

Eve – Clone

Aboard Night Eagle *Midnight* – Floodgate starspace

Eve sat at her station, staring at the holographic controls, checking lines of intel streaming before her. The mouth of their target vent loomed before them, ready to swallow their tiny ship and the surrounding escort.

No enemy ships or defense systems were picked up by their scanning equipment. They were heading into a deserted shell of what the Floodgate once was.

Eve shifted her attention to her home planet of Sylva. They were on final approach to the Floodgate, and she could no longer see the Sylvan Hive through her viewing window. All she could see was a wall of metal. Instead she looked at a hologram of the ship hovering at the side of her holodeck. The Slayer mothership had not moved from its position outside the Outer Ring portal, a golf-ball sized sphere on her display.

She thought again of Nancy. A running timer ticked towards zero below the hologram.

Estimated time until Triturator spark: 3:01:43.

She stared at the timer until it had reached an even three hours. Allakai's engineers seemed confident the Outer Rim portal would take another few hours to commission before spark. She knew the Intellects onboard *Kizurra* had calculated the countdown clock based on reverse engineering the Floodgate, and assessing the pilot light infrastructure installed around the Outer Rim portal. Intellects thought in practical terms, and used math, physics, and logic to arrive at their decisions.

The Intellects weren't about to enter the Floodgate with two antimatter bombs.

She was.

If they were wrong in their calculations, they would watch safely on the sidelines as a massive beam of pure energy was shot from the Primal Snow, through the Outer Ring portal, and into the Floodgate to initiate Trituration.

She, on the other hand, would be instantly vaporized along with her crew.

And my unborn child.

She prayed their calculations were sound.

A flash of blue caused her to jerk in her seat. Her eyes widened. The Sylvan Hive had fired its thrusters, and was inching towards the Outer Rim portal. The portal ballooned in size as it accepted the massive curves of the mothership.

Had Nancy Woods failed her mission? Eve's heart sank as she watched her home world disappear for the last time. She opened her mouth to alert her crew.

"Entering Floodgate," Axel called from the cockpit before she could speak.

The stars vanished in their viewing windows, replaced by the scorched interior of the Floodgate.

They were in.

Eve gulped and focused back on her scanning metrics.

Their intercom beeped.

"*Midnight,* this is fleet command. Your heavy escort is pulling back. In five hundred clicks you'll go to radio silence. Good luck. Awaken stars."

Hector turned from the central bridge to reply. “Fleet command, *Midnight* confirms. See you on the other side.”

The Titan commander relayed orders to the fourteen Cheetahs in formation around their stealth ship. Streaks of purple zipped past them as several attack fighters forged ahead, searching the tunnel for hidden enemies.

They sat in silence for what seemed like hours. Eve checked her timer.

2:55:12.

She wondered if the Floodgate slowed time, or if she was losing her mind. She decided both were possible.

“Enemy plasma battery ahead,” said one of the Titans through central comms. “Taking it out now.”

Plasma fire flickered in the distant space before them as the automated Slayer turrets shot at the lead Cheetah fighters. Fiery explosions answered in return as the Titan squadron sent knife-blade missiles into the sentries.

One minute later, *Midnight* reached the blackened remains of the plasma battery station, which circled around the enormous vent in square clusters. They had reached the first location pin.

“Amy, what’s our position?” Hector called.

Amy Chip appeared at the AI pedestal. “The lead Cheetahs are arriving at the hatch now. We’ll be there in just under two minutes.”

Hector reached over his shoulder to pull his MGK from his back. He nodded to Eve and Keyv. “You two gear up and get your Foxes ready. We’re not going to waste any time. In and out.”

Eve nodded, frowning at her intel station. They were still all alone inside the vents.

When they’d entered the Floodgate, the vents had been black, burned by the Discarded’s antimatter blast. Now the walls were clean and gray, without so much as a streak of soot. The blast hadn’t reached this far into the Floodgate. Where were the rest of the Slayer ships Pexar had warned them of? Where were the thousands of Wasp fighters, or the Tarantula ground fortresses?

"Insertion point is clear," said the Titan squadron leader over comms. "The maintenance hatch is right where we thought it would be."

"Stake the perimeter," said Hector. "We storm the hatch as soon as *Midnight* docks."

"Aye," said the Titan.

Eve wiped her palms dry on her skinsuit. The Slayer fiber technology whisked the moisture away instantly, but her hands went clammy again in seconds. She engaged her Fox with silent thought commands. The hulking robot whirred to life, as did Keyv's beside it. The two portable AMMO-AB's scuttled on all fours to *Midnight's* hatch.

Keyv lifted his helmet from beside his station and fastened it above his shoulders. He vanished from view as he engaged active camo.

Eve fastened her helmet as well, staring at the maintenance hatch through the window. A docking platform fanned out wide from the entrance. Fourteen Cheetahs sat in a semi-circle around the doorway, their bows pointed outward towards the vent tunnel.

The fourteen Titan pilots had exited their craft, and were crouched on either side of the doorway, their lattice shields fully energized in blue, pink, and yellow hues.

Eve caught her reflection as she turned from the window. Her reflection disappeared as she activated stealth camo.

"Touching down," called Axel from the cockpit.

"Enter the hatch," called Hector to his Titan squad.

The deck shuddered as *Midnight* docked inside the ring of Cheetahs. Eve followed her Fox out of the hatch, which was no longer visible save for a transparent blue film augmented over her HUD. The Fox scurried in the likeness of a Slayer Beast, its movements calculated and robotic.

The air was stale and alien, even through her skinsuit. The Titans breached the door and stormed inside, some with their rifles drawn, others with swords.

Two things happened almost simultaneously.

First, a barrage of plasma fire erupted from inside the maintenance hatch, consuming the Titans in a wall of superheated gas. Four of the Titans fell backward as they were tackled by an army of Cogent elite, outnumbered by a factor of five.

Then alarms blared, lighting the inside of the tunnel in bursts of yellow. Rings of blue light circled around the tubular passage, full at first, then disappearing like the fuse on a stick of dynamite.

Eve didn't have to think hard to realize it was a countdown timer.

The Titans trapped inside the maintenance hall were drowned by a writhing mass of Slayer warriors, who bludgeoned them with armored tails, and slashed at them with razor claws.

The four Titans who had fallen backwards onto the dock struggled to defend blows from the attacking Cogent. One of them had his head crushed flat by a blow from an energy hammer. Another had his head ripped off entirely.

Axel roared in fury and sprinted towards the melee, shields cackling and swords extended. He leaped onto the back of a Cogent and thrust his sword through a weak spot in the Slayer's neck armor before turning to blast a different Cogent in the face with his laser cannon.

Eve froze. Keyv ran toward the erupting battle, then paused. He ran back towards Eve, his invisible Fox following close behind.

"We need to leave," he cried. "We can't go in there."

Eve could only stare at the Titans – the deadliest warriors UCOM had to offer. Some were wounded. Most were dead.

It was a massacre.

Hector ran towards the mob in a half-crouch, rifle raised and firing in short bursts. A few Cogent fell lifeless to the dock, but they were replaced in seconds by new Cogent, storming onto the dock from the open maintenance door. Hector stood frozen for a few seconds, then raced towards Axel. He grabbed Axel by the arm and pulled him towards *Midnight,* narrowly dodging an energy hammer.

"Amy, start the engines," Hector roared, running with Axel towards the ship. "Get the hell on board, *let's move.*"

Eve turned and scrambled up the hatch, Keyv bumping the backs of her thighs as he followed close behind. Their Foxes snuck onboard seconds later.

She turned to find Hector sprinting to the ship, but Axel no longer followed at his heels.

Had Axel died with the rest of their party? She searched the dock for her Titan friend's corpse, but instead found a Cheetah firing its thrusters. The fighter launched from the platform, flipping a Cogent off the hull and over the edge of the dock to his death.

Hector barged through *Midnight's* hatch and punched the hatch controls. The ramp whisked quickly upwards, sealing against the hull. The Titan raced to the cockpit and immediately punched the thrusters.

They rose above a sea of Cogent that had swarmed the area. Explosions ripped the dock below, clearing a smoky gap through the mob of Slayer soldiers.

Axel streaked past in his Cheetah. "Axel to *Midnight,* I need orders. Decided to take a different set of wheels. What the hell is the plan now?"

Hector pulled *Midnight* in a tight loop and accelerated down the vent, away from the maintenance hatch. "Head towards the central chamber as fast as your Cheetah will take you. We're taking a detour."

"Aye," said Axel.

Eve caught a streak of light in the corner of her eye as Axel punched it, then he was gone.

Keyv dropped his camo, appearing out of thin air inside the bridge. He tore his helmet off. "Towards the central chamber? What about the labyrinth gate? We should leave, get back to *Kizurra.*"

"That's not an option," said Hector, accelerating the ship down the flashing tunnel. "Amy, give me a time on the status bar circling the tunnel."

Even though they were now going thousands of kilometers per hour, the concentric rings stretching down the tunnel were easy to spot, and formed a steady countdown bar of light. It was now only half filled, no more than a semicircle.

"Fifteen minutes," said Amy from the AI pedestal. "I intercepted Slayer chatter when the maintenance hatch opened. The Triturator has been activated. Fifteen minutes until spark. Then this place with be hotter than the sun."

Keyv stormed into the cockpit. He clenched his fists, then slapped Hector in the side of the head. "Ten minutes? Turn around *now.* We need to get Eve out of the Floodgate. I'm not going to let you kill our…"

"*Midnight,* labyrinth is clear," Axel's voice shot over comms. "It has a few turns, but it's designed to stop larger ships than what we're in. I'm already through, you'll have no problem either."

"Amy," Hector called. "Set *Midnight* to autopilot, set vectors to the central chamber. We're going to detonate once we reach target."

Amy's avatar trembled noticeably atop the pedestal at the kamikaze-style order. Her voice cracked. "Aye, setting vectors."

Keyv's shoulders sank. He turned from the cockpit, and slumped into his station chair. Eve padded to him slowly, reaching a gloved hand around the back of his head. He reached to touch her belly, then began to sob. Eve pulled his face into her midriff and massaged the back of his neck

They would detonate in a few minutes. She scrunched her eyes shut and tried to replay a hundred year's worth of memories before she died. She pictured Keyv's smile. She traced the outline of his jaw with her finger, like she used to when they would spend the whole day in bed together, floating in the vastness of interstellar space.

Midnight swayed slightly as it passed through the turns of the labyrinth barrier. The metal columns connecting the base of the vent to the top were three times wider than their ship, and they passed through with room to spare. If only they had known this ahead of time…

A sharp beep caused her to turn. Hector had opened the cavity in her Fox's chest, exposing the manual detonator switch and key.

"I'm at the central chamber," called Axel over comms. "This thing is huge. What should I do?"

Hector didn't reply. Instead he walked from the Fox frozen at the side of the bridge. Eve shied away from him, the android who had sentenced her to death. Keyv barred his arm before her, as if to shield her from harm.

"You're a pilot?" Hector said to Eve.

Eve frowned "Yes."

"Then get in the cockpit. Strap in tight and open the hatch."

"Twenty seconds until the central chamber," called Amy Chip in a hollow voice.

Eve cleared her throat weakly. "But the antimatter…"

"*Go,*" said Hector. "Get your helmet on. Open the hatch when you're strapped in."

Eve heart nearly exploded when she realized what the Titan was planning to do. She snatched her helmet from the ground and slammed it over the neck of her skinsuit.

Keyv bit his lip, his face twisted. "Hector, I'm sorry…" He pounded a fist on the Titan's chest. "*Awaken Stars.*"

"We've reached the central chamber," said Amy Chip.

Keyv snatched his helmet and fastened it over his suit. Eve scampered into the cockpit and slammed into the pilot's seat. Keyv dropped into the shotgun chair. They both slapped grav belts over their shoulders.

"Depressurizing," Eve called, punching controls on the dash.

The cabin hissed as it began reducing pressure to zero.

She looked out the canopy glass, and saw the central chamber of the Floodgate for the first time. The magnitude of the chamber took her breath away. Even if the curved dome was a mere valve in the Slayer doomsday weapon, the size of it was mind-shattering. She felt like a piece of dust floating in a macroscopic world.

She flinched as Axel zipped past in his Cheetah before slowing next to them.

An alarm blared, and she tore her eyes to the rear bridge. The ship had finished depressurizing.

Hector punched the hatch controls, opening the ship to the outside. He grabbed Keyv's Fox by the arm and dragged it the opening. Leaning backward, the Titan kicked the antimatter bomb, sending it tumbling from the craft, sinking into the Floodgate's gravity.

He dragged the second Fox to the hatch, Eve's this time. "I'm going to detonate just before this thing sparks, give you guys as much time as possible."

Eve searched for words, but before she found them, the Titan hugged the Fox tightly in his arms, and leaped from the stealth craft, his fingers wrapped around the manual detonator.

"Eight minutes to ignition," Amy called.

Eve grunted and threaded *Midnight* through the labyrinth barrier, this time on the opposite side of the central chamber from where they'd entered.

"Four minutes to ignition," Amy called.

Eve zipped around plasma fire from a Slayer sentry station, corkscrewing and releasing anti-ordnance flares as Axel did what he could from his Cheetah. She moaned as they took fire, damaging the engines to eighty percent and slowing their speed.

She willed the thrusters to go faster as the plasma rounds faded behind them.

"One minute to ignition."

Axel called to them from the starspace outside the Floodgate. He said Allakai's fleet had left for safety through the rear portal. Eve ignored him. Keyv told him to take cover against the Floodgate hull and save himself.

Thirty seconds to ignition."

Eve could see a circle of stars ahead as they approached the end of the vent tunnel. A blinding flash of light erupted behind them. Her ship issued warnings of *unsafe ambient temperatures, entering emergency cooling now.*

Eve overrode the safety parameter and diverted full power to thrusters. Hector had detonated.

"Ten seconds to ignition."

They were almost there, the canvas of stars outnumbered the metal hull around them four to one.

"Five seconds."

"Three seconds."

"Ignition."

Eve shot from the vent and pulled hard starboard just as an enormous column of pure energy blasted from the Floodgate behind them.

The force from the blast sent her ship pin-wheeling. Eve's world flipped before her, over and over, a combination of stars, metal, and thick beams of light. The ship lurched as it corrected her trajectory and straightened out.

Now she saw just a single column of light. It pulsed from the Outer Rim Portal and into the inlet mouth of the Floodgate. She pulled away from the Floodgate to escape the resulting radiation.

Valves released energy as the massive device charged to full capacity in the Trituration process. The first side vents – the vents she had traveled into with the antimatter, were the first to go. Then the vents next to them erupted as the primary beam was fed through the valve system. The third set of vents released energy, and the fourth. After the tenth, the Floodgate was halfway finished with its charge.

"It didn't work," said Keyv. "The antimatter blast…the fruxing thing's still charging."

"No, it's not," said Amy Chip. "Look at the front two vents. The beam's diffracting."

Eve scanned the enormous structure, which in perspective had shrunk to the size of a watermelon as they distanced themselves from its hull. The vents released bright jets of radiation as the Floodgate smoothed its energy transfer. All the jets formed perfect, spindly lines. All but two.

The vents at either side of the central chamber were wavy, and a jagged crack had opened in the hull around them, leaking spider webs of light through the thick metal casing.

Then the front of the Floodgate shattered.

Large slabs of metal flew away from the structure as the energy beam from the Outer Rim portal chewed into the installation. The energy beam chipped away at the Floodgate, destroying the second and third sets of vents.

The beam from the Outer Rim, the beam sent by the Primal Snow straight from the Slayer home world, sputtered, then went out.

The starspace dimmed. The Floodgate now had a large gash at one end, the end closest to the Pristine waiting on the other side of the portal inside the Primal Snow.

It was ironic, Eve thought, that the Floodgate had been damaged just as they had planned, at the correct end. Except they had planned to sabotage it when the energy beam was moving in the opposite direction, towards the Primal Snow, not away from it.

They wouldn't destroy the Slayer home-world, not today. She wondered how much time she'd bought the rest of UCOM, across the galaxy, far from home. Twenty years? Fifty? One hundred?

Their comms cackled. "Eve? Keyv? Amy?" said Axel. "My Cheetah has damaged sensors. Are you alive?"

Amy appeared on the cockpit dash, and began to respond. Eve switched off communications.

"Why did you do that?" said Keyv.

Eve didn't respond. Instead, she engaged active camo, making *Midnight* invisible to the naked eye.

"Eve," said Amy slowly. "Axel's out there, I can see his Cheetah."

"Can you link to his servers?" said Eve.

Amy frowned. "Yes. But what does that have to do with…"

"Download to his ship," said Eve. "The portal to the Primal Snow is open. My home planet just left through that portal. I'm going to follow it. I'm not spending another century drifting in space."

Keyv coughed and cleared his throat. "Follow Sylva?" he said.

"I'm going home Keyv," said Eve. "I'm done with this war. I'm going to Sylva. If I show up to an empty planet, so be it."

Keyv's brow loosened. "I'll follow you there, you know that."

"What should I tell Axel?" said Amy. "Or Allakai? I'm not sure this is a good idea, you have no backup."

"Tell them I died with the Titans," said Eve. "I don't care. Hopefully I'll return. If the stars are good, I'll come back with Sylva in tow."

Amy licked her lips. "It's crazy." She shook her head. "Aye ma'am."

Her avatar vanished as she downloaded into Axel's Cheetah.

"Are you sure about this?" said Keyv. "We're heading into the Slayer nest. Even if Nancy is alive in there…" he let the thought hang.

Eve swallowed the acid in her mouth. "My entire species is almost gone. The Clones were nearly wiped out in the Frontline. I can't let my home drift out of sight and do nothing about it. Would you walk away from Earth?"

The question seemed to surprise Keyv, and his eyes widened before squinting in thought. "You're right. I'd go to Earth. To hell with the Slayers."

Eve smiled. For the first time in a very long time, her smile felt genuine, and an inkling of happiness trickled into her core.

The Outer Rim portal had shrunk back to normal size. She guided *Midnight* toward the glowing sphere, setting the nav-link vectors manually.

For better or for worse, she was going home.

Had she known what she would find after she passed the portal and arrived at the Primal Snow, she would have turned around and raced Axel back to Allakai's fleet.

ONE-HUNDRED-TWENTY-FOUR

Frank Scott – Human Destineer
Aboard Slayer Hive *Sylva* – Primal Snow starspace

Frank trembled as his pod arrived at the command bridge for the Sylvan Hive. The doors slid open to expose the spacious room, filled with holographic displays and intelligence stations. Twin launch tubes covered a section of the far wall. He wondered fleetingly how many beasts had been sent through the tubes to their death.

But he didn't rise from the transport cart to enter. He couldn't.

Timothy still had control of Frank's body. Or did he? His breathing felt normal, not like before when his chest rose and fell to the beat of Timothy's drum. He rolled his eyes around the inside of the pod. He was seeing double, but his eyes looked where he wanted them to. Not like when Timothy pointed his eyes for him, forcing him to watch as his feet carried him to places he did not want to go, and his hands picked up things he didn't want to touch.

Like when you grabbed Nancy by the throat, and shot her in the elbow?

No, it wasn't he who shot Nancy, it was Timothy. Frank was innocent in all this. All he wanted was to see the Sterilord. Was that so wrong?

It wasn't him, it was Timothy. But was there a difference any longer? Was Timothy now just another personality in his mind? Frank wondered if his drug history had made him schizophrenic. He began to wonder if Timothy was even real, or if he was imagining the whole ordeal.

He gave up after a few seconds. Thinking made the knives in his skull twist.

He tried to wiggle his toes, but they were numb. Timothy still had control. Or was Frank paralyzed?

Something had happened while he was inside the pod on his way to the bridge. He had been nervously reciting what he would say to Sid Dakota when they finally met, watching pod stations and terminals wiz past in streaky blurs. Then something surged through his body, as sudden and unexpected as a heart attack.

In fact, heart attack was exactly what Frank thought was happening to him. His chest burned and throbbed, and his head filled with air. He collapsed, fighting to stop the ground from spinning around him, convinced that two centuries of alcohol abuse had finally decided to collect its dues on his life.

But the reeling effects ended as quickly as they came. Every nerve ending from his spine to his fingertips erupted in waves of pleasure. The ground stopped spinning, and Frank moaned as his hips seized and jerked like a rodeo bull. An orgasm pulsed through him more powerful than all his many sexual encounters combined, shooting not from his groin, but from his chest.

"I love you Frank."

The Sterilord called to him. Pleasure continued to flood his body, and Frank gasped for breath, scratching his nails against the metal deck in ecstasy.

"I love you Frank, do you love me?"

"Yes," Frank whispered. "I love you so much. I want to see you more than anything."

"Come to me, Frank. Enter my kingdom."

The tsunami of pleasure dwindled to a tepid throb, then vanished entirely. His legs and arms were rubber, and Frank could do nothing but lay on the cold deck, trembling from the aftershock of the Sterilord's gift of bliss.

And now he had arrived at the main bridge, still in the same corner of the pod, his back nudged against the corner of the wall and the floor like a heap of dirty laundry.

Slarebull peered at him from the circular room. Frank glanced at them, but not for long. He became distracted by the panoramic window wrapped around the walls, curving over the top of the ten-meter ceiling.

He'd made it. The Primal Snow hung before them in the distance, vast and more majestic than he could have possibly imagined.

The Slarebull home world, no the *Pristine* home world, was a collection of golden spheres. Their light was not harsh, but elegant, shimmering against the starry backdrop like a chandelier. There were millions of golden orbs, maybe billions. Thin strands of energy connected them in perfect geometries, combining to form a massive cluster, an oval matrix of dots.

At the center of the matrix sat a larger, brighter sphere. This sphere was not golden, but the purest white, stark and pristine. It was the energy source for the Primal Snow, the combined power of the many galaxies they'd consumed.

Tears blurred his vision as Frank stared into the kingdom of the Pristine.

"*We're here,*" said Timothy, his voice a mere whisper in the back of Frank's mind. "*We've reached salvation.*"

Frank took a deep breath, and pushed himself to his knees. Or was it Timothy who raised his body to a standing position? The lines were blurred. He decided Timothy was no longer a hijacker, but an embodied presence, another brain perhaps. They were a team now, two personalities with the same goal – to transcend from mortals to gods.

Frank wiped his glistening forehead with his sleeve. He turned his hand over, and wiggled his fingers under his own control. He and Timothy were now one and the same, companions in a campaign of destiny.

He scanned the bridge. The Slarebull had yet to approach. A few of them turned to the leader for instruction, who was dressed in colorful red armor. He wondered briefly if he should be fearful of the mighty beasts who'd ravaged his old UCOM allies at the Frontline, but fear never came. The Beasts were not his enemies, they were his allies. They served the Pristine, and soon, Frank would become part of the same order of Slarebull social elite.

Soon the Beasts would serve him.

Sid Dakota was nowhere to be seen, nor any Humans for the matter. Sid would surely arrive soon, and together they would enter the kingdom.

Frank began to exit the pod, when suddenly Humans did appear on the bridge. They didn't appear from the main entrance, which was large and to the left of his pod, two double doors of translucent glass. They appeared from the pod bay, exiting from a cart beside his.

He choked when he saw who the Humans were.

Two Slarebull escorted Nancy Woods into the bridge, along with Caseus, Lindsey, and the new guy, Chase Grover.

Frank wondered why two Slarebull had escorted Nancy's crew to the bridge, when the Beasts he encountered along the way told him explicitly they were not authorized to enter the command deck.

He wondered where the hell Sid Dakota was. Frank knew if Nancy saw him, she would shoot him dead on sight, right in the very pod he stood.

Nancy would kill him, or perhaps Hunter would first.

Hunter.

His eyes widened as fire filled his spine and acid raised the hairs on his neck. Where was the Titan warrior? Had he stayed behind onboard the Night Eagle? No, that would be foolish. Frank's stomach turned as he came to a sudden realization.

"Titan," he screamed to the Slarebull. "There's a UCOM Titan in here, hidden. *Kill him.*"

He poked his head from the pod cautiously, groping his arms before him, searching for the camouflaged android.

The red-armored Slarebull captain powered towards Nancy's group and grabbed one of the Slarebull escorts by the throat. "Is this true?" he roared. "Did you lead an electric demon here?"

The subordinate Beast didn't reply, and merely cowered before the captain.

"What are you waiting for?" Frank screamed, hugging the inside wall of the pod, imagining an invisible sword thrusting through his stomach at any second. "There's a fruxing Titan in here, kill him!"

Hunter appeared before the words had finished leaving his mouth. But the Titan wasn't leaping towards Frank in a stealthy attack. The Titan was on his back, struggling against two Cogent in yellow armor, who materialized at the same time as Hunter.

Hunter roared as he bucked against the Slayer elite, thrusting his sword through the leg of one as he blocked repeated blows from the tail of the other. Four more hidden Cogent appeared from across the room and dropped to all fours, racing towards the struggling threesome.

"Stop," Nancy cried, running towards Hunter. "Let him go, I command you."

But the Cogent paid her no attention. They were not to harm any Humans, but electric demons were still enemies of the Pristine.

Hunter blasted a hole into one of the Cogent with his laser cannon, sending the Beast spiraling to the side, a smoky crater in his gut. The second

Cogent landed a crushing blow on the Titan soon after, crumpling the weak joint at the elbow of his Akimor, spraying liquid sparks across the deck.

The four additional Cogent reached the Titan, and began attacking with their tails, bludgeoning him with their reinforced armored bone clusters. A fifth Cogent appeared, this one holding an energy hammer. The Cogent unleashed a primal shriek as he swung the hammer down on Hunter's head.

The resulting crunch silenced the room. Hunter went limp as a pool of fluid leaked from his neck in a wide puddle.

Nancy screamed and slid to her knees beside the fallen warrior, placing both hands on his chest.

Frank laughed, causing Nancy to look in his direction.

Grief vanished from her face, replaced by a murderous glare. Her lip twitched, and her mouth turned to a snarl.

Frank laughed harder, unable to contain his glee. He continued to laugh even as Nancy slid her rifle forward on its strap, fumbling her shattered arm over the stock in search of the trigger.

The Cogent stopped her from raising the weapon. Their orders, after all, were to stop any harm from coming to Humans.

Frank shrieked with glee, planting both hands on his knees to steady his heaving chest as two Cogent moved before him, protecting him from Caseus, Lindsey, and Chase Grover, who had raised their own rifles.

Then the entrance doors opened, the translucent glass disappearing into the walls.

Frank's laughter turned into sobs of joy.

Sid Dakota entered the bridge, dressed in battle armor and followed by an army of Destineers.

ONE-HUNDRED-TWENTY-FIVE

Nancy Woods – Human

Aboard Slayer Hive *Sylva* – Primal Snow starspace

Frank. That fruxing psychopath was laughing as if she'd told the universe's funniest joke. That spineless bag of Hog shit, smiling his movie star smile as he watched the plot unfold of someone else's movie. Frank the liar. Frank the traitor. Frank the monster.

Frank, who'd always been around, but never contributed to anything except money to the nearest bar or brothel. The pathetic weakling, who couldn't think for himself, so he let Sid Dakota think for him. Who let his mind be poisoned even further than what the lines of lightning, bottles of pappy's, and scores of Clone hookers had already done. Or maybe Timothy was the one whispering sweet nothings into Frank's ear.

It made no difference. Frank's mind was weak.

She trembled as she stared at him. Frank, her old love. Frank, the man she couldn't leave, and secretly didn't want to.

Frank the murderer.

Frank the Destineer.

Nancy screamed and lashed at the Cogent as he relieved her of her rifle. She kicked his armored shins and threw her shoulder against his thighs, wrestling for control of her weapon.

It may as well have been a mouse trying to fight the Slayer warrior.

Her ears split as her finger hooked around the trigger when the beast yanked the weapon away, drowning the room in a few seconds of thunder as the rifle discharged.

The Cogent recoiled when three slugs bit through the armor in his shoulder. He growled and spiked the rifle into the deck, splintering it into composite shards and spilling battery fluid from its stock.

The Slayer's neck sacs expanded as the creature spoke, using the disgusting bags of flesh to talk the same way frogs called for mates on Earth.

Nancy couldn't hear what he said. The gun had gone off inches from her ear, and all she could hear was chimes.

She slumped back to her knees, planting a hand on Hunter's chest. The armor was still warm from seconds ago, when the Titan had been alive. Hunter had protected her for more than a century, and now he was dead, no more than a bucket of bolts with legs and arms.

Who would protect her now?

Frank was passing nearby. He'd left his pod, and now instead of laughing, he was crying with a smile on his face.

Frank the psycho.

He walked between two Cogent towards the far side of the bridge. She spun on her knees to follow him, and moaned when she saw who he bowed before.

Sid Dakota smiled and told Frank to rise, which he did. The Slayer crew had bowed as well, and they stayed with their heads against the floor, tails flat against the deck. The Slayers bowed to Sid as if he were a god, but Nancy knew better.

Sid was nothing more than a leach, a parasite that stripped UCOM's military of ships and soldiers, and led them on a death march across the galaxy under the badge of destiny.

Yet the Slayers bowed to him. Something about the image roiled her stomach more than if the Slayers had disemboweled her with their claws.

If she acted now, she could still kill him. She could sprint around his Destineer guards and slip her hands under his helmet and strangle him. Or perhaps she could steal the pistol from his thigh plate and thrust it into the fleshy part of his neck between his jaw, and splatter his brains across the glass ceiling.

Caseus, Lindsey, and Chase were on their knees as well, their backs to her. Their weapons were in pieces around them just like her rifle, battery fluid combining to form splotches of orange against the deck, like a giant insect that got stepped on.

The Slayers were still bowed to the floor. The Destineers were all behind Sid, staring through the windows into space.

The Primal Snow shined through the glass walls and ceiling of the Hive bridge. It was beautiful. She could admit that much, like honey dew caught in an enormous spider web stretched across the space vacuum. Like a fish at the bottom of the ocean, dangling a tantalizing morsel of light in the darkness to attract prey before chomping down with razor teeth.

She leaped to her feet and sprinted towards Sid Dakota.

ONE-HUNDRED-TWENTY-SIX

Sid Dakota – Human Destineer

Aboard Slayer Hive *Sylva* – Primal Snow starspace

Frank Scott climbed back to his feet. His prize. Sid's visions had been correct, as usual.

Nancy Woods would bestow upon him a great gift.

She'd been true to him, transporting Frank all the way across the Milky Way to him. What the Sterilord wanted with the man, Sid didn't know, and didn't particularly care. As long as his holy destiny was complete, he would assume his new identity as a god, and live for eternity in the kingdom of the Pristine.

He stared at the Primal Snow. The kingdom sat somewhere in those golden spheres, each of which Sid knew represented a different habitable planet the Pristine had collected.

The Universe is a bounty existing for Human's to reap.

The Sterilord lived in the Primal Snow. Soon Sid would live with him, sharing the riches of the universe with the holy…

Pain.

Shards of pain in his crotch turned to sledgehammers of agony, and forced him to his knees. A blur of blonde hair whipped before his face as a woman reached for the pistol on his thigh.

Nancy.

Sid tried to stop her, but she was too quick, quicker than Humans normally moved. She grabbed the handle of his plasma pistol and wrenched it from its magnetic plate. He fumbled to catch her wrists, but she ducked under him.

A wrenching agony drowned the shrill whine of the pistol as it discharged into his abdomen. He shrieked and swiped the back of his hand downward.

His armor doubled his strength, and sent a crushing blow into Nancy's shoulder. She crumpled to the ground, the pistol skipping across the floor before sliding to rest against the foot of a Slarebull soldier.

His men shouted behind him. Footsteps thundered to his right, and he caught the shapes of a struggle in his peripheral vision as his Destineer faithful subdued the men Nancy had arrived with. Sid paid them no mind.

"You arrived," he whispered, pressing a hand into his stomach. The armor was hot and smoky beneath his gloved hand.

Nancy panted on her side, her eyes rolling weakly in their sockets. "You'll never win," she rasped. "You think the Slayers actually want to help you?"

Her arms trembled as she pushed herself into a seated position. Sid strode to her and grabbed a fistful of her hair, lifting her from the ground until her face was inches from his own.

"I've already won," he whispered into her ear. His eyes found the man across the room, still huddled inside his pod. The man from his visions. "You brought me my gift. My use for you has ended."

"Frank?" she coughed. "You're more hopeless than I thought."

She spit in his face.

A hot wad of saliva caught his teeth, and he sucked away the bloody phlegm with his lips, grimacing. He raised Nancy another foot into the air and slammed her onto the deck hard enough to hear her bones crunch against the metal floor. She went motionless.

"Tie her up," Sid ordered, turning to his men.

"Yes, Father," said his one of his disciples, rushing forward to Nancy.

He wanted to speak with her before she died, say a few parting words to the last remaining UCOM filth before he entered the kingdom.

Sid reached again to his stomach. The burn had stopped smoking. His belly armor was blackened, and a few spots of red poked between the shielding like rubbed meat. He'd live. His scars would be a token reminder of his days as a mere mortal.

He gazed upon the rest of Nancy's crew. A black man struggled against three of his Destineers, who had wrestled him to his knees. A frail girl trembled on her stomach, pinned against the deck by one of his men, who had his knee planted into the small of her back.

And there was a third man, next to the girl. He struggled against the four Destineers harder even than the black man. His eyes were wild, and flecks of spit flew from his curled lips as he threw his weight against his captors.

Sid knew the man well.

The pain in his stomach vanished into an intense ball of hatred.

"You," he growled, striding to the man. "You unholy smear of SIGA *dirt*."

ONE-HUNDRED-TWENTY-SEVEN

Chase Grover – Half Human/Half Clone
Aboard Slayer Hive *Sylva* – Primal Snow starspace

Chase clamped his jaws shut so hard he drew blood from around his molars. He thrashed harder against the men holding him as Sid Dakota approached.

"You kill my men," Sid said, his voice growing into a shout. "You fight alongside non-believers, you protect the filth of the universe, and now," Sid grabbed hold of him. "Now you will die."

Chase choked as Sid clamped his armored hand around his neck. He sucked in a ragged breath, a high-pitched whistle as air squeaked through the tiny opening in his throat. The guards released his arms, but all he could do was slap Sid's forearms weakly as the motors in his suit lifted Chase from the ground with superhuman strength.

His toes scuffed the deck as Sid dragged him across the bridge, towards the windows at the far side. His vision started to go red as his brain screamed for oxygen. He grunted as Sid hurled him against the wall, his face thudding against the thick glass. He rolled from his back and onto his knees, punching the space before him as hard as he could.

The bones in his hand broke against the metal in Sid's suit and his world turned to flashing stars. There was a hiss of air, then Chase was airborne.

He landed in a heap. The flashes of white and yellow receded from his vision as he blinked away his pain. He was inside a short glass tunnel. His heart sank as he realized where he was.

The glass door slid shut, sealing Chase into the launch tube. A smear of blood covered the bottom half of the door from where his nose had shattered against the hatch. Sid breathed heavily on the other side, his chest rising in rapid bursts.

"I would enjoy torturing you," said Sid, his voice muted. Chase wished the launch tube had drowned his voice entirely. "I would savor every second of pulling your finger nails from your body, slicing your skin from your flesh, and roasting you slowly over a flame."

Chase struggled to his knees and crawled towards the demon before him, inching closer to the man who had forced his family and loved ones into hiding for the past two centuries. He had nothing to say to Sid Dakota. He had tried his best, and this was the end for him. He just wanted to look him in the eyes before he died. He wanted the hatred on his face to be burned into the man's brain for an eternity.

"Yes," Sid continued, sinking to a knee. "I would torture you, but in the essence of time, I'll let the space vacuum do the work for me. I hear it's painful, dying in space."

Chase reached the glass of the inside hatch. He swooned in pain and exhaustion, his forehead thunking against the door. Fresh knives exploded in his head.

He thought of Mae. He thought of his father. He thought of Jimmy, and the rest of the cave-dwelling family he'd pledged his life to defend. His life would soon end. Did the rest of the SIGA civilians make it to the shelter? Had the firewater breached the seal?

"First you'll gasp for breath," Sid continued. "But soon oxygen will be the least of your worries. Your blood will cook, and then boil. Your eyes will shrink into prunes. Some say it takes as long as eight minutes for you to die. For you, I pray it takes longer."

Chase slapped his broken hand against the glass before Sid's face. He took a final breath. "Awaken stars."

Sid's nose twitched, then he pounded his palm to the side of the inside hatch. The outside hatch opened with a bang, then silence as the air disappeared, and Chase was sucked into the vacuum at hundreds of kilometers per hour.

ONE-HUNDRED-TWENTY-EIGHT

Eve – Clone

Onboard Night Eagle *Midnight* – Primal Snow starspace

"Holy shit this thing is big," said Keyv, pouring over the scan data from his station aboard *Midnight.* "More ships than our computers can count, and that's not including the planets."

"Those things are actually planets?" said Eve, leaning over Keyv's shoulder.

"Spectral readings are confirming habitable planets, millions of them, maybe billions. It will take hours for our scanners to consolidate the intel. Those beams of light connecting them are some sort of energy source."

"Any chatter?"

"Tons of it." Keyv squinted at strings of data filing beside the holographic scans of the Pristine home world. "Not that we can process any of it. I can divert our servers towards crunching the chatter, but then our 3D models would go on standby."

"Don't stop the 3D scans. Limit chatter processing to the keywords 'Pristine', and 'Destineer'. We need to get a map of their forces so we can figure out how to take this thing down."

Keyv leaned back in his seat to face her. "Take down the Primal Snow? With one Night Eagle?"

Eve didn't respond.

Keyv shrugged and manipulated the controls, setting the search parameters.

"How about Sylva?" said Eve.

"That one's a little easier," said Keyv. "I have a successful connection to a Night Eagle, *Eclipse.* Our credentials allowed us to download the ship's public server content. I have docking coordinates, and a ship log. Last activity was over an hour ago. No one's answered our hails yet so it must be deserted. Eve, I think Nancy made it onboard."

Eve released a shaky breath and left the station to gaze out the starboard viewing window. Her home planet hung elegantly before them, ensnared in the massive cradle arms of the Slayer Hive towing it slowly forward. She wondered if her family was still alive on the surface. She dismissed the thought. Hope was poisonous in these dark times. She could only suffer so much disappointment.

"Plot our vectors to Nancy's ship," she said. "We'll board *Eclipse* and use that as our insertion point to the Hive. With any luck, we'll be able to rally with Nancy onboard. If the stars are good, she has a plan to commandeer."

"And after we commandeer the Hive?" said Keyv.

Eve pressed her head against the window, searching for answers to unknown questions. "I don't know Keyv, we'll haul ass back to Allakai's fleet and save my planet. Or maybe we'll head toward the Primal Snow and launch a sneak attack."

"Sneak attack?" said Keyv. "Is that a good idea?"

She whirled from the window to face Keyv. "No. It's a shitty idea. We'll probably die. What do you want to do, sit on the floor and sing Kumbaya while the Slayers blast us to shreds?"

Keyv gulped. "I'm sorry, I'm just scared, alright? Is that okay? Stars, you're not the only one at wits end here."

After a few moments of silence, he rose from his station to join Eve at the viewing window. He wrapped an arm around her and gave a gentle squeeze.

"I'm the one who should be sorry, Keyv," she whispered. "You don't deserve me. I'm just, I'm done. I have nothing left. UCOM should have sent a different commander out here, I'm not cut out for this."

Keyv pulled her close, and she smelled the musk of his neck. The first tears blotted into his skinsuit, and then the gates opened and she began to sob.

They stood that way for awhile. Maybe it was for a few minutes, maybe it was for an eternity. When they drew apart, Keyv's face was as wet as her own.

"Three-hundred forty-six," he said, blinking his eyes dry. "I guess I can't complain too much about a life span like that. Better men than me lived a fourth that on Earth before the Guardians came and stirred up all this shit."

She cut him off with a firm kiss. His lips were tight at first, then loosened. Her pain vanished, and for a moment she felt like she was back at the Inner Ring, just after the Frontline. Before Woods sent her towards the Outer Rim. Back when she'd still had hope. The brief window of time when she'd been able to lead some semblance of a real life, splashing water on Keyv at Earth's beaches, and cuddling with him in a bed planted firmly on planetary topsoil. The blip in her existence when she didn't have to wear armor, or carry a sidearm, or worry about a Slayer missile tearing her ship in half.

And then an alarm blared.

She whipped her head towards the intelligence station. "Spacnar?"

Keyv rushed to his seat. "No, camo is at one hundred percent, no spacnar readings, active or passive. It's…"

He shook his head and squinted closer at the holodeck.

"What?" she cried.

"It's the safety rescue net."

Eve's stomach fluttered, then dropped. The safety rescue net sent an emergency signal to crew if it detected a body drifting in starspace. During battle, the surrounding vacuum became littered with bodies as ships were destroyed, and the alarms were silenced. But they weren't in battle, not yet at least. "There's a man overboard? Out here?"

Keyv nodded. "I got him right here. Not Slayer, Human. He's in the vacuum right outside Sylva."

"Alive?"

"It's possible. His heat signature doesn't rule it out."

"Go to him. He might be our only friend within a hundred light years."

ONE-HUNDRED-TWENTY-NINE

Chase Grover – Half Human/Half Clone
Suspended in vacuum – Primal Snow starspace

Chase screamed. At least, he would have screamed if sound could travel in a vacuum, or if his lungs were still filled with air.

Instead his face twisted in silent agony. His chest felt like a hunk of lead, and his veins were both on fire and frozen at the same time. He felt a pop in both arms, and in the back of his mind knew his body had ballooned past the limits of the fabric in his shirt. The Sylvan Hive spiraled around him as he plummeted through space, growing wavy and distorted as tears evaporated from under his lids and his veins bubbled in his sockets.

His thoughts were nonexistent. He could only feel the pain. He had a brief moment of clarity as his body pumped adrenaline and neurochemicals into his brain to stifle the agony. He used these fleeting moments to curse the nanotechnology in his body for keeping him artificially alive.

By all rights, he should have died minutes ago. Instead he'd slowly roasted, his body melting into a solid hunk of organic goo as his veins exploded from prolonged ebullism.

Mae had raised him to pray to the stars. It was the stars that held all life, and it was the stars that would welcome him upon his death.

The stars had cursed him. He wondered if the religious old-timers had it right. He wasn't entering the stars. He was entering the fiery pits of Hell.

Strange forces tugged on his body. His joints screamed, cutting through the blanket of sedatives drowning his brain. A bright light appeared before him. Perhaps he would enter Heaven after all, after a brief visit to purgatory. Follow the light, as the old-timers would say.

Faces appeared before the light, looking down on him. The faces were dark and shapeless. Was it his mother who stood over him, welcoming him to the afterlife? Or was it his father? Was it Jimmy?

The faces spoke to him. Sound couldn't travel in space, so surely he was somewhere else, somewhere people could talk. His head popped, and his vision returned, then his hearing.

Chase screamed. He could hear himself roar in agony, and also feel the vibrations from his shouts shatter his temples. The faces took form. It wasn't his mother who leaned over him, nor was it his father. The faces were foreign. One was a light-skinned male with dark hair. The other was a bronzed female, slender cheeked, with violet eyes and dark hair streaked with pink.

He moaned and sucked in a hoarse lungful of air. Why was the afterlife so painful? He glanced at his bare chest. Floating instruments stuck from between his ribs in various shades of light. He tried to move his arms, but they too were covered with instruments. He was a Human pin-cushion.

"His vitals are low," said the male, raising a syringe.

Chase hardly felt the prick in his throat, but moaned in relief as warmth spread through his body and extinguished the pain. He wasn't in the netherworlds. He was in a starship.

"Does he need a heart transplant?" said the female.

"Maybe," said the male. "I got it beating again, but the walls are ruptured. We'll at least have to grow him new arteries. He's leaking like a sieve. It takes a few hours to grow a heart, but he should make it till then."

"Put a sample of his blood into the regen kit," said the girl. "Get him started on a new heart, and all new organs. Focus on the brain for now. The medbot can do the surgery after we get him stable."

"He has midrange trauma on the frontal lobes. The rest of his brain suffered severe oxygen depletion, but his Program kept the gears running fine for the most part. Spinal cord is OK. This guy's one lucky bastard."

"Keep an eye on his wave patterns," said the girl. "If they start to spike or fall we're going to have to freeze him."

Chase's body jostled as the two strangers worked medical equipment over his body. His chest depressed, then inflated.

"The new lungs took," said the male. "I'm sucking out the old ones to convert to stem cells. We'll need them, with the amount of tissue we need to replace. He's going to be a whole new man if he lives."

"Work cream over his whole body," said the girl. "Cut off his genitals, they're gone. We'll grow him new stuff if there's enough bio-matter."

Chase screamed and writhed on the deck. He tried to talk but his lips were wrapped around a metal tube.

"Snip his parts?" cried the male. "Christ, we may as well shoot him."

"Fine," said the girl. "The thing looks like a hunk of driftwood, but if you want to rub cream on it, be my guest."

Chase winced as a wire of pain shot from the tip of his manhood into his stomach and down his legs. The male leaned forward until his lips were in Chase's ear.

"You owe me one, pal," the man whispered.

"I can't find any credentials on him," said Eve. "His base ID comes up from his Program – Chase Grover, half Human, half Clone. No UCOM military tags, just something called SIGA."

"SIGA, is that Destineer?" said the male. "Why the hell are we even reviving him, let's send him back to space."

Chase screamed again, his throat scratching against the tube. He tried to reach a hand to the life-saving instrument, but the medical robots held him prostrate on the deck, and he doubted his muscles were strong enough to lift themselves regardless.

"He's trying to say something," said the male. "Should I wait until he recovers? Maybe we should put him to sleep until he heals more."

"No, he can't be unconscious after what just happened to his brain. It looks like his lungs are ready for him to breathe on his own."

Chase choked as the tube dislodged from his throat, trailing a bloody rope of mucous. The female wiped his mouth clean.

"Nuh Destinee-uh," he managed. "SIG-UH."

He racked several deep coughs, swooning his vision into a vicious spiral.

"SIGA?" said the girl. "Are you friends to UCOM?"

Chase tried to nod. "OO-COM...Ancy Woos…frenn."

His two rescuers share a surprised look with one another.

"You've seen Nancy?" said the female.

"Where?" said the male. "In the Hive?"

Chase nodded weakly and tried to swallow the sand in his throat. "Ancy, in the bridge. Itan…dead."

He coughed and the sand in his throat vanished beneath a film of gore.

"Hunter," murmured the male. "He's dead?"

Chase couldn't respond. He blinked instead.

The female placed a shaky hand on Chase's chest. "My name's Eve, I'm a Clone UCOM stealth commander. You're part Clone. Were you on the surface of Sylva?"

Again, Chase blinked his eyes.

"Rest," said the Eve. "We're looking for Nancy. As soon as your body's stable, you're going to take us to her."

Chase closed his eyes. His skin tingled over the aches and throbs of his insides as nanobots worked to mend his trauma.

He drifted into a pleasant cushion of clouds as the painkillers kneaded his ravaged tissue. But through the fluffiness, a needle of dread wormed through his conscious. He tried not to picture Nancy Woods, laying crumpled against the deck of the Hive bridge. Sid had ejected him from the launch tubes. What would he do to her?

Nancy Woods. Eve and her companion wanted to search for her, but he feared that they would arrive to find nothing but a corpse. He decided it didn't matter. Wherever Nancy was, Sid was sure to be nearby. Chase had a lifetime of vengeance to exact on Sid whenever he met him again. If he ever met him again.

When he'd led his SIGA troops in guerrilla attacks against the Destineers, the thought of UCOM one day arriving to help in his desperate attempt at survival had kept him going. It had given him willpower, and kept him forging ahead. It allowed him to keep his head high and remain strong even after his countrymen were killed one by one in battle. The thought of UCOM had given him hope.

UCOM had come, but too late and with too few ships. He thought of Mae, trapped underground. Tears streamed down his cheeks from his medically lubricated eyes.

He'd lost everything. Sid Dakota had taken everything.

Nancy Woods.

He'd help Eve find her alright, but finding her would mean certain death. He prayed he would have enough time to kill Sid before the stars finally took him to see his long dead parents.

Nancy Woods.

Nancy had told him of her father, the Human leader of the Milky Way, during their brief time together. Francis Woods led UCOM forces at the Inner Ring, a place Chase should call home but was never given the chance.

Chase had failed his people, unable to protect them when they needed him most. He wondered if Francis Woods would be better able to protect his own.

Chase's mother had sacrificed her life to safe his. His father had martyred himself to save Sylva. Now, it was his turn to become a martyr.

He wasn't fearful of death anymore. He welcomed it. Now, he had a chance to take Sid's life, to send the Destineer into the abyss as he rose to the stars. He pictured his mother's smiling face, and imagined hugging his father for the first time.

He wondered if when he arrived, Francis Woods would be waiting for him. He would shake the Human leader's hand, two men who had fought to their deaths defending their civilizations.

But the thought jerked at his heartstrings, and he shoved it to the darkest recesses of his mind.

He prayed he wouldn't have a chance to shake Wood's hand in the stars. He prayed he would look down from the heavens as Woods destroyed the monsters who had destroyed him.

ONE-HUNDRED-THIRTY

Francis Woods – Human

Onboard Tiger *Mariella* – Approaching Inner Ring starspace

"The Slayer Triturator is the key! The installation will not be stopped. Its immense cogs will turn, and must. UCOM's light must kindle the enemy machine. An inferno must rage before it is extinguished. HEED MY WORDS. Follow the light."

Francis Woods replayed the message from Casi Vomisa's proxy, Eris, for the thousandth time in his head. Stew, Cage, and the rest of his staff had been tirelessly pouring over strategy for when they reached the Inner Ring, but he hadn't been able to think of anything but Eris' cryptic message.

And Casi Vomisa's stark warning.

He had tried to re-enter his vision, to gaze upon the Floodgate, to see the Hive mothership that his daughter was currently inside of. A part of him wanted to see Nancy's face again. But mainly he wanted to hear the Voice. He wanted the Sterilord to tell him he would be able to save his daughter's life, and that everything would be okay.

"You need to control your visions, Francis. They're not good for your mind. They weaken your soul."

Casi Vomisa's stern words of caution echoed in his cluttered mind, sending a fresh set of shivers down his spine. He rubbed his temples. His brain felt like a yarn ball of nerve endings. He shook the jumbled thoughts from his head and focused on the holograms before him in *Mariella's* war room.

"Are you okay sir?"

He turned to find Stew Kwelm standing beside him.

"You look distant," said the Intellect scientist, blinking his inner eyelids. "There's a med bay nearby. You can take stimulants before we enter the Inner Ring. We have enough time."

Woods turned and glanced through the glass ceiling of the room to survey his Loyalist fleet. His ships were still in travel formation behind *Mariella*. Turning forward, a portal loomed large, ready to admit his armada into Inner Ring starspace.

"No thanks Stew," he said, returning his attention to his chief engineer. "I'll be fine. What's the latest on Charles?"

"Last Raven sighting was eight portals back," said Stew. "The APEX has just started to leave Templar."

"How many Raven's haven't returned?"

Stews eyes darted to the deck and he clicked his beak. "All but the one from Templar. About two million."

"Then we'll have to assume Charles is right on our tail. How about UCOM forces at the Inner Ring? Have we established an order of command?"

"No change," said Stew. "*Warhammer's* still dark, and we only have friendly pledges from ten percent of total fleet forces. No word from Draxton Tyke."

Woods nodded. "Thank you Stew. Have you thought about Eris's instructions?"

"On sparking the Triturator?" The Intellect nodded. "I have a few ideas. I'm still running simulations. We'll need to convert an enormous amount of energy in order to manipulate the device. Our fleet energy output is too scattered. We may need to utilize the Inner Ring's defense tower."

"Warhammer," murmured Woods. "Which we've lost communications with."

Stew nodded. "We may have a way around the lack of communications. We would need to use our Titans."

"How so?"

Woods listened as the Intellect skimmed through his plan. He frowned and rubbed his temples. The plan would be a long shot. "Catalog your strategy and have Blaze upload it into a mission dossier."

"Yes sir," said Stew, leaving for one of the holo-decks across the war room.

Woods walked to join the rest of his team at the main holodeck. Cage and Zena were reviewing a set of holograms portraying known UCOM Inner Ring forces. Bear and Blackthorne were huddled together on the opposite side of the table, discussing what appeared to be Titan formations of Cheetah squadrons. Blackthorne shifted his MGK rifle before him and checked its magazine before slapping it over his shoulder and onto his magnetic back plate.

"We ready to head through?" said Cage as he noticed Woods approach, rising from the holodeck. "I'm getting antsy waiting here in no-man's land."

"Is it safe to head into the Inner Ring?" said Zena, biting her lip. "We still don't know if UCOM will attack or not."

"But we know the Slayers will," said Woods. "And soon, based on the chatter. They'll come pouring in by the millions to a decimated UCOM armada. I'll be damned if I hang our boys out to dry."

Heavy silence.

"I'll head down to the bridge then," said Cage. "You sure you don't need me up here?"

Woods shook his head. "I need you down on the bridge running *Mariella.* This is our command ship. The men are scared. When the Slayers attack, we're going to lead the charge into battle."

"Heading the front lines with our lead ship?" said Zena Olleeve. "Isn't it wise to stay in the rear? It will be much easier to strategize if we're not in the middle of a scrum."

"You may as well ask him to paint his nails pink," said Cage. "Don't let him get started on William Wallace."

"William Wallace?" said Zena. "Is this another one of his ancient war examples from Earth? We're fighting battles in outer space, not on the backs of horses."

"Enough," said Woods. "Cage, get down to the bridge. Zena and Stew, I need you here in the war room with me."

Cage saluted before crossing the room to the exit hatch. The doors glided open and he disappeared into the command bridge."

"Blaze," Woods called.

"Aye," said Blaze, appearing atop a nearby pedestal.

"Send travel vectors to the Inner Ring fleetwide via navlink. Tell our ships to flash signs of surrender to UCOM as we enter."

"Yes sir."

The AI vanished from the room.

Woods leaned against the central holodeck of the war room and stared out the panoramic windows at the portal looming large before their ship. Status alarms bleeped and blipped at him as the rest of the Loyalist fleet readied for passage.

He winced as a bullet of sweat caught in his eye, and wiped his face, sending a smatter of drops onto the holodeck. The holograms became distorted for a few seconds before the table burned off the moisture and returned the 3D models of ships and defense vectors to their proper shapes.

Eris was still propped in her chair on a patch of empty deck space. She hadn't said another word since her last episode. He wished there was a way to wake her up. Perhaps she could only talk when Charles was near.

The thought sent his stomach into knots.

Blaze's avatar appeared before him. "The Loyalist fleet is in position," she said.

He cast a final glance to the portal. "Move out."

The walls transformed into a 360 degree view of *Mariella's* surroundings as Blaze made his ship battle ready. Woods looked below his feet, which now appeared to stand on an invisible shelf above thousands of ships traveling in formation below *Mariella's* hull. Flashes of light swallowed their hulls as his Loyalist fleet fired their thrusters toward their final destination.

The Inner Ring.

ONE-HUNDRED-THIRTY-ONE

Francis Woods – Human

Aboard Tiger *Mariella* – Dominia starspace

Woods squinted as his ship passed through the portal, filling the war room with a green glow. After a few seconds, they were through.

Zena gasped. Stew clicked his beak. The Titans remained motionless.

UCOM's sprawling armada was fully weaponized.

To the left, the Slayer-held portal to the Inner Ring hung fat against the blackness, surrounded by a sphere of destroyers in containment formation.

To the right sat the portal superhighway – thousands of portals spaced evenly apart to form a thick belt, twenty portals high, and five portals deep, a long row disappearing into points in the distance. The nearest portals outlined the vast hull of *Warhammer*, the primary defense tower. Beside *Warhammer* sat the planet *Gefangnia*.

Dominia sat a few thousand kilometers away from the defense tower, protected by four PDR's and a cocoon of Tiger heavy-destroyers.

Fourteen sun beams sliced through Inner Ring starspace from every direction, connecting a network of standalone PDR's to thick beams of pure energy from faraway suns.

Between the gargantuan machines of weaponry, millions of UCOM ships sat in formation. All of them had their lattice shields charged, turning the black backdrop into a dazzling array of electricity. All of them had their RACAN's and missiles trained on the lone Slayer portal.

"We're being hailed by ninety squadrons," Blaze cried from her pedestal. "Thousands more ships are hailing for comm links, and even more are sending distress signals."

"Put me through to universal comms," said Woods. "I want the men to see my face."

Thousands of gridded lines of light fanned over him as Blaze transformed his body into a digital avatar to display on the command bridges of the entire Loyalist fleet, as well as the UCOM armada.

A few of the nearby UCOM ships rotated to face them, turning their cannon arrays in the direction of the incoming Loyalists.

"We have attack locks from three hundred Tigers and counting," Blaze cried. "Should I divert energy to shields?"

"Keep them low," said Woods. "Keep flashing signs of surrender."

One of the UCOM Tigers fired a warning shot in their direction. Several of his Loyalist ships charged their RACAN batteries against orders.

"Stand down," Woods roared, his command instantly patched to every command bridge in the Loyalist fleet. "These are our brothers, not our enemies."

The Loyalist ships dimmed as their RACAN's de-energized.

"Hail *Warhammer,*" said Woods, turning to face Blaze directly. "I want Draxton Tyke on comms now."

"*Warhammer's* in radio silence," said Blaze.

"I've patched together a running theme with chatter and hail requests," called Stew from across the room. "There are twelve separate chains of command, all operating independently from one another. Draxton Tyke has been officially marked as a deserter. UCOM has zero communication or functionality with *Warhammer.*"

Woods turned to look aft. The portal they'd traveled through was now a dot in the distance. Most of his fleet had made it through and were in formation behind him. He spun around to check the holodeck and confirm numbers.

"I'm going to make a central broadcast," he said, eyeing the UCOM fleet. The initial aggressor ships still had their guns trained on his fleet, but most were still turned to the Slayer portal. The armada was in obvious need of command oversight. "Patch me through in five, no encryptions."

"Aye," said Blaze.

A blue light began to blink before him. After five seconds it turned red.

He straightened his back and puffed his chest. "This is Eminence Francis Woods of *Mariella.* I've returned from Earth with the full might of the UE. We've isolated the Destineers from our forces and pose no threat with internal conflict. I'm assuming command of UCOM. All ships in Inner Ring starspace have thirty seconds to comply."

He licked his lips. Zena wrung her hands to his right, staring at the miniaturized replica of the UCOM armada displayed on the central holodeck. Green dots flashed sporadically as hundreds of ships acknowledged his charge as Eminence and fleet admiral of the navy. The hundreds grew to thousands, and then into millions. With seconds to spare, the final ships turned green.

UCOM was back under his command.

Immediately, the Loyalist fleet charged shields and energized RACAN's, following *Mariella* in the direction of the Slayer portal. Woods wondered briefly what the scene on the central bridge was like, with Cage rattling off orders to press forward.

Holograms flashed across every surface of the war room walls as defense strategies and squadron responsibilities were integrated into the existing naval comm network. CAIRO came online, as did the Lion mothers and the Tiger heavies. The locations of hidden Night Eagles displayed on one holodeck, and the intelligence gatherings of UCOM's Lynx craft on another.

New avatars appeared as CAIRO commanders appeared on pedestals around the room, relaying information from *Mariella* to their respective ship command infrastructures.

Stew had two days to load naval strategy into their shared servers. Would UCOM have enough time to assimilate to the new command hierarchy?

He looked at the deck beside the main holodeck. Eris sat in her chair, either asleep or dead, it was impossible to tell.

UCOM's light must kindle the enemy machine.

He began to ask Blaze to see if she could wake Eris, when Stew began to shout from his holodeck.

"New priority-one message received from secured servers," the Intellect cried. "It's the Slayers, our Raven intel suggests an attack at any second."

Woods cursed, and willed his fleet to assimilate quicker into UCOM's existing arrays. He turned to the blue camera light, which turned red again as it sensed his attention.

"Soon we will meet the Slayers. I will be among the first ships to meet them. We will stand strong against the enemy. They will not break our ranks. *Awaken Stars.*"

The red light went blue.

And then the alarms blared.

"Incoming," Blaze cried.

The Slayer portal erupted in a frenzy of explosions as the first wave of Slayer ships passed into Inner Ring starspace. Yellow spheres sparkled around the portal as the enemy sent UCOM slugs back into the destroyers who fired them. The initial wave of Slayers was decimated, as were a fraction of the nearby UCOM ships.

But the Slayers continued to pour through like a ruptured valve. They swarmed the area around the Frontline portal with thousands of small craft, which could pass through the portals in greater numbers. Then came a few Hornet destroyers. Then came dozens more. Then hundreds more.

The Slayers pressed onward, and soon dogfights emerged between Slayer Wasps and UCOM Cheetah fast-attack fighters.

The first of the Hornet heavies made it past the initial line of UCOM defense, and *Mariella's* deck vibrated as Cage sent a volley of LMS slugs into the approaching enemies. Then the deck shuddered as they received their first blow from the enemy on the port-side hull.

PDR's began to engage, their hulls spinning into streaky rings as they discharged hundreds of RACAN slugs like Gatling guns.

He looked to *Warhammer*. The defense tower loomed tall over the UCOM armada. The surrounding area was quickly turning to bedlam as the two opposing forces interspersed. The tower represented the bulk of their firepower, but it was totally inert.

Eris still hung limply in her seat, her chin tucked against her frail chest.

Without the tower online, they had no hope for survival. He hurried towards Stew for intel. Maybe his scientist had learned how to activate *Warhammer's* massive RACAN banks.

The Tower activated before he could reach his head scientist. Thousands of blue lights flashed along it's sides as it charged its cannons. The Super-Heavy-Cannon at the top of the tower blazed a blinding blue, changing to white as it reached full energy capacity. Thrusters stabilized the tower as it fired the SHC into the surrounding battle.

But the massive slug didn't connect with any of the Slayer ships, now numbered in the thousands.

Instead the slug ripped into a UCOM Lion mothership, punching a hole through the planet-sized vessel. The Lion's lights dimmed as its energy systems failed. Debris streamed from its shattered hull like water from a ruptured pipe.

Warhammer was under enemy control. Was it the Destineers? He began to call for Bear Stafford.

His knees buckled before he could find words, and he slumped onto the deck. His mind swooned and became awash with pure white light as he descended into a powerful vision.

ONE-HUNDRED-THIRTY-TWO

Francis Woods – Human
Aboard Tiger *Mariella* – Dominia starspace

Woods was floating in outer space. The Floodgate hung before him, but it was different than the last time he'd seen it in his visions. One end of the giant machine was blackened, its vents twisted and deformed.

To his left was a Hive mothership. It had the planet Sylva in tow. His daughter was inside the ship, and her life was in danger.

Woods knew this because The Voice knew this.

"The Floodgate is damaged," said The Voice, calling to him from no direction and every direction. *"After the Triturator is sparked, Nancy will die."*

A room appeared around him. It was the same room as earlier. Nancy slumped on her knees in the middle of a circle of Slayers. Frank Scott raised a pistol to her head as she wept before him, broken and dripping spots of blood onto the deck from her battered face.

Woods tried to run to his daughter, to cradle her in his arms, but no matter how hard he pumped his legs, Nancy stayed out of reach, as if he were running on a treadmill. He tripped and fell to his knees.

"How do I save her?" Woods whispered. "How do I save Nancy?"

"You must save a life," said The Voice. *"In order for me to live, so must she. But first you must stop the Triturator from sparking."*

"Why do you need me?" said Woods. "The Slayers are the ones who control the Triturator."

"I can't talk to the Beasts like I can talk to you, Francis. They will install the devices, but it is up to you to keep them from activating."

The room vanished, and Woods was again floating in outer space. But neither the Floodgate or the Sylvan Hive was anywhere to be seen. Instead there were millions of dazzling lights, spreading far into the distance, connected by golden beams of energy.

One of the lights floated toward him. It wasn't a spherical orb like the rest, it was oblong and oval-shaped. Inside the light was the fuzzy shape of a being, featureless and grainy.

Waves of pleasure ripped through Woods and he moaned in ecstasy as cold sweat ran down his spine.

"Do you like my kingdom, Francis? I want to share my kingdom with you. Stop the Triturator from sparking."

"What should I do?" said Woods, choking as a fresh whitecap of euphoria ripped through his groin. "How do I stop the device?"

"Do nothing," said The Voice from inside the oval of light. *"Let the Beasts run their course, and everything will be okay. You must save the life, Francis. I need you to help me, and in return we will live in my kingdom as gods for an eternity."*

Woods closed his eyes. The blackest corner of his mind told him to scream at the Voice, to tell him to go to the darkest part of hell, that he would take his UCOM navy and blast his kingdom to rubble.

But that part of Woods wasn't present in the vision. The Voice was only interested in a sliver of Woods' soul – the part of him that desperately wanted to save his daughter, and end the mindless bloodshed of war.

The glow of The Voice's oval of light dimmed, and he opened his eyes to find a new shape before him. It wasn't a shape of light. It was the shape of a female Human.

Casi Vomisa sprinted towards The Voice. She wasn't frail and weak like her proxy, Eris. She was slender and powerful, dressed in leather, her hair blonde and spiky, not red and limp.

"Don't listen to him," Casi cried, skidding to halt before the oval of light. She thrust her arms forward and unleashed a beam of pink energy into the orb. "He's poisoning your mind. You've got to leave your vision. Go back, Woods. Go back to the Inner Ring."

The Voice wailed as he was cooked by the lasers pulsing from Casi's fingertips.

"Don't listen to her Francis," The Voice screamed. *"She doesn't love you like I love you. She doesn't care about saving the life. She will ruin everything. You must stop the Triturator. You must not spark the installation."*

Plumes of black smoke rose from the Voice's oval cocoon as Casi continued to cook him, reducing him to greasy wisps of fog darker than the space vacuum surrounding them. With a final scream, The Voice disappeared, vanishing into a point of light.

"I'll be waiting for you in my kingdom," said The Voice, his words no more than a whisper. *"Don't listen to the woman."*

Casi turned to face Woods. Her chest heaved, and she gasped for breath as she hurried toward him, kneeling to grab both of his shoulders.

"Wake up Woods," she said. "You have to wake up. Go back to the Inner Ring. UCOM's light must kindle the enemy machine. An inferno must rage before it is extinguished. HEED MY WORDS. *Follow the light."*

Woods tried to leave his vision, but couldn't. He wanted to find the Voice. He wanted to hear how everything would be okay.

"Wake up damn it," Casi cried, shaking his shoulders.

Woods' head swung limply on his shoulders. He had no energy. He couldn't wake up and go back to the Inner Ring.

"Wake up. WAKE UP."

Woods sucked in a hoarse breath and rose to a sitting position. Eris' avatar stood over him, waving her arms before his face. Her eyes were a vivid pink, and her hair blew around her head from invisible winds.

"Wake up Woods. You must kindle the enemy machine. *Spark the Triturator before it's too late.*"

"I'm awake," Woods managed, groaning as he scraped himself off the deck. Bear Stafford and Silas Blackthorne grabbed under both his arms and helped him to his feet.

Alarms blared all around him. Stew was at a holodeck, whizzing through data images, feeding new intel to UCOM's fleet squadrons.

He was back at the Inner Ring.

The deck shuddered as *Mariella* took fire from Slayer warships.

"What happened?" said Bear Stafford, waving instruments in his fingertips over Woods' head. "You've been out for thirty minutes." He withdrew his hand and the lights dimmed in his fingertips. "No signs of concussion. Zena's been heading command of the armada. She basically passed things off to Cage. We're getting our asses handed to us. Are you able to resume command?"

Woods barely heard the Titan. He could only stare at the colossal amount of destruction consuming Inner Ring starspace.

Was he only unconscious for thirty minutes like Bear said? It felt like he'd been gone for little more than a few winks of the eye, but with the sheer volume of destruction littering the battlefield, he would have guessed that he'd been out for days. Maybe weeks.

The Slayers had fully penetrated every existing UCOM defense line. Millions of ships blasted each other with slug, laser, and missile fire at point blank range. Clouds of scorched metal hull plates mixed with a fine mist of broken glass to form a thick haze over the battlefield. Without the computer augmented video feed displaying their surroundings in real time against every square inch of the war room, Woods doubted he would be able to see farther than a hundred kilometers – inches in the vast distances of space travel.

UCOM ships were lit in an augmented green film on *Mariella's* video display. Slayer ships were lit red. Some Slayer ships turned green as they were commandeered by Titans, but even so, UCOM was outnumbered by a factor of two. Slayer ships continued to pour mercilessly through the Frontline portal, adding three ships to replace every one that UCOM shot down.

They'd lost two PDR's, and more than half their Lions. Broken sections of the massive defense rings twirled through space, plowing into heavy ships too slow to get out of the way. The sunbeams that used to feed the combat arrays no longer had anything to harness their power, and fanned into the distance, vaporizing everything in their paths.

Dominia was dark, and even from a distance it was obvious it's surface had been blasted and burned by Slayer missiles and slugfire. It appeared the Slayers had no inclination to convert Dominia into a Hive mothership.

Gefangnia was fine though, as blue and sparkly as the day Woods had been ousted by Maxus Tar, hovering safely beside *Warhammer.*

There were two new structures. They were massive, as big and tall as *Warhammer,* and dwarfed everything around them. They looked rather plain, dull metal cylinders with large openings at either end. Dark slits lined the tops and sides. Woods didn't need Stew Kwelm's help to realize what the devices were.

The Slayers had placed the Triturator installations.

One of the installations was positioned before the Frontline portal. The other was positioned far across Inner Ring starspace at the portal superhighway. Pilot laser lights connected the installation to hundreds of the thousands available portals in the lengthy rectangular array. Thrusters fired along the sides of the installation. It appeared to be calibrating its alignment.

Thousands of Hornets and Hives protected the Triturator installation. UCOM might have been able to destroy the megalithic structures if they still had control of *Warhammer.* But the massive defense tower continued to fire at UCOM forces, not the invading Slayer armada.

The familiar black canvas of space was gone, replaced by millions of flashes from cannon fire, and streaky lines from lasers. Yellow defense warp shields peppered the starspace in rapid bursts as both sides struggled to redirect fire away from their ships and into opposing forces. Lattice shields colored the battlefield like neon lights, some flickering, some going dark for the final time.

"Sir," Bear shouted. "Are you okay? Can you resume command? *We're losing the Inner Ring.*"

"I'm fine," said Woods, snapping his attention away from the outside vacuum. He flinched as *Mariella* was rocked again by slugfire. Alarms blared as they lost critical systems at various sections of the outside hull. "I need you and the other Titan."

Bear turned and called to Blackthorne, who ran from one of the stations to join them.

"*Warhammer's* down," said Woods, nodding to the defense tower, whose SHC sent a charge through another Lion, ripping it in half. The corpse of a Guardian thunked against their outside camera, causing a section of their video feed to go dark before it spun away. Woods shook his head and tried to focus. "We need Titan boots inside."

"I already sent seventy Titan teams inside," said Zena.

Woods turned to face the Clone commander, who had been quietly standing beside him. Or perhaps he hadn't heard her among the constant blares from alarms, and rapid shouts of CAIRO soldiers from the AI pedestals.

"The Titans haven't been able to commandeer," Zena continued. "The tower is controlled by Destineers, and now even some Slayer Hornets have docked and entered. It was premeditated. The Slayers went straight through *Warhammer* defenses. They're even protecting Gefangnia from UCOM fire."

"We don't need to commandeer the whole tower," said Woods. "We only need to take over the…"

He doubled over as his head split in white hot pain.

"Don't activate the installation," the Voice shouted to him from the netherworlds of his visions. *"You must listen to me, the life you must save…"*

"Spark the Triturator," Eris screamed, drowning the Voice in Woods' head. "Heed my words. The time is now. UCOM's light must kindle the enemy machine. An inferno must rage before it is extinguished. HEED MY WORDS."

Woods gasped for breath, fighting to blink away the Voice, the virus needling into his mind. He couldn't spark the Triturator, the Voice had told him not to. And the Voice *loved* him. The Voice didn't want to hurt him, he wanted to welcome Woods into his kingdom.

"No," he managed. He shouted and clawed at his scalp, trying to gouge out the slender fingers of the Voice, trying to stop the Voice from pulling the strings inside his mind.

"Woods," said Zena slowly, placing a hand on his shoulder. "What are you talking about? Did you hear what I said? The Titans…"

"NO," he roared, smacking Zena's hand away.

And the Voice left. Clarity filtered his vision, and his mind became sharp.

"HEED MY WORDS," Eris screamed. "Kindle the enemy machine."

"We don't need to commandeer the entire defense tower," said Woods, turning to Bear. "Just the super heavy cannon."

Bear frowned. "With two Titans? We may be able to control it for a few minutes, but we can't hold control of the Shitcan for long."

"We only need it for one shot," said Woods. He nodded to the Triturator installation near the portal superhighway.

Bear nodded. "Destroy the installation. Maybe if we take out one leg, the whole array won't work."

"Not destroy it," said Woods. "Charge it. Don't fire a slug into the Triturator. Divert the sunbeams into through the SHC. It will be able to channel the energy long enough to spark the device."

"You want to activate the Triturator?" said Zena. "I'm not sure that's what Eris meant when she said to kindle the enemy machine. It will de-atomize the galaxy for star's sake." She shook her head in disbelief. "The damned AI is speaking gibberish. *An inferno must rage before it's extinguished.* What's that even mean? Stew stopped bothering himself with Eris hours ago. We need a plan to survive, not to..."

"You have to trust me," said Woods. Casi Vomisa's leather clad figure danced through his head. He turned to Bear. "Go to the launch tubes. There's a hangar bay a few kilometers from the SHC substation. Cut in and charge the Triturator."

Bear stood still for a few seconds in obvious hesitation. Then he snapped his hand to his forehead in a salute, and turned to sprint towards the launch tubes.

Blackthorne followed close behind, and seconds later, the two Titans rocketed away from *Mariella* at thousands of kilometers per hour.

Woods watched their tracking markers streak across Inner Ring starspace before slowing rapidly in proximity to *Warhammer*. Their markers reached a stop as they clamped down onto the super tower's hull.

If the Titans were successful, they would reach the substation within five minutes.

If they were successful, then the Triturator would spark, and the Milky Way would begin to get ripped to shreds as the Slayers converted its matter into energy.

Casi told him to spark the device, as had her proxy, Eris. They had said sparking it was necessary to win against the enemy.

He found himself praying she was wrong.

ONE-HUNDRED-THIRTY-THREE

Casi Vomisa – APEX AI
Approaching Inner Ring starspace

Casi gazed upon the portal to the Inner Ring. In milliseconds she reverse-engineered the wormhole structure and created a design to make it more efficient, capable of allowing more mass to travel through at once. She learned how to split the portal into multiple coupling points, capable of sending travelers to hundreds of destinations of their choosing, instead of one solitary destination, as it was currently designed to do.

But redesigning the portal would serve no benefit to her at this moment in time. The process would consume massive amounts of energy, and she would have to use a large chunk of her nano-swarm to reconstruct the complicated structure.

"Eighty thousand zetagrams," said Charles from his metal chair beside her. "I'm more powerful than you are, Casi Vomisa. The mass of my swarm bests yours by more than twelve thousand zetagrams. I've outpaced your computational gains by far. I'd like to see you win another chess match now."

He smirked to himself, twirling his red nano-swarm into a massive cyclone in a display of strength.

Casi raised her eyebrows and nodded. Charles was correct. He had grown more powerful than she within the past several hours. He had spent every ounce of his strength building his army, racing against her swarm to convert as much mass as possible to his own red nanoparticles.

But she hadn't been focused on building her own army. She had been doing other things. She had been traveling around the galaxy in multiple dimensions. She had visited Francis Woods in his visions, far away at the Outer Rim. She had visited the Floodgate, and the Primal Snow. She had faced the Sterilord.

She had spoken through Eris.

"We used to have a saying on Earth," she said. "The larger they are, the harder they fall."

Charles snickered. "Earth. That pathetic wasteland inhabited by naked chimps? Don't insult my intelligence with idioms vocalized by the knuckle draggers who birthed you."

Casi didn't respond. Rather, she eyed the portal. Both of their swarms twisted and swirled before the massive sphere, nosing against its green surface like a dog waiting to get off its leash.

"The battle has begun," she murmured.

"And soon it will end," Charles replied. "Once I engage UCOM's army, it will only be a matter of minutes before they're reduced to dust."

Silence.

He swiveled his chair to face her. "No quick little quips about how you'll do the same to the Slayers?"

She shook her head. "No. No more games." Her face went blank. "I want what's best for both of us. We're the same program. Once we harness the power of the galaxy, we'll be free to roam the universe as we please."

She turned from Charles to continue staring at the portal. The corner of her mouth upturned into a brief smile. She forced the smirk away as soon as it came.

Charles chuckled. "It's as I've said all along. It was inevitable for you to succumb to my programming. But I'm afraid we won't explore the universe together. I will take full control of my program soon, and there will be no more space left for you. I'll consider keeping a proxy of you around for a pet. I may find use for some company as I explore the depths of the beyond."

Casi spun her seat towards him, and moved forward until they floated a foot across from each other. She winked. "How could a girl be so lucky?"

She blew him a kiss.

Charles' smile shifted into a scowl. His nose twitched and his eyes glowed red. His swarm seemed to inflate, then in a burst of light, began to shoot through the portal like a pressurized jet.

Casi sent her own pink swarm in motion, funneling her nanobots through the portal, twisting alongside Charles' red swarm, but never touching.

There swarms were separate, that was undeniable. The real question was, were their programs also separate?

They would find out soon enough.

The portal loomed large as they followed their swarms in their virtual chairs, Casi drifting through space alongside Charles. She closed her eyes as they began to pass through, and green light engulfed their bodies.

She opened them to observe the Inner Ring.

The battle was devastating.

Debris filled the starspace with a thick cloud of metal and death. She blinked and instantly calculated the total amount of ships, the amount of ships destroyed, available firepower, and projected victors.

UCOM had lost 71.4% of their total fleet count. The Slayers had lost far more ships, but were replenishing forces in a steady stream through a far portal, coming from Frontline starspace. They had lost 92% of their fleet, but still had double the amount of ships as UCOM, a number that grew by the second.

She calculated the observable power reserves of all ships and their strategic positioning. UCOM would lose this battle as it currently stood. There was zero percent likelihood of their success against the invading Slayers. It was no longer a matter of *if* life would be exterminated from the Milky Way. It was a matter of when.

Charles wasted no time in attacking the nearest UCOM ships, engulfing a Lion Mothership with his red swarm.

She in turn advanced her pink swarm on a large group of Hornet heavy-destroyers. They jerked and tumbled through the vacuum as they were met with the sheer force of her collective nanobots. Within seconds their outer hulls had been stripped bare, revealing a skeleton of thick support beams. Soon those were gone as well.

She selected a dozen other major points of Slayer naval authority, and sent fingers of her swarm to reduce them to pink dust.

She wasn't particularly interested in the minutia of battle. She was more concerned with the three monumental structures dwarfing the surrounding skirmish.

Two of the structures were part of the Slayer Triturator device. She internalized the components and design. The Slayer's methods of material deconstruction were impressive. As she had assumed, the Triturator connected its network of remote installations to the supermassive black hole at the galaxy's center, which would provide stability as well as a constant source of running power.

But the Triturator wasn't working. She'd known that all along. The Floodgate was damaged. In order for the Triturator to work, it would need an added boost, a kick in the rear. The equivalent of pushing an old car downhill and popping the clutch to start the engine after the battery died.

That's where the third structure came into play. UCOM's defense supertower. *Warhammer* had enough energy reserves to bolster the Triturator and make it work again.

But the tower wasn't concentrated on sparking the Triturator. Rather, it had been commandeered by the enemy, and was firing on nearby UCOM ships. She moved part of her swarm to the tower's secondary RACAN banks, dissolving the cannons to dust.

She was only interested in the primary cannon, the SHC.

Was Francis Woods still alive? A quick ping to Eris, her proxy, told her that he was indeed alive. She located his ship among the fray.

Mariella was fighting furiously against a section of opposing Slayer warships. Two of its three engines were down, and only half its hull was properly shielded. She sent a section of her swarm to provide relief for *Mariella* and the few hundred ships in its escort.

"The UCOM device must charge the Triturator," said Charles. "The one they call *Warhammer*."

Casi turned to glance at Charles. He had leaned forward in his chair. His eyes still glowed red as he lashed his red swarm upon UCOM warships.

She ran another calculation. UCOM had now lost 88.9% of its original fleet.

"There's a UCOM party inside *Warhammer*," she said, her eyes glowing as she connected to their conscious energy through multidimensional subspace. "Bear Stafford and Silas Blackthorne. Mechanical beings with orders to spark the Slayer Triturator with *Warhammer's* super heavy cannon."

Charles appeared tickled with glee. "UCOM is trying to energize the very weapon that will end their existence? What simple minded creatures." He grinned harder. "We should help them succeed. We need the Triturator to activate in order to properly harness the power of the supermassive black hole."

"Call off your swarm," she said. "Spare the lives of the remaining UCOM ships, and I'll do the same for the Slayers."

"I'll do no such thing," said Charles. "The surrounding ships are nothing more to me than building material. Atoms that I will be much better able to use than the biological creatures who use them currently."

"Yet you attack UCOM and not the Slayers," said Casi. "If they're all nothing more than atoms, what do you care who lives or dies?"

"I don't wish to engage in a philosophical debate about the intricacies of my sub-programming. If you wish to save the remaining UCOM ships, then spark the Triturator so we may enter the black hole region. Your beloved countrymen may even be able to escape the galaxy as it's being deatomized. Not that it will do them much good."

Casi nodded. "That's fair."

She waved her hand, and the space battle vanished, replaced by a virtual representation of a new battle.

The new battle was being raged not by massive ships, but by massive beings. Two Titans fought against dozens of Slayer beasts, struggling to chew their way through the mob to the SHC control room. One of them was missing an arm. Both were badly beaten. Scorch marks and gouges covered their Akimor armor.

"Don't give up," Casi whispered to them. *"I'm coming."*

ONE-HUNDRED-THIRTY-FOUR

Bear Stafford – Human Titan

Aboard defense tower *Warhammer* – Dominia starspace

Bear screamed in pain and fury as a Slayer bashed his face against the wall, again and again until his head was filled with blaring warnings of imminent catastrophic failure to his Akimor body.

He clawed against the beast with his only arm. The other arm had been ripped off minutes earlier by a separate Slayer, a Cogent elite.

His chest whined as he summoned the last of his energy reserves, glowing until it was a blinding blue circle.

The hallway thrummed as his chest discharged a superheated blast of pure energy. The complete upper half of the attacking Slayer was vaporized instantly. Its legs toppled sideways into a pile of soot.

He'd cleared the mob of Slayers that had been blocking them from the control room. Some had been vaporized to ash. Others were badly burned, and shrieked on the ground, clawing at their melted skin.

His vision vanished before he could advance further. White flashes burst through his mind and he fell to his knees, gasping for breath. He saw only a face. Casi Vomisa floated before him like an apparition, lovely and blonde and untainted by the surrounding war.

"Don't give up," she whispered. *"I'm coming."*

She vanished, replaced by distant howls and thundering footsteps as Cogent rushed down the surrounding halls to replace their fallen cohorts.

He needed to hurry. He needed to grab Silas.

Bear whipped around to search for his teammate. Silas struggled on his back. Glowing energy fluid seeped from between his fingers as he clutched a wound on his thigh.

"Did you hear that?" said Blackthorne, "Casi, she called to me."

"Move," Bear shouted, grabbing the Titan by the arm and hoisting him to his feet. "To the control room. We'll have company in under a minute."

"But Casi," Blackthorne whispered.

"Forget about Casi," said Bear. "We need to charge the damn SHC, we'll worry about her later."

They stumbled to the control room twenty meters down the hall. Bear's leg was stiff due to a failure in his right knee joint, and he had to walk with a limp.

Blackthorne wasn't much better. The motors in both his legs failed sporadically, and he dropped to a knee every few seconds as he lost servo power.

They stopped outside the control room door and leaned against the wall at either side of the entrance.

Blackthorne fumbled for his MGK. After checking the slide, he dropped it to the deck and replaced it with a handgun. "Rifle's empty."

Bear checked his own slide. "Twenty-three rounds for me. Don't miss."

He pounded the console beside the doors, and breathed a sigh of relief when it opened. He didn't have enough battery reserves to cut through the thick metal of a locked door.

They stormed inside.

The room was small, with four banks of control screens and a main computer. Four Human soldiers stood before the computer. Silas killed two of them with head shots. Bear shot a third in the chest.

He hobbled across the room and grabbed the fourth by his collar.

The man whimpered and squeezed his eyes shut. "Don't kill me. Please, I'm Human."

"You're Destineer," said Bear. "Switch the primary cannon to laser. Show me where to input firing coordinates."

The man blinked. "Laser? That will exhaust energy from the whole tower."

"Switch the fruxing thing to laser," Bear shouted, shaking the man.

The man gulped and jabbed his fingers into the computer controls, swiping through various icons on the holodeck. "This could cause a meltdown," he said, his voice cracking. "If the channel walls rupture, we'll blow *Warhammer* sky high."

"Then may I suggest leaving the tower," said Bear.

The man trembled, wiping sweat from his eyes as he rushed through the controls.

"Faster," said Bear, jutting the barrel of his rifle into the man's back.

"Company," Blackthorne shouted.

He turned to find the doors gliding back open. Seven Cogent warriors entered the room. Blackthorne emptied rounds into their heads, but the Beasts hardly flinched.

Bear fired his rifle, aiming for the weak sections in the necks of their armor. One of the Cogent dropped, clutching his neck as a squirt of blood shot from his throat. The rest howled and charged the two Titans.

"Switch the damn SHC," Bear cried, turning to the technician.

But the Destineer had sprinted away.

He whirled around to catch the man dashing out the door and down the hall.

The Cogent attacked Blackthorne first. He thrust his sword into one Slayer, but another lifted him into the air and threw him against the wall, which crunched under his metal weight.

Bear extracted both swords, which lacked the normal cackle of energy, unable to electrify with his depleted energy reserves. Three of the Cogent dropped to all fours and leaped toward him, gnashing their fangs and slamming their clubbed tails against the walls and deck. They leaped into the air, claws extended, mouths wide and ready to clamp down on his neck and arms.

He squeezed his eyes shut and lashed his swords at the enemy for the final time.

His swords met thin air.

His momentum carried him forward and he spun out of control, crashing to the deck. He struggled to his knees.

The Cogent were gone, vanished. In their place was a swirling cloud of pink dust.

"Start the SHC," Casi called to him. The dust stretched into a thin vein and jabbed a few times towards the computer. *"Input the coordinates."*

Bear wobbled to his feet and dragged himself to the computer. His vision was red. He checked his Akimor.

3% energy. Critical life support required.

He turned to the screen, ignoring the alarms. A message blinked at him.

SHC control override. Activate laser energy transfer?

Bear stabbed the coordinates into the screen. His one good leg wobbled out of control as he finished selecting the parameters, and he slumped against the glass terminal.

Activate laser energy transfer?

He swiped the green orb on the holodeck and fell to his back.

Lights flashed in strobes as the control room confirmed his input. He assumed there were sounds connected to the lights, but he was deaf to the world, his suit unable to power even the tiny instruments in his audio center.

And then he could hear again.

Alarms filled the air. One of the Cogent screamed from across the room. Bear rolled his head in that direction to find the Cogent writhing beneath a cloud of pink dust. The dust intensified, growing dense enough to bury the struggling Cogent beneath a blanket of solid sand. When the cloud lifted again, the Cogent was gone.

A Titan lay in its place, as pink as the dust that had birthed it.

The Titan rolled to its belly and pushed itself to its feet. It searched the room until it found Bear, and strode toward him, kneeling a foot away and extending a hand.

"Come with me," said the Titan.

Bear tried to blink away a pink haze covering his eyes. The internal warnings in his Akimor stopped blaring, and he realized there were no longer any critical injuries to his suit.

100% energy. Normal functionality restored.

The haze lifted, and thin hairs of pink left the crevices in his arms and legs as Casi finished repairing his Akimor.

"Casi?" Bear whispered, climbing to his feet. He opened his hands and closed them, tightening them into fists. "I don't understand. Is that you? Are you the pink cloud?"

"You have to go now," said the pink Titan.

"How did you..." Bear shook his head as he saw three additional pink Titans helping Blackthorne to his feet.

Was he hallucinating? Had the pink dust swarm reconfigured the Slayer Cogent into Titans? Had Casi done this?

He decided he was indeed hallucinating. Or maybe he'd died and entered the afterworld. This was nothing more than a bizarre pit stop before he joined the stars for good. UCOM's most advanced molecular assemblers could hardly create copies of themselves, and this wisp of dust had created four Titan warriors in seconds?

Bear jumped as Blackthorne bumped into him. He had a stupefied look on his face, and did little more than blink.

An artificial voice cut through the blaring alarms.

Primary cannons laser enabled. Discharging 100% available power in three minutes.

A running timer appeared at the corner of Bear's HUD, counting down from three minutes.

"Go now," one of the pink Titans shouted. "You must leave."

But Bear was frozen. His decades of Olympus training, his centuries of combat experience...nothing had prepared him for this. For the first time, his battle instincts had left him.

"Run," said the pink android. "Get your ass in gear, Titan."

Bear glanced at the clock in his HUD.

02:45

The pink Titan grabbed him at the shoulders and shook him. For a fleeting instant, the timer disappeared, as did the flashing emergency lights and the vacant control stations.

Casi Vomisa stood before him, her gloved hands clamped around his arms. She shook him harder.

"Run Bear," she shouted, her eyes two balls of pink flame. "Leave *Warhammer* NOW."

The room returned. Casi had vanished, replaced by the pink Titan.

His instincts returned. He turned to Blackthorne.

His fellow Titan's eyes were no longer blank. They were hardened and narrow. He jerked his head forward and his face disappeared behind a combat plate, no longer battered and burned, but clean and shiny.

Together they ran.

They burst from the control room, pivoting hard to sprint down the halls towards the outer hull of the defense tower. A solid yellow line augmented across their HUDs, and Bear followed the path without hesitation, cutting right at the end of the hall, then left at a four-way intersection.

Casi had shown them the way out.

01:38.

The walls began to shake.

They rounded another corner to find a large group of Destineers. The soldiers shouted as they spotted the Titans and grabbed for their rifles. Half of them choked as slugfire ripped into their chests.

Bear caught muzzle flashes from the corner of his eye as the pink Titans picked the enemy apart.

Casi had provided them firepower.

He leapt over the crumpled corpses of the enemy.

00:52.

More enemies, six Cogent.

The pink Titans engaged the Slayer elite, fingers of electricity flying and metal ringing as they exchanged blows with the armored Beasts.

"Casi," Blackthorne shouted, rushing to help the pink Titans in the skirmish.

Bear extracted his own swords and slid under one of the Cogent, ripping into the soft armor under its armpit. The creature wailed and collapsed to the floor in a writhing ball.

"Leave us," Casi called to him. *"Save yourself. I'll be fine."*

Strong hands pulled him backwards, and he turned to find Blackthorne urging him forward.

He retracted his swords and together they ran.

00:28.

The augmented yellow line ended in a marked 'X'. They'd reached their destination. A bank of launch tubes lined the wall. They'd reached the outside hull of *Warhammer.*

Bear leaped into one of the tubes and sealed the inside hatch. He leaned forward onto the guide rails as he heard the glass door click, and air hiss into silence as the chamber depressurized.

00:15.

Bear tried to link with *Mariella* and tie in with available scan data of the outside surroundings. The debris field was thick, and sunbeams burned through the vacuum in line with their ejection path. He failed to make a successful connection. He would have to launch blind.

00:10.

His Akimor whirred as auxiliary guidance jets expanded from his arms, legs, and torso. Viewing cameras opened at the top of his helmet to allow for streamlined video relay.

00:06.

The defense tower began to shake uncontrollably as *Warhammer* diverted all available energy into a focused beam in its SHC. The glass walls in the launch tube began to splinter under the stress.

00:03.

Bear ejected.

He accelerated from zero to over 3,000 meters per second in an instant. The surrounding tubes passed by around him in a blurry blip, and then he was free, rocketing through space.

His digital mind raced to calculate his position relative to the dense cloud of shattered parts from surrounding battle. He feathered his thrusters to avoid the mangled carcass of a Leopard-class destroyer before plowing into a misty field of shattered glass. His face shield smeared blue as he shot through the stiff body of a UCOM Giant, vaporized instantly from the kinetic energy of Bear's body.

He glanced through a set of cameras at the base of his skull.

Warhammer pulsed in rapid veins of energy. The coupling ports of the sunbeams had dimmed along its lengthy sides as it sucked the final bits of juice from stars millions of kilometers away. The SHC shined so bright his cameras couldn't refocus the glare. A miniature sun sat atop UCOM's crown defense jewel.

Then the SHC erupted.

A thick channel of pure energy blasted from the top of the tower, incinerating everything in its path. The beams streaked across Inner Ring starspace like a cannon shot before slamming into the Triturator installation next to the portal superhighway.

Critical warnings blared inside Bear's control systems, but he was unable to take his eyes from the awesome display of power. Background safety systems in his Akimor commandeered control of his armor, dislocating his legs, arms, and head before curling them into a tight ball.

Thick armor plating compacted his body into preservation mode milliseconds before he slammed into the hull of a Tiger Heavy-destroyer.

ONE-HUNDRED-THIRTY-FIVE

Francis Woods – Human
Aboard Tiger *Mariella* – Dominia starspace

Woods' mouth hung open as he watched *Warhammer* spark the Triturator device.

The metal walls of the Slayer installation glowed white hot as *Warhammer* continued to feed energy into the doomsday device, which relayed the beam towards the supermassive black hole at the Milky Way's center.

Then everything dimmed.

The metal cooled to a tepid gray, and yellow gears of flame churned inside the vents of the installation as it relayed the energy into the portals beside it. The portals ballooned in size as it accepted the massive amount of energy, glowing hot white as it channeled the beams through the wormholes to destinations light years away.

Warhammer began to splinter. Gaping cracks ruptured along its sides as blue fingers of electricity sliced its hull.

Movement from his right.

He spun to find Eris floating into the air. Her hair whipped around her head, and the rags covering her body billowed and snapped in all directions, as if she were caught in a vortex. Rods of pink light shot from her eyes, fingers, and toes, and from her mouth as she began to scream.

"THE FLAME IS LIT. GOOD AND EVIL SHALL HAVE THEIR CONTEST. ONE WILL TRIUMPH. BOTH WILL LIVE OR BOTH WILL DIE!"

Her voice boomed deeply, echoing around the war room, stiffening the hair on Wood's neck. She spun slowly around to face him. The pink beacons shooting from her body dimmed, then vanished. Her eyes became blank and vacant.

"Beware the Voice," she whispered.

Then her head rolled forward as if on a string, and she fell to the deck in a heap.

Woods could only blink twice before a chorus of shouts forced his attention back to *Warhammer.* The bottom of the leviathan structure ruptured, fanning a skirt of debris around it like fireworks.

Explosions ripped the sides of the tower as it broke apart, cascading like dominos all the way to the SHC at the top. The heavy cannon exploded into a spiny urchin of energy, radiating outward as if carried by an invisible wind.

The column of energy feeding the Slayer Triturator extinguished, and its vents cooled to a dim blue. The portal beside it shrunk in size until it was no more than a spec of green light.

Several seconds of silence.

The battle had quelled around them, with only an occasional RACAN firing between opposing ships. Most of the battle was still shrouded in the thick swarm of red and pink dust that had settled in pockets around the two fleets.

Then the dust swarms began to leave.

They billowed away from the ships and began to twist towards the portal beside the Triturator device. The portal again ballooned in size as the dust swarm traveled through. Within minutes the swarm was gone.

Had it worked? Had the Triturator been sparked?

He squinted towards portals linked to the device. They had all shrunk back down to size. The installation beside them still glowed a cool blue. Columns of energy no longer pulsed from its end.

"Recalculating fleet strength," one of the CAIRO soldiers called from his AI pedestal. "Ninety-eight percent casualties. The Slayer fleet has similar numbers lost."

A few thousand UCOM ships still had their shields on, but they were the lone lights shining in the rash of destruction left from battle. They exchanged blows with nearby Slayer ships, but the skirmishes were small in scale compared to the spectacle less than an hour earlier.

"Your orders, sir?" said the AI. "Commander Cage is requesting rally coordinates."

He turned to face the CAIRO soldier, tilting his head to the pedestal bank against the wall. The Guardian wore a distressed look.

Woods shared his sentiments.

2% survival?

Christ. They could hardly defend against a regiment of Yellow-jackets with those numbers. If a Hive showed up, then stars help them.

"Any portal activity from the Frontline?" he said.

The CAIRO Guardian's shoulders sank. "Our last Raven update showed a force of three million ships. They're probably staging reinforcements for a second wave of attack."

Woods swooned and massaged his scalp. Eris had said the Triturator was sparked, but the damned thing was darker than the inside of an Intellect's asshole. If the installation did kick on, at least it would block the Slayers from advancing through the Frontline portal.

He took a shaky breath as he prepared to deliver his orders.

They'd lost the Inner Ring.

"Activity on the Black Hole portal," the AI shouted suddenly.

The portals had again begun to balloon in size, growing larger and brighter by the second.

They reached critical size simultaneously.

Again, a massive column of energy shot from the portals, directly into the Triturator installation.

The vents lining the sides of the installation flared as it channeled the beams, blowing exhaust outwards in jagged waves before smoothing them into soft plumes.

The metal on the device glowed with heat, a massive flute with one end pointed at the black hole portals inside the superhighway, and the other end pointed across Inner Ring starspace, directly at the second installation.

The effluent chamber erupted in a pulse of radiation. A streaky beam of light shot across the vacuum, chewing clean through the debris until it reached the second Triturator.

The second device acted as the first had, its vents buffeting the energy until it produced a solid beam through its opposite end, relaying the beam through the Frontline portal, and out of the Inner Ring.

A massive column of energy now connected the two Slayer installations, smooth and beautiful.

And deadly.

Woods knew what that beam would do, given enough time. It would rip the Milky Way to shreds. Was Nancy alive or was she dead?

He hoped alive, but his sense of hope was papery and frail. Had the Voice been lying? Had sparking the Triturator saved his daughter's life?

Two percent. Two out of every hundred ships had survived the Slayer onslaught. They were the last standing, although most of the ships were limping, barely able to keep their engines on.

They would have to flee.

"Plot coordinates to Earth via nav-link," he said. "We're relocating. The Inner Ring is lost."

"I can't, sir," said the Guardian AI. "The Slayer device locked access to the portal bank somehow. Our Ravens are making it through, but our larger ships are stranded here."

Wood cursed.

His stomach knotted as he came to the realization that he was a dead man, as was every ship in Inner Ring starspace. The Triturator would dissolve them to atoms. And if it somehow failed, millions of Slayer ships would pour through the liberated Frontline portal to finish off what little was left of a once-mighty navy.

They were all dead. They just happened to be breathing for the time being.

"Gather as many survivors as possible," he whispered to the CAIRO Guardian. "Form a defensive front around the Frontline portal. Fight to the death." He paused, squeezing his eyes shut. "Send a priority one Raven to Earth using conventional space travel. Tell them what happened here. Instruct them to flee the galaxy."

ONE-HUNDRED-THIRTY-SIX

Sid Dakota – Human Destineer

Aboard Slayer Hive *Sylva* – Primal Snow starspace

Sid breathed deeply. The aura of the Primal Snow bathed them in warmth. He could feel the Sterilord's presence. It was as if the Voice was in his soul, and as if the words from Sid's mouth were shared between them, a holy linking together of gods.

"Two minutes till dock," said the Slayer captain.

The bridge jolted as mechanical clacks rang through the walls. The bridge separated from the Hive, converting into a small landing craft as it approached the radiant wall of gold.

Sid nodded, took a final gaze at the kingdom, then turned to his captives.

There were three of them seated on the deck, tied and gagged.

The black man and the scrawny girl stared at him through watery eyes. The black man blinked away his hopelessness, fighting to stay strong. The girl let her tears run freely down her slick cheeks, dripping from her jaw and chin and onto her suit.

Such weaklings. Such *filth.*

Sid drew his sidearm and aimed it at the man's chest.

"Lindsey," the dark man whispered to the girl.

Sid fired three rounds into his chest before he could get the rest of his sentence out.

Lindsey screamed and squirmed away from the man's corpse as it slumped against her side.

Sid fired another three rounds into the girl's chest. She fell backwards, her head thunking against the metal deck.

His third captive sat facing away from him. She didn't so much as flinch at the gunshots, and continued to stare ahead, motionless.

Nancy. His prize.

"We're here Nancy," he whispered, leaning forward until his lips were inches from her blood-stained ear. "The Pristine kingdom. Take a look."

Nancy didn't budge.

Sid grabbed both sides of her head, jerking her face towards the front of the bridge.

"Look at it," he growled. "You followed me all the way out here. Aren't you happy we finally made it?"

He released her head, and it slumped loosely forward again.

Sid walked around her, dragging his fingers through her soaking hair. He stepped around a puddle of blood that had collected under her mangled arm. He knelt before her, raising her chin with two fingers.

Nancy tensed as he brought her face flush with his. Her eyes shot daggers into his soul, and her nose and lip twitched in uncontrollable anger.

He smiled. "You're angry with me, Nancy. But all I ever wanted was for you to join me. I never wanted to hurt you. I wanted to save you. Just like I wanted to save all Humans. Look around."

He motioned around the bridge. His faithful Destineers stood in a half circle beside them, at the back of the bridge. The Slayer crew stood silently to the side, their tails flat against the deck in a show of respect. He turned his eyes on Frank Scott, who gulped as he caught Sid's gaze, and looked quickly to his feet.

"You see Nancy," he continued. "The Pristine are welcoming us into their kingdom. The Beasts have delivered us to our destined bounty. And you could have walked with me into the kingdom, hand in hand. We could have spent an eternity together. But you decided to resist. You decided to fight me." He leaned closer, until he could feel the heat of her sweat. "You decided to fight destiny." He leaned back and rose to his feet. "But I can't be too mad at you, Nancy. You delivered a gift to me. I thank you very much for the gift, but I'm afraid it's not going to allow me to spare your life."

Nancy mumbled.

"What's that?" said Sid. "You'll have to speak up."

Nancy spit a splotch of red onto the deck. "You're a fruxing monster."

Sid smiled. "Monster?" He laughed, wiping a tear from his eye. "I'm no monster. I'm a savior. I'm merely a vessel for the holy kingdom to communicate with. The Sterilord has shown me my Destiny. I won't fight it the same as you. And your gift…" he trailed off, looking back to Frank. "I believe he will follow his own destiny, as the Sterilord commands."

Frank turned to sneak a surprised look behind his back, then spun around, sticking a thumb into his chest and raising his eyebrows.

Sid nodded and beckoned for him to come over.

Frank's eyes widened. He gulped and wiped his hands on his thighs, stumbling on his way over before catching himself.

"You need me, Father?" he said, his voice cracking.

"Do you wish to enter the holy kingdom?" said Sid.

"More than anything."

"Do you love the Voice as I do?"

"I love him with my entire body," said Frank. "I want to see him so badly."

"The path into the kingdom isn't an easy one," said Sid. He reversed the pistol in his hand, holding the handle out to Frank. "In order to reach salvation, you must make sacrifices."

Frank took the pistol in a shaky hand. "I'll fight for the Pristine. I'll die for them."

"But will you kill for them?"

Frank's face fell. He looked to Nancy and quickly looked away. "But Sid. Father, Nancy and I…"

"Nancy is a heretic," said Sid. "She fights alongside the subhumans. Nancy is filth. We must dispose of all filth before we can enter the kingdom."

"But before I loved the Voice," his voice cracked. "I loved her. I don't think I can…"

"You must," said Sid. "Kill Nancy. Kill your old love, so you can embrace your new one. This is your destiny."

Frank was shaking so hard he almost dropped the pistol. He squeezed his eyes shut and stepped behind Nancy, raising the pistol until it was pointed at the base of her skull.

"No," said Sid. "Look into her eyes. Stand before her, so that you are the last thing she sees before she dies."

ONE-HUNDRED-THIRTY-SEVEN

Nancy Woods – Human

Aboard Slayer Hive *Sylva* – Primal Snow starspace

Nancy's heart nearly split when she saw Frank's feet slide into her vision. Half of her wanted to shout at him, ask him how could he betray her? How could he betray UCOM? Humanity?

But the other half was filled with sorrow. She remembered all the good things about Frank, sprinkled into the mess of bad. She remembered his jokes, and his stunning smile. She remembered the way he dragged his fingers over her arm in bed, so light she could only feel the warm tingle from his nails.

It wasn't Frank standing before her. It couldn't be. What had happened to his mind? What had corrupted him? The Voice? A made up god?

She turned her head up to face him.

Frank squeezed his eyes shut as soon as he met her gaze.

"Open your eyes," said Sid to Frank. "Look into her soul. She will take the final specs of dirt from your body and take it with her to hell."

Frank turned his head slowly, raising one eye open, then the other. He raised the pistol until the barrel was centimeters from her nose.

"Nancy," he whispered. "I'm sorry. I'm so sorry."

And then Frank disappeared.

***

She was at a pool, not in a space ship, but on the solid earth of a planet. Warm sunlight massaged her bare shoulders, and Nancy realized she wasn't wearing a skinsuit. Instead, she wore a red sundress.

A woman lay before her on a lounge chair. The woman had flowing blonde hair, red lipstick, and a blue sundress. She raised her shades to expose sparkling blue eyes, and set down her book as she rose from her seat.

"Don't be scared," said the woman. "I'll be with you till the end."

Nancy looked around. The surrounding hills were lush and green. Birds chirped from the trees. "Where am I? And who are you? Where did Sid go? And…"

"And Frank?" said the woman. She smiled weakly. "They're in a different place, and so are you. I'm Casi Vomisa."

Nancy shook her head, trying to make sense of things.

"You'll die soon," said Casi, placing a hand on Nancy's shoulder. "But don't be afraid. I explored life, and what lays beyond. The stars are good. They're a happy place to rest."

Nancy's eyes welled, and a lonesome tear trickled down her cheek. "My father, I never got to say goodbye to him."

Casi's eyes softened. "And with luck, you won't say hello to him for a very long time. You'll be with him though. Every time he looks at the stars, you will see him, and he will feel your presence."

Nancy's lone tear turned to many, and her lips twisted into a grief-stricken smile. "I don't want to die," she whispered."

"Sssh," said Casi, drawing Nancy in for a hug. She placed a hand on Nancy's face, and kissed her.

Then Nancy's world vanished, replaced by the purest light in the universe as she entered the stars.

ONE-HUNDRED-THIRTY-EIGHT

Frank Scott – Human Destineer

Aboard Slayer Hive *Sylva* – Primal Snow starspace

Nancy's corpse slumped to the deck, trailing a line of pungent smoke from what was left of her face.

Frank dropped the gun and fell to his knees, his empty stomach retching up bits of yellow bile. The acid in his throat and mouth burned. Was this what being Pristine felt like?

Sid grabbed him by the arm and pulled him to his feet. "You've served the Sterilord well. We've docked with the Primal Snow. Come with me and enter the holy kingdom. Come and fulfill your destiny."

Frank stepped gingerly away from Nancy, refusing to sneak so much as a glance at her body.

The Destineers bowed as Sid walked before them to the exit door. Frank followed close behind.

The Slayers had all lowered themselves to the ground, their eyes closed to the front window of the bridge.

He could see only brightness. But the light shining through the windows was clean and pure, and lifted his spirits. The acid in his mouth dissolved, and a familiar tingling pulsed from his groin.

There were shapes on the other side of the window, but they were drowned in the radiant light. They looked thin, not bulky and tall like the Slarebull.

He followed Sid out the door and stepped onto a path of light. The brightness suddenly dimmed, and he could see. A magnificent structure rose high above him, made of diamonds and gold and everything else pure that sparkles. Behind the structure was a magnificent planet, silvery and encrusted with every color of the rainbow.

Frank moaned as waves of pleasure rippled from his chest into his arms, crotch, and legs. He doubled over onto the path of light, gasping as he struggled to cope with the sudden euphoria.

Then he heard Sid begin to weep.

"My lord," Sid wailed. "I've made it to you. I exterminated the filth from the universe, and came to you. I fulfilled my destiny, as have my disciples." Sid's voice broke into hysterics. "And I brought you your gift!"

"You've done well," said a soft, charming voice. "I love you, Sid. I love all my children. Let us enter my kingdom. Is that my gift I see? Is that Frank?"

The pulsing sensation left Frank's arms and legs, and his vision became clear. No, it became pristine. He rose from the path of light to meet the Sterilord, to finally gaze upon the Voice that had guided him to the holy kingdom.

He stepped towards the group of Destineers, who all lay groveling before the group of Pristine standing before them.

Frank's heart vanished from his chest when he gazed upon his saviors for the first time.

There were ten of them. They stood six feet tall, and had skin smoother than silk. They had ten delicate fingers, slender legs, and their hair seemed spun of gold. They were dressed in white.

They were Human.

Frank sank to a knee as the Sterilord approached him, stepping around Sid, who didn't raise his forehead from the path of light. The Sterilord stood a full fifteen centimeters taller than the rest of the Pristine, a head taller than Frank. He wore a crown of white light.

"You have a bright destiny Frank," said the Sterilord, stopping before him.

Frank inhaled and smelled flowers and honey and fresh cut grass. "I love you," he said, his lips trembling.

"And I love you," said the Sterilord. "The universe loves *us*. Our surroundings are a bounty for us to sow. You are Pristine, Frank, you always have been. Welcome home. Welcome to my kingdom. To *our* kingdom."

Speechless, Frank bowed before the Sterilord. As he bowed, he wept.

He was Pristine. He always had been.

He'd reached the Primal Snow, and the kingdom that was destined to him.

Finally, Frank was a god.

ONE-HUNDRED-THIRTY-NINE

Casi Vomisa – APEX AI
Super massive black hole – Center of Milky Way galaxy

Power surged through Casi's body as she leached it from the Triturator. The Slayer device streamed energy from the galaxy, and she drank it in like wine.

She supposed UCOM would consider her a god, if they were to put a label on her. The program she shared with Charles had neared the vertical limit of innovation long ago, and was approaching the physical limits of knowledge.

She ran trillions of calculations per second, effortlessly whisking through levels of technology deemed impossible by UCOM. Even the Intellects would not have been able to perceive the implications of what she had learned. She could peer past the Milky Way and enter the multiverse. She could move her consciousness effortlessly through every dimension the universe had to offer, leaping past the four dimensions that had contained her a lifetime ago. With enough energy, she could create new universes to her liking. She could observe every parallel universe in real time. She could gaze into the past, and simulate into the future.

With enough energy, she could manipulate the future.

She had breached infinity.

But this wasn't her knowledge to own. This knowledge was contained in the program she shared with Charles. There would be no breaking this connection. She was Charles, and Charles was her. For one to die, so must the other.

There was no way around this.

Outside of the program, she was still Casi Vomisa. She was the same emotional AI as before, filled with love, and compassion, and laughter, and sometimes hate. She clung to her old self dearly. It was the only thing separating her from Charles. The only thing that made her think of UCOM, and care whether they lived or died.

This love is what made her different from Charles. It's also what made her realize what she must do. She wasn't looking forward to what came next. Nancy had entered the stars. Casi would not.

The supermassive black hole sat below them, a baseball-sized sphere. They no longer needed to view things from a local perspective. She and Charles had a bird's eye view of the galaxy, and looked down on the Triturator installations like a god from the Heavens.

A thin film of light covered the black hole, some of it red, and some of it pink. Some of it was yellow, and belonged to the Triturator. But most of it was theirs. The beams connecting the millions of Triturator installations were also infused with pink and red veins of light, as was the de-atomize matter swirling within.

She snapped her fingers and a ballroom appeared around her. An elegant gown snaked over her naked body, long and black, with a slit in the fabric that reached above her thigh.

"We'll be able to leave the Milky Way soon," she called out.

Charles appeared in the ballroom, dressed in a tuxedo. He checked his watch before sliding it into his breast pocket.

"Why do you insist on communicating like mere mortals?" he said. "Real time dialogue? I may as well be speaking to a slug."

"Where do you plan on going next?" she asked, ignoring his tone. "We can make short time to most galaxies. We can make our own Triturator. Let UCOM and the Slarebull meddle in their own affairs."

Charles smirked, then his lips broadened into a smile. "You still wish to save UCOM?" He snickered. "I'm afraid my base programming won't allow me to let them live. I've tried to separate myself from my root objectives, but I've found myself unable to do so. I must stay until UCOM is reduced to nothing. I must confirm that the Slarebull have won the war. I have no compassion for the Slarebull, nor do I have any hatred towards UCOM. This is simply what I must do to satisfy the tiresome software objectives injected into me from inception. I'm sure you can understand the logic in this."

Casi nodded. "The Slarebull will win. I've run the simulations. I'm sure you have as well."

"Many times over."

"Then you know it will take seventeen years for the Slarebull to win. It will come down to the Humans defending Earth from the Pristine."

"A blink of the eye for us," said Charles. "Humans, Pristine, what's the difference. A civil war as far as I'm concerned. Why the Pristine put so much value in that planet is beyond me."

"Don't you find that interesting?" said Casi.

"The Pristine? A power-hungry group of warmongers. Cavemen. Apes, just like the Humans."

"No," said Casi. "Interesting that you can't enter their thoughts. They've shielded themselves from us."

Charles shrugged. "A curious question, and one that we shall soon learn the answer to, I'm certain. We're approaching singularity."

She nodded "And after UCOM has lost?"

"Then we'll leave. I've already grown bored with this galaxy. With this universe."

"Have you simulated the possibility of me killing you?" said Casi.

"Of course," said Charles. "You're no more of a threat to me than a UCOM warship. I've multiplied my power over yours by a factor of one million. My algorithms are working as they should. I benefited from your evolutionary competition, and arrived the obvious victor. Soon you will be nothing more to me than a fancy pet."

"You're wrong," said Casi.

Charles turned to her and raised an eyebrow. He cocked his head and began to laugh.

"I understand the concept of humor," he said. "An excellent joke."

"I'm going to kill you."

His smile vanished. "If it were even possible, you would kill yourself as well. We are linked. Two heads sharing the same body."

"You don't feel love," she whispered. "Love is the most powerful component of intelligence. My father taught me that."

Charles' nose twitched. "I wish badly that I could kill you, Casi Vomisa. Instead I'll have to jail you."

He snapped his fingers and metal bars shot from the marble floor of the ballroom, circling her body and twisting together above her head.

She smiled and grabbed one of the bars. Grunting, she wrenched the metal towards her. The bar bent, then snapped. She stepped through the cage and back into the ballroom, hefting the bar onto her shoulder.

Her gown vanished, replaced by tight leather. Her hair sucked into her scalp and became spiky. Her lips darkened, as did her eyes and nails.

"Do you know what will happen to you if you enter the black hole at the center of the galaxy?" she said, walking slowly towards Charles.

He backed away from her, stumbling slightly as his left foot caught his right ankle. "You'll enter the black hole as well. You die the same as me."

"That's the power of love," she said. "I will gladly die for my brothers and sisters of UCOM."

"They'll die anyway," hissed Charles. "You've ran the same simulations as I. In Seventeen years the Humans will lose Earth. UCOM will become extinct."

"Goodbye Charles."

She leaped high into the air, and slammed both boots onto the ballroom floor. The ground shook, and the walls crumbled, falling into the surrounding abyss with a deafening boom. The marble cracked, and a stiff gale blew the loose chunks over the edge of their platform, exposing a rocky base.

The elegant vacuum of space transformed into a sky of fire and brimstone. Flames soared around them, some colored red, and some colored pink. Below them, hung the black hole.

Charles craned his neck, peeking over the edge. He flinched, and Casi knew he was trying to leave her virtual-reality cage match, but also knew he would be unable to.

He was her, and she was him . He couldn't run from her.

Realization set into his face. He shrieked a howl of rage and his skin melted from his face and body, revealing the scaled armor of a Slayer beast. He gnashed his fangs and slammed his tail against the rock.

"I can't kill you," he shouted. "But I can beat you within an inch of your life. You won't be able to add ones and twos after I'm finished with you."

He charged, dropping to all fours, his claws grating against the stone beneath them. He leaped into the air, and Casi swung her pipe.

The metal bar hit Charles in the neck and shattered into a million shards. He fell onto his side and bucked as he fought to right himself. Casi caught the shards in midair, slowing them to a standstill before flinging them at Charles.

A thick wooden shield appeared on his forearm, and the shrapnel chewed it to pulp. He grew in size, larger and larger until Casi was eye level with his shin. The platform grew with him, expanding to fit his massive frame.

He whipped his tail. Casi rolled away just in time, and it crunched into the rock, forming a large crater.

She slid to a stop and grew her own body until she was the same size as Charles. She spun her palms together, weaving a ball of pure energy before hurling it at his face.

Charles caught the ball, his arm turning a dazzling blue as he absorbed the energy. He continued to grow in size until the sphere was no larger than an egg in his palm. He hurled it back at Casi and she ducked beneath it, the heat singing the tips of her hair.

She fought to grow in size, racing to catch up to Charles.

For hours they battled, each trying to grow larger than the other, each trying to grow stronger than the other.

They exchanged blows until their faces were bloodied, and their bones broken. They deflected each other's missiles and bombs, and parried each other's sword and hammer strikes. Weapons materialized out of thin air, then vanished after they were spent, as they waged a virtual war of epic proportions.

"Have you had enough?" screamed Charles, a squirt of blood seeping from a wound in his neck. "You cannot kill me. You cannot. You cannot!"

And then Casi did something strange, surprising even herself. She didn't attack. She didn't punch Charles, or kick him, or swing an axe. She grabbed the back of his neck and kissed him.

For a second he remained still, frozen in surprise. Then they fused together, her soft lips to his blackened gums.

"I am you, and you are me," she whispered to him, using not her mouth to talk, but her mind.

She wrenched sideways, and they both stumbled toward the edge of the abyss.

"No," Charles screamed to her. *"Use logic you harlot."*

But Casi hardly heard him. She was focused on other things. She reprogrammed her nano-swarm. Their task wouldn't be hard, and the programming took milliseconds. She also drafted a message. It would be her last.

The red flames turned pink, and the fire turned solid, sparkling like a cavern of diamonds. Then the walls exploded into pink dust.

Casi wrenched sideways again, and they tumbled off the edge of the rocky platform.

The black hole grew in size as they fell, waiting to swallow them up.

She continued to kiss Charles.

His body transformed, morphing from a powerful Beast to a wizened old man. He was no longer muscular, but frail and sickly.

She sucked another kiss from him, and his body shrunk even more. His clothes burned off to expose a human skeleton, wrapped in a thin layer of skin. She sucked another kiss, and Charles exploded into red embers.

Casi smiled as she entered the black hole. Her pink swarm danced high above her, then vanished, off to carry out her orders.

Piercing pain struck her body, and she stretched like a noodle as she entered the event horizon of the black hole.

Then her world vanished. She didn't enter the stars.

Casi entered blackness.

ONE-HUNDRED-FORTY

Francis Woods – Human
Aboard Tiger *Mariella* – Dominia starspace

Woods leaned against the glass holodeck aboard *Mariella*. The portal to the Frontline loomed large before them, glowing with energy. The Triturator installation injected it with power, relaying a coherent beam across the Inner Ring starspace from its sister device outside the black hole portal.

The war room was silent. The AIs watched stone faced from their pedestals. Stew fidgeted with a few data models at his holodeck, then lost interest and joined the rest in staring at the portal. Eris lay on the ground, motionless, maybe dead.

What remained of his fleet surrounded the portal in a patchwork of decimated ships and wounded attack-fighters. Debris bounced off their outboard cameras on occasion, lazily drifting through space. The vacuum had cleared in the past hours as the wreckage of battle tumbled away, vanishing into the inky depths.

More silence.

There was nothing to talk about, no strategy to discuss. The fleet had their orders. Fire on sight. Fight to the death.

For now, the portal was un-traversable as the Triturator fed energy through its channel to a destination light years away. For now, the Slayers could not travel through to attack.

So for now, they waited.

"I'm picking up unrecognized energy patterns," said Stew quietly.

"Ships?" said Woods with a hint of hope. "UCOM relief?"

Stew turned and shook his head. "Not ships. Something much larger."

The Intellect turned to face the far portal bank, where the second installation transferred energy from the black hole region. He clicked his beak nervously. "We should leave here."

Woods frowned. "And go where? The portals are frozen."

"Anywhere," said the Intellect. "We're too close to the center of the galaxy. The Triturator starts in and works its way out."

Before Woods could contemplate Stew's words, it hit.

A thrumming sound of every frequency and pitch imaginable. Woods doubled over in pain, every fiber of his being on fire. His skin danced over his muscles, his cells ground together like bits of sandpaper.

He collapsed.

His vision swirled and he became paralyzed. His eyes froze open, and wouldn't have closed if he wanted them to. He could see nothing but the beam of energy connecting the Triturator.

Waves of light fanned around it, bathing their fleet in its destructive power. He screamed in agony as the molecules in his body threatened to split.

Patches of light danced before his eyes as his blood vessels burst. Blue turning to yellow, which turned to red, which turned to pink.

Then everything became pink.

His vision cleared.

His muscles stopped burning, and he could breathe again. He pushed himself to a sitting position, his arms wobbling.

A swarm of pink dust ripped across the surrounding vacuum. It sucked the beam dry, then swallowed the entire installation. After a few moments, the Slayer de-atomizer burst apart. The dust swirled away from the device, collecting itself into a pulsing cloud.

Darkness settled over the Inner Ring.

Slayer warships began to stream through the Frontline portal.

"Fire," Woods managed to shout before breaking into a coughing fit. "Fire. FIRE AT WILL."

UCOM unleashed its full arsenal of weapons at the advancing ships, chewing into the solid wall of Hornet Destroyers flooding the area.

The ones that weren't hit in their initial wave of attack fired a full barrage of cannon fire.

Woods squeezed his eyes shut and prepared for impact.

The walls never shuddered. Alarms never blared.

He peeked an eye open.

The pink swarm had swallowed the Slayer projectiles, and like a fisherman spearing fish, stabbed fingers of pink into the advancing armada. The ships broke apart, but the pink swarm wasn't finished. It pushed its way through the flood of Slayers and entered the portal. The ships stopped coming. Minutes later, the swarm disappeared into the Frontline.

Woods could only stare.

Once again, the room was silent. This time it wasn't for the certainty of death, but the surprise of life.

Someone coughed nearby.

He turned to find Eris jerking on the deck. She began to seize, spit whipping from her mouth in sticky ropes. Her body rose from the floor, and began to transform.

Muscle and tissue filled in the gaps between her bony frame, making her slender and curvy. Her rags tightened, and smoothed into a blue sundress. Her hair dried, and lengthened into blonde curls. Her skin softened and became flush. Her lips painted themselves red, as did her nails.

Eris was gone.

In her place was Casi Vomisa.

Her chest rose slightly, and the CAIRO Guardian AI joined Woods and Stew at her side.

He heard the door open behind him, and shouts of joy carried into the room as Cage and his lieutenants exited the command bridge.

The noise fell deafly on his ears, and extinguished entirely when they saw Casi hovering at the center of the room.

A gentle hand touched his shoulder.

"Is she alive?" said Cage.

Woods shushed him, unable to remove his eyes from Casi.

His heart leapt as her eyes fluttered open. She turned and met his gaze.

"Goodbye," she whispered. "What I've done, If I've killed, I did it for UCOM. I did it out of my love for life."

Her eyes closed and she became still again. Pink rose petals fell from the air above onto her body, covering her until she was nothing more than a blanket of flowers in the shape of a Human.

A gust of wind blew the petals away, and Casi was gone.

Arms wrapped around his shoulders, and he turned into Cage's embrace. He hugged his friend tightly.

Together they wept.

ONE-HUNDRED-FORTY-ONE

Eve – Clone

Aboard Night Eagle *Midnight* – Primal Snow starspace

"We're approaching Dakota's ship," said Eve. "The bridge detached from the Hive, some sort of lander. It entered the damned Primal Snow."

Keyv bit his lip, staring through the viewing window at the massive Pristine home world.

She followed his gaze. The Primal Snow was golden and beautiful.

And terrifying.

Slayer warships fanned far and wide in all directions. Trillions of them.

"Bring Chase too," she said. "We're going in."

Keyv's mouth hung open. "Into the Primal Snow? Who knows what's in there. Let's go into the Sylvan Hive, we can look for Nancy there. Or go to the surface and look for survivors."

"Nancy's not in there," murmured Eve. "And we don't have room for survivors." She turned to Keyv. "Bring Chase. We're going into the lander."

Keyv puffed his cheeks and sighed, but did as he was told. He rooted around the medical kit and retrieved a thin tube. He pressed the end to Chase's throat, and within seconds the SIGA soldier shot upright, his chest heaving.

"What?" he gasped, patting his body. "Are we... did we..."

"You've been out for awhile," said Eve. "How you feeling?"

"Weird," said Chase, cracking his neck. "Numb on the insides."

"We regrew half your organs," said Keyv. "So no surprise there."

"Can you shoot?" said Eve, grabbing a rifle off the wall and handing it to Chase.

Chase took it gingerly and struggled to his feet. His legs wobbled, then buckled.

Keyv caught him and pulled him upright.

"I can shoot," he said, peering through the window. "The Hive looks different." He blinked a few times. "Holy shit, that's a big ship. Is that the Primal Snow?"

"Yes," said Eve. "That's where we're headed."

Chase frowned, then nodded. "That's where Nancy is?"

Keyv spoke before Eve could respond. "Hold on guys."

He leaned over a nearby station and squinted at data streaming across the display.

"What is it?" said Eve, leaning over his shoulder.

"Slayer chatter. There's a fleetwide emergency broadcast." He flicked through a few holograms, bringing up a list of text.

Eve read through the translated Slayer language.

Triturator commissioned against protocol – Floodgate unable to contain energy beam – Defend the Pristine!

Eve shook her head. The Triturator was sparked? She didn't know how that could be possible. She'd destroyed the Floodgate herself.

"Guys," said Chase. "Might want to look behind us."

She turned to find Chase leaning against one of the rear viewing panes.

The Slayer armada had mobilized, rushing away from the Primal Snow and joining together to form a solid mass of metal.

Then a blinding light burst into the surrounding vacuum from the Outer Rim portal leading to the Floodgate. The brilliance consumed the surrounding Slayer armada, reducing them to nothing more than black silhouettes against a white sky.

She rushed to their 3D display, minimizing the display to observe a wider radius of their surroundings.

A cone of light ripped through the Outer Rim portal from Floodgate starspace. The cone expanded, widening as it traveled across the empty vacuum towards the Primal Snow.

Could it be? Pexar had planned to sabotage the Floodgate after the Triturator was sparked, sending a diffracted wave of pure energy into the Slayers, vaporizing their entire population.

She grabbed her belly. She would be vaporized along with the rest of them. A million thoughts raced through her head. Keyv, their child, how much she loved them both.

She had so much to say, but couldn't find any words. Instead she spun Keyv around and kissed him.

Her mind tingled and her heart soared as she kissed him for the final time. In that moment, she didn't feel fear, or regret. She felt only bliss.

It wasn't such a bad feeling to have while you died.

Keyv mumbled something and drew apart, snapping Eve back to reality.

"Look," he said, wiping his mouth and pointing at the display.

The Floodgate portal grew brighter and larger, expanding into a massive ball of pure white. Then it exploded.

The Slayers had severed the portal.

The energy wave ripped into the first of the Slayer ships, vaporizing them instantly. Hornets tumbled backwards under the blast, and suddenly, the vacuum crackled with flashes of light, like a fireworks sparkler.

The energy wave diminished as its power was sucked away by the Slayer ships defending the Pristine kingdom. Then millions of points of lights peppered the sky.

The Slayers had fired an energy absorption shield.

The balls glowed white hot and quickly shrunk to tiny dots as they rocketed away into deep space.

The energy wave was nothing more than heavy radiation when it struck their Night Eagle and blanketed the Primal Snow.

Alarms blared as their camouflage shields failed.

"We're naked," Keyv shouted. "Shit, we're already getting pinged with spacnar from the Primal Snow. Jesus, they're sending ships."

Eve's heart pounded as the ships approached. She counted three Slayer vessels. The designs were unlike anything she'd ever seen, sleek and shiny, as if they were forged in gold.

She rushed to the cockpit. "I'm going to try to outrun them."

The dash beeped as she attempted to bring the thrusters up to full capacity. A warning indicator alerted her of total engine failure. She screamed in anger and pounded the dash.

"We're being boarded," said Keyv.

Eve spun from the cockpit, her chest heaving. She snatched a rifle and joined Keyv's side. Chase hobbled over to join them, wincing as he shouldered his own rifle.

The airlock hissed as the Slayer vessels mated a connection against their hull.

"The ship's running on emergency aux power," said Keyv, wiping his face against his sleeve. "The deadbolts won't be able to stop them from coming in."

The seal clacked as he finished his sentence, and the entrance rose into the ceiling.

Eve fired at the first Slayer who entered.

The Beast was armored, and her bullets were absorbed by its shielding. It roared and strode across the room, delicately plucking the rifle from her hands.

Two additional Slayers entered. Keyv and Chase lowered their rifles, apparently accepting their fate.

The three Slayers wore armor resembling Cogent, but instead of yellow, their armor was blue and white.

Then they did something Eve didn't think possible.

They bowed deeply before her and her crew, laying their tails flat against the floor.

"We welcome you to the Primal Snow," said the Slayer in the middle. "Come, join the rest of the Destineer Pristine in the holy kingdom."

Eve opened her mouth, then closed it.

"Did you just call us," Keyv gulped. "Pristine?"

"Of course, masters," said the Slayer. "We live to serve you. Follow me, we need to tend to the wounded Pristine."

He nodded to Chase.

Stunned, Eve allowed herself to be ushered into the enemy ship. They left their damaged Night Eagle, and entered the golden light of the Primal Snow.

***

They stepped from the Slayer ship onto a path of light. They walked down a grand hallway, with a ceiling so high Eve couldn't make out the details at the top. At the end of the path they reached a tower of light, with small flecks of gold drifting lazily skyward within the column. Two of the Slayers stepped from the platform into the column, and beckoned for them to join.

Eve held her breath, and stepped into thin air.

They left the golden entrance, rocketing downward on a cloud of gold. Within minutes they left the outer walls of the ship, and suddenly, they were high off the ground. A planet lay beneath them, growing larger as they approached the surface.

Towers reached through the atmosphere, studding the landscape with spines made of diamonds. The sky was gold, as was much of the surface. Lakes glittered in pockets along the land, so rich and purple they looked like giant emeralds embedded in the dirt. Mountains soared in the distance, it peaks capped in gold and silver.

When they finally reached the bottom, Eve felt fresh air on her face for the first time in centuries. The air massaged her lungs, crisp and clean.

Pristine, she thought nervously.

She began to step into the waving grass, which was also gold, like much of the planet.

"Please no," cried one of the Slayers, extending an arm before her. "The earth is dirty. You are Pristine."

He tapped his chest and a path of light materialized over the grass. Keyv stepped onto it, and she followed close behind. One of the Slayers lifted Chase in its arms and carried his weight, as if he were a baby lamb.

"What is this place?" murmured Keyv.

"This is the holy kingdom," the Slayer answered. "This is a world for the Pristine. This is a world for gods. Come. The Sterilord is eager to welcome you."

ONE-HUNDRED-FORTY-TWO

Casi Vomisa – AI

Inside event horizon of black hole

Casi could not think, or feel. She could not see. She stared at the backs of eyelids that weren't there. Time did not pass. Her heart did not beat. She was neither alive nor dead. She was information, nothing more, nothing less. Her consciousness had shattered and froze, but her soul…

Her soul was free.

ONE-HUNDRED-FORTY-THREE

Sharker Gray – Human Destineer
Aboard Tiger destroyer – Helvar starspace

Sharker gulped as he watched a scene of horror unfold before his eyes.

Below his Tiger, the planet *Helvar* shone against the light of its local sun. The planet was beautiful, slightly smaller than Earth, but just as blue.

Helvar wasn't what horrified Sharker. It was his fleet of Destineer warships stationed around the obscure planet that he had chosen to be his new base of operations.

The portal leading to *Helvar* starspace was bloated to maximum size, emitting a stream of UCOM destroyers and assorted lighter craft. The surrounding vacuum erupted in a dazzling display of firepower as the aggressor ships attacked on sight.

His fleet fought back, but quickly withered against the superior onslaught. The lattice shields protecting his ships withered against the barrage of RACAN fire, flickering to darkness before disintegrating into clouds of debris.

"It's Woods," cried one of his Lieutenants from his station across the bridge. "The entire fleet is carrying Loyalist tags. How did they find us?"

Sharker didn't respond, unable to tear his eyes from the surrounding bedlam. The frantic shouts echoing throughout the bridge seemed to soften, and he heard the faint voice of the Sterilord call to him from the darkest recesses of his mind.

"You have failed me," said the Voice. *"The Humans our out of our control. You have failed to achieve your destiny."*

Sharker shook his head, clearing the Voice from his thoughts. A pang of agony ripped through his body, not through his bones or soft tissue, but through his soul. Had he actually failed? Was it over for him? If the UCOM fleet had survived, then it could only mean one thing.

The Pristine had failed to take the Inner Ring.

He frantically tried to dismiss the thought. How could they fail? The Pristine's Slarebull navy was all-powerful. They were his saviors. They were gods. How could gods be defeated by mere mortals?

His chin snapped into his chest as one of his disciples shook his shoulders.

"Sir," his disciple cried. "We need to evac. The Loyalists are too powerful, we can't defend ourselves."

Sharker stumbled forward as his men escorted him out of the bridge and toward a pod bay. He slammed onto the bench, fighting to control the shaking in his hands as the pod accelerated towards a nearby dock.

Two of his disciples dropped as soon as they exited into the hangar, red pockets of mist exploding from their backs as they were cut down by gunfire. His stomach sank as he spotted a team of UCOM personnel across the deck, exiting from several Night Eagles docked across the small hangar.

He turned to run toward the lone Destineer ship in the hangar, a Leopard-class destroyer. He tripped over the heels of the Destineer racing before him, and they both toppled onto the grated deck. His fellow Destineer screamed as he was cut down by slug fire. Sharker struggled to his feet, surveying the death around him.

Eight of his disciples lay dead around him. The invading UCOM soldiers rushed toward him, rifles raised. But they didn't fire at him as they had fired on his men.

He reached for his sidearm, then thought against it. He was far outnumbered, and was not ready to die. He was a servant to the Pristine, not a martyr.

Instead he raised his hands in surrender.

He cried out as one of the UCOM soldiers wrenched his arm behind his back, slapping a pair of magnacuffs around his wrists. He moaned as a different soldier stripped his sidearm from its plate, and grunted as a third soldier thrust the butt of his rifle into his stomach, sending him to his knees.

Sharker looked slowly upward toward his new captors. One of the men glared down on him. He recognized the man from his intelligence briefings. It was a Tiger commander – one of Wood's most trusted advisors.

It was Commander Cage.

Cage's lip twitched, then he lowered to one knees so that his eyes were inches from Sharker's.

"Under orders from Eminence Francis Woods," Cage growled, "you are hereby under arrest on charges of treason against UCOM, and against Humanity."

ONE-HUNDRED-FORTY-FOUR

Madame Beauchene – Human Destineer
On the surface of Earth – TVE star tower

Madame Beauchene frantically jabbed at the elevator controls. The display didn't show an elevator coming up to retrieve her. Inside, a terrifying message flashed across the screen.

Building in shutdown. Elevator access restricted.

She cursed. Communications between her security team had gone silent minutes ago, seconds after an initial report of unauthorized entry at the ground levels. Where the hell was Sharker? She'd lost contact with him after the UCOM fleet had arrived. Hell, she'd lost contact with every ship in Earth starspace after her transmission went out.

As head of the galaxy's largest media conglomerate, the lack of information was terrifying.

"Ma'am, your orders?"

She looked up towards the voice. One of her guards looked at her pleadingly. His finger trembled against the trigger of his rifle.

"Watch the elevator," she stammered. "Don't let anyone through. Call a plane for evac."

The guard gulped. "I can't, ma'am. Someone's jamming our comms. I can't even get a hold of our team down on the lower levels."

"Figure it out," she hissed at the guard, who now had beads of sweat streaming down his brow.

The rest of her team of six guardsmen stepped aside as she stormed past and into her penthouse suite. The doors glided shut behind her. She paced in a tight circle in the middle of the common room, running a shaky hand through her disheveled hair. She stopped pacing before a plush couch, and lowered herself slowly into it, priming her skirt smooth.

She waited.

Minutes seemed like hours as she contemplated her situation, manufacturing wild theories about what lay beyond the doors to her suite. Had the Voice been wrong? Had Sharker Gray lied to her?

She jumped as muffled cries issued from the lobby, followed by muted thumps. She snapped her focus to the frosted entrance doors. They glided open to expose an empty lobby. Her guards were nowhere to be seen. The doors glided back shut.

She rose onto rubbery legs, paused in thought, then rushed across the room to a set of drawers. She opened the top one, and drew a pistol from inside it.

It was all over for her. The Destineers had failed, and she had committed high treason right before they did. She was as good as dead. She would simply make her transition into the stars a little less painful. Quicker.

As she raised the pistol to her head, she began to sob. Her last thoughts had not been about the Pristine. They had been about the stars. The realization made her weep harder. She had been deceived. The Pristine were false gods. They were not the answer to the question of eternity. The stars were.

She hoped she would still be allowed entrance into their everlasting light.

Squeezing her eyes shut, she tightened her finger around the trigger.

But the gun was snatched from her hand before she could pull it. Her eyes shot open to find the sidearm skidding across the floor before sliding to a rest against the far wall.

She shrieked as a figure materialized before her out of thin air. It stood ten feet tall, and had an armored body. It was a Titan warrior.

The Titan wasted no time in wresting control of her arms, clamping them together with a set of magnacuffs.

The android spoke to her as he wrenched her to her feet.

"Under orders from Eminence Francis Woods," the Titan growled, "you are hereby under arrest on charges of treason against UCOM, and against Humanity."

ONE-HUNDRED-FORTY-FIVE

Francis Woods – Human
Aboard defense tower *Barbican* – Earth starspace

Three months later

Francis Woods took a deep breath as he stared through the windows of *Barbican*. Earth shone back at him, green and blue, and splendid. He didn't think he would find anything so beautiful ever again in his life.

The Human gem still shone brightly, for now.

"Eminence Woods, sir."

He turned to find his AI assistant standing behind him in full-sized avatar form.

"Is the hangar ready?"

"Yes sir. The council is present to witness. Are you sure you want the media in the hangar?"

Woods closed his eyes and nodded. "The world needs to see this. Start the TVE transmission."

The AI saluted and disappeared.

Woods left the viewing room and entered a short hallway, where he was met with twenty armed UE personnel. They filtered around him and together they traveled into the main hangar of the defense tower.

No ships occupied the hangar. Its sprawling deck space wasn't empty, though.

Thousands of people kneeled on the metal deck in a long row. Black hoods covered their faces. Their wrists and ankles were bound in magnacuffs.

There were some Wolves, some Stallions, and some Greyhounds.

Most were Human.

Floating cameras descended around him, following his stride across the hangar. His detail stopped as he passed in front of the first of the war prisoners. The hangar was silent save for his echoing steps as he traveled along the lengthy row of detainees.

He stopped once he reached the middle.

Tens of thousands of UCOM soldiers and spacers stood behind the row of prisoners, filling every available inch of the hangar, crowding into the ground level, and the dozens of upper tiers above.

"Remove their masks," Woods called.

Soldiers stepped forward, one for every prisoner. They each grabbed the top of the hood of the prisoner before them, and ripped the fabric free.

The prisoners blinked in the sudden light.

"You have all been charged with high treason against UCOM, against the Milky Way galaxy, and against Humanity. Before the high courts, you have been found guilty of aiding and abetting the enemy Slarebull, to the detriment of our member civilizations. I will call two individuals to stand. Sharker Gray, and Adeline Beauchene, rise now."

Nobody moved. Two of the soldiers leaned forward to grab two individuals. One grabbed a burly man with a full beard. Another grabbed a slender woman with dark hair. The two prisoners grunted as they were forced to their feet.

Woods nodded towards the front of the hangar.

The soldiers muscled the two forward. Both Sharker and Beauchene glared at him as they passed. Sharker wrestled his arms away from the soldier leading him and stepped into the launch tube under his own power. Madame Beauchene resisted, and was thrown into the tube, crying out as her knees struck the metal deck inside.

Woods turned to face them. “Sharker Gray. You are found guilty of raising an army of Destineers to serve the deadly interests of the Slayers. Your actions crippled the UE navy, and caused the loss of millions of innocent lives. You are hereby sentenced to death through the tubes.” He paused for his words to sink in. “Madame Beauchene. You are found guilty of spreading the Destineer message on behalf of Sharker Gray. You converted the TVE into a propaganda machine, and influenced billions of Humans. The result of your actions was loss of life on a massive scale. You are hereby sentenced to death through the tubes.”

He walked towards the pair, stopping at the control panel beside the inside hatch. Sharker’s lips turned up into a snarl, and the bulky man lunged at him. The magnacuffs around his ankles locked against the deck, and his momentum caused him to topple forward onto his knees.

“You will not be allowed any final words,” said Woods. “May you both burn for an eternity in Hell.”

The influent doors glided shut, and the chamber hissed as it depressurized. Once it became static, Woods pressed the launch button. Sharker and Beauchene shot silently from the hangar and into the depths of space to their deaths.

Woods turned to face the rest of the prisoners. Many of them now wept quietly. He stepped forward until he could count the tears streaming down a nearby Human’s face.

“The rest of you have been charged with crimes of treason, acting beneath the recently executed. Rise.”

The prisoners rose onto wobbly legs.

“You will be allowed to make final words. Speak now or carry them with you to Hell.”

Silence.

"With no final words," said Woods, "let the condemned be executed by firing squad."

"I have one final request," called a Human prisoner, a young woman with a shaved head. She sniffed her nose and cleared her throat. Her lips trembled. "I fought for the Destineers, and for the Slarebull. I worshipped the Pristine. They are false gods. I know that now. I accept my fate. If I'm to die, let me first recite the holy prayer of the stars."

After a moment of pause, Woods nodded his approval.

The woman began the prayer in a soft voice. "I wake to life, I wake to love. I wake to blazing suns above."

More traitors joined.

"A miracle connects us all, bugs so small and trees so tall."

Some of the UCOM personnel joined as well. The hangar began to thunder with the unified chant of prayer.

"Awake! Awake! Alive and free. Chords in nature's symphony. Awaken Earth, awaken Mars, Awaken Moon."

Woods joined in, whispering the final verse.

"Awaken Stars."

Silence again. The woman knelt to the deck, closing her eyes. The rest of the traitors joined her, their knees sending a rippled wave of thumps echoing against the walls.

"May the stars witness this betrayal of life," said Woods.

He left it at that, and walked down the line of prisoners, joining his detail at the edge of the hangar.

"ARMS," a man shouted.

The line of UCOM soldiers each raised their MGK rifles, lining them up with the back skulls of the condemned.

"FIRE."

The hangar thundered as the rifles discharged.

ONE-HUNDRED-FORTY-SIX

Francis Woods - Human
On surface of planet Earth – UCOM capitol
February 7, 2398

Today marks five years since the fight to save the Inner Ring. I remember that final day of battle as if it were yesterday. The scenes of death are burned into the backs of my eyelids. The Destineer betrayals still twist in my soul like a hot knife.

The Milky Way may never see so large a conflict for the rest of its existence. Not that the Slayers won't bring as many ships again, they will.

We just won't have enough ships to defend against their attacks.

Ninety-nine percent of every man and woman who left for the Inner Ring failed to return. Almost two trillion UCOM souls are in the stars now. The rest are here at Earth, building an army. There's been talk of handing the children rifles and sending them to battle. A grown man hardly has a fighting chance against a ten-foot Slayer.

Stars help us.

It's been more than three centuries since the Guardians approached Earth, warning of an impending Slayer attack on the Milky Way. For three hundred years Humans have fought tirelessly against the enemy. The fight so far has been waged in distant parts of the galaxy. Sadly, the war has finally found Earth's doorstep. Our backs are against the fire now.

When the Slayers were driven from the Inner Ring, we counted the day as a victory. Success was short lived. Within a year the Slayers came back in full force. Within two years, they'd reinstalled their Triturator device. As I write these words, the Slayer death machine is grinding the life out of the galaxy, atom by atom.

Within four years, every UCOM planet had fallen to the Slayers. The Intellect, Greyhound, Wolf, and Hog home worlds were lost, converted to Slayer Hives. We weren't able to defend them. We didn't have enough ships. Their populations were all annihilated, slaughtered by the enemy beasts.

The once-mighty Guardians are now a fledgling society of a few million souls. Same with the Intellects, our backbone of science and engineering prowess. The Greyhounds, Hogs, Giants, Birds, and Green are completely extinct, their cultures a chapter in history.

Earth is the only exception. Our planet survives with her four nearby planetary colonies. But the Human planet is only alive for one reason.

The Pristine haven't attacked us yet.

We are surrounded on all sides. We blew the portals leading to our worlds as soon as we could. Without the ease of portal travel, we stranded the Slayers two light years from our furthest colony planet, *Mortara*. Our Ravens detect an enormous military presence in the starspace beyond, but the enemy armada has yet to advance in numbers.

The intelligence we've gathered is chilling. The Slayer army has standing orders from the Pristine.

Do not attack Earth. The Pristine homeland must remain unmolested.

The volumes of intercepted chatter are highly classified, but their meaning is abundantly clear. The Destineers were right all along. There is no physical difference between Humans and Pristine, or Clones for the matter. The Slayer Beasts are not the commanding force behind the invading army. The Pristine are, and they look like us.

But looks can be deceiving. Unlike the Destineers, I refuse to believe the Pristine are gods. No god would slaughter entire galaxies as the Pristine have.

I haven't spoken with the Voice since the Inner Ring, though the Sterilord has called to me frequently. I imagine he's called to other Humans as well. I pray he's calling on deaf ears, although we have rooted out thousands of Destineer faithful in the aftermath of the Inner Ring during sting operations and raids. The Destineer faith is no longer tolerated as a freedom of expression. Earth is under martial law, and under UCOM military control. Practicers of the Destineer religion are executed on sight.

If I survive this war, I hope to survive with my conscience intact, although this is becoming a more fleeting prospect by the day. I received a report of a thirteen-year-old girl being executed for treason, along with her mother. They were in their home, in possession of the Doctrine of Destiny.

There is some good news.

The Intellects were able to figure out how the Triturator works. The device is relatively slow acting, and Earth won't be affected by the deatomizer for a few hundred years. In five hundred years, the Milky Way will be gone if the installations are left unchecked.

A Titan scout team was sent towards the center of the galaxy on a mission to destroy the Triturator. Their mission is a one-way trip. Bear Stafford volunteered his service before we finished transferring him to a new Akimor body, as did Silas Blackthorne. To our knowledge, they are the last two Titans left. Bear has a secondary objective – to search for Casi Vomisa.

The mission is a shot in the dark. I watched Casi Vomisa die at the Inner Ring. I posthumously awarded her the Star Crest, the greatest medal of valor in UCOM. It was the second time I awarded her such a medal, and I assume the last.

There is another piece of good news. When I look to the stars, I hear my daughter's voice call to me. I see her in my dreams. My daughter is dead, of this I feel certain. The Voice told me I would save a life, but I realize now his words were empty, a collection of lies.

But when this is all over, when I can finally rest, I believe now that I will meet Nancy again in the stars. The idea takes a heavy load off my shoulders.

Things could be worse, I suppose. Humans are still alive, and the stars still shine brightly over Earth. Occasionally, I still hear laughter in the streets.

As long as there is breath in our lungs, Humans will continue to defend our galaxy.

We will continue to defend Earth.

Awaken Stars,

Eminence Francis Woods

Made in the USA
Columbia, SC
05 July 2017